THE UNDEAD. DAY FOURTEEN

SEASON TWO

RR HAYWOOD

THE UNDEAD
Season Two
Day Fourteen

CHAPTER ONE

'This is nice,' Mum grins at me as she places the steaming bowl of broccoli onto the table, 'we haven't had a family dinner for ages.'

I smile back, pleased to see her happy. Dad walks in and takes his seat at the head of the table. A kind man with an easy nature. He raises his eyebrows suggestively as he picks up the carving knife and sharpening steel.

'Oh, Dad,' Sarah sighs theatrically, 'are you going to go through the whole routine again?'

Dad smiles slowly and starts to run the knife blade up and down the steel, quietly humming to himself. The way he does it always gets me laughing, his comical expression adopting a serious face as he focuses on the sharpening.

'Howard,' Mum calls from the kitchen, 'don't you sit there, playing with the knife. That meat won't stay hot forever.'

'Yes, dear,' my dad replies in a singsong, faraway voice that sets me off grinning again. I watch the knife glinting from the sunlight streaming through the net curtains. Up and down, with a soft sound as the blade is gently stroked along the steel.

'Here, Howie, your favourite,' another bowl is placed down, this one being strategically placed closest to me and filled with Mum's crispy roast potatoes. Just the sight of them makes my mouth water. I know they'll be crunchy on the outside but fluffy and white on the inside.

'Favouritism,' Sarah mutters with a smile. She then looks up as Mum places a bowl of corn on the cob in front of her, bright yellow, with butter melting down the sides.

'You were saying?' I ask her.

'No favouritism in this house,' Mum laughs. 'Howie has his roast spuds, and Sarah has her corn.'

'What about me?' Dad looks up with an expectant expression.

'You, dear,' Mum smiles, 'get the sprouts.'

'Urgh,' he grimaces and returns to his knife-sharpening.

Mum takes a seat, pulling her chair in as she swipes the sharpening steel from Dad.

'So how's work, then?' she directs the question at Sarah as she lives in London now, and they don't get to see her much.

'Good,' Sarah nods, 'very busy, but yeah, it's pretty good.'

'And life in the big city?' Dad asks.

Sarah half smiles and sighs. 'It's okay,' she replies slowly, 'not the nicest place in the world, but it serves a purpose for now.'

'So?' Mum asks pointedly.

'What?' Sarah replies with a blank expression. 'Oh, not that again,' she adds as realisation dawns. 'Noooo,' she smiles, 'no men.'

'Want some beef, Howie?' Dad asks. I look up to see

him standing over the joint of meat, holding the blade just above the surface of the meat. 'It's lovely and juicy, Howie.'

The blade bites in, slicing a thick wedge of beef. The outside of the meat is charred to perfection, and the inside is pink, with dribbles of blood forming on the serving plate.

'Look at that,' Dad says, impressed at the quality of the meat.

'You do like your meat, don't you, Howie?' Mum smiles. I glance at her, but my eyes snap back to the bloody joint. The cooked flesh that bleeds onto the plate. The knife that saws back and forth, slicing deep, peeling the layers away.

My stomach revolts at the sight, and a wave of nausea passes through me. Breathing hard, I realise how hot it has suddenly got. Sweat pours off me, dripping onto the table-cloth, and I sweep my hand through my hair, brushing the perspiration away. My hand is filthy, encrusted with grime and dirt.

I shove it under the table, feeling ashamed that I never washed my hands before sitting down to dinner. I don't think they notice as Dad keeps sawing at the meat, carving and chopping thick wedges of flesh away. Blood spurts from the joint, spraying onto the pristine white tablecloth.

They don't notice but keep chatting. The blood sprays higher, splashing against the wine glasses and into the bowl of roast potatoes.

Dad smiles, but he doesn't look happy now. He looks mean and angry, hacking at the meat harder and harder. Sawing away as his lips purse and a light film of sweat covers his forehead.

'Go on, Dad,' Sarah urges, 'kill it ...'

'It's already dead,' I blurt out. They all stare at me like I'm five and have just said a swear word at the table. 'What's happening?' I glance round, fear escalating into terror. Pure, unadulterated horror, a feeling of impending doom that something terrible is about to happen.

'Gee, Howie, you don't look so good.' My head snaps to the other end of the table. He smiles with big, perfect, white teeth, framed by flawless skin and that world-famous face.

'Paco?' I whimper.

'Hey, buddy,' he stares at me, 'you taking care of my dog? Eh, buddy?' He grins with good humour, winking at me.

'Oh, Paco,' Mum slaps him gently on the arm.

'W-what ...?'

'Mum,' Sarah stands up, tapping the side of a glass with a fork, but she does it too hard, and the glass smashes. Shards embed into her fingers, slicing the flesh open. Thick streams of red blood drip down, but she doesn't stop, just carries on smashing the fork into the glass to get everyone's attention.

'I have an announcement,' she grins. 'Paco and I are getting married!'

Mum and Dad are on their feet. Mum hugs Sarah as Dad claps Paco manfully on the shoulder.

'What about Clarence?' I call out, but my voice sounds weak.

'Hey, buddy,' Paco grins down at me. He's very tall, with huge muscles that bulge out from a tight top. 'Don't bring it down, Howie. You know what I mean?'

'Yeah, Howie,' Sarah snarls at me, 'why can't you be happy?'

'Fuck,' I shout in alarm at the sight of her extended, huge pregnant stomach.

'Howie,' Dad tuts, 'watch your language in front of your mother.'

'Sorry, Mum,' I look over, but she looks away disdainfully, making a point of ignoring me.

'We did look for you, Howie,' Dad says as he stabs a serrated commando knife into the joint of beef. 'We did look for you.'

'Yeah, Howie,' Sarah adds spitefully. She sticks her tongue out and looks down at the newborn baby in her arms. Paco joins her, staring down at the figure swaddled in a blood-soaked blanket. Mum and Dad move in closer and together they all stare down, making cooing noises and smiling proudly.

'Look, Howie, this is your nephew,' Sarah smiles at me. Standing up, I move in and look down. My heart hammers in my chest as another wave of fear rips through me. Horror creeps up my spine at the squelchy mess of body parts my sister hugs in the blanket. Torn off limbs, fingers, teeth and bits of brain, grey things and intestines, and on top of it is a big heart. The tubes are snapped and torn off, but it beats strong and solid, pumping out thick, oozy blood with each bass-filled beat.

'We should eat before it gets cold,' Dad sighs and moves back to the joint. A big, shapeless lump of black fur now rests on the serving platter. Dad turns the platter slowly, the face of Meredith coming into view. 'Tongue, Howie?' he asks, pulling the dog's long, pink tongue out.

Whimpering, I slump down and cover my face with my hands, rocking back and forward on the chair, tears streaming down my face. It's so hot in here. I can hardly breathe.

'Howie,' Mum's voice calls out. Dropping my hands slowly, and everything is back to normal. Dad carving the beef, and Mum taking a sip of wine. No blood or baby parts, no dog's head, and no Paco.

'Howie,' Mum calls again. I look up to see tears rolling down her face.

'We're so proud of you, Howie,' her hand reaches across the table, grasping mine tightly. 'We are both so proud of you.'

'We are,' Dad reaches out and grasps my other hand. 'We never got to say goodbye, Son.' He smiles sadly, and I can see the love in his eyes. 'But we've been watching you, and we are so, so proud of you,' his voice is hoarse with emotion.

Sobs rack my chest, tears streaming down my face, 'I'm sorry,' I whimper. 'I'm so sorry ...'

'Howie,' Sarah moves to my side and puts her hand onto my arm.

'I got everyone killed, Sarah ... I'm sorry ...' I can't speak from crying so hard.

'Shush,' Mum urges, 'it wasn't your fault.'

'It was ... I should have stayed there ...'

'Son,' Dad interrupts me, 'listen to me, Son. We are so very proud, but you have to wake up now.'

'I don't understand.' I glance between them, unsure of what he means.

'Howie, you have to wake up,' Dad urges again. 'This is a dream, Howie ... You know that, right?'

'No,' I whimper, 'I want to stay here with you.'

'No, Howie,' Mum whispers softly, 'you don't belong here yet. Not yet, my Howie ... my beautiful Howie ... my son ...'

'Please, Mum, let me stay with you and Dad and Sarah ...'

'We all love you very much, Howie, and we're watching over you, but you have to wake up now ...' Sarah urges me.

'They need you, Howie. Dave needs you,' Dad adds, 'the lads need you ...'

'Lani needs you,' Mum smiles sweetly. 'She is very beautiful, Howie.'

'She is,' I grin through my tears. 'You would like her.'

'I do like her,' Mum laughs softly, with fresh tears falling down her face, 'and one day we will meet, but not now, not here ... You have work to do, Howie ...'

'You have to wake up now, Son,' Dad says firmly, but his voice is choked as he stifles a sob. 'You're not here, Howie. You're in the car park, in the tunnel. There's bodies on top of you,' he speaks quickly, staring at me with earnest. 'You will die if you don't wake up and move. You have to wake up and move ...'

'I ...'

'Get up, Howie. You must wake up ...'

So hot now. There is no air, and I know I have to do what they say, but I don't want to go. I'm safe here, safe, and with my family. Why should I go when I can just rest now. The last two weeks have been brutal, and I am tired, so very tired.

'Wake up,' my father jolts me hard, snapping my senses back, but they drift off again as the lure of the long sleep starts pulling me back under. He shoves me again, harder this time, and he keeps doing it, shoving and pushing at me, rocking my body with hard jolts as he refuses to let me sleep.

CHAPTER TWO

He fights harder than he has ever fought before. Controlling his fear, he uses it to drive his arms out, spinning left and right, forward and back. He drops and pirouettes as graceful as a ballet dancer. Leaping higher than an acrobat, the deadly blades swipe across throats, opening arteries to spray hot blood into the packed, dense ranks.

Hands slick with blood, but his grip doesn't falter. Every step is placed exactly where it needs to be. The infected are slow and cumbersome, and they cannot hope to match him.

Dave was born for this. The very essence of him is designed for this purpose. To kill without hesitancy and to keep killing.

Howie is in there somewhere. Howie is alone and surrounded. Dave knows they want Howie. This swirling motion has worked perfectly and has been expertly executed. Rings of infected moving clockwise against a counter flow moving the opposite direction. Swirls and rings all moving at different speeds and making it near-on impossible to gauge a sense of direction of distance.

With each high leap, he clocks the location of the

entrance to the ramp, instinctively knowing that is the direction Howie has gone. The infected simply move without attacking, and Dave ploughs on. Killing faster, driving harder. His face determined and utterly ruthless. A glint of fear in his eye, fear of knowing what will happen if Howie is truly gone. If that is the case, he vows deep within his soul that he will not rest until the last infected has fallen under his knife.

Something changes. A ripple of energy pulses through the infected, changing the way they move. Dave senses it has something to do with Howie. He knows something has happened. The infected retaliate and get faster, the swirls move quicker. The placid faces change into the ferocious expressions of hunger.

He knows that they're about to attack again. It's obvious. They're being pumped full of chemicals, getting primed and ready to go. Dave keeps on, willing them to turn and start.

When they do, he grunts in satisfaction. The swirling motion ends suddenly, and they turn to attack, lunging forward with wild howls that fill the air. Clarence roars from somewhere, voices scream, and orders are shouted, but Dave has one objective in mind, and now they're not swirling, he can finally make progress and use the momentum of their attack against them.

He feints left and right, the blade in each hand whipping out to slash as he jigs and dances through them. Dropping low to scoot between legs, using the falling bodies to leap high and get closer to Howie.

Slash, swipe, stab, hack, and each blow given is a killing blow. Each step taken drives him closer to the ramp. The darkness grows as he gains the entrance. The press of bodies is pumping out an intense, fetid heat that makes even his brow break out in a light sweat. Down the ramp and into the tunnel enclosure. Dark now, almost too dark to see, but Dave doesn't falter. He knows the human form better than he knows himself. He knows through instinct and long years of solid combat and training exactly where to place the knife, and he knows how each strike will cause the opponent to fall or react in a certain way. It is all preordained. There are no surprises for they are slow and dull-witted. They lack individual thought, and each one follows the same pattern of rushing in and lunging with teeth bared, thereby exposing the soft flesh of the neck.

His foot hits something hard. He slides the edge of his boot along the object, feeling the shaft and broad double blade. Howie's axe. He must be close. Whatever took place happened here.

'MR HOWIE,' he roars, his voice edged with fear. 'MR HOWIE,' he screams again, casting about to peer into the gloom. Bodies still thrust into him, only to drop and die quickly as the ground becomes soaked with pints of blood spurting out from so many cut arteries.

In the distance, the constant staccato thud of the GPMG fills the air and the sound of the Saxon engine roaring to life. Clarence must be organising an attempt to retreat and leave.

There are bodies on the floor here, but Dave can't tell if they're from the previous battle or something to do with Howie. Too dark, and his arms are kept busy killing as he gains fleeting glimpses of the corpses littering the floor.

'HEADLIGHTS,' Dave roars with unbridled power. 'GIVE ME LIGHT.' Seconds pass before the tunnel is lit. The press of bodies blocks the light from flowing through, but just enough reflects from the ceiling of the tunnel for him to see what he is doing.

The engine of the Saxon raises in volume. They're going to be bugging out which means they'll be coming down here, and the only way to do that is to fire into the central part of the packed ranks of infected.

He has to find Howie. He must be here somewhere. He drops down, using one hand to pull bodies over while his other flicks out, keeping the lunging infected at bay.

Sweat drips from his red face, breathing becoming harder from the heat. Bodies get turned and kicked aside. Heads grabbed to be examined for the briefest of seconds.

Frustration builds as the infected press their attack harder, keeping him too occupied to concentrate on finding his leader.

Dave rarely feels anything. His mood is level and constant in the most trying of times. But tonight he has felt fear, and right now, he starts to feel rage building up. Rage that these things are preventing him from doing what he wants to do. They just keep coming and coming in a relentless wave, and there is no space to do anything.

Every time he tries to shove a corpse, he finds another zombie lunging in. The rage and frustration build and finally explode. Dave reverses his knives and goes to work, spinning with utter savagery to slice into every throat he can reach. Arms spin, and his body weaves and dances. The blows are harder now, much harder than normal as he uses the violence of the rage to drive him on.

Within seconds, he's cleared a space, and the mound of cadavers slow the ever-advancing horde. Taking the few seconds he has created, he moves swiftly back to the pile of bodies, driving his hands deep into the soft corpses.

There. A patch of dark, curly hair that he would recognise anywhere. Howie buried under two huge bodies. Dave yanks them away and stares down at the blood-encrusted face of Howie. His fingers prise the human heart from his mouth and flings it away. Howie is inert and without response. Dave wipes the filth and gore from Howie's face and turns with a snarl as the horde gain the ground he just cleared.

Howie is here, and he'll be damned if they're having him back. Dave doesn't know if Howie is alive, dead, or turned, but what matters is that Howie is by his side again. Grasping his shoulders, he quickly heaves him to the side of the tunnel and turns back as the attack surges in. Standing his ground, with Howie's lifeless body behind his heels, he fends them off, refusing to let them have his beloved leader.

The Saxon screams out and starts moving, the lights wavering and dancing, and bodies all around start being ripped apart from the heavy-calibre bullets flying through the air.

The infected turn and start towards the new threat, intent on preventing the vehicle from escaping. Dave drops down, grabbing ruined corpses and dragging them over to pile on top of Howie, taking care to keep his head and chest clear so he can breathe.

He gets in close, using his own body and those he has just killed to create a protective barrier over Howie's form. The GPMG drops more infected which Dave grabs and heaves over to pile up. As the vehicle comes into view, he hunkers down. His quick mind has already thought of trying to get Howie into the vehicle, but he knows that only by keeping the forward momentum will the Saxon get through. So he does the next best thing and protects him from the heavy bullets whilst waiting in the stifling darkness.

More bodies fall under the constant firing, the sounds become muffled and distant as both Howie and Dave start getting crushed under the bodies. Dave fights to keep the pressure from Howie's chest and keep his mouth clear. He uses the bodies as a shield, leaving just enough space for Howie to breath.

The crush of the bodies builds as the death given out above sends the corpses onto the pile, but Dave refuses to give in. Bracing himself with tears of pain streaming down his face, he holds still, taking quick gasps of heated air as he desperately fights to keep the press from Howie's upper body.

Pitch darkness now and time passes slowly. Just the muffled thud of the GPMG as it sweeps by, voices distant and weak. He waits, holding steady with a fierce grimace.

The weight on his back is immense and pushing him down harder and harder. Time stops.

Seconds become minutes, and gradually the sound of the GPMG drifts further away. Mr Howie will be pleased to know the vehicle got away. Only a few lives may have been saved, but that's enough.

He waits and holds steady, knowing that the tunnel and parking levels will still be thick with the infected. His knives are gone, dropped somewhere during the desperate movement to drag the bodies into a shield. He has one more knife attached to his belt, but that comes later. All he has to do now is wait and hold these bodies away from Mr Howie. One hand planted either side of Howie's head, his knees driving into the hard concrete, and he holds them off. Hands burning with pain, his back feels like it will snap in half any second, sweat pours from his face, and tremors start shaking through his limbs.

In the absolute silence that follows, he becomes aware of a very faint feeling of air being moved in front of his face. There are too many bodies packed in to allow any form of breeze or wind, so there is only thing it can be. Dropping his head to listen, then feels the softness of warm breath blowing against his ear. Faint but there.

'Stay alive, Mr Howie,' Dave murmurs as quietly as he can, 'just stay alive.'

CHAPTER THREE

Lani's method of ignoring the infected and simply driving through them works well. In fact, it works too well. Keeping low and moving fast, she ducks and weaves through the swirling ranks, letting their momentum carry her a few feet before forcing into the next ring and being swept along. As Dave slaughters, she gently works further in, plunging into the darkness of the ramp, knowing Howie was taken in this direction.

The heat within the enclosed ramp is staggering, making her wilt and gasp for breath. Groans from every direction, and the constant shuffle of feet scraping along the floor. Course shouts and voices screaming out from further back on the top level, but she pushes on, feeling and groping her way through the ranks.

As a human heart is forced into Howie's mouth, stifling his screams and filling his throat with fresh blood, Lani stumbles by. Just inches away, but with the dense ranks, the lack of light, and the ground already covered in bodies, she has no hope. But still she works on with an ever-growing fear of failure inside her stomach. Even if she finds him, it might be too late. He could be dead or turned, and with so many, hundreds, possibly thousands of infected still surging in, she has no hope.

Down the ramp, and she finds herself on the second level of the car park. The infected here don't swirl or turn but simply push on, driving the train further to the top level.

They don't attack, and they pay no attention to Lani as she pushes and shoves through them. The outer wall ends as the ramp gives way to the second-level parking zone. Like an unwanted guest, she is forced to the side and away from them.

The relief is immense. The crushing sensation of being trapped within so many rotten bodies is lifted, and the stench of the infected breath becomes fresh air. Filthy, bedraggled, and gasping for oxygen, she staggers free, walking further into the car park level. Moonlight streams through the open sides; orange flickering from the ceiling and walls from the flames of the burning buildings in the High Street.

Maybe Howie got here and broke free like she did. She casts about, searching the shadows and running through the many sections. Tears stream down her face at the thought of losing him. It doesn't seem real or right. Howie wouldn't go down like that, not like this. He was the one to fix these ranks away from everyone else.

Nobody could survive against that many. Maybe Dave, but they weren't after Dave. They were after Howie. He was gone, lost, dead.

Shaking her head, she refuses to accept it. Howie is alive. She can feel it. She doesn't know how, but something deep inside tells her that he is alive. They fear him for a reason, for something he has that no one else has got. What that might be is beyond her frame of mind at this time, so she runs on, continuing to search for Howie.

Light and sound fill the distance behind her. The sound of firing and the powerful headlights of the Saxon. The GPMG blasting into the ranks to force a path. She spins round, catching sight of the vehicle as it powers down the ramp, forcing swathes of infected out the sides to spill onto the parking level.

'WAIT,' Lani screams and starts sprinting towards the ramp, cursing herself for going so deep into the parking area. Shouting again and again, but she knows the sound of the machine gun and the close quarters fighting going on behind the vehicle will be drowning her out.

The infected forced out from the ramp fill the space between her and the descending Saxon. Almost too late she realises that they're not just swirling and moving now but have reverted back to the full-on attacking monsters, teeth bared and faces contorted with primeval rage.

Coming to a hasty stop, she grips the handle of the meat cleaver and starts moving away. Several break free from the group to surge towards her.

With a vicious backswing, she takes the first one down, driving the sharp edge deep into the throat. Dropping and spinning round, she comes up behind the next one, slamming the cleaver into its ankle and almost driving the blade clean through the bone. As the body falls, she kicks it hard, forcing it into the path of another one lunging in. It goes down with limbs entangled, and Lani wastes no time in slicing its throat as she backs away.

They keep coming, charging towards her, but she's fast and light, and like Dave, she moves with power and grace. Feinting left to get them lunging that way only to jolt right at the last second and chop down, severing through a spinal column.

Grunts of exertion sound out as she keeps backing away, sensing the ever-increasing size of the horde spilling out from the vehicle ramp. The Saxon has gone, and even the thud of the GPMG is dull in the distance.

They surge in as fast and as mean as ever before. The silvery moonlight giving them a look of pure horror. Yellow flickers dance from the flames still raging, and she fights quickly, knowing she's about to be overwhelmed.

Three come in fast, two males and a female. She ducks and slices deep into one of the males' groin, driving the blade deep to open the vein. Coming up from a spin, she grabs the female infected by her long, blood-soaked hair and yanks her head back, forcing the infected to stagger backwards and using her as a shield. With one hand guiding the zombie woman, she feints and moves as more come in hard. The female she grips lashes out, thrashing her hands with violent motion, which serves to batter at those lunging in.

Losing ground with every second, Lani keeps swinging out and finally shoves the woman into two more lunging in. They all go down in a heap, but the size of the group coming in is just too much. Alone, separated from her team, she screams with fury and charges in for the attack, refusing to let herself be cowed by the presence of so many infected.

Howls rip the air apart, low growls that rise in pitch and volume. Animalistic and guttural. Body after body falls under her cleaver, but more fill the space, backing her closer to the wall where there is no further space to retreat.

They sense her fear. They know she will be taken. There's nowhere else to go now, so they come in for the final charge, unabated fury pumped by harsh chemicals released from glands on overdrive. The infection raging and pushing the hosts to get this finished, take them all, destroy them and be done with it.

A nasty place to die, Lani muses to herself. A filthy multi-level car park in some shitty seaside resort that had its heyday thirty years ago. Alone, without Howie, without any of her group. Having survived being bitten once and to end like this. Fuck it. Fuck them all.

Lani roars with defiance and fights back, swinging her cleaver with wild abandon. Adrenalin courses through her body, her heart pumping to drive her on and overcome the fear of her imminent death. Howie must be alive. He must be. So every one of these killed means one less that can hurt him.

But as strong and as fast as she is, the numbers are simply too great, and their violence simply too strong. The adrenalin eases off, the rage burns out, fear grows, and a sudden longing to be anywhere else rises. Somewhere warm and beautiful. Images of her homeland fill her mind–the lush, green jungles and the white, sandy beaches lapped by crystal clear waters.

No coming back from infection this time. She beat it once, and god only knows how that happened, but this time they will tear her apart. She can see from the violence of the charge that there will be no gentle nip, no sensual kiss of death while they hold her gently. Her form will be ripped apart as hundreds of filthy mouths take deep, savage bites.

Her arm becomes heavy and slow as the finality of her life becomes apparent. If she was on the line with her team, she would never falter, but the very fact of knowing she is done for saps her strength faster than ever before.

A new sound reaches her tired ears, and her sad eyes look up as she strikes out feebly. Sweat stings her eyes, hair plastered to her forehead.

Barking. Deep, powerful barking coming from the beast that never tires. Meredith barks loud and strong, letting Lani know she is coming. Lani's heart beats stronger, fresh energy pulses into her limbs. Meredith barks and fills the air with her growls; then, she's upon them with a snarl. Several infected are removed from their feet as the almighty power of the dog drives into them at a flying leap.

Her jaws go to work: grip, savage, and shake, grip, savage, and shake. Her snarls and growls are louder than theirs, her strength greater, her speed faster. Lani is the only other female in the pack, and Meredith fights to protect her.

Her pack are separated and spread out, but now they are two, and two can fight better than one. Meredith gives voice and tells them who she is. She tells them she has killed many and will keep killing them.

Lani fights with vitality, just knowing Meredith is with her. That pack instinct is as strong in the human mind as it is within the animal. Something to fight for, something else to protect and defend.

The two females of the pack destroy the horde coming at them. Big infected males, strong and pumped up with testosterone, but they all fall from the deadly cleaver and even more deadly teeth. Two females, hot, tired, and pissed off, unleashing hell within the parking level.

The infected find that they are no longer gaining ground but are being forced to give it. Pushed back as the energy of the two bursts from their souls. Lani screaming with defiance and working straight ahead while Meredith bounds in loops round her, keeping her flanks and rear safe.

Onto the vehicle ramp, and they fight down, plunging further into the darkness. The heat of battle surges through them, and just enough light comes through the open sides to see the foes as they present themselves.

Having gone after the fleeing Saxon, the crowds of infected have thinned out considerably, and the two find themselves dealing with less and less adversity as they work their way slowly down onto the first level and move away from the ramp into the parking area.

Breaking free from the fight, they move quickly, running to gain distance before turning at the far corner and realising none of the infected have come after them. Gasping to gain control of her breathing, Lani spits and bends double, the meat cleaver hanging from one hand as sweat pours from her brow.

Meredith pants noisily, dragging ragged breaths in, and her long tongue bounces as it lollops down from her mouth. An incredible thirst rages in Lani, a dry throat that sucks all the moisture from her mouth. The heat is unbearable, truly draining, and her legs feel week, shaking from the aftereffects of the constant fighting and running.

Meredith's stare is fixed towards the ramp. Every few seconds, she holds her breath and cocks her head to listen, and only when satisfied there are no threats does she continue the noisy panting.

Feeling dizzy and faint, Lani backs to the furthest corner of the parking level and rests her back against the wall. Her legs give out, and she slides down with fresh tears making tracks to join the rivulets of sweat pouring down her cheeks.

He is alive. She knows it. He must be alive, but the only problem is–where? Completely drained and unable to summon the strength to keep going, she wills herself to get up and find him, but the energy expended from her body is claiming the high cost. Hands shake as she lifts the bloodied meat cleaver, and even Meredith sags down next to Lani, positioning herself to face the ramp.

Lani reaches over to push her fingers through the long thick fur of Meredith's back, feeling the hair and the warmth coming from her body. Licking her dry lips, she tastes the filthy metallic tang of blood in the air. Dreaming of fresh, cool water, iced lemonade, or a cold can of coke, she feels the first pull of sleep tugging at her eyes.

The darkness, the heat, the exhaustion all working in conspiracy to lull her senses into a relaxed state. Her mind fooling her into believing this little dark patch right here against the wall is safe. Quiet now too. No sounds of fighting, just the distant sound of voices shouting and the far-off crackle of fire burning.

With one hand buried in Meredith's hair, she closes her eyes and drifts off. Her last conscious image sees Howie safe and well, holding a cold bottle of water out for her.

CHAPTER FOUR

'Where did he go?' Blowers shouts amidst the carnage of the battle.

'Dunno,' Cookey yells back as he swings out with his axe to take another one down, quickly twisting the shaft in his hands as he takes the backswing and cleaves another skull open.

'Why aren't they attacking?'

'Dunno that either,' Cookey replies, hacking at a female with half her face missing.

'Can you see him?' Blowers asks after a pause of glancing between the swirling ranks. 'He went that way,' he motions with his head as Cookey glances round, nods, and starts attacking in the direction indicated.

The two lads hack a path through the rotating circles of infected, scoring kill after kill, but for every one taken down, there are scores more. The constant motion confuses them. The ranks are too dense to see anything else or to gain an idea of direction, and again, within seconds, they've lost the route they thought they were taking.

'BOSS?' Cookey yells out. 'MR HOWIE? DAVE? CLARENCE?'

'LADS?' Clarence's deep voice floats from somewhere, but again, the actual *where* is lost in the confusion and chaos surrounding them.

'This is like fucking fog,' Blowers curses and takes a vicious swing as though to chop them away and create space to see, but again, they fill the gap and keep moving round and round.

'What do we do?' Cookey shouts as he slams the end of his axe shaft into the nose of a big male zombie with a bald head.

'What you asking me for?'

'You're in charge, aren't you?' Cookey shouts back.

'Me? Fuck off!'

'You are. Mr Howie said you were like in charge ... so do something.'

'Er ... fuck it ... we'll pick a direction and just keep going.'

'I thought that's what we were doing,' Cookey exclaims.

'This way,' Blowers roars and starts attacking with fresh vigour, pausing to let Cookey fall in at his side. Always side by side. Blowers on the left, and Cookey on the right. They never changed, and it was instinct to fight this way. When Blowers lunged hard left, Cookey kept an eye on the front. When Cookey swept and hacked towards his right, Blowers would take a step forward to offer a degree of protection.

Blowers had a habit of just slightly overextending with some of his swings, something that Cookey recognised and covered for. Blowers also reverted to his boxing training and several times had started punching out when they were cornered. Cookey knew he did it through instinct, and he would shout and step in front for fear of his friend cutting his knuckles open.

For his part, Blowers watched Cookey like a hawk. Cookey was jovial and funny and brought light to their group in the darkest of times. But Cookey also wore his heart on his sleeve, and it reflected in the way he fought. If he was happy and buoyant, the lad would swipe and hack with ruthless precision. When Cookey was upset, he became a tiny bit uncontrolled, taking wilder swings and exposing himself to greater risks. It was only by fighting alongside him for so many days that Blowers had picked up on this, and now with Mr Howie gone, Cookey was starting to show his anger and fear.

'Shit,' Blowers shouts, picking up on the energy change rippling through the infected. The faces becoming warped and contorted with rage. They fight harder, hacking side by side to forge a path through the ranks. Not knowing which direction they're going but knowing that staying in the middle is no longer an option.

'Oh dear, oh dear, oh dear,' Cookey replies, desperately trying to keep the fear from his voice. Mr Howie is gone, sucked into the darkness to be taken away. Right now, there isn't time to think, just to fight and get away before they turn and start.

'NOW,' Blowers screams as area around them erupts into a frenzy of savage beasts lunging to take wild swipes and bites at the lads. Pressed in on all sides, they go back to back, each one of them swinging out left and right. Blowers still trying to forge a path through the ranks as Cookey keeps back-stepping.

'Don't fucking push me,' Blowers seethes from the constant pushing of Cookey walking into him.

'Well, fucking hurry up, then.'

'I'm fucking trying.'

'Try harder, fuckhead.'

'Cookey, you twat, that big fucker almost got me.'

'I had him!'

'Fucking hell, you are slow as shit.'

'Get fucked, Blowers, stop looking at their arses and try killin' them instead.'

'Where the fuck is everyone?' Blowers shouts after a few seconds of frantic fighting.

'No idea,' Cookey grunts, 'just keep going.'

The axe shafts become slick with blood, the two lads gripping with tight fists. The edges of the axe blades start to dull, the constant hacks and swipes through thick cartilage and bone taking their toll on the weapons. They still do deadly work, but each strike needs more force to bludgeon and chop. The relentless action drains energy, sapping strength from arms, burning coursing through shoulders. Sweat drips into eyes, causing blurred vision. Legs stumble, and feet trip over the downed corpses. The banter is gone. Just loud grunts expelled as they keep hacking and cleaving into the never-ending flow of lunging zombie faces coming in harder and harder.

Then they're free, bursting from the side, into open space. The force of the ejection sends Blowers staggering several steps and only just managing to right himself. Cookey, feeling the sudden loss of Blowers behind him, doesn't fare so well and goes down onto his arse. The lad never misses a beat and doesn't flinch but keeps hacking away.

Several come after him, lunging in at seeing him down. Blowers is there in an instant, charging in to buy his friend the few seconds he needs to get up. Cookey springs to his feet and goes back in, fury and anger pulsing through his body.

Dave screams out for headlights, his voice carried loud and clear from the entrance ramp. Seconds go by before the powerful headlights of the Saxon are on, casting fractured illumination through the ranks.

A split second later, the GPMG starts up. Both of the lads yelping as they dive away from the crowd, cursing whoever is firing for not shouting a warning.

The familiar noise of the engine bursts into the air, filling the roof space of the car park with sound.

'Who the fuck is that?' Blowers shouts.

'Why do you keep asking me stupid questions?' Cookey whines, shaking his head. 'How the fuck do I know who it is?'

The Saxon starts pulling away, the GPMG firing into the dense central section of the crowd to create a path. The two lads stare at each other, both of them sensing they are about to be left alone on the roof.

A piercing scream breaks the air behind them. The lads spin round to spot a thick wave of zombies pouring through the door to the stairwell. The few youths left on position are overwhelmed. Several taken down to be bitten and savaged, screaming with pain and horror.

Within a second, they are full-on sprinting, both of them reacting at the same instant. The vehicle might be pulling out. It might be forging a path to escape this utter terror, but the sight of children being taken down to be ripped apart causes an instinctive reaction.

Axes gripped and held high, legs pumping, and faces fixed with determination. They roar, side by side, as they plough into the infected. Using momentum and violent swings, they force the infected back, kicking, punching, lashing out left and right.

More come through the door. Blowers glances round, catching a glimpse of the Saxon pulling away, with a line of survivors behind it, fighting out. If these infected get through the stairs' door, they'll be attacking the rear of that line. Within that line, Blowers spots the huge form of Clarence swinging his double-bladed axe. They lock eyes for a split second. Blowers nods.

'THE FORT,' Clarence bellows. Blowers nods again. If the Saxon stops, they'll lose the momentum and get bogged in. If Blowers and Cookey try to run for them, this lot from the stairs will surge in.

No choice, this line has to be held. Turning back, he shoulders in next to Cookey and joins him at the wooden double doors. They fight on, slowly pushing through until they gain the top of the wide concrete stairs, using the height advantage to hack down into the horde coming up.

The bodies mount and again create a natural obstacle for those infected still trying to clamber up the stairs. The lads take the opportunity and drop down to the next landing, taking ground and fighting on, dropping more bodies to fall and encumber those coming up.

The stairwell is darker, and as with the vehicle tunnel, the hot, foul air is trapped, building the heat to a staggering temperature. Losing valuable fluids with every second, they fight and swing, step and swing, trip and curse with increasingly dry mouths. Unable to spit or speak, their throats burn, and their eyes sting. Heads pound with pain as the dehydration builds. The ferocious action is relentless, but they don't falter. They have the upper hand, and they press that advantage home. Both of them ignoring the intense discomfort to wreak havoc and drive the infected back down the stairs.

The concrete walls, the concrete steps, the handrails all drip with blood, gore and bits of body. Blowers feels the dampness of hot blood on his trousers. Cookey scowls as his top clings to his frame from sweat and fluids.

Down they go, reaching the next landing, winning their small war against the infected. Snarling with fury, they hack and kill, bursting skulls apart and kicking out to ram the soles of their boots into noses.

Past the doors to the next level, with no idea that Lani and Meredith rest across the expanse. Believing everyone else has gone with the Saxon, they press on, determined to reach the bottom. Fuck it, there might be another thousand of them waiting, and they'll probably end up just fighting back up to the top, but they can do it. The two of them can take these stairs. Their own private battle. The two lads acting as one against the infected. Both of them refusing to let the utter exhaustion slow them down, and sheer, stubborn pride pushes them on.

The last flight and the darkest part, with no ambient light coming in. Sordid and dirty. The gritty reality of the situation starts to hit them. What happens when they reach the bottom? How the fuck will they get away? Neither Blowers nor Cookey blame Clarence for leaving. The children had to be saved, and they know the chances of walking away from something like this are very slim.

As a unit, together with the others, they have survived incredible odds, but that was as part of something special with Mr Howie and Dave. When Mr Howie went into *that zone,* nothing could stop him. They'd all seen it time and again. But Mr Howie isn't here. Dave and Clarence aren't here. Or Nick or Lani or Meredith with her strong jaws.

Just the two of them, fighting with an ever-growing sensation that all is not well. The team have fractured and splintered, and for the first time, they both genuinely feel this really might be it.

The last few steps down, and a sliver of light comes through the dirty glass panes of the double doors leading out onto the street. They cut the last few down and stagger those final few steps to the doors. Both of them staring with hard eyes, waiting for the next surge to come powering through.

'I ain't going back up,' Blowers growls. 'Fuck that, mate.'

'Kay,' Cookey mutters, too exhausted to argue or even reply with anything funny.

'We're going out,' Blowers adds.

'Kay.'

'Fuck 'em.'

'Kay,' Cookey tries to spit, but his mouth is too dry. He coughs to clear his throat, but it is too dry. Even swallowing causes pain now. No longer sweating either. His body has ceased to waste fluids and instead diverts them to the essential internal organs. With no ability to sweat, his body will soon become overheated. Heatstroke and exposure are setting in, and any further dehydration will lead to hallucinations. The thought of doing anything is beyond him, so instead, he'll follow Blowers because Blowers is his mate, and that means something.

It means the exhaustion and the dehydration can go fuck themselves. The pounding headache can kiss his arse. The thirst can piss off and annoy someone else. He nods, a grim act with a pursed mouth and a brow set. He won't fail now. Not yet. Maybe in a few minutes when they charge outside and hit the enormous horde waiting for them. Maybe when his arms can no longer swing, and his legs can no longer kick. Maybe when he falters and goes down, and they come in for the bite. Maybe then he will fail.

But not now. Now he readjusts his grip on his axe and looks over at Blowers. Blowers stares back at his friend for a second. He feels exactly the same way, his own body mirroring that of Cookey and no longer sweating.

They turn to face the doors, lips curling up into snarls. They could stay here and wait it out, maybe go back up and try to find some fluids. There are several options that do not involve charging out of these doors and into certain death, but that is not the way this team works, and that is not the way Mr Howie led them to be.

The infected are out there. The dirty, fetid, diseased undead. And not too far away, there will be an old British Army armoured personnel carrier travelling slowly back to the fort, with a trail of desperate children running behind it. So for that reason, they will go out and create merry hell. They will scream and roar and bring the attention onto them. That is the team's way, and that is what Mr Howie would do.

'Ready, Cookey?'

'Yes, Mr Fucktard,' Cookey replies.

'HAVE IT,' Blowers screams, launching himself at the doors with a violent yell. His axe hits the doors first; then, his body slams into the hard wood and bounces back off to fall into heap on the bloodied and mangled corpses.

'It open inwards, you fucking idiot,' Cookey bursts out laughing, hard guffaws that bring him to his knees at the sight of a demented Blowers screaming blue murder, only to bounce off and fall flat on his arse. 'It ... fucking hell ... you fucking dick ...' Cookey gasps for breath, bent double as the laughs bursting from his throat cause him physical pain, 'opens inwards ... oh, fucking hell ... that's the best thing ever ...'

'Fuck off, twat,' Blowers slowly gets to his feet, retrieving his fallen axe. He stares at Cookey for a second, a small smile twitching at the corners of his mouth at the sight of his mate bent double, crying with laughter, and he starts to chuckle at himself. Feeling a slight burn in his face at the heroic image of bouncing off the doors.

'Have it ...' Cookey repeats his final words through ragged breaths, 'he said have it ... Oh, it's too much ... I fucking wish everyone else was here ...'

The laughter is as infectious as the virus carried by the undead, and within seconds, Blowers is exhibiting symptoms, tears streaming down his face as the nervous energy is expended. Both of them leaning against the wall, laughing harder and harder, and the more they go, the more they set each other off.

Nearing hysteria, with a few genuine tears mixed into the ones caused by laughing, they start to bring themselves back down. A deep sadness pervading their souls as they take stock of the awful situation. With no idea where any of the others are and facing a huge horde outside the doors, the few minutes of laughing drop them lower than before.

'Why haven't they come through?' Cookey asks. If the doors open inwards, the horde could have come in with ease. Blowers grabs one of the handles and tugs it open. A stupid move, considering what could be on the other side, but exhaustion clouds their normally alert minds.

'Fuck,' Blowers mutters, staring at the empty scene. Cookey steps through, joining his friend to stare out, at the street. The flames of the burning High Street flicker and dance off the sides of the car park. Bodies litter the ground everywhere, crushed and shot to bits, but other than the odd crawler pathetically dragging itself on bloodied stumps trailing long, black, glistening innards, there are no undead, no zombies, no walkers.

'Where have ...?'

'Dunno,' Cookey cuts him off, his axe still gripped, raised, and ready to fight. Slowly, he lowers his arms and lets the axe hang at his side. 'You must have scared 'em off, mate.'

Blowers turns slowly to stare at Cookey, too exhausted to ask and knowing he doesn't need to.

'That commando entry there ...' Cookey turns to look at him. 'They knew they were outmatched.'

'Or they fucked off from sheer embarrassment more likely,' Blowers snorts.

'You think they took Mr Howie with them?'

'Fuck knows,' Blowers shrugs. 'Don't seem right, though.'

'What doesn't?'

'Mr Howie going like that. It's ... well, it's fucked up ... like ...' he shrugs again, his mind foggy and feeling numb.

Cookey pauses, then takes the thought process up, 'Dave went after him. I saw him.'

'Yeah?'

Cookey nods. 'Dave won't let anything happen to him. He'd kill the lot with his bare hands ...'

'So where are they, then? And where the fuck are the zombies?'

'Dunno,' Cookey sighs, 'or anyone else. Clarence was behind the Saxon. What about Lani and Nick? Did you see the dog?'

'Maddox was with Clarence. I'm sure I saw him,' Blowers replies, staring round and settling on the closest crawler trying unsuccessfully to clamber over a pile of bodies. 'Why doesn't it just go round?' Blowers asks.

'Eh?'

'That thing,' he nods at the crawler. 'He's trying to go over when he could just go round.'

'Oh,' Cookey turns to watch, 'yeah ... Stupid fucker. Mind you, they ain't all that dumb. Lani went flying off when Mr Howie got pulled away. I thought Nick was with Clarence tonight. He must have got out with the Saxon.'

'Yeah, hope so,' Blowers nods. 'Lani must be with Dave and the boss, then.'

'Yeah, yeah, definitely ...' Cookey mutters, both of them trying desperately not to think of the consequences of the other option.

'I'm fucked, mate,' Blowers sighs deeply.

'Really? I must have missed that. Big, was he?'

'Very funny, come on ...'

'Where we going?'

'Find a drink. I'm gagging.'

'Kay, we get a drink then and grab a car, yeah? Head back to the fort. Or should we stay here and look for the others?'

'Drink first,' Blowers steps off, still staring at the crawler who almost makes it to the top of the pile before slipping back down with a groan. 'Drink first and then think about it,' Blowers pulls his knife and stabs down, driving the point deep into the skull before placing his foot on the zombie's neck and yanking the blade out.

Cookey walks by, looking down at the bare arse of the zombie exposed to the air from the clothing torn away. He grins quickly, looking at Blowers with a sudden glint in his eye.

'Don't,' Blowers groans, 'please ... just don't fucking start ...'

'Fuck it ... I'm too tired,' Cookey coughs and rubs his throat, trying to swallow and feeling the pain spreading across his forehead. 'Your legs shaking?'

'Yes, mate,' Blowers replies, 'feel like shit.'

'We need to drink, fuckhead. Let's head away from the town and find a house.'

'Yeah, great plan, cockchops.'

'What? What's wrong with it?'

'No, seriously, it is a good plan,' Blowers says with as much sincerity as he can muster.

'Oh, thought you were being sarcastic.'

'Me!?' Blowers asks. 'Oh, fuck it ... I'm too tired, mate. Can we banter later?'

'Kay.'

Stepping over bodies and around the dark patches of gore, they move slowly away from the town, pushing deeper into the dark streets and away from the flaming town centre. With the car park already at the far end of the High Street, it takes them just minutes to reach the first residential street. Signs of devastation everywhere–not a window intact or a door not ripped off. Cars smashed up or burnt to a molten lump.

Exhausted, they plod on in silence. If it wasn't for the raging thirst burning, they would happily fall down on the spot. But thirst, proper thirst, raging thirst takes over everything else. It pushes the body and fills the mind with a never-ending claxon. All other thoughts are meaningless when the body needs water, feelings of loss and grief mean nothing. Even the possibility of Mr Howie being killed or taken is now not the primary thought. Just the thirst.

The day's solid, strength sapping heat, the fires raging

nearby, the fighting, the running and firing, close quarters battle have all taken their toll.

Like the infected they kill, the two lads stagger up the first path to the dark house, clumsily kicking the broken door aside and threading their way through the hallway and to the kitchen at the rear.

Cupboards ransacked and emptied of food, and a foul stench emanating from the fridge freezer is ignored as they go straight for the tap. One filthy hand twists the metal, and they both feel a slight thrill as water bursts from the tap, cascading noisily into the stainless steel bowl. It's the sweetest sound they've ever heard, and for a second, they just stare down and watch the water flow. Cookey dips in, mouth already open.

'Let it run,' Blowers mutters, blocking his path. 'You got a torch?'

'Yeah,' Cookey digs a small flashlight from his pocket as Blowers retrieves a glass from a shelf. He fills the glass and holds it up as Cookey shines the torch into it.

'Looks clear,' Blowers croaks. 'Here, mate,' he offers the first glass to Cookey.

'You have it,' Cookey urges. There are more glasses, but the act is symbolic, a gesture of their closeness and the sacrifice they would both make for the other.

Blowers pauses, then slowly lifts the glass to his mouth, taking that first slow sip as the cooling liquid floods his parched lips and tongue. The water instantly soothes his throat, and he can feel the chill of it tumbling down into his stomach. Reflex action kicks in, and the glass is lifted higher as he downs it, opening his throat to take noisy gulps and letting the water spill down his chin.

Glass drained, he slowly takes it away, opening his eyes to look over at Cookey and give him a satisfied smile.

However, Cookey is already bent over the sink, with his mouth stuck to the end of the tap, slurping the water as it runs.

'Greedy fucker,' Blower burps. 'Move over.'

'Fuck off. Go upstairs,' Cookey gurgles.

'Bastard,' Blowers grumbles and pulls Cookey's torch from his hand to shine a path back down the hallway and up the stairs, to the bathroom.

For long minutes, the lads remain in silence, mouths stuck to the ends of the taps as they slurp and drink, filling their stomachs with the lifesaving liquid.

Energy starts to flow back into them. Normal cognitive function resumes as the pressing urge to stay alive abates.

They strip tops off, letting the water run over their filth-encrusted faces. Hands are scrubbed with washing-up liquid and shower gel. Faces are rubbed, and hair is rinsed through. Chests are soaped and rinsed off. ` Neither of them paying any attention to the black water running from them onto the floor.

Once cleaned, they drink more, and Blowers heads back downstairs to find Cookey sat in the dark, with his back to the units, the orange glow of a cigarette dangling from his mouth.

Blowers slumps down next to him, taking the offered smoke and lighter, shielding his eyes from the glare as he takes the first pull.

'You smell nice,' Cookey comments quietly.

'Shower gel. Found it in the bathroom.'

'Oh.'

'You smell of Fairy washing-up liquid.'

'That,' Cookey replies, 'is because I used Fairy washing-up liquid ... but I am not surprised you recognised the smell of Fair–'

'Fuck off,' Blowers cuts him off.

'That water was fucking nice,' Cookey says after a quiet pause of smoking.

'Yup,' Blowers replies, blowing smoke away. 'I'm fucked, mate, utterly fucked ... I don't think I can move for a minute.'

'We'll give it five, then go back out,' Cookey yawns, stretching his aching legs out.

'Don't ...' Blowers tuts, then yawns himself, rolling his sore shoulders and craning his head to one side, easing the pain in the back of his neck from swinging the heavy axe so much.

Just as Lani convinced herself that she will rest just for a minute, the lads do the same and start to feel the tug as eyelids get heavier. There is no weakness here. They are young and strong, but the body can only function for so long before it is ordered to rest by the brain.

So rest is given, and breathing slows as they fall into a deep sleep that is close to being unconscious.

CHAPTER FIVE

The Roman Empire was strong and held power for a long time. Tribe and country fell before it as they sought to dominate the known world. Using military tactics still deployed in modern times, they fought battles with opponents many times their number.

But then the giants came. They came from the north where the countries were cold, and you had to be big to survive. They landed on the shores of England, saw the green, lush, fertile land, and they took it.

Nothing could stand before them. Physically huge, with legendary strength. They fought with passion and feeling. They had honour and unity, and those genes passed through the generations, and still to this day, the gene of those peoples is as pure as it was before.

He stands a head taller than most. Shoulders wide and powerful, arms thick with muscle, legs solid and unbreakable. A warrior born and a soldier made through years of training and discipline. A sense of honour runs through him, and a deep instinct to protect those unable to defend themselves.

If time went back a thousand years, and he was dressed in a sheepskin sleeveless jacket, with course woollen leggings, he would perfectly match the giants from the North. Now, in this modern time, he grips the double-bladed axe and watches as Mr Howie is taken away.

His keen eyes watch as the boss is ripped away, deep into the ranks. His heart pounds, pumping his muscles with rich, oxygenated blood. Adrenalin pumps, testosterone pours into his system as his body makes ready to charge and take the boss back.

But his feet do not move. Instead, his eyes glance back to the children scattered in front of the Saxon. They still hack and kill with blind fury, and they do deadly work, but the giant knows these things will turn, and when they do, these children will fall.

Conflict rages within him. Mr Howie must survive. He has an ability to unite the people around him into a fearsome machine, flawlessly using people's strengths to cover others' weaknesses. Without Howie's power, the risk is they will falter and become just another band of survivors trying to get by.

Movement catches his eye–Dave spinning to leap high and watch the direction Howie is taken. Clarence nods, a tiny movement done without conscious thought. Dave is going after him. As strong and as powerful as Clarence is, as much as he has the nature of the Viking Berserker within him, he knows he can never hope to match or equal what Dave can do.

Decision made. The soldier once more makes the rational and right decision, overpowering the urge of the heart.

'MADDOX,' Clarence roars, spinning round to pick

out the adults nearby, 'GET EVERYONE BEHIND THE VEHICLE ... NICK?'

'Here,' Nick screams back from a few feet away, slicing his axe into the back of a male infected.

'Get on the GPMG and make ready.'

'What about the boss?'

'NOW!' Clarence bellows. 'Dave is going after him. Get on that gun.'

'The others ...'

'Nick,' Clarence glares over, 'we have to get these kids out while we can ... We're going now.'

Nick spins round, viewing the children armed to the teeth as they hack and slaughter away. They look ferocious and deadly, but it was only a short time ago most of them were crying and looking terrified at the body parts being flung out and the fucked-up laughing from the infected. Clarence is right, the team might be splintered, but Dave is going after the boss, and the others are hard enough and experienced enough to fight their way out.

He nods and starts back, threading his way through the youths towards the vehicle already loaded up with the youngest picked by Maddox.

'What?' Maddox shouts as he gets closer to Clarence, the flush of battle is evident on his face, a long-bladed knife held tight in his hand, thick blood dripping from its blade.

'Get everyone behind the vehicle, facing out. ROY ... get behind the wheel and get ready to drive ... PAULA, get inside with Roy ...'

'Why?' Paula demands.

'Protect the kids inside, the two of you,' Clarence barks as he starts pushing children to the back of the vehicle. 'NOW ... MOVE NOW ... GET BEHIND THE SAXON.'

'Come on,' Roy tugs at Paula, pulling her towards the vehicle.

'I can stay outside and fight,' Paula shouts.

'He's right,' Roy replies. 'Get in.'

'No, Roy,' she pulls her arm free.

'Just get in,' he urges in the same calm voice, half ushering and half pushing a protesting Paula towards the door.

Maddox works with Clarence, ordering the children to the back. Darius, Jagger, and Mohammed quickly work out what is needed and run back and forth, getting the strongest kids to the outside, facing out and the youngest behind them.

'HEADLIGHTS ... GIVE ME LIGHT,' Dave's voice booms across the top level of the car park. Roy fumbles with the controls, finding the switch to flick the lights on to full beam. The engine rumbles into life, and Nick shoves his way through the packed interior to climb up and make ready with the machine gun.

'Roy, just keep going straight and don't stop,' Nick shouts down. 'If we keep momentum, we'll punch through.'

'Got it,' Roy shouts back, his tongue probing along his gum line at a new sensation and a possible swelling at the back. 'Is my Corsodyl here anywhere?' he asks mildly.

'Look at me,' Paula snaps. 'Open,' she adds as he turns to face her. She shines a torch into his mouth, quickly glancing to the top, bottom, and sides. 'Nothing there, Roy, looks clear.'

'Sure?'

'Totally,' she nods with sincerity.

'NOW,' Clarence bellows. The GPMG commences firing, eliciting a yelp of alarm from the young children crowded into the rear. Nick aims high for a short burst, giving a warning shot to any of the team still within the ranks of infected.

Roy pushes his foot down, feeling the immense power and weight of the vehicle as it pulls away with a throaty roar. Nick holds for as long as he dares, grimacing with fear while praying the team aren't in the way.

'NOW, NICK,' Clarence shouts.

He squeezes the trigger, feeling the solid recoil of the weapon as it starts thudding. Sending the large calibre rounds whipping through the ranks. Bodies burst apart as he focusses on a narrow section immediately in front of the vehicle. With the weapon slaughtering them down, Roy increases the speed. Driving into the ranks and watching with delight as the solid front wings batter the zombies away.

'I fucking love this vehicle,' he shouts, earning a quick puzzled look from Paula. She turns back, watching with interest as the power of the heavy machine gun cuts swathes of zombies down. Heads exploding, chests bursting apart, limbs torn off.

Behind the vehicle, the youths move quickly to keep up, travelling at a half running pace while facing out. Within a few seconds, the Saxon is deep within the infected. Clarence watches as they change, the energy pulsing through them.

'GET READY,' he shouts to those around him, 'STAY CLOSE AND KEEP MOVING ...'

Faces contort with rage. The hunger takes over as the infection makes the horde ready. A split second later, and they're charging, thundering into the sides of the vehicle and the lines of youths facing out.

Several children go down from the initial impact, overwhelmed by the ferocity of the attack. The rest fight for their lives, trying hard to keep up with the vehicle while fending the zombies off.

Maddox moves amongst them, shoving youths into gaps that open up as children get taken down.

Into the tunnel, and the ranks press tighter, the vehicle gathering speed, which causes the youths to run faster. Clarence feels the urge to shout to slow down, but he knows speed is of the essence now, and they must maintain the progress.

Within the enclosed tunnel, the fighting eases off until they reach the first opening for the second level. The Saxon batters huge sections of infected out to the sides, who then thrust back in to attack the strung-out lines at the rear.

Nick fires intelligently, knowing the last magazine is being rapidly depleted and trying to hold back for when they reach the bottom.

Down they go, turning round the circular road to descend ever closer to the ground level. The youths pant and gasp for air, sweat pours from faces, and hands become slick as they grip weapons. Children trip and fall from the broken bodies underfoot. Maddox, Darius, and the older ones run to drag them up and get them going again.

Clarence takes the far rear, holding the huge following off with his almighty strength, swinging the double-bladed axe with his grip right at the end of the shaft as he makes full use of the length of the weapon.

Counting off the levels, he knows they're on the final section now, praying to any god listening that they can punch through the thick horde at the bottom.

Nick stares with unblinking eyes as the road twists round to reveal the bottom access ramp. Thick ranks push forward and drive into the opening, desperate to prevent the vehicle from leaving.

Nick sees the opportunity. With the height advantage and the position, he attempts to '*do a Dave*' and sweeps the aim at head height, watching with satisfaction as skull after skull pops open.

Seeing the dense crowd, Roy knows speed and power is the only way through. Pushing his foot down onto the accelerator, he surges the vehicle into the crowd, slamming the hard front into the front ranks. Nick switches back to firing directly in front, cutting a path for Roy to follow.

As soon as the back end of the vehicle leaves the relative safety of the tunnel, the infected once more surge into the lines at the rear.

Maddox jumps onto the back of the Saxon, heaving himself up to look ahead. There are too many to fight out like this, but up ahead are two side junctions, one either side of the road.

Dropping down, he works to the middle of the lines. 'WHEN I SAY,' he shouts, his voice rich and deep, 'STARBURST ... YOU GET ME? YOU FUCKING STARBURST AND DO ONE ...'

'What?' Clarence shouts.

'We don't stand a chance like this, trust me ...' Maddox replies. The crews cannot stand toe to toe with so many adult zombies coming in like this. Their strength won't hold out. But they're fast and nimble, years spent legging it from police and angry shopkeepers, other gangs or whatever threat they perceived.

Maddox stares to the side, willing the junction to come into view.

'ALMOST OUT,' Nick shouts. He keeps the pressure up, doing his best to cleave a route for Roy. Then it's done. The weapon clicks empty, and without a further thought, he prises himself out and shouts for someone to pass his axe up. Grasping the shaft, he scurries across the back and drops down to land within the lines, quickly moving to the back to fight with Clarence.

'They're starbursting,' Clarence grunts.

'Who?'

'This lot. They're gonna leg it when Maddox says ... LISTEN IN,' he shouts, 'STAY LOCAL, AND WE'LL COME BACK FOR YOU OR HEAD SOUTH TO THE FORT ...'

'NOW,' Maddox clocks the first junction coming into view, 'GO ... STARBURST ... GO ...' The line breaks as the youths do what they do best and make it look like they were never here.

Small bodies that duck and weave through the packed ranks, scooting between legs. Heads down and legs pumping. They burst away in every direction possible. Some don't make it and get taken down instantly. Some get several strides only to be savaged, but many break out. Council estate living giving them good skills.

Clarence and Nick are caught out. The protection of the line is gone, and the infected surge in. Within seconds, they're separated and fighting individually. Clarence, being that bit taller, manages to keep an eye on Nick's position for a few seconds, bellowing for the lad to join him.

Overwhelmed and sensing he has just seconds to either do something or die, Nick follows the course of action taken by the youths and breaks out, pushing and fighting his way to the side to break free.

Clarence watches him go and starts going after him, but Nick moves faster than he is able to, and then he's gone from view, absorbed into the darkness and chaos.

'NICK?'

'GO,' Nick screams back.

'GET TO THE FORT.'

'GO ... I WILL ... GO ... I'M OUT ...'

Clarence nods and starts running for the back of the vehicle, using his massive hands to simply swat the infected aside. With a leap, he gains the back ledge and heaves himself up onto the roof, banging down hard on the solid metal casing, 'GO, ROY ... PUT YOUR FOOT DOWN.'

Roy heeds the order and pushes the vehicle harder. Ploughing the hard front into the bodies to batter them down.

The infected try the same grounding tactic and move quickly to drop in front of the vehicle in an attempt to ground it out, but Roy changes direction, simply turning the wheel to weave and snake through them.

'Clever bastard,' Clarence mutters, wishing he'd thought to do that. Gripping the GPMG hole, he watches as the front of the horde starts thinning out, craning his head to see hundreds and hundreds of them still charging after them. Nodding with satisfaction, he wills them to keep coming, giving those that have escaped a fighting chance to get to safety.

Finally they're out, bursting the last few apart as the Saxon gains free ground and speeds up.

Reminding himself that Dave went after the boss, he still feels the same sense of fear and desperation the others feel. The first time they've been split apart like this, and they each feel it. That sense of loss, of strength and unity. The big man wills them to just hunker down and survive, find a hole to dig in and wait for him to come back.

He pats the roof of the vehicle gently. The Saxon is as much part of the team as anyone else, and between them, they are the strongest, and they will come back.

Nick shouts for Clarence to go. He knows those youths will need him if they stand a chance of surviving. He breaks free of the horde, swinging his axe to make a path of broken bodies. Once out, he sprints, pumping his legs as fast as possible to gain distance from the horde.

The youths are gone, vanished from sight as they ran towards the darkest shadows. Nick gets into the side junction and keeps going straight for as long as his legs and lungs will allow. With a hasty, snatched glance behind, he realises only a few have come after him, so he slows down and works to control his breathing.

Head pounding with pain. The same effects felt by Lani and the other lads flood through Nick. Dry mouth, burning throat, legs shaking, and the sweat no longer coming.

Slowing to a walk, he forces himself to take deep breaths, turning to walk backwards and gripping the axe as he watches them run down the road. His keen eyes sweep the small group, picking out the fastest and strongest. One sprints forward, streaking ahead of the others. Nick starts jogging backwards, hefting his axe and making ready. At the last second, he charges forward, taking the fight to the infected. Axe up and swinging; its head detached from the neck to roll off into the gutter.

He spins round and swings out, slicing deep into a shoulder before wrenching it free and snapping the shaft back to ram the hard end into the face of one lunging in. As the infected starts to drop, he slams the blunt edge down, fracturing the skull and sending shards of bone into the brain.

The next one is taken off her feet by the recoil of Nick's

previous swing. She sails through the air to slam down onto the windscreen of a car, the alarm warbling out noisily into the near silent street.

Just a few left, and Nick starts going backwards again, letting them come to him and chopping them down as they come in for the attack.

With a long, strung-out line of chopped-up corpses, he works further into the quiet residential street. Hacking with increasingly tired and heavy arms, he takes the last few down and then stands with chest heaving at the empty street ahead of him.

With those last ones killed, the silence hits him hard. After the constant noise of the battle, it doesn't seem real, and for a second, he wonders if he died and this is the after-life. It just doesn't seem right. The stars twinkle bright in the night sky and the moon shines silver, the same as ever. The houses look normal, and he realises the car alarm has stopped.

Looking down he takes in the layers of gore on his hands and clothes. With a sigh, he turns and walks further into the street. This area isn't safe to stop.

Two streets down, and he picks a dark house with an undamaged front door, checking the rooms before he goes back to lock the door. Into the kitchen, and he does the same as Cookey and Blowers, twisting the cold tap on to suck the water into his parched mouth.

He drinks and drinks, sucking water into his stomach before holding his head under the tap to start washing the filth and dried sweat away.

Legs shake as his mind sends signals that the danger of imminent death has gone. With trembling hands, he scrubs and washes, using washing-up liquid which gets into his eyes and makes them burn.

Unlike the others, Nick has that last bit of strength left to strip off and scrub his top in the running water, rinsing the worst of the filth away before wringing it out and draping it over a chair. Then his boots come off, peeling away the stinking, sodden socks. Lifting one foot in turn, he holds them under the water, then makes his way upstairs to root through drawers until he finds clean socks.

Sitting on the edge of a big, soft double bed, he stares down at the filth on his trousers. Infected blood will be all over them, so he strips them off too. His exhausted mind isn't thinking straight as he strips off and heads back into the bathroom to wash his legs. Moving like a robot, he finds himself back in the bedroom, unable to remember the last ten minutes.

Drunk on water and drained to the point of passing out, he sinks back, feeling the softness of the bed envelope him. The smell of laundered sheets drift into his nose, clean and dry now. Where are the others? Are they alive?

It takes little more than a few seconds before his mind shuts down.

Lani sleeps with her back to a grimy wall in the car park. Cookey and Blowers side by side in a dark kitchen. Nick flat-out on a double bed in a quiet, dark house. Meredith sleeps with ears pricked and listening.

Two more of the team are within the car park. One small man that walks slowly back up the ramp. In his hand, he carries a double-bladed axe, and over his shoulder, he carries the unconscious form of his leader.

He stands at the top and sweeps the view of broken bodies. There will be weapons here, so he gently rests

Howie in the corner and moves quickly round, collecting all the fallen weapons.

Moving back to Howie's side, he works through them, ejecting magazines as he looks for rounds. Between all the dropped guns, he scavenges enough unused rounds for a few full magazines, loading two of the weapons up and pocketing the rest. Back on his feet, he straps the two rifles to his back, then manhandles Howie up and over his shoulder before squatting down to scoop the axe up.

Pain doesn't factor, exhaustion doesn't matter. He feels the same as the others, but Dave is different. He just ignores it and carries on the same as before.

Carrying the heavy load, he makes his way quietly down the stairs, into the street, and then away from the town. Each step is taken as gently as possible to prevent causing discomfort to Howie, and slowly he gets into the side streets.

Like Nick, he finds a dark house and gets inside, laying Howie down on the sofa before checking each room.

Back at the front door, he stares out for long seconds, listening intently. He lets his mind absorb the natural sounds as he glances up to view the same sky that Nick looks at.

Like a sentinel, he stands strong and quiet. The team is separated, but they've been taught well, and they're capable. They'll survive. Dave knows this.

But will Mr Howie survive? Will he come through whatever happened to him before Dave found him?

A rare look of worry settles on his face as he glances back into the lounge doorway. Sighing, he quietly closes the door.

CHAPTER SIX

'Oh no, said the brown bear. How will I eat my porridge now? I will have to find another spoon. So the brown bear set off to find another spoon ...'

'Dad.'

'Yes?'

'I'm hungry, Dad.'

Holding the picture book open on his lap, Andrew looks down at the young face staring up at him. Pain shoots through his heart at the thought of his child going without food for another day.

'I'm sorry, but we'll have something in the morning.'

'Where from?'

'Pardon,' Andrew asks, surprised at the question.

'Where will the food come from, Daddy? We don't have any, and you said the shops have all run out.'

'Well,' Andrew smiles, 'I will just have to find some, won't I?'

'When, Daddy?'

'Tonight. I will find something yummy tonight.'

'But ...' the child stares with frightened eyes.

'Hey now,' the man soothes the child. 'Lilly will stay with you, and when you wake up, there will be something nice to eat.'

'Like sweets?'

'Maybe not sweets but ...'

'Cake?'

'Well, maybe not cake either, but something ... something nice, I promise.'

'You promise, Daddy?'

'I promise,' Andrew closes the book and leans forward from his chair beside the bed, kissing the boy on the forehead. 'Now go to sleep and have nice dreams.'

'I'll try,' the boy yawns and smiles up at his father.

'And remember, what happens if you wake up in the night?'

'Don't make any noise and don't call out,' the boy replies sleepily.

'Good boy,' Andrew kisses his son's head again and gently moves out of the room, leaving a single small candle burning on the dresser. With thick curtains and even thicker blankets fixed across the window, he knows none of the light will escape, and the candle will be blown out as soon as the boy nods off.

Moving quietly across the landing of the large flat, he stands in the doorway of the lounge. The soft flicker of candlelight dances across the walls. Desperately hot, he wipes the sweat from his forehead and starts wringing his hands, knowing what he has to do and dreading it.

'I've got to get food,' he says quietly. Stepping into the room, he looks down at his daughter using the meagre light to read. She looks up with an instant worried look, her brow knotting in concern.

'Wait till tomorrow,' she whispers.

Shaking his head and wringing his hands, he then realises the worry he is displaying to his daughter, quickly dropping his hands to his sides before smiling broadly. It's a fake smile, and he hopes she won't notice the lack of humour in his eyes. 'Neither of you have eaten today,' he replies.

'We can wait till tomorrow,' she repeats, 'and you didn't eat yesterday, so I should go out–'

'No,' he cuts her off firmly.

'Dad, you're exhausted ... I can find something just as ...'

'I said no,' he snaps, holding a hand up.

'Dad,' she pleads with an urgent tone, 'you look terrible. You haven't slept for three days. I can go and find something.'

'Lilly, I said no,' he repeats with an increasingly firm tone.

'Well, where are you going, then?'

'I don't know,' he shrugs, frantically thinking of where to try next. All the houses locally have been looted. The local shop was cleared out the day after it happened, and now, twelve days in, finding food is getting harder.

At first he was simply running to one of the many local houses to raid the kitchen, but increasingly, he found someone had got there before him and taken everything edible. He knew he'd have to go further out, but that meant exposing himself to greater risk, and the thought of leaving his children alone terrified him more than going out.

'Dad, I haven't been outside for what ... twelve days now ... Please let me go,' Lilly begs. Even in the dark shadows of the doorway, she can see the deep bags under his eyes. His face looks ashen and sallow, his cheeks sunken from lack of food and sleep. His hair looks greyer than ever before, and the normally jovial, kind, loving man was slowly being replaced by a nervous wreck barely holding it together.

He doesn't reply but just shakes his head. Thinking of where to try next, which street to go to and trying to remember where he last saw those things. But the lack of food and sleep are taking their toll, and his mind finds it harder to fix onto anything more than a simple thought process.

'Your mother wouldn't want that,' he says at length. 'She will never forgive me if she found out I left you alone. When she gets back, she will ask if I left, and you know I can't lie to her ...'

'Dad,' Lilly says softly, 'Mum isn't coming back. She's gone, Dad ...'

'No,' he hisses, 'she will come back ... I promised William she'll be back.'

Standing up slowly, she crosses the room to stand in front of her father, folding her arms as she gets ready for *the conversation* again.

'Dad, you have to tell him the truth. How long can we stay here for? The food is running out, and the water could end any minute. We don't even know if it's clean anymore ...'

'Of course, it's clean.'

'No, it looks clean, but there could be anything in it now. We did a lesson in biology and the teacher said–'

'I don't care what your teacher said. The water is fine.'

'Okay,' she softens her tone. 'What about Mum? She isn't coming back, Dad. We have to accept that and find somewhere else to stay.'

'Lilly, we are not leaving. How will she know where we've gone to? How will she find us? We have to wait here until she–'

'Dad, please,' Lilly pleads, 'you said there's no food. We haven't eaten today, and you haven't eaten for ages ... It's not safe here. William can't make any noise. He can't go outside ... He looks ill, Dad. Have you seen how pale he is?'

'We just have to wait,' he replies quietly. Lilly stares at him, sensing his resolve weakening. He usually would have bitten her head off by now for pushing the point so much.

Seizing the chance, she presses on, speaking in a low but urgent tone, 'We're too close to the town here. They stagger past all the time. What if they hear us? We can leave a note for mum and tell her which direction we're going. Tell her we'll get to someplace and wait there for a week.'

'Like where?'

'The harbour where the boat was kept,' she replies, referring to the small inlet on the coast where her father used to keep his speedboat. But that was before the recession and before he lost his business and before they had to move into this flat because of the house being repossessed and Mum going back to work while Dad became increasingly depressed.

'She knows where that is, and it's in a rural place with only a few houses ... Leave a note saying we'll go there every day at twelve and wait an hour ...'

'You've thought this through, then,' he comments drily.

'Yes,' she keeps going, sensing he is really listening this time, 'we'll take the first car we can find and just drive away. We can get food on the way, and we might, like, meet other survivors or families ... There might be soldiers or something.'

'Lilly, you haven't seen what it's like out there,' he whispers.

'If it's that bad, then why are we staying here?'

'We are waiting for your mother,' he replies in a tone

that implies she is being stupid, which forces Lilly to take a deep breath and stare in sadness at the father she loves so much. She thinks about his rapid decline since he went bankrupt, the depression and loss of self-esteem and now this–left on his own to take care of a young child and a teenager.

They have been cooped up inside the flat since the day it began. With her mother working nights at a care home, something she hated, but the rate of pay was higher than the day shifts. Lilly and her father watched the events unfold on the television. Watching at first with almost amused interest at the crazy people running around, biting each other.

But as with many millions who watched the same news channels, they soon edged closer to the television. Watching as country after country fell to the violent epidemic sweeping across.

Then it was upon them. The town centre exploding which such ferocity that her father went into virtual meltdown, running between the rooms with his mobile and landline, trying over and again to call the police and the care home.

The internet went down with the phones; then, the television channels stopped reporting. Her father tried to tune the radio in the kitchen, but it was a digital thing with pre-set channels, and try as he might, he couldn't figure a way of tuning it across the frequencies.

So they hid and stayed quiet. Taking a chance the next day, they fortified the flat. This consisted of sticking blankets over the windows and shoving some furniture against the front door.

Days passed slowly as Lilly's father tried to hold it together, pacing from room to room as he constantly took his glasses off to clean the lenses on his shirt tails. A medium built man with medium brown hair that was greying as rapidly as it was receding. A slight paunch showing the middle-aged spread, and he was every wealthy businessman suffering from the recession and plunging into depression.

Lilly, being fifteen, was old enough to know what was happening outside. William however, being six, was not. So at first, it was a game. Hiding quietly and pretending to sneak about. William loved the game and became the ultimate spy, crawling between rooms with a ski mask over his face. Rolling under the windows to avoid the spy satellites, and the mystery and wonder of using candles at night was amazing.

But that only lasted a couple of days. Then it became weird, and William missed his mother. He missed watching cartoons and playing in the field nearby. He missed playing on the Wii and the DS. He didn't like candles anymore, and now he was hungry and growing increasingly listless from being cooped up for so long. He knew something was wrong as normally his big sister would snap at him when he annoyed her, but now she didn't. She was being so patient and kind that without knowing it, it freaked William out.

When the power went off, they used the gas oven to feast on the contents of the fridge and freezer. Three hungry mouths soon devoured that, and then it was down to snack food. Once that was depleted, Lilly's father was left with no choice but to venture out to scavenge for supplies.

As the days went on, the pickings got worse, and the last time he went out, just two days ago, he found all the local houses had been ransacked. Being so close to the town centre, the location chosen simply because of the size of the old property and the low rent, he saw first-hand the devastation wrought from the event. Dead bodies rotting, shops smashed and looted, cars burnt out, and those *things*. He, like everyone else, knew what zombies were, but the thought of actually calling them that was too much.

'Dad,' Lilly prompts, snapping her father back to reality.

'You're right,' he sighs deeply.

'I am?' she asks with genuine surprise.

Nodding, he sags and rests one shoulder against the frame of the door. Removing his glasses to once again clean the lenses on his shirt tails, he repeats himself, 'You're right. We have to go.'

'Christ, Dad,' Lilly exclaims. 'What ... what changed your mind?'

'Everything you said,' he looks up, pushing his glasses back up his nose. 'Sensible, just like your mother,' he smiles sadly. 'She was always the sensible one, you know, always had common sense, whereas I,' he looks down at the floor as Lilly feels the first prick of tears forming, 'was just a bloody fool.'

'You're not a fool, Dad,' she whispers.

'I was, love. I was greedy and wanted more. Your mother knew the recession was coming and told me to ease back, but I didn't listen. I kept pumping the money back into the business ...' he trails off as Lilly listens intently. He never spoke about it. He was just quiet and tried acting like everything was okay. For the first time in her life, she saw her father as a man, not just a dad.

'So now you're the sensible one,' he grins quickly, and this time with real humour in his eyes. Sadly, the look drains away as quickly as it came.

'We'll be okay, Dad. We'll leave notes so Mum knows where to look ... When are we going?'

'Tomorrow, first thing in the morning,' he replies. 'We'll

make a game of it with William. Then once we're somewhere far away, I'll try and tell him what's happened.'

'Okay,' she nods. Her choice would be to tell William as soon as possible and before they leave the house, but it was enough that her dad was finally relenting.

'I'll go out now and get us some supplies,' he says more to himself than to Lilly. 'Er, ... Billy wants some sweets or cake, yeah ... should definitely look for some sweets. Maybe find a comic book or something for him? What do you think?'

'Er ... yeah, you could,' Lilly replies slowly, 'or just ... get whatever you can grab quickly. Anything will do until we're out of the town.'

Andrew straightens up and visibly tries to stiffen his resolve, nodding with firm action as he looks towards the barricaded front door.

Lilly follows him about quietly as he prepares to leave, changing from a white shirt to a black one used for funerals. Taking an empty rucksack, he quietly starts moving furniture away from the door.

'Dad,' Lilly calls, holding the long-bladed knife out to him.

'We've discussed this Lilly,' Andrew turns back, ignoring the knife to carry on making a path to the door.

'Just take it, Dad.'

'No, I don't plan on getting close enough to use it, and besides, if I brandish a weapon, then other people might think to use one. Violence doesn't solve anything, Lilly. Diplomacy, talking, and making sure you don't get caught out are the best strategies.'

She drops the hand holding the knife, knowing she would take it if she was going out there, but her father was a staunch pacifist. She had always admired this trait in her father, in his belief that a non-violent resolution should always be sought. Lately, however, along with the growing frustration she felt, she started to internally question if it really was pacifism or just plain cowardice.

After pausing to listen for long seconds, he slowly prises the letterbox open and peers outside. Only when absolutely sure the area is clear, does he crack the front door open, sliding through the small gap.

'I'll be a couple of hours at most.'

'Okay, Dad ... Dad?' She calls out quietly but too late, the door is closed. Standing there for a second, she places the knife on the kitchen side before locking the front door, pushing the bolts home and heaving the barricade back.

With the candle in the kitchen extinguished, she pulls back the thick blanket covering the window, staring down at the quiet, deserted street. As they lived on the first floor of an old house, they had a private front stairwell going down to their own front door. Apparently that made the flat a maisonette, something her mother kept saying whenever she spoke to family or friends.

Lilly watches as her father comes into view, crouching down between the brick pillars at the end of the garden path, cautiously checking the street before proceeding up and out of sight.

Staring out, she takes in the view of the darkened houses, all of them looking foreboding and eerie. Dark shadows, and just the moonlight giving illumination.

Twelve days stuck inside, and she longs to be outside. With the windows closed and covered by thick blankets, the heat within the flat became oppressive, and the long, sweaty hours passed even slower with nothing to do. All the books had been read, all the magazines flicked through. Clothes had been tidied and made neat. Everything that could be done was done.

With her father gone, she waits a few more minutes before sliding the clasp back on the window and pushing the wooden-framed lower pane up. In disappointment, she realises the outside air is pretty much the same as inside. Hot and listless. No breeze or cooling quality at all. But it still felt different.

She thought of school and her friends. Well, the friends from her old private school. She hadn't seen that much of them lately. Moving to the comprehensive state school was a necessity that she understood, so she did it with minimal complaint. She was a good student with high grades and tried to keep a low profile. At fifteen, she looked older, with a developed body and a figure most models would die for. Long, naturally blond hair and striking blue eyes. The years at private school had taught her to speak properly, pronouncing each letter of each word as they should be pronounced. Her looks, the way she spoke, and her high intelligence made Lilly a perfect target for bullying. The local girls detested her on sight. The lads adored her and flocked round her whenever possible, which only heightened the perception of arrogance and the other girls believing she thought she was better than they were.

Even trying to dull her looks didn't work. Wearing baggier tops to hide her figure, not wearing any make-up and stopping styling her hair just served to make her more attractive. She was a natural beauty and couldn't be anything else.

Lilly took it without complaint. Her parents had enough worries to deal with without having her bullying issue to sort out too.

Thankfully, Billy was young enough not to notice the

change in lifestyle, and as young children do, he adapted easily and loved having his dad at home every day.

Closing the window, she tucked the blanket back in place and moved into her bedroom, pausing at the door as she thought of what to pack. They had to stay light and only take essentials. She would have to be brutal with her choice, but it had to be done.

Placing the candle on her dresser, she commenced sorting and packing, moving between the rooms to sort clothes into piles, and then digging bags out to see what would fit and what wouldn't.

It was boring and dreary, but it passed the time and pretty soon her mind was occupied enough not to notice the how long it had been since her father had left.

CHAPTER SEVEN

Breathing hard, he pauses at the end of the street. Fear and exertion made his heart rate rocket, and he fought to get it under control, convincing himself that it must actually be audible it was hammering so loud.

So far he had seen nothing of concern. Just dark streets with dark houses, dark cars, and even darker sections of deep shadows.

Since the breakdown, everything had terrified him. Realising that his strong, successful business could be taken away so easily made him question everything about his life. Fundamentally undermining every facet of his existence. Guilt was the worse one. Guilt that his daughter was forced the change schools. He had seen the change in her. Going from a vibrant young lady wearing figure-hugging clothes to the plain attire she now dressed in. But he simply didn't have the mental strength to deal with the reasons. That added to the guilt. His wife, forced to go back to care work. That added to the guilt. Losing their home, the cars, the boat, the lifestyle. It all added to the guilt and ate away at his soul.

This event, as bad as it might be, served to put all people back on an even keel. Wealth and prestige no longer mattered. Who you were before the event was no longer relevant. What mattered was what you did now, what decisions you made. Andrew could have seized this and gathered his former strength, but the rot was too deep and the fear too strong. Now, with his wife gone, he was barely holding it together.

Moving down the street, he knew he had to keep going–these houses had all been checked. Someone had been through them all, removing every trace of food from every single one of them. Nothing was left. It was systematic and thorough, and that worried Andrew. Somebody was organised and making efforts to gather supplies, and they were prepared to kill for it.

Finding the homeowner of one of the houses stabbed through the chest in the kitchen made him realise that. The body was a normal man. Not a zombie, and he was old too. And old man dressed in pyjamas, with thin, grey hair. Not a threat to anyone.

It was image that sprung to mind when Lilly was urging him to take them away. Accepting the fact that his wife was now gone was too much, so he clung to the belief that she was trapped or stuck somewhere and would eventually make her way back. In the meantime, they would have to leave and get somewhere safer.

At the next street, he approached the first house, tentatively staring all around in case of movement or sound. The front door was like the previous street, battered open to hang from the near broken hinges. He knew this house had been ransacked before going inside. When he did finally reach the kitchen, a cursory glance told him it had been emptied.

The next house was the same, and the next. All the houses had been done, and he was forced to move further away from his home in search of food.

With a sizable distance between him and the town centre, Andrew follows the twisting lanes and avenues until he reaches an old estate, the kind of place heavily populated by the elderly with perfectly manicured gardens and older-style small cars on driveways.

Hardly believing his luck, he spots the small corner shop near the entrance to the estate. A family run convenience store, somewhere the locals could get bread and milk, play the lottery, and get the newspaper.

The door was open, but otherwise it looked intact. The windows weren't smashed in, and even the houses round here didn't look in that bad a state. Maybe whoever was gathering all the food hadn't reached this far yet or had just carried on by on the main road.

Tracing a route down the street, he clings to the side, staying in the shadows. His hands tremble, and his nervous eyes dart furtive looks in every direction. With yards to go, he keeps his eyes fixed on the door set into the corner, pauses to check and steps round, yelping with fright at the other man stepping round from the other side of the street.

With a startled cry from both of them, they quickly back up and hold still, both of them ready to turn and flee. Andrew feels his heart bursting with fright and quickly takes stock of the other man. Middle-aged, with greying brown hair, medium build, with a paunch, and wearing glasses. He looks just as frightened as Andrew and stares back wide-eyed.

'Hello,' Andrew whispers, his voice quavering.

'Hi,' the other man nods back, his voice also full of fear.

'Er ...' Andrew stammers.

'Um...' the other man stutters.

'I'm looking for food,' Andrew finally manages to blurt out.

'Me too,' the other man replies. 'Where you from?'

'By the town centre. You?'

'That way,' the man points off to the opposite direction. 'Nothing up your way then?'

'No,' Andrew shakes his head, still keeping his distance.

'Same,' the man says. 'I haven't been out for a few nights, but we've run out.'

'Me too,' Andrew whispers. 'My kids are starving.'

'Yeah, mine are too.'

'How many you got?'

'Son and daughter. You?'

'Same,' Andrew nods. 'No wife?'

'We split up. It was my weekend with the kids,' the man shrugs.

'No word from her?'

'No, nothing. Have you seen any police or army or anything?'

'Nothing,' Andrew shakes his head, 'just dead bodies and ...'

'Yeah,' the man says softly. 'You heard about the fort? That's where we're going.'

'No,' Andrew says, staring at the man.

'I bumped into a bloke a couple of days ago. He said one of the forts on the coast is up and running. They got police and soldiers, like a proper government place with medics. Chap called Mr Howie runs it.'

'Mr Howie? Never heard of him. Is he like a minister or something?'

'The impression I got was that he's from the army, got

soldiers with him and army vehicles, you know, with proper machine guns and everything.'

'Wow,' Andrew blanches at the news, 'we were going to head south tomorrow just to, you know, get away from the town.'

'Come with us,' the man urges quietly, 'got to be safer travelling together.'

'Well, er ... wow ... er ... that's very kind of you.'

'I'm Norman,' the man takes a step forward with his hand held out.

'Andrew. Very nice to meet you, Norman.'

'Likewise, Andrew. Er ... have you checked inside yet?'

'Not yet. I was going to, but er ... well, you scared the life out of me.'

'I jumped rather high myself, er ... Shall we then? After you.'

'Oh, er ... thank you, Norman.'

'So we'll just have to agree where to meet. Oh dear ... I think we're too late.'

'Yes, certainly looks that way,' Andrew replies sadly, looking at the empty shelves, the metal cover for the tobacco counter ripped back, and the cash register lying on the ground.

'Worth checking under the shelves, do you think?' Norman asks in a soft whisper.

'Might as well,' Andrew starts forward, dropping down to peer into the void between the base of the units and the linoleum floor. 'We could meet here if it suits you.'

'I was just thinking that,' Norman replies. 'The motorway is only a few miles away, so we could aim for that. Probably the quickest route.'

'Hmmm, yes, but er ...' Andrew lies down to grope into

the empty space, the shadows too deep to see clearly, 'bit dangerous, though, don't you think?'

'Good point,' Norman grunts. 'How about we follow the motorway then, you know, stick to the side.'

'That could work,' Andrew shifts position to reach under another unit. 'Oh, I think I've got something here ... definitely a tin, no ... two tins ... maybe more. I say, could you reach in from the other side?'

'Hang on. Where are you?'

'Over here, at the end.'

'Oh right. Yes, got you now. Just by the middle? Is that right?'

'Yes, that's it. They're just out of reach.'

'Okay, got something.'

'Er ... that's my hand.'

'Oh, my mistake. Sorry, Andrew.'

'No problem, Norman. Just there, off to my left.'

'Oh yes, got something. Hang on, I'll prod it your way.'

'Got it!'

'There's another one here. I'll prod again. You ready?'

'Yes, got it ... That's two. Any more there?'

'Something here, Andrew. Can't quite reach it.'

'Oh yes. I can prod it your way if that helps?'

'Please do ... Yes, got it.'

'Think that might be it. I can't feel anything else.'

'We've got three, though, Andrew. Not too bad. Can you see what they are?'

'Too dark,' Andrew replies, grunting to his knee. He gets up and moves towards the door and the light of the moon shining down. Joined by Norman, they stare down at the prizes held.

'Baked beans,' Andrew remarks of the first tin held up, 'and plum tomatoes.'

'Oh, well done, old chap. Let's see ... er ... spaghetti hoops, I think,' Norman reports.

'I feel bad now,' Andrew comments. 'I've got two, and you've only got one, and we've both got two children.'

'They can have half a tin each. It'll keep them going until we find something else tomorrow,' Norman replies.

'What about you? When did you last eat?'

'Me? Oh, I'm okay ...' Norman says in a forced light tone.

'No, this isn't right, er ... Well, what about we share one tin between us now and each take a tin back for our children?' Andrew suggests.

'Oh, I couldn't do that,' Norman replies.

'No, no, I insist,' Andrew presses on. 'What about the plum tomatoes? I know my two would rather have the beans or the spaghetti.'

'Well, if you're sure ...' Norman stares hungrily at the tin held by Andrew. 'Have you got an opener?'

'Hang on, no, look, it's got one of those pull things. Come on, what do you say we share some plum tomatoes?'

'Well,' Norman grins, 'I would love to share the plum tomatoes with you.'

'Here, would you hold this,' Andrew passes the tinned beans over while he carefully pulls the lid back on the plum tomatoes. The smell hits them instantly, a rich tomato scent that gets their mouths watering.

'After you,' Andrew holds the open tin towards Norman.

'Oh no, old chap, you go first.'

'I insist, you have the first one,' Andrew prompts.

Placing the two tins down, Norman gently pushes his fingers into the rich sauce, groping to grip a peeled tomato. 'Slippery blighters,' he comments as the tomato drops back in. 'Got it.' He scoops it out and into his mouth, murmuring with delight at the taste.

'Nice?' Andrew asks.

'Mmmm,' Norman replies.

Andrew delves in, taking one of the big fruits and grappling it into his mouth. First savouring the rich taste as it soaks into his tongue and then drips delightfully down his throat.

'Oh god, that was nice,' Norman sighs. Andrew holds the tin out for him to take another one. Norman plunges in, scooping another to quickly mouth the morsel.

On Andrew's second tomato, he closes his eyes, thinking in amazement at how life has changed. To be stood in a ruined shop, with a polite stranger, sharing a tin of plum tomatoes and really enjoying them.

With the tomatoes gone, they each take a sip of the remaining juice, sharing the tin back and forth until the last is drained away.

'That,' Norman says, sucking the sauce from his fingers, 'was lovely.'

'Truly,' Andrew agrees. 'How old are your children?'

'My boy is six and my girl is fifteen.'

'Never,' Andrew exclaims, 'mine are the same. Lilly and William, well, Billy.'

'You don't say,' Norman stares over in wonder. 'Well ... small world. Samantha just turned fifteen a few months ago, and Todd is six and a half now.'

'What's that word?' Andrew screws his face up in concentration.

'Fortuitous?'

'Yes!' Andrew beams. 'Very fortuitous. I don't mind admitting I was petrified coming down here.'

'Me too,' Norman says. 'Utterly terrified I was. Glad I bumped into you like that, though.'

'Oh, definitely, shame we can't all get together tonight.'

'I wish we could,' Norman agrees instantly, 'but I don't fancy bringing my two out in the dark. Sam would be okay, but Todd wouldn't like it.'

'Oh gosh, no,' Andrew adds. 'I wouldn't chance it either.'

'So we meeting here, then?' Norman asks.

'If that's alright with you?'

'Sure,' Norman nods. 'You got a car?'

'No, unfortunately not ... er ... had some financial problems so, er, kind of had to give it back.'

'Oh dear, recession, was it?'

'Yes,' Andrew replies grimly, 'bloody awful.'

'Did my marriage in,' Norman states. 'I'm only hanging on by my fingertips. Well, I say that, but er ... don't think it really matters now.'

'No, guess it doesn't.'

'Well, we can walk to the motorway if we don't find something on the way.'

'Agreed,' Andrew nods. 'Well, I better be getting back. Nice to meet you again, Norman.'

'You too,' shaking hands, they nod and smile, both of them feeling a huge sense of relief at meeting the other, both of them feeling the tug to return to their families, and both of them not wanting to go.

'Have you got bags and things?' Andrew asks quickly as a way of dragging it out for another minute.

'Oh yes, we've got rucksacks. How about you? Anything you need?'

'No, I don't think so. I was going to pack a couple of books for Billy.'

'I'll do the same,' Norman replies. 'We can share then.'

'Great, Lilly will be pleased. I think she's getting rather fed up of just having her dad for company.'

'Sam too,' Norman grins. 'Well, er ...'

'And you,' they shake hands again as they step through the door, into the moonlit street.

'Oh, the tins,' Andrew laughs.

'Oh, crumbs,' Norman chortles as Andrew retrieves them from the ground just inside the door, passing the spaghetti over.

'That wouldn't have gone down well,' Andrew says.

'No, definitely not. Right, well ... er ... see you here first thing, then? You okay with that? If we go first thing?'

'Absolutely, we'll set off as soon as the sun is up. It shouldn't take long.'

'Same. See you in the morning then, Andrew.'

'Yes, see you, Norman. Nice to meet you again.'

'You too, take care on the way home.'

'And you, Norman.'

CHAPTER EIGHT

'You sure about this, Dad? I mean, we don't know them or anything.'

'Honestly, Lilly, he was a really nice man. We shared a tin of–'

'Plum tomatoes. Yes, you said, but how do you know he isn't some axe-wielding murderer?'

Andrew stops and stares at his daughter. There was a time when he would have stared down at his daughter, but now it was more or less straight across. He could, however, still look down at his son.

'What do you think, Billy? Do you want a new playmate?'

Rolling her eyes, Lilly shrugged her heavy bag higher up her back and tried to adjust the straps. It was a glorious morning with bright sunshine and already high temperatures. They were all sweating freely, but that didn't matter. Being outside, in the open air was incredible. She felt like a prisoner being released into freedom, and Billy was smiling properly for the first time in days too.

Clutching his rucksack, he looked every inch the

intrepid explorer, with a sun hat perched on his head and wearing his blue knee-length shorts, he tottered along, clutching his father's hand while he picked a route that avoided the worst atrocities.

By the end of their street, those atrocities simply couldn't be avoided, and both Lilly and Billy saw their first dead bodies. The lightness of their mood plummeted instantly, Billy squeezing his dad's hand tight as he stared in wonder at what looked like humans, only they had all the inside bits on the outside in a gooey mess, with flies and writhing maggots feasting on the rotting cadavers.

Trepidation stole through Lilly as she both thanked the heavens for the change in her father's behaviour but worried deeply about the coming days.

On his arrival home last night, he was noticeably different; clutching a single can of beans like a hunter from the old days returning with a freshly killed deer. He spoke at length about Norman and how they'd worked together to find the food, and what a lovely chap he seemed. He had two children the same age, and they were going to meet up and head south. Andrew spoke about the fort and survivors and how a man called Mr Howie from the government had everything running properly and their mother was probably at the fort now, waiting for them.

Lilly listened to the repeated tales through the night as they packed and prepared, and she didn't mind that he failed to notice she had mostly got everything ready.

By the time the sun was up, they were ready, packed, dressed, and set to leave. Billy had demolished the tin of beans with gusto. Lilly could see how hungry he was, so only took a small mouthful, insisting that she wasn't all that hungry really. The hunger pangs were almost painful, but she knew that Billy would need the energy most.

Andrew's mental state manifested during the packing process, displaying an inability to think rationally and trying to pack far too many bags. It was almost as though he was planning a holiday for two weeks in the sunshine instead of it being a desperate fleeing away from the horrors of the town centre and to stave off the risk of starvation.

Fifteen years old, still a child herself, but Lilly became the maternal figure, using sound common sense and judgement to pack the real essentials. Light clothing, seeing as it was hot. Lots of water and personal keepsakes. Her mother's jewellery that could be used to barter for goods, and despite her father's protests, she shoved the kitchen knife into the top of her bag too.

'So we'll head for the fort, and your mother will know where we are,' Andrew repeated again. It seemed he was going over the same thing more for his own benefit rather than either of theirs. *Maybe guilt for leaving,* Lilly thought as she watched her dad nervously glancing up and down the street.

Looking round herself, she could see just how bad it was. The area looked like a warzone or something from the movies. Houses were smashed up, windows and doors ripped out, cars left abandoned in the street, and bodies everywhere.

The smells were weird too. The fetid, foul meat stench from the corpses was just awful. Even from a distance, it made her want to gag. But away from the death, the air was different. Somehow more clean and pure. Like the sudden loss of mankind and all the fumes was already having an effect.

Billy swept his gaze from house to house, his young face lingering on the bodies in the street and doorways.

Although he was quiet and withdrawn, he seemed more interested than he was frightened.

'It's hot, isn't it?' Andrew remarked to break the silence, his voice low and muted.

'Very,' Lilly replied, equally as quiet.

'Do you know any girls called Samantha your age?' Andrew asked again.

'Yes, Dad,' Lilly answered with forced patience, 'quite a few.'

'Got a brother called Todd. Their father is–'

'Norman. I know, Dad. You've said a few times now. No, I don't know ...'

'You alright, Billy? Not too hot?'

'I'm okay, Daddy. Who killed those people?'

'Killed? How do you know they're dead? They might just be sleeping.'

'Their insides have come outside, and that one doesn't have his head on. It's over there, by that red car.'

'Oh, right ... yes, his head is over there, isn't it?'

'Why Daddy?'

'Why what?'

'Why is his head not on? Do heads come off?'

'No, Billy, heads are not *meant* to come off. I think he had an accident.'

'Oh ... did they all have accidents?'

'Dad,' Lilly intoned, 'we talked about this ...'

'Yes, I know, Lilly,' Andrew hissed. 'Can we just wait until we're away from here.'

'It's going to be everywhere. He might as well know now.'

'Know what, Lilly?' Billy asks, looking up at his sister. She stares at her father for long seconds. He returns the look but sags and just looks away, clearly not willing to say anything yet.

'Nothing, Billy,' Lilly smiled.

'Not nothing,' Billy shakes his head. 'Did Mummy have an accident, and her head fell off too?'

'No, Billy,' Andrew snaps, 'your mother is just stuck. That's all.'

'Stuck where, Daddy?'

'At work, Billy, she's stuck at work.'

'Why doesn't she drive her car?'

'The car doesn't work.'

'Well, she can get on a bus just like we do, Daddy, when we go to the duck pond.'

'The buses are all broken, Billy.'

Silence for a few seconds, then followed with, 'Why Daddy? Why are the buses broken?'

'They just are ... We have to be quiet now, Billy. Daddy needs to listen.'

'What for, Daddy? Lilly? What is Daddy listening at?'

'*For*. Daddy is listening *for* something, not *at* something.'

'What then?'

'Shush now, Billy, be quiet for a minute,' Lilly says quietly, picking up on her father's rapid increase in nerves as they pass down a street where all the doors have been battered in.

Andrew nervously leads the way, threading through the deserted and silent streets. The oppressive heat only serves to enhance the ominous feeling as their feet crunch and step noisily along.

'Are we there yet?'

'Not yet, Billy. Be quiet for now, please.'

'Can I have something to drink, please, Lilly?'

'Now, Billy? Okay, hang on,' she rummages through his backpack as he walks along, drawing a bottle of water out to hand down over his shoulder.

'Water? Haven't we got any juice?'

'Just water, that's all we have.'

'We always drink water now. Mummy used to give me juice and milk.'

'We only have water for now,' Lilly says quietly.

'I need the toilet.'

'We only left a few minutes ago. You said you didn't need to go,' Lilly sighs.

'I didn't ... but I do now.'

'Okay,' she groans, 'use that wall.'

'Mummy said I wasn't allowed to do a wee wee outside.'

'I know, but we're allowed to now. They changed the rules.'

'Did the teachers change the rules?'

'Yes, Billy, come on ... hurry up.'

'Ha, look, Lilly. I can wee really high ... Dad ... Dad ... Daddy ... look.'

'That's great, Billy,' Andrew says without looking, scanning the houses nearby for signs of movement. The walk was taking ages, with Billy going so slow, and he worried that Norman wouldn't wait for them.

Hustling his young son, he picks the pace up, urging Billy to keep going. Billy, after too many days of being stuck inside, is full of wonder and awe at the outside world. Asking question after question. *Where is everyone? Are all the cars broken? Is that car broken? What about that red one, is that broken?' Who broke all the doors? Will the man get in trouble for breaking the doors? Is he a burger man because they said at school that burger men go into houses and steal toys? Can we get a burger now?' Can we go to MacDonald's later? Where do baby ducks come from?*

Lilly fielded the questions deftly, speaking quietly as she too kept a constant vigil of the surrounding area.

'That's it,' Andrew points ahead to the shop on the corner. 'Oh dear ... no sign of them ... Maybe we're too late.'

'We should just keep walking,' Lilly suggests, 'or one of these houses will have keys for a car.'

'Daddy said all the cars are broked.'

'Broken, not broked,' Lilly corrects automatically.

'Andrew?' Norman asks, stepping out from the shop doorway.

'Norman! Glad to see you. Sorry, it took us longer than planned,' Andrew smiles and waves, sounding to Lilly like he was apologising for being late for a game of golf. 'Norman, this is my daughter Lilly and my son Billy.'

'Nice to meet you,' Norman offers a weak handshake to Lilly before tussling Billy's hair. 'Hello, young man.'

'Hello,' Billy looks up, 'is your car broked too? My dad said all the cars and buses are broked, but we're going to MacDonald's. Are you coming to MacDonald's?'

'Ah, er ...' Norman smiles, unsure of how to respond.

'We're not going to MacDonald's. We're going for a long walk until we can find a car that isn't broked. I mean broken ...' Lilly explains. She takes in the middle-aged man. He looks the same as her father. Brown hair greying at the sides, medium build, with a paunch and the same pale and worried look.

'This is Samantha and Todd. Say hello, Todd,' Norman turns as two more figures step out of the shop. A young boy clutching a teddy bear and an older girl staring at them through scared eyes.

'Hello,' Andrew nods, holding his hand out to the girl, 'I'm Andrew ...'

'Hi,' Samantha mumbles quietly. She nods to Lilly, then looks away. Dark-haired and younger-looking than Lilly, wearing jeans and a black t-shirt.

'Were the beans nice?' Norman asks Lilly with a forced grin.

'Fine, thank you,' Lilly replies politely.

'How about your spaghetti?' Andrew asks.

'Oh, they enjoyed every mouthful, although it didn't really last very long, did it, Sam?'

'No,' Sam shakes her head.

'Well, this is better, isn't it?' Andrew smiles round, the same forced smile that Norman keeps stuck to his face. 'You girls can talk about girly things ...'

'And us men can talk about manly things,' Norman adds as Lilly struggles not to roll her eyes. *How can they be so fake and forced? Don't they see what's going on around us?*

'Well, everyone ready, then? I was thinking of staying on foot until the motorway and then trying to find transport once we're away from the town ...' Norman says, his voice dropping to a low tone. 'Didn't want to make any noise here ... you know ... engine sounds and drawing attention ...'

'No, quite,' Andrew nods, 'I agree, on foot we shall go, then.'

'We should take a car,' Lilly interjects. 'We can get keys from one of these houses ... It'll be faster and safer in a car.'

Samantha stares at Lilly in surprise, nodding in agreement.

'No, Lilly,' Andrew says as though embarrassed by her suggestion. 'We should stay on foot until we get somewhere safer to get a car.'

'Absolutely,' Norman nods.

'If here isn't safe, then why are we walking? We should be getting out of here,' Lilly continues, making sure her tone is soft and easy. 'There are loads of cars on these driveways. We should just take one and go.'

'Thank you, Lilly, but I'm sure Norman and I know what's best,' Andrew says stiffly, glancing with admonishment at his daughter.

'Oh, I'm sure young Lilly here means well,' Norman offers a weak smile. 'And you're fifteen, Lilly?' he asks with a fleeting glance at her developed chest.

'Yes,' she looks away, feeling embarrassed, and tries to cross her arms, an awkward movement hampered by the thick straps of the rucksack on her shoulders. She blushes instead as she has to half cross them, feeling both stupid and exposed and wishing she hadn't worn the tight vest top. She was used to men glancing down there. Her mother was buxom and had told her from early in life to get used to it.

Samantha, seemingly unaware of her father's glance at Lilly's chest, stares at the new members of their group, flicking her gaze between her father and Andrew, at the similarities between them.

'Are we ready, then?' Andrew asks the group in general.

'I took the opportunity to mark out a route on a map,' Norman produces a folded ordnance survey map to show Andrew the thick black line indicating the proposed route to the south coast.

'Very good,' Andrew nods eagerly, 'very good, indeed. Well done, Norman ... I, er ... well, I didn't have a map, so I couldn't ...'

'I don't think anyone does anymore,' Norman adds.' I foolishly went for my satnav before realising I couldn't charge it up. Luckily I had this old thing in a cupboard. I should imagine a lot has changed in the years, but the route should be the same.'

They set off, and within a few paces, the dynamics of the group are obvious as Andrew and Norman take the front, chatting politely between themselves in their newly formed mutual appreciation society. Both of them clutch the hands of their young sons who totter along beside them, staring furtively at each other.

Lilly and Samantha bring up the rear, letting a few paces develop between them and their fathers. In awkward silence, they move along through the debris-strewn streets. Lilly wishing they would see sense and take a car to get out of here quicker. Samantha wondering why she didn't look like Lilly instead of her very slim, almost boyish physique.

'Sorry,' Lilly remarks quickly as she stumbles on a broken kerb stone, rubbing her shoulder against Samantha.

'S'okay,' the other girl replies instantly.

'This bag is so heavy,' Lilly tugs at the straps again, rotating her shoulders to try and ease the pressure.

'Yeah, mine too. It's, like, well killing my shoulders.'

'Did you get packed last night?' Lilly asks, glancing across at Samantha.

She nods and stares forward at her father and brother. 'Dad was well weird when he got home last night,' she whispers. 'He was, like, all excited at meeting your dad and kept going on about a tin of–'

'Plum tomatoes?' Lilly cuts in with a wry smile.

'Yeah, like, well going on about it,' Samantha half grins.

'Mine was too,' Lilly steps in closer to drop her voice. 'He must have told me the same story like a hundred times, how they were trying to reach under the shelves and prodding tins at each other.'

'Yeah, that was it,' Samantha snorts. 'Where's your mum? Er ... if er ... like, you know ... Is it okay to ask that?'

'Of course,' Lilly replies. 'She was at work when it happened,' she shrugs. 'Just didn't see her again. No contact or word from her ... We left notes at home saying where we are going. I thought Dad was going to keep us there forever. We haven't eaten properly for days.'

'Same,' Samantha nods. 'It was our weekend with Dad. Mum lives miles away, so, like, we don't know anything that has happened with her. Dad's kept us in the house all the time. We were, like, going crazy ... and starving too.'

'We should have taken a car,' Lilly whispers. 'I don't know why they want to walk. It's boiling out here, and I know Billy won't last long in this heat. He had most of the beans yesterday but still ...'

'If your dad is like mine, then he won't listen. I don't like it here ... all these houses all, like, smashed up and like ... bodies everywhere ... It's well creepy.'

'We can suggest it again when the boys start whining,' Lilly conspires.

'Okay, you like ... you speak well nice ...' Samantha blurts out, then blushes furiously.

'Dad sent me to a private school. We had elocution lessons ...'

'Oh, you from like, you know, a posh house and all that?'

'God no,' Lilly shakes her head, 'not now. Dad had a business, but it went under. We lost the house and cars, and I had to leave the private school. I was going to the high school here.'

'Oh, right,' Samantha says, 'my mum and dad split up cos he was working so much. She's got a new boyfriend now.

He's really nice. Dad just works and gets, like, well depressed and ...'

'Is he on pills? Mine is,' Lilly interjects.

'Yeah, takes 'em every morning. They make him all monged-out and weird for like an hour.'

'They should get on well, then,' Lilly smiles, staring ahead at the two fathers talking away in hushed tones as they both nervously glance round the area.

'Yeah right,' Samantha smiles back, 'he wouldn't even, like, take a knife or anything. He said violence was never the way.'

'I got one,' Lilly whispers. 'Mine wouldn't take one either, so I put one in my bag. It's at the top.'

'Mine's here,' Samantha pulls her top up an inch or so, revealing the handle of a small knife tucked into the back of her waistband. 'He might not like violence, but we got Todd with us, so Dad's got to protect him, you know ... those things are well nasty.'

'Have you seen them?' Lilly asks.

'Only outside, going past the house. They were, like, well slow in the day and really fast at night, but we haven't seen any for a day or ...'

'Same,' Lilly nods. 'Dad said all the food was gone too. I don't think he realises how hungry we are.'

'Todd had the spaghetti,' Samantha cuts in. 'I was starving. I still am, like, but his little face when he saw them ...'

'We'll give it an hour and get them to find food, or we can do it,' Lilly says.

'Yeah, okay,' Samantha nods eagerly, smiling across at Lilly.

They walk on, quietly talking sense between them while their fathers discuss golf clubs, cars, and business projects. The two small boys still taking furtive glances at one another and now playing a game of poking tongues out and blowing raspberries.

Both girls realise within a short time that their fathers are too engrossed talking to keep a decent look-out. They add it to their list of duties, constantly scanning ahead and to the sides and taking it in turns to turn round and check behind them.

As with many towns in the south of England, the urban sprawl soon gives way to suburbia, which in turn gently transforms into the picturesque rural spread of fields, lanes, and meadows. With the heat blasting down, they trudge on. Lilly and Samantha cajoling both the boys to drink and then taking the boys' hands, leaving their fathers to merrily lead the way, almost painfully ignorant of the dangers they face.

CHAPTER NINE

Why was I being punched repeatedly in the stomach? They weren't hard blows, but they were consistent. Hazy dreams flooded my mind, images of my family and that actor Paco Maguire.

At some point, I drifted back to the present and looked down to see the back of Dave's heels. I realised I wasn't being repeatedly punched–it was his bony shoulder digging into my stomach as he carried me along. I think I puked at that point. The jolting, the dehydration, and the metallic taste of blood in my mouth all conspired together to bring burning bile up my throat and onto the back of Dave's legs.

I didn't know where we were going. I wanted to ask, but speaking was beyond me. Consciousness was like trying to grasp a greasy bar of soap, and it kept slipping away. I felt the sensation of being carried for what felt like a long time; then, I was on something soft. When I opened my eyes, it was pitch black, and I couldn't tell the difference between my eyes being open and closed.

All I could think about was that heart being pushed into my mouth. It was dark when that happened, so I didn't see the heart, but there was no doubt what it was. The fucking thing was still pumping as it was stuffed between my teeth. Thick blood shot out of the ventricles to fill my throat. I felt it die, like a wounded animal, slowly pumping the life out of itself.

At that point, I wondered if my own heart recognised the beat of this heart in my mouth. I don't know if was still alive if I'm honest. I really couldn't tell. I could have been one of the infected, being carried off by Dave to have my head removed from my body.

Why was Paco holding a baby? Oh, right yeah, he's the father of Sarah's child, isn't he? Is he? Was that real? Jesus, I can't tell. I thought Sarah liked Clarence, and I guess a person has the right to change their mind, but wow–that pregnancy must have flown by. Still, Mum and Dad will be pleased. They always wanted a grandchild, and they knew the chances of me finding a suitable partner were pretty slim.

I hope they like Lani. She's nice. I like Lani. She's way better than Marcy. Whatever happened to Marcy? Does she know Paco? Maybe they're friends or something. Oh, that could be awkward in the future if we all get together at a family function. What with me being with Lani and Marcy being good friends with Paco. How will that go down?

I shouldn't worry about that now. Sarah is switched on, and she can smooth it over. Hmmm. Actually, it's probably best I don't go to the function, yeah ... I can say I've got work or something. Mum and Dad won't mind. They'll understand.

I'm sleepy now. Really tired. It's quiet in my flat tonight. I'm surprised the drunks aren't making loads of noise going back from the town. Have I got work tomorrow? Did I set the alarm?

It'll be okay. Dave will cover for me if I'm late in. My new bed is lovely and comfy.

I'm glad I got it.

'Shush, sleep now.'

'Okay, Dad,' I didn't realise Dad was staying over. That's nice of him. We can spend the day together tomorrow, maybe go to that cake shop he likes in the next town. No, that burnt down, didn't it? Did I burn it down? Shit, maybe the police will arrest me for arson or something.

'Sorry, Dad, I burnt your cake shop down.'

'Drink this,' my head is lifted up, which is a strange thing to do to someone when they're sleeping. A cup is pressed to my lips and cold, and beautiful water pours into my mouth. My god, I'm so thirsty. I didn't realise I was this thirsty.

'Slow down,' my father intones, but I want more and drain the cup down greedily. My head rests back. A second later, it's being lifted up, and more water is being poured into my mouth. I try to say something but end up spitting water over my dad.

'Drink ... Good ... Now rest.'

'Thanks, Dad. Love you.'

Dave watches Howie closely, that worried look still on his face but slowly easing off. His vital signs were good, his heart and pulse were strong, his breathing normal. His pupils looked right, and he wasn't too hot or cold.

Shock. Shock and dehydration. He needs rest and fluids. Checking his eyes, he notices the absence of any redness. Just normal white, with the dark iris barely discernible against the blackness of his pupils.

Sitting back on his haunches, Dave thinks hard. Drawing his knife, he taps the blade against his leg, considering the options.

Mr Howie is immune. Infected blood went into his mouth. A whole heart was in his mouth, and you can't get more-infected blood than from a still-beating heart.

Mr Howie kissed Lani. Lani is immune. Who passed the immunity to whom? Lani turned, so that suggests she had a weaker strain of immunity than Mr Howie. Shaking his head, he realises that doesn't mean anything. Genetics, mutant strains of DNA, and cell structure simply didn't work like that.

Mr Howie and Lani could both be uniquely immune. The chances of that are very slim, but it is possible.

But the infected fear Mr Howie. There is something different about him. Something unique. They don't fear Lani, and she's immune now, or is she? Maybe she is carrying the virus but just not showing it.

It makes sense to Dave that the reason they fear Mr Howie was because he couldn't be turned. He is the key to ending the infection. He is the natural antibody.

Dave's mind was unique. He wasn't stupid, and he didn't have low intelligence. His brain was simply structured differently to most other people, and right now, he knew the limitations of his knowledge and figuring this out was beyond him.

So with nothing else to do, he drank water, washed, and kept a very close eye on Mr Howie. Taking regular trips to the front door to listen intently for sounds of approaching infected.

When they did come, he showed no reaction. First

moving to the back door and double-checking it was locked and secure. He pulled the lounge door closed and then opened the front door to stand in the frame. Listening. Waiting.

Two new knives sourced from the kitchen and sharpened to his exact standard were gripped in his hands.

They must have spread out after the Saxon went off. That was the most logical thing to do. They couldn't chase a moving vehicle, so they filtered off to hunt the others down.

Bare feet slapping against the road made a distinctive noise, and lots of bare feet slapping against the road made an even more distinctive noise.

Standing stock still, Dave watches as the infected run past the gate. There was quite a few of them, but none had picked up on Dave's or Mr Howie's scent. Scratching his head with the handle of a knife, Dave considers this.

He and Mr Howie were immersed in the bodies of the fallen zombies. So they were saturated in their stench. That must be why Mr Howie was left alone after the heart was shoved in his mouth. In the darkness, the confusion, and the cramped space, they couldn't find him. They couldn't smell him.

It had been a long night already, and the preceding few days have been non-stop. Dave can feel the ebb of fatigue just starting to gnaw away, but an idea steals into his mind. The infection is a conscious entity. It must be. It drives those hosts like they are part of a super-organism. It reacts with increasing speed and is constantly developing and evolving, changing tactics and strategies.

Mr Howie is down right now. He needs rest, and if the rest of the team are out there, fractured and alone, they will need rest too. The last thing they need is to be running and fighting all night, for as fit and strong as they are, they will soon drop from exhaustion.

With an almost imperceptible shrug, Dave reaches the conclusion. He doesn't fear the decision, nor does he question it. The action he must take is logical, and besides, it will give him a chance to test a theory.

Turning round, he gauges the door behind him and the length of the path, judging distance and special awareness. He takes a step forward and checks again, reaching an arm out to ensure he can reach the door from this distance, making small precise adjustments to gain the perfect position.

Once satisfied, he fixes his gaze on the garden gate and the low wall running either side of it. His mind works out the routes they will take and tracks back to his position. The window negates this position. A big bay window designed to allow maximum light into the front room. A body crashing through that will take out most of the large panes, leaving a perfect route in.

No good. Instead, he locks the front door, making sure it is firmly closed before making his way down the path, to the gate, pausing until the last of the infected have staggered past. Only then does he step out into the road, taking purposeful strides to the middle and then moving a short distance along, double checking that he still has a view of the house within which Mr Howie rests.

They can't smell Mr Howie, so they don't know which house he is in, nor do they know if he is in this area.

'Here,' Dave calls out and watches as the horde react as one, stopping to turn and face back down the road, towards the small man illuminated in the silvery light of the moon.

Dave turns to check behind him, sensing movement and spotting the next lot coming up the road.

The first horde start moving back, but they don't run. They walk steadily. Turning his head, he spots the horde coming from the other direction have also slowed to come in at a slower pace.

Interesting. Another change of tactic. Not running full-on to charge in but taking a steadier pace to ensure they all come together at the same time.

The knives in his hands are flicked up so the reverse side of the blade presses against his forearms. Slowly he flicks his gaze left and right, watching and tracking each horde as they move in.

Rolling his head, Dave stretches his neck and starts rotating his shoulders. At the same time he brings first one knee to his chest, then the next.

'My name is Dave,' he says out loud, his clear voice carrying with ease into the quiet street. 'You went after Mr Howie,' he adds, pausing as he rotates his wrists, circling his hands gripping the knives. 'So now I will go after you,' he continues, 'and I won't stop ...' He stares to one side, fixing his eyes on the approaching horde. 'Bring more,' he turns his head to face forward, using peripheral vision to monitor the approach but appearing to stare away unconcerned. 'Bring many more ... bring all of you ...' They're close now, edging in with slow, deliberate movements. The sheer hunger pours off them. The raging violence pulses through the hordes, visible and tangible. The electric atmosphere would make the strongest, hardest men piss themselves in fear. The sight of the drawn creatures with clawed hands, sunken, hollow eyes, thin lips pulled back to show blood-encrusted teeth, hair thinning, wounds festering and writhing with maggots that eat away at the flesh.

At the last second, Dave pushes his left foot back and brings his right arm across his chest. He takes a slow, deep breath and waits. That rare thing crosses his face as he starts to smile, a slight tugging of the lips that blossoms into a big grin the very second they release and surge forward.

He holds until the very last split second of impact, then spins round, stretching his arms out to scythe the blades across many throats. The first corpses fall as the first of the blood is spilled onto the hot surface of the road.

He moves as water through a dam of twigs and stones, finding holes and gaps to move through. All the time, his knives thrusting and sweeping. He uses his legs to trip them, cutting throats as they fall. Each time they lunge to where he is, he is simply not there anymore. He is where he needs to be, in that space there between the two big males. They twist with rage to lunge, but that space is empty, and those big males are losing their life blood as it spurts out from the severed arteries in their necks. By the time this is even realised, several more have gone down.

Alone now, and he fights the best way he knows. He doesn't have to monitor Mr Howie or any of the team. It is just him and them. His sole focus is which space to slide into and which throat to penetrate next.

When they surge in too hard and close the gaps, he uses the falling body of an infected as a stepping stone to leap high and plummet down further away. Creating confusion and mayhem. It's dark, and it takes them seconds to know where he is, just a trail of bodies that fall one after the other, after the other.

Those fallen bodies create trip hazards, and Dave tracks his own progress, working in certain direction to force the oncoming ranks to go over those bodies, knowing some will trip and create gaps he can use to his advantage.

His energy is relentless. His life force unstoppable. He knows that while they are coming for him, they are leaving the others alone. This gives them something to focus on and lets the everyone else have a chance to rest, wherever they might be.

On the tips of his toes, he pirouettes, one knee bent to provide balance for the centrifugal force as his outstretched arms rip through neck after neck.

Down he goes, dropping to take an apparent bow, but he slides several steps back into the space he had already seen. The knives are thrust backwards, driving the points into two throats. He drops again and takes more steps back, hacking left and right through Achilles heels to force them down onto the ground.

Like playing cards, they drop, and Dave is no longer in that space. Two huge strides, and he is deep within the ranks again, weaving and dancing. His face looks serene and content. His breathing, although harder and faster than normal, is controlled.

He gives bursts of energy, driving his body to work to the maximum capability, sensing his heart rate bursting higher. That burst of speed and power allows him to fell many within a few seconds and create a much larger space.

Then he rests, sliding back into the ranks to allow his heart rate to recover, controlling his breathing with deep breaths. All around him, they growl and roar, they howl and snarl, but they die.

Howie once joked that all they ever needed was Dave with his knives, and looking down, there is a small man in the middle of a huge pressing horde of writhing bodies driven by the virus within them to destroy this thing that cuts so many hosts down.

CHAPTER TEN

On her feet, meat cleaver gripped tight and ready, eyes wide and staring as her heart races. Meredith jumps to her feet instantly, growling at the sight of Lani going from full sleep to fighting pose. The dog stares about, looking for the threat that the woman must be seeing. She spins, checking all directions, but her excellent eyes and ears detect nothing.

Lani breathes hard and becomes aware of her actions, not knowing why she leapt to her feet, but here she is, up and ready. Legs shaking, and her mouth so dry she can barely swallow. Her head pounds from dehydration as slowly she lowers the weapon and looks about.

Strong sunlight streaming through the open sides of the car park forces the shadows of the night to retreat in. The ever-continuing battle between light and dark. A noise behind has her spinning round only to see Meredith squatting to take a long piss, the urine pooling out between her back legs. Finished, she stands up and turns to sniff at the puddle. Seemingly satisfied, she walks closer to Lani and stares up.

Where is the team? What happened to Howie and the

others? Those thoughts flood into her mind only to be trounced by a raging thirst that burns through her insides. Throat dry and painful, mouth drier, and even her eyes feel sore and dry.

Neither of them will be any good if they don't drink and rehydrate, and with the threat of another scorching day, that action needs to be sooner rather than later. Walking towards the vehicle ramp, she takes in the mangled bodies with an instant over-powering feeling that she will see Howie or one of the others amongst the corpses.

Lani stops, her eyes screwed tight, dreading the view of seeing her team amongst the corpses. With a deep breath, she opens her eyes and scans the bodies, searching for any tell-tale sign of them. Nothing here, and she pauses, wondering if to go higher or head out for a drink. The thirst is severe, but what if one of them were lying injured, unable to move or crawl away. With that thought imprinted in her mind, she doesn't hesitate but starts back up the ramp, towards the top.

Meredith moves over the bodies without concern, her natural four-wheel drive giving her excellent traction control. She views the remains with relative ease, checking what's left of ruined faces, hair colour and clothing. Lani keeps moving up to the top level, grimacing at the sheer numbers taken down during the fighting. The twisted body parts that were thrown at them still litter the area, spent ammunition cases and useless weapons thrown aside as the youths went for hand weapons.

She spots the large, circular swathes cut down by Clarence wielding his double-bladed axe and the never-ending amount of throats slit open from Dave's knives.

A sadness steals through her heart at the sight of the first youth, easily recognisable from the cleaner clothes and fresh look of the corpse. Taken and turned, only to be cut down minutes later. More of them lie fallen amongst the piles, and a sense of guilt adds to the conflict of emotions that she feels.

Meredith is nose down, following familiar scent tracks to the door leading to the stairwell, whining as she paws at the closed doors. Lani moves over, spotting the small pile of assault rifles stripped of magazines. The sight suggests someone gathered the fallen weapons to use whatever ammunition was left.

Would Maddox think to do that? It smacks of something Dave would do or maybe Nick, and it's a good idea. She pulls her pistol out and checks the magazine. Still full. The hand weapon was unused during the fight, so at least she still has a sidearm. She picks one of the rifles up and checks the breech and moving parts before starting to sift through the bodies, searching for any magazines left.

Everything has been spent and used, but she keeps the rifle with her, pushing an empty magazine in before looping it round her back on the strap. Plenty of weapons here, shotguns, rifles, and some of the weapons sourced from the refinery too. Biting her bottom lip, she worries about leaving them here, knowing how hard it was to find them in the first place.

Too many to carry, that's for sure. Instead, she gathers them up, wincing as the pain in her head explodes every time she bends down, followed by a wave of dizziness when she stands back up.

A flash of memory, of Tom in the back of the Saxon complaining about feeling sick and weak and Clarence telling him about heat exhaustion. He said to drink loads of fluids and rehydrate, and that's what she needs to do now. The feeling is distracting to the point of being unable to focus on anything else. Drink. Find water. Her body screaming out that she may be fit and small, she may have greater stamina than most, but even she needs fluids.

With the weapons stacked on the inside of the doors to the stairwell, she starts heading down, clocking the injuries sustained to the corpses. Clear axe marks, skulls cleaved open, and limbs hacked through. No doubt about it. After days of fighting alongside the others, she would recognise the wounds better than any pathologist.

Someone came down here and fought their way out. The thought gives her hope, propelling her to move faster, which just brings on a fresh wave of nausea. Biting it down, Lani snarls with contempt, refusing to let the ill feeling take over.

At the bottom, she stares in wonder at the big pile of bodies and feels a deep sense of pride that whoever came down here took so many down. Out into the sunshine, and she thinks of who it could have been, which only serves to enhance the feeling of pride. It could have been anyone, apart from Dave. Their fighting abilities are now so good it's almost impossible to tell them apart.

If she had to guess, she would say Blowers and Cookey, simply for the fact the number of bodies that have been taken down suggests two worked together. Could have been Clarence? No, she saw Clarence at the rear of the Saxon going down the ramp. So it must have been one of the lads.

Shielding her eyes from the sun, she steps through the bodies and takes in the surrounding view. The High Street still burns fiercely, with long rows of shops now well alight, and thick, black smoke billowing up into the sky. Several junctions lead off to residential side streets with rows of houses on either side.

Lani stares up at the thick smoke pluming into the air, a

perfect smoke signal, and something everyone can aim for. Clarence got away with the Saxon, so it's only a matter of time before he gets back. Turning round, she takes in the surrounding streets, looking at each junction in turn. A long line of bodies marks the route the Saxon took down the main road. If the lads got away from here, they would head for the shelter of the side streets, somewhere they could hunker down and get water.

Nodding to herself, she sets off for the nearest junction, purposefully keeping to the middle of the road and watching Meredith as she runs round in large loops with her nose to the ground. With luck, the dog will pick up on the scent of the lads and lead her to them. But didn't Howie say the dogs had to be trained to do that? Maybe all dogs have the natural ability but have to be trained to show the handler where the trail leads.

Into the first street, and she stares closely at the first houses, looking at the doors and windows. She wouldn't choose one that was too smashed in as it would be indefensible. Likewise, something that was completely intact would stand out too much. The first few are discounted simply for the sheer amount of damage they have sustained, but the further from the town she goes, the less the damage is apparent.

Meredith stops and spins back, her nose just millimetres above the ground. Lani watches her closely as she loops round and round, then stays still for long seconds, sniffing one spot over and over. Then she's off, tracing a route down the pavement and actually weaving in the pattern someone would take if they were running.

There are no bodies here, which suggests whoever came this way managed to evade any infected coming after them.

The dog veers a sharp left, turning into a front garden

where she pursues the scent trail to the front door, then stops, and looks back at Lani as if to say '*well, open it, then*'.

Smiling, she gently presses down on the door handle. The front door is intact, with just some minor signs of damage, and it opens inwards. With one hand clutching the dog's collar, she steps in quietly and stares down the hall to the two bodies slumped against the kitchen cupboards.

The smile stretches into a grin as she notices Cookey has slumped down to rest his head on Blowers' shoulder. A thick spool of saliva drips from his slightly open mouth as they both snore peacefully. She pats her pockets, searching for her iPod to use the camera, remembering it's in the Saxon, rigged up to the loudspeaker. That would be perfect–a picture of these two slumbering together like this.

'Good morning!' she booms instead, watching with glee as they both jump out their skins. They are instantly awake and on their feet, both of them staring with wide eyes at the fright of being woken like that. 'You left the door unlocked,' Lani continues cheerfully. 'What would Dave say? Both of you sleeping like that? Tut-tut ...'

'Eh?' Blowers stares as though entranced. His face a picture of shock and surprise at the sight of Lani stood there grinning. She lets the dog go, watching as she sprints down the hall to the lads, whining with pleasure as she snakes round their legs.

'Lani,' Cookey eventually says, blinking hard as he tries to shake the sleep from his mind, 'what you doing here?'

'Meredith found you,' Lani replies. She heads straight for the sink and lifts the plastic bowl out, emptying the contents before twisting the tap on to refill it. 'I figured it was you two that went down the stairs ...'

'Yeah,' Blowers nods, still clearly reeling from the rude awakening.

'I saw Clarence going off with the Saxon and some of Maddox's lot. He must have had Paula and Roy with him ...'

'Yeah, he did,' Cookey cuts in. 'We were on the top when all hell broke out. Poor kids got taken down at the door, so we took it ...'

'I saw the bodies,' Lani replies grimly. Placing the bowl down, she watches for a second as Meredith dives straight in, her long, pink tongue lapping at the liquid. Grabbing a glass, she fills it and starts drinking, savouring the perfection of cool water cascading into her dry mouth and soothing her burning throat.

'That's so nice,' she mutters, refilling the glass to drink again.

Blowers rubs his eyes and stretches, groaning from the ache in his tired muscles. Cookey, watching Blowers, catches the yawn and follows up with one of his own before ferreting through his pockets for cigarettes.

'You seen the boss?' Blowers asks, his voice low and worried.

Shaking her head, Lani finishes the second glass and slowly moves it away from her mouth. 'No, I went through the bodies as best I could, but nothing ... Someone had taken all the weapons apart on the top level. Looked like they were going through them for ammunition.'

'Dave?' Cookey asks.

'Sort of thing he'd do,' Lani nods.

'Or Nick,' Blowers adds. 'He's switched on like that. Any sign of him?'

'None,' Lani shakes her head again.

'Fuck,' Cookey sighs, placing his hands on the top of his head as a deeply worried look crosses his face. 'What now?' he asks quietly.

'What happened to you, then?' Blowers cuts in.

'I went after Howie but lost him,' Lani explains. 'I got down onto the second level and got stuck with a group coming after me. That's when Meredith found me ... We kept looking round, and I saw the Saxon go down but couldn't get close to it ... We backed off and ...'

'You been there all night?' Cookey asks. 'Bloody hell. Didn't they find you?'

'They've all gone,' she replies. 'I did the same as you and passed out. Woke up, and the place was deserted ... I reckon they went after the Saxon.'

'Clarence will come back,' Blowers nods to himself.

'That's what I figured. Get some water, and we'll head back to wait. There's loads of weapons left there too but no rounds.'

'That empty, then?' Blowers nods at the assault rifle strapped to her back.

'It's for show,' she gives a quick grin, refilling the glass for another long drink.

'Fuck,' Cookey groans again. 'So Clarence went off with the Saxon. Dave went after the boss ... What about Nick? Where did he go? Did he get out with the Saxon? Hang on ... Shit, it was him up top, firing ... Yeah ... yeah, definitely he was up top.'

'You saw him?' Lani asks.

'Definitely,' Cookey nods firmly.

'Thank fuck for that. So just Dave and the boss, then?' Blowers says.

'Did you see the way they went after him?' Cookey asks. 'Just fucking swirling round all crazy and shit ... He got sucked right in ...'

'He was still fighting, though,' Blowers says, 'and Dave was right after him.'

'We need to get back,' Lani urges. 'Get some water while I use the bathroom.'

'There's no bog roll if you going for a poo,' Cookey calls out.

'Thanks, Cookey,' Lani shouts as she heads up the stairs.

'Use some of the clothes they left,' Cookey shouts helpfully.

'I don't need a poo. Thanks all the same, though.'

'You are a fucking nightmare,' Blowers shakes his head. Filling two glasses, he passes one over and starts drinking his own down, burping noisily as he finishes it off.

'Look at the state of her,' Cookey nods at the dog still lapping at the water. Blowers glances down, grimacing at the fur matted with dried blood, and the water in the bowl now a pink colour from the blood that had dried and congealed round her muzzle and made wet again from her messy drinking.

'Any cloths in there?' Cookey points to the cupboard under the sink.

'Check the garden, mate. Might be a hose we can use.'

'He's a bossy fucker, isn't he?' Cookey says to the dog. 'Always bossing me about, isn't he? Yes, he is ...'

'Fuck you. Have you found a hose yet?'

'Does it look like it?' Cookey asks, his hand still on the closed door handle.

'What about now?'

'Fuck off!'

'What about now?' Blowers repeats as Cookey gets the door open, stepping out into the bright sunshine.

'Shit, it's hot out here.'

'It's hot in here,' Blowers counters.

'It's fucking hot everywhere. Here, mate, bring her outside.'

'She's still drinking,' Blowers replies.

'Well, duh! Bring the bowl out, then.'

'Clever fucker,' Blowers mutters. Picking the bowl up, he heads into the garden, throwing the contents onto the dried-up flower beds as Cookey twists the hose on. They fill the bowl first, then start on Meredith, the cool spray hitting her flanks and soaking into her matted coat.

'She's filthy,' Blowers comments.

'Just like your mum, then,' Cookey quips.

'She's filthier than my mum.'

'Not possible ... Sorry, mate, but it's–'

'She alright?' Lani calls out, walking through the kitchen, to the back door. Her face freshly scrubbed and hair rinsed of the gore from the night's events.

'You wearing a different top?' Cookey asks with a puzzled glance.

'Found it in one of the drawers. Fits okay,' Lani looks down at the plain, black t-shirt. 'There's more stuff up there. You had a look yet?'

'Not yet,' Blowers replies, pushing his finger over the end of the hose to make the spray come out harder.

'Er ... well, maybe you should,' Lani says in a blunt tone. 'You're both filthy ... On second thoughts, keep doing that, and I'll find something ... You should get those trousers rinsed off. They'll have dirty blood all over them.'

'Oh my god,' Cookey gives a theatrical cry, 'you're both so bossy.' Shaking his head, he carries on muttering to himself.

'I'm not standing in my pants, waiting for them to dry,' Blowers screws his face up.

'Fine, I'll find something you can wear on your bottom half then too.'

'Ha, get him a skirt,' Cookey laughs. 'That'll be funny.'

'You're in a good mood,' Blowers says quietly after Lani has walked off.

'Not really, mate,' Cookey replies with a sudden downcast look. 'I'm shitting myself about the boss and the others.'

'Yeah,' Blowers says. He goes to add something but just shrugs and starts working along her coat, using a dustpan brush to scrub at the matted fur. Meredith stands patiently waiting for them to finish. This seems to be a normal occurrence now. They let her get filthy and then insist on giving her a bath. Still, she enjoys the fuss and attention, and the cool water feels nice in the high heat. Disappearing inside, Cookey starts going through the cupboards, ransacking the contents in search of food.

'Will she eat cat food?' he calls out.

'Why wouldn't she?'

'She's not a cat, is she? She's a dog,' Cookey replies as if the answer is obvious.

'She doesn't know that,' Blowers scoffs.

'What, you reckon she thinks she's a cat?'

'No, you plank, she doesn't know its cat food.'

'Hmmm,' Cookey considers the reply for a long second, 'good point. Here, moggy, try this.' Upending the box, he scatters the contents onto the ground. Meredith moves round, first sniffing the biscuits before digging in and taking big mouthfuls. 'Bloody hell, she's hungry ...' Cookey pours the entire contents out, letting the dog work her way through it as Blowers finishes off washing her.

Staring down at the bloody water, Cookey thinks back to the previous night and the horrible feeling tugging away inside of him. This is the first time since they met that they've been separated, and it's horrible. He's thankful for being with Blowers and Lani and Meredith, of course, but it feels like a deep part of him is missing.

'We'll find them,' Blowers says softly at seeing the worried look on Cookey's face.

'Yeah, yeah, okay ...'

They work quickly, using the hose to scrub the worse of the filth and bits of body from their clothes, spraying detergent onto them to disinfect the bacteria.

By the time Lani returns, they're both stood in boxer shorts, their clothes washed, wrung out, and now stretched out to dry in the sun. Smoking away, they act completely normal, not batting an eye when Lani steps out, carrying a bundle of clothes. She rolls her eyes at the sight and shakes her head, trying desperately to keep the normal behaviour up whilst having that gnawing feeling of panic inside her, panic that they should be doing something, anything. Searching or waiting back at the car park. But Dave's lessons have been installed deep–clean your kit whenever you can. Take care of your kit and yourself.

They'll know to wait in the area close to the car park, and they're probably doing the same thing they are, washing and cleaning up from the previous night.

Convincing herself that that is the case, she stands watching the dog eat and wishing they had some food too.

'I just said to fucknuts,' Blowers calls out, 'that they'll be okay ... We'll find them. They know to wait near here for Clarence to come back.'

Nodding back, Lani stares up at the sky and bites her bottom lip with the same feeling both Blowers and Cookey have, that something deep is missing, something vital taken away. The whole has been made less than whole. A part of her is missing.

CHAPTER ELEVEN

'As soon as we get inside, get everyone out and get ready to go back out.'

'We need fuel.'

'Right,' Clarence growls, rubbing one large, meaty hand over his large face in a vain attempt to knead the tension away, 'we get fuel and get back out.'

'Er ... the fuel truck is back in the town,' Paula twists round, wincing as she sees the dark look spreading across his face.

'Right, listen in,' Maddox booms. 'You lot will go find some vehicles that use diesel and syphon some fuel off. Get it back here, you get me?'

'Will do, Mads,' one of the youths replies quickly. Squished into the side bench seats, with the huge form of Clarence standing over them, the rear of the Saxon is both exceptionally hot and exceptionally cramped. The youngest of the crews, handpicked by Maddox, were not happy at being taken away from the fighting. It was a sign of weakness, of being younger and vulnerable, and their backgrounds dictated that you never showed a weakness.

Whilst the rest starburst from the hordes of infected pressing in, the Saxon gained speed and was soon out of danger, speeding down the main road and onto the motorway. All of them feeling wretched at leaving their comrades, mates, friends, and colleagues alone with that load of filthy, diseased, and violent zombies after them.

Clarence took charge, the professional soldier doing the right thing by working to save and protect the youngest. All of them were exhausted, drained from heat and constant action, and it wasn't long before some of the children started dropping off, their young heads lolling with eyes closed, instantly transforming their young faces to look like the children they really were.

Now, with Clarence and Maddox shouting orders, they snap awake; eyes wide as they realise where they are.

'Maddox, can you grab another vehicle? Get a van or something big that can carry lots of people.'

'We'll do that,' Paula shouts back. 'You get the fuel, and we'll find the vehicles. Have you got any more weapons?'

'Maybe some shotguns left, but I think it got stripped out,' Clarence mutters. 'Grab what you can, but we've got to be quick.'

'How will you know where to look for them?' Roy calls out from his position driving the Saxon.

'My lot will stay close. They'll know we're coming back.'

'We left a lot of those zombies there, though,' Roy replies. 'They could have forced them further out ... It could take some doing to find them.'

'Then doing is what we'll do,' Clarence growls, his voice deep and hoarse.

'Those children need some sleep,' Roy continues. 'They're exhausted. You can't expect them to go back out.'

'We're alright. We ain't fuckin' staying,' one of the louder children shouts.

'You are,' Clarence glares them into submission. 'One, we need the space in the vehicles to bring the others back. Two ... you need rest and fluids ...'

'We ain't pussies,' the youth scoffs.

'And three ...' Clarence continues. 'The fort has been left undefended. We need people back there to guard it ... You get me?' he adds caustically. The edge in his voice and the sheer size of the man drops the children into silence.

'He's right. Stay there and help Lenski,' Maddox adds. 'I'm coming with you. Darius too.'

'Fuck yeah,' Darius adds from the far back of the Saxon.

'Okay, so fuel and weapons ... then straight back out ... any water down there?' Clarence asks.

'Can't see a fucking thing, bruv,' Darius replies, 'and we're too stuffed in to get anythin' from the floor too.'

'We're not far off,' Roy replies.

'What happened back there?' Paula asks. 'Why did they do that?'

'They wanted the boss ...' Clarence replies, his glare fixed.

'Never seen 'em do that before,' Roy cuts in, 'swirling like that. Worked a fucking treat, though, didn't it? Christ, that Howie got sucked right in ...'

'Roy,' Paula warns in a low voice.

'How anyone can survive that is beyond me. He must have gone right into that tunnel. Poor man ...'

'Roy,' Paula warns with an increasingly loud voice.

'What?' he turns to ask, a look of innocence on his face. 'Oh ... er ... yeah, but you know ... he'll probably be okay,' he adds weakly.

'Dave went after him,' Clarence mutters, his voice dropping several more octaves.

'Yeah, but one man against that many,' Roy carries on, oblivious to the glare from Paula.

'Dave will find him. Nothing can defeat that man,' Clarence says louder this time. 'Dave will find him,' he adds more to himself.

'I think we're close now,' Paula calls out, tactfully changing the subject. 'Yep, we're onto the long road ...'

'Good,' Clarence mutters. Dave did go after the boss, and nothing can defeat Dave. Dave is unstoppable. He'll defend Howie to the last breath in his body. Clarence repeats these thoughts to himself, fending off the rising feeling of fear gripping his insides.

A steel core runs through the giant man. He won't rest or stop until he's found every member of the team. They'll stay close and wait. He knows this is what they will do. Words and instructions weren't needed. They never actually discussed what to do if something like this happened, but they know he'll go back.

'Flash the light,' Maddox calls out, 'let them know we're coming in.'

'Righto,' Roy shouts, fiddling with the controls to figure out the right button to use. The powerful beam of light starts alternating between full and dipped, signalling ahead to get the gates open.

'Er ... there's a chap stood outside,' Roy shouts back. 'He's got a shotgun or something ...' Clarence forces his bulk forward to stare out the window, looking ahead at the solitary figure picked out by the lights. One man stood there, holding a long-barrelled weapon. Legs planted apart, with a stocky physique.

'Who is he?' Maddox asks.

'No idea,' Clarence replies, a feeling of dread coursing through him.

The Saxon pulls up a short distance from the gates. The man holding the gun uses one hand to shield his eyes from the glare of the lights, waving to turn them off. Roy obliges, switching them to side lights and watching as the man lowers his hand and resumes the solid stance.

'Get the doors open.' Clarence urges the youths out the way as he drops down out the back doors and strides round the vehicle. Maddox and Darius running to join him either side. Paula and Roy are already out the front doors and walking ahead.

'Stay there,' the man calls out in a warning tone, bringing the weapon to aim forwards.

'Who the fuck are you?' Maddox calls out.

'Watch your tone,' the man snaps back. 'You must be the returning heroes then.'

Clarence doesn't break stride but keeps heading towards the man, his peripheral vision picking up the movements of the rest as they fan out to present a much wider target. The man sweeps the gun side to side, a double-barrelled shotgun that Clarence notices is held with steady hands.

'Who are you?' Clarence asks, his voice menacingly low.

'I'm the man holding the big gun,' the man replies, trying to match the menacing tone but failing.

Roy drops back to the Saxon, reaches in to draw his compound bow and a single arrow and tugs the night-vision goggles over his face. Once done, he steps away to the side, absorbing into the shadows, banking on the fact the man will be watching Clarence and the others.

'This is our place now,' the man adds quickly, seeing the

big man coming at him. 'We've got armed men inside, and we'll fucking kill everyone if you ...'

'What?' Clarence asks, 'I don't have time for this ... Get out the fucking way.'

'Keep coming, big boy,' the man raises the weapon to aim at Clarence, 'come on ... see what happens ...' He tries to sound tough, but this isn't going how it was meant to be. This man is massive, and he looks angry, but above all else, he doesn't look scared at all. The others are moving out quietly to the sides too, making it harder for him to track everyone. So instead, he keeps the gun trained on the big fella.

'Toby? You alright?' a voice calls out from the other side of the gate. 'What's going on?' Toby doesn't answer. The slight distraction of the voice calling out was enough for Clarence to deftly step in and grip his throat, virtually lifting the man off the floor.

'Toby? Toby?' the voice calls out again, more urgent this time. Toby drops the weapon. His primal instinct kicking in to draw oxygen into his system–something he is unable to do due to the pressure being applied.

'Your man is fucked, bruv,' Maddox shouts. 'Come out, or we'll kill him.'

'Toby?' the voice shouts with alarm.

Gently, Clarence lowers Toby to the floor, just the one hand gripping his throat. His baleful eyes stare deep into Toby's soul. Toby sees the eyes of a killer, the eyes of a man who has seen everything there is to see.

'I'm gonna let go,' Clarence whispers. 'Make a sound ... one fucking sound, and I'll rip your larynx out ... Understand?' Toby nods, a quick, firm motion done with a bright red face starved of air, eyes bulging out, and tears streaming down his face.

Roy, having heard the second voice runs back to the Saxon and draws his rucksack out, tugging the straps on and making sure he can reach overhead to grasp the shafts of the arrows. Once armed, he again steps away into the shadows, nocking an arrow to take aim at the gate.

'If you kill Toby, we'll do everyone in ... er ... in here ... We'll do everyone in, in here,' the voice shouts, somewhat puzzled by his own choice of words.

'How many men have you got?' Clarence whispers, releasing the pressure from Toby's neck. He sucks air in, gulping it down as he regains some composure. Clarence feels the wet patch spreading underneath his knee and shifts position, avoiding the spread of urine from Toby pissing himself.

'Please,' Toby croaks, and the pressure is immediately reapplied.

'I asked you a question. Answer me ... How many men you got in there?'

Once again, Toby feels the pressure being released from his throat and sucks air in. 'Seven,' he gasps.

'Seven?' Toby nods, his wide eyes fixed on the bald man looming over him.

'Are they all armed?' Toby nods again, his head hardly stopping from the constant bobbing. 'What with? What guns do they have?'

'Shotguns, rifles ... er ... one's got a pistol.'

'How did you get in?' Maddox asks, dropping down to speak in a low voice.

'Toby? What the fuck is going on!?' the voice shouts. A muted conversation starts up behind the gate; arguments and hasty whispers being thrown about.

'We just walked up,' Toby replies. 'Some Polish bird tried to ... Urgh!' Toby winces as his nose is broken from

Maddox's powerful punch, hot blood spurting out down his front.

'That Polish bird is my missus,' Maddox hisses. 'If she's been hurt, I swear I'll slit your fucking throat.' He presses a blade against Toby's face, digging the point in for added emphasis.

'Maddox, back off, mate,' Clarence mutters quietly. Maddox is strong, but he doesn't have the knowledge for this. By telling Toby he'll be killed if he says anything happened to Lenski, he's just inviting the man to lie, which isn't the point of this.

'She's fine,' Toby wails, holding his hands to his face.

'We haven't got time for this,' Clarence seethes. Glancing over his shoulder at the gates, he can sense the danger Howie and the others have been left in. The urge to find his team and bring them back to safety presses in. This is an inconvenience that needs resolving quickly.

'Roy, with me,' Clarence stands up. One hand clutching Toby by the hair, dragging him with ease to the gate. Roy runs forward, joined by Paula drawing her pistol. Maddox and Darius both move ahead to join the ex-soldier dragging the man across the ground. Darius pauses to scoop the shotgun up, breaking it open to check it's loaded.

'Open the gate,' Clarence shouts out. His voice loud and flat.

'Toby?'

'Toby's with me. Now open the fucking GATE,' Clarence roars, his voice building to a bellow.

'Get fucked,' the voice shouts, braver now he's been joined by more men whispering with him.

'Open this gate, or I swear to god–' Clarence warns.

'What? What you gonna do? Make a battering ram? Yeah, good luck with that.'

'Don't tell him that, you twat!' another voice shouts.

'Why?'

'Giving him ideas. That's why. What if he drives into the gates?'

'Fuck's sake. He probably heard you say that,' yet another voice joins the internal arguing.

The voices are cut off by the impact of Toby being launched bodily at the smaller walk-through gate. Clarence remembering it is held shut by just a couple of bolts. With every ounce of strength in his enormous muscles, he grasps Toby and flings him hard at the gate. Watching with satisfaction as it caves in, screams of panic and alarm sound from inside as they see the mangled remains of Toby flying past them.

Clarence bursts through, using their surprise to his advantage. Shots ring out, but Clarence dives deep, flinging himself to the ground as the idiots shoot each other from either side of the gate, adding more screams to the air.

Roy takes position just on the outside of the gate, using the enhanced vision of the goggles to take perfect shots at those huddled inside. He takes two down with arrow shots, wrenching them off their feet.

Clarence is up and charging into the other side, using his big frame to slam multiple bodies against the hard inside of the vehicle gate.

Paula runs in, pistol up and ready. She spots a man running for the inner gate, firing several times into his back.

The shotgun blasts out as Darius opens up with both barrels at figures running in panic. Maddox runs past Paula, heading straight for the inner gate, going into a quick dive as shots fired from inside splinter the wooden frame.

Shots keep striking the door and ground just inside;

then, someone slams it shut, and the sound of thick bolts ramming home is distinct.

Twisting round, the leader of the former compound spots Clarence snapping a neck by twisting the head. All those inside are dead or dying slowly. The weapons kicked away and taken up by the children from the Saxon running in to join the melee.

'Fucking seven, my arse,' Darius spits. 'There's five out here, plus that Toby motherfucker.'

Clarence seethes with the failure of the hurried assault, taking down so many in such a quick incident was staggeringly good, but it still failed. More armed men were now inside the locked gate and taking up position.

These fools out here were stupid enough to stand either side and then shoot each other, but those inside are clearly set back and aiming at the gate. The first one through will be cut to bits. For a second he considers using the downed bodies to throw through, but he heard several distinct shots taking place–that means several different guns.

'You,' Maddox points at several of the children crouching nearby, 'get down there and get some fuel out them vehicles ... We need diesel and get it into that army truck.'

'What you doing?' Clarence asks quietly.

'You gotta get back. Those are my crews out there too,' Maddox says quickly. 'We'll sort this. You get the fuck out of here.'

'What?' Clarence stares back open-mouthed. 'Seriously?'

'Yeah, seriously,' Maddox nods, 'get going, take Paula and Roy, leave this to us ... but don't just look for your own team ... find my crews too.'

Nodding back, Clarence goes after the youths to the

many parked vehicles rammed into the section between the gates. The children work quickly, identifying those vehicles with diesel and getting the fuel caps opened. Hose is found, along with fuel cans, and within seconds, diesel is being sucked up and out to fill the cans.

Clarence wanders between them, feeling the urge for action but not being able to do anything. The experienced children work quickly and make him redundant. So he paces back and forth, waiting without patience for the first fuel can to be filled. When it is, he snatches it off the children and gets it to the Saxon.

'What you going to do?' Paula asks Maddox, watching Clarence run past.

'We'll figure it out,' Maddox replies gruffly. Paula twists round, staring at the Saxon and Roy, then back to the inner gate.

'Maybe I should stay with you,' she suggests. 'Clarence and Roy can get the others and–'

'Up to you, lady,' Maddox cuts her off, his face a picture of concentration as he stares at the high gates with such intensity as though his will alone will see it fall.

'That cunt lied,' Darius spits again, unable to get over what Toby said. His mind whirring with worry for Sierra trapped inside with Lenski.

'I'm staying,' Paula says to Clarence running past to grab another fuel can. He doesn't answer but just keeps going, his sole focus on getting the fuel.

'Oi,' Maddox shouts, 'you hear me?'

'Okay,' Clarence gasps at Paula, running past with another fuel can, 'me and Roy will do it. You stay here ...'

'That's what I just said,' Paula mutters at the man running back to the Saxon.

'I said ... do you hear me?' Maddox shouts, cocking his

head to listen for any replies. When no reply comes back, he stares over at Darius, a very rare look of worry on his face that serves to convince Paula of the need for her to stay here.

'We're done,' Roy jogs over. 'He said you're staying here.'

'Yeah,' she replies.

'Want me to stay with you?' he asks quietly, finally pushing the goggles up from his eyes. 'I, er ... I don't mind staying with you,' he adds.

'Roy,' Clarence runs in, 'you ready?'

'Go,' Paula urges, 'you need to get those children back here.'

'I know,' Roy nods, but he still hesitates, 'but er ... well, you know ... we're like a team and er ...'

'Are we?' Paula asks with genuine surprise, then realises the tone of her reply. 'That's really sweet,' she grins. 'Thanks, Roy.'

'What? Oh no, don't mention it ... just, you know ...'

'Roy, I'm going ... Stay here if you want,' Clarence strides off.

'Actually, I rather think I should stay,' Roy calls after him.

'No, Roy, you go,' Paula cuts in. 'Clarence will need you.'

'What about here? You've only got a couple of shotguns which are no good over range. I can use my bow in the dark ...'

Clarence stops mid-stride. Turning round, he stares up at the fort. These people don't know who Big Chris is, they don't know about Sergeant Hopewell or Ted, they don't know about Sarah. They know nothing of the sacrifices made to keep this place. The fort has to survive. It has to be the safe place that survivors can go to. Howie is adamant about that, about how important it is, that it has to be a free area without fear or dictating rule.

The people stuck in the town are important to Clarence and the others, but the numbers of survivors who will need somewhere safe outweigh that importance.

'Roy's right,' Clarence adds, his deep voice penetrating the hushed conversation taking place. Striding back to the group, he keeps his voice low. 'He can use that bow better in the dark than anyone of us with a rifle. Stay here and do what you can ...'

'You going alone?' Paula asks.

'Yep, I'll be fine.'

'What about taking another vehicle?' she asks.

'These are no good,' he replies, pointing down the alley at the parked vehicles. 'The keys are in there,' he nods to the fort.

'Don't need keys, bruv,' Darius comments.

'There's enough vehicles left out there to use,' Clarence says. 'Stay here and get this sorted ... I'll get everyone else and meet you back here.'

'Are there any tunnels or other ways in?' Paula whispers before he walks off.

Shaking his head, Clarence looks up at the high walls. 'Just the door at the rear. That's the only one I know about. Might be another way in somewhere but ...' he shrugs, deciding enough time has been wasted. 'See you in a few hours at most. I'll signal with the headlights when I come through the estate. Three flashes ... If everything goes wrong, then we'll meet at the little village across the bay.'

'Got it,' Maddox nods, exchanging a quick handshake before Clarence double-times it back to the vehicle. Once behind the wheel, he takes a brief second to stare at the fort.

Shaking his head at the turn of events, he eases the big armoured personnel carrier forward to turn in a wide arc.

The others, standing silently in the alley between the high walls, watch the retreating vehicle. All of them feel a sense of despondency at the Saxon leaving. All of them, apart from Roy, who mid-way through scratching his right upper arm detects a small lump and goes into meltdown. For the first time since the fighting started and all through the events of the evening, his heart finally notches up above normal. His breathing increases, and a sense of panic starts to grip his insides.

Tugging the night vision goggles down, he twists his own arm, trying to see the back of it and the giant tumour growing out of his arm. This is it. This is the big one. The start of the serious illness. He feels round the lump, craning his head while whimpering softly. An angry, red lump. Shit, that has come up quick. It must be growing fast, spreading through his entire body. This lump will be the tip of the iceberg.

'Roy!' His attention snaps up, yelping in pain from the retina burn of the torchlight glaring into the lenses of his goggles. 'It's an insect bite ... We've all got them,' Paula says quietly.

'A bite?' he gasps, the feeling of relief starting to flush in.

'Yes, Roy,' she says softly, 'just a bite. Maddox has got them too ... and Darius ... Haven't you?' She turns round, glaring wide-eyed at the two lads.

'Have we?' Darius stares at her, then at Maddox.

'Er ... yeah ... my arm. It's like ... well itchy,' Maddox picks up on the contorted facial expression of Paula, quickly rubbing an imaginary bite on his arm.

'Me too,' Darius rubs his leg. 'Got me on the thigh. Itchy as fuck ... You lot been bitten too?' he asks the youths.

Slowly, they understand the glares being sent their way from the combined forces of Paula, Maddox, and Darius. All of them start scratching at various parts of their bodies, making noises of pain and relief.

'See,' Paula smiles back at Roy, 'just a bite.'

'Fucking good job,' Roy beams. 'Got me scared that one did ...' Paula stares at him for a second, full of admiration for the way he is and the skills he brings with the bow. Even in the car park when it was time to go hand to hand, he didn't hesitate but wielded that sword like a demon. He was so fit and athletic, driving round to thrust and slice. His courage and skill were undeniable, but that propensity to swear just doesn't suit him.

Vowing to ask him where that comes from, she steps back to join the others staring up at the locked gates with the perfectly silent fort behind. All of them now scratching various parts of their bodies.

CHAPTER TWELVE

'Dad, we need to stop. The boys are getting tired ... or we should find a car,' Lilly calls ahead to her father and Norman walking side by side down the country lane.

'Norman, what do you think?' Andrew asks. 'Stop here, shall we? Or press on a bit further?'

'Oh, I don't know, Andrew,' Norman replies. 'I rather think we shouldn't stop in the middle of a road. What do you think if we keep going and find somewhere?'

'I think I would agree,' Andrew nods blithely. 'The committee has designated that we should press on for a short while,' Andrew grins back at the girls, clearly proud of his humorous statement.

'Yes,' Norman agrees in the same annoyingly patronising tone, 'the committee says to push on for a little while. You boys are okay, aren't you?'

'I'm tired Daddy,' Todd replies.

'Hungry, my tummy is making noises,' Billy adds.

'Well, yes, we're all hungry, Billy,' Andrew comments. 'Just a bit further, eh? There's a good boy. So, Norman, you were saying?'

'Oh yes, well, up to the recession, I would say our output was matching that of the big players in the business, and to be truthful, we didn't notice any downplay in customer orders for quite some time ...'

'The committee?' Lilly whispers to Samantha.

'God knows,' the other girl rolls her eyes. 'Listen to them. You'd think they were playing golf or something.'

'Lilly,' Billy pipes up, 'where are we going?'

'I've told you already,' Lilly snaps, tired from the heat and the worry of walking in the middle of nowhere with two men completely engrossed in discussing business models. Taking a breath, she softens her tone, 'We're going to a big fort where other people are living.'

'Will we have a house?' Todd asks.

'With a puppy?' Billy grins excitedly.

'A puppy? Where on earth did you get that idea from? No, we're not having a puppy.'

'I want a puppy,' Billy says sulkily.

'Can I share your puppy?' Todd asks.

'Yes,' Billy nods seriously.

'There's a house up there,' Samantha points ahead to the flashes of roof appearing between the trees.

'Dad, there's a house up ahead. We can stop there,' Lilly calls out.

'Where? Oh yes. I see it ... Well, I shall put it before the committee and get back to you,' he grins again before turning back to discuss it with Norman.

'You okay?' Lilly asks, watching as Sam rubs her stomach and winces.

'Period,' Sam whispers, 'really hurts.'

'Cramps?'

'Yeah,' Sam replies. 'It's okay,' she shrugs it off, trying

her best to ignore the pains. 'Er, have you got any, er, you know?' Sam asks, aware that young ears are listening.

'In my bag. Do you need some?'

'I will when we stop. I couldn't ask Dad to get me any.'

'Mum had loads at home,' Lilly explains, her face dropping at the memory of her mother not seen since the event started.

'The committee has agreed to stop at yonder house,' Norman beams.

'Gee, thanks,' Sam rolls her eyes again, shaking her head in embarrassment of her father.

Getting closer, they start to see more of the house, a large, detached stone-built cottage set back from the road with large front gardens. Picturesque and quaint, with dried-up flower beds and a large willow tree shading an old, wrought iron bench embedded into the grass.

'Very nice, must cost a pretty penny,' Norman admires as they walk closer.

'Think of the heating bills in the winter, though,' Andrew comments. 'Those old-style windows, no double glazing.'

'Must be listed,' Norman nods. 'These old buildings are a bugger to alter if they're listed.'

Lilly stares hard as the two men stroll through the gate and start heading up the path, both of them still chatting away amiably and not paying the least bit of attention. The two girls stare at the windows and front door, scanning the area while listening intently.

'Dad,' Lilly whispers, 'we shouldn't just walk up!'

'What? Out here, Lilly? Come on ... this house looks fine.'

'Sam, get my knife from my bag,' Lilly says in a low

voice, pausing while the girl opens the top flap to pull out the bladed weapon.

Checking her father and Norman haven't seen, she tucks the knife into the waist band at the back of her jeans, adjusting it to make sure the blade doesn't dig into her backside.

'Stay here with the boys, Sam.'

Sam grabs the hands of the two boys, preventing them from walking any further as Norman reaches the front door and uses the big brass knocker to announce their arrival. Lilly spins round, checking the road behind them before walking to the corner to view up the side of the house, constantly scanning the windows for movement. Still, the fathers just stand there, chatting, not even stepping back from the door. Lilly grimaces, her heart beating harder at the blasé way they are treating this. Like a walk in the woods or a country stroll.

'No answer,' Norman states loud enough for them all to hear.

'It's locked,' Andrew reports on trying the handle. 'Shall we go round the back?'

'I'll do it,' Lilly strides off, not giving her father a chance to disagree.

'Headstrong like her mother,' Andrew tuts.

'They grow up quickly these days, Andrew,' Norman adds sagely.

'They do, Norman,' Andrew agrees, trying to make himself sound as sagely as Norman.

Keeping to the far side of the garden to gain a better view of the house, Lilly walks towards the rear, her eyes roving from window to window. At the corner, she stops and takes in the view of the rear gardens. Large and mostly laid to lawn, with ornamental pots bordering a long gravel path weaving between more flower beds.

Silence. She edges forward, one hand gripping the handle of the knife in her waistband. At the window, she slowly eases round to peer inside, seeing an old farmhouse-style kitchen with a large pine table. About to press on, and she spots one of the pine chairs lying on its side. That's not right. She peers on closer, spotting the cupboard doors have been left open.

Something's wrong here. Her instincts scream out to move away, this place is unsafe. Supressing the reaction and knowing they need food, she edges on past the window to the back doors set back from view.

Metres away, and a solitary shoe stands alone on the path. Dark coloured. She didn't see it because it blended in with the ornamental pots, except for the small bloodstain next to it.

The knife is out, held in front as she breathes harder and leans round to see the open back door. The corpse of an old woman lies across it. Dried blood is smeared down the flagstone floor hallway where she tried to crawl away before slumping on the threshold never to move again. Lilly takes it all in quickly–the inner hallway with the knocked over furniture, the opened cupboard doors, and the dead body.

They need food desperately, but this place has been done over. She can see the cut throat from here. The ragged flesh of the knife wound deep in the throat that caused the blood to come out so quickly. Murder. This wasn't defence or zombies but plain murder. Gasping with shock, she spots the old woman's knickers are round her ankles and the old flannel skirt pushed up high.

The sight sickens her, and she turns away as her stomach flips over. Jogging quickly round the side to the others, she waves them away, urging them to get back on the road.

'We need to go,' she whispers urgently. Both the men stare back in shock at the knife in her hand, the two of them too stupid to respond. 'We have to go,' she presses in a forceful voice.

'Why?' Andrew asks dumbly.

'Come on,' Lilly strides away to join Sam and the two boys already retreating out onto the lane. The four of them start walking off, and Lilly notices the knife held in Sam's hand down at her side.

'Lilly,' Andrew calls out, 'what's going on?'

'There's a dead woman at the back. She's been murdered and ... er ...'

'Oh gosh,' Norman blanches, 'really? Oh dear ... yes, well, maybe we should press on then.'

'And what?' Sam asks, picking up on Lilly's voice trailing off.

'Raped,' Lilly mouths the word silently. Sam nods with a firm glance and picks her pace up, gripping Todd's hand to urge him on.

'How sad,' Andrew says after a few seconds, 'out here too, in the countryside. I expect those things got to her. Poor old dear probably didn't know what they were.'

'She was murdered, Dad, not bitten,' Lilly replies.

'Oh, I doubt that,' Norman adds. 'Murdered out here? For what?'

'Food, clothes, medicines ...' Lilly explains, shocked at the reaction of the two adults.

'Suicide?' Andrew asks Norman.

'Most likely,' Norman replies in his sagely voice.

They didn't see her, Lilly thinks. Neither of them actually saw her with her throat cut, but they're convincing themselves that it was some accident or self-inflicted injury. Sam glances across at her, managing to convey the same thought process in a single look. Lilly nods, an affirmation between them that their fathers are incompetent idiots.

The boys, although picking up on the nervous fear of their older sisters, soon forget the drama and return to complaining about being hungry, something that plucks heavily at the heartstrings of Lilly.

Ahead lays a wide junction. One side branches off to a leafy side lined with large, detached old-style houses set back, and the other side opens to pasture and thickets of trees.

There is no choice. They have to find food or risk the boys becoming sick from starvation or malnutrition. It's one thing to be inside a house where the rate of energy consumption is low, but now they're walking and in this heat, they'll be using up valuable energy very quickly. The water is almost gone too, all of them using it as a way of warding off the hunger pangs.

But still the two adult men, who should be leading and guiding the others, are slipping further into their deep conversation. They share life stories and trade anecdotes. Ill-equipped and never designed to withstand this kind of hardship, they find solace in the company of a like-minded person.

'We're going to have to try those houses,' Lilly stops at the junction, completely aware that her father and Norman have strolled right across it without a second glance.

'What?' Oh yes, up there,' Andrew turns and nods. 'What do you think, Norman? Worth a go?'

Shaking her head in disbelief, Lilly stares daggers at the two men, willing them to firm up and be decisive. Can't they see they have two young children here that are starving and are getting quieter with every passing hour.

'Well,' Norman rocks back on his heels, 'I think it's probably worth a go. See if we can't find us a tasty morsel or two to snack on.'

'They look intact,' Andrew comments, walking towards the first house. So did the last one, Lilly muses, seeing that neither of them have learnt anything from the previous address. What was her father doing those nights he went out? He kept coming back saying how bad it was, the bodies and the destruction, but meeting Norman has seemed to dull his wits.

She lets them lead the way this time. Both her and Sam stare with alert eyes at the windows and door, rotating round to view the road and surrounding area, heads cocked as they listen.

'Locked,' Andrew reports on trying the door again.

'Blast,' Norman replies, 'shall we try the back?'

'Yes, lets,' Andrew moves away to join Norman as they tread noisily along the gravel path to the rear. Lilly winces, willing them to take a step to the left or right and walk on the grass. They let her take the back on her own last time, but now they have to go together.

'Stay here,' she whispers to Sam, moving off silently across the grass, one hand tucked behind and holding the handle of the knife. She watches the two adults stroll into the back garden, both of them commenting on the layout and design before they even glance at the back of the house. Lilly clocks the windows are fastened closed, but the back door is wide open, same as the last time, and the hairs on the back of her neck prickle with the sensation that something isn't right here too.

But the food is desperately needed, even a packet of

crisps to give the boys some energy. It has to be risked, so she watches the men walk up to the back door and politely call out, hanging around and waiting as if some kind old granny wearing an apron and carrying a freshly baked apple pie is about to appear and invite them in to drink home-made lemonade.

Eventually they go inside, which prompts Lilly to move closer. They're not even aware that she's with them. They didn't look about or check behind them, nor did they take any notice of the large shed in the garden with the door hanging open. Holding position, she watches both the back of the house and the shed, staying quiet to listen for any unusual sounds, but the only noises are her father and Norman plodding around inside as they chat happily away.

Gritting her teeth, Lilly heads over to the shed and checks inside. Nothing there, just tools and gardening stuff. Satisfied, she walks over and through the back door, heading straight into the kitchen where she instantly spots the open cupboard doors. Again, the cupboards have been looted, but at least there's no body slumped on the floor this time.

'Oh, you came in too,' Norman comments, leading Andrew into the kitchen.

'There's no food here,' Lilly ignores the remark, biting down the reply that they should have bloody heard her coming in.

'Oh dear,' Andrew tuts, checking through the cupboards that Lilly just went through. She looks over to see Norman smiling at her. A fatherly gesture, but there's something odd in his eyes, and she notices his gaze drops down to her chest before he coughs and starts checking the same cupboards that Andrew is going through.

'They're empty. I checked,' Lilly states, staring at the back of Norman's head and feeling very uncomfortable.

'Certainly appears that way,' Andrew steps back. 'On to the next one, then.'

'Er, we could still get some water, though,' Lilly suggests.

'Oh, water, of course, yes ... Hang on, I'll call the others in.' Andrew goes straight to the front door, unlocking it and calling out loudly to Sam and the two boys. Lilly winces at his booming voice, tutting to herself.

'Right, I suggest, Andrew, that we go to the next house while these get some water. Good idea?'

'Agreed!' Andrew beams. The two men start of, walking out the front door, leaving a stunned Lilly in the kitchen while Samantha fills glasses with water for the boys.

'Where are we meeting?' She rushes to the door, calling out in a low voice, 'We staying here or coming after you?'

'Good point,' Norman points a finger in the air. 'Well said, that girl, yes, er ... Stay here?' he asks Andrew.

'Yes, yes, stay here and get some water. We'll be right back.'

'Clever girl, your Lilly,' Norman comments audibly.

'Like her mother,' Andrew replies, 'old head on young shoulders.'

'Hmmm,' Norman glances back at Lilly standing in the doorway, a furtive glance that takes in her developed figure. 'Quite so.'

Lilly moves away quickly, hating every second of this ridiculous plan. Storming back into the kitchen, she can barely conceal her anger, something which Sam picks up on straight away.

'They didn't even tell us what to do. I mean if we should stay here or go with them,' Lilly replies after Sam asks her what's wrong.

'They're in a world of their own. That's for sure,' Sam comments.

'My dad had a nervous breakdown. He's been a bag of nerves since this started, but he changed completely meeting your dad last night. Look at them now ...'

'Mines the same,' Sam cuts her off. 'He would only go out when we were desperate, just kept us inside, hiding behind the curtains and not making any noise. The nights were the hardest ... Todd was having nightmares, and I had to stay with him to make sure he didn't cry out.'

'Jesus,' Lilly stares at the girl. Taking the offered glass, she drinks it down quickly before taking the empties from the two boys and refilling them. 'Come on, you two, drink it down.'

'Is there any juice?' Billy asks. 'I don't like water.'

'I know, Billy, but no juice here. Maybe we'll find some later.'

'And some sweets?' Todd asks.

'Maybe,' Sam smiles sadly. 'There's some cars up that road. I saw them as we came up ... Do you think they'll let us take one?'

'Probably not,' Lilly sighs. 'We should. We should be getting out of here ... That last house was all emptied, and that lady was ...' she glances down at the boys.

'Yeah, I know,' Sam nods.

'Well, someone has been in and taken everything here too ... and if they're going to do that to an old lady, then what about us? We shouldn't be here.'

Sam leans back against the worktop, clutching her glass with two hands and a very worried expression. 'If it was just me and you, we would take a car. Can you drive?'

'No, can't be that hard, though ... If them two can do it,

then how difficult can it be?' She laughs, a soft sound that makes the boys stare up smiling.

'True,' Sam snorts. 'Well, we might have to give it like the full-on nagging mode, you know, like proper whining ...'

'Ha, like when your phone needs topping up,' Lilly laughs.

'Yeah, or there's a sale on at TK Maxx.'

'Oh, seriously full-on whining. Got it,' Lilly nods.

The four of them wait, drinking water until bladders are full and taking it in turns to use the toilet. The delay is worrying, causing concern to both girls who do their best to keep the boys' spirits up, playing 'I spy' and guessing games until a dull silence descends.

Not being able to stand it any longer, they head outside. Two fifteen-year-old girls leading two small boys. Hands firmly gripping knife handles. In the sunshine they move down the path and into the road, staring up and down for a few seconds.

'Come on,' Lilly nods, leading the way up the road and past the houses. Scanning windows, doors and straining for any noise coming from anywhere. The heat is incredible, searing down with scorching sunshine that threatens to burn any exposed fair skin. The boys go quiet, simply beaten into submission by the oppressive heat.

'There,' Sam points ahead at the two figures coming out from a driveway, into the lane. Lilly breathes a sigh of relief and notices instantly they're carrying bags in their hands.

'Hey, hey,' Andrew calls out in a voice that carries easily down the lane, 'we got some goodies.'

'Oh my god,' Sam seethes quietly, 'tell him to shut up!' The girls spin round, knowing his voice would have been heard from every direction.

'Did you hear?' Norman shouts down. 'We got food!'

'Ssshhh,' Lilly pushes a finger to her lips while waving the other hand at them.

'Oh, Lilly. You are a worrier, aren't you?' Andrew remarks. Her mouth drops open at being called a worrier. This coming from the man going through a nervous breakdown and medicated to the eyeballs.

'You're so loud. Anyone could hear you,' Sam cuts in, staring at her own father.

'There's no one here,' Norman looks at Andrew with an expression that begs forgiveness for his stupid daughter.

'Where did you get the food?' Lilly asks.

'Er ... a few houses up,' Andrew replies. 'We got beans and spaghetti, tinned vegetables, corned beef er ... some spam ... tuna, and look,' he pulls a bottle out of the bag, 'some salad cream too. Not even opened.'

All thoughts of noise and safety are gone at the sight of the food, both the men holding the bags up to show the delicious goods inside. Lilly feels the pangs of hunger stabbing at her stomach, and an image of ripping the bag from her father to start devouring the food now flits through her mind.

'Come on, then,' Andrew grins. 'Who's up for some lunch? Billy? You hungry?'

'Yeah,' Billy grins excitedly, running alongside his father as they head back towards the first house. In the kitchen, they empty the contents of the bags onto the dining room table as Lilly and Sam ferry plates, cutlery, and a tin opener from the kitchen.

'Look at this,' Norman smiles with triumph, pulling a tin of custard out to show off proudly. 'Eh? Doesn't that look nice?' he asks the two boys, glancing again at Lilly. She keeps her eyes downcast and places the plates down before moving to the other side of the table next to her father.

Tins are opened, and the contents spooned out. Tuna is mixed with salad cream and placed with tinned vegetables and cold baked beans. Weird mixtures and contrasting flavours, but the food is delicious. The hungry mouths devour every morsel placed in front of them. Speaking ceases as the focus becomes solely on the food.

Stomachs that are starved of food shrink fast and take far less to be filled than they were once used to. Within minutes, the group are struggling to finish what they've opened. Even the grown adults struggle, with Andrew and Norman feeling that their eyes were bigger than their bellies.

'That was lovely,' Andrew sighs, rubbing his stomach while looking round the table. 'All that walking has made me a bit sleepy, you know,' he adds, yawning with a big stretch.

'Our two little soldiers look a tad snoozey too,' Norman comments. 'Perhaps a short break for them to rest is in order.'

'We should keep going,' Lilly cuts in quickly. 'If we take a car, the boys can sleep in the back.'

'And how do you propose we fit six people into one car?' Andrew asks with eyebrows lifted.

'Er ... two cars?' Lilly shrugs. 'There's enough of them left here.'

'Oh, right, yes, of course ... Makes sense, I suppose,' Andrew sniffs while Norman gives Lilly a sly smile that makes her skin crawl.

'I think we're better off on foot,' Norman drops the smile and leans forward. Deepening his voice to sound serious, he looks round the table in a weak attempt to add gravitas to his manner, but again, his gaze lingers on Lilly. 'Several reasons for this thought process,' he continues in the same forced tone. 'One, we are quieter and less intrusive on foot so we can stay undetected. A car engine makes noise. Two, er ...' he stops, thinking frantically for another reason. Now he's said there are several reasons, he can't just offer one. 'Er ... it would mean dividing our party, which I am uncomfortable with. What if we take a wrong turn or get separated?'

'How would that–' Sam starts to ask.

'Three,' Norman exclaims, excited at thinking of another reason to offer, 'we've all been cooped up for days on end, so er ... the fresh air and er ... sunshine will be good for us. Yes ... er, we need the exercise too.' He looks to Andrew for help, imploring him with his eyes.

'Right,' Andrew replies slowly, unsure of the way this was going, 'yes, er ... um ...' He holds Norman in high esteem, and already the two of them are getting on so well. Andrew, being a nervous and fearful man was only too happy to find a like-minded individual to team up with. To disagree with him now might invoke a negative reaction, which he is desperate to avoid. Taking a car was the original plan, and it does make sense not to walk the whole journey, but Norman has obviously thought this through.

'Well, yes ... there are some serious merits to your proposal, and yes, I guess we could all do with the exercise and fresh air, so, er ... well, I don't have any problem with continuing on foot for a while. Maybe if the boys get too tired, we can find a car later?'

'Agreed,' Norman beams, 'the committee has passed the motion, and we'll stay on foot for now.'

Lilly stares at her father. She saw the concern flash across his face, then just as quickly disappear as he blithely agrees with Norman. She drops her gaze, berating herself for thinking of her father as a weak and pathetic man. He's just doing his best. He was a businessman, not a soldier or survivalist expert, and besides, he's had all those problems with the breakdown. She suppresses the urge to speak out and disagree, simply for not wishing to oppose her father.

A thought reaches her. The common sense genes passed down from her mother's side work quickly to spur her mind into overdrive. That woman was murdered. No doubt about it. Her throat was cut, and she'd been raped too. What other reason would there be for her knickers being round her ankles?

'Dad,' Lilly speaks up, making sure her tone is light, 'those other houses, the ones you checked before you found the food, were they all empty?'

'Of course, they were,' Andrew replies. 'We haven't seen anyone.'

'No, I mean the food? In the kitchens? Were they all gone, and how did you get in?'

'Eh? Oh, er ... the back doors were open, and yes, some of them had been emptied, but we found one that wasn't so ...' he shrugs. She can see he is thinking the same thing but just doesn't want to admit it.

'Didn't you say someone was going through the houses in our town? Like, taking all the food and things?'

'Well, yes,' Andrew concedes, 'but we're in the country-side now, not in the town.'

'Saw those too,' Norman cuts in. 'Just other survivors like us, getting food and getting out.'

Nodding back, Lilly absorbs into her own thoughts. That house with the body of the old woman had been entered from the back, and all her food taken. These houses have been entered from the back too, and all the food taken, apart from that one where they got this food.

An image fills her mind of men going from house to

house to strip it clean. Filling a vehicle, leaving when it's full, and returning to continue. They'll come back, then. Not all of these houses have been cleared yet.

'We really should go,' Lilly says quickly, looking up to stare directly at her father.

'We just agreed to let the boys get some rest,' Norman replies.

'No, now ... and we should take a car and go quickly ... Someone is clearing all these houses of food, so they'll be back to carry on with the ones they haven't done yet.'

Her father agrees. She can see it in his eyes. The risk of being confronted by other men terrifies him. A man of average build and physically out of shape. She doubts he's ever had a fight in his life. 'Dad, they'll come back,' she repeats. 'We don't want to be here ... We have to go.'

'Maybe Lilly is right,' Andrew turns to Norman. 'Of course, your idea of being on foot was good but er ...'

Thinking quickly, Norman stares round, his mind whirring to come up with reasons to keep them on foot. The last thing he wants is to get to this fort straight away. Not today and certainly not tonight. His gaze flicks to Lilly again, unable to help himself from glancing at her chest straining against that flimsy vest top.

'She's right,' he adds seriously. 'Well done, Lilly,' he nods at her, trying to convey a serious adult to adult acknowledgment. 'We should go right away, er ... but I'm thinking we shouldn't take a car from here. If these people come back, they'll know we've taken one and be looking out for us. Yes, good idea,' he says out loud, rushing on to cover the slip up. 'Let's get this cleared up and hidden and get away quickly. We'll go into the countryside and keep going until we've got a good distance between us ... bloody hell,' he stands up, nodding again at Lilly. 'Good thinking, Lilly,' he starts grabbing plates and tins, piling them up to carry out to the kitchen.

Andrew jumps up, the thought of a returning group propelling him to work as fast as possible. 'Lilly, grab a bin bag, and we'll get this lot cleared up.'

'Who cares about a bin bag?' Sam asks. 'Just shove it somewhere. They've already been in here, so they won't come back.'

'Good point. Well done, Sam. You girls are clever cookies, aren't you? Eh, Norman? Glad we've got two clear thinkers with us.'

'Definitely,' Norman strides back in, still holding the items in his hands, realising he was just about to do what he has always done and start washing up.

With everything shoved into cupboards out of sight, they get ready and start heading out the back door, snaking round the house to walk quickly down the lane and onto the country road.

'We need to get off this road,' Norman says quietly, playing up to feed the fear and nerves rippling through the small group. 'We're not safe,' he adds, keeping his gaze serious and far away, trying to affect the look of someone brave and serious.

'Good idea,' Andrew agrees quickly. 'There's a footpath up there. We should take that and go across the fields, stay out of sight.

Norman leads the way to the narrow opening in the hedgerow, standing back as though to usher the others through and to bravely bring up the rear. Off the road they go, onto the narrow footpath that snakes along the edge of the fields running adjacent to the road but hidden from view by the thick brambles and trees.

Staring ahead, Norman finds his eyes flicking between

his daughter's backside and that of Lilly. Noticing the difference between Sam's slim, boyish figure and Lilly's natural hourglass curves. He'd certainly never viewed his own daughter in anything other than fatherly love, and never any of her friends either, but Lilly was different. For a start, she didn't look anywhere near fifteen, more like eighteen or nineteen, and she acted older too. She didn't use all the slang teen speech that Sam used. She spoke properly and had a serious look in her eye.

Society had gone, and the need to reproduce was important now. In olden times, it was natural for older men to go with younger girls. The law to protect vulnerable girls was only ever brought in as their culture evolved. Anyway, in some parts of Europe the age of consent was still something like fourteen, he thought, because girls are physically able to have sex at that age. Loads of girls get pregnant at that age. He'd seen all those council estate girls who have two or three kids by the time they're sixteen.

Lilly keeps glancing at me anyway. Her own father is a bit wet and weak, so it's only natural she would feel an attraction to him, maybe the start of a crush. Norman keeps going, each tread of his feet signifies a further effort to justify his desires.

Walking behind her father and holding Billy's hand, she can feel his eyes boring into her. It feels almost like a hot tingling from the stare he is directing at her, but those thoughts are pushed away. Her dad is here, Billy and Todd, plus Samantha, and the danger is coming from everything else, not this mild-mannered man who is so similar to her own father, trying to be serious and manly but just looking stupid in the process.

And it was a good idea of not taking a car from there. Those people–whoever they might be–would spot a missing car and might come looking. Something about that doesn't feel right. There must be loads of survivors all heading to different places, which would mean lots of cars being taken. One doesn't make a difference. It could be another group of men, armed with guns or knives that took the car. Just because a car was taken doesn't mean that the group were vulnerable, nor would they know which direction they took it.

Still, they were heading away from there, and that was the main thing. Keep going cross country for a few hours and find somewhere else to get a car and more food too. Thinking it through reminds her Samantha asking for a tampon. They shouldn't just get food but medicines too, like aspirin and antibiotics and those creams you use for insect bites and rashes. All those sorts of things should be taken.

The people at the fort will have thought of these things, surely. If they've got a whole commune going with loads of people, then, of course, they'll be considering all of these things and have stockpiles of medicines and things. They might even have a vaccine or something or know what this is all about. Maybe her mother is there now. Lilly knows the odds of that are very low. If she was able to have got away from the care home, then she would have come home and not to that fort.

They just need to get there as quickly as possible.

CHAPTER THIRTEEN

'I thought this was the next one.'

'It is, we did the others ... I remember, it was the one with the big, red Honda outside.'

'It's been done, though. We must have done it.'

'We didn't. I know we didn't. We did all those and stopped before the house with the big, red Honda.'

'Well it's been done.'

'Not by us.'

'Eh? Who else would do it? This is our patch. Peter and his lot wouldn't come this way. The Doc said we had to stick to our maps. If those cunts have come onto our patch, I'm going fucking spare–'

'They wouldn't. Maybe it was already like it ... Yeah ... must have already been emptied by whoever lives here.'

'Yeah, that makes sense. Fuckers ... Why didn't they take their car then?'

'How the fuck would I know? Probably had two cars. These rich bastards out here have all got loads of cars.'

'Cunts.'

'Wankers.'

'Do the next one, then?'

'I'll get the van.'

'Ere, look at that.'

'What?'

'That, you blind twat, down there, on the ground.'

'What?'

'Fuck's sake, are you fucking blind? That packet of custard creams ... See it?'

'Got it, shit ... Did we drop that?'

'No, we didn't come up to this house, did we? We stopped at that one ... We just fucking discussed this. We didn't do the one with the big, red fucking Honda, and the custard creams are outside the house with the big, red fucking Honda.'

'Alright, smart arse. Don't get chippy.'

'So? Someone's been here, ain't they? We'd have seen them biscuits ...'

'Would we fuck? As like, they could have been there for days.'

'In the countryside, with all the foxes and badgers and shit?'

'Fucking foxes don't eat custard creams. How they gonna open the packet?'

'Have you seen badgers eat? They're strong as fuck. They'd have that open in seconds. Nah, someone's been through here.'

'Bollocks ... So what if they have!'

'You know what the Doc said.'

'Yeah but ...'

'What if he's testing us?'

'Really? You think he'd do that?'

'Pete said he did it with Chris's lot.'

'Fuck, so what do we do? Take 'em back or something?'

'Yeah, we take the custard creams back. He's testing us with a packet of fucking custard creams ... He wants to make sure we're not eating them.'

'Alright, don't get chippy, you sarcky fucker.'

'We'll have to check them houses. The ones we did already.'

'Seriously? Fuck ... It's hot as fuck, and I just want to get done and go back.'

'Alright, but you explain to the Doc that we found a packet of custard creams and didn't do fuck all about it.'

'Fine, fucking fine. Come on, then ... We'll work down from here.'

'Fucking hello.'

'What?'

'Glasses on the side. They still got water in 'em too, like wet round the top.'

'Oh yeah, someone been in here then.'

'Today too. This wasn't like this before. Check the rooms.'

'You check the fucking rooms.'

'I did the last one.'

'No, we both did the last one ...'

'You're fucking hard work, you are. Eh ... smell that?'

'What?'

'Fish ... no ... tuna. That's fucking tuna, that is. Hang on, someone wouldn't take food from that house and eat it in this house ... Why not just eat it in that house?'

'I dunno. Fuck do you think I am? Uri fucking Gellar? Or that bloke who guessed the lottery numbers, what's his name?'

'Russell Grant.'

'Fuck off! He does the stars and shit on the telly. No, that bloke with the little beard ...'

'Chuck Norris? He had a beard.'

'Jesus, help me. Yeah, Chuck Norris guessed the lottery numbers ... Brown or something. He's got that first name?'

'That helps, someone with a first name.'

'No, like he's got a first name but spells it different ... Darren. No, Derren Brown! Yeah, him.'

'What about him?'

'What?'

'Derren Brown? What about him?'

'Er ... can't remember now. 'Ere, they've shoved all the dirty shit in here.'

'Let's have a look, messy fucking weirdos. Who puts dirty dishes in a cupboard?'

'Freaky.'

'Fucking right.'

'A few of 'em too, by the looks of it. They've opened everything.'

'Is that Spam? I love Spam ... Is it all gone?'

'Yes, mate, and we've got enough Spam to last like for-fucking-ever.'

'Good, I love Spam.'

'Fucking bean juice is still wet. That shit dries fucking quick, especially in this heat. We must have only just missed 'em.'

'Ain't no one on the road, though. We'd have seen 'em.'

'We gotta go look. The Doc said other people are more important ...'

'Not just people but ...'

'Stop it.'

'What?'

'It don't matter what he wants ...'

'I didn't say anything.'

'But you were going to. Don't ... don't say fuck all.'

'Fine ... What's he want them for anyway?'

'I don't know, and I don't want to fucking know. Just do as we're told and get on with it. That's my motto.'

'He who dares wins. That's mine.'

'That's the SAS. You can't use their motto.'

'Why not? It's a good motto.'

'Cos it's their motto. Get your own.'

'Alright! Don't get chippy. I'll share yours, then.'

'No. Get your own.'

'Every little helps, then.'

'That's Tesco, and that's lame as fuck ... You might as well have hands that do dishes can be as soft as she wishes ...'

'I'll think of one while we're looking for these fuckers.'

'Good, you do that.'

CHAPTER FOURTEEN

Eyes wide open, and I'm sat bolt upright. Where am I? Where is everyone? Where's Dave? What the fuck just happened? Paco has had a baby with my sister. Shit, how the hell am I going to tell Clarence? No, hang on. That was a dream. Shit, that was a strong feeling. It was so real. Like I could feel their presence. My mum and dad were there too. I spoke to them like they were really there.

A memory, a real memory of the dream is in my mind now, like it really happened. I know it didn't happen, but it feels like it did, so I'll cling onto it with everything I have. Sadness rushes through me as I realise that if my parents are with Sarah and Paco, they must be dead.

Get a grip, you idiot, it was just a dream. It wasn't some message being relayed by the gods for the sole purpose of Howie, the supermarket manager. It was a combination of dehydration, exhaustion, and some wanker shoving a heart in my mouth.

The thought makes me gag. I can still feel the rubbery, fleshy texture of it. Hot and wet, and still pumping. Oh, and the blood that came out of it. Shit, that was gross. Leaning over, and I retch as my stomach joins my head in agreement at the revolting memory of it. Water comes out, which surprises me as I figured my stomach would be empty.

That means I've been drinking. My face is clean too. No dried blood or scabby remains of the diseased zombie heart sticking to my stubble.

Shit.

Diseased zombie heart.

That was in my mouth. Fuck, maybe I am one of them now. They brought me here and washed me off. No, it was Dave. I puked down the back of his leg. Or was that part of the dream?

And where the fuck am I? It's very dark in here. Is it still night? The same night or another night?

Confused is an understatement, so I clamber to my feet, expecting a wave of dizziness, but there isn't anything. I feel fine. I feel completely normal. Well, a bit sore and tired but nothing other than that. I must be a zombie, then. Marcy said it takes away all the bad feelings.

Sighing, I resign myself to the thought and grope round for my pistol. It's still there, hanging from my belt, and in the dark, I eject the magazine and feel the resistance of the rounds. Slotting it back in, I know what must be done. Shot to the head. Bang, and it's all over. Shame, but what can you do? I'm not going to start rampaging round the country like Darren or Marcy.

Will the infection let me shoot myself? What if it like freezes my finger or something so I can't pull the trigger? I could jump out of a window, I guess, but then it could stop me from doing that too. Oh, this needs some creative thinking. How do you do yourself in if you can't do yourself in?

Shit, that hurt my head. Maybe I should check before I shoot myself in the head. Yeah, need a mirror. Groping about, I try and feel my way to the door and end up crashing into what I think is a television, then a set of chairs and a table. Completely disorientated and cursing foully, I somehow end up back where I was, falling over the sofa I just woke up on.

I catch some weird noises coming from outside. Sounds like someone having sex with loads of grunting. Do zombies have sex? I'm not having sex with any zombies. Bugger that.

Where the shitting hell is the sodding door. Am I in a cave or something? Wall, got a wall, so follow this, and I should find the door. Corner, more wall, bloody television again. Oh well, that's broke. What's this? Something soft and velvety. A curtain? I give it a yank and end up spinning away at the searing pain in my eyes from the strong sunlight burning through.

Stupid black-out curtains. Who puts black-out curtains in a lounge? Shielding my eyes, I find the door and stagger through, slowly blinking as my vision works to adjust. Mirror, there's one–big one by the front door so the vain buggers could check their important image before they went out for the day.

Oh.

Well.

Interesting.

Appears I'm immune, then. Shock hits hard, so hard that it pretty much wipes out my tiny mind from thinking of anything ever again.

Dropping my head down, I run through what happened last night. We were on the top level of that car park, having a big scrap. Then they started swirling, and I got dragged into that tunnel area. Then that one that was on top of me; I got my hands into his stomach and ripped his innards out. I check my hands to find them surprisingly clean. Someone has washed me.

Then my hands on its face. Didn't I pop its eye out? Then the heart. Wasn't just the heart, though. There was loads of shit going in my mouth. The eye juice went in, and blood was definitely going in as they were right on top of me, and I was facing up.

So I look up to double-check, using the tips of my fingers to stretch my eyelids back. Rolling my eyeball up and down, then side to side. Definitely white. I poke my tongue out, then wonder why I am poking my tongue out. What do zombie tongues look like? I have no idea, so it was a pretty useless action.

'Immune,' my voice is rough from being asleep for so long. I check my eyes again, just to be sure. Still white.

Lani passed me that cigarette last night in the Saxon too. I should have got infected from that, surely?

Without realising it, the nicotine receptors in my brain have got all excited at the memory of cigarettes. They direct my hands to start groping around for some cigarettes, but I never carry them. I always pinch them from the lads.

Where are the lads? And everyone else? Bloody hell, I could murder a coffee. Strolling into the kitchen, I try and wrestle with the understanding of being immune, but it's just too great to think about right now. I prioritise the important stuff like having a piss and getting some coffee.

Nice toilet down here, very nicely decorated. I stare round at the little ornaments on the shelves while I urinate into the bowl. They've got one of those old Spanish ladies with the big skirt to hide the toilet roll under.

Bladder emptied and back into the kitchen, examining the stove and grinning when I find it's gas and not electric.

'Come on, come on ... be good to me,' I whisper to

myself, still trying to avoid any thought process of dealing with what happened last night and what it means.

'Yes!' The low hiss of gas escapes from the nozzle, so I press the ignition button, hoping its battery run and not mains.

'You beauty.' Blue flames pop up in the circle, and within a few seconds I've got a big pan of water on the hob and searching the cupboards for coffee. I know I'm ignoring the big issues, but I need coffee. Today, this morning, right now. I am going to have a cup of coffee before I do anything.

The world can sod off, and all the big decisions can just wait until I have had that coffee. Nice, they've got Millicano coffee. I like Millicano. Shame there's no milk, but you can't have everything, I suppose. They've got sugar, though.

Popping the lid open, I inhale deeply at the rich aroma, savouring a smell that doesn't involve rotten corpses or rotten bodies or rotten corpse bodies trying to shove rotten body parts into my gob.

The water boils as water does when heat is applied. Nice and simple. A chemical reaction that is the cornerstone of a civilised world. I shall make this coffee and then work out where everyone else is, then get some food and maybe later, much, much later, after I have found some smokes, I will try and consider the possibility that I am immune.

Immune. Wow. Lani is immune, but then she turned and then went back to normal, whereas I have just stayed the same. Does that mean anything? Did I pass something to her when we kissed that night? Or did she pass something to me? Shit, I'm not snogging Dave and the lads if that's what has to be done. Sod that.

Coffee. Focus on the small things first and let the big

things piss off for a bit. Water into the mug, stir and smell the goodness of strong caffeine floating in the air.

Ha. I have coffee. I did it. I actually got to make coffee after waking up. But it's too hot to drink. Without the cooling effect of milk, it will take longer to get down to a temperature that doesn't peel my lips off.

Cold water is added, just a little trickle to bring the heat down a little. Perfect.

Mug in hand, I stroll down the hallway, humming away to myself as I ignore the pressing urge to think about serious things. In the lounge, I spot my axe and an assault rifle next to the sofa.

After what happened in the fort, I vowed never to be without my axe, so it gets taken with me as I walk slowly back to the front door, gently sipping from my mug of coffee. The mug of coffee that I just made. In the kitchen. Like civilised people do.

Looks like another beautiful day. Mind you, it has been too hot lately. Don't get me wrong, I love the hot weather, but this? Too hot, far too hot.

Staring at the door handle, I contemplate that I have no free hands left to open it, and the process of trying to decide if I should put the mug or the axe down is relegated to the file labelled "too difficult to think about right now". So I use my elbow and try to avoid spilling the contents of the mug everywhere.

My whole body freezes, my elbow half pushing the door handle down. I don't move, but I stare down at the coffee mug. Something just crashed through the lounge window. Something big and heavy, and the air is filled with the sound of breaking glass. Now that there is a stonking big hole where the window used to be, I can hear the grunting outside a lot more clearly. Lots of grunting.

Sighing deeply, I push the handle down with my elbow and wriggle my foot into the slight gap to pull the door open. It takes a few seconds for my eyes to adjust again to the sunlight, so I just stand there with my axe and my coffee mug.

'Morning, David,' I call out when my eyes have adjusted.

'Dave,' he responds instantly. Not looking round, not hesitating, no welcoming, love-filled yell of '*Oh, Mr Howie, you're alive and immune ... I'm so pleased*'.

Stepping out, I look left, down at the body that has just fallen from the window frame. Shards and splinters fall down to shatter on the ground. A bit of wooden frame drops down, which makes me think they spent all their money on the downstairs toilet when maybe they should have invested in double glazing.

'I got coffee,' I call across.

'Okay,' he replies.

'I just made it.'

'Okay,' he replies again.

'The hobs are gas, so I boiled some water.'

'Okay.'

'The ignition runs from a battery too, so I didn't need a flame.'

'Okay.'

'It's Millicano too.'

'Okay.'

'Do you want one? The water is still hot.'

'Not right now, Mr Howie. Can I have mine in a bit.'

'Fair enough, mate. Just say when, and I'll get it done.'

'Thank you, Mr Howie.'

'You're welcome, Dave.'

I sip my coffee. The coffee I just made whilst I pretend this is a perfectly normal start to a perfectly normal day.

'Do you need a hand?' I call out reluctantly and feeling a bit guilty.

'No, thanks, Mr Howie. Enjoy your coffee.'

'Cheers, Dave. Don't suppose you got any cigarettes, have you?'

'I don't smoke, Mr Howie.'

'Okay, never mind.'

'Wait just a second, and I'll have a look round.'

'Don't worry too much, mate.'

'It's not a problem, Mr Howie.'

'Only if you're sure. I know you don't like smoking.'

'Here's some, er ... They say menthol on the front. Are they okay?'

'Fine, mate, thank you.'

'Catch ...'

The packet drops at my feet. Again, I am stuck with the dilemma of not having a free hand to pick them up with. In the end, the axe is propped against the wall whilst I pick the packet up and slide one of the slim, white sticks out.

Patting my pockets down for a lighter, I start to think maybe I will have to go back into the kitchen to use the hob when a red-coloured Clipper lighter lands at my feet.

'Cheers, Dave.'

'Okay, Mr Howie.'

Coffee and a cigarette. Standing outside the front door on a gorgeous, hot summer day. Not a cloud in the sky. The nicotine and caffeine do their evil work quickly, firing my brain up until it's happily buzzing away.

'You on your own?' I shout across.

'Yes, Mr Howie.'

'Where are the others?'

'I don't know.'

'Did you see them?'

'Clarence got out with the Saxon ...'

'One behind you, Dave ...'

'Thank you. I knew he was there. Clarence got away with Nick. I saw Lani somewhere near where you got taken down ... Didn't see Simon or Alex.'

Simon and Alex. I love the way he keeps using their first names. I don't feel worried. Something is telling me they'll be okay and somewhere nearby. I can't explain why I feel like that. I just know.

'They'll be okay,' Dave adds. 'They know to stay nearby.'

Finally, I mention the huge elephant in the room, the one I've been stoically avoiding since I stepped out. 'You killed all these, then?' a mild comment given the utter sea of bodies layering the ground. Bodies piled up in heaps, strewn about. Corpses all mangled and very dead. Lots and lots of bodies.

And Dave stood in the middle while they keep stupidly charging at him. They haven't reacted to my presence but just going for him. Like they have a personal vendetta to take down the small man with two knives.

'I'm glad you're up, Mr Howie,' he yells out.

'Oh, thanks, Dave. Yeah, I feel ...'

'These knives are getting blunt. Could you throw me two more from the kitchen please.'

'Oh, right. Yeah, hang on,' I stroll back inside and open the drawers to select two long, straight-bladed knives before quickly pouring the still hot water into another mug of Millicano. Back outside, I place the mug down as he shouts for me to throw them one at a time, not together. As if I would!

He catches them deftly and takes a split second to step back and stare down at the blades and the handles before shrugging and going back to slicing throats open.

'Almost there,' he shouts with just a few more to go.

'Come and get your coffee. I can finish them off.'

'No, no, Mr Howie. I started, so I will finish.'

'You sure, Dave?'

'Quite sure, Mr Howie.'

'Suit yourself.' I light another cigarette and sip at me coffee. He doesn't look the least bit tired. He looks completely the same as ever. Not sweating, not struggling, with heavy legs. Just perfect movements that place him exactly where he needs to be.

'Done,' he exclaims proudly.

'What about him?' I nod down the road to the solitary zombie shuffling in, arriving late to the party.

Dave looks round casually and shrugs before spinning to throw both the knives with incredible ferocity. The sun glints off the spinning blades that embed straight into the thing's head, driving him off his feet to fall back with two handles poking out his face.

Dave turns back and, with a small smile, takes a bow. The shock of it makes me spray my coffee all over the path. Whilst I choke and laugh all at the same time, he strolls down the path, gingerly stepping over bodies until he reaches the front step and lifts his coffee mug, giving me a polite nod as he takes a sip.

'It's going to be hot again,' he remarks as I compose myself from the ridiculous bow.

'Are you making small talk?' I ask him.

Shrugging, he turns round and stares out at the devastation he has wrought.

'Are you even human?' I ask him. 'Have you slept?'

'Of course, I have slept.'

'No, Dave, I mean last night. Did you sleep last night?'

'No.'

'You've been up all night?'

'Yes.'

'Did they attack us, then?'

'No.'

'Oh. So why did you kill them all? How did they find us?'

'They didn't, Mr Howie.'

'They're dead, Dave, all of them ... right there ... I can see them ...'

'I know. I killed them.'

'Okay, so how did you end up killing them?'

'With knives mostly,' he looks at me, and I swear he knows full bloody well what he is doing.

'How did you end up killing them outside this house?'

'They were running past.'

'Right?'

'What?' He looks at me again.

'They were running past and then what?'

'I killed them.'

'Why?'

'They're zombies.'

'Fucking hell, Dave, you do this on purpose.'

'I didn't kill them by accident if that's what you mean.'

'No, I meant you talk like this on purpose. Never mind ... So they were running past, and you decided to kill them? Is that right?'

'Yes, Mr Howie, I just said that.'

'Okay, so why did you kill them? Other than them being zombies or infected or the enemy ... Specifically, why did you kill them at that point ... when they were running past and didn't know we were here?'

'I figured the others had got away, so it cuts the numbers down and keeps them occupied on me. Plus, you were asleep so ...'

'Right, got it,' I take a sip of coffee and stare out into the street. 'So, did you just charge at them or ...?'

'Oh no,' he replies, 'I called out and got them to come back. Then more started coming and more ... and it just sort of went on like that really.'

'Righto, makes sense, I guess.'

'I ran out of knives a couple of times,' he explains nonchalantly. 'Some of these people don't use proper knives, you know,' he looks over with a frown. 'They're cheap and snap easily, or they're not kept sharp. I had to go into a couple of houses and find better ones.'

'While they were chasing you?'

'Well, not chasing me ... I sort of took them with me.'

An image of Dave fending off hordes of screaming zombies with one knife-wielding hand while he casually sorts through someone's knife drawer springs to mind, lifting them out one after the other and tutting while shaking his head.

'Not good,' he adds after a few seconds.

'What isn't?'

'The standard of knives used in this country,' he replies quickly. 'Really not good. The government should have done something about it.'

'Like what? Insist that everyone has high-tensile commando blades in case of the zombie pandemic?'

He shrugs but doesn't answer.

'We'll have to get some more,' he finally says.

'Knives?'

'Yes, Mr Howie.'

'We'll get some, Dave.'

'Okay, Mr Howie.'

'Did I puke down your leg last night?'

'Yes.'

'Sorry about that.'

'It's okay. I washed it off.'

'Okay, and er ... thanks for getting me out.'

'That's okay.'

'And thanks for cleaning me up too.'

'You're welcome, Mr Howie.'

'And I guess it was you that removed the zombie heart from my mouth.'

'It was.'

'Thanks for that.'

'Okay.'

'Well ...' I pause, letting the silence fill the air. He glances round and raises his eyebrows before sipping at his coffee and adjusting his position.

'Immune, then ...' I add casually.

'Looks that way.'

'Whole heart in my mouth. It was still beating ... Did you know that?'

'Was it?'

'It was.'

'They do that.'

'What do?'

'Hearts, Mr Howie, they keep beating for a little while after being ripped out.'

'You've done that, then? Ripped hearts out, I mean.'

'Couple of times.'

'Oh.'

'Only when it was needed, you understand, not you know ... for fun.'

'Of course, Dave.'

'And the blood? Did it go down your throat?' he asks.

'It did, lots of it. And eye juice too.'

'Eye juice?'

'I popped an eye, but the bugger was right above me, so the juice went into my mouth, and I think I might have bitten a finger off too.'

'A finger? Did you swallow it?'

'No idea, mate. I was busy at the time, you know, what with the heart thing going on.'

'I understand,' he nods.

'What do you think it means?' I ask him.

'Means, Mr Howie?' He stares with what I have come to know as his puzzled expression.

'Yeah,' I shrug, 'what do you think it means?'

'I think it means you are immune.'

'And Lani?'

'Not sure,' his reply is quick, telling me he's been thinking about it. 'It could be that she passed it to you, or you to her ... or you are both resistant or immune separate from each other.'

'I kissed her,' I say, more to myself, 'but things like that don't get passed by kissing, do they? Even some diseases don't get passed from just a kiss, let alone the vaccine for them ...'

'I don't know,' he shakes his head, a small movement but done firmly. 'We will need doctors and ...'

'Yeah, I know, scientists and machines and generators and then fuel for the fucking generators, and then some bugger will just come along and ruin everything.'

'It does explain one thing, though. Why they are scared of you,' he adds.

'Maybe,' I don't deny it this time. No point. They do fear me. Not enough to make them run away quivering like jellies, but it's there. 'And I didn't turn. Lani turned ...'

'She did,' he agrees. Silence stretches between us.

'Did you know?'

'What?' He avoids the stare I direct at him.

'Dave, did you know?'

'Know what?'

'You know full well what. Did you know?'

'I thought about it,' he says quietly. 'That it was a possibility,' he adds slowly.

'But you never mentioned it to me.'

'No, what good would come from it? It was just a thought process, a factor that was considered along with many others. If I had mentioned it, you might have done things differently.'

'I see.'

'No, Mr Howie, I don't think you do. There's a reason why they fear you. There's a reason why we all heard you that day outside the fort when you said the prayer. There's a reason why everyone is following you and doing what you say ...'

'Okay,' I nod slowly, waiting for him to continue.

'That's it,' he says. 'I don't know what the reason is, but there is a reason. This outcome, that you are naturally immune, was one of the factors I had considered.'

'Right. What other factors did you consider?'

'I considered that you were mentally unstable for a while,' he says without any trace of humour, 'or just a natural leader or ...'

'Mentally unstable?'

'Yes.'

'Why?'

'Caltrops? Using cannon? Charging into the enemy when they outnumbered us by so many?'

'But they worked,' I cut in, not quite sure how to react.

'Which is why I don't think you are mentally unstable now.'

'Cheers then, mate.'

'You're welcome, Mr Howie.'

'What if I was?'

'What?'

'Mentally unstable?'

'I don't know. You seemed to get things done so ... I don't know.'

'Maybe we all are, you know ... a bit weird in the head. We must be. We could just sod off and find somewhere quiet and safe.'

'We could.'

'But we won't.'

'We won't.'

'Why not?'

'Because,' he turns to me, 'the fight isn't over yet. We've got you and Lani and the dog. That's three living creatures that appear to be immune to the infection. So we have to work out what we do with that and how we use it to our advantage.'

'Speaking of which, we better go find them. You reckon they'll be near the car park?'

'Yes, Mr Howie.'

CHAPTER FIFTEEN

'YO!'

'What the ...' Blowers mutters, all three of them spinning round while grabbing pistols, Meredith jumping round quickly to sound a warning bark.

'Jagger?' Cookey calls out at the youth striding down the street.

'Nah, bruv. Mohammed, innit. Jagger back there,' he thumbs behind him. 'Oi, Jagger,' he yells, 'it's clear, bruv.'

They watch as Jagger sneaks out from a front garden, leading several younger children to catch up with Mohammed.

'Sweet,' Jagger grins, his wide smile and white teeth visible even from that distance. Moving at a steady jog, they soon reach the others. Meredith standing her ground for a few seconds before moving off to the side. She is aloof and watchful, picking up on the non-threatening vibe from the newcomers and recognising them from the previous day, but they're not the pack, so she won't attack, but she won't immediately accept them either.

'What you doing here?' Blowers asks, looking at the small group.

'And why haven't you cleaned up?' Lani adds, taking in the filth- and grime-covered children still wearing the dirt from the battle.

'We had to starburst,' Mohammed explains, 'getting out from that car park. Fuckin' things were everywhere ...'

'No choice,' Jagger continues. 'They's comin' in so hard we had to do one.'

'What about the Saxon?' Lani asks.

'That went. Your big, hench fella got 'em away.'

'Clarence?' Lani leans forward, staring intently at the young lads.

'Yeah, him,' Mohammed nods.' He got them out, said they'll come back.'

'You seen the others?' Jagger asks, Lani switching her gaze between the two slightly older lads.

'Others?' Lani probes.

'Loads of us ran off,' Jagger says.

'Went off every direction. They's runnin' like the feds was coming,' Mohammed cuts in.

'Will they stay here? You know, like in this area or what?'

'Guess so,' Mohammed shrugs, 'dunno.'

'Car park first; then, we can start looking,' Lani says clearly, with an air of authority. Leading them off, she heads back down the road. Meredith going ahead in her natural role to scout the ground, sniffing and running in circles while constantly glancing back to check the position of the group.

'You not seen Mr Howie, then?' Jagger asks the lads. 'What happened to him?'

'No idea,' Blowers replies. 'He got pulled into the ramp …'

'I checked but couldn't find him,' Lani cuts in. 'Dave went after him so …'

'So what?' Jagger asks.

'Dave would have got him out,' Blowers says confidently.

'Out where?'

'Don't know. Anywhere away from that lot. He'll stay close, though …' Blowers explains.

'You don't think he got done, then? Mr Howie? Like, you know, got bit or sommin?'

'No,' Blowers shakes his head.

'Kind of weird,' Cookey cuts in. 'Can't explain it but … dunno, just don't think he has.'

'How?' Jagger pushes the question. 'He was fucked. They's all on him.'

'Maybe,' Cookey trails off, the worry evident on his face but still with that indescribable feeling inside that Mr Howie is okay, that Dave got to him. He tries to rationalise the feeling, give it a name or words, but it's so fleeting and intangible that he can't seem to grasp it solidly enough. He just *knows*.

'You alright?' Blowers asks him, seeing the deeply puzzled look.

'Eh? Yeah fine, just thinking …'

'About the boss?'

'Yeah, like he's okay, but I'm still shitting myself that he's not okay, but I know he is okay and …'

'Me too,' Lani adds, 'same thing.'

'Really?' Cookey asks.

'Not just Howie, though, but all of us–Nick and Clarence too, even Dave.'

'Yeah,' Cookey exclaims, 'yeah, same thing. Like I'm worried and scared and stuff, but at the same time I kind of know they're okay ... Can't explain it.'

'Fuckin' freaky,' Mohammed comments. Following the conversation, he looks at each one. First at Lani, then at the two lads. They're different and have an air of survivors about them, that nothing could stop them, completely and utterly dependable. All three of them constantly scan the area, checking the flanks and rear. Weapons ready but held relaxed. He and Jagger have a closeness built up from years of friendship and both know they can rely on the other.

He thinks of Maddox, of the devotion they all feel towards him. That he has that same thing that Howie has, that ability to lead and inspire everyone else.

'Shit,' Cookey comments as the car park comes into view, taking in the bodies and the raging fires of the High Street in the near distance beyond. 'We gotta stop burning everything down.'

'Nah, it's fun,' Blowers replies.

'Motherfucking shit,' Jagger spits. 'Look down there. What the fuck?' Crossing a junction and while everyone else stares at the High Street and car park ahead, he glances down to the hundreds of bodies lying strewn across the road.

The group stop, all of them taking in the view of the corpses littering the ground. They're piled up and stretched out in long lines, tracing the route Dave took through houses and gardens and then back to the road.

'Dave,' Blowers says.

'Dave?' Jagger asks.

'Dave,' Blowers nods. 'Come on.' Entering the road, they head towards the first corpse, spotting the cut throat, then the next one and the one after that. Each throat cut open has a severed artery, and while that body still lived, it pumped pints of blood out until the heart ceased to function. Hundreds of bodies, hundreds of hearts, thousands of pints of blood, and the road is thick with the stuff. So dense and thick it remains wet and sticky even in the heat, and the stench is terrible. Rotting corpses, bowels voided, metallic tang of blood. Flies and insects have already moved in, taking advantage of the bodies to generate whole colonies of breeding grounds. A massacre, like something from a movie. Too much to be taken in and made sense off by the naked eye. They've all seen death and lots of it, but the blood is something else.

'Look,' Cookey points to the corpse lying a short way off with two knives sticking out of the face. 'Dave.'

'Definitely Dave,' Lani nods.

'All of these?' Jagger asks. 'No fucking way ...'

'All the throats are cut. That's Dave,' Lani shrugs. 'No one else can do that.'

'One man?' Jagger says dubiously.

'You saw him, Jagger,' Mohammed says, 'last night. He was like a ninja or sommin'.'

'Where are they, then? Some of these are fresh ... very fresh,' Blowers asks, kneeling close to a corpse to inspect the surgical-like cut administered to the neck.

'Must be close,' Lani looks round, staring at the houses.

'Here,' Cookey calls out. Standing at a garden gate, he points to the window fractured and splintered, with the body slumped at the base of the house wall.

'Boss?' Blowers calls out, making his way down the path. Pushing the door open, he spots the two empty coffee mugs on the doorstep and bends down to feel the sides of the mugs.

'They warm?' Lani asks.

'Not really,' he replies. Inside the house, they search through the ground-floor rooms, spotting the sofa and the red-stained cloths Dave used to clean the filth from Howie.

'They made coffee,' Cookey calls out from the kitchen. 'Gas is still on, and this pan is still a bit warm.'

'Just missed them, then. Two mugs, though, so Mr Howie must be okay,' Blowers says, his hard face staring down at the pan held by Cookey, then looking up to the open coffee pot and the stained teaspoon on the side.

'Tobacco,' Lani sniffs the air. 'Someone's had a smoke.'

'Dave doesn't smoke,' Blowers nods firmly. 'They must be at the car park.'

Moving faster now, they exit the house and thread carefully back over the corpses, making their way to the end of the road and back towards the car park in the distance.

Thick smoke billows from the burning High Street, giving the area the look of a warzone. Bodies lie everywhere, and the stench of death, of rotting flesh clings to the area.

Heat like nothing ever felt by the young people bears down, oppressive and suffocating, and the combined effect makes it feel like they are walking through hell.

Taking a breath, Blowers gets ready to call out for Dave and Mr Howie, but the oppression of the scene and the heat makes him hesitate, instead exhaling to keep walking silently.

Meredith runs ahead with her nose down, circling in large loops as she scours the ground and constantly glances back to check the position of the group behind her. All eyes scan the area ahead, eagerly trying to pick out the two figures that should be there.

Reaching the ugly, grey building, they pause at the start of the vehicle ramp, all of them casting about and looking to each other.

'Check round the back,' Lani instructs as she stares round at the silence of the scene.

Blowers and Cookey peel off, quickly moving round to the side entrance of the stairwell. They check inside before continuing round the back and finally to the front. 'Nothing,' Blowers reports.

'Nothing?' Lani asks.

'No, nothing,' Blowers affirms. 'Inside?'

'Probably, I'll go with Meredith up the ramp. You two take the stairs.'

'On it,' Blowers nods, striding back round the side of the building with Cookey.

'We waiting here, yeah?' Jagger asks.

'Please,' Lani gives the one-word answer. There's no doubt those bodies were Dave's work, and Dave wouldn't be there without Howie. They've had coffee and even a cigarette, and they'd know to stay at the car park. Maybe they didn't know everyone splintered and ran off. They could have grabbed a car and be heading for the fort right now. No, they wouldn't do that. They would be here, checking and searching for a while before moving off.

Heading up the ramp with Meredith, she takes greater care to check the bodies. Convinced that Howie and Dave are both safe but needing that added reassurance. Slowly, she climbs higher, passing the openings for the levels as she scours the floor, shoving bodies over with her foot and pressing on.

'Lani?' Cookey calls down, having reached the top using the much quicker stairwell.

'Here,' Lani shouts back from the depths of the tunnel. 'You got anything?'

'Nope. You?'

'Nothing,' she shouts back. A minute later, and they all stand, looking round, feeling lost.

'Any ideas?' Lani asks eventually. The two lads stay quiet, shaking their heads as the worried looks come flooding back.

'Where are they?' she asks out loud.

'They'll come back,' Blowers says after a few seconds of silence. 'We'll wait at the bottom for them. They'll come back.'

CHAPTER SIXTEEN

Sometimes, you get pushed just too far. A sequence of events can lead to the loss of control. Those events could be individually insignificant, and taken separately, they wouldn't raise an eyebrow. However, lack of sleep affects moods very quickly. Heat, constant, sustained, and oppressive, will also sap away at the energy reserves. Fear will start with a tight knot in your stomach, then swell to drive all other thoughts. Suddenly, you're in a nightmare.

Clarence is a big man by any degree. A strong man too. Stronger than normal humans, and it is argued that such men possess a gene that is different to others, a gene that changes the way the deep muscle fibres adhere to the bone and tissues, giving them larger, denser muscles that are capable of far greater feats than other men.

But these men are normally gentle in nature. They do not feel the need to dominate nor control others with their size but rather they become natural protectors of those who are less able to defend themselves.

Once in a while, though, even those men can get pushed

too far, and the resulting explosion of rage is something that will frighten even the toughest of minds.

Take, for instance, a big man with such capability. Take away his sleep for almost two days, give him crap food without the proper nutrition that drops his blood sugar. Give him heat, sustained and constant. Put his friends in peril. Give him an added pressure that the safe place is now under danger. Give him a task, a task that requires him to drive to what was the safe place, deposit one group, and then return to the scene of one of the hardest battles he has known to find his team.

He can cope with that. He will not only cope, but he will rise to the challenge. He can fend off the tiredness, the fatigue, the heat sapping at his mood. He can worry about the dire threat at the place of safety later. All he has to do now is return to the car park and find the others.

What he cannot cope with, what will cause the explosion of rage, is the Saxon breaking down. The Saxon, which has been as much a part of the team as any of them, with so much heart and soul that it almost makes it an entity with conscious will, something on their side, a machine made from moving parts but with a desire to help. The Saxon that has never failed now fails. One of the many moving parts doesn't work.

Clarence explodes. The anger, rage, sheer, uncontainable pressure bursts out like a nuclear detonation. A small town with a relatively small High Street. And Clarence launching litter bins through the windows of those shops. Clarence ripping benches from the ground to swing round and through more shop windows. Clarence, who takes something long and hard, too angry to even see what it is and uses the object to beat more objects. Vehicles, cars, vans, trucks, windows, doors ... anything in his way is destroyed.

The Saxon sits nearby, forlorn and alone. It has ceased to function and will not keep going. Despite the prayers, the curses, the threats, and more prayers, it simply stopped. It could be something simple, something that would take five minutes to fix. But Clarence is a soldier, not a mechanic. He can give field triage and treat battle wounds. He can fire probably any weapon ever designed or made, but mechanical stuff, that's left to the engineers.

He doesn't speak or make any sound, but his eyes blaze as the air is filled with smashing, crashing, breaking, splintering, ripping, and tearing sounds. If this was normal society with normal rules, the first attending officer would be standing back and using the police radio to summon back-up. He would be telling them to bring everyone. Bring dogs and Tasers and helicopters and shields and guns. Call the army and request they send a tank. Phone an elephant vet and ask for a shit load of tranquilisers because there is no way, not on God's green earth, that the officer is going anywhere near the giant man going nuts.

Alas, this is not normal society. This is the apocalypse, and there isn't anyone to help or possibly hinder. So time does what time does, and lets the big man play out his anger until the blind rage starts to ebb, leaving him a little shaky, a little bit more tired, but feeling a whole lot better.

Coming to, he realises just how far he travelled from the Saxon, standing down the street and looking back at the trail of destruction to the Saxon.

Chest heaving, muscles pumped from heavy use, sweat

pours from his red face. The rage has burnt out to leave his mind calm, more able to rationalise and think through the dilemma.

The Saxon doesn't lock, or if it does, they have no keys to lock it. That means leaving it here with all the weapons and equipment. Unless he can find something else to use that is big enough to transport everything and still bring the team back, plus all those kids.

His hand unknowingly goes to his chin, rubbing across his thick stubble in the same manner Big Chris did whenever he was in deep thought. Mind you, he muses, all he has to do is get there; they can find other vehicles in that town.

What they cannot afford is for the Saxon to stay here with all the equipment in it, so no mechanic can come along and take it or strip it clean.

But that is going to take time. Consider the options. Shit, Howie and Chris are far better at decisions like this.

The team are scattered but strong. They'll know to head back to the car park and wait, or if the area is crawling with the zombies, to lie low and wait nearby. The children will hopefully do the same. He thinks through his options. Finding someone to fix the Saxon is instantly negated by the simple fact of how to find someone. Leaving the Saxon loaded up here cannot be done, so it has to be stripped, and the weapons will have to go with him.

'Right,' he says firmly, 'need a van.' Staring round, he spots several that would have been perfect if they hadn't just been completely trashed by a berserk, bald-headed giant going crazy with heavy litter bins and wrought iron benches.

Feeling more than a little ashamed of his actions, Clarence walks back to the Saxon. He takes a long drink from one of the water bottles as he looks up and down the road, trying to decide which direction to go to find a van.

Shrugging, he goes left, breaking into an easy jog whilst he offers more prayers to keep the others safe.

CHAPTER SEVENTEEN

'Which way?'

'Don't know. I lost her.'

'Shit,' I bend over, gasping for breath, spitting on the ground as I let the sweat drip from my forehead.

'Could be a trick,' he says again. Glancing up, I shake my head. Unbelievable, Dave's hardly even breathing fast and still looks perfectly composed. I've slept all night, had a coffee and water, and I'm blowing out my arse. Still, I had a heart shoved in my gob, and he didn't. Not that that makes any difference.

'Could be,' I concede.

Standing up, I take in the view. It's just another street with more houses. The girl could be anywhere, in any of them, or gone into the gardens at the back or even kept going. She was a fair distance off when we saw her. Just a small, blond-haired child, who we assume is female from the long, flowing locks and the brightly-coloured summer dress. She was standing at the end of the road, watching us as we came out of the house. Both of us saw her and stood there, watching for a second as though expecting her to walk down or be joined by adults.

Of course, the fact that she could be one of them was considered very quickly, but the act of standing there and watching and waving back when I lifted my arm to her suggested that she wasn't.

Dave isn't convinced, though. I can see it in his face and the way he keeps saying *it could be a trick.*

When she didn't walk towards us, we started walking towards her. She started backing away, so I waved and called out, which seemed to prompt her to run off.

We gave chase, and now we're here. In another unknown residential street, staring at more houses after running through hell knows how many other bloody streets until we lost sight of her. Even Dave, running ahead to keep a decent view, lost sight of her.

'She must have gone to ground here.'

'Probably,' he replies.

'HELLO!' I shout out, but my voice is weak and doesn't carry that far, 'Dave, you call out ...'

'Okay,' he takes a deep breath.

'Dave,' I interrupt.

'What?'

'Try not to sound angry.'

'Pardon?'

'If she's on her own, she isn't going to come out to you bellowing about finding her house and burning it down, is she?'

'I wouldn't say that,' he stares at me.

'Yeah, right, well ... just try and say something nice.'

'Okay,' he sucks the air in again, pauses, then blows it out before looking at me. 'Like what?'

'Er, I don't know. Just sound nice,' I shrug.

'Shall I say we've got sweets?'

'No, Dave, we're not paedophiles. Er ... say we're from the army, and we're here to help. Yeah ... say we're soldiers, and we won't hurt anyone.'

'Okay,' he nods and draws the breath in again, then again blows it out.

'What now?'

'You shouldn't lie to children,' he says.

'Eh? How are we lying? You were from the army and ...'

'Yeah, but we do hurt people. We hurt lots of people.'

'They're zombies, Dave. They're not people.'

'They were people.'

'Yes, they were people, but they're not people now.'

'Okay.'

'And you were about to say we had sweets. That's lying.'

'It isn't. I have got sweets,' he replies.

'Where?'

'These,' he pulls a sealed tube of fruit pastilles from his pocket. They're all bent out of shape and somewhat squashed but easily still recognisable.

'What the fuck, Dave?' I stare at him. 'What ...? Why have you got them?'

Shrugging, he stares down at them, then back up at me. 'I like fruit pastilles.'

'Right, so why haven't you eaten them?'

'I was saving them.'

'What for? The apocalypse?'

'Don't know, just saving them ...'

'Okay, well, er ... great,' I offer a quick, confused smile. 'Best stick with the soldiers' bit and not hurting people, though. Shouting we've got sweets to a little girl running away is a bit creepy.'

'Okay,' drawing breath, he raises his head, 'WE ARE

SOLDIERS ... WE ARE NOT HERE TO HURT ANYONE ... I SAY AGAIN ... WE ARE SOLDIERS ... WE ARE NOT HERE TO HURT YOU ...'

Stock still, with mouths open, we strain to listen for any sounds. Silence. Then, a door closing somewhere off to the left.

'That way,' I nod. We set off, walking steadily to keep quiet as we scan windows and doors. Another slight banging noise comes from the houses, so we cross over the road, staring ahead but unsure exactly where it is coming from.

'We can't just leave a little girl here,' I whisper.

'I didn't say we should,' he replies quietly.

'But you said it's probably a trick, so you must be thinking this is a waste of time, and we should be trying to find the others.'

'No,' he lies badly. 'Well, maybe,' he admits just as quickly.

'What was that?' I ask at the sound of something creaking, then juddering.

'Garden fence?' he suggests.

'Shout again.'

'WE ARE SOLDIERS FROM THE ARMY. WE ARE NOT HERE TO HURT YOU ...' Immediately followed by another bang. We set off at a jog, knowing the noise was somewhere up ahead from one of the houses on the right side. All of the front doors have been pushed closed, and the curtains drawn at the front. Veering off, I trace a path through to one of the doors and check the handle.

'Locked.'

'Okay,' Dave replies. Jogging into the next garden, he checks the door to find it swings open. He waits whilst I run round, joining him looking at the damaged front door and the lock busted off.

'Hello?' I call out. 'Don't be scared. We're here to help you.' Treading softly, we head into the lounge area, spotting a makeshift den made on the floor with food wrappers and comic books piled up. Empty glasses, bags of crisps, chocolate bars, and a torch. The air smells of body odour, of someone unwashed.

Into the kitchen, and the back door is open. We head out into the garden to find a small ladder has been propped against the fence on the left side and a bigger ladder on the right, offering an easy escape route from the garden to either side.

'Hello? Are you there? We're not here to hurt you. We just want to make sure you're okay.'

Nothing, no response, no noises either. 'She must be terrified,' I add quietly.

'If she isn't a zombie, you mean,' he replies.

'With a den in the lounge and comics? And these ladders?'

'Could be,' he shrugs.

'Try that one. I'll do this one,' I make for the bigger ladder, scaling the rungs to the top of the fence to peer over into the next garden. With the height advantage, I can see there are ladders, stepladders, chairs, tables, and storage boxes all stacked against each of the garden fences for at least the next four houses down.

'Same here,' Dave replies when I tell him.

'She must have been here since it started, eating shit food and waiting for family or something.'

'Check inside?' be asks. Leading the way, he enters the back door and into the house. The dining room looks untouched, with a fine layer of dust covering everything.

The kitchen is the only other downstairs room, other than the lounge, that shows signs of life. More empty cups by the sink and empty bottles of squash left on the side. The bin is overflowing with wrappers and packets.

Upstairs we find the bathroom in a shit state, with faeces stuck to the side of the toilet bowl and shit-smeared hand towels in the bin. The empty toilet roll holder suggests the paper tissue ran out some time ago.

Closing the door quickly to keep the stench inside, we check the other rooms. One big double room that must be her parents' room. No signs of disturbance other than a few drawers opened and the bed sheets all messed up like someone got up quickly and didn't return.

Another bedroom looks like an older child uses it, posters of teen boy bands and homework stacked on a desk. The smallest room must be the girl's. The bedding is filthy and stained with piss and smeared with what could be either chocolate or more shit.

'Poor sod,' shaking my head, I take in the sight of the unkempt room, clothes strewn about and toys everywhere.

'Milly,' Dave says, nodding at the glittery name stencilled on the door.

'Come on,' heading back downstairs, we go into the back garden and stand quietly for a few seconds. 'Milly?' I shout out. 'Can you hear me, Milly? My name is Howie, and my friend is called Dave. We're here to help you ...'

Still nothing. She must have stayed very quiet and very hidden to survive this long. Her instinct to stay away from others has to be strong, so no wonder she's staying quiet now.

'Milly, we have to make sure you are okay ... That's all we need to do. We won't try and grab you or do anything, and I promise we won't touch you ...' Still no response.

'Any ideas?' I ask Dave.

'Could threaten her,' he suggests, which prompts a long and awkward few seconds while I conjure the image of Dave holding a knife to the throat of her favourite doll while screaming he'll do her in if she doesn't show herself.

'No, mate.'

'I'VE GOT FRUIT PASTILLES' he bellows, causing me to jump out of my skin from the lack of warning. Bloody hell. I wouldn't come out with some maniac screaming about fruit pastilles, let alone a little girl.

'Too much?' he asks.

'Just a bit, mate,' I reply. Instead, we climb the ladders and sit atop the fences, scanning the area. Lots of garden sheds, greenhouses, playhouses, and tarpaulins that could all easily hide a child.

'Dave, can you see my side from there?'

Perfectly balanced on top of the ladder, he nods. 'I'll go this side and start checking. You keep watch.'

'Maybe I should search, and you keep watch, Mr Howie.'

'It isn't a trick, Dave. She's not a zombie.'

'How can you be sure?'

'Zombies don't read comics, and they don't shit the bed either ...' jumping down, I start in the first adjacent garden, checking all the places that could hide a small body. The shed is clear, as are the playhouse and the recesses, so I move into the next garden.

'Milly?' I call out repeatedly. 'Don't be scared. We're not going to hurt you, I promise ... Just shout out, and we can make sure you're okay.'

There is no response, but I keep going, keeping my tone light and soft and wondering if my shouting is just scaring her more. But then what would be more frightening? Me searching in silence, and the little girl hearing me getting closer, or calling out nicely so she can tell where I am. I make noise too, not banging or anything loud. But just making sure I don't go too soft.

'Anything, Dave?'

'No.'

'I think she must be terrified of us,' I shout out. 'I feel sad that we are scaring her. I don't want to scare anyone. Do you, Dave?'

'Sometimes,' he replies. I curse foully under my breath and give him a hard look.

'But not children, though? Eh, Dave?' Please don't say anything bad, Dave.

'Er ... no?' he shouts back, clearly struggling to keep up with the layered conversation.

'Milly?' I was just about to call out that she can meet our big dog called Meredith, but I realise that would be about the same as shouting we've got sweets and a puppy. Creepy. Very creepy.

'Other way,' Dave bellows. 'MILLY ... STAND STILL,' he orders with that parade ground voice booming out. It scares me, and I know him, so god only knows the effect it must have on the little girl.

Back over the fences, vaulting, clambering, and a whole lot of falling whilst trying not to use really bad swear words. Dave, as ever, goes off like a gazelle, gracefully leaping any obstacle in his path. He sees this as a challenge, not as a rescue mission of a little girl.

'Dave,' I yell, 'ease up, mate ... don't frighten her.' Bit late for that, but he does slow down a bit and seems to realise he's not going after an armed, insurgent baddie. Again, out of breath and sweating freely, I join him at the last point he saw her, several gardens down from our original point of access.

'Which way?'

'Lost her again.'

'Really?'

'Yes, Mr Howie.'

'You telling me we're being outwitted by a little girl?'

'Seems that way, Mr Howie.'

'Dave, the scourge of the British Army, the uber trained secret ninja commando has now been outwitted twice by a little–'

'You told me to slow down,' he says rather defensively.

'True,' I accept with a slight nod. 'So it's either over that fence ...' I point across the garden. 'Or over that fence,' I change my pointing direction to the rear of the garden, 'or through the house.'

'Yes.'

'Three directions and two of us. Right ... Would you mind getting up on that fence to have a look while I check the house?' He goes off, getting up the stepladder onto the top and examining the view while I make my way to the back door, dripping sweat and snot everywhere.

Luckily there is a nice, thick roll of kitchen towel on the side which I make great use of, noisily blowing my nose and mopping my brow and even taking the opportunity to grab a drink of water, which earns me a haughty glance from Dave.

'Milly?' Calling out softly as I thread through the downstairs rooms, checking in each one. I feel terrible at scaring the girl, but she can't stay here alone. She might be able to get by now while food is easy to find, but once that's gone, she'll struggle, and this hot weather can't last forever either. The thought makes me think how many children have been left alone and frightened, desperately waiting for their mums and dads to come back.

Poor kid. She must have been so terrified, but what choice do we have? We might scare her a bit more now, but then we can get her to a safe place with people that care for her.

Suddenly, small feet go thudding down the stairs, flying across the hall and out the open front door. Twisting round, I catch a flash of blond hair as I start running.

'Milly, just hang on ... Please stop running ...' Out the front door, and she's already at the gate, turning sharp to sprint across the road. Sucking in air to shout for Dave, I bite it away at the last second, knowing it will only keep the fear factor high if I'm screaming while chasing her.

'Milly, please ... It's too hot to keep running ... My god, you are so quick!' By the time I'm at the gate, she's across the road and increasing her pace. Nothing for it but to speed up, so I try and push my legs faster.

Luckily, she goes for a straight sprint and tries legging it straight down the road. She's quick, but my legs are longer, and I start to reduce the distance between us. She glances back, but surprisingly she doesn't look that scared, just utterly determined to outrun me.

'Milly,' I gasp, 'please stop running.' Gradually, painfully, I gain closer and start to reach out. Being this close, I can see how filthy and lank her greasy hair is and how the bright summer dress is covered with stains. Running in her slipstream, I can smell the musty, stale odour of an unwashed body.

Finally, my hand just catches the top of her small shoulder. She stops dead, spins, and sinks her teeth into the top of my knuckles. I yelp and pull my hand back as she swiftly kicks me in the privates. I drop to the floor as stars and colours explode in front my eyes, the searing pain in my bollocks obliterating all other thoughts.

A shadow falls across my closed eyes. Glancing up, I see Dave standing there shaking his head without the slightest trace of sympathy on his face.

'What?'

'Nothing,' he shrugs.

'Don't just bloody stand there, get after her.'

'I don't need to,' he replies, which earns him a confused glance until I prise my head up to see her stood off at a respectable distance, watching us.

'Oh god, that hurts.' Letting my head rest on the hard surface of the road, I wait for the pain to abate before stumbling back to my feet, shaking my sore hand with a perfect imprint of teeth across the back of it.

Dave stares at the hand, then shakes his head again. Fortunately the skin isn't broken, but it still bloody hurts.

'You sure you've never had kids, Dave?' I ask him at the sight of the fearless girl watching us closely.

'Quite sure,' he replies.

'Sister, perhaps? Cousin? Niece?'

'No, Mr Howie,' he answers seriously.

'Milly? Is that your name?' calling out, but she doesn't reply or show any signs of hearing me. 'Listen, we're not here to hurt you ... I promise ...' She looks maybe seven or eight years old, small and slight build. 'You can't stay here, Milly. This place isn't right for you. We have a, er ...' Shit, what do I say now? *Come with us to our big fort?*

'We have a place, a big place with lots of people and lots of children with their mums and dads, and we have food ... lots of food ...' As we take a very slight step forward, she takes a very big step backwards. Making it clear she is more than happy to turn and run.

'Please don't run again,' I call out. 'We're both old and can't keep chasing you.'

'I can,' Dave cuts in quickly.

'Ssshhh. Milly, we just need to make sure you're okay ... Do you live with anyone?' No response. 'Mum or Dad? Do you have any brothers or sisters?' Still no response. 'Is that your house?' I point back up the road, but again, she shows no response.

'You want to me grab her?' Dave asks, not quite quiet enough, and she bursts away.

'Bloody hell,' groaning, we start after her. 'Just keep her in sight until she gets tired.'

'That might take a while,' he replies.

'Get off,' I scoff, 'she's only little ... How long can she keep going?'

CHAPTER EIGHTEEN

'Do you think we've gone far enough off the beaten track, Norman?' Andrew asks, stopping to wipe the sweat from his red brow. His thinning, brown hair clings to his scalp, giving him a look of a thirties' gangster with greased-down locks.

Norman stops and makes a point of looking around, narrowing his eyes in that hard look he has been trying to perfect throughout the day.

'Not sure, old chap,' Norman replies quietly. 'This terrain is quite open, so we could still be easily spotted. Maybe we should find some cover somewhere for the night.'

'For the night?' Lilly cuts in. 'It's only half past three, and we need more food and water ... We should find a house and a car.'

'And we will,' Norman is quick to reply, 'most definitely, but er ... well, I am just a little concerned at showing ourselves, so maybe a few more hours away from the, er ... populated zones would, er ... be ... er ... beneficial.'

'Really?' Andrew asks quizzically. 'Well, yes, I suppose there is some merit in your suggestion.'

Shaking her head, Lilly again feels a wave of shame at

the bad thoughts she has of her father, at his weak disposition and the way he seems to hang off every word Norman says. It's quite obvious to Lilly that Norman is making it up as he goes along, and god knows why he wants to be out here in the countryside for so long. But it does feel a bit safer out here, especially after finding that body in the house and all those other houses with their kitchen cupboards stripped.

'So, onto the next matter at hand,' Norman nods round at his little group as he asserts his position as leader. 'What's our supplies situation like?'

'Supplies?' Sam asks as she stares at her father and wonders why he's being so weird and why he keeps glancing at Lilly.

'Water and ... food,' Norman explains.

'We just ate it all,' Samantha says, 'like in that house we were just in ... I mean, duh, Dad!'

'Yes, thank you, Samantha,' Norman huffs. 'I am quite aware of the meal we just had. I was just asking what we had left.'

'Nothing,' Lilly says. 'Few bottles of water, but that's it.'

'Right, so we do need some more supplies, then. I suggest we keep going and hopefully find a farmhouse or ... you know, like a country cottage or something.'

'Or something?' Samantha mutters.

'What was that, Sam?' Norman snaps.

'I said–or something.' Samantha rubs her stomach as the dull ache from her period, the heat, and the constant walking take their toll and drive her already precarious mood down even lower.

'You boys, alright?' Norman beams, quickly moving on from having to deal with his awkward daughter in one of her awkward moods. 'Good,' he adds, not giving them a chance to reply, 'let's press on, then.'

So they do. They press on. Walking down footpaths and country lanes that weave and snake through the sun-parched countryside. Passing fields that should have been lush and green but are starting to show the first effects of such a prolonged dry spell with extraordinary temperatures. Forests in the distance look dark and inviting, offering shade against the glare of the sun.

The unmade lanes are rough and undulating, and all of them are feeling the effects of wearing inadequate shoes within a few hours. Feet become painful and sore, legs aching from the sustained walking after so many days of barely moving. Sweat is pumped out from pores, but not enough fluids are put back in. Dehydration starts to set in, only mild at first, and the group ebbs into silence as their bodies subconsciously work to preserve energy.

Dull headaches then start to nag, eyes become irritated at the hot sun and lack of shade. Skin feeling itchy, sore, and dry, and they all find their minds flashing with images of swimming pools, of the cooling sea, of glasses of cold coke and juice, water fountains, and waterfalls. Their brains sending messages, urging their bodies to get water.

The water they do have is sipped and conserved, Lilly making sure the young boys get what they need before anyone else.

Billy and Todd being so quiet worries her. They don't complain but keep going, with tiny feet plodding along in the dirt road, kicking up dust, and sending small stones skittering into the verges. Samantha rubs her stomach, wincing at the dull pain and cramps shooting through her insides. The two men stay at the front and neither of them are looking round often enough, both seemingly absorbed into their own thoughts.

Lilly takes all of this in. Scanning the vista herself and periodically checking behind them. When the shade from trees offers some minor relief, she gently guides the boys over to the dappled shade. She holds them there for a couple of minutes to drink water and to wash their hot faces off.

'I'm tired, Lilly,' Billy mutters, his voice muted and sounding far away. The concern is etched clearly on Lilly's face as she strokes his cheeks and tells him they will stop soon. She turns to Todd to do exactly the same as she notices neither Norman or Samantha step forward to offer words or actions of encouragement.

'Come on,' she takes their hands, 'let's play "I spy" ... Shall I go first? Okay, I spy with my little eye something beginning with T.'

Silence as the boys stare around, suspiciously looking at the ground, then the verges, then the sky, and over to the rolling meadows sweeping into the distance.

'Come on,' Lilly smiles, 'it's an easy one.'

'Tree,' Norman calls out.

'Dad!' Sam snaps. 'That was for the boys.'

'Was it tree?' Todd asks.

'Yes, yes, it was,' Lilly stares at the back of Norman, wondering why on earth he'd do that.

'Dad, it's your go now,' Todd pipes up.

'I spy with my little eye something beginning with ... B'

'Bumble bee,' Billy calls out.

'No,' Norman doesn't even look round.

'Nice try though, Billy,' Lilly lifts his hand up and smiles down. 'Come on, try again ... What about you, Todd?'

'Er ...' Todd stares about, 'billy goat?'

'No, Todd, can you see a billy goat?' Norman asks.

'Good try, though, Todd,' Lilly smiles again.

'Give up?' Norman asks. 'Barley corn!'

'Dad! How are they supposed to know that?' Samantha hisses.

'The field ... it's full of barley corn.'

'I didn't even know that. How are they supposed to know it?' Samantha continues.

'Oh dear, I've upset the apple cart here, Andrew ... it seems my daughter is having one of her *moods*.'

'I am not having a mood!'

'Todd, why don't you have a go now?' Lilly asks.

'But no one got Dad's B.'

'I'm sure he won't mind,' Lilly replies.

'Of course not, Todd, you have a go,' Norman says in a weak attempt at being gracious.

'I spying with my little eye something that begins with R ...' Todd says proudly.

'Road,' Norman almost shouts.

'Dad!' Sam warns.

'Road?' Billy asks, realising Todd neither said yes or no to his father's suggestion.

'Roof,' Andrew shouts.

'Dad, it's for the boys,' Lilly's tone, while carefully restrained towards Norman, is unleashed on her own father.

'No. A roof. Over there, look,' Andrew points ahead at the slate grey roof clearly coming into view.

'Looks like a farmhouse,' Norman comments. Lilly stares ahead, at the single detached building and thinks that although she doesn't know much about farming, surely a farmhouse would be in a farm? This one is just a big, old house with a low wall running round the garden. No outbuildings or barns. Definitely no tractors that she can see, and a distinct lack of any farm-type animals. In fact, no animals at all.

What she does see is the white top and blue sides of an old-style Land Rover. Clear and distinct and big enough to carry all of them. Lilly moves to alert Sam, stopping when she spots the look of agony on the other girl's face. She looks pale and drawn, sweating freely but looking cold and shivery at the same time.

'You okay?' Lilly asks as she breaks away from holding the boys' hands to step closer.

'Fine,' Sam whispers, 'just hurts.'

'They always this bad?'

'Yeah, like pretty much,' Sam rolls her eyes, wincing as the next round of cramps hit deep.

'They might have some painkillers,' Lilly says softly. 'You see that car too?'

'What car? What, like that blue thing? Yeah ... Dad ... they got a car there.'

'Yes, thank you, Samantha. Andrew and I can see the vehicle clearly.'

'Wanker,' Sam hisses, staring daggers at the back of her dad's head.

'What's his problem?' Lilly whispers.

'He's just a prick,' Sam shrugs. 'That's why mum left him.' She goes to say something else but stops and rubs her stomach instead. Lilly looks up, staring at the windows of the house as she sweeps her gaze across the front.

Norman stares at the Land Rover, cursing the luck of finding a house now and one with a vehicle big enough to carry all of them. This wasn't what he had in mind. He wanted a night out under the stars, maybe in a forest with lots of trees and deep shadows. Willing himself to keep staring forward and stop glancing back to watch Lilly, his mind goes into overdrive as he tries to think of a way out of it.

'I don't like it,' he announces quickly, even though he hasn't thought of a plausible excuse not to like it yet.

'Why?' Andrew asks, coming to a sudden stop, thinking that Norman has seen something.

'Too quiet,' Norman does the narrow-eyed look again, pursing his mouth and staring around, 'just too damn quiet for my liking.'

'Oh,' Andrew says in a tone of mild surprise, 'er ... well, what did you, er ... expect?'

'I don't know,' Norman replies, 'but something just doesn't feel right.'

'Looks perfectly right to me,' Lilly cuts in, striding past the two men as she heads towards the house.

'Lilly,' Andrew calls out in a low whisper, 'get back here.' She keeps going, blindly ignoring the protests of her father.

'You stay here,' Norman whispers quickly. 'I'll go with her and make sure it's safe.'

'You sure?' Andrew blanches. 'I don't mind going, you know, she is ... er ... well, my daughter,' but the words are lost to the back of Norman as he jogs forward to catch up with Lilly.

'You're very brave,' Norman says quietly, 'very brave, indeed.'

'Thanks,' Lilly mutters, keeping her eyes fixed on the windows and front door.

'I think this is going to be down to you and me, Lilly.'

'Pardon?'

'Keeping this lot safe. It appears you and I are the two leaders emerging in our little group, eh?'

Why is he staring at me and not at the house? Pausing at the gate, she takes a final stare from window to window, then down to the front door.

'And for my part, it's nice to know someone here has my back,' Norman continues, still oblivious to the dangers of approaching an unknown house. 'We've got to watch out for each other.'

'Can you hear anything?' Lilly cuts him off.

'Hear anything? Er ... no, well, er ... no.'

'Good,' she moves through the gate and up to the door, one hand gripping the knife handle tucked into the rear of her waistband. Tentatively, she tries the door handle, pushing it down slowly as she increases pressure against the door.

'Locked,' she reports, stepping back to stare up at the house. 'I'll try the back.'

'We'll both go,' Norman scurries after her, giving a quick thumbs up to the waiting group. Following the building line, they make their way to the rear garden, Lilly coming to an abrupt stop as it comes into full view.

'What is it?' Norman asks in a hurried whisper, ready to flee.

'Nobody lives here,' Lilly announces.

'How on earth do you know that?'

'There's a big sign there saying Primrose Holiday Cottage.' She points to the large, wooden sign erected at the rear of the house next to a gravel parking area.

Norman stays quiet, cursing himself for not appearing to be the observant one. Instead, now knowing the coast is clear, he boldly steps out to make his way to the rear doors.

Lilly watches him pass the rear ground floor windows without even looking inside them. Sighing, she rushes forward and checks the view inside. Just plain, old-style pine furniture. The kitchen clean and tidy, with no debris or personal effects on display.

'Locked,' Norman tuts, stepping back with his hands on his hips. He turns to the nearest window, sizing it up before casting about for a rock to smash the glass.

'There will probably be a key somewhere,' Lilly suggests, 'unless the owners meet them here every time guests arrive.' She shrugs as Norman stares at her with a weird expression on his face.

'Course,' he nods, 'that's what I was looking for.' He goes back to his searching, ignoring the big rock he was heading towards and veering off to check under plant pots. 'Got it,' he announces within a few seconds. 'Yep, knew there'd be a key here somewhere ...' he says, shoving the long key into the lock opening. 'That's what I was saying, Lilly. It looks like you and I are the brains of the outfit here. Brains and the beauty, eh?' He winks, sending a creeping shiver down her spine.

No law now. No police. No rules. Norman walks straight into the kitchen, his mind completely absorbed with thoughts of Lilly. Going straight to the sink, he twists the tap, watching for a second as the pure clean water pummels into the ceramic bowl. A night in the forest. No law. No police to call. No phones, no anything. All he has to do is get Lilly away on her own, maybe under the pretence of talking about how to lead this group. Alone and away from the others. She might even give herself willingly.

'It's clear,' Lilly announces, making him jump. Standing over the sink to rinse his head off, he sprays droplets over the floor between them, wondering if he looks macho and tough with wetted hair.

'Yeah, I was just going to do that, er ... You get some water, and I'll call the others in.' He pauses at the sink, rinsing his hands as she gets closer, waiting to see if she will stand close next to him. She doesn't and holds back, feeling extremely uncomfortable and not knowing quite what to do.

'I'll get them,' she walks off quickly with a burning sensation flooding her cheeks. Although she is still young, she is old enough to know, or suspect, what he is thinking.

Opening the front door, she waves and steps outside, making out like she's waiting for the rest before going back in.

'Everything okay?' Andrew asks.

'Holiday cottage. Nobody here,' she replies, moving forward to lead the boys into the cooler kitchen. At the sink, she finds glasses and gets the boys drinking while soaking a cloth to rinse their hands and necks with cold water. Both of them look far too red and flushed and shouldn't be out in this heat anymore.

'Dad, can you look for some painkillers,' Lilly asks, earning a horrified look from Samantha. 'I've got a headache,' she adds.

Giving her a thankful smile, Samantha waits her turn for the sink, leaning over the boys to fill a glass with water.

'All clear,' Norman announces walking into the room, 'all the rooms have been checked. We're safe for now.'

I just did that! Lilly carries on washing the boys and bites down the urge to say something. With their bags dropped, she gets the boys onto chairs at the table, urging them to drink more water. Turning back to the sink, she notices a knife handle poking out of the top of Norman's waistband, the same style of knife she has. He spots her looking and winks, once and quickly. Oh, shoot. It looked like she was just looking at his bum.

'Here,' Andrew pulls a packet from a cupboard, 'er ... ibuprofen? They any good?'

'Perfect, thanks, Dad,' Lilly makes a point of popping two from the blister pack before handing them to Samantha, asking her to look after them.

'Any food?' Lilly asks.

'Pasta, rice ... just dried stuff,' Andrew replies, leaning into another cupboard to sort through various packets.

'That's good,' Lilly responds, remembering her mother saying how pasta and rice were full of carbohydrates. 'Can we cook them?'

'Electric hob, I'm afraid,' Norman announces sadly. 'No good.'

'We can build a fire outside and heat water,' Lilly suggests.

'Good idea! Well done, Lilly,' Andrew grins.

'Er, I thought of that, but er ... smoke! Yes, the smoke will be seen for miles ...' Norman nods quickly. 'We couldn't cook it here,' his mind racing as it struggles to adapt the new circumstances, 'but ... we could take the pasta and rice with us and wait until we're somewhere, er ... discrete and then light a fire ... How about that?'

'Do you think we need to do that, Norman?' Andrew asks. 'I mean, we're pretty far from anywhere here, and if the wood is dry, then the smoke should be clear ... They might even have a barbeque or something.'

'Too risky,' Norman shakes his head. 'We've got to think of the boys here, Andrew, and the girls too,' he nods at Lilly, not noticing that his own daughter left the room a few minutes ago. 'We don't know who those people are, going around, murdering old ladies.'

'Hey!' Lilly winces, nodding towards the boys sat just feet away.

'Sorry, Lilly,' Norman holds one hand up, showing he is willing to be chastised, 'you're absolutely right. Yes, so er ... I don't think it's a good idea to have a fire here. We'll be fine outdoors in this weather and far safer too.'

'What do you think, Lilly?' Andrew asks.

'I think we should take that old car and get away,' she replies, 'get to the fort where we'll be safe. Have a look for the keys.'

'Great plan,' Norman nods. 'Yes ... the keys ... They must be here somewhere. Come on, boys. You going to help us find the keys, eh?'

'No, you stay there and rest,' Lilly cuts in quickly. Their faces were still flushed, and Billy hadn't drunk much water. The search begins in earnest, drawers and cupboards opened and rooted through. Samantha comes back, nodding thanks again at Lilly as she joins in. All of them moving through the rooms, looking for the vehicle keys. They find plenty of old keys but not car keys. Even outside and under flowerpots, checking the wheel arches of the locked Land Rover and all the other hidey holes, but all to no avail.

'Shame,' Norman shakes his head ruefully, staring at the Land Rover as though he so wished they had the keys. The keys which were safely in his pocket, having been nabbed quickly from the hook in the hallway before anyone spotted them.

'Nothing we can do about it,' Andrew sighs. 'This place would be perfect to spend the night, though.'

'Very true, Andrew, if it wasn't for the, er, other situation, we would be making camp here, but alas, just not to be.'

'No, no, I guess not.'

'In fact, I would advise we move off as soon as possible,' Norman lowers his voice to a conspiring whisper, affecting the narrowed-eye *man-to-man* look. 'I know you agree, Andrew, and are just as keen as I am to protect our group.'

'Yes, yes, of course.'

'You and I share a great burden, Andrew, looking out for these souls, our children ... We must do everything we can to protect them.'

'Goes without saying,' Andrew nods.

'Whatever it takes, Andrew. I know I can trust my children with you, and I can only hope you feel the same.'

'Of course, Norman. You know, we only just met, but well, I think you can get a vibe from someone straight away, and I certainly feel an element of trust with you.'

'Good,' Norman nods. 'Down to us, then.'

Hustling the small group, Norman urges and harries them to make ready. He leads them out of the house while exchanging knowing nods and winks with Andrew and Lilly. Andrew rises to the sense of sharing the load with a strong character, at being seen as an equal alpha, ready to lead and take command. Lilly, on the other hand, feels an increasing discomfort around Norman and works hard to retain a neutral expression and avoid eye contact.

Out of the holiday cottage and into the fields they go.

Norman leads them deeper into the countryside, using unmade tracks and narrow lanes to thread a route further into the rural pastures. All the time, he scans ahead for the perfect spot.

By late afternoon, it comes into view. A wooded copse nestled into a small valley between meadows of long grass. At first it looks too small, but the closer they get, the more he realises it stretches away, becoming less of a copse and more like woods.

Big trees with thick trunks and dense foliage provide cover whilst low bushes dotted amongst them restrict the view and deaden any sound. By night, it will be dark in there–dark with plenty of hollows and dips.

Without mentioning anything for fear of Lilly or Andrew objecting, he leads the group towards it. Samantha wouldn't say anything. He loves his daughter, but she's not blessed with deep intelligence. Neither is Andrew, too meek and willing to be led. Lilly, though, she's a strong girl with a strong character. Another few years will see her blossom into a very capable young woman.

Norman's imagination serves to impose a warped image of himself being a rugged survivalist. He has a short beard with a hard, faraway look in his eyes, lean muscles, and defined stomach. He stands outside a wooden shack, dressed in furs and holding a spear while a scantily clad Lilly stands behind him, still trembling from the emotion of their love-making.

His own children don't factor in the daydream. Maybe they have been packed off to live in the fort with Andrew and Billy, leaving a love-struck Lilly to serve her master in isolation.

Turning round, he smiles at her, noticing the shy way she looks down at the ground. Bless her, she doesn't want the others to know of their *special* relationship. But who can blame her? They only met a few hours ago, but true love is like that. It doesn't care about time or age, and anyway, the times have all changed. This isn't about dating and getting to know someone. This is a new world with new rules where the strong get the best girls, and by god, Lilly surely is one of the best girls he has seen in a long time.

A wave of revulsion passes through Lilly at the sly grin he throws her way. He is creepy and dirty, with lank, brown hair that clings to his scalp. His thin limbs remind her of twigs, and his soft belly strains against his shirt. She looks down, determined not to show him any attention as she struggles to hide her revulsion.

In a funny kind of way, she agreed with him that staying at the cottage would be a bad idea. It looked lovely now in the daytime, but come night, it would be pitch black, and any light they use will be easily seen from miles around.

No, until they can find a car, they are better off away from anyone else. Weird about there not being any car keys at that house. The thought that Norman might have taken them did flit through her mind but was just as quickly disregarded.

Why would he do that?

CHAPTER NINETEEN

'What's up there?'

'How the hell would I know?'

'You're from around here, ain't ya?'

'Nope, not really ... few miles away. No sign of 'em anywhere else, so let's give it a go.'

'There's a sign there. What's it say?'

'Why? Can't you fucking read?'

'It's slanted towards you. I can't fucking see it.'

'Tilted, not fucking slanted ...'

'Fuck off, it's slanted ... Tilted is when it, like, hangs facing down and shit.'

'Is it bollocks.'

'What does the fucking sign say?'

'Oh, er ... holiday cottage, Primrose Holiday Cottage.'

'Oh, right ... Worth a look, I suppose.'

'It's on our patch, and the Doc will be pleased we found it.'

'He'll be even more pleased if we find those fuckers that been snooping through our houses.'

'Well, they ain't technically our houses, are they?'

'They's on our fucking manor, ain't they?'

'Yeah, yeah, fair enough. Ere, watch out!'

'Sorry, didn't see it. Fucking potholes everywhere.'

'Break my spine in half if you keep driving into 'em.'

'Well, it's getting fucking dark, and I can't see anything.'

'Use the lights then. No ... actually, don't use the lights.'

'You reckon?'

'Alright, you sarcastic twat. Aye, up there it is. Land Rover outside. Might be someone at home.'

'Might be. Fuck 'em.'

'Ha! Yeah, all the lights are off, though.'

'Move quick, go straight for the door.'

'I'm on it. Back door is closest. I'll go for that.'

'Right behind you.'

'It's unlocked.'

'I can see that for myself.'

'Hello? Anyone home?'

'Avon calling!'

'Avon, ha! Nice one ...'

'You like that one?'

'Yeah. My old dear always had Avon.'

'They still about. Well, not now obviously, but you know what I mean.'

'Think so, dunno really ... Guess no one here, though.'

'Power's off. You got your torch?'

'Yeah, hang on ... Hello! Someone's been thirsty.'

'Six glasses used. Still wet too.'

'They must be sticking to the fields then, avoiding the roads.'

'I reckon you could be right.'

'Can't be that far away. They ain't gone down that lane, so there must be another way.'

'Footpath or something? Let's have a look.'

'Hold on then, wait up ... Aren't we checking for food first?'

'Nah, we got loads. Doc'll be chuffed to bits if we track 'em down.'

'Fair enough, mate. Is that a footpath sign there?'

'Bloody hell, you're a clever one, aren't you?'

'And you're a sarcastic fucker.'

'Yeah, footpath. Must have gone that way.'

'No doubt. Come on, then.'

'Oh, this is gonna be fun. I can feel it. You reckon there might be girls with 'em?'

'Might be ... with a bit of luck. You got the shotgun shells this time?'

'Yes, smart arse, I have the fucking shotgun shells.'

'Just checking ...'

CHAPTER TWENTY

'Something isn't right. Clarence and Nick should be back by now, and where is Mr Howie and Dave? This isn't right. I'm telling you ...' Blowers shakes his head. 'We've been here for a couple of hours now. We can't just keep waiting.'

'We can't just leave either,' Lani cuts in. 'They'll turn up as soon as we leave; then, they'll be here for ages, looking for us.'

'Mr Howie and Dave, though,' Blowers continues. 'Maddox's lot are all coming back here,' he says with a nod to the group of youths gathered nearby–their numbers continually growing as they drift back from wherever they sought refuge after running off. 'If they can make it back here, then the boss and Dave should have too.'

'I agree,' Lani says quickly, 'I really do, but what else can we do? Clarence and Nick will know we'll wait here. Howie and Dave too.' She shrugs and looks down, thinking frantically of what to do next.

'Me and Blowers will go look for them. You stay here and wait for Clarence and Nick,' Cookey suggests.

'We should stay together.'

'I get that, Lani, but what if they're surrounded or something?' Cookey asks.

'Dave? Surrounded? Behave,' Blowers scoffs. 'Nah, it won't be anything like that. Something must have happened if they're not here. Maybe the boss is sick or something. We all know that Dave would never leave him.'

'He could be injured and hurt,' Lani bites her bottom lip, 'if they hurt him last night, and Dave got him out ...'

'So we should go look,' Cookey urges. 'You stay here with this lot.'

'Take Meredith then.'

'Meredith? Why?'

'She found you in that house, didn't she?'

'Not a bad idea, but that leaves you here alone,' Blowers cuts in.

'Well, I'm not exactly alone, am I?' she peers round at the children standing in the one area next to the car park not covered in bodies.

'Yeah, well ... maybe you should keep the dog,' Blowers suggests tactfully.

'Or maybe I go looking for them with the dog, and you two stay here,' she retorts with a flash of temper.

'Alright, take it easy. We'll go ...' Cookey mutters softly.

Sighing deeply, Lani massages her forehead and takes a deep breath. 'Sorry, it's so hot, and I'm worried sick now.'

'We'll find them. Just stay here until we get back,' Blowers urges.

'Er, maybe we should like set a time limit or something. Like, stay here, and if we're not back by whatever time, then make for the fort. Just a suggestion,' Cookey looks to both of them.

'Okay, what about five, then? That gives you several hours to find them and get back. If Clarence and Nick get here, they can either hang on or do a run back to the fort while I wait.'

Frowning and with pursed lips, Blowers stares first at the ground, then up at Lani. 'No,' shaking his head firmly as he changes his mind. 'Mr Howie would want us to stay together. There must be a reason they haven't got back to us. We have to just stay here and wait.'

'Blowers, we just agreed ...' Lani mutters.

'No, no, it's not the right thing,' he replies. 'Cookey, he'd want us to stay together. We're weaker when we're apart. Dave is with him, and Dave can handle anything ...'

'See your point,' Cookey rolls his eyes with frustration. 'Maybe ... yeah, maybe you're right.'

'I am right,' Blowers continues. 'We stay together. When Clarence and Nick get back, we can send this lot off and search together, but we have to stay together.'

'Okay,' Lani nods slowly, fighting the urge to do something, to do anything other than just stand here, surrounded by corpses and the acrid stench of the blazing High Street. A desolate scene of carnage that saps any positive energy they have. But Blowers is right. Howie has always been adamant about staying together, and to separate again now goes against everything they have evolved to be. 'Okay,' she repeats, more for herself than the others.

'They'll be okay,' Blowers says softly.

'They will,' Cookey agrees, moving one hand out to touch her shoulder. 'Like Blowers said, Dave can handle anything, and the boss is fucking indestructible.'

CHAPTER TWENTY-ONE

How far can a little girl run?

Turns out, it's bloody far. Very bloody far. She's like a Duracell bunny, just going on and on. The heat and constant running have me drained, sweating and gasping for air. Even Dave has broken out into a sweat, albeit a light one, but there is still moisture on his brow.

'Where?' gasping the word out, I round the corner to see Dave standing there, looking left and right. I know what the answer will be, and I'm already regretting asking it.

'Lost her.'

'Again!? Fucking hell, Dave, she's running rings round us. I thought you were Special Forces and trained to–'

'She's got skills,' he interrupts me.

'Skills?' Bent over with my hands on my knees, I glance up at him, wondering how a little girl can have Special Forces skills.

'Not taking a straight path but weaving left and right. It makes her much harder to track. Plus, she's using her small stature to her advantage by going through obstacles that pose problems to us.'

'Oh, right, yeah, that's the new commando training they're doing in pre-school these days. I read about it in the paper.'

'Really?'

'No, Dave, how the hell is a little girl going to know all that stuff?'

'Natural instinct,' he shrugs.

'Natural instinct? Jesus, she's only what, seven or eight? Imagine her grown up. She'll be like you. God help us.'

He stares at me, clearly unsure how to respond. 'I meant that nicely,' I add quickly.

'Okay,' the calm look reappears instantly.

'MILLY,' he bellows without warning me first, causing my heart to thud faster than the GPMG, 'GET SOME WATER. WE'LL WAIT HERE FOR A MINUTE ... DRINK SOME WATER.'

'What the fuck?'

'It's hot, Mr Howie. She could dehydrate.'

'Yeah, but ... it's just ... Okay, no, good idea ... fair enough.'

'Up there,' he points to the small figure stepping out of a driveway much further up the street, clearly visible, holding a glass which she lifts to her mouth.

'Do we get a water break too?'

'No, Mr Howie, she'll be off again in a minute.'

'Have you got any?'

'What?'

'Fuck, Dave, have you got any water?'

'No, Mr Howie.'

'Bollocks, yeah, you drink that nice, cold glass of water, you little shi–'

'Mr Howie!'

'What?'

'You can't call a little girl a little shit.'

'Sorry, Dave.' I blush with the shame of being told off. 'Hang on a minute, you were going to shoot those kids in Portsmouth.'

'Yeah, but ...'

'And when we met Maddox! You wanted to get out the van and attack them.'

'Yeah, but I wouldn't call a girl a little shit.'

'Oh, so it's fine to slaughter them willy nilly, but we can't call them little shits?'

'Well ...'

'Fucking hang on,' I say, standing up to rest my hands on my hips, the axe and assault rifle on the floor next to my feet. 'You're always shouting stuff. *I am Dave ... I will kill you,*' I mimic his voice. He goes to speak, but I keep going, '*I will burn your house down and murder your goldfish ...*'

'That is different, Mr Howie,' he says pointedly. 'That is a tactic designed to induce fear and thereby cause the enemy to make mistakes, which I can then use to my advantage.'

'Oh, that's what it is?' I ask with a raised eyebrow.

'And I never said I would murder a goldfish.'

'I was joking, Dave.'

'Dogs, cats, and I've done a ferret but not a–'

'What?'

'What?'

'A ferret?'

'What about it?'

'Dave, did you just say you murdered a ferret?'

'No, I said I threatened to murder a ferret.'

'Oh right, why? Why would you threaten to murder a ferret?'

'The man I was after loved his ferret,' he shrugs.

'Not his wife or ... mum ... or brother?'

'Oh, I tried those. He didn't react, so I went for the ferret.'

'Did it work?'

'Straight away,' he nods eagerly. 'He rolled over instantly.'

'What? The ferret rolled over?'

'No, the man rolled over.'

'Why would he roll over? Was he doing tricks?'

'It means he gave us the information we wanted.'

'So he didn't actually roll over?'

'No, Mr Howie.'

'Did the ferret roll over?'

'I never saw it roll over. Maybe it could have done. I couldn't say it had never rolled over.'

'So what happened?'

'To who?'

'The man! What happened to the man?'

'Nothing, we let him go.'

'The ferret?'

'We gave it back. We weren't heartless animals, Mr Howie.'

'No, mate, clearly not. Bloody hell, she's taking her time with that water.'

'Probably thirsty, Mr Howie.'

'Yeah, I know, Dave, I was ... Oh, never mind ... What she waving at?'

'Us, I think.'

I wave back, extending my arm high to sweep it back and forth. This is surreal, like a giant game of hide and seek.

'Milly?' I call out. 'Can we stop now, please? We're both knackered.' She doesn't respond to my pleas but walks slowly back towards the house she came out of. Cursing, swearing, muttering foul oaths, we start jogging again. Determined to try and catch her again.

'Morals, Dave, that's what it comes down to.'

'What does?'

'This, chasing her ... We could just sod off and leave her, but we won't because we have morals.'

'Oh,' he replies like he knows what I'm talking about.

'We'd never forgive ourselves if we just gave up now.'

'Okay, Mr Howie.'

'I mean she's tiny. I can see how she's survived this long, running like that, but she can't stay here.'

'Okay, Mr Howie.'

'Bloody hell, look at that,' we stop dead at the garden gate leading to the house she ran inside. There, on the doorstep are two big glasses of water. She obviously struggled to carry them as half the contents have sloshed over the ground. Dave goes forward, grabbing them both to sniff and taste before he hands one to me.

'What was that?' I ask him. 'You checking for poison?'

'You never know.'

'By a little girl? Where she going to get poison from? Or know what poison is? Maybe she did the poisoning assassination course with the commando training?'

'Very funny, Mr Howie.'

'Thanks, Dave.' We down the water in a couple of thirsty gulps before proceeding inside and heading straight to the kitchen sink for more water. Both of us deciding to forget the chase for a second and grab more fluids.

'Thank you, Milly,' I call out, 'very nice water. Thank you very much.'

'THANK YOU,' Dave roars, scaring the shit out of me again and making me spray water over the kitchen window.

How he makes the words '*thank you*' sound like '*I want to kill you*' is beyond me.

'Back?' I ask, nodding at the open back door.

'Yes,' he replies, and I swear there is a glint in his eye. If I didn't know better, I would start to think he was enjoying this.

CHAPTER TWENTY-TWO

Blowers, Cookey, and Lani wait at the car park, fretting and worried.

Howie and Dave chase a little girl through the sun-parched streets in a desperate attempt to get her somewhere safe.

Clarence seeks a van, something big enough to carry all the kit from the broken-down Saxon and still be used to ferry the remaining children and team from the burning town.

Maddox, Paula, and Roy remain outside the fort, locked out, with no response from those inside.

One member of the team remains blissfully asleep. Flat on his back in a king size double bed, snoring peacefully. The increasing heat of the morning raises the temperature in the room. Sweat trickles down the side of his face to soak into the pillow.

Alone and unaware that his team think he is with Clarence, Nick murmurs quietly in his sleep. Oblivious to anything apart from the dreams playing in his mind.

CHAPTER TWENTY-THREE

The day is oppressive and gloomy but thankfully a couple of degrees cooler. Looking up at the canopy overhead, Lilly shudders from the sensation of the trees pressing in. They are surrounded by thick trunks; their leaves spreading out to form a dense canopy overhead. The ground is barren from the lack of sunlight, apart from a few hardy-looking bushes scattered around.

It's still unbearably hot and sticky, but at least there is shade. The canopy masks the smell of the wood smoke too.

'No, didn't work,' Andrew sighs. 'We'll just have to hold the handle and keep the pot over the flames.'

'Dad, it takes fifteen minutes to cook pasta.' Lilly moves towards the fire burning on the ground. They made it out of the dead wood they found strewn about and quickly managed to build a decent sized blaze over which to cook their pasta. Several attempts have been made by Andrew and Norman to fashion something to hold the pan in place, all of which have failed dismally.

The first one was made from sticks and twigs, neither of them making the connection that putting a wood-made cradle over a fire wouldn't work that well. Then they tried using stones, but they just served to cut the airflow out from the fire, which in turn reduced the flames to the extent they would never heat the water in the pan.

'Well, there really isn't any choice,' Andrew replies.

'We can just take turns to hold the handle,' Norman adds. 'Use some cloth or something to grip it ...'

Lilly nods, watching the two inept men convince themselves they are equipped with the necessary skills to do this kind of thing. Frowning with concentration, she stares at the flames flickering up. Wood burns, so that's straight out. The pan is metal, metal doesn't burn. No, some metal will burn, but it has to be really hot.

They need metal to make a cradle to rest the pot on. But they're in a forest, which doesn't exactly have lots of metal lying about. Maybe a wire fence? That might do it, but there haven't been any fences for a few miles.

Do they have any metal? She heads over to the bags, examining each of them in turn. Norman's rucksack is larger than the others and rigid too. Feeling along the back and seams, she finds something hard contained within the material. A frame used to distribute the weight of the bag evenly.

Without thinking, she opens the top of the bag to try and find a way to get to the frame, not for a second realising she is effectively rummaging through Norman's bag. Slowly, she becomes aware of the silence in the group as all the chat stops. Three pairs of eyes turn to stare at her as Norman, Andrew, and Sam all notice what she's doing.

'Sorry,' she blurts, 'I was looking at the frame ... it's metal ... for the saucepan ...' Feeling her face blushing, she stands there, holding the open bag. 'I wasn't going through your bag.'

'Good idea!' Norman bursts up, quickly taking the bag from her. 'There's a metal frame in the bag. Well done, Lilly,' he beams and winks again, and this time she doesn't feel revolted but is thankful that he isn't offended at her going through his private belongings. Smiling back, she notices he cocks his head to one side with a weird look on his face.

'Will it work?' Andrew steps closer, lifting the bottom of the bag up to feel the stiff rods within the material. 'It's stitched in,' Andrew reports.

'Here, try this,' Norman passes him the knife pilfered from the holiday cottage. Together the two men butcher the rucksack, slicing through the material with long gashes that makes Lilly bite her lip at the clumsy ham-fisted way they do it.

The frame is pulled out, two long metal rods held out in victory by Andrew. He grabs one at both ends and tries bending it, his weak arms struggling to hold the thing still while he exerts force.

Going even redder in the face, he grunts and strains, barely bending the bar. Giving up with a shake of his head, he looks over at Norman trying the same with the other one and also failing dismally.

'Stiff little buggers,' Norman grunts, feeling a loss of pride at being unable to bend the bar in front of Lilly.

Use your feet. Use your bloody feet. Lilly wills, reluctant to keep making suggestions that only serve to show the inadequacies of her father.

'Here, you grab one end Andrew, and I'll try this one ...' Together they start pushing and pulling. Uncoordinated and working more against each other, they stagger and trip round the little hollow as the thin rod refuses to be bent.

Lilly looks down at the ground, simply staggered at how

two grown men can be so incompetent. She loves her father deeply and knows how intelligent and caring he is. He may not be the strongest or the biggest man, but he loves his family and tries hard despite his own failings.

A yelp lifts her head up to see Andrew rubbing his arm where the rod slipped out from his grip to whack him across the elbow.

'Not going to work,' Norman tuts. 'What a bloody shame.'

'Er ... maybe you could use your feet or something?' Lilly finally suggests. 'Er, use leverage to ... er ... gain more force?'

A look of annoyance flashes across Norman's face. Andrew, looking at his elbow misses it. Samantha, staring at Lilly, misses it too. Lilly doesn't. She clocks the expression and gets that overwhelming feeling of being distinctly uncomfortable again.

'Good idea again, Lilly,' Norman smiles, but this time the smile is forced and doesn't reach his eyes. 'I say, Andrew, your daughter really is a switched-on little thing, isn't she?'

Little thing? Patronising bastard. Right there, at that point, Lilly comes to the rapid conclusion that she does not like Norman. That he is slimy and weird, lecherous and emits a foul, pervy signal that sets alarms off in her head.

Placing one foot in the middle of the bar, Norman heaves on one end, grunting and straining again as he pulls his own foot off the ground.

'Stand on one end,' Lilly instructs.

'I'm sure Norman knows what he is doing,' Andrew is quick to say at the tone from his daughter.

'No,' Norman grunts, 'it's fine ... Another good idea,'

sliding his foot down the pole, he grips and starts to heave again.

'And brace the end against a tree,' Lilly adds in a strong voice that snaps Norman's head up to glare at her.

'Lilly, that is quite enough,' Andrew harries back and forth.

'Well, it's obvious,' Lilly huffs, 'brace one end, stand on it, and pull the other end up ...'

'Lilly!' Andrew snaps.

'Or,' Lilly continues in full flow now, 'just build the rocks up either side of the fire and rest the unbent bars across the top to put the pan on ... Saves bending them.'

Norman freezes, bent over with his face going red from the downward slant of his body and the flush of anger coupled with embarrassment. Samantha stares with an open mouth in awe at the other girl standing her ground proudly. Andrew goes into mild panic, fretting to and fro while wringing his hands.

'Right,' Norman says slowly, standing up to wipe his hands together as though removing dirt from them, 'why don't you show us, Lilly?'

Lilly ignores his barbed tone as she gathers the previously used rocks to build two sturdy platforms either side of the fire. Going back to the rods, she walks past Norman without a glance, grabs both, and heads back to make minor adjustments. Within minutes, the bars are wedged between rocks, providing a stable platform for the saucepan now resting on top, over the flames.

Standing back, she looks down at her work, then up at her father. His face is devoid of expression, but the atmosphere in the camp is now sliding rapidly downhill. Moving her gaze, she observes Norman and the baleful look on his face, one that is mixed with disgust and contempt at being shown up so easily.

'It works,' she shrugs and turns away, busying herself with cooking the pasta.

'The water isn't boiling,' Norman comments acidly.

'Doesn't need to be boiling,' Lilly replies instantly. 'Mum said the consumption method works just as well–the pasta cooks as the water heats.'

'Lilly, I think your tone is rude,' Andrew complains.

'No, it's okay, Andrew, she's a growing lady, and it's only to be expected,' Norman sneers.

'What was that?' Samantha edges closer to Lilly.

'The consumption method. It means the water doesn't have to be boiling to start cooking.'

'Wow, how did you know that?'

'Mum told me, and then showed me the packet that it was written on,' Lilly adds with a smile.

'I, er, I got some sauce from that house,' Samantha says quietly. 'Just like, you know, some ketchup, but I thought it would, like, be nice for the boys instead of, er, you know, plain pasta.'

'That's brill,' Lilly grins. 'Hear that, boys? You got yummy ketchup flavoured pasta for dinner.'

'Are we sleeping here?' Billy asks, glancing up at the trees.

'Yes, Billy,' Andrew answers, 'just for tonight. Thought we'd camp outside for fun.'

'I don't like it,' Billy carries on staring at the trees. 'Can't we go home now?'

'Not now, Billy, we're going to a big place with lots of other people,' Lilly explains.

'On the topic of camping,' Norman seizes the opportunity. 'I suggest we take watches during the night. Two at a time so we keep each other awake.'

'You think that's necessary?' Andrew asks mildly.

'Oh, definitely,' Norman says in a deep voice, 'we've got to stay alert ... and it's a good opportunity to get to know each other too, you know, have a chat and things.'

'Hmmm, yes, I can see the merits of that,' Andrew nods amiably. 'It would give us a chance to bond.'

Lilly focuses on the saucepan, knowing what's coming next. 'Maybe,' she cuts in first, 'Sam and I can take the first watch, then.'

'Great!' Sam grins broadly. 'Yeah, Lilly and me will do it.'

'Lilly and I,' Norman corrects, 'and, no, Samantha, we need one adult awake at all times.'

'We're fifteen, Dad,' Sam whines. 'We can stay awake the same as you.'

'Decision made, Sam. One of us men will be awake at all times, and it will be a good time for you to get to know Andrew.'

'Me?' Andrew asks.

'Well, yes, Andrew. Sam's my daughter, so I know her very well, but I hardly know Lilly or Billy, so it will be a good opportunity for us all to get to know each other.'

'I can't see Billy staying awake very long,' Andrew chuckles.

'Be that as it may, I would be honoured if you would take this time to get to know my daughter. God forbid anything should happen to me, but if it did ... then I would want my children to go with someone they know and are familiar with.'

'Ah, yes ... when you put it like that, yes, that does make sense,' Andrew nods seriously.

Norman nods back and walks away in an effort to hide the look of victory on his face. His own feelings shifted during the last few minutes. Gone were the fantasies of a life spent with Lilly in the wooden shack. Now, after being shown up like that, he felt a strong sexual desire to dominate and control her. She's a wild little thing, full of ideas, and she needs to be tamed.

The first pan full of pasta is made and carefully drained out, causing Lilly to chastise herself for not bringing a second pan to use to capture the already hot water. Instead, they have to refill with cold, add more pasta, and wait for it come back to the boil.

With ketchup mixed in, giving the food a lovely tomato tang, the boys get stuck in, using forks to stab at the chunks and shovel into their small mouths.

The two men and two girls watch hungrily as the boys devour the food, licking their lips and getting sticky sauce plastered round their mouths.

'Dad, you ready?' Lilly starts draining the next pan.

'I certainly am!' Norman says with forced cheerfulness.

'No, girls, you go next. We men can wait a minute for the next lot,' Andrew cuts in with a loving smile towards his capable daughter.

'Oh yes, of course, that's what I meant,' Norman adds quickly.

Sauce is added, and the girls tuck in, eating just as fast as the two boys did. The taste is amazing. Just simple pasta with tomato sauce, but for hungry bellies emptied from so much walking, it is divine and finished quickly.

'Look,' Sam nods at the two boys already nodding off. Lying back on the soft undergrowth of dead leaves, their eyes droop, and their breathing becomes deeper.

'Bless,' Lilly replies quietly. Contentment from eating

proper food spreads through her. That and standing up to Norman too. She is sensible and full of common sense, more than her father and Norman, and if it means ruffling his feathers to keep the boys and Sam safe, then so be it.

Lilly cooks more pasta, setting some aside for the boys in the morning. It might be not the tastiest cold food, but it will give them energy for the next day. She and Sam share another pot; then, Andrew and Norman get stuck in.

The afternoon draws to evening as the small camp relaxes into quiet chat. Sam and Lilly talk about school and life as they knew it. The men go back to business and how the recession screwed everything up. Shadows grow longer, and the yawns become more frequent. With the heat still so high, it sucks what little energy they have out from their already exhausted bodies.

Norman wills the sun to go down, wills those shadows to get longer and deeper. It frustrates him having to make polite small talk with this idiot when he has something much more important on his mind. Allowing himself a glance over at Lilly, he notices the way she stretches out on the ground. The contours of her body and the obvious swelling of her chest.

His own daughter, by comparison, still looks wan and thin. Ungainly and very childlike, more like a boy than a girl. The biting anger from earlier subsides, leaving him with the returned fantasy of living in the wooden shack with Lilly. But now she isn't demure and standing behind his rugged form. She is wild and full of passion, making love with a fiery intensity as she rakes long nails down his back.

'You alright?' Andrew chuckles. 'You look a million miles away.'

'Eh?' Startled and worried in case he inadvertently said something out loud, Norman shakes his head and thinks quickly. 'Oh, you know, just, er ... thinking about everything.'

'Yes,' Andrew yawns again, the third time in the last few minutes. *Come on, you old man, go to sleep.*

But he doesn't. He seems perfectly content to chat away, talking about god knows what that involved god knows who. Norman smiles and nods as his mind drifts back to the fantasy. *Must be this heat and the exercise making me all horny*, he thinks. *Soon I'll have this belly fat burnt off and should maybe cut my hair too. Shave it off so I look tougher. Exercise? Yeah, that's not a bad idea. I'll do some push-ups and things to make my arms bigger. I'll need the strength and energy for all the sex too.*

'And so I said, you know, we just cannot compete with the Chinese anymore ... We realised it was time to pack up, but I kept going, and well, the rest is history ... If only I had got out when I had the chance.'

'Oh yes, of course,' Norman nods, catching the tail end of the long monologue.

'Well, I think I'm going to drop off any minute, and it's looking very dark now ... Yes, I would say this is nighttime ... Who's up for the first watch?'

'You rest, old chap,' Norman says kindly. 'Your bag is heavier than mine, so you've had more work today. You sleep first, and I'll wake you up in a couple of hours. Hear that, Sam? Lilly and I will take first watch so you get some sleep.'

'You sure, Norman?' Andrew asks with another yawn. 'Feel awful having the first sleep. Maybe we should let the girls get some rest, and we stay up, eh? Carry on with our interesting business chats.'

'No,' Norman says too quickly, 'I mean no, you look beat, Andrew, and we're going to need our senses about us tomorrow. Sam looks about done in too, eh, Sam? I said you look about done in.'

'I'm falling asleep now,' Sam groans. Lilly stares across the dark camp. The small flames flicker illumination at the faces of her father and Norman, contorting their features to make the eye sockets deep and hidden. Norman's face looks slick with sweat and almost predatory.

Silence descends as first Andrew slips into slumber, audibly snoring as he drifts deeper from exhaustion. Sam is close behind, her soft breathing becoming longer and deeper.

Lilly settles and listens, first focussing on the sounds of the sleeping forms next to her, before tuning into the natural noises from the forest. She can hear animals moving through the undergrowth; a fox far away and distant calling out for her young. With no breeze, the branches don't creak, and nor do the leaves rustle against each other.

Slight crackles and hisses come from the small fire, and she becomes painfully aware of Norman sitting across the camp and staring right at her.

'You okay?' he whispers in a low, hoarse voice.

'Fine,' she nods, then realises he won't see the nod. 'Yeah, I'm fine, er ... You can sleep if you want, Norman. I'm happy to stay awake.'

Hearing his name said by her sends a thrill through him, a tingle into his groin that makes his heart beat a bit harder. 'No, I'm fine too ... Never did need much sleep,' he whispers softly, aware his voice is becoming slightly deeper as the lust builds.

Silence again. Awkward and sustained. Lilly shifts position and stifles a yawn. She thought the forest would scare her, but strangely, it doesn't. Actually, in self-reflection, she doesn't feel that scared at all. Having Billy and now Todd to think about pushes the fear away.

'Hear that?' Norman whispers urgently, snapping her from the deep thoughts.

'No, what?'

'Something ... not sure ...' he gets up slowly and carefully, the soft light reflecting on his form as he stands listening intently. 'Thought I heard someone moving about.'

'Really?' Lilly is on her feet. 'We should wake everyone up.'

'No!' Norman whispers. 'Not yet. Don't scare everyone. It might be an animal or er ... a deer or something, maybe a badger ...'

'We can't take the risk,' Lilly urges.

This isn't the plan. Not the plan at all. Norman carries on pretending to listen while he thinks frantically. 'I'll go look,' he says eventually. 'Yeah ... you stay here, and I'll have a quick walk about.'

'I'll wake Dad up.'

'No, don't, not yet. It's probably nothing, and it's not worth disturbing him unless necessary. Just wait here for a minute.'

Unsure and thinking they really should be waking the others up, Lilly concedes and pauses. Holding still whilst listening to Norman quietly slip out of sight into the undergrowth. She tracks his movements, suddenly aware of just how quietly he is moving.

Minutes pass as she stands completely still, craning her head round to listen and focus on the noises. One hand gripping the handle of the knife held ready.

'Lilly,' Norman's voice comes softly through the undergrowth, 'come here.'

'Why?'

'You've got to see this.'

'What? See what?'

'Ssshhh, don't wake the others. Come and look.'

'Look at what?'

'Er ... some lights, but er ... in the distance, like far away.'

'Lights? What kind of lights?'

'I don't know. Come and look but stay quiet.'

'Okay, wait there,' she slips into the darkness. She loses her sense of direction within seconds because of the blackness of the forest. 'Where are you?'

'Over here,' his voice sounds further away now, but she follows the sounds, carefully stepping to avoid tripping over roots.

'I can't find you,' she whispers, wondering what lights he can see. Maybe a commune or some people all together, might be a safe place they could head for tomorrow.

'Keep coming. You have to go right over here to see them,' again, he sounds further away, but she ploughs on, intent on seeing the lights for herself.

'Norman? I really cannot see a thing.'

'Just here, down this bank. Watch your step, it's quite steep, that's it ... I'm right here.'

With his voice now a lot closer, she finds her way to him. Some slivers of moonlight finding their way through the trees to offer gloomy, indistinct shadows. 'Just over here,' he adds, his voice low and hoarse again.

'How far? We shouldn't leave the others alone.'

'I know, but I want you to see this.'

'Maybe we should wait till morning or wake the others up first.'

'Just have a look first and see what you think.'

'Where are they?'

'Just a bit further.'

Following Norman, Lilly starts realising that something isn't right. They shouldn't be out here, so far away from the others. The need to say something builds slowly, the need to know what the hell is going on.

'We have to go back,' she says finally, proud of the strength in her voice.

'Lilly, there is something I want to talk about,' Norman turns quickly, standing too close.

'What?' Stepping back, she detects his movement as he moves in closer again.

'You and I, Lilly ... I saw the way you were looking at me. Now, I know I'm older, and you are only fifteen, but times have changed suddenly, Lilly, and ...'

'What!?'

'Ssshhh, keep your voice down!'

'I'm going back.'

'No!'

'Take your hand off me! Let go. I said let go. You're hurting me ...'

'Lilly, just be quiet and listen for a minute ...'

'Get off me. Let go of my wrist now. Let go, or I'll scream for my dad.'

'No, please just listen, Lilly. I'll only take a minute, please ...'

'You're scaring me. Please let go ... DAAA ...'

'Shut up! Shut up, you stupid bitch,' clamping one hand over her mouth, he stifles the scream before it wakes anyone up. Lilly squirms and bucks against him, fighting to get him off, but his grip on her wrist is too strong. In the darkness and the ground littered with organic obstacles, they go down, tripping over roots and each other to land in a heap amongst dead leaves.

'Ssshhh,' Norman hisses, 'just shut up ... I saw the way

you were looking at me ... I didn't mean to scare you, but my god, Lilly, you are so beautiful ...'

Fear grips her stomach. This cannot be happening. She tries to bite his fingers, moving her mouth against his hand. Norman feels the warmth of her lips and tongue against his hand, which only serves to drive the lust deeper into his groin.

'Oh god, you've got such a hot body,' Norman gasps, pressing his mouth close to her ear. 'There's no way you're only fifteen ... We'll be together, Lilly. Just me and you, yeah? Would you like that? Just us two living alone in our wooden house ...'

Squirming and fighting, she tries to feel for the knife she dropped when they went down to the floor.

'Oh, Lilly, I know you like me. You do like me, don't you? We'd better not say anything to your dad yet ... I'll take my hand away, but don't scream ... please, just talk for a minute.'

'Norman,' Lilly gasps, 'please get off me ... please just stop it ...'

'Lilly, but you like me ... I know you do.'

'No, no, I don't ... not like that ...'

A loud scream reaches them through the forest. Long and terrified, high pitched and full of pain. Norman freezes, Lilly stiffens as they listen to the drawn-out sound.

'Sam,' Norman hisses. 'Oh god ...' On his feet instantly. All thoughts of Lilly gone from his mind as his fatherly instinct finally kicks in. 'Todd ... Sam ...' whimpering, he plunders through the bushes, snapping twigs as he powers through the dark forest.

Shocked to the core, Lilly scrabbles up and starts after him. She tries to remember the route they took to get here, but the darkness is too intense. Her vision is rendered useless by the lack of light, so instead, she focuses on following the sounds of Norman as he runs ahead, screaming the names of his children in blind panic.

Another scream rips through the foliage, plunging Norman into greater panic. Thrashing his way through low branches, he trips time and again, falling hard onto the ground. He snags his ankles and bruises his hands, face and knees. More screams, unearthly and filled with pain. Male voices shouting now, too far away to be clear.

In his consuming panic, Norman races ahead of Lilly, leaving her to find a route through the blackness of the night. The screams and shouts are her markers to aim for. With the knife still on the ground somewhere, she has no weapons and is utterly defenceless.

Norman bellows for all he is worth at hearing the unmistakable sound of a girl in dire pain, the fear for his children coursing through his veins.

Trying her best to keep up, Lilly listens to the noise ahead, identifying the instant Norman bursts back into the camp from the rise in volume and chaotic noises, shouting, aggressive male voices, and someone screaming. It could be Sam or the boys. She can't tell who.

Forcing her tired body to run faster, she races towards the noise, seeing the light of the fire flickering through the undergrowth and trees. With just metres to go, she catches the tip of her foot on an exposed root. The power of her legs driving her forward sustain the momentum as she goes down hard, sprawling into the hard, compacted earth.

Winded and stunned, she has no choice but to lie still and wait for the dizziness to pass. Hands and knees bruised, but the pain is ignored. Slowly, she lifts her head up to try and see into the clearing.

What she sees freezes her to the spot. She is unable to

move or respond. Her heart jumps around erratically as she stops breathing . The sounds come a second later, filtering through to her stunned ears and foggy brain.

Everything has slowed down. Movements are slower than they should be. In shock, she blithely notices the fire has been built up and is now bigger than it was. Flames dance as they cast orange light against the branches. Faces shadowy, then bright, giving the eye sockets a hollow, empty look. The contrast of the brightly coloured rucksacks piled together against the muted colours of the vegetation.

The screams don't mean anything to her. She is at home, watching a movie. The remote control must be here somewhere. She can just switch over and end it.

But this isn't a movie. This is real.

Norman has run into the camp and gone straight to the man on top of his daughter. Lilly notices the naked backside of the man lifting and thrusting between the pale, skinny legs of Sam. Her father on his knees, staring up into the barrels of a shotgun held by another mam. His arms wrapped protectively round the shoulders of the two young boys screaming with fear.

Norman is felled quickly, stunned by the blow of the butt of the shotgun smashing into the side of his skull. Sprawled out on the floor, he sluggishly rises, only to slump back down as through drunk.

The man holding the shotgun laughs and shakes his head, prodding the barrels into Andrew's chest when he squirms in panic. The naked backside keeps rising and thrusting going from gentle, almost loving movements to a harder, urgent action. Samantha screams and screams, but the noise seems to whip the rapist into a frenzy. He has pinned Sam's wrists to the ground, making it impossible for her to do much more then squirm. The glow from the fire reflects from his demonic face, the twisted features contorting as he thrusts harder and harder, slamming his groin into the girl.

On all fours now, Norman tries crawling to his daughter. Screaming with terror, pleading for the man to stop. Dark blood pours from one ear, and he keeps losing his ability to move. His fatherly instinct is the only thing keeping him conscious and moving.

Andrew begs and pleads, wailing as he pulls the boys harder into his chest. Suddenly the noise is overwhelming–a cacophony of voices wailing, screaming, yelling, and laughing.

The man on Samantha lifts his hand to grip her chin, squeezing it harder as he thrusts with violent power. He starts hitting her, slapping her across the face with blows that increase in force until he is punching down, driving his clenched fist into her nose. Blood bursts, spraying up as she screams through broken teeth. Like an animal, he climaxes at the same time as Sam falls unconscious, pulverising her face to a bloody, ragged mess.

Instead of flopping down with the afterglow of climax, he jumps to his feet, standing there and roaring with triumph as his still erect penis stands proud off his body. With arms raised high, he whoops and bellows, a guttural primeval noise that echoes through the trees of the forest.

'CUNT ...' he spits down on the girl. 'CUNT, CUNT, CUNT ...' he screams the words over and over and spits phlegm onto the bloody, pulped remains of her facial features.

'You are fucking sick,' the man holding the shotgun laughs. Like watching his mate flick a bogey.

'Watch this then,' the rapist nods, his head bobbing up and down. Possessed, the boundaries of law and civilisation have been ripped away. He can do what he wants. He is powerful, god-like, and no one can stop him. Grabbing his semi-erect shaft, he grunts and focusses for a second, wriggling his body to get the piss flowing. It spurts out, thick and foul.

It coats her face, the acidic liquid burning the exposed wounds. The action snaps her awake, screaming with pain as he sprays his piss down on her.

Laughing harder, the man with the shotgun has to focus to keep his aim on Andrew, the end of the gun waving back and forth. 'I take it I ain't having a go, then,' he shouts.

The man pissing whips his aim off to the side, suddenly aware of what he is doing. 'Oh fuck, sorry, mate ... shit ... I didn't think of that. I can wash her off if you want?'

'Fuck off! I'm not going after you. Sloppy seconds? No way, keep her, mate.'

'Seriously? Her pussy is alright, bit tight, but like, I loosened it up now.'

'Urgh! Fucking gross, mate, really fucking gross.'

'Suit yourself. You'll only regret it later,' the rapist shrugs, tugging his trousers up to cinch the flies and belt closed.

'Sam,' Norman wails, his voice weak and pitiful, 'oh, Sam ... Sam ...'

'That your daughter, is it?' the rapist asks conversationally.

'Sam ... oh, my Sam ...'

'Shit father you are,' the rapist shakes his head. 'Fucking off to take a dump and leaving her alone ... that other bloke was asleep,' he says with indignation, pointing at the sobbing Andrew. 'What father leaves his kid asleep in the forest with all this going on ... shame ... fucking shame ...'

'Please ...' Andrew blurts, 'please just go ...'

'Oh, he's awake now,' the rapist comments. 'You didn't exactly do anything either ... Now, if it was my daughter, I would go fucking apeshit. Honestly, you'd have to shoot me to get me to stop. I wouldn't fucking stop ... but you two ... crying and begging, tut-fucking-tut ...'

'Oh god, Sam ... Todd? Where's Todd?'

'He's here, Norman ... please ... please just let us go ...'

'Or what?' The man holding the shotgun says. 'Ain't no piggy snout filth now, mate. Who you gonna call?'

'Ghostbusters!' the rapist shouts.

'Ha! Fucking love it when you do that ...Ere, we ought to, like, have that as our thing ... like that bloke in Pulp Fiction when he does the bible speech at the start ...'

'Oh, er ... yeah ... Oh fuck, what was his name? Samuel Jackson?'

'Yeah, him. We do that from now on?' the man with the shotgun laughs.

'Yeah, alright,' the rapist giggles. 'Ere, you sure you don't wanna have a go?' he nods at Sam squirming quietly on the ground. 'I'll give her a rinse out if you want.'

'Er ...' the man with the shotgun thinks for a second, 'nah. Nah, thanks, mate, but like, you know ... girls that age don't do it for me ...'

'What you saying?' the rapist challenges in a hard voice.

'Nothing, no, nothing, mate ... Fuck no, I don't mean that ... She's old enough, ain't she? I just meant I like 'em a bit older, with some, like, meat on their bones and big old tits, you know, not all scrawny and shit.'

'Every hole's a goal,' the rapist shrugs, placated from the suggestion that he likes young girls.

'Yeah, you know, fair one, mate, but ... nah, I'll pass ... Anyway, we better get these two back for the doc.'

'He'll be chuffed as fuck,' the rapist grins.

'Yeah,' the shotgun man nods, a dark look crossing his face as he stares down at the two boys being held by Andrew.

'Oh, give over,' the rapist huffs.

'What?'

'Your face, that's what ...'

'I didn't say anything,' the man with the shotgun replies quietly.

'Didn't need to, your face says it all. Don't let him see that. The Doc won't like it if he sees you do that ...'

'I didn't do anything,' shotgun man protests, but his voice is low and muted.

'I couldn't give a fuck what you think,' the rapist shrugs. 'Really don't bother me ... but don't show the doc. He'll go fucking nuts ...'

'Fair enough,' shotgun man nods quietly, his face now devoid of expression. 'Come on, we gotta go ... You two, come with me,' he nods at the boys.

'Please, no ... just go ... I'm begging you ... don't hurt them ...'

'We ain't gonna hurt 'em,' shotgun man replies. 'Really, we ain't gonna touch hair on their heads ... They'll be safe enough ...'

'Where you taking them?' Andrew gasps, gripping the boys harder.

'The Doc wants 'em,' the man with the shotgun says quickly.

'Please ... just go ...' Andrew begs again. 'My god, I'm begging you. Please just leave us and go ...'

'No can do, mate. We's got orders, ain't we? Hand 'em over now, mate. They ain't gonna get hurt or nothing ...'

'No! No ... just leave ... please ... oh my god, please no ...'

'Ere, mate, I ain't standing here all night, fucking

discussing it. Give 'em here now, or I'll fucking shoot your face off." He pushes the shotgun into Andrew's face, leering at him from above.

In desperation, Andrew releases Todd, pushing him away as he clutches Billy with both hands. Lilly, watching from the undergrowth clamps her hand over her mouth at the callous action of her father.

'Take him ... Please not Billy ... please ...'

'DAD!' Todd screams.

'You nasty fucker!' the rapist shouts. 'That's fucking cold, that is ...' Striding forward, he grabs Todd by the wrist, wrenching him onto his feet before giving him to the man holding the shotgun. 'What a nasty cunt.' Shaking his head, he marches back to Andrew, punching him hard in the face. 'Let him go,' the rapist shouts as both Billy and Andrew scream in terror. 'I said ... fucking let him go ...' The thumps get harder as Andrew takes the blows, refusing to yield his son to the two men.

'Stubborn cunt ... fucking let him go!' the rapist bursts into violent rage, using both hands to reign blow after blow into Andrew.

Screaming, Andrew pushes Billy away with a hard motion before lunging up at the rapist. Caught by surprise, the rapist falls back as Andrew powers into him, roaring with blind fury as he lashes out, landing punches and slaps into the rapist's face.

'Ere, fucking get a grip,' the shotgun man shouts.

Andrew, pumped with rage, presses the attack harder. Lilly catches a glimpse of her father's face, a mixture of terror and berserk anger twisting his normally mild features. The rapist goes down, unable to fend the blows off and tripping on the uneven surface. Andrew surges in, sensing the opportunity to cause damage. Like the infected they are running from, Andrew clamps his mouth onto the rapist's cheek, gnashing his teeth as he drives both clenched fists into the side of his head.

The sudden boom of the shotgun is deafening in the small enclosure. The force of the explosion sends Andrew flying off to the side, his head a bloody pulp, with half the skull removed, brains and bones mixing with bloody goo down the foliage around them.

Lilly stifles the scream, pushing her own face into the dirt and biting down. Tears sting her eyes, her whole body tensed completely rigid.

'Jesus fucking Christ,' the man with the shotgun complains. 'Where did that come from? You alright?'

'No, I'm not fucking alright ... cunt bit my fucking cheek ... shit, that hurts ...'

'Let's have a look ... Oh fuck, that's right through ...' he sucks in a sharp intake of breath. 'Nasty, mate ... that'll need stitches.'

'Cunt ... fucking cunt ...' rapist stands up unsteadily, swaying as he clutches his bleeding face. Grabbing a piece of cloth from his pocket, he presses the material to the wound, pushing hard as he stalks over to the boys and grabs a screaming Billy by the hand.

'Shut the fuck up!' the rapist bellows, spraying blood over the young boy's face.

'Don't!' shotgun man shouts at seeing the rapist raise a hand to strike Billy. 'Doc'll go fucking spare if they're marked ...'

Holding his hand above Billy, rapist struggles to bring his temper back under control, 'Yeah, but he don't know we got two, does he? We can just take one back, and he'll be happy.'

'Nah,' shotgun shakes his head, 'come on ... take the gun, and I'll take the boys.'

'Fine, you take the fucking brats, then. Fuck that hurts ... CUNT!' he screams with temper, running over to slam the front of his boot into the mess that was Andrew's head.

'Sam ...' Norman bleats pitifully, swimming in and out of consciousness.

'What you wanna do with him?' shotgun man asks.

'Fuck him, skull's fucked ... He'll be dead in a bit ...'

'Sure?' shotgun man asks. 'Just shoot him now.'

'Nah, fuck him, let him die slow, the cunt. His fucking mate bit my cheek, didn't he?'

Without further words, the rapist takes the gun as the other man grabs the boys, one big hand gripping one wrist each. Pulling them to their feet, they start walking off, leaving the devastated camp behind them and one girl frozen in fear as she hides in the undergrowth.

CHAPTER TWENTY-FOUR

The silence is only broken by the ragged death rattle of Norman. Lilly forces herself to get up, pushing with her hands until her feet take her weight, and she staggers from the perimeter into the camp.

Standing still, she stares at the ruined body of her father. His head unrecognisable from the blast of the shotgun. Norman twitches and murmurs quietly.

From instinct, she goes first to Samantha, kneeling down at her side as she takes in the pulped mess of her face. Nose clearly broken, and her lips split and torn from being driven into her teeth which are snapped and bloodied. One side of her face has completely caved in.

Bending over, she tries to listen for breathing, her own heart pounding with abject terror. No sounds, nothing. She remembers the first aid training the school made them all do and gropes the girl's bloody neck, feeling for a pulse.

Checking wrists and then finally resting her head on Sam's bony chest, she is forced to accept that Sam has been beaten to death. The sheer number of overwhelming, hard blows caused serious brain injury.

Standing up, she staggers towards Norman, then pauses. A small voice permeates her brain, forcing her to listen. The boys have been taken, but they're alive. Those men said they couldn't hurt them.

Norman is dying. Thick blood oozes from one ear, and his breathing comes with ragged gulps. Turning her head, she stares at the direction the two men went, then back to Norman.

Quickly, she darts forward and scrabbles at Norman's belt for the knife he had there. Her elbow digs into the top of his thigh and something hard within his pocket. Thinking it might be another useful weapon, she pushes her hand in, grabs the object, and pulls it free. A wave of nausea surges through her as she realises it's the keys to the Landover from the holiday cottage.

Any sense of sadness towards Norman vanishes in that second. They could have loaded up and gone, be far away and safe. This man, this foul, perverted, sick man hid these keys just so he could have a night outside with her. They didn't need to be here. Her dad, the two boys, Sam.

For a second, she imagines herself plunging the knife into his chest, finishing the job the other men started. Instead, she gets to her feet and moves away, heading out of the camp and into the darkness of the forest.

Without a look back, she leaves the scene. Her father is dead. Sam is dead. Norman is dying, and her brother and Todd are being dragged terrified by two rapist, murdering men.

Forcing herself to think straight, she creeps after them, knowing that going too slow will run the risk of the men getting too far ahead, but too fast, and they'll hear her.

How did they find them? It cannot be an accident. They must have found the holiday cottage and then followed the footpath. The smell of the fire would have drifted, and then all they had to do was wait until dark and find the light of the fire.

The shock is deep and repressed. Her mother is almost certainly dead. Her father is dead. Everyone she knows is probably dead or one of them things. The one remaining person is now being dragged away to some doctor somewhere. Todd too. So both the boys are now the sole reason to keep going. The image of her father launching the attack at the rapist summons a rare feeling of pride towards her father. That he had the courage to go out fighting for his children, and if nothing else, he hurt that man badly. A weak, mild man, best by problems that hampered his own life and that of his family, but at the last second, he really did show he was a man.

The tree line ends suddenly. The darkness eases up as moonlight floods the scene before her. The figures are ahead, moving slowly away. Two big figures gripping two smaller ones. If she can see them, they will be able to see her.

Stay low and be ready to drop. Common sense takes over as she moves off at a crouch. As they navigate the meadows and fields, she periodically loses sight of them. She takes the opportunity to get upright and run faster until they once more come into view, and she's forced to go low again.

Get ahead and do something to their car. That is the best plan. Prevent them from driving off and buy time to get the boys back. But in the dark, in a strange place, and not knowing the direction they are heading, she has no choice but to follow them. If she deviates, she runs the risk of becoming lost and being no use at all.

What about when they drive off? They'll see her behind

them in the Land Rover. How can she follow them without being seen?

She could call out and go with them, but after seeing what they did to Samantha, that idea is disregarded very quickly. She'll be no good at all if she's dead, and the other man said he liked them with more meat on their bones and some tits to grab.

There is no other option but to keep going. So she does. Staying low and hardly daring to breathe, she follows them back to the holiday cottage.

When it comes into view, she has no opportunity to get ahead of them but again has to wait and hold back, taking care not to walk on the dirt track and run the risk of kicking a stone or pebble.

'You need to wash that cheek,' shotgun man says.

'Yeah,' rapist replies, 'fucking hurts. You reckon they might have painkillers there?'

'Where?'

'At that fucking house!' rapist snaps.

'Might do. Worth a look. You wash that cut, and I'll have a look. You boys thirsty? Eh? You want some water?'

Too terrified to reply, the boys get dragged along, quietly sobbing. Lilly feels her heart breaking at the sight of Billy and Todd being so close but being unable to do anything to help them. As they near the cottage, torches get switched on and used to find the way to the unlocked back door. The four of them disappear inside.

Lilly takes the chance to run ahead into the small parking area and find their car. She finds a big, white van and goes for the driver's door. Locked. Same with all the doors.

How do you disable a van? She has no idea but runs round the vehicle, looking for anything that could be broken or snapped. The walls are sheer-sided. The lid to the engine bit is closed and sealed. The underneath wouldn't mean anything to her. Even the fuel flap is locked.

Tyres! She can puncture the tyres with the knife, but then they would know someone had done that. What is the choice? Do nothing and run the risk of losing them.

With a faint grunt, she stabs the kitchen knife at one of the tyres, blanching when the blade bounces off to skitter to one side. Retrieving the knife, she tries again, amazed at how much force is needed to puncture an almost rigidly inflated tyre. She aims for the top where the tread is thicker, not knowing to attack the thinner side wall of the tyre.

Eventually, out of sheer frustration, she slams the knife at the wheel. Missing the top and hitting the side. The point sinks in, only a small amount but enough for the hiss of air to let her know she's hit the right spot. Yanking the blade free, she visibly watches as the van sinks a few inches as the air escapes the pressurised tube of the tyre.

'Where's this place we going, then?' the rapist asks as they leave the cottage.

'South somewhere, some old manor house. Chi ... no ... Chantsworth House? Can't remember what he said now.'

'Chapsworth House, that was it.'

'What the fuck you asking me for if you already know it?' the man holding the hands of the two boys says, coming into view. Lilly scrabbles backwards to the Land Rover, dropping down on the far side to stay out of sight.

'Because,' the rapist sighs, 'I fucking forgot, didn't I? What with my face being fucking bitten off and all.'

'The others will already be there. We're late as it is.'

'Yeah, but he ain't gonna moan, is he? What with us getting these two.'

'Hope not,' the man with the boys replies. 'FUCK IT!'

'What?'

'Puncture ... look ...'

'Fuck ... Must have been them potholes, shit ... shit ... We got a spare?' Rapist feels at the freshly washed wound to his face, pressing a clean tea towel against it.

'Yeah, underneath. I'll do it. Hold these.' The rapist takes the boys, using one hand to hold their two tiny wrists while he presses the cloth to the side of his face.

'He's gonna get shitty as fuck at how late we are,' the rapist comments.

'Yeah, I fucking know he will, but it isn't our fault, is it?' the other man snaps.

'Not saying it is, but ... just saying ... that's all,' rapist mumbles, wincing at the pain in his face.

Lilly watches the man work, not realising the spare wheel was held there. It only takes the experienced man half an hour to get the damaged wheel off, pushing it aside and fitting the spare one. Grunting with the exertion of tightening the bolts. She wills them to keep speaking, to give her information or details of where they are going. But rapist is too sore to speak and snaps angrily at the boys when they cry too loud, and the other man is pre-occupied changing the wheel.

'Done,' he stands back, wiping his filthy hands down the front of his jeans.

'Thank fuck for that,' rapist mumbles. 'Get in ... go on ... get in the fucking van!' he snaps at the two boys, manhandling them into the passenger side before clambering up and slamming the door closed.

The other man climbs in the driver's side, starts the engine, and pulls away. He sweeps round the car park before pulling out onto the road. Lilly runs round to driver's door of the Land Rover, fumbling with the keys to get the door unlocked. Inside, she stares down at the basic controls. The gear stick too worn and faded now to show the numbers of the gears.

Shoving the key in, she turns it too quickly, not giving the coil a chance to warm up and start the diesel engine. When it fails to start, she keeps trying, eventually getting the loud engine spluttering as it rumbles to life.

Grinding noises wrench into the night as she shoves and pulls at the gearstick, trying to find a slot for it to go in. It takes time to figure out how to hold the clutch down, find the gear, and lift it at the right time while lifting the gas pedal for the engine to move and then even longer to find the handbrake and release it.

False starts as the engine stalls again and again. Lilly, refusing to let the frustration take over, keeps trying, learning from each mistake until, gingerly, the vehicle moves off. It doesn't have power steering, and she grits her teeth at the strength needed to turn the steering wheel, learning it's much easier to do when the vehicle is moving.

Onto the lane, and she bounces along, first trying to fumble for the headlights, then realising that's the last thing she wants to do. Inside the van, they might not hear the engine, but at night, they will definitely see the lights.

So she pushes on in darkness, bouncing the vehicle over the potholes and ruts as she keeps it in first gear. The engine screams out, begging her to change up, and eventually, she gives it a go. Losing all power as she fails to find the slot and is forced to start again from scratch.

Juddering, failing, stopping, and starting, she gets to the end of the lane, to the junction with the main road and no sign of the van in either direction.

Trying to think, she imagines the direction they came

from would be left, back to the houses they found earlier. Maybe she should go right then to find Chapsworth House?

The tears start to fall, she's lost them already. With a fifty-fifty chance of them being in either direction, she pulls out and heads right, again juddering the vehicle as she clumsily tries to push through the gears.

She refuses to sob. The tears can stream down as much as they want. That's a physical reaction that she has no control over. But sobbing? Weeping? Not now.

If she doesn't find them, then that is the place to head for. At least Sam took the painkillers from the holiday cottage. That rapist scum can suffer a bit longer. Hopefully he will get infected from the bite and die a slow, painful death.

Her mind fills with images of stabbing the two men repeatedly, cutting their throats, and watching them die slowly. But none of that matters. What matters is getting Billy and Todd away from them, away from here, and somewhere safe.

Fifteen years old, and she pushes the Land Rover on, determined to do what her father and Norman failed to do and protect her family.

CHAPTER TWENTY-FIVE

'BOSS!'

His own voice snatches him from the final layers of sleep. His voice but not recognised. He knows he shouted, but the yank from sleep to awake was too fast and has left the mind unable to differentiate between reality and dream.

Sat bolt upright, with wild eyes staring round the room, he tries to remember what he was seeing just before he woke up. But the images have already faded and disappeared. Mr Howie? What happened to him?

Scrabbling to the end of the bed, Nick gets quickly to his feet. Too quickly. The waves of dizziness pulse through his head, forcing him to sink back down onto the soft mattress.

Slow down. Slow down, get a grip.

Last night. Clarence got away with the Saxon. Everyone else had to run for it. He got into the street and was chased. He killed the infected and got in here. Right. His head makes the connection to the universe. The built in sat-nav telling his brain where he is in time and space.

'I slept here,' muttering to himself, he looks round the room, at the pink bedding and the lace pink covers on the bedside lamps and the faded pink rug and the cream and pink dressing table.

'Nice choice,' he repulses at the shock of pink on display. Almost thankful that the lads won't know he chose an overwhelmingly pink room to sleep in. It was dark, though, and he was knackered, and that bed was very comfortable.

Nodding, he tries getting to his feet again. This time his heart works in synchronisation with his body, and the pressure is stable enough to sustain the movement. Moving quickly, he exits the room and opens doors until finding the bathroom, grimacing at the sight of more pink. Pink washbasin, pink bath, pink toilet seat cover. Everywhere is bloody pink.

Toilet seat up, zipper down, and release. The jet of piss is joined by the sigh of relief as his bladder is allowed to empty the contents.

Eyes track the room, his upper lip twitching in horror at the vibrant shades of pink. His own reflection makes him look twice, a literal double-take done at the sight of the man staring back at him.

Not a boy or a youth anymore but a man. His thick, dark hair stand up straight from his head, stubble coats his set jawline, any fat that remained has been sluiced off from the constant running, fighting, and lifestyle of the last two weeks. What remains is a lean man with defined muscles, a narrow waist that flares to a wide back and the promise of powerful shoulders.

The stream turns into a sprinkle as he finishes up, giving a shake before zipping and automatically reaching for the handle to flush.

Even his own hands look alien. The slender fingers that were only good for taking things apart have now been responsible for thousands of deaths. They give death time and time again. Taking bodies apart instead of electrical appliances.

Glancing up, he examines his own reflection again. Never given to vanity or conceit, Nick had battled with dyslexia and low self-esteem for much of his life. It wasn't narcissism that held his gaze at the mirror. It was the realisation that the eyes of a killer stared back at him. The hardness that all the team had was there and clearly evident. A coldness that will never lift. The ability to take life in an instant.

The team. They were his family now and far better than the family that he belonged to in his previous life. Loyalty and devotion to one another was a new concept for Nick. He had always had a kind, loving heart. But years of self-degradation, of self-perception that he was something less than average, that he was thick, dense, lacked intelligence, all of those things had imprinted into his psyche, making him prefer the company of solace to that of others.

Is it wrong to use someone else's toothbrush? Lifting an eyebrow at himself, he ponders the question, then takes the subject matter and compares it against the horrors of pain, suffering, torture, and death has witnessed. But the two cannot relate. Death and suffering are one thing, but using someone else's toothbrush? Nah, that's just gross. A step too far.

Shuddering with the thought of it, he avoids the bristly tool propped in the glass next to the sink and instead rinses his face, cleansing the sweat built up from his sleep.

And it was a long sleep. His limbs feel tired and achy,

but on the whole, he feels good. The sleep has rejuvenated his mind and body alike.

After his face, Nick washes his armpits, then drops his trousers and undergarments to clean his privates, enjoying the sensation of the cool water on his body.

'I've got a great arse,' he chuckles to himself as he cleans between the cheeks. 'Hey, you got a great butt there,' he mimics an American accent, making himself chuckle again.

What happened to the boss? The question pops back into his head and stops his joking around immediately. The question hasn't left, and it won't leave until the answer is known.

Clarence will go back to the car park, so that is exactly where Nick needs to be now. Surprisingly for someone so in love with gadgets and gizmos, Nick doesn't wear a watch. The essence of the day, however, is not that of early morning. Or is it?

The heat makes it impossible to tell. The light is always so strong now, and the heat is relentless. Speaking of which, Dave's voice drives into his mind. *Drink when you can.*

So he does. Bent over at the tap, he sucks the cool water into his throat and keeps going until it starts to get uncomfortable. Standing up, he belches and wipes the back of his hand across his lips.

At least the water has gone someway to filling his ever-hungry stomach. Always hungry. Always starving. Nick loved food almost as much as he loved taking things apart.

Grunting at the thought of food, he hurries downstairs, clutching his axe and checking the pistol on his belt, then feeling in his pockets for the spare magazine.

In the kitchen, he grins with satisfaction. Miss Pink has a well-stocked kitchen. Tinned meat, tinned fish, beans, and tinned fruit.

He should get going. Really should get going. But Dave always says to drink when you can, so that probably extends to food too.

Definitely extends to food.

Drawer: opened.

Tin opener: found.

Tins: opened.

Food: removed.

Mouth: masticating.

Throat: swallowing.

Stomach: getting fed.

Nick: stuffing his face.

Fish is mixed with fruit, which is mixed with spam, which is mixed with beans, and all of it washed down with warm but fizzy coke from an unopened bottle.

Sugar and salt levels go through the ceiling. Glucose soars. His body gives a standing ovation to the carbohydrates being taken in. Muscles nod seriously at one another as the protein is absorbed.

Food. Real food. Really real food that has to be chewed and has flavours and everything! Rummaging while chewing, he gives a muted yell of victory at finding the box of Coco Pops cereal. They get poured into his open mouth and mixed with the fish, beans, fruit, and spam to make a meal that at any other time would have most people gagging.

His stomach fills far quicker than it used to. A direct result of the reduced diet and the infrequent meals has seen the stomach lining reduce in size.

The feeling of being full is nice. The energy that pours into his body is even nicer. Mind fully awake now as it buzzes from the nutrition absorbed.

Only two things remain that could make this morning perfect. Well, three things if he was going to be completely true. One, a cigarette. That can be dealt with. He fishes in his pockets for the crumpled and battered packet, and he draws one out. Holding the lighter to the end, he inhales to savour the harsh bite of smoke.

Two, a coffee. But nothing can be done there. The hobs are electric, and pretty short of building a fire to heat water, he will simply have to go without.

Three, a beautiful woman to wake up with. Now that is never going to happen. Not now, not tomorrow, and probably not ever. The world is suddenly lacking in beautiful women. Lani is beautiful but not in that way. Like a sister, and besides, Lani and Howie are meant for each other. That's pretty obvious.

Marcy was nice, very beautiful, but she was a dirty fucking zombie. Other than that? Well, they all keep getting killed, so probably best not to go there.

One out of three isn't bad, though. It's better than none out of three. Fed, watered, and now with a cigarette, and it's time to leave this house of pink and make his way into the bright, hot weather waiting outside.

Exiting the front door, he squints into the sky, letting his eyes adjust to the glare. Out the front garden and into the street, staring down the road and trying to remember which way he came. He was killing zombies; then, he ran for a bit before finding this house.

Shit, must have gone some distance. Can't even see the smoke from the fires in the High Street, unless they've gone out. Who would put them out?

Wondering if any of these houses have gas hobs to heat water and make coffee with, he starts strolling down the street. Biting his bottom lip as he tries to resist the temptation to start checking and keeps going.

Why aren't I worried for the boss? Because he's okay.

That's why. How does he know this? How can he possibly know this? A connection, a feeling, something intangible and fleeting that cannot be grasped. Mr Howie is okay. Dave will be with him.

What about everyone else? Blowers and Cookey? Did they get out? No, they were at the door to the stairwell. Lani? She went after Mr Howie. Meredith? No idea, but that dog is like Dave and indestructible.

The connection is there with all of them. He worries because they are separated, but deep down, he knows that they're ok. It doesn't make sense.

But it is what it is, so Nick walks on, still resisting the temptation to find a gas hob and make coffee.

At the end of the road, he pauses, looking first left, then right as he still tries to figure out which way he came in. Turning round, he considers the possibility that he came in from the other end. *Shit, can't even remember if the house was on the left or right when I got here.*

That's bad. And clearly down to a lack of coffee. Should have a coffee. Shrugging, he walks on, choosing to go left simply because he is closer to that side.

The problem with these places is that they all look the same. All the houses are made from brick, with slate roofs and small front gardens. Nick used to look at magazines and watch programmes of the houses in America, at how big they were and made from wood too. All of them seemed huge, with massive gardens, and each one was unique.

Axe over one shoulder, he pauses to light another cigarette before glancing up to look around at the houses. Less signs of the devastation here. Some doors smashed in, and windows broken, some of the cars have been dented or set on fire, but mostly the area looks to have escaped the worse of the carnage.

He wonders if there are survivors cooped up inside the intact secure houses. Maybe watching him now and wondering who he is, and why their town centre has been set on fire, and who was doing all that shooting last night. Mind you, still can't even see the smoke from the town centre from here.

They could have just slept through it all without any idea that such a battle was taking place just a short distance away.

No way, they must have heard the explosion Paula set off before they got back with the Saxon. Judging from the destruction caused, they must have been big bangs. Cocking his head to one side, he thinks that he will have to ask Dave to show him how those bombs are made and anything else like that.

What was that? Focussing, he inhales purposefully, detecting the scent of smoke in the air. Not cigarette smoke from the one in his hand but wood smoke mixed with chemicals. Staring up into the sky, he rotates fully round, catching sight of a slightly darker area in the distance. Like a dirty mist hanging in the air.

With a direction to follow, he sets off, thinking how far away he is and again amazed at the distance he ran last night. He comes to the end of the residential area and moves into the next one. More houses, more front gardens, more low brick walls, and more cars.

All these lives just poodling along, doing whatever normal people do. Going to work and coming home, watching television and eating dinner before going to bed and doing the same again. Family issues, falling out with people over comments made on Facebook. Texting, emailing, computer games, and all the time sitting down and waiting to die.

Years must go by without the routine ever changing. The only excitement is the annual holiday to somewhere hot and sunny just to come home and return to the same lifestyle that just goes on and on. Buy food, eat food. Go shopping. Buy clothes. Text. Email. Facebook. Watch movies, go to work, go to sleep, and get up again. Own your house, don't rent. Get a mortgage, buy a car. Oh, and don't forget to exercise and don't smoke and don't drink and don't eat fatty foods or even look at MacDonald's.

The lessons of life drummed into society, told how to live, how to think, how to buy, and how to work. And now? It's all gone.

His keen mind works fast, processing thoughts into a seamless flow that swims through his conscious. The last two weeks have been a living hell. Watching people die every day, watching mates die. Fighting and fighting. Running away or chasing after the infected. But somewhere deep inside, his heart, it feels better than it was.

He belongs to something that is important. He enjoys being a part of it. Not an observer stood on the outside, looking through the window, being unable to join because he can't read or write, wishing he could join that group or be a part of that team. Wishing he didn't have the issues he had.

But now none of that matters. He adores Howie. As with every member of the team, he deeply respects the man and knows there is something incredibly special about him. Same with Dave, Clarence, all of them. Even Blowers and Cookey are closer to him now than any of his own family were before this happened.

To put your life in someone else's hands, to trust them implicitly with every facet of your existence, knowing that if they fail, not only will you die, but many others will too.

Knowing they trust you just as much, and to handle that responsibility and step up to the plate, that means something.

Normal life frightened Nick. The future was uncertain. How he could find a decent job that didn't just involve carrying or moving things or cooking fast food. Shit, even cooking fast food was a problem as it meant reading the computer screen to see the orders. He could read, but when pressure was applied or people were watching, he felt an overwhelming sense of freezing, of drying up and being unable to put the letters together. The same with writing. Alone and without anyone watching, he could put pen to paper and form words. It was slow and bloody hard work, but it could be done. As soon as anyone tried to watch him do it, he lost the ability.

Rachel, the special needs teacher, always told him it didn't matter, that he was deeply intelligent, and not everyone has the same skills in life. The small amount of respect he has for himself comes from Rachel. She told him that brains are wired up differently. Some people are brilliant with maths and numbers, others can play instruments, and some can read many languages and write beautiful words. What Nick could do with taking things apart and understanding how they worked was something incredibly special and a skill many people simply didn't have.

Leaving school and leaving the support Rachel gave him, was one of the hardest periods of Nick's life. That structure was gone, and with it, the constant coaching and mentoring that Rachel offered.

It was meaningless. His family didn't take any interest in what he did, until something broke, and then they got him to fix it. But that was never done with any form of compliment or reward, not even an acknowledgment that he could take the thing apart and work out why it wasn't working.

He'd spend hours on the computer, mindlessly playing games or wandering the streets. Drinking cans of lager, getting into scraps, and just dossing. It wasn't a lack of ambition or motivation that held him back. It was a lack of knowledge and how to find a way out.

Now though, he was dressed in army gear, carrying a fucking big axe, with an army pistol strapped to his belt, walking through the apocalypse whilst trying to find his ragtag bunch of mates who have proven to be possibly the hardest fighting force left in the country.

That ragtag bunch of misfits: the supermarket manager leading the autistic Special Forces soldier, the Thai girl who worked in a nightclub, the giant ex-paratrooper, the two lads always taking the piss, and of course, the dog. Together they have killed hundreds of thousands of those things.

Many have died, but many lived because of what they did, because of the action they took, and because they made a stand against the infected.

Wishing Rachel could see him now, of how far he had come and how integral he was to the team. Of how proud she would be. That brings a small, sad smile to his face. Thoughts of his family don't enter his mind. If they saw him now, they'd just ask where the food was, where the fort was. Where's the booze? No, it was Rachel that would give him that huge grin and tell him how proud she was.

She talked about the kickboxing she did out of work, so maybe she survived? Maybe she is leading another small group somewhere, killing zombies while yelling at small children for running in the corridors.

This new world needs more Rachels. It doesn't need

greedy, spiteful, selfish idiots who only want to take. It needs those that work and work hard.

'Fuck,' snapping to attention, he realises how far he has walked, drifting through street after street without registering the direction.

Shaking his head, he walks on, spotting the main road ahead and the dirty smoke pluming into the air further on.

Maybe he should tell the others about the pink bedroom. That would get a laugh and a few solid days of piss-taking too.

'Shit, it bloody hurts,' rapist moans again at the pain in his bitten cheek.

Rolling his eyes, the other man stares at the road ahead. Driving now for several hours, and all he has had to listen to is him yacking on about how much his face hurts and how that *fucker bit him.* Even the two boys fell asleep a couple of hours ago and haven't moaned as much as him.

It does look bad, though, with blood seeping through the now dirty rag pressed to his face. The Doc will be pissed off that they've been so long, but what can you do? It didn't make sense that he sent them so far north to work the towns further away before doing these. Why not do the closest towns first and work out? But the Doc said everything was for a reason.

'I need a wee,' one of the little boys pipes up in a scared voice.

'Hold it,' the rapist snaps.

'Can't,' Todd whines.

'Just shut up and hold it!'

'Can't,' Todd squirms, the pressure on his small bladder too much to take.

'We'll pull over,' the man driving sighs.

'No, he can bloody hold it,' the rapist shouts, then curses from the angry movement flaring the pain in his cheek. 'I need some fucking painkillers ...'

'And you think the Doc will give you some if we turn up with two kids covered in piss? If the boy has to go, then he has to go.'

'Well, he can fucking piss out the window then. Come here ...'

'NO!' Todd squirms away from the bleeding man reaching out to grab him.

'Hang on,' the driver interjects, 'he ain't pissing out the window. Just wait. I'll pull up. Ere, do you need to go?' He glances down at Billy. Shaking his head, Billy looks up at the man. Even the young boy can detect the differing energy between the two men. The bleeding man who hurt Sam is nasty and keeps shouting. The man driving isn't that bad. He's still a bad man but just not as bad as the bleeding man.

'Sure? Cos we ain't stopping again.'

'No, thank you,' Billy replies, remembering his manners.

'Okay,' the driver shrugs as he brings the speed down, naturally drifting over to the side of the road from long habits of driving. 'Go with him,' he says to the rapist.

'Really? You think?' rapist sneers. 'Fucking well done, Einstein ... Would never have figured that out on my own.'

'Alright,' the driver placates.

'Hurry up,' rapist snaps. Pushing the door open, he clambers down and stretches before swearing again as even that movement causes pain in his cheek. Todd drops down and shuffles over to the edge of the pavement.

'Where you going?' rapist demands.

'For a wee wee,' Todd replies meekly.

'Do it, then,' rapist shouts.

'Take it easy,' the driver calls out. 'He ain't gonna piss with you yelling at him, is he?'

'Just ...' Biting the anger down, the rapist takes a breath, pressing the rag harder to his cheek. 'Just hurry up, then.'

Todd carries on to the side of the pavement, followed by the bleeding man watching him closely. Standing in front of a wall, he fiddles with the zip on his shorts, struggling to get them undone.

'Come on,' rapist mutters.

Todd glances up, tears starting to burn his eyes in terror at the man glaring at him. He struggles and tugs at the zip, finally yanking it down before pausing before drawing himself out.

'Well, get on with it,' rapist shouts.

'I can't,' Todd sobs. 'You're watching me.'

'Fucking what?'

'Oi,' the driver leans over the passenger seat, yelling out the open door, 'stop yelling at him.'

'Or what?' Rapist spins, unleashing his temper on his mate.

'Or the Doc'll find out you been a wanker, and then what'll happen? Think about it, you moron. If these kids go back saying you were being an arsehole ...'

'Fine,' rapist snarls, taking a step away from Todd, and standing with his back to him, he folds his arms. 'Happy now? This far enough away, is it?'

Todd glances round, spotting that the bleeding man has moved away and is shouting with the other man in the van. Billy stares out, locking eyes with Todd. Todd holds his gaze for a second, looks at the driver; then, he stares at the back of the bleeding man and decides to run. His little legs pumping furiously as he starts running. An instinct booming in his mind, telling him to get away, run, run, and keep running.

'GET HIM!' the driver yells. Rapist spins round, cursing foully at the sight of Todd running down the road. Starting after him, he yells hoarsely, threatening to split the kid in half if he doesn't stop right now.

Pain burns in his cheek, his head banging with pain and waves of dizziness. Growling, he runs on, trying to open his stride to go faster. He is tired, though, exhausted even and has had no sleep for a long time. He struggles to sprint, so he drops back to a jog, knowing the boy has nowhere to go and he'll stop running soon. Then when he catches him ... well, the Doc won't know any different if they just bring one boy back.

'You little cunt!' rapist shouts. 'I'll fucking kill you like I did your old man ... and that fucking bitch ...'

Sobbing, with his chest heaving, eyes misted from tears, Todd runs and runs, following the natural bend in the road until he reaches a junction. A long wall follows the contour of the road as it bends into the side street. Sticking close to it, he tries his best to run as fast as he can, but the long walk yesterday has left him tired, and his energy levels are already starting to drop. Pure fear pushes him on, forcing his little legs to keep going.

'Keep running, you little cunt!' rapist bellows. 'I'll fucking kill you ... I'll fucking stab your face off ...'

Rapist spots the junction. The lack of anyone running down the road means the kid must have gone down the side street, 'OI ... FUCKING LITTLE WANKER ...' The rage in him explodes. Nothing will stop him getting that little kid and hurting him bad. The psychotic fury, the same psychotic fury that has seen him serving many prison sentences for serious assaults, makes his eyes go wild, the red mist descending in his mind. In the past, when that mist has lifted, the rapist has genuinely struggled to recall the events of what he did during that "episode". In many interviews with the police, he has sat there listening to evidence of witnesses put before him, shaking his head with confusion. Even when shown security camera footage of his own actions, of beating a man unconscious outside a pub, he struggled to recognise himself. His own mind refuses to accept that he wasn't the easy-going, fun-loving person he thought he was.

The rape last night wasn't a psychotic episode. That was just a necessity. He is a man, she was a woman, so he took it. Simple. No rage needed there. Until the end, of course, when he was smashing her face in with his fists.

'I AM GOING TO FUCKING KILL YOU ... HERE ME? YOU ARE GONNA DIE, YOU LITTLE WANKER CUNT PRICK ...'

He rounds the corner into the side street and skids to a stop.

'Pardon?'

'Who the fuck are you?' the rapist shouts with enough rage left to contort his features into an evil sneer.

'I'm the man holding the gun,' Nick replies. Holding the pistol with one steady hand, he uses the other to push the weeping boy behind him, forming a protective barrier. 'What did you just say?'

'What?' rapist demands.

'You said you were going to kill him. You said that ...' Nick repeats, his voice soft and deadly.

'What? Eh? Nah ... fucking hell, mate,' rapist swallows and tries smiling with a quick, dirty leer. 'He's er ... he's my kid, ain't he? Little fuc– er ... little sod got told off, so he legged it ... You know what kids are like, eh, mate? Ere, hand him over.' Rapist extends one hand, beckoning Todd to come.

'Your kid?' Nick asks.

'Yeah, s'what I said, innit? Come on, nipper, mum's waiting,' he beckons harder, trying to smile again as he ignores the pain in his cheek.

'What happened to your face?' Nick asks. 'Looks like a bite mark.' Nick steps back, forcing the child to move with him, still with one arm wrapped round his shoulders.

'Eh? What? Oh, er ... you mean this?' The man gingerly touches his face. 'Yeah, er ... fucking dog, yeah, a dog ...'

'A dog? Wasn't a big German Shepherd, was it?'

'Eh? What? No, er ... a, er ... staffy, yeah, a staffy got me ... Our staffy actually ... fucking thing just turned, you know.'

'Turned?'

'Yeah, turned. No ... not like them things. Fuck, mate, no. Just, you know, snapped and went for me.'

'Not surprised,' Nick says. 'You threatening to kill children and all that.'

'Ha! Yeah, got a temper on me,' rapist forces a laugh. 'He's the same, ain't you, nipper? Take after your old man, don't you, nipper?'

'What's his name?'

'Er ... Spike.'

'The kid, not the dog.'

'Oh, ha! Thought you meant the dog, mate, yeah ... ha! Er, the kid ... yeah, his name is, er, Brian, yeah, Brian ... Come on, Brian. Mum's waiting, and we gotta get a move on, come on, Bri–'

'What's your name kid?' Nick asks.

'Ere, mate, don't be getting all fucking weird.' Rapist takes a step forward. 'What you some kind of peado or sommit? How old are you anyway? And where you get that gun from? You in the army or something?'

'What's your name?' Nick nudges the boy while keeping his eyes locked on the man with the injured cheek. 'Is he your dad?'

'Don't question my nipper,' the rapist protests. 'That's fucked up, mate. You don't go round questioning other people's kids.'

'Oi, mate,' Nick nudges the boy again, 'is this man your dad?'

'Now, listen here ...'

'No,' Todd whimpers, terrified and frozen to the spot as he clings onto Nick, staring down at the big axe on the ground.

'Brian!' rapist shakes his head.

'What's your name?' Nick nudges the boy, prompting him to answer.

'Todd.'

'Oh, you little shit,' rapist snarls. His cheek hurts, his head hurts, he is tired, and that all takes its toll. The one chance he has to protest, his one chance to act out the role of the stunned father and try to blag out of it, that moment passes. The moment that follows is the one with Nick staring through the eyes of a killer, holding a 9mm army issue pistol whilst staring at the man with the injured cheek.

'He killed my dad and Sam,' Todd whimpers in a soft voice that carries only too well into the silence of the street.

'When?' Nick asks bluntly, watching the facial features on the injured man change. Anger replaced by indignant surprise replaced by confusion replaced by fear that seeps across his features.

'And Billy's dad too but not Lilly.'

'Billy? Who is Billy?' Nick asks.

'Listen, mate,' rapist finds his voice as he starts back-stepping, holding his hands out in front with the palms facing out, 'things happen, don't they ...? All this going on, and you know what I mean, yeah? We's just trying to get some er ... some food, and things happen ...'

'Who is Billy?' Nick asks, this time directing the question at the man. He starts walking forward, maintaining the distance between him and the retreating man.

'Billy? I don't know,' rapist shrugs. 'Never heard of him.'

'Todd, who is Billy?' Nick asks, eyes still locked on the man in front.

'Lilly's brother,' Todd whimpers. 'Down there. Billy didn't need a wee ... I weed in my pants.'

'That's okay,' Nick replies softly. 'Don't worry about your pants.'

'Come on, mate, keep the kid, yeah? You want to keep the kid, he's all yours,' rapist holds his hands up, giving a magnanimous gesture. 'Everyone happy, yeah? You keep him, and I'll go ... No problems here, mate ...'

'Where is Billy?' Nick presses, speeding up as he walks at the man. 'Stop moving back.'

'Come on, mate.' Rapist keeps going, back-stepping while talking in a pleading tone, 'Come on, mate ... take it easy ... things happen, don't they? You know that ... Me and you, we're men, ain't we, yeah? You get me, don't you, nipper?'

'Don't call me nipper, and if you keep walking away, I'll shoot you,' Nick speaks bluntly.

Rapist makes a mistake. His fear of dying stops him from properly seeing Nick. He sees a nipper dressed like a soldier, young and lean. What he doesn't see are the eyes, the hard stare that fixes unblinking.

A lot can happen in two weeks. Over three hundred hours. Some of them have been spent sleeping, eating, and walking, but many have been spent in battle, firing weapons and becoming lethal. More rounds have been fired by Nick than most platoons do during a tour of overseas warzones. Nick is intelligent. He learns quickly. Years of playing computer games, of working on small things that require focus and concentration have made his hand to eye co-ordination phenomenal.

The man is only a few yards away. The distance is small. One minor adjustment to his aim. One single solitary squeeze of the trigger. The retort is loud and instant, bouncing off the houses as it rolls down the street. The round exits the pistol, crossing the short distance and striking the man in the thigh, tearing through muscle and tissue before exiting the other side.

Shock hits the rapist faster than the pain from the gunshot. The nipper only made a quick twitch, and bang! Staring down, he spots the blood spurting from his leg. That didn't just happen. No way did that young nipper just shoot him in the leg.

He falls down, the leg suddenly unable to take his weight. Clutching the wound, the pain hits, and for the first time in a few hours, the injury to his cheek is completely forgotten.

'I'll ask you again,' Nick says, still holding the trembling boy close. 'Where is Billy?'

'Down there ... fuck, you fucking shot me ... He's down there ... in the van ... down there ... VINCE!' rapist bellows. 'VINCE ...VINCE ...'

Nick glances up at the sound of an engine coming from

ahead. A big, white van crosses the end of the junction, pausing as Nick clocks sight of the man behind the wheel and the young boy sat on the double passenger seat. The passenger door swinging open.

As Nick lifts his aim, the engine screams louder. The driver has spotted his mate on the floor and the soldier stood over him with the kid.

'BILLY?' Nick bellows, catching sight of the boy lifting his arm before the van speeds off, accelerating down the street and out of view.

'VINCE ...' the rapist bellows, twisting round to see the van driving off. 'VINCE! GET BACK HERE ... VINCE, YOU FUCKING CUNT ...' his voice trails off at the same time the noise of the van tapers away. Whimpering, he stares down to the junction, at the void where the van was just seconds ago. 'Vince ...' he whimpers. Slowly, he twists round, wincing from the pain exploding up his leg. Now he can see the hard eyes staring down at him. The face is young but holds no compassion for him, and that shot, it was so fast and completely brutal.

'Shit,' the rapist mutters, 'please, mate ...'

'Your mate has fucked off,' Nick observes.

'Please, mate ... come on ...'

'What?' Nick shrugs, slightly confused at what he's being asked. What does he do now? The shot he took to stop the man getting away was done from instinct. But now, the man lying there with a gunshot to his leg, and there is a young kid stuck to his side.

'It wasn't like that,' the rapist blurts out. 'His dad went for me. I swear it ... It was self-defence, and I kept the kid to keep him safe. I didn't mean what I shouted ... I wouldn't kill a kid, mate ...'

'Todd,' Nick asks, 'what happened with your dad?'

Todd doesn't reply. Terrified witless, he clings onto Nick, only too aware that the man with the bleeding cheek is right there, so close and able to reach out and grab Todd again.

'I'm telling ya, His dad went for me,' the rapist pleads. 'Really, mate ... it was him or me ... We had some food, and his dad wanted it ... Fuck, mate ... You gotta believe me ...'

Suddenly, it isn't so clear. A few seconds ago, and relying on pure instinct, Nick knew what to do. This was a bad man. He was threatening to kill a child. Easy, that's black and white. Man threatening to kill child equals bad man. But now, he's on the floor, giving a plausible reason for it, explaining why he killed the kid's dad. The kid himself is too scared to say anything.

'So what happened?' Nick asks, wanting to know more details before he decides what to do next. If he saw someone holding a gun, he would probably drive off too, so that reaction doesn't mean anything.

'Me and Vince, we had this camp in a forest ... You know, mate, like keeping our heads down,' the rapist gasps in agony. 'They came in and tried to take our stuff. It all got bad, and like his dad got it ...'

'They?' Nick probes.

'What?'

'You said they?'

'Yeah, they ... fucking they ... them ... the fuckers that tried to steal our food,' the rapist snaps.

'So not just Todd's dad, then?'

'Eh?'

'How many came into your camp?'

'What? I don't fucking know ... Shit, mate ... you get shot in the leg and see if you can remember everything ... Have some mercy, mate ...'

'How many?' Nick asks again.

'I don't know!' the rapist wails. 'They raped Vince's daughter, and it all went fucking bent ...'

'What?'

Too late now, it's been said. Rapist curses himself internally for egging it too far, but now it's out, it can't be taken back. 'Yeah ... Vince's daughter ... She's in the back of the van all cut up and stuff, poor cow ...'

'Why didn't you say that before?' Nick asks.

'Er ... fucking scared, mate ... You waving that gun about and saying you gonna shoot me and ...'

'I never said I was going to shoot you.'

'You did, I swear you did ... shit, mate ... I haven't eaten for days, and my cheek got bit, and I'm confused ... You're confusing me.'

'You said they came for your food.'

'Yeah.'

'But you just said you hadn't eaten in days.'

'Eh? Look, you're confusing me. You're doing it on purpose just cos you got that fucking gun ... This is torture, this is ... You're torturing me ...'

'So,' Nick asks slowly, 'you hadn't eaten the food that they came for, and they managed to rape Vince's daughter before you–'

'Fucking hell!' Rapist screams in agony, cutting Nick off. 'My god, this fucking hurts ... I think you got the bone ... Shit, I'm gonna die here.'

'You ain't bleeding that much,' Nick peers down at the leg.

'Bullet is still in there,' the rapist rolls over for effect, clutching his leg as he writhes on the ground.

'Nah, it came out,' Nick says. 'I heard it bounce off the pavement.'

'Oh god ... my poor wife ...' rapist wails.

'Wife?' Nick scratches the side of his head. This is all getting too much. What would Mr Howie do? He knows what Dave would do. This bloke wouldn't have been shot in the leg for a start. But what would the boss do? *Christ, this is difficult*, Nick thinks to himself.

His instinct is telling him the man is lying. Lying about everything, and his story has more holes in it than a sieve. But what if he's telling the truth or really is just confused?

'Can you walk?' Nick asks, deciding to get him back to the car park and leave the decision to someone else.

'Eh? Er ... yeah ...' the rapist spots the glimmer of light. He can sense the young lad's indecision. His leg hurts like hell but not that bad. The bullet missed the bone, so the pain could have been a lot worse.

'Get up, then,' Nick orders.

'Where ... where we going?' the rapist mutters. Moving slowly, he uses his good leg to take his weight as he eases himself upright.

'Just get up,' Nick replies. 'Todd, you alright?' No answer, but Nick feels the boy nodding against his side. 'Todd, we're going to have to walk for a little while.'

Todd nods but doesn't let go. Nick doesn't know what to do, so starts walking awkwardly over to his axe, scooping it up whilst navigating the small child clinging on and keeping the pistol aimed at the other man.

'Can you move off a bit?' Nick asks softly, prompting Todd to squeeze harder. The young boy, like Billy did with the rapist and the driver in the van, senses the difference between Nick and the injured man. Nick looks like a soldier, and soldiers are like policemen. He speaks softly and holds him close. They wear a uniform and are the goodies. Mummy always said *if you get lost, then find someone in a uniform.* Seeing Nick walking down the street prompted

Todd to run straight for him, grabbing him tight as he listened to the screaming threats being bellowed from behind.

Nick doesn't push the boy off but starts walking with him holding on, hoping that it's as uncomfortable for Todd as it is for him and that he'll soon relax a bit.

Grunting with pain, the rapist limps slowly forward, using both hands to squeeze the wound. Nick notices there isn't that much blood; the bullet must have missed any arteries and gone straight through the muscle. In this heat, with the amount of dirt and filth about, the wound will get infected if not treated quickly.

'What's your name?' the rapist grunts, glancing up at Nick with what he hopes is a friendly look.

'Nick,' for a second, he was going to tell him to mind his own business, but what harm can knowing his first name do?'

'Nice to meet you, Nick,' the rapist nods with a quick, puzzling grin. 'In fact, mate, I'm glad it was you we met, you know. Even though you shot me, eh?' With a chuckle, the man carries on limping. 'Nice young lad like you, yeah ... Soldier, are you?'

To save giving the long explanation, Nick just nods but makes sure to keep a good distance between them and the pistol held ready.

'Good for you, nipper. Wanted to serve myself, but life got in the way. Shame really. I was always told I'd have made a fucking good soldier. Cor, fuck me ... that hurts some ...'

Nick lets him speak, using the time to gain the measure of the man. He is larger than average and covered in faded, old-style tattoos. Messy, lank hair, thick limbs, and a big gut that, no doubt, was somewhat bigger two weeks ago. This man doesn't take care of his appearance. He screams bully with the hard look and icy, thousand-yard stare.

Two weeks ago, Nick would have done everything he could to avoid people like this and the rough, brutal, bullish attitudes they always had. They were always too ready to fight and pick on those smaller than them.

But that was two weeks ago, and now, even without the pistol, Nick would have stood his ground.

'Yeah, you know, Nick, the last two weeks have been hell, ain't they? Just hell ... Keep hoping the government will sort it out, but it don't look good, does it? What's your orders then, Nick?'

'Orders?' Nick asks, not liking the way this man keeps using his name.

'Army orders. What's the score then, Nick?'

Nick is unsure how to answer, so he doesn't. He remains quiet, reluctant to get drawn into a conversation.

'Oh, I get it,' the rapist gives a knowing wink, 'yeah, course, Nick, can't be telling everyone what your orders are, can ya? Nah, course not. Guess you must be in the Special Forces or something, eh, Nick?'

'Just keep walking,' Nick prompts. His tone tells the rapist his constant, inane chatter is starting to work. He can wear this lad down, get him comfortable and safe, make him think there is no malice and no threat.

'Poor lad, he alright, is he?' the rapist nods at Todd. 'Going through all that must have scared him half to death ... Didn't mean to scream all them bad words at the poor mite, but I was shitting myself that he'd run into those things and get bit ... I tried asking nice like, Nick, but the lad kept running, so I figured I might try and scare him into stopping ... You can see that, can't you, Nick?

'Quiet one, ain't ya, Nick? I get that ... I like the peace

and quiet myself. Yeah, I can see a young me in you, Nick. Very good the way you handled that gun there, very quick ... and a good steady arm too ... well trained, but then the British Army is the best in the world, ain't it, Nick?'

'You remembered what happened last night, then?' Nick asks quickly. 'How many came into your camp?'

'Cor, bloody hell, Nick, it was so dark. I'm a big fella and all, but I don't mind telling you that I shit myself. Frightened half to death I was ... begging 'em to just go and take what they wanted but ...'

'But what?'

'They wouldn't have any of it, would they? Did that to Vince's daughter, the poor sod. Then Vince, he like went for one of them, and it all kicked off ... One bloke went for me ... His dad, I reckon, it was ... Anyway, so he went for me, and I was begging him to stop, but ... things happen,' his voice trails off, as though the memory is too hard to handle.

'So how many were there?' Nick asks again.

'Well, there's his dad,' he nods at Todd, 'then, er ... the other fella, so that's two ... and er ... well, Todd there, he was sort of, you know ... er ... behind them and er ...'

'Just two of them? Against three of you?'

'Three?'

'Vince's daughter?'

'Eh? Oh yeah ... well, she's only a wee one herself.'

'How old?'

'Eh? Oh er ... fourteen, I guess. Yeah, she's fourteen.'

'What about Sam?'

'Who?'

'Todd said you killed his Dad and Sam? Who was Sam?'

'Oh yeah ... that was the other er ... the girl,' the rapist grimaces, realising Sam must be the name of the girl he raped.

'Girl? A girl attacked you too?'

'Yeah, bloody hell, Nick, she was going crazy ... like a ... a ... banshee or something. Just nuts. Shocking, really shocking ...'

'Todd, who is Sam?' Nick asks quietly.

'Sister ...' Todd replies, his voice muted and muffled.

'Your sister?' Nick confirms, feeling the boy nodding his head.

'How old is Sam?'

'...teen.'

'What did you say, Todd?'

'Fifteen,' Todd pulls his head away to answer, then promptly pushes it straight back into Nick's side.

'Fifteen? You were attacked by a fifteen-year-old girl?' Nick asks in a suspicious voice.

'Was she fifteen?' The rapist shakes his head in shock. 'No way ... not fifteen. Bloody hell, she was a big unit ... I would have put her at nineteen or maybe even twenty ... Fuckin' hell ... gotta be drugs, high on drugs–'

'I think,' Nick speaks up in a strong voice that cuts the rapist off mid-sentence, 'that you are full of shit, mate.'

'Eh? Hang on, Nick ... you weren't there, mate ...'

'And if you don't stop talking, I will shoot you in the other fucking leg. Trust me. I will shoot your other fucking leg.'

'Nick, just listen, mate ...'

'Don't believe me? Up to you, fucknuts. Keep going and see what happens. I ain't that intelligent. Really, I ain't, but even I can spot bullshit like that.'

The rapist hobbles on, his nasty, little eyes scanning the road ahead like a hungry rat looking for food. Opportunities present themselves all the time; just got to be ready to make the best of it when it happens. They're obviously going somewhere specific, probably to meet other people, maybe more soldiers. If that little shit starts speaking and tells a good tale, he's done for. They'll either shoot him outright or string him up like they used to in the old days. Ain't no law or fair trials now.

The going is painfully slow as the rapist makes a meal of his injury, painfully limping and grimacing. However, as time goes on, the pain increases until he is genuinely struggling, with real pain flaring in his leg and his cheek.

'Nick, I need to rest a minute,' he wheezes, still adding a bit on for effect, hoping the young lad will be lured into thinking he is worse than he really is.

'Nope,' Nick replies cheerfully, 'keep going.'

'You just shot me in the leg. Have a heart, Nick, come on ... just a quick rest ...'

'Alright,' Nick concedes, thinking he could do with a drink of water and a cigarette. Checking the area, he spots a house with a front door torn from the hinges, leaving a gaping hole into the hallway 'Over there,' Nick points, directing the limping man across the road.

'Up the path,' Nick prompts, walking slowly behind while the man takes his time, muttering and grumbling with pain. 'Stop there. HELLO? Anyone home?' Nick calls out, ready to shift his aim from the man to the hallway should anything present itself.

Fuck. Now what? They can't all go into the kitchen, can they? He can't leave Todd outside with this man, and he strongly doubts that Todd will want to go inside on his own to get them all a drink of water.

An easy solution presents itself as Nick nods, thinking this is what Mr Howie would do. 'Right, mate, you go down and get some water ... I'll be right behind you, and if you do anything other than get water, I'll shoot you in the bollocks.'

'Course, Nick,' the rapist nods eagerly, 'course, mate, you're in charge.' He stumbles over the front doorstep, wincing as a fresh jolt of pain soars through his thigh. They go down the hallway and into the kitchen at the end. Nick is right behind him, watching every move. Having learnt first-hand from Dave how dangerous knives are, Nick does a quick visual sweep of the kitchen, making sure there are no potential weapons lying around. The rooms have been turned over, with signs of intense fighting taking place. Dried blood is smeared across the beige walls, and a long stain leads away, towards the open back door. Glancing outside, Nick spots the corpse on the grass with a garden fork impaled through its face.

'Get some water,' Nick nods at the sink. The man sighs as he rests his backside against the work top and lifts a mug from the draining board. Twisting the tap on, he rinses the mug out, ensuring all his movements are slow and controlled, doing everything he can to drag it out. Eventually, he fills the mug and takes a long swig, gulping it down noisily.

'Todd, you need to drink some water,' Nick urges.

'Here, mate,' the rapist holds his hand out, extending the filled mug towards the small boy. Todd flinches back to quickly get behind Nick.

'He doesn't like you, does he?' Nick comments drily.

'Can't blame him,' the rapist shakes his head sadly, 'poor kid ... It's alright for us as we know what's going on, don't we, Nick? But these poor little blighters, eh?'

'Put the mug down and go over there.'

'Yeah, course, Nick ... mind if I sit down on that chair, Nick? My leg is hurting somethin' proper, mate. Cor, you got me a right good shot there, Nick ... No hard feelings, though, eh, nipper ...?'

'Todd, get some water, mate,' Nick urges, gently pushing the lad towards the mug and taking a relieved stretch when Todd finally let's go of him.

Keeping one eye fixed on the seated man, Nick gets to the sink and finds another mug to fill. The rapist stares at him with interest whilst gripping his thigh.

'Take your drink, Nick. I ain't going nowhere, mate. Go on ... get a nice drink ... Bleedin' hot out there, it is.'

Nick gulps the water quickly, his thirst not that great since his hearty breakfast this morning. Fishing a packet of cigarettes out from his pocket, he taps one out and watches a greedy glint come into the other man's eyes.

'Got a spare one, Nick? Left mine in the van.' Pondering the request, Nick shrugs and chucks the packet over, noticing the deft catch and the quick movements of the man as he pulls one out and starts patting his pockets down.

'Ere, nipper,' the rapist says to Todd, 'you'd best go and stand by that back door if we're smoking in here.'

A passing comment said in a kindly voice, but Todd looks at Nick with wide, scared eyes, unsure of what to do.

Nick doesn't want to be seen agreeing with the man, but at the same time, the child should stand by the back door while the room fills up with smoke.

'I hate it when people smoke round kids,' the man comments, inhaling deeply to blow the smoke out into the air above him.

Nick doesn't reply but flits his gaze between Todd and the man, taking care to blow his own smoke towards the open back door.

'So you been about much, Nick?' the rapist asks conversationally. 'Ere, nipper, can you pass me that towel there?' he points to the tea towel hanging from the cooker front.

Todd doesn't move, refusing to even look in the direction of the man and keeping his gaze fixed firmly on Nick. Leaning over, Nick grabs the towel and throws it over. The man ties it round his injured leg, wincing at the pain before gingerly touching the wounds in his cheek.

In silence they stand, sit, and smoke. Nick wishes Mr Howie was here to deal with this. The man is talking shit about what happened, but shooting him in cold blood just doesn't feel right. Leaving him here is another option but not one that Nick is comfortable with.

'Let's go,' Nick speaks up. The man nods amiably and struggles to his feet. With the rapist in the lead, Nick follows with Todd glued to the back of his legs. The small group shuffle down the hallway, out the door, across the garden, and once more into the road. The heat slams into them like a wall.

'Eh, Nick, you ever felt heat like this before?' the rapist comments in a tone that suggests they are now acquaintances. 'Hotter than fucking Malaga, this is. Bloody terrible it is ... Be nice resting on a beach with a can of lager, watching the birds, though, eh, mate? Cor, I bet the birds love you in that uniform, eh? Ha! Takes me back ... being young and handsome ...'

Nick zones out, letting the man waffle on in his pathetic attempt to build a relationship between them. He's trying to bridge that gap and show the human side of his manner, show that they're all in this together. Nick might struggle with the written language, but his perceptions are good, very good, and he understands exactly what the man is trying to do.

Todd remains silent and stays very close to the back of Nick's legs, keeping him as the barrier between him and the man. He saw what the man did to Sam, how they were both almost naked and wrestling on the floor. He knew the man was hurting his sister, and he knew it was a very bad thing. Todd had never seen anyone wrestle with their clothes off before, and his mum was always saying you shouldn't be naked in front of anyone, apart from your mum and dad, and Sam was okay too, and doctors and nurses, but other than that, you shouldn't be nudey.

Todd also heard what the man said about last night, but the connection wasn't made. Todd didn't understand what the man was talking about, and he was too scared to say anything.

With a growing impatience, Nick keeps glancing up at the sun. Time is ticking away, and the pace they are going at is too slow. What if the others can't wait or something else happens that means he misses them?

Worst case scenario is that he has to find a vehicle and head to the fort. They all know that is the fall-back position.

The smoke pluming into the sky edges nearer, but it doesn't look right. It's not big enough for a start. Initially, he thought the distance made the smoke appear small, but it is small. Far smaller than it should be for a whole High Street on fire. However, the fires could have died down during the night, leaving just small sections smouldering.

A nagging feeling grows. Are they heading in the wrong direction? Surely they should be close to the town centre by now. No signposts, no directions, and no features that suggest they are getting closer. If anything, the houses are getting bigger and are set back further from the road, suggesting they are moving towards the outskirts of town where the more expensive houses are built.

The cars on the driveways become less working man and more Mercedes and BMWs. Keeping his eyes glued to the smoke, Nick waits for the road to open up to gain a better view.

Maddox's kids ran off in all directions last night, so it's possible they got this far and something happened that resulted in another fire or something else.

Unsettled and starting to worry, the normally easy-going Nick stays close to Todd, making sure the boy is within arm's reach.

The rapist picks up on the change. The atmosphere is now that bit more charged than it was. The soldier lad is worried, something isn't going right for him. Pick your moment and wait for the opportunity.

His leg hurts like hell but nowhere near as much as he makes out. Slowing down again, he gives it a good act of struggling to walk. He clutches his leg while holding his breath, which he knows will make his face go red and push the veins out in his neck.

Voices? Maybe? A fleeting sound that fades as quickly as it came. Noise, maybe a car door. Nick keeps his eyes fixed firmly on the road ahead, wishing that bend to straighten out so he can see what it is and hoping it is some of the team.

An engine, definitely a diesel engine spluttering noisily. Jesus, the thing is being hammered in second gear, protesting with a loud whine that builds to breaking point. Whatever vehicle it is backfires, a loud boom that causes the rapist to twitch and Todd to rush closer to Nick.

Rapist stays quiet, his own gaze watching keenly as the bend ever so slowly opens up.

The screaming engine cuts out suddenly, spluttering as it dies off. They can hear more voices now–someone laughing, and another car door being slammed shut.

With a quick glance, the rapist notices Nick is focussed

on the road ahead, his steady gaze holding as firm as the hand which grips the pistol. *Luck of the devil,* his mother used to say as she shook her head in disgust at the wayward child she couldn't help but love.

Land Rovers are sturdy and robust vehicles, used by police, military, and emergency services all over the world. Easy to fix and famous for being able to navigate the most treacherous of terrain. As strong as they are, as robust as they are, being held in second gear for hours of driving over long miles does nothing to maintain that reliability.

If Lilly had been driving a modern vehicle, she would have easily worked out how to change up through the gears. The Land Rover, though, was something else. She could find first and second, but third? No way. I just wasn't there. She tried and tried again to make the shift, but it just wouldn't budge and resulted in a loss of whatever speed and momentum she had gained.

Her only choice was to stay in second. She could have, with knowledge and experience, brought the speed up and block-changed from second to fourth. But she didn't know that.

The Land Rover struggled on, doing what it was designed to do. Already an older vehicle with many faults, dodgy electrics, and a damaged gear box, it was simply unable to sustain the high revolutions forced by the constant second-gear driving.

It got hot. Too hot. Things started to break, small things that made thunks and bangs, but as long as it kept going, it didn't matter.

Lilly was tired. The long walk in the blistering heat the

day before. Then being up all night and getting by on pure adrenalin. The lack of proper food and sleep had taken its toll. Even with the window open, there was no fresh air, and as the sun came up, the interior got hotter and hotter.

Heat sapped at her eyes, forcing them to become drowsy to the point of the vehicle swerving side to side until she snapped awake. The high drone of the engine dulled her senses until she felt sleep tugging at her eyes.

It got hotter. The sun became brighter. The windscreen magnified the rays and increased the temperature. Sweat poured down her face. Her hands were slippery on the hard, plastic steering wheel. The seat was sticky and uncomfortable, the vehicle bouncy and uncomfortable.

There was no choice but to push on. To find Billy and Todd and work out a way of getting them back. Ideas and thoughts raced through her mind. Maybe she could offer herself for their release, but without her to take care of them, they wouldn't last five minutes. Find them first and work out the plan after.

Into the outskirts of another town–this one larger than those travelled through before. Big houses set back from the road with expensive-looking cars on the front drives. Coming down from higher ground, she had seen the big, dirty smudge of smoke hovering over the town centre. Another smaller trail of smoke hung nearby.

This was the time to find another vehicle. Plenty of modern cars left on driveways here. It would just be a matter of getting the keys, and job done.

Snapping awake, she spots a red van double-parked ahead and two men walking towards it from a nearby house, carrying bags of food.

The men from last night had a white van, and even from this distance, she can see these men are different.

Trying to decide whether to turn off or approach them, the Land Rover makes its own decision and calls for help by backfiring. A sound like a shotgun blast that booms into the street, echoing and rolling off the houses.

The two men come to a sudden stop, heads snapping towards the Land Rover.

Too late now. Have faith, Lilly, not everyone is bad. There are good people about who can help. These men might have children of their own and understand her plight. If nothing else, they might help her find a car or tell her where this place is.

Bringing the Land Rover to stop just short of the red van, she finally switches the engine off, sighing with relief at the cessation of the awful noise. Dropping down, she notices the steam hissing from the front, realising the vehicle couldn't have gone much further anyway.

'You alright?' one of them shouts over. Standing still, he watches as the blond girl jumps out and moves position to get a clearer view of the Land Rover; no one else with her.

'Christ, love, you ragged that thing a bit,' the second man laughs. Shaking his head, he strolls to the back of the van and deposits the bags before waiting for his mate to join him.

'I need help,' Lilly calls out, heading straight towards them. 'Some men killed my dad last night. They killed Norman and raped Sam and took–'

'Slow down!' The taller of the two men steps forward, waving his hands slowly. 'Who did what to who?'

'My dad!' Lilly replies, fighting the hysteria threatening to take over. She takes a breath and starts again. 'Two men in a big, white van got into the place where we camped. They killed my dad and Norman and raped my friend Samantha ... She was only fifteen ... Then they took my brother Billy and another little boy called Todd ...'

'Shit,' the tallest man says, 'that's awful,' love ... What about you?'

'I hid,' Lilly blurts. 'I was in the bushes. They didn't see me ...'

'Big, white van?' The shorter man walks closer with an interested look on his face. Lilly nods, slowly taking in the details of the two men. Their large build and tattooed arms and necks look too familiar.

'Two blokes you said, yeah?' His interested look slowly morphs into a wry smile. 'One of 'em had a shotgun by any chance?'

Lilly stops walking, looking between them as alarms start ringing in her head. She nods slowly as the tiredness abruptly ends and the hysteria ceases. Calm floods through her as she thinks the situation through.

'You know them?' she asks quickly.

The two men exchange a quick glance. 'Er ... no, love . Saw a big, white van go through here a couple of hours ago ... didn't we, John?' the shorter man says.

'Yeah, yeah, er ... couple hours ago at least, Terry,' John replies. 'Two blokes in it, yeah ... two blokes ...'

'Which way did they go?' Lilly snaps.

'That way,' John replies, nodding down the road behind him.

'They got your brother, have they?' Terry asks in a concerned voice.

'And Todd,' Lilly nods quickly.

'How old are they?' John asks, taking a step forward and affecting the same concerned tone.

'Six.'

'Both of 'em?'

Nodding back, Lilly struggles with the internal debate raging. Her instinct says to run and get away, but they seem really concerned and said they saw the van a couple of hours ago. She suppresses the natural reaction to flee, thinking it's just because they're big, hard-looking men, the sort that normally wolf-whistle and make comments.

'Terrible,' John shakes his head sadly. 'Are you alright, love?'

'Yeah,' Lilly says weakly, 'I got to find them ... They said they were going to, er ... Chapsworth ... Chapsworth House. That was it.'

'Chapsworth House?' Terry says.

'Do you know it?' Lilly asks, seeing the flicker of recognition in the man's eyes.

'Yeah, it ain't that far from here,' Terry says quickly. 'Couple of hours maybe. That about right, John?'

'I'd say so, yeah, probably couple of hours at least ... That's awful, love ... and this was last night, was it?'

'Yeah, I been driving all night, but that car is ...'

'I can see,' John cuts her off, 'poor you, you must be knackered, love. We gotta take her with us, Terry, get her back to our camp and speak to our ... er ... men ...' he gives Terry a stare while saying it, a message passed along with the words.

'Definitely,' Terry gets the message loud and clear, 'listen, love, we got some ...' his voice trails off as Lilly snaps her attention to something behind them. Three figures, two big and one small, and all of them walking towards them.

Terry and John exchange another glance but remain silent. Walking slowly forward, Lilly strains to see the figures. One of them is limping like he has a bad leg. The other man walks behind him, holding hands with a small child. It's the child she fixes her gaze on, staring hard as she feels her heart starting to hammer.

'Are they with you?' she asks quickly, not taking her eyes off the figures, missing the quick shake of the head that John gives Terry.

'No, love,' Terry replies.

The figures move painfully slow, which prompts Lilly to start walking towards them. Terry and John follow close behind.

Lilly watches the child. A boy, definitely a little boy. She speeds up, unaware that John and Terry are right behind her.

'Todd!' she screams at recognising the boy, breaking into an all-out sprint. 'That's them,' she screams at Terry and John, 'that's them ...'

'Slow down,' Terry shout, but Lilly is charging forward, her face a mask of rage as she flits her gaze between the man hobbling on the injured leg and the other man walking behind him.

'Todd! Where's Billy? Get away from him ... get away from him ...'

Nick stares in surprise at the woman charging towards them. They watched the girl talking to the two men at the back of the big, red van for a couple of minutes as they edged closer, seeing the parked Land Rover with the steam hissing from the front end.

The rapist stayed quiet, hardly believing his luck, but then mum always said he had the luck of the devil. Too soon to show any reaction, so he kept his mouth shut and his eyes open. Waiting for the two men to get closer.

The girl he didn't recognise and didn't pay too much attention either. She was a stranger to him and right now was no more important than one of the stationary vehicles parked nearby. What was important was Nick walking right behind him with that fucking pistol held in his hand.

The girl screaming out, then running towards them, shouting the boy's name was a surprise and one that he quickly tried to put to his advantage. She knew the child's name, so she must have been part of their group.

Ducking his head down to hide his face, he makes out his leg is hurting, grimacing in pain as he clutches at the thigh.

'Get away from him!' Lilly screams. Racing across the road, she makes straight for Nick, seeing Todd behind his legs. Todd stares in confusion at first; everything too much for his mind to cope with. This man is nice. He doesn't shout or say much at all. Hearing his name called out, he looks up, recognising the voice. Lilly! She was the lady from yesterday, Sam's friend.

Stepping out, he watches as she runs towards them. Her face looks angry, and she's shouting. Everyone keeps shouting, and it scares him. Nick doesn't shout, so he stays still, unsure of what to do now.

Nick is lost in a momentary lapse of focus at seeing the stunning woman running across the road. She's gorgeous, with flowing blond hair and golden skin. The fact that she's shouting and looks extremely pissed doesn't register immediately.

Self-consciously, he drops the pistol, not wanting the girl to think he is holding the boy against his will. Glancing down, he notices Todd has stepped out a little but isn't running towards the girl. Maybe she is one of this bloke's group? Shit. Too late.

Lilly, not seeing the pistol, goes straight for Nick, ramming straight into him and taking him off his feet.

'Lads! Quick.' The rapist bellows at the two men still coming across the road.

'Derek? What the fuck, mate?' John shouts with a puzzled look at the girl attacking the other bloke on the floor, the young child standing there, screaming, and now Derek shouting at him.

Derek and Vince were in the white van sent north to do the houses up there. That girl saying what happened last night could only have been Derek and Vince, especially Derek with his seedy mind. The two men quickly decided to keep that information to themselves in the hope of getting the girl comfortably into their van without issue.

'Get off,' Nick yells, 'I saved him ... get the fuck off me ...'

'You dirty fucking murdering bastard ... You like raping girls? You nasty pervert ...' Reaching round for her knife, she hisses with anger, realising it must be in the Land Rover. Instead, she starts pummelling blows into Nick's head.

Nick dodges and weaves, trying to peer out from under the attacking girl to the man shouting loudly while hobbling away.

Despite the punches, he squirms and leans over, catching the sight of two men shouting at the one he shot. They seem to know each other, the way they respond and look at each other.

'NOT ME ...' Nick bellows, refusing to look at the girl who slams her fists down again and again, striking his arm with such force it smacks into his own head.

One of the men turns and runs back towards the red van as the other two turn to face Lilly and the bedlam taking place.

'Get his gun,' the rapist shouts, 'he's the one that did your dad in ...'

'NO,' Nick screams, catching a glimpse of a man running towards them. Gritting his teeth and taking the blows without flinching, he tracks the target and squeezes the trigger. The gun booms with a loud retort. As the man goes spinning off to the side. Nick drops and fires again. The girl on him screams and lunges off to grab Todd.

Todd screams as the violence explodes around him. Rooted to the spot, he gets quickly smothered by Lilly diving on top of him, driving him to the ground as she protects him with her body.

Freed of her weight, Nick twists round on his back. No time to get up, so he stays down, eyes flitting between the three targets. One down on the ground, one with a bullet through his leg, and one running towards the red van.

'JOHN,' the rapist screams, 'HE SHOT TERRY.'

Nick takes the information in. They know each other, they know each other's names. The man he just shot writhes on the ground, clutching his shoulder in agony.

The third man reaches the van and opens passenger door. Grabbing something from the front, he starts to turn back, and Nick catches sight of a long barrel.

Without hesitation, he fires, holding the pistol in the two-handed grip Dave taught them. The shots are true, striking their target and slamming the man against the side of the van. The shotgun falls from his hands to strike the floor with a thud.

On his feet in an instant, Nick tracks the pistol between the three downed men. Eyes fixed, breathing hard, mouth set and pursed.

What the fuck is going on? Who are these people? He

checks to the side to find the girl laying across Todd with her face turned towards him.

'Is he alright?' Nick yells. 'Todd? Is he alright?'

'I ... He's fine ... I ...' Lilly stammers. 'Todd, are you okay? Are you hurt?'

'Are you with them?' Nick tracks the pistol wider, taking a few steps to the side so he can keep a clear view of everyone.

'What ...?'

'Todd, who is this girl? Todd, you gotta answer me, mate. Who is this girl?'

A muffled voice, lost under the protective layer of Lilly keeping him covered.

'Easy now, Nick ... well done, lad ... good shooting that,' the rapist shouts.

'SHUT UP,' Nick roars. 'Todd ... I need you to tell me, who is this girl? How do you know his name?' Nick glances at the girl, the pistol still held two-handed.

'He was taken last night with my brother,' Lilly manages to blurt out, her own mind a whirling mess of panic and confusion.

'Brother?' Nick asks. 'What's his name?'

'Billy!'

'Todd, tell me who this girl is,' Nick demands, unsure of what the hell is going on. These men know each other. The girl was with them, and she bloody attacked him. Is she on their side? How did she know Todd's name? Already he can feel a trickle of blood dripping down from his scalp, and his face feels tender.

'Todd, tell him ...' Lilly urges. Slowly removing herself from the boy, she keeps herself between him and the armed man. 'Todd, it's okay ... It's okay, Todd, tell this man who I am ...'

'Lilly,' Todd blurts.

'Lilly? Who is Lilly, Todd?' Nick asks.

'Nick, take it easy ... those two cunts are the ones that got us last night ...' the rapist takes advantage of the chaos to try and create another opportunity.

That voice. *Nah, fuck him, let him die slow, the cunt ... His fucking mate bit my cheek, didn't he?*

Last night, that voice. That same voice. She stares across the road to the man lying down, clutching his leg. The position of him means his face is turned away, but that voice.

Snapping her head towards Nick, she finally looks at him properly. She sees a young man dressed like a soldier, with straight, dark hair that stands up from his head and a voice she doesn't recognise. Not one of the voices from last night. It was dark, and with only the firelight to use, she knows she might not easily identify them, but the way they spoke will stay with her forever. Deep and mature from years of hard living, with rough accents. Nothing like this man with the gun.

'Nick,' Lilly calls out, bringing his attention to her, 'is that your name?'

'Yeah,' Nick nods, 'and I don't have a fucking clue what is going on right now ...'

'Nick!' the rapist shouts. 'Thems the cunts that got us last night, that bitch is one of 'em ... Get her away from that boy, Nick ...'

Standing up slowly, Lilly once more stares over at the man on the ground. That voice is distinct, the way he speaks, the dropped letters. The image of him thrusting into Sam fills her mind, of the way he beat his fists down into her face. The way he screamed and laughed.

'You,' she hisses. Nick snaps his head round, thinking she is talking to him and spots the intense look of hatred on her face as she stares at the rapist. 'You ... you evil ... nasty ... evil ...' Words are not enough. The foulest of oaths cannot match the sheer rage bursting from her soul. She stalks towards Nick, her eyes still fixed on the man. Scooping down, she lifts Nick's axe up, hefting it in her hands.

Nick watches, completely stunned at the pure rage showing on her face, at the way her eyes are fixed.

'You ... you killed my dad ... you killed Todd's dad ... you raped Sam ... You did that ...' Lilly walks slowly towards him. 'I watched you ... I saw you hurting Sam. You beat her to death.'

'What? Fuck off, you crazy bitch. We's the ones that got attacked. Nick ... don't fucking listen to her ...'

Nick holds his position, listening intently as the girl speaks. 'My dad is dead because of you ... He bit your face. That was my dad that did that, and he did it to protect us ... Now he's dead.'

'You're fucking barking, love. Nick! She's fucking nuts ... Don't listen to her, Nick.'

'Where's Billy?' Lilly pauses just a few feet away, holding the axe two-handed as she stares down with malice.

'Eh? Now, hang on, love,' the rapist squirms to sit upright before slowly working his weight onto his good leg. 'Now slow down, eh? I don't know what you on about ...'

'Where is Billy?' she seethes, the question coming out dangerously low. 'Where is my brother?'

'Now, see, love,' the rapist gets to his feet, wincing at the pain shooting through his leg. 'Now, if you kill me, you ain't gonna find out, are ya? See? I know where they got him but ...'

Nick strides over, his head cocked to one side as he listens to the exchange.

'You want to find Billy, you gotta make sure nothing

happens to me firs–' his words are lost in the gunshot from Nick's pistol as he fires into the man's good leg. This time the bullet doesn't pass through but strikes the bone, embedding deep within the marrow.

Dropping down into a squat, Nick pushes the gun into the man's face, pressing it hard against his forehead. 'Where is Billy?' Nick asks bluntly.

'Oh fuck ... oh fuck ... my fucking legs ... Don't kill me, please, don't kill me?'

'Answer the question,' Nick replies. The decision to take the side of the girl was made from instinct. That instinct, however, was self-consciously drawn from many facets. The way she spoke, the way she moved in contrast to the way the injured man moved and spoke, their body language, and the information they imparted during comments they made. All of these things were absorbed instantly and naturally. Reading other people is something done every second of interaction, so when an instinctual reaction takes place, it is based on many, many factors all of which are understood within the blink of an eye.

So he squeezes the trigger, squats down, and uses force to elicit the information that is required. The dynamics change within that split second. Choosing a side and taking it, taking action that tells the others within that situation who you trust and who you don't believe.

Within the same blink of an eye, Lilly grasps the shift in the atmosphere. The shot startled her, followed quickly by the understanding that this young man is now on her side.

'If you kill me ...' the man begs for his life. He too understood the change in power. The time trying to win an advantage through needling chat designed to undermine the other's thought process is over. His life is now very much at stake. He has one hand left to play, that he knows where Billy is, and they don't. 'You'll never find him ...' he adds. 'They'll keep him, and you won't see him again ... You need me alive ...'

'Chapsworth House,' Lilly blurts. 'They said they were taking them to Chapsworth House.'

Rapist glares up in shock, frantically thinking as his last ace is trumped by the young lady.

'Why?' Nick asks calmly. 'Why did you take them?'

Another opportunity presents itself. 'I can help you,' he gasps. 'Help me, and I help you, yeah? You need me ...'

At this point, Mr Howie would step back and let Dave ask the questions, Nick thinks. Dave would get the answers quickly. Dave wouldn't hesitate. Be Dave.

'FUCK!' the rapist screams as Nick digs the point of his knife blade into his thigh just inches from the gunshot wound. Nick slowly pulls the knife out, then gently rests it on the ragged hole caused by the bullet penetrating the flesh.

'OKAY ... OKAY ... FUCK.'

Pulling the knife out, Nick waits for a second as the man struggles to compose himself.

'Too slow,' Nick says, pushing the point back into the wound.

'THE DOC! Thedocwantsthem ...' he blurts, the words coming out in a solid stream of noise.

'Keep going,' Nick twists the point of the knife.

'SHIT ... PLEASE ... dunno, I dunno ... He wants the kids ... He just wants them ... We get food and kids, and that's it ... I don't know why.'

What else would Dave ask? What information would he want to know?

'How many men you got?'

'Loads,' the man whimpers, 'loads of them ...'

'Guns?'

'Lots, shotguns ... fuck, please stop ... rifles ...'

'Machine guns?'

'Couple,' he wheezes, almost at the point of blacking out.

'Does he hurt the kids?'

'NO!' Rapist screams, a long, drawn-out sound full of agony and pity.

'What does he do with them?'

'I don't know ... I don't want to know ... We get food and women and ...'

Would Dave ask anything else? Yeah, he'd ask about entry points, ways of getting in, who the doc is, where this place is, the range of the weapons, if they get drunk at night, and loads more questions.

All of which are now rendered obsolete as the man slumps unconscious. His mind shutting down as the pain grows to a point that cannot be handled.

'Shit,' Nick mutters. Standing up, he stares down at the still figure. He raises the axe. 'Shit ...' he mutters again. 'FUCK!' he shouts as the axe swings down, the blade biting deep into his knee joint and cleaving through bone and cartilage.

Lilly, in her young years, has never heard a human make a sound like the rapist does now. Nick has heard the same thing many times. He has heard the infected laughing and goading. He has heard death in all its many forms.

The pain snaps him back, his eyes snapping open as he realises what just happened. Lilly tugs at the axe, the blade wedged in the dense bone of the knee joints. Placing one foot on his thigh and pushing in, she levers the axe out. Torturing the man with savage intensity, she wrenches the axe free, lifts it high, and stares down. Holding her poise for a second, she locks eyes on the rapist. He stares back completely frozen in fear. As the axe swings down, his system floods with regret that his life was not a good one. There will be no guiding light for him, no angels singing in welcome, and no loving embrace that eases the pain.

Screwing his eyes shut, he whimpers like a child as the axe ploughs through his skull, instantly smashing the bone apart as grey, sticky brains burst out.

Lilly sobs, a sudden pitiful sound as she drops the axe. The sight of his head exploding was worse than she expected. Realisation hits her that she just killed a man.

'Oh my god,' her hands raise to her mouth as she staggers back, 'oh no ... no ... what did I do?' Tears stream down her face. The action is irreversible. He's dead, and his death came from her. She killed him. She took his life whilst he begged and pleaded. She saw the fear in his eyes and heard the soft whimper.

Nick moves quickly, just catching the girl as she sags to the ground. Good lessons learnt well as the pistol is kept in hand, pointing towards the ground. He guides her down, then quickly checks around for anyone else that might want to jump out and join in.

Todd rushes over, his own face a mess of tears and snot as he sobs uncontrollably. Wrapping his small arms around Nick's neck, he holds on for all his worth.

Smothered by a child, trying to hold the woman's head up, and still holding the pistol, Nick goes with the flow, managing to get the pistol back in the holster before freeing the other arm to wrap round the boy.

With Lilly down and quiet, Nick focusses on the boy. Rubbing his back and wondering what to say. He never had experience with children before. Mr Howie is good with kids, Clarence is brilliant with kids, Lani too. Shit, even the other two lads are better than him. Maybe not Dave, though.

'Er ... it's okay?' Nick ventures for a start. When the child doesn't explode, he keeps going. 'Just calm down, mate, it's all okay now ...'

Seconds tick by. The child cries and cries. Nick gets hot from the face pushing against his neck. Uncomfortable crouched down like this, but the boy just keeps crying.

Her eye lids start to flicker. Slowly they open to reveal the bluest eyes Nick has ever seen. Deep oceans of pure water surrounding perfect, white clouds.

'Thank fuck,' Nick sighs, 'he won't stop crying ... What do I do?'

Lilly takes a few seconds to swim back to the surface of reality. Opening her eyes, she sees the handsome young man comforting the boy. Sweat covers his face; his eyes are dark and mysterious. With the blue sky behind him, she is captivated by the sight. Slight stubble covers his young face, giving him an older look. Tanned and smooth, lean, and after what just happened, very dangerous too. Then he speaks, asking her what to do with the boy.

Blinking hard, she shakes her head. 'Here, Todd, it's okay, come here.' Sitting up, she gently prises the boy away from Nick. Todd releases, turns, and clamps on with a fresh round of sobs. 'It's okay,' Lilly soothes. 'We're all okay now ... You're safe ... I'm here, and nothing will hurt you.'

Slowly standing up, Nick automatically digs into his pocket for his cigarettes, pulling one out to light up as he listens with interest to the words the girl says. He was close, he almost said all of what she's saying.

Exhaling, he stares about. Three men killed. Well, definitely two of them are dead, and that one with the shoulder wound might be alive.

With the action over, he takes stock of the events, at how fast it all unfolded. One thing is clear, Dave would be impressed with the shots he got off. With that girl battering his face, he managed to keep track of the real threats and negate them before it got worse.

Speaking of which, he fingers the edge of his scalp, wincing at the tender spot and the small cut there. Stretching his face, it feels a bit tender. She got a few good shots there, but thankfully, nothing broken.

'Sorry,' Lilly offers an apologetic half-smile half-wince.

Nick chuckles easily, grinning sheepishly as he rubs his face. 'It's okay,' he shrugs. 'I've had worse.'

'Are you a soldier?' Lilly asks, still rubbing Todd's back as his loud wailing subsides to a quiet weeping.

'Er,' Nick pauses, suddenly self-conscious at being stared at by this beautiful woman. Is he a soldier? He joined the army when it all happened, but that was like the first training weekend. It's been Mr Howie, Dave, and Clarence that taught him everything. Does that make him a soldier?

'I, er ...' he stammers, 'sort of?' He blushes, realising what an idiot he sounds like.

'Sort of?' Lilly asks. 'How can you sort of be a soldier?'

'Er, well, er ... Shit, that's hard to explain ...'

'Sorry,' Lilly looks away. 'Didn't mean to pry,' she adds quietly, sensing his reluctance to answer and misconstruing the signs as something to hide.

'No, you're not prying,' Nick says quickly, seeing her turn away and drop her tone of voice. 'It's, er ... complicated sort of ... We joined the army but were only on our first fucking weekend when this happened ... But Mr Howie and Dave came, so we, er, went with them, and er ... fuck ...' he trails off, blushing deeper as she turns those deep blue eyes on him.

'Oh, right,' Lilly replies, wondering why his face is going bright red. 'Mr Howie?'

'The boss,' Nick nods, not really providing any helpful information, 'he's ... in charge ... nice man, really nice man ... You'd like him. Everyone likes him ... Dave's a bit odd, but he's very fucking good.' *Gabbling, definitely gabbling.* 'Then there's Lani. She's great and from Thailand.' *Still gabbling.* 'And the lads, Blowers and Cookey. They were in the army with me, really funny, and Clarence, he was in the army too, but he's huge like, er ...' Nick blushes even deeper as he realises his hand is held high to show the height of the big man. 'Like really ... big.' Why can't he stop gabbling? Christ, he wishes some zombies would attack right now. Anything to stop the girl from staring at him.

'Okay, they sound really nice,' Lilly smiles, trying to ease his discomfort. Why do some men get like this when they talk to her? All tongue-tied and weird. He's just killed two men, shot another one, then stabbed him in the leg without blinking, and now he's standing there, squirming and blushing like a schoolboy. 'Are they close?' she asks lightly.

'Should be,' Nick nods, overwhelmingly glad of the change of direction. 'Not far ... Do you, er ... want to meet them?' his voice cracks as he thinks he just sounded like he was asking her out on a date. Fucking hell, three dead men lying nearby, gunfights, stabbings, fucking zombie apocalypse, but he still can't talk to a pretty girl? Christ.

'I need to get my brother,' Lilly stands up, her voice suddenly strong and resolute.

'We can help,' Nick says quickly. 'Mr Howie won't let something like that happen, no way ...'

Biting her lip, Lilly considers the options. Time is ticking away and pulling at her like a giant elastic band, urging her to move now and find Billy. But this man just shot three men, even with her battering him, and he seems to have a plan. She could use some help.

She told herself a few minutes ago that not everyone is bad, that people will help, and look what happened. Unsure of whether to trust her instinct, she stares in shock as Nick walks towards her holding the pistol.

'Take this,' he offers. 'Have you used one before?' She doesn't reply but stares at the gun. Black and solid-looking. It's familiar from watching so many movies and television shows, but so strange to see one in real life. Nick holds it out, butt first. 'You don't have to trust me,' he adds. 'I wouldn't trust anyone ... Take this, and then you don't have to trust anyone,' he shrugs.

'What about you?' she asks, hesitating to take the gun.

'I got my axe,' he shrugs again, 'and my knife.'

Taking the pistol, she holds it in her hand, completely unsure of what to do with it. Nick digs into his pocket and draws the spare magazine out.

'Here,' he steps in closer. Absorbed in showing her how it works, he relaxes into his natural easy manner. 'That's the safety. Keep it on until you need to use it; otherwise, you'll probably shoot yourself in the fucking ... I mean the foot. Sorry, I didn't mean to swear.'

'It's okay.'

'Er ... yeah, so ... this is how the magazine comes out, and this is the other magazine. You push it in and ... Here, can I show you? It's easier to fucking see it ... shit ... sorry ... Dave is always telling me off for swearing .'

'Honestly, it's okay.'

'So it goes in like this, slide this back, and it gets the first bullet from the magazine into the ... er ... barrel, and that's it ... Have a go.'

'Like this?'

'Yep, that's it ... Then push it back in really hard and pull the top back ... Yep, got it. Er ... take the magazine back out.'

'Okay, er ... got it.'

'Right, now point it away like over there and pull the trigger, go on ... It's empty,' he adds as she screws her eyes shut and looks away. 'See, that's how much fucking pressure you got to ... sorry ... got to apply. Try it a few times and hold it with both hands. Are you right-handed?'

'Yes, like this?'

'No, er, keep your, er ... right hand on the grip, and the left goes like this ... er ...' Nick tries to position her hand the right way, moving in closer until his hand covers hers to move them to the right positions. 'That's it ... Two-handed as it kicks like a fucker when it goes bang. Shit! Sorry.'

'Don't worry,' Lilly says.

'Try it with a bullet so you know what it feels like. We can only use one as we don't have a lot but ...'

'Oh, don't worry then ...'

'No, you should know what it feels like,' Nick replies. 'Get the magazine back in. Yeah, that's it, slide the top ... point away ... See that window of that house? Aim for that ... don't close your eyes and just relax and squeeze the trigger ... Well done! Good shot! Fucking hell, that was good.'

'It kicks a lot,' Lilly lowers the gun, then lifts it back up to push the safety on. 'Are you sure?'

'What? Yeah, course I am, you should have it ...' Nick nods firmly, distracted as he works at his belt to slide the holster off.

'Do I need that?' Lilly asks. 'Don't they just go down here?' She shoves the gun into the waistband of her jeans.

'NO!' Nick reaches to pull it out without thinking. 'You'll shoot your dick off! Oh ... shit ... Fuck, I'm sorry. You don't have a dick. Oh my god!' He goes bright red, staring in horror at the way his mouth keeps going while his brain is screaming to shut up.

Lilly laughs at the absurdity of it all. Surreal is not the word. He turns away from sheer embarrassment and slides the holster off before handing it over.

'Thanks,' Lilly holds the heavy gun in one hand and the holster in the other. 'Er ... what do I do with it?'

'Put it on your belt.'

'I don't have a belt.'

'Oh, er ... shit ... um ... fuck ... wait here,' he yells and runs off towards the nearest house, running up the path and into the open front door.

Staring after him, Lilly shakes her head in amazement. She looks down to see Todd is still clinging onto her legs, although he's stopped crying now.

'Todd,' she drops down to face him, 'that man, er ... Nick?' Todd nods slowly. 'Did he hurt you at all? Did he shout or do anything to you? Todd, you have to be honest now ...'

'No, he was nice,' Todd mumbles. 'He gave me a drink.'

'Did he? That's good. He didn't hit you or shout or anything like that?' Todd shakes his head, the snot hanging from his nose swaying side to side. Using her hand and used to snotty boys, Lilly wipes it away and flicks her hand to rid the sticky bogeys before wiping it on her jeans.

'No belts!' Nick shouts. Exiting the first house, he jumps the wall into the next garden and heads for the front door. Finding it shut and locked, he pauses, then knocks. Standing back, he turns and nods to Lilly, waiting patiently in case anyone decides to answer.

'No one home,' Nick reports needlessly. 'Er ... yeah ...' Turning back, he kicks at the front door, doing what Clarence taught them and aiming for the lock. It goes in easy enough, and Nick offers a prayer to the gods of kicking-in-doors for not letting him look like a total twat.

Less than a minute later, he runs out, clutching a belt like a triumphant warrior, 'Got one!'

'Great,' Lilly smiles. Handing the belt over, he stands there, grinning away while she threads it through the loops on her jeans, then remembers the holster, and pulls the belt back out of the loops to attach to the holster.

'Ha,' Nick snorts, watching her fumble. Glancing up, she smiles at him and watches as he blushes again and finds something else to look at.

'Ready,' she says simply. Pushing the pistol into the holster, she feels the reassuring weight of it tugging on one side. She is armed now, armed with a gun that has bullets. If only she had this last night, things would have been so different. A lump of metal that makes other bits of metal fly out the end, that's all it is. Knowing she could pull the pistol out and shoot someone right now sends a funny feeling through her. She's fifteen years old, walking around with a gun and has killed a man with an axe.

Breathing in deeply, she tries to settle her nerves. She is exhausted from lack of sleep, lack of food, and the terrifying horrors she has witnessed, but there isn't time to rest now.

'Just realised ...' Nick walks off towards the red van and retrieves the shotgun from the ground next to the body. He breaks it in half, checking the barrels are loaded before snapping it shut and mooching around in the cabin. Finding the box of shells, he stuffs his pockets full.

Lilly watches the way he moves, the constant scanning

as he lifts his head up slightly to check the area. His hands move quickly with a focussed, concentrated look.

'Got this.' Walking back, he lifts the shotgun as though she might not have seen the big gun in his hands. 'Next, we need a fucking car and ... shit! Sorry.'

'Honestly, don't worry,' Lilly says.

'Yeah, but you know ...' Nick nods at Todd. 'I'll really try not to swear. Just tell me if I do, okay?'

'I don't think he's that worried.'

'Maybe,' Nick shrugs, 'anyway, we need a car and then the town centre.'

'The centre?' Lilly asks. 'Why?'

'That's where we got split up last night. Everyone will be heading there to wait so we can get back to the fort.'

'Sorry, what?' Lilly snaps, her keen eyes locking on Nick.

'What?' Nick stares back, momentarily mesmerised by the blue eyes before glancing away.

'Fort? What fort?'

'Oh, sorry, yeah, we got a fort, er ... on the coast ... er ... south,' he trails off again.

'That's where we were heading,' Lilly sighs. 'The place with the army.' She rolls her eyes at Nick as if it suddenly makes sense.

'Not quite the army,' Nick mumbles. 'We did have a lot more but ...' a dark look flashes across his face, his voice dropping in tone, 'but things went wrong ... We got some more people now.'

Lilly stares back, detecting the sadness in his manner. Nodding softly, she waits for him to lead the way, checking to make sure Todd is okay.

'We'd better go,' Nick nods, 'find a car and–'

'That van has loads of food in it,' Lilly nods to the

vehicle behind Nick. 'Those men were going from house to house, stripping all the food out. I saw it.'

'Really? Fuck ... might as well have it then. Nice one,' he grins with a sudden easy motion that lifts his features completely. 'We'll get your brother, I promise. We just gotta find Mr Howie and the others first.'

Nodding, Lilly takes Todd's hand and starts walking towards the van. This is the third time within the last few hours that she trusted someone else. Norman in the forest and being groped, then these two men, and now Nick. He seems genuine and nice, and he does keep blushing and looking away shyly.

Patting the gun on her belt, she walks on, knowing this time she'll be keeping a very watchful eye on everyone.

CHAPTER TWENTY-SIX

'Where is everyone?' Blowers frets again.

'They'll be here,' Lani reassures him. The roles have switched, with Lani moving to the role of calming the other two while they get increasingly worried.

'Something must have happened,' Cookey shakes his head. 'They'd be back by now. It's been hours.

'Maybe Clarence has already found a load and taken them back,' Lani suggests.

'No way,' Blowers says dully. 'He'd come here first.'

'This place fucking stinks,' Cookey grumbles, 'fucking stinks of fucking dirty fucking dead fucking zombies and dirty fucking fire ...' Turning round, he once more stares with disgust at the scene of carnage all around them. Bodies fester in the staggering heat, flies and insects buzzing between them. Pools of blood congeal into crusty scabs; unrecognisable body parts start shrivelling as though in an oven.

'I know,' Lani replies softly. 'Maybe we should start walking then, stay on the main road and ...'

'We can't,' Blowers shakes his head. 'If the others come here, they won't know where we are.'

'Leave a note then,' Lani suggests again.

'Where? What, pinned to one of them? Dear everyone, we got fed up waiting so we're going to–'

'Blowers,' Cookey shoots his mate a dark look in reaction to his bitter tone.

Breathing slowly, the hard-faced young man dips his head. 'Sorry,' he mutters.

'Forget it,' Lani says. 'Heat, bodies, fire ... this is a shit place.'

'Whoa! Lani just swore,' Cookey jokes feebly. 'She must be getting mad.' The joke falls flat as their surroundings start sucking the life from them. They still all feel that Howie and Dave are okay, but they aren't back yet. They should be here by now. The feeling must be wrong, something has happened.

'YO!' Jagger walk quickly towards them.

'What?' Blowers snaps impatiently.

'Hear that?'

'No, what?' Blowers stands up, his face suddenly focussed and interested.

'Van, diesel engine ...' Jagger cocks his head to one side.

'What?' Cookey stares at him. 'I can't hear anything.'

'He's right, bruv,' Mohammed steps in. 'Jagger got some freaky fucking hearing skills going on.'

'Transit,' Jagger nods, 'big fucking transit van coming this way.

'Yeah,' Lani nods, 'I got it ... Yeah, I can hear it.'

'Really?' Cookey looks about, spotting the dog now standing up with her head cocked to one side. Shoving fingers into his ears, he wriggles them about before trying again. 'Can't hear anything,' he shrugs.

'You's deaf, bruv,' Mohammed comments.

'Yeah, I got it,' Blowers nods.

'What the fuck?' Cookey takes a couple of steps forward as though decreasing the distance by a few feet will aid his hearing.

Finally, the sound reaches him. The low, throaty rumble of a diesel engine rattling along the roads comes closer. Used by delivery companies and workmen all over the world, the sound is intrinsic part of what modern life was.

When it appears at the far end of the main road, the youths start to gather round Lani, Blowers, and Cookey. Talking ends as they all watch with interest, none of them recognising the vehicle.

'You got your pistols?' Blowers asks in a low voice, already noting that Cookey has drawn his to hold low and ready.

'Is that ...?' Cookey takes another step forward, squinting as he presses the side of his palm to his forehead to reduce the glare of the sun. 'Yeah ...' he laughs, 'that's Clarence!'

'Is it?' Blowers steps forward, doing the same as his friend. The big, bald head is unmistakable, the broad grin that spreads across the driver's face even more so.

'Where's the Saxon?'

'Dunno,' Cookey shakes his head. 'Big bloody van, though,' he adds at seeing the size of the extra-long jumbo-sized van.

Coming up the road, Clarence notices the size of the group gathered there and feels a sense of relief that they all had the sense to wait.

Getting closer, he starts picking faces out. Lani, Blowers, Cookey, and the dog are instantly recognisable. No sign of Howie or Dave, and no Nick either. The grin starts to fade as he brings the speed down, leaning forward to scan the group. With the time it took him to find another vehicle, get back to the Saxon, and transfer all the kit, means everyone should have been back here.

The delay just added to the growing sense of frustration and urgency. Knowing that the fort is occupied by another armed group, he knows that he has to get the group back there as quickly as possible.

'Where are they?' all greeting pushed aside, Clarence jumps down to shout the question while striding forward. The initial relief at seeing some of the group alive has faded as he now starts to worry why the others aren't back as well.

'Don't know.' Lani looks sick, the composure she held before now slipping at the sight of the older, more experienced man.

'Where's Nick?' Cookey asks, stepping round to see if another vehicle is coming up behind.

'He went with them,' Clarence points to the children standing nearby. 'We were bugging out. All hell breaking lose ...'

'What?' Blowers exclaims. 'What the fuck?' Spinning to face Jagger, his face crosses with anger. 'Why didn't you fucking say?'

'I didn't know,' Jagger replies, looking confused. 'We thought he went with you,' he says to Clarence.

'No, we were getting swamped ... He went off with you lot.'

'Was chaos, bruv,' Mohammed pipes up. 'Everyone legged it every direction ... Pitch fucking black too.'

'So Nick is missing too? What about the boss and Dave?' Clarence asks.

'No sign of them,' Lani replies.

'Have you searched?'

'Yes, we've searched,' Lani says.

'Have you searched properly?'

'Clarence! We've searched every inch of it and checked all these bodies too. They're not here.' Lani's voice grows stronger with frustration, the worry now evident on her face.

'We figured they'd be back by now,' Cookey shrugs. 'We didn't know Nick was gone. We thought he got out with you. Shit ... shit ...'

'Alright,' Clarence forces his tone to be calm as he senses the rising panic, 'we'll find them. Don't worry. Dave went after Howie ...' He stops to think for a second, replaying the fight from the previous night through his mind, 'He went into the vehicle ramp. That's the last I saw of him.'

'Who?' Blowers asks. 'The boss or Dave?'

'The boss. Dave was going that way. He shouted for light. Yes! He shouted for lights, so we put the headlights on. Remember?'

'Not really,' Cookey shakes his head. 'We were at the door to the stairs.'

'I heard it,' Lani nods quickly. 'If Dave shouted for lights, he must have seen something.'

'Then got Mr Howie out,' Blowers takes the train of speech up, 'but where? And why aren't they–'

'More problems now too,' Clarence interrupts. 'Fort's been taken over.'

'What?' Blowers shouts.

'We got back. Some bloke with a gun was outside, and the gates were all locked up. We got into the first gate, but that was it ...'

'Who are they? What? I don't ...' Blowers demands.

'Don't know, don't know anything ...' Clarence explains.

'Left Maddox there with Paula and Roy. I came back here for you lot.'

'Fucking hell!' Cookey groans. 'What the fuck? Why does this keep happening?'

'We'll deal with it,' Blowers growls. 'We gotta find the others first. The fort can wait.'

'Agreed,' Lani nods firmly. 'Why wouldn't they come back here? What would stop them? We need to think clearly so we can figure out where to look.'

'The boss could be injured somewhere,' Cookey suggests. 'Dave looking after him.'

'They wouldn't get lost,' Blowers adds quickly. 'Same with Nick. They'd know to come back here.'

'Nick can't read,' Cookey says quietly.

'So? What difference does that make?' Blowers snaps.

'He can't read the road signs. What if he legged it really far away? Or got chased or something?'

'The fucking High Street is burning down,' Blowers exclaims.

'There isn't that much smoke,' Clarence cuts in, 'not really ... It looks worse from here, but I didn't see it until a few minutes before I got here.'

'Fuck, so he could be lost then ... No way, not Nick!' Blowers shakes his head, refusing to accept the possibility.

'He'd go south, for the fort,' Lani says. 'They all would if they couldn't get back here or ... I don't know, something's stopped them.'

'Okay,' Clarence growls, his deep voice grabbing everyone's attention. 'The plan ... You lot get back to the fort,' he points at Jagger and Mohammed. 'Take this van and get them back. We'll stay here and start looking.'

'Plenty of cars about,' Cookey says. 'We'll grab a couple and drive about.'

'Good,' Clarence says, 'do that. Can you lads drive that van?'

'You're joking, right, mate?' Mohammed says as he rolls his eyes.

'No time for jokes, son,' Clarence glares. 'Get your lot back to the fort. Wait at the estate and make sure it's safe to go down. Do not just drive down, you understand? Good. Tell Maddox and the rest we're going to find Howie and our team; then, we'll come back. If any of them get there, tell them to wait. Understand? Don't let them come looking for us. It'll get confusing otherwise. Tell them to wait until we get back. Got it?'

'Yeah, course,' Jagger nods seriously.

'You two,' Clarence points one thick, gnarled finger at Jagger and Mohammed, 'are in charge of that lot.' He motions the group behind them. 'You get them back safely, and no fucking about on the way.'

'Yeah,' Jagger continues to nod, sensing this isn't the time for flippant remarks or stupid comments.

'Go then. Lani, you're with me. Lads,' Clarence turns to Blowers and Cookey, 'you two together in a car and searching, windows down and drive slow ...'

'Radios?' Blowers asks.

'FUCK IT!' Clarence roars, making everyone jump back. 'They're in the Saxon. I didn't get them.'

'Don't worry,' Lani says softly. 'We'll meet back here in two hours. Agreed?' She looks at the two lads nodding. 'Two hours from now, whatever happens, we all meet back here.'

'And don't touch any of our kit in that van,' Clarence glowers down at the children traipsing past him.

Waiting for the others to squeeze into the van and then watching the minor squabble between Jagger and

Mohammed over who will drive the van, they stand quietly, each absorbed in their own thoughts and worries. That pervading feeling of being separated nags stronger as time wears on. The bond between them, so strong and seemingly unbreakable, now feels under threat. The saving grace, the one thing they each cling on to, is that Dave would never let anything happen to Howie, and Nick is very switched on and highly capable.

They'll be okay.

Please, let them be ok.

CHAPTER TWENTY-SEVEN

'Jesus, I'm fucked ... no more ... please ... Even you're sweating now, Dave.'

'Yes,' his voice just one pitch lower than normal. That and the sweat are the only signs that he's having any difficulty at all.

'How? Just fucking how?'

'How what, Mr Howie?'

'How can a little girl keep going like that?'

'Well ...'

'Dave, it was a rhetorical question. You don't have to answer it. Were you like this?'

'Like what?'

'Like that girl?'

'I'm a boy, Mr Howie.'

'No, Dave, I mean could you run like that and never ever need to pissing well stop and rest.'

'Yes,' he answers firmly.

'Then we're fucked.'

'We'll catch her, Mr Howie.'

'When? Today? Next week? She's playing with us.

She's more evil than Darren and Marcy and all the fucking smart bastard zombies put together.'

'I don't think she's evil, Mr Howie.'

'No? Why is she not stopping then?'

'Scared?' he ventures.

'Scared? Fuck off! She bit my hand and kicked me in the bollocks, then runs off and leaves two glasses of water for us.'

'A game, then?'

'A game?! A fucking game? What kind of game is this? Really? Tell me? I want to know what kind of game this is?'

'Mr Howie.'

'Yes, Dave?'

'You are starting to rant.'

'I know!'

'Okay,' he shrugs, 'just thought I would mention it.'

'Right, so,' I take a breath and let the sweat pour down my face, 'if that was you running from us, what would it take to make you stop?'

'Getting caught,' he answers instantly.

'Helpful,' I comment drily.

'You asked,' he shrugs again.

'Other than getting caught?'

'Injury or getting trapped.'

'As much as I hate her right now ... I hope she doesn't get injured. As for trapping, we could do that if we knew which way she was going ... but seeing as she's ahead of us all the time, we can't do that either.'

'No.'

'No.'

'That's what I said, Mr Howie.'

'I know. I was repeating it, as in, yeah, I agreed with you.'

'Oh, okay.'

'Keep going, then,' I sigh, a long, drawn exhalation of breath. A little girl. Small and sweet, in a summer dress, but judging by the state of the house she was in, she'll also be covered in shit and filth. We can't leave her. Leaving her now, as much as wish to, just isn't an option.

Another day gone to rat shit, and it started so nicely, too. Waking up rested, having a coffee, and watching Dave slaughter loads of infected. What could be better? But oh no, it has to fuck up within the mandatory twenty minutes, doesn't it?

Somebody up there is watching all of this and clearly thinking *oh look, Howie and his merry bunch of men and Lani have woke up. Now, what shit can I throw at them today? Maybe I should just make it rain actual shit? Big, stinky, wet turds falling from the sky. No, I know ... I will make that innocent, little girl run and run all day long while they try and catch her.*

'Turds?' Dave looks at me.

'What?'

'How can it rain turds?'

I stare at him. I said all that in my head. I am sure I said that in my head.

'Dave?'

'Yes?'

'Was I speaking out loud?'

'Yes, Mr Howie.'

'Like properly out loud? You know, words coming out of my actual mouth?'

'Yes, Mr Howie.'

'I don't think I was, Dave.'

'You were.'

'I was thinking it but not saying it.'

'You said it.'

'Hmmm,' looking away, I ponder the idea that either I am losing the plot completely or Dave lives inside my head. I don't know which option is scarier.

'Mr Howie.'

'What?'

'Why did you just pinch my arm?'

'Just checking.'

'Checking what?'

'That you're not imaginary.'

'Okay.'

'You're not, are you?'

'Imaginary? No.'

'How would we know? I mean, if you are figment of my imagination, then pinching your arm could just be another, like, mirage or something ...'

'I'm not imaginary.'

'Really?'

'Really. I am not imaginary.'

'Prove it.'

'How?'

'I don't know ... Do something unexpected.'

'Like what?'

'I don't know. If I told you, then it would be in my head, wouldn't it, and you would do it anyway ... What are you doing?'

'Jumping.'

'Why?'

'You told me to do something unexpected.'

'Oh yeah, I did, didn't I? Okay, fair enough, mate, cheers for that.'

'Okay, Mr Howie. MILLY!'

'Fuck, Dave ...'

'Sorry, Mr Howie, I didn't warn you ... I am now going to shout for Milly, okay?'

'Bit late to warn me after the fact, mate.'

'MILLY,' he roars, ignoring my comment, 'PLEASE STOP RUNNING.'

'What?' I ask him as he cocks his head to one side.

'Nothing,' he answers too quickly with a slight worried look on his face.

'Dave, what?'

'She's laughing.'

'What?'

'I heard her laugh.'

'Laughing.'

'Yes.'

'At us?'

'I don't know what she is laughing at, but she laughed.'

'She laughed?'

'Yes.'

'You heard that?'

'I did.'

'Tell her this isn't a game ... tell her this is serious, and she must come back right now or she will be in lots of trouble ...' Taking a hasty step away as Dave bellows into the air, I try to bite down a flare of righteous anger and have to admit my pride is starting to get seriously dented.

This time even I hear it. The distant giggle of a little girl who finds something funny. Not creepy like a horror movie or anything like that. In fact, it's a nice sound, and at any other time, I would be smiling at hearing it.

'Right, we need a cunning plan.'

'There are none, Mr Howie.'

'I know.'

'If there was a plan, I would have done it by now.'

'I know. It just made me feel better saying it.'

'We just have to keep running after her.'

'I know.'

So we do. We keep running and running. I've lost track of the streets and the direction. All I know is that we're heading further away from the town and closer to the countryside.

The girl has skills. Not taught or probably even skills that she is aware of. She has survived this long on her own. Yes, she's been eating shit junk food, but she had the gumption to at least eat and stay close to home. Even now, with running like this, she's deviating the route and going through houses. The glasses trick has been repeated a few times. Dave and I staggering into a house, well, me staggering, and Dave jogging lightly, to find one glass emptied and two full ones next to the sink. As a point of principle, I don't want to drink the water, but we do. We down it thankfully and very gratefully before setting off again.

Both of us take turns in shouting out, calling and begging her to come back and to stop running. A couple of times, Dave has run ahead, confident at being able to catch her on his own with his exceptional speed and agility. Couple of minutes later, I come chugging round the corner to find him standing there, scratching his head with an expression of *how did that happen?*

Jesus, no wonder the infected haven't got her. They probably tried for a few nights, then gave up to find an easier target, staggering away all grumbling and sulky at being outfoxed by a little girl.

Which is what I want to do right now. Except, like I said, we can't. The junk food will run out soon, and guessing at the state she's in, well, the state of her bedroom and the house, she could get any number of diseases. The streets are littered with rotting corpses, which doesn't seem to bother her, but they will also be spreading diseases.

There is no choice. No person with a conscious could walk away and leave her.

Street after street, house after house, garden fences, another house, and back into the street. It's also hampered by the fact that so many of the houses have ruined front doors, so unless we catch a sight of her, we don't know which one she's run into and have to wait and listen, prowling quietly for the creaking of a fence or a back door being opened.

'Getting near open land,' Dave observes as we jog along. Looking up, I can see what he means by the absence of rooftops and houses.

'Hopefully,' I pant, gasping the word out, 'she'll go that way.' Open land with nowhere to hide. She doesn't stand a chance against Dave in the open; even I might be able to catch her on open, flat run.

'There,' Dave points. A vehicle moves slowly across the junction at the far end of the street. Without thinking, I draw my pistol and loose a shot into the air, causing Dave to snap his head round at me in shock.

'It's the others,' I blurt out, hoping the gunshot didn't scare the girl. Hopefully, she won't know what a gunshot is and just think it's a loud bang.

'Might not be.' His face morphs into a serious expression, which is the same as all the other expressions. Except I know Dave now, and I can tell the difference. It's just a subtle change in the way his eyebrows lower, his eyes narrow, and he becomes more focussed.

'It is,' I reply flatly. I don't know how I know it is them, but the vehicle reverses back into sight and stops. One of the doors opens, and something long, big, and black jumps out.

'Meredith!'

'HERE,' Dave booms, and even from this distance, I can see the dog's immediate reaction as she spins round and locks on. Then she's off, head low and ears flattened as she sprints flat out towards us. With all thought of the girl gone, we both start running, with a big grin spreading across my face.

My god, she is fast, and she covers the ground within seconds. She bounds up to us with high-pitched barks of excitement. When we meet, she goes nuts, running round our legs while making little yelping noises as her tail wags faster than helicopter rotor blades.

Both of us drop down to give her fuss, rubbing her head and back as she snakes round and round. Looking up, I can see the vehicle has manoeuvred to head up the street, towards us. The unmistakable shiny, bald head of Clarence is behind the driver's wheel with one huge arm waving out the window.

With the dog jumping at us and yelping in glee, I miss seeing who else is in the vehicle until it comes to a stop and both front doors open up. The sight of Lani running towards me makes my heart drop through my stomach, and I'm off, running towards her while my axe clatters to the ground.

She rushes into my arms, and the sudden warmth of her, the contact is spellbinding. Her strong, lithe arms wrap round my neck, pulling me close as I do the same. I literally lift her off her feet to spin her round.

'I thought something had happened,' she sobs into my neck, the wet tears pouring down her face. 'I was so scared ... Why didn't you come back?'

'Lani ...'

'Don't do that again, not ever ... You hear me ...?'

'I won't.'

'Promise, Howie ... you promise me ...'

'I promise, Lani ... not ever ...' We cling on tight, and right now, at this very second, nothing else matters. The world can do what it wants. It can go to hell as I am holding the woman I love in my arms.

'Are you okay?' I gasp as my own tears stream down my face to mingle with hers.

'Fine, fine ... Are you crying?'

'I don't care. Yes ... yes, I am ...'

'I'm crying,' she half-laughs and sobs again. Lani is a tough woman, of that there is no doubt. She is like Dave in so many ways, holding a straight face and voicing her opinions. She laughs easily and is stunningly beautiful, but she is also incredibly smart and not afraid to voice her opinions. This can make her intimidating at times, but I feel all that melting now. The raw emotion pouring from her is so beautiful and so strong it takes my breath away.

'I came after you ... I tried, Howie ...'

'It's okay,' I whisper softly.

'I lost you,' she cries again. 'I couldn't find you ...'

'I'm here, Lani, right here.'

'What happened? It's so hard not to kiss you, Howie.'

'Kiss me, then.'

'I can't ... Don't, Howie ... What happened? Where did you go?'

'Lani, look at me ...' Her brown eyes lock into mine, the red tinge from crying adding to the softness and love coming from her. 'I'm immune,' I whisper.

She doesn't reply but stares in wonder. Pure shock crosses her face as she blinks slowly and swallows. 'What?'

she gasps, but I don't reply. Instead, I gently move my mouth towards hers. She stares at me in disbelief at first, like it's some sick joke that will play out, but at the last inch, she melts, closes her eyes, and moves in until our lips touch.

The soft, tender feel is beyond words. The contact, the connection, the chemistry that fires and releases inside of me is intense. All I know is that it feels amazing. Totally and utterly amazing. Just lips touching, that's it, but it's so much more than that, and I truly hope she can feel the love pouring from me.

Tenderness evolves into passion as the kiss becomes harder, like something we have been denying ourselves that we can now have. Our tongues probe gently with loving caress as we wrap our arms more firmly round each other.

Breaking away, her eyes remain closed for long seconds until slowly they flicker open. Pupils dilated and warmth emanating from them as an easy grin stretches across her face.

'Ahem,' Clarence says pointedly, 'did you just say immune?'

'Yeah,' I nod, still looking down at Lani and not wanting the moment to end.

'Oh right, nothing important then,' he remarks.

Finally I have to step away, suddenly conscious of being in front of Dave and Clarence. Clumsily, I go to retrieve my dropped axe and start to worry until Dave holds it up for me.

'Cheers, mate.'

'Immune?' Clarence prompts with forced patience. Lani just stares at me with her head shaking slightly side to side.

'Only you,' she says softly, 'only you could get taken like that and walk away.'

Chuckling self-consciously, I check the axe head and start to explain what happened. Most of it they know, about the circling motion of the infected and getting drawn in. After that, the bit with the fight and then the heart being shoved into my mouth they didn't know.

As I tell them, Lani stares at me in fascinated interest which slowly blends into horror at the thought that she just kissed a man who only hours before had a still-beating zombie heart rammed in his gob.

'That,' she spits, 'is disgusting ...' She spits again, 'You could have said something.'

'What?' I ask just a little offended at the way she keeps spitting.

'Oh, I don't know,' she snaps. 'Maybe *Hey, Lani, nice to see you. I would kiss you, but I had this still-beating heart IN MY MOUTH.*'

'Well, it's not there now, is it?' I exclaim.

'Have you brushed your teeth? And if you have, then how? Because your toothbrush was in your bag, which was in the Saxon.' Another look of horror crosses her face. 'Don't tell me you used someone else's brush?' She steps away and spits again.

'No!'

'No, you didn't brush, or no, you didn't use someone else's brush?'

'No, I, er ... didn't brush.' I mutter as Clarence starts looking at me with distaste while shaking his head.

'Gross, boss,' he rumbles.

'I used mouthwash,' I shrug sulkily.

'Did you?' Dave asks. 'I didn't see any.'

'Cheers, Dave,' I groan.

'Oh, Howie,' Lani says, 'urgh, there could have been bits of heart in your mouth.'

'Don't be daft! Anyway, I used toothpaste and my finger so ...'

'Well, that makes it alright, then,' she still shakes her head. 'Listen, I'm glad you're okay, really, I am ... I love you, Howie, but that,' she grimaces, 'was gross.'

'You love me?' I ask with a big grin.

'Yes,' she laughs, 'but I am not kissing you again.'

'Hear that?' I face Clarence. 'She loves me.'

'She does,' he nods, 'but that was disgusting. I would have punched you if you kissed me.'

'Really? Wanna try it?' I take a step forward with my mouth puckered-up and ready.

'Fuck off!' He steps back quickly.

'Howie, we're missing Nick,' Lani cuts in, the humour gone in an instant.

'Eh?'

'Nick, he's missing.'

'What? What happened?'

So they tell their story of how Clarence and Nick got out with the Saxon and the youths while Lani got stuck on the levels searching for me. On the road out, they got swamped to the point of being overrun, so everyone had to starburst and run, including Nick.

Then Clarence hits home with the double whammy, telling me about the fort being occupied by another group.

Dave and I listen intently, absorbing all the information quietly until they've finished.

'Right.' I switch on and get down to business. 'Blowers and Cookey are looking for him, yeah?'

'And you. We've got to meet them back at the car park.'

'Okay, so Nick ran off into this town somewhere. Knowing Nick, he would choose a safe place for the night, then sleep for hours, especially if there was no one there to wake him up. We find Nick, then get down to the fort.'

'The girl, Mr Howie,' Dave prompts.

'Girl?' Lani asks.

'Shit, the girl. Fuck it. Right, that throws another spanner in the works.'

'What girl?' Lani asks again.

'Little girl. We saw her running off earlier. She's just a tiny thing, so we went after her. Her house is a complete shit tip with actual shit everywhere. Poor little bugger has been living on junk food. Doesn't look like she's washed or changed her clothes either.' Both of them make faces while I pause for breath. 'Anyway, turns out she's like some distant relation to Dave ...'

'Really?' Clarence glances at the small, quiet man.

'No, not really, but she bloody should be as we can't catch her. We've been chasing her for hours now. She just keeps running.'

'Like a game,' Dave adds.

'Yeah, and,' I point emphatically, 'she keeps running through houses and out the back, but get this! She puts two glasses of water out for us.'

'No way,' Lani leans forward in surprise.

'Yep, just heard her laughing a minute ago too.'

'Hasn't Dave got her?' Clarence asks.

'Nope, not even Dave,' I say with a furtive look at Dave who chooses that second to glance away. 'I did grab her, but er ... well, she bit my hand and kicked me in the bollocks before running off again ... What? That isn't funny, Lani.'

'It is,' she laughs. 'Serves you right for kissing me with a dirty mouth.'

'I'm struggling here,' Clarence rubs one big hand over his big, bald head. 'So you're immune, we're missing Nick, and now we've got a little girl to catch. Oh, and the fort has been taken over ...'

'Yeah,' I nod, 'that's about it, mate.'

'I need some sleep,' he moans.

'You not had any?'

'No. Oh, yeah ... by the way,' he mentions casually, 'the Saxon is fucked too.'

'Oh, what?'

'Broke down on the way back. I got a van back here, but that was it. It's left in some shitty, little town.'

'Did you strip–'

'Yes, Dave,' Clarence growls. 'I stripped it.'

'Good.'

'Easy,' I step in at the glare from Clarence. 'Another busy day then,' I comment.

'Still,' Lani beams at me, 'you're immune! Oh my god, Howie ... Did you pass it to me when we kissed before?'

'You could have passed it to me?' I reply.

'So have we got to kiss everyone else? I'm not sure they'll mind doing that with me, but you?'

'I'm not kissing you,' Dave says quickly. 'Either of you.'

'No offence, boss,' Clarence agrees.

'Truth is, we don't know anything more now than we did before. We could be uniquely immune, resistant, carriers. Fuck knows ... Either of us could have passed immunity to the other, but that doesn't mean we can pass it on again.'

'Still fucked, then,' Clarence says.

'Yep, business as bloody usual really.'

'Until we find a doctor,' Lani prompts. 'That has to be a priority now.'

'Funny that,' I smile. 'That's kind of what we've been trying to do for days now.'

'True,' she nods. 'I am so happy to see you again."

'Oh, stop it,' Clarence grumbles. 'Have we got to put up with you two going all gooey now?'

'Gooey?' I ask.

'Yeah, gooey.' He shrugs, which is like watching two massive bowling balls raise a few inches before plummeting back to earth at terminal velocity.

'Plan?' Dave brings us all back to reality.

'Right. Lani stays with us to help find this girl. Clarence, can you head back to find Blowers and Cookey and bring them back here? We get the girl, get everyone together, and then find Nick who will no doubt be fast asleep in some comfy bed somewhere, the lazy shit. Once we've done that, we'll go find the Saxon, figure out what's wrong with it ... which Nick can hopefully do, then go rescue the fort. Ha! No problem.'

'Jesus, you're happy,' Lani says.

'I am,' I grin. 'The sun is shining, and I just had a big, wet kiss with a beautiful girl.'

'Don't remind me,' she spits again, ruining the moment.

'If you're chasing this girl,' Clarence asks, 'how will we find you?'

'We'll break car windscreens,' Dave says flatly. 'Follow them.'

'Got it,' the big man says. 'Dog staying with you?'

'She could get the girl,' Dave says, looking down at Meredith taking a piss a few feet away.

'No, Dave, we can't send a dog after a little girl.'

'She wouldn't hurt her,' he replies.

'You sure?'

'Yes, I am,' he says firmly.

'Well what good would it do then?'

'She could bark and tell us where she is.'

'And she's trained to do that, is she?' I ask.

'Maybe,' he mutters.

'Clarence, can you take the dog with you,' I ask before he climbs into the car.

'Keep her,' he replies. 'Dave's right, she wouldn't go for a child. She's had plenty of chances, and she hasn't done anything like that yet. She loves kids by the looks of it.'

'Hmmm, yeah, okay then.'

'I'll keep her with me,' Lani says.

'Right,' I straighten up, 'where is she?'

CHAPTER TWENTY-EIGHT

Red everywhere. Red from the blood spilled on the ground. Red from the bodies split open and torn apart. Red flames that eat into the buildings they consume.

The red van matches the scene, like it belongs there as one of the varying shades of death. Nick stands at the rear with his hands on his hips, staring round.

Lilly walks slowly towards him, having told Todd to remain in the front of the van with his eyes closed to shield him from the scene of utter carnage.

'No one here,' Nick comments quietly.

Lilly stares in awe-struck wonder at the scale of the battle. Bodies stretched out in every direction and killed in every way possible. Limbs strewn about like twigs, heads separated from bodies, torsos with innards hanging out, thick layers of corpses, with spent shell casings glittering in the bright sun. The stench is something never known before. Rotting, charred meat mixed with the metallic tang of blood and chemical smoke from the burning High Street.

'They should be here,' Nick turns round, the first real signs of worry evident on his face.

'Maybe they went,' Lilly speaks softly, hardly daring to break the silence of this oppressive area.

'No,' shaking his head, 'they'd wait here ...'

'But they're not,' Lilly states the obvious. The urge to do something to find her brother nags constantly at her. She can see he wasn't lying; the bodies and the fires are testament to that. The bullet casings indicate fierce fighting too, but he also said they would be waiting for him.

'Nick, I can't wait,' Lilly says.

'But they should be here,' he repeats. 'They'd know we'd come back.'

'Something must have happened,' she replies. 'Maybe they went to the fort.'

'Maybe,' he sighs. 'There'd be a reason. They wouldn't just fucking leave me here.'

'What do you want to do?' she asks. Staring from the side, she can see the concern etched into his face, the way he stares about as if he will find his mates any second.

Shrugging, he carries on looking, staring for any sign that they were here. 'I don't know ... fort, I guess ... Fuck it. Why didn't they wait?'

'How do you know they came back here?'

'Because ... just because that's what we'd do. We've never been spilt up before, but I know that that is what they would do ...'

'But you think they're okay?' she asks softly.

'Yes, I do,' he replies firmly. 'Yeah, I don't know how, but yeah ... fucking yes ... There's no way they'd all get ...'

'Okay,' she steps closer to him, 'Nick, you stay here if you want. I've got to find Billy.'

'We need the others first.'

'They're not here, Nick, and I can't wait.'

'Lilly, I know they'd come back, but it's already late and …'

'Then something must have happened. Go to the fort and find them … Listen, Nick, thank you for everything you've done but–'

'You can't go on your own,' he turns to face her. 'You can't do that.'

'I don't have a choice,' she shrugs. 'He's my brother.'

'What about Todd? You can't take him with you … No. We have to find the others first.'

'Nick, thank you, but I have to find him. Anything could happen …'

'Mr Howie can–'

'He's not here, though,' Lilly cuts him off, her tone kind but firm. 'Keep the van, I can find something else, but er … can I keep the gun, please? I'll bring it back once I've got Billy.'

'No,' Nick shakes his head.

'What do you mean?' Lilly feels the first nagging worry. 'Nick, I have to go,' she takes a step back, creating distance between them.

'Eh?' Nick stares at her, confused, seeing the hard look cross her face. 'Take your bloody hand off that gun …' he sighs. 'I didn't mean I was going to stop you.'

'You can't stop me,' she says firmly.

'I don't want to fucking stop you,' he says quickly. 'I just meant you can't do it on your own.'

'I'm fine.'

'Did you go to public school?' he asks suddenly. 'You speak really nice and posh.'

'What? What relevance does that have?'

Shrugging, he looks away. 'Just asking.' He blushes at the stern rebuke.

Seeing his face flushing, she softens, realising he wasn't trying to force her into something. 'Yes. Yes, I went to a private school before my dad was made bankrupt.'

'Shit, really?'

'Yes, really,' she looks down at the memory of her father, of the way his body blew apart from the shotgun blast. 'Look, you might be used to this,' she starts speaking quickly, 'all this ... this death, but up until yesterday, we were hiding at home ...'

'Lilly ...'

'My dad was killed last night,' she chokes on the tears, 'and Sam was raped and ... and ... I saw it all happen, and now Billy is ...'

'It's okay,' Nick moves in as the tears start pouring down her face.

'I can't ...' she gasps, roughly trying to wipe the tears away with the back of her hand. 'I'm so tired, and I've got to find Billy.'

'Okay,' Nick says softly.

'No, it's not okay,' she snaps. 'It's not okay at all ... not at all ...' she weeps hard and quick, the tears streaming down her face.

Instinct moves Nick close and sends his arms around her. Stroking her back, Nick stays quiet for a few minutes, letting the girl weep without words.

'We'll find him,' he says eventually. 'I promise ... we'll find your brother.'

'How? I can't do it ... but I'll have to ... I can't wait, Nick.'

'It's okay, come on ... it's going to be okay ... I'll come with you. We'll go together.'

'But you said ...' she sniffs.

'I'll come with you,' Nick repeats. 'This is our way. That's what Mr Howie would say.'

'What?'

'Our way, this is our way of doing things,' he explains. 'You can't leave someone on their own like this.'

'You don't have to,' she regains some composure, her voice strengthening in resolve, but she doesn't move away. The warmth and contact from another person, from someone tall and strong with a soft voice and a calm manner, is needed too much to break away.

'I will,' he says firmly. 'I'm coming, and that's fucking that.'

'You do swear a lot,' she comments in a quiet voice.

'I know. Dave keeps telling me off for it. If it wasn't for Cookey fucking up all the time, I'd be making the brews for the rest of my life.'

'They sound nice, the people you keep talking about.'

'They are. They're the best,' Nick replies without shame or embarrassment.

'I'm so scared,' she admits. With her eyes screwed tightly closed, she presses against him, feeling the warmth of his body against hers. His voice is deep like a man, and he speaks so kindly to her that she is reluctant to move away from the safety of his arms.

'That's normal,' Nick strokes her back, the scent of her hair filling his nose as he feels an overwhelming sense of shame that someone like this has to experience all of this death and carnage. He and his team have been doing it since the first day, since it happened, and they've had each other to rely on and stick with. She only came out yesterday, and already her life has been ripped apart. 'Lilly, I promise you. I will do whatever it takes to find your brother. I promise.'

'Thank you,' she whispers.

'Come on, we'll do it now.'

'Don't you want to wait longer?' She steps back, looking up at the dark-haired young man with kindness pouring from his eyes.

'No, they'll be okay ...'

'You should leave a note,' she suggests quickly, 'leave a note and say where we're going.'

Panic grips Nick. To admit now that he can't write is a shame too far. Telling this woman he will do anything he can to save her brother only to admit now that he can't write. On his own, away from everyone, he could do it slowly, but not under pressure and no way in front of her. His mind can't think quick enough to ask her to do it.

'No, it'll be okay,' he stammers quietly. 'Er ... no ... they must have gone to the fort.'

'Sure?' she asks, confused at the change of his mind.

'Yeah, sure,' he berates himself internally for not just admitting it and asking her to do it. However, Nick, for all his strengths and presence, is but a young man full of a young man's pride, and Lilly is so beautiful that the admittance of such a thing cannot be expressed.

The blood red van starts moving away from the car park. With the streets so littered with bodies, they have no choice but to detour into a side street, away from the town and away from the car park.

Within minutes of their exit, another vehicle drives into the area from a different side road. Two young men sit within, driving slowly so they can scan the area before coming to rest near the car park.

CHAPTER TWENTY-NINE

'Nice choice,' Cookey comments.

'Stop going on about it.'

'Well ...'

'It's fine. Stop fucking whining,' Blowers groans.

'It's not fine. It is shit.'

'Does it matter?' Blowers asks for the umpteenth time.

'Well, duh!' Cookey says. He stares out the open passenger window, scanning the houses and area while Blowers slowly navigates down the street, back to the main road. 'Oh, nice one, brainache. We're back at the car park now.'

'Yes, because that is where I was going,' Blowers explains with forced patience, 'to see if the others have got back yet.'

'Fair enough,' Cookey holds his hands up. 'Still a shit car, though.'

'It doesn't fucking matter,' Blowers exclaims.

'We could have had that nice BMW ... It was only three doors up, but oh no ... You've got to get the fucking Fiesta, the shittiest heap of shit rust bucket fucking Fiesta in the entire fucking country. I mean, look ... it still has a fucking tape player ...'

'So? We're only using it for a bit.'

'A fucking tape player ... Who has a tape player in their car these days?'

'Fuck me,' Blowers groans.

'And they've got fucking tapes in here,' Cookey says as he opens the glove box. 'Look ... actual fucking music tapes.'

'Look out the window, not in the glove box.'

'I'm looking,' Cookey glances up and round before delving back into the music selection, 'Ha! Duran Duran. Get this ... Duran Duran.'

'Who are they?'

'Who are they, he says,' Cookey laughs, 'like he doesn't know.'

'I don't know.'

'Yeah, fuck off, you're like they're biggest fan.'

'What are they doing back here?'

'Who?'

'You'd know that if you were looking properly,' Blowers comments, checking his side mirror to see the car taken by Clarence and Lani driving up behind them. Cookey cranes back and forth, staring forward, then left and right before looking across with a puzzled glance.

'Behind us, you twat,' Blowers shakes his head, sighing again as Cookey twists round to wave at the car behind them

'What's up? Where's Lani?' Cookey shouts, climbing out to see Clarence already out and striding towards them.

'We got the boss and Dave. Lani's with them now. Any sign of Nick?'

'Really, where?' Cookey shouts.

'On the outskirts,' Clarence replies. 'Where the hell is he?'

'Nick? Probably asleep somewhere,' Blowers stares around, betraying the confidence of his voice.

'I bloody hope he is. He'll be making the brews for the next ten bloody years, though,' Clarence growls. 'Follow me.'

'What about Nick?' Cookey asks. 'He might come back here.'

Clarence stares at the ground around the car park with a look of distaste. Being back here is offensive, a hell hole that should be burnt to the ground. He glances up at the flames licking at the buildings in the High Street with narrowed, tired eyes. With luck, the fire will destroy everything and leave nothing here. Wipe it off the face of the planet and let nature reclaim it.

'Leave a note for him. Make it obvious,' he snaps before walking off, leaving a quiet Blowers and Cookey staring after him.

'He's not happy,' Cookey comments quietly.

'He must be knackered,' Blowers replies. Clarence gets back into the car and reverses. He goes too fast and slams the back of the vehicle into an old Renault before slamming his fists down on the steering wheel so hard the thing snaps off to disappear from view.

Both lads watch as the giant exits the car holding the steering wheel in his hands, a face flushed with anger as he stares at the object with pure venom. Titanic self-control exerts itself, and he just lets the plastic steering wheel fall from his hands.

'Get on with it,' he barks at the two lads, then turns to march to the nearest house. As he walks through the already broken front door, the lads glance at each other with looks of worry, neither of them knowing if they should be doing something.

A car in the street clunks audibly, the indicators flashing as the alarm is deactivated.

'Why are you still here?' Clarence asks, walking out the house towards the car he just unlocked.

'Going now ... Er ... you alright, Clarence?' Cookey calls out. He winces as the big man stops dead and slowly turns, his face a picture of anger mixed with worry and near exhaustion.

'Yeah,' Clarence sags on the spot, 'sorry ... I'm just fucked ... no excuses but er ...'

'Okay,' Cookey says. 'Just worried about you, that's all.'

'I'm okay,' Clarence nods, 'I shouldn't have snapped at you. The boss is safe with Dave. They've got some good news for once ... See you in a minute.'

'Clarence,' Blowers calls out, 'we don't know where to go, mate.'

Once again, he lifts a huge hand to rub his smooth head. The feeling of being out of control floods through him. He is a professional soldier, trained for combat and high-stress situations. Losing it now is not an option, but the exhaustion is starting to sap his mental functions.

'Come with us,' Cookey urges. 'We can get another car later.'

He nods, knowing the time is right to take help from those around him. A team is a team for a reason–they help each other through the hardest parts. Ditching the keys, he walks towards them with a small smile before coming to a sudden stop at the side of the car. Looking down, he takes in the tiny car before glaring up at Blowers.

'A Fiesta?'

'What?' Blowers rolls his eyes.

'I bloody told you, Blowers,' Cookey yells. Wrenching the passenger seat forward, he clambers into the back. 'And only three fucking doors too.'

'Stop moaning!' Blowers snaps.

Cookey holds his breath as Clarence tries to ease his bulk into the passenger seat, his enormous shoulders and wide back dwarfing the seat. As athletic and fit as he is, getting both legs inside, even with the seat pushed back develops into an ordeal that threatens to eclipse the snapping of the steering wheel a few moments ago.

'Get the other car,' Cookey shouts, but Blowers is already off, retrieving the keys from the floor where Clarence dropped them.

'Better?' Blowers asks. Five minutes later, Clarence is sprawled across the back seat of a much bigger car as he sticks a finger up at a grinning Cookey.

'A Fiesta,' Clarence mutters.

'That's what I said,' Cookey replies. 'Er ... has anyone got any note paper?'

'Fuck,' Blowers brings the car to a stop, gently resting his head on the steering wheel as he counts to ten.

'I'll get it,' Cookey jumps out, feeling the charge as two angry men start fuming quietly. Running into the first open house, he rummages through kitchen drawers before finding an old-style lined notepad and black pen. Pen and paper in hand, he moves quickly to the cupboards.

'Here, found these,' he hands out cans of warm, fizzy lemonade, 'only cheap supermarket stuff but ...'

'Nice one,' Blowers accepts it with a quick smile, 'thanks, mate.'

'Well done, Cookey,' Clarence takes the can, patting the young lad on the shoulder with his hand.

With the two grumpy bears busy drinking to replenish their blood sugar, the trio move off while Cookey scribbles a note. Changing his mind, he rips the first attempt from the note pad before starting again. Nick struggles to read, so writing small won't help. Instead, he writes big and clear, using capital letters.

EVERYONE OKAY. STAY HERE. WILL KEEP CHECKING. IF WE DON'T FIND YOU, GO HOME. COOKEY.

'Nice and simple,' he muses, reading it back quietly. Plus no one else will know what it means in case some meandering zombie with the ability to read comes tottering along. Nick will know what "home" means. The fort is their home now.

With the other two out to keep watch, Cookey runs around the area trying to find somewhere to put the notice, deciding in the end to use the doors to the stairwell.

'So what's this news?' Cookey asks, back in the car as they drive through the quiet side streets.

'I'll let the boss tell you,' Clarence replies with a smile, 'but there is something else you should know.' Sitting upright, he relates the events at the fort during the night and then this morning's event with the Saxon breaking down. He finishes by telling them they found Howie and Dave chasing a little girl. The lads listen quietly, nodding as they absorb all the information.

'So why are Mr Howie and Dave all the way out here?' Cookey asks.

'Don't you listen?' Blowers snaps. 'They're going after that girl. Clarence just said.'

'Oh right,' Cookey nods, 'ha, yeah, got it now.'

'Bloody hell, Cookey,' Clarence sighs.

'What! Sorry.'

'Never mind, mate,' Clarence mutters. 'Is this heat ever going to stop?'

'Getting worse by the day,' Blowers comments.

'It can't keep getting hotter, can it?' Cookey stares up at the clear sky. 'I know it gets hot here sometimes but not like this.'

'Fuck knows,' Blowers replies. 'We won't be able to keep going if it does. We're struggling enough as it is now.'

'Down there,' Clarence points. 'Keep going, then left at the bottom.'

'Got it,' Blowers turns the wheel. 'So the fort is fucked, the Saxon is fucked, we're going to be chasing some little kid in this heat, and Nick is fast asleep somewhere.'

'Pretty much,' Clarence says. 'We hope Nick is asleep anyway.'

'Either that or he's blowing something up or setting fire to something,' Cookey laughs. 'Wish I could do what he does. Shit, that didn't make any sense,' Cookey laughs at himself. 'I mean I wish I could understand electrical shit like he does.'

'I think we understood you the first time,' Clarence chuckles. 'The lad's got a gift, though.'

'What gifts have we got then?' Cookey asks Blowers. 'I know what yours is,' he smirks.

'Don't tell me,' Blowers grins. 'Something to do with bumming zombies?'

'Ha! How did you know? You must be telepathy too.'

'Telepathic, you thick twat. So what's your gift?'

'Me?' Cookey asks. 'I make you laugh,' he grins.

'Do you fuck!' Blowers laughs.

'See, you're laughing now.'

'At you. I'm laughing at you, not with you.'

'Same difference,' Cookey shrugs.

'There,' Clarence calls out, 'Lani and Howie ... See?'

'Got it,' Blowers glides the car down the street, grinning while Cookey waves out the window at Lani and Howie turning round.

'Morning!' Howie grins. 'Where the bloody hell have you two been?'

'Morning,' Cookey yells, running forward to greet Howie. 'What happened? Where did you go? Clarence said you had good news?'

'Easy, mate,' Howie laughs. 'Blowers, you alright, mate?'

'Boss,' Blowers nods seriously, but a huge grin stretches across his face, 'good to see you again.'

'You too, mate, both of you,' Howie grins back. 'You up to speed, then?' He looks at Clarence for confirmation.

'Saxon, fort, girl, and Nick,' Clarence says curtly, 'but not the other thing. Thought I'd leave that for you.'

'What other thing?' Cookey asks excitedly. 'What? What is it?'

Howie smiles and looks at them both, their faces eager as they wait for some good news for once. Pausing for effect, he nonchalantly pushes a hand through his hair.

'Oh for god's sake,' Lani sighs, 'stop messing about.'

'I'm immune,' Howie blurts. He grins as their jaws go slack.

'What the fuck?' Blowers mumbles in shock. 'How?'

'Lost her again,' walking out into the street, Dave nods casually at Blowers and Cookey. 'You two alright?'

'Fine, Dave,' Blowers replies. A temporary distraction comes bounding over as Meredith greets the lads.

'Again?' Howie groans. 'How?'

'Over the fences,' Dave shrugs. 'Couldn't figure out which way she went.'

'What about the dog?' Lani asks.

'She took a crap on the grass instead,' Dave explains.

'Sorry,' Cookey says loudly, 'immune?'

'Yeah,' Howie grins, then launches into the story of the previous evening all the way through to waking up this morning to watch Dave slaughtering the entire remains of the horde.

'Fuck,' Cookey grimaces, 'in your mouth?'

'Yes, mate.'

'A whole heart?'

'I think so,' Howie replies.

'Really?' he grimaces again.

'Still beating too.'

'No way,' Cookey exclaims, 'a beating heart? Urgh, that's so gross.'

'Slightly,' Howie accepts.

'What did it taste like?'

'Cookey!' Blowers snaps.

'What? I never met anyone who ate a heart before.'

'I didn't eat it,' Howie says.

'What happened to it, then?'

'I took it out,' Dave cuts in.

'Was it a whole heart?' Cookey probes for the gory details.

'It was,' Dave replies.

'Ah,' Cookey spits, but unable to help himself, he asks again, 'what did it taste like?'

'I don't know,' Howie shrugs. 'It was hot and rubbery and ...'

'Urgh, no, stop!' Cookey shouts. 'No, don't stop ... Was blood coming out?'

'It was still beating,' Howie explains, 'pumping blood into my throat.'

'Ah, no ... don't ...' Cookey steps back in horror. 'Shit. Did you drink it?'

'Either that or drown, mate.'

'Worst thing,' Lani says in a matter-of-fact voice, 'he kissed me when he saw me earlier.'

'You didn't!?' Cookey recoils. 'Oh, that's awful ... Could you taste it too?'

'No,' Lani scoffs.

'Did you brush your teeth?' Cookey asks. 'Was there like bits of goo in–?'

'Stop it,' Blowers shouts, 'fucking disgusting.'

'Hang on,' Cookey shakes his head. 'So you're both immune ...'

'And I bit a finger off,' Howie adds, enjoying the gory story and watching the lads' faces.

'Clean off?' Blowers stares in horror.

'Think so,' Howie nods, 'and popped an eye, so the juices went in my mouth.'

'Shit, Howie,' Lani glares at him, 'it's not something to boast about.'

'Wait, wait,' Cookey shakes his head again, trying to snap his own attention away from morbid curiosity, 'so if you're both immune, then ... well, how did that happen? Is it when you snogged at the fort?'

'How does everyone know about that?' Howie asks.

'Does that mean we've got to snog you?' Cookey asks, taking another step away, 'Blowers might like it but ...'

'Fuck off,' Blowers snaps.

'I'm not snogging any of you,' Howie points out.

'What about Lani?' Cookey grins with a mischievous glint in his eye. 'Will Mr Howie beat us all up if–'

'In your dreams, Cookey,' Lani laughs.

'Can we get this girl?' Dave cuts in seriously.

'We don't know anything more now than we did before.' Howie nods at Dave before continuing quickly, 'I could have passed on immunity, or Lani could have ... or we could both be resistant or carriers or ...' He shrugs, 'We just don't know.'

'You can't pass immunity for something by kissing,' Blowers says. 'That's not possible, is it?'

'I've never heard of it,' Howie nods, 'so we don't know anything.'

'Are we all immune?' Cookey asks.

'No idea,' Howie replies. 'Not the sort of thing we can find out really.'

'Maybe we can't catch zombie,' Cookey says to himself more than anything. 'That would be cool ... Oh fuck!'

'What?' Howie asks as an angry look crosses Cookey's face.

'April,' the lad groans. 'Fucking hell! I could have been immune, and she was right there ...'

'Don't be a twat,' Blowers snorts.

'Oh, April,' Cookey sighs ruefully, 'the love of my life ... What could have been between us ...'

'Yeah, twenty seconds of grunting probably,' Blowers laughs.

'Stop,' Lani warns. 'I do not wish to be reminded of that night, thank you.'

'Oh shit, yeah, Marcy,' Cookey says quickly as the rest groan at him mentioning her name.

'Little girl?' Dave prompts.

'Yes,' Howie seizes on the distraction, noting the glare now being offered by Lani. 'Any news on Nick?' he asks.

Shaking his head, Cookey explains about the note as an uncomfortable silence descends.

'We get this done and head back, then,' Howie says firmly. 'Nick's switched on. He'll be alright.'

'He's a hard lad,' Clarence offers in his deep voice. 'He can fight alright.'

CHAPTER THIRTY

'I've never heard of it,' Nick says. 'Chapsworth House? Nah, no idea.'

'Then we need to find a guidebook,' Lilly replies, 'or a map or ... I was about to say a computer so we can access the internet.'

'I wish,' Nick remarks. Leaning forward, he looks down at Todd fast asleep in the middle of the double passenger seat. 'Maybe you should sleep too.'

'Not yet,' she says quickly. 'I couldn't sleep anyway. Listen, Nick, thank you for doing this.'

'Don't worry,' he says, 'we'll get your brother and go to the fort but just ...' he pauses.

'But what?'

'Fucking hell, listen, if there's like loads of people there with guns and stuff, we might have to go to the fort first and get the others.'

'But ...'

'We'll see, okay?' he says. 'I'm just saying that we don't want to bundle into something we can't handle.'

'Okay,' she replies quietly, with a worried frown.

'I know he's your brother, but we've got Todd with us and ...'

'I get it,' she nods. 'I do.'

Nick stops himself from glancing over at her again. The way the sunlight was behind her reflects from her hair and casts a golden glow on her skin. Amidst the horror, he can't help himself from admiring the natural beauty of the woman. It is an organic reaction and one which cannot be resisted despite the circumstances. Lilly is terrified yet determined to do the right thing and do it as fast as possible.

'Were you in the army, then?' she breaks his train of thought, and the expression of interest in his life, as casual as the question is, makes his face flush once again.

'Yeah, sort of,' he replies, 'we were on our first weekend when it started.'

'Oh,' Lilly nods, 'so you didn't get to do all the training and, er, things, then?'

'No,' he replies.

'But what you did back there, shooting those men so quickly even though I was attacking you ... How did you know how to do that? Why didn't you shoot me?'

Nick snorts with a humourless laugh, 'That's Dave.' He shakes his head and smiles wryly, 'Target perception is probably what he'd call it.'

'Wow, sounds good,' she smiles, noticing the way he keeps blushing and trying to keep the conversation going casually.

'No offence, but I didn't really see you as a threat,' Nick explains. 'You didn't have a weapon, and the punches were good, but you were just like fucking smacking them down all over the place. The other blokes were the dangerous ones, especially the one with the limp.'

'Okay,' Lilly adjusts position, 'what should I have done then?'

'What do you mean?'

'When I attacked you, what should I have done?' she repeats. 'Say the same thing happens again?'

'Well, for a start, don't go attacking some bloke with a fucking gun ... shit ... sorry ...I am trying not to swear.'

'It's okay,' she laughs gently.

'But if you do have no other choice, then, well, I guess you do what we do, you have an explosion of force but direct it.'

'You mean the punches, yes?'

'Punches, kicks, slaps, gouging ... Remember you are a woman, so that means you got less strength than a bloke, so don't just punch, go for the eyes, the ears ... shit, go for his nuts if you can.'

'Nuts?' she laughs, a pleasant sound that fills the van.

'Sorry,' Nick smiles slowly,' I meant his private bits.'

'I know!'

'Okay, yeah, don't just try punching but go for whatever you can see. If you got a knife, then stab and stab and don't stop until he's dead. Same with the zombies, if you have to fight them then go for it ... don't be holding back.'

'Have you killed many of them?'

'Thousands,' Nick replies. 'Between us, I mean, not just me ... Probably tens of thousands, maybe more,' he shrugs.

'All with guns?'

'Fuck, I wish it was,' Nick laughs. 'No, half of 'em were with bloody axes and whatever else we could find.'

'Oh my,' Lilly stares in surprise, 'with your hands?'

'Yeah,' Nick half grins and grimaces at the only too recent memories.

'Do you just go round, killing them?' Lilly asks, genuinely interested.

'Not quite,' Nick explains, 'we got the fort after getting out of London and sort of decided to try and set it up as a safe place. Then they all came to the fort ...'

'Sorry, who did?' Lilly leans forward, staring at him with keen interest. Glancing over, he catches sight of those deep blue eyes staring at him, and for a second, he becomes flustered again, trying to change gear where no gear change is needed.

'What was that?' Lilly asks as the van jolts from being pushed into fourth when fifth was perfectly okay as it was.

'Oh, nothing,' Nick covers it up, pushing the clutch down a few times and wiggling the gear stick, 'just seemed a bit sticky ... the gear stick ...'

'Sticky stick,' Lilly observes, making the poor lad blush even more. Laughing at the sight, she looks away and leans closer to the open window. Men are so funny, the way they either try and boast about everything and show off or get like this, all tongue-tied and flustered.

Something about the lad makes her smile. Very good-looking, tall and dark, with lean, hard muscles and that shy grin that hides how very capable he is. The quickness of his reactions, the shots he took when she was hitting him. He could have battered her aside with ease and just apologised later, but he didn't, he took the blows to save them all.

A feeling of guilt rushes through her that she's even thinking about Nick like that at a time like this. Billy is god knows where, with strangers that could be doing awful things, and here she is, thinking like this.

'Gift shop,' she announces, startling Nick into snapping his head round.

'Eh?'

'We need a gift shop or something like that, for a map or guidebook,' she explains with perfect pronunciation, her voice strong and cultured.

'Okay,' Nick replies, 'a fucking gift shop it is.' Wincing at himself for not being able to stop swearing, he focusses on driving. *Stop fucking swearing,* he thinks, *you sound like a twat.*

Shame hits him, shame that he can't read or write and now can't stop swearing for more than a few minutes. This poor woman, lost in this wasteland of horror, trying to rescue her brother, and all she gets is an uneducated, thick idiot who swears all the time.

'What?' he asks, aware she was speaking but so absorbed in self-depreciation that he missed the actual words.

'I said how can we find one?' Lilly says and watches whilst a confused look etches onto his face. 'A gift shop?'

'Gift shop, oh, right, yes ... A gift shop ... er ... not back there, that's for sure. Everything is on fire so ... er ... maybe the next village or town probably.'

'Wow,' she smiles.

'What?'

'You said a whole sentence without swearing.'

'Ha, sorry,' he grins, 'do you want me to say it again with some curse words?'

'Curse words?' she laughs. 'I haven't heard that for years.'

'My nan always called them curse words,' Nick says.

'Did you like her?'

'My nan? Yeah, loads,' Nick nods. 'She pretty much raised me on her own.'

'Oh, what about your parents? Were they working?'

'Working? My parents? No way, getting pissed more like, oh, and watching Jeremy Kyle.'

'That's sad,' Lilly frowns, 'but it's good you had your nan.'

'Yeah, yeah, it was. She died a few years ago.'

'Oh, that's awful.'

'At the time but now,' he motions out the window, 'I don't know. Maybe she is better off now all this has happened.'

'Well, I am sorry Nick,' she says politely.

'Thanks,' Nick glances across. The way she speaks is so nice, all the letters being pronounced properly like someone off the telly when they read the news. 'What about you?'

'Me?' Lilly asks. 'Er, I lived with my mum and dad, and Billy of course. Dad ... well, he, er ...'

'Shit! I'm sorry, Lilly, I just don't fucking think sometimes.'

'No, don't be silly,' she says quickly. 'Er, well, my mother worked in a care home. She was working when it happened, and she just never came home.'

'Fuck,' Nick groans sadly, 'that's awful.'

'Yeah, it was. Dad went to pieces. He just couldn't cope without her. We stayed there for ages, well, until yesterday actually, but I kept going on, saying we should leave and find somewhere else. I nagged and went on and now look what happened.'

'You didn't know that,' Nick interrupts. 'None of us know what will happen.'

'I know,' she whispers.

'How did you escape last night?'

'I didn't escape,' she says quickly with a change in tone that Nick picks up on instantly.

'Oh,' he says when she doesn't elaborate, 'okay.'

'We met this other family,' Lilly says in a low tone. 'Norman and his two children. Sam, the girl I said about previously, and of course Todd. We found a forest, and Norman said we should stay there the night to stay out of sight. Norman and I took the first watch while everyone else slept ...'

'You don't have to explain,' Nick says at hearing the pain in her voice.

'No, it's okay,' she says more for herself. 'Norman said he heard something and went off into the forest and then called me. He said he could see lights in the distance like a town or something like that.'

'Okay,' Nick listens intently.

'But he couldn't see any lights. There were no lights. He just wanted to get me on my own, away from the others.'

'What?'

'He started touching me and ...'

'Fucking prick,' Nick explodes, fighting the urge to speak louder for fear of waking Todd.

'He was ...'

'It's okay,' Nick says, 'you don't have to say.'

'Oh, nothing happened,' she continues. 'He was saying that I wanted him, and he could see it. He had his hands all over me,' she shudders at the memory, 'then we heard screaming, and he took off, running through the forest until he burst back into the camp. I tripped and fell down and just stayed there ... watching it all happen.'

'Jesus,' Nick shakes his head, 'that is fucking terrible. Dirty fucking wanker.' He grips the steering wheel harder at the thought of some dirty pervert groping the terrified girl in the woods.

'Yes,' Lilly says primly, 'he was a dirty fucking wanker.'

An instant reaction, and Nick laughs, a sudden sound that fills the van and earns a reproving look from Lilly.

'Sorry,' he drops his head to stop laughing, 'just the way you said it.'

'What?'

'The way you said dirty fucking wanker,' he laughs again. 'I never heard anyone say it like that before.'

'Like what?'

'You know, all nice and posh like that, *you dirty fucking wanker,*' Nick puts on his poshest voice, mimicking the girl.

'I do not sound like that,' she snaps but with obvious humour and very glad of the change of subject.

'You do,' Nick grins.

'Really?' she asks, biting her bottom lip. 'Should I stop it, then?'

'What? Speaking like that? No ... why should you?'

'You know, so I sound tougher and, well, not so posh and soft.'

'What you gonna talk like instead, then?' he laughs.

'I don't know,' she replies in the prim voice. 'I hadn't thought that far ahead when I suggested it.'

'Go on, then,' he prompts.

'What, now?' she asks in mock horror.

'Yeah, give it your best shot.'

'Well, what shall I say?'

Nick laughs again, a pleasant sound that makes her grin broadly. '*Well, I say, dear, whatever shall I say?*' Nick mimics.

'Stop that,' Lilly gives him a stern glance, 'we shall have no ribbing here, thank you.'

'Okay, sorry,' he says with a forced apologetic tone.

'Right, you ready? Ere, wot' all this, then?' she says in a

deep voice, causing Nick to burst out laughing again, which wakes Todd up.

'Sorry,' Nick laughs, 'that was brilliant.'

'Ssshhh,' Lilly strokes Todd's head, 'you sleep now. Are you thirsty? No? Okay, try and sleep.'

'Sorry,' Nick says quietly, 'my fault.'

'It's okay,' Lilly replies. 'I take it my attempt wasn't very good, then?'

'No,' Nick says bluntly but with a smile, 'bloody awful if I'm honest.'

'Really?' she asks lightly. 'That bad?'

'You sounded like a copper from the old movies.'

'I was trying for those gangster movies, er ... Snitch?'

'Snatch?'

'Yes, Snatch, I was trying for that.'

'Didn't work,' he chortles.

'Then I shall practise,' she smiles, 'but quietly in my head.'

'Village,' Nick nods ahead, spotting the rows of houses breaking up the rolling countryside. 'Might be a shop we can check.'

The humour dies off, but the good nature remains as they both peer ahead, scanning the rows of buildings for the ubiquitous village stores.

When they see it, their hopes dwindle at the sight of the smashed-in windows and signs of looting. Bloodstains on the ground, and a rotting corpse lying half out of the door. Nick holds the van way back, sitting quietly with the engine off and the windows down, listening intently. Lilly notices the change in him straight away, the easy grin replaced with a hard look as he stares round at the scene.

'Nick.' She blanches slightly at the hand he holds up, a clear indication for silence and done without a glance at her. The minutes tick silently by as she waits patiently. The engine cooling, and Todd's deep breaths the only noise.

'Okay,' Nick nods, 'sorry, what's up?'

'I was just going to say I can go look,' she whispers.

'No, stay here and keep watch,' he orders with a natural air of authority, 'use the step so you can get a bit of height and watch all directions. If you see anything, just shout, and I'll come running, ok?'

She nods quickly, 'Do I hold the pistol now or ...?'

Smiling, he nods, 'Yeah, I would. I'll be in and out.' He slides out the door and pulls the long-barrelled shotgun out, once more checking the barrels are loaded before walking quickly towards the shop.

Glancing back, he nods at Lilly standing on the passenger step with pistol in hand, carefully looking around. He glances down at the corpse but has no way of knowing if the body was human or infected, seeing as the skull has been smashed completely in. Looks old, though, so he steps forward, gently easing into the store before pausing to listen again. His eyes move quickly over the emptied shelves, to the counter at the end and the cigarette display. The sight reminds him he hasn't smoked for a while. It didn't feel right lighting up with Todd in the van.

All quiet, so he creeps to the magazine rack, scanning the covers for anything that might look like a guidebook. He thinks of the word, spelling the letters out in his head. G-U-I-D-E.

It's okay now with no one watching him. He knows Lilly is waiting, but at least she's not watching, so he can afford a few minutes. Most of the magazines are still here, brightly-coloured glossy covers showing smiling women and men that all looked tanned, fit, and healthy. Some actors and celebrities too that he recognises from movies. A jarring feeling kicks in at the sight of Paco Maguire on the front of one cover. The big, white smile and his arms folded to show his bulging muscles. Remembering the night they fought together, Nick smiles sadly and feels a sudden overwhelming sense of loss.

Taking the magazine was a natural reaction, something to remember the man and show the others when they get back together. Exhaling deeply, he returns to scanning the shelves until finding a stack of local maps. He smiles at the memory of Cookey and Blowers taking the piss in the back of the Saxon when he was trying to read the directions out.

Grabbing a load of them, he quickly walks the aisle, checking for any food or drink left over. Everything stripped and gone. Behind the counter, he peers down to the floor, grinning at finding several packets of cigarettes gone unnoticed. Lighters too. Maybe Mr Howie will finally take his own instead of asking him all the time.

Lilly visibly relaxes at the sight of him coming out of the shop, smiling with genuine warmth as he clambers into the van to dump the cigarette packets, magazine, and maps on the floor.

'Here,' he hands her several maps. 'Mind if I have a quick smoke?' he asks politely.

'You don't have to ask me,' she replies with a smile.

'I guess you don't smoke?' he ventures.

'No, but you carry on,' she says, flicking through the map covers to see the selection.

Breathing a sigh of relief at not being required to read the maps in front of her, he jumps back out and lights up, inhaling the smoke deep before blowing it out and checking all sides.

With Lilly absorbed in the maps, he smokes quietly and finds himself as equally absorbed in watching her. Long strands of blonde hair hang down from her forehead, slender fingers flick through the pages, and her face expresses what she thinks. A slight puzzled frown crosses it now as she deciphers and works out each geographical area, followed by a quick nod when she finds the right one. She makes funny shapes with her mouth too, pushing her bottom lip out then sucking it back in. The loose strands of hair get pushed back, only to fall back down a few seconds later.

Lilly senses being watched and glances up, catching Nick staring at her with a look of rapture on his face. He balks and turns away, quickly sucking on his cigarette and making a meal out of checking each direction.

'Chapsworth House,' she muses audibly, trying to put him at ease, 'do you think that could be a stately home?'

'Fuck knows ... I mean, I don't know,' Nick corrects himself.

'English Heritage site maybe?'

'I, er ... I don't know, sorry,' Nick replies.

'Nothing here,' she says, reading through the index of places of interest. 'Maybe another map,' she talks more to herself, picking up the other maps to scan-read the indexes, running a finger down the columns.

'Chapsworth Park,' she says quickly. 'What do these numbers mean, Nick?'

'Which ones? Er ... they mean the page number and the er ... here,' taking the map from her, he reads the numbers, thanking god that his problem with words doesn't extend to digits. Finding the right page, he flicks back to check the numbers before working along the boxes. 'Walk before you climb,' he says quietly.

'Pardon?'

'It means you go along the bottom first when you read

the number from the map, like this, see,' he shows her the number along the bottom of the page before finding the corresponding value for going up the page, 'then you go up ... See, like climbing, and that's the box ...'

'Can you see Chapsworth House there?' she asks, trying to peer at the map. Nick stares down at the tiny words as they suddenly start swimming across the page.

'Er, here, you have a look,' he pushes the map back quickly before stepping back out into the blazing sun.

'Got it,' she exclaims. 'Right here, see?' she holds her finger over a big, green splodge with what looks like a building in the middle and some words printed in black, words that Nick cannot read.

'Great,' he grins. He might not be able to read, but he can view a map and work out what the colours mean. The shades of green and the swirly lines represent the gradient of the land. 'Open flat land,' he mutters, 'big too. Look at all this green area. What's that?' He holds his finger over a lighter shaded section within the green.

'Let me see,' she pushes her head so close next to his that he can smell her hair and feel the warmth coming from her. 'Golf course,' she smiles up at him. 'See, it says there,' she points at the small, black printed words.'

'Oh yeah,' Nick says, long practised at covering his inability up, 'sorry, didn't see it.'

'That's okay,' she manoeuvres closer to view the map. 'Golf course,' she says again, holding her finger over the word. 'Main house,' she points to a square section with more small words.

'What's that say?' Nick squints at the page.

'Er ... copse, Chapsworth Copse. See the little tree symbols?'

'Yeah, course,' Nick grins quickly while nodding.

'Do you need glasses, Nick?' she asks softly.

'No,' he replies, dropping his head quickly to avoid eye contact. His tone also drops, which Lilly detects in an instant.

'What's wrong?' she asks with concern. Nick bites down the urge to lie and make something up. This is all too important to try and avoid it. What if something happens that needs him to read words. Shit, he can't even read the words on the map.

'I can't read,' he blurts out, and despite the embarrassed blush, he lifts his head to stare directly at her. 'I'm dyslexic, really fucking dyslexic ... sorry.'

She stares at him, reading the signs of his intense discomfort on his face. Refusing to yield to the shame, he holds her gaze with a mixture of defiance and apology.

'It doesn't matter,' she smiles slowly. 'I can't shoot a gun,' she adds, 'or sound very tough, but you can, and I can read.'

'It does matter,' Nick softens his stare, looking down at the map. 'I didn't want to say anything but ... well, something might fucking happen that, you know, means I've got to read or something, and I can't do it ... Well, I can on my own but not when someone else is watching me ...'

'Hey, it's okay,' she reassures him with genuine warmth. 'Honestly, Nick, I can read anything that needs ... er ... reading?' She pulls a face as her own sentence becomes convoluted.

'Don't blush,' she adds, seeing the red tinge burning in his cheeks. Reaching out, she rests her hand on his forearm, squeezing gently. 'Honestly, Nick, it doesn't matter.'

'Thanks,' he mumbles, looking down again.

'Do your friends know?' she asks with the hand still on his forearm.

'Yeah,' he nods. 'They take the piss all the time,' he grins, showing there's no offence.

'Well, then,' she grins, 'think of me like that.'

'Yeah right,' he laughs. 'You look a lot fucking better than Cookey and Blowers,' the words come out faster than the control gate in his head can slam down. His mouth drops open in a comical expression as she laughs in delight. 'Shit, Lilly, I didn't mean to be a perv or anything.'

'Thank you for the compliment,' she says graciously.

'Well, yeah ... er ... so I can't read any of these little fucking words on here. They're like those things the Egyptians used.'

'Hieroglyphics.'

'Yeah, them. It's just all weird shit that swims about ... If I'm alone and I picture the word first, then try and recognise it, I can do it, but ...'

'But you can read the map signs, yes? You know what all these lines and things mean?'

'Yeah, they're easy. These ones are the gradient of the land, the closer they are, the bigger the fucking hill.'

'The bigger the fucking hill,' she repeats seriously. 'Got it.'

'The roads are easy, and these ones are footpaths, and those other things that horses go on.'

'Bridleways.'

'Yeah, them.'

'So between us, we can find it easy,' she proclaims. 'Team work.'

'I guess,' he laughs.

'So stop worrying, and let's go. Is there anything else I should know?'

'What like?' he asks, climbing into the driver's seat.

'I don't know ... Are you blind or deaf, maybe have a false leg?'

'No,' he laughs, 'none of those. Just reading and writing, that makes me useless enough.'

Watching him and the way he speaks, she can tell he isn't fishing for compliments. The man, as amazing as he is, is genuinely lacking from self-confidence and esteem. How hard it must have been to survive in a modern world without being able to read or write. That would pretty much rule out the internet, even text messages, probably. But then, so far he hasn't shown any shock at anything that's happened, and Lilly feels nothing but genuine gratitude for meeting him.

Feeling like a weight has just been lifted, Nick drives the van, amazed at how naturally she accepted what he said. There was no hesitation either, no pause as she tried to cover the sneer or stifle the laugh like so many girls had done before.

With Todd fast asleep, Lilly reads the map, directing Nick through the leafy country lanes, towards Chapsworth House.

CHAPTER THIRTY-ONE

'There,' Blowers shouts, 'straight ahead. She's running into that house on the left.'

'On her,' Cookey sprints away.

'Dave, pass the house and get into the gardens, cut her off. Lani, likewise, this side. Clarence, stay in the street and be ready if she comes back out.'

'Got it,' Lani sprints hard, turning quickly to get down a garden path before bouncing off the locked front door with a yelp. She vaults the low fence and goes into the next one along.

Dave goes up the road, away from us, heading past the house Blowers saw her going into, and easily overtakes a running Cookey giving it his best shot. Clarence jogs towards the last location she was seen in to stand ready in the street. Meredith leaps about, barking while running between everyone, obviously detecting no threats, so seeing this as a great game of let's all run about like idiots in the blistering heat.

We've got her this time, though. Dave sails past the house, followed by Blowers and Cookey reaching the front gate. I hold back to see which one Dave goes for and watch him vault the wall with ease and disappear into a door a few houses up.

'Milly,' I shout, 'come on now ... No more playing ... You have to come out now.' I sprint into the back garden to find Blowers and Cookey running round to check all corners with exasperated looks on their faces.

'Over the fence,' I shout clearly.

'Which one?' Lani's voice drifts over. I stare at Blowers, hoping he can answer, but the lad just shakes his head.

'No idea,' I shout back.

'I'll get upstairs and look out the windows.' Cookey runs back inside.

'Did you hear anything?'

'No, boss,' Blowers shrugs. 'She's fucking quick.'

'Isn't she?' I reply.

'You see anything?' Blowers shouts up at Cookey opening an upstairs window. The grinning lad leans out, checking left and right, waving at Lani and Dave.

'Nothing,' he calls out. 'Oh shit! There ...'

'Where?' I spin round as though expecting to see her pop up.

'Over the back,' he shouts, 'going into the house over the back.

'THE BACK,' I bellow as Blowers and I make a run for the rear fence.

'CLARENCE ... THE BACK ...' Dave roars.

'ON IT,' Clarence's deep tones reach us easily.

'Where's the dog?' I shout.

'With me,' Lani yells back. Reaching the back fence, we leap at the same time, which is stupid as our combined weight just about obliterates the thin panel.

'What was that?' Lani shouts.

'Blowers and Mr Howie need to lose weight,' Cookey shouts, running past us with a grin.

'Wanker,' Blowers growls. Getting quickly to our feet, we run to catch up with Cookey.

We aim for the side of the house and the open garden gate left swinging from the girl. Gasping for breath and sweating buckets, we burst through and into the front garden. All of us, me and the two lads, Dave and Lani all emerge into the street at the same time, albeit several houses apart. She outfoxed every single one of us.

Watching the other female of the pack, she pants hard from the exertion of running and jumping fences. Her strong heart beats fast, and her lungs work quickly. This is a great game. Spotting the other pack members further down the road, she bounds to greet them, yelping with glee that everyone is running together.

There is someone else here. A little one that is running away from the pack. She doesn't sense hunger or threat from the pack to the little one, but nor does she detect fear from the little one either. So it must be a game. A game of chasing the little one, just like she used to do with her old pack.

Her ears are sharper, her nose much stronger, so putting these to use, she snuffles along the ground until she picks up the track. The scent is strong, a female little one that smells of human waste, and the track hovers above the ground like a different colour, an almost tangible thing that can be sorted separately from the other background smells.

The pack leader makes loud noise, but the track is strong and wills her on. Nose to the ground, she weaves the route taken. Over the hard surface and through this gap towards an old pack den. Another pack lived here but not now. Into the old den, and the track is strong, through the rooms and into the rear with the soft surface under her feet.

Snaking the route, she heads straight across the grass, to the rear fence. The little one has learnt to go over obstacles. With a running leap, she uses her paws to drive her off the top of the fence and land easily in the next garden.

Noise ahead, a noise that sends a feeling of happiness through her body. A familiar noise the little one from her old pack used to make. The noise he made when he was happy.

Nose down and tail wagging, she runs across the soft grass, down the side of the house, and out into the street. With a yelp, she opens her stride. The scent is no longer needed as the little one comes into view running down the street.

Bounding up next to her, Meredith yelps and wags her tail. The little one makes noise and stops to stroke her.

She likes the touch from the little one and can sense her happy energy. The little one is covered in dirt. Dirt like this is bad, so she tries to remove it, using her rough tongue on the girl's face and hands which makes the little one do the happy noise again.

The pack leader shouts from nearby, so she makes noise back, telling him to come this way. The little one makes the happy sound and starts running again.

She stays with the little one, running alongside her, but this time the little one doesn't go into any of the old dens but keeps running down the street.

This game is great fun, so she makes noise, telling the pack where she is so they can chase them.

The hard surface ends as the little one climbs over to get onto the open soft ground the other side. She spins round, making noise. This isn't a good place to hide, they will see us too easily here, but the little one carries on anyway.

Springing over the obstacle, she once again lands with ease on the soft surface and runs alongside the little one. Her long tongue hanging out as she watches the little one show her teeth and make noise.

Already checking the route ahead, and she can see the high thing, too high for either of them to climb. The game must end now as the pack will find them easy. Maybe another one from the pack will run and hide?

The pack leader makes loud noise from behind them. He sounds angry. Something is wrong. She turns to see the rest of the pack running towards her, all of them making loud noise like they do when there is a threat.

Spinning round, she checks the area. Nothing here, no threats. Confused at the noise being made, she checks again. There, on the air, a faint smell.

It is a scent unknown to her, a familiar animal scent, but this is stronger and much more potent.

'MILLY, NO,' I scream as she runs towards the high chain-link fence. Dave breaks away, running as fast as he can, legs and arms almost blurring as he opens his stride fully. Lani is only just behind him, and the rest all stretched out, every single one of us screaming at the tops of our voices for the girl to stop before she hits the fence. The electrified signs are clear as day even from this distance, and no way of knowing if the power is off.

Behind the fence, thick bushes obscure whatever lies beyond. Meredith is watching us, and I will her to have the intelligence to grab hold of that girl, but that is asking too much, even from her.

I think we all gasp as the girl jumps to start climbing, a tiny tot going hand over hand as she climbs with the dexterity of a monkey, scaling the fence like it was made of rope. Thankfully, she doesn't burst into flames or go flying thirty feet into the air in a shower of sparks.

She must be superhuman, running all that distance and now going over a fence that has to be at least six metres high.

It took us a little while to figure out which direction she went after getting through the next row of houses and into the street. It was only Dave hearing Meredith barking in the field that got us in the right direction.

Sweat is pouring from me, my legs feel like lead, and my lungs want to burst apart, but if nothing else, I'm still going. If I tried to do all this two weeks ago, I would have collapsed in a crying heap. Even now I know there is a bit of final speed and power left, that hidden reserve that is only ever to be used in the event of a dire emergency, such as a little girl about to jump onto an electrified fence.

Milly scales the fence and with ease starts down the other side, the little sod actually pausing when she drops to the ground to wave at us before legging it out of sight, into the bushes.

A few seconds later, and Dave hits the fence with a running jump, his deft movements have him reaching the top in a matter of seconds. Lani is pretty much the same, the two athletic bodies scaling the structure with ease.

Us four? Well, we get there alright, then stop to get our breath just as the other two drop down the other side.

'You alright?' Lani asks at seeing us huffing and puffing with bright red faces.

'Fine,' I just about manage to squeak. 'Get her ...' I wave them on needlessly, seeing as Dave has already started forcing a path through the bushes.

'No way,' Clarence looks up at the fence with his huge chest heaving up and down, 'not happening ...'

'Get ...' I try and speak, but my lungs demand more air. 'Get a car and ram it,' I finally manage to gasp.

'We don't know what's on the other side,' Cookey says through ragged breathing.

'Who cares,' I shrug. 'He'll never get over it,' I nod at Clarence. The fence is strong and high, but the chain link is tight together. There is no way he will get his hands through the gaps enough to pull his heavy frame up, and his feet are too big to gain purchase in the loops too.

'Fuck, gotta run back now,' Clarence groans. 'Come on,' he calls the dog after him before turning to start jogging off.

'Up we go,' I leap for the fence, slide down, and start again from the ground. The lads join me, all three of us grunting and swearing in pain from the thin wire digging into our fingers. Several minutes later, we're dropping down the other side, clutching our sore hands and swearing even more. Our axes, thrown over before we started climbing, lie nearby in wait to be taken up.

'You got any water?' Blowers asks.

'No, mate,' shaking my head, I know what he means. The heat is fucking horrible, and despite taking water on several times this morning, I am already gasping for more.

'Dave?' I call out as we head for the bushes and start pushing our way through. 'Oi, Dave?'

Still no response, so we push harder until we break through the bushes. We see the ground falling away in a long, gentle slope to a wide vista of open land dotted with clusters of bushes, trees, and small lakes. The sight is beautiful, lush and just eye-wateringly gorgeous. What's more, it seems to stretch on without a break into the distance.

'Jesus,' Cookey gapes at the view.

'There,' Blowers points off to the right at the little figure still running along. Dave and Lani now not too far behind her. We set off at a steady jog, knowing they'll catch her easily enough now the ground is open and flat.

Watching ahead, I can see both Lani and Dave look like they're holding back a little, as though waiting for the girl to get tired and slow down instead of just catching her outright. That, I guess, will be Lani's thinking so they don't scare her too much.

'This is amazing,' Cookey stares about at the view. 'Must be some rich fucker's garden. Why's he electrified the fence, though?'

'Stop us rough types getting in probably,' I reply. The heat is unbearable. Out here, in this flat, open land, it feels even hotter, with absolutely no breeze.

'She just doesn't stop,' Blowers groans as we watch the girl happily running along with the occasional casual glance over her shoulder. She does start to slow down, almost as though she knows the game is finished and there is nowhere to go.

With the distance between her, Dave and Lani diminishing, we all start to relax a little. Then she stops and simply waits for the other two to reach her.

Lani quickly takes the girl's hand to stop her running off again and bends down to talk to her while Dave stands nearby, watching closely and ready to react if she bursts off.

By the time we get there, we are wilting from the running and the oppressive heat. We are three red-faced, gasping blokes practically falling down to rest.

'Milly?' I ask with a glance from the girl to Lani.

'Yes,' Lani nods, 'this is Milly. Say hello, Milly.'

'Hello, Milly!' the girl laughs happily. 'Can we play again now?'

'No!!!' we all shout. Well, the three of us do while Dave and Lani just stand there, looking stupidly fit.

'Hello, Milly,' I grin while shaking my head, 'Good god, you can run.'

'I like running,' she announces to us all proudly, 'and I like climbing, and I like chocolate, and I like ponies, and I like ...'

She goes on, describing all the things she likes, chattering away happily while holding Lani's hand. The rest of us don't get a word in as she talks with no discernible break for breath. Her hair is matted with filth, thick strands all stuck together, and a firm layer of grime on her skin, especially round her mouth, with various layers of chocolate and god knows what else. I'm guessing we all smell pretty bad, but my god, she pongs to high heaven. Body odour, faeces, and stale urine, her bright summer dress is filthy too, and her bare legs are almost black from being unwashed.

'Hi, Milly,' Cookey grins and holds a hand out, 'nice to meet you.'

'Hello! What's your name? My name is Milly,' she beams, staring at the hand as though wondering what to do with it. 'My mummy said I shouldn't talk to strangers. Are you strangers? Where's the doggy?'

'I'm Cookey,' Cookey grins but does drop his hand. 'And this is Blowers,' he points at Blowers while Milly laughs.

'That's funny,' she giggles, ''Blowers ...'

'And that is Mr Howie,' he nods at me.

'Hello, Milly, you've led us on a merry dance, haven't you?'

'I like dancing,' she grins a toothy smile. 'And I like jumping,' she adds. 'Why are you called Mr Howie?'

'Er, I ...'

'Because he's in charge,' Cookey explains, 'like a teacher.'

'I like teachers,' Milly announces. 'Do you like teachers, Lani?' Milly looks up at Lani. We all look at Lani who just shrugs.

'I already told her my name, and yes, Milly, I do like teachers.'

'Dave?'

'Yes, Milly?'

'Do you like dancing?'

'No.'

'Do you like ponies?'

'No.'

'Do you like running?'

'Yes.'

'I like running. Can we run now?'

'No.'

Shaking our heads in stunned amazement, we watch the girl chatter away with no hesitation. The confidence just pours from her.

'Can we pet the doggy now? I'm hungry,' she adds with a serious glance that implies we should be giving her food right now at this very second.

'Come on,' standing up straight, I nod to head back the way we came. 'Have you, er ... said anything to her yet?' I ask Lani.

'Not had a chance,' she shakes her head. 'She hasn't stopped talking.'

'And we can have some cake and biscuits and read

comics, and then we can play hide and seek again ... It's Dave's turn to hide now.'

'Why Dave?' Cookey asks.

'Because he catched me, silly billy,' she laughs, 'and if you catch Dave, then you can hide, and if Lani catches you, then she can hide, and if I catch Lani, then I can hide, and if Mr Howie catches me, then ...'

'Got it,' Cookey laughs.

'Milly?' I ask, interrupting her mid-flow. 'How long have you been alone for?'

'Um ... some days,' she says quickly. 'Mummy and Daddy went out, and I waited at home, and they didn't come back, so I ate the chocolate and the crisps and the sweets, and they didn't come back, so I went to next door to see Carol, but she wasn't there, so I ate her chocolate and her crisps ... I know where Carol keeps her chocolate and crisps, and I can show later when we go to my house and then ...'

'Whoa, Milly, slow down,' I laugh. 'Have you seen anyone since your mummy and daddy left?'

'I played chase and hide and seek with the strangers, but they didn't do talking. They make funny noises,' she laughs, 'like daddy did one day when he fell over.'

'Did they catch you?' Lani asks lightly as we all listen intently.

'No!' Milly laughs. 'They were slow and silly, silly, silly,' she sings the last few words.

'Christ,' Blowers mutters, staring down at the happy girl.

'Silly, silly, silly billy,' Milly sings. 'What's that?' she points to the pistol on Lani's belt.

'That's my gun,' Lani replies.

'What does it do?'

'It shoots the ... er ...' she looks round at us all for help.

'It shoots bad people,' Dave says flatly.

'Bad people?' Milly thinks for a second. 'Are the strangers bad people? I don't like them ... They don't talk, and they don't play, and they look horrible, and they keep getting cuts, but they don't put plasters on, and Mummy said you should put a plaster on if you cut yourself.'

'That's right,' Lani says.

'What's that?' She points to Lani's meat cleaver now held in the other hand. 'Mr Howie has a gun, and Dave has a gun, and Cookey has a gun and ... Blowers, do you have a gun?'

'Yes, it's here,' Blowers pulls it out to show her.

'Can I shoot the bad people with the gun?'

'No,' Blowers says, quickly putting the gun away.

'You're good at remembering names,' Cookey says with a grin.

'I am, I am, I am,' Milly sings.

'Shit!' Blowers snaps.

'You said a rude word,' Milly laughs with delight. 'Mr Howie will tell you off.'

'Oh shit ...' Blowers spins round as we all stop to look up. 'Big fence ...' he mutters, 'big electric fence.'

'What?' Cookey asks.

'Keeps them in,' he hisses.

'Keeps what in?' Lani asks as we turn round, staring at the view.

'There,' Blowers points to a cluster of trees away to the right.

'Behind too,' Dave reports.

'What?' I ask, unable to see anything other than trees and bushes.

'Oh,' Lani whispers.

'What!?' I ask again. Staring in the same direction as Lani, I watch a cluster of trees. Something moves, then something else moves. Then they start moving away from the trees, towards us. They break free from cover and stroll out into the open. It's a sight so familiar from television but not something I have ever seen with my own eyes in real life.

'Five that side and four behind,' Dave announces. 'The big male is behind.'

Turning round slowly, I spot the four others behind us. The big male is easily distinguishable from his size and shape.

'Lions ... fucking lions ...' I mutter in shock. 'We're in a safari park ... in a bloody safari park ...'

'Oh, Lani, Mr Howie said a rude word too,' Milly gasps. 'Who tells Mr Howie off?'

'I do,' Lani replies in a distracted voice. 'Don't say rude words, Mr Howie.'

'Sorry,' I reply, turning to look at the five coming from the right, then back to the four behind us.

'Probably not had any food for two weeks,' Cookey decides to share his thoughts with us, 'so they'll be hungry ... really hungry ...'

'Thanks, mate,' Blowers mutters.

'Dave?'

'Yes, Mr Howie?'

'Any experience with lions?'

'Pistols shots will just annoy then unless you get a clean shot to the heart,' he replies.

'That's good to know. You reckon you can get the hearts?'

'No, I don't know where the heart is.'

'In the middle?' Cookey half-says and half-asks.

'Where in the middle?' Dave asks.

'What about the head?' Lani asks.

'Their skulls are very thick,' Dave replies. 'Might be okay up close ... but that will mean being very close.'

'Right,' I say quietly, 'this all going swimmingly then. The Saxon is broken down, the fort has got some new people taking it over, we've lost Nick, and after having a human zombie heart shoved in my mouth, we're now in a safari park with a pack of hungry lions.'

'Pride,' Dave says.

'Dave, we have pride, mate. I'm just saying what our current situation is.'

'Pride of lions, not pack, Mr Howie.'

'Oh, right ... yeah, got it ...'

'I wanna see the lions,' Milly says. 'Pick me up,' she tugs at Lani's wrist.

'Here,' Cookey bends down to lift her high.

'HELLO, LIONS!' she waves, calling out in a high-pitched singsong voice.

'Get her down!'

'Sorry, boss.' Cookey lowers the girl to the ground.

'Milly, you have to be quiet now,' Lani urges.

'They're moving slowly.' I watch the two groups slowly stroll towards us in no apparent hurry. 'They're probably used to people, must have seen them every day.'

'Yeah, when they're being fed,' Lani states. 'They might associate us with food.'

'Do we move or stay still?' Blowers asks, his pistol out and being held ready.

'Move slowly and don't make any noise,' I whisper. We start moving slowly back the way we came, slow steps one after the other as we stay huddled together, with Milly in the middle.

The fence now looks much further away than it did a second ago, much, much further away. With the lions advancing from all sides, it's our only viable escape route.

'They're coming but very slowly,' Lani whispers. The two prides keep the same pace, seemingly intent on tracking us from a distance but with no effort to move in.

'They're flanking,' Dave states as one lioness breaks away from the group to move off to the side.

'Same at the back,' Lani whispers. 'It's the lionesses that do the hunting, isn't it?'

'I think so,' I reply, trying to remember watching the documentaries.

'Typical,' she sighs, 'always the women doing the work.'

'Can we stroke the lions?' Milly asks.

'No,' Lani replies. 'Milly, you have to be really quiet now.'

'Why, Lani?'

'Er ... because we're playing a new game,' she whispers. 'We are only allowed to whisper until we get back to the fence ... Do you think you can play that game?'

'Yes,' Milly whispers, 'I like whispering. Dave, do you like whispering?'

'Yes,' Dave whispers.

'Cookey, do you like whispering?'

'I do, Milly.'

'Blowers, do you like whispering?'

'Yes.'

'What about Mr Howie?' Lani asks when she doesn't ask me.

'Teachers don't play games,' Milly whispers. 'Teachers watch and say the rules, and they have a whistle, and they write things on the board.'

'Mr Howie likes playing games,' Lani whispers. 'Is it okay if he plays with us?'

'Okay, Mr Howie, do you want to play with us?'

'Yes, Milly, thank you.'

'You are only allowed to whisper until we find the fence, Mr Howie.'

'Okay, Milly.'

'This seems to be working,' Lani says. 'They're not coming in any faster.'

'Flanking, though,' Dave reports.

'Just keep going like this and stay together. We look bigger together,' I whisper, thinking about how herds of zebra and other prey animals stay as one.

The progress is painfully, achingly slow. Shuffling along with whispered voices, we gradually cross the open land back towards the slope. The lions stretch out into lines that gradually surround us. Other than that, they don't speed up or try and move in, and they are walking upright too which gives me a sense of confidence as I thought they normally went into a crouch when they were hunting.

'We might just make this,' I whisper softly as the distance between us and them stays the same.

'Where's Clarence?' Lani asks quickly. 'Didn't he get over the fence?'

'Clarence!' I groan at the same time as Blowers takes a sharp intake of breath and Cookey swears.

'What?' Lani asks. 'Where is he?'

'He's, er ... about to ram that fence down with a car,' I offer meekly.

'What?' Lani hisses. 'Why would he do that?'

'Er ... cos I told him ...'

'Why?' she groans softly. 'Why would you tell him to ram the fence down on a safari park?'

'We didn't know it was a safari park,' I protest.

'What did you think it was?'

'I don't know! Did you know it was a safari park?'

'No, but I figured a big fence would be used to keep something safe inside.'

'Stop whisper-shouting at me!'

'I'm not whisper-shouting,' she whisper-shouts.

'They're moving in,' Dave cuts in. The lions pick their pace up, only by a fraction, but enough for us all to spot the change.

Then we hear the engine. The otherwise silent environment is gradually interrupted by the loud roar of a powerful vehicle coming towards us.

'Shit,' Cookey whines, 'what do we do?'

'Nothing we can do, mate' I reply, listening to the roaring getting closer. He must have chosen something big and heavy to get that fence down.

A horrific, metallic wrenching noise rolls around the open ground. The impact sends the lions scattering off a few meters. They drop low, then burst apart before coming to a standstill and watching nervously as the bloody great big four-wheel drive comes slamming through the bushes.

'Fight or flight,' Lani says.

'Yeah, but which one?' Cookey asks.

Born into captivity, the pride is used to seeing humans, but with high fences surrounding their territory, the vast grounds and the structure implemented by the expertise of the safari staff meant the actual contact from human to animal was minimised in every possible way. The tours through the grounds were strictly controlled, with staff on hand to prevent any of the drivers or their passengers from opening windows to call out, shout, or make any noise other than simply driving through.

Music from car stereos was forbidden, and repeated requests made for mobile phones to be switched to silent.

Feeding was done by careful means of establishing where the pride was located before depositing the food in another location, thereby encouraging the animals to scour for it rather than become lazy and dependant on the humans coming to them with food.

The owners of the safari park had also established another form of revenue that assisted with the incredible expense of keeping such a large pride of big cats. Arrangements were made with scientific study groups and filmmakers that the pride could be used for observation and filming. Both groups were often intent on studying or capturing footage of the cats when they hunted and caught their prey. At key times, when the park was closed to customers, live prey was released into the grounds. Sometimes this would be a single sheep or goat, other times larger numbers were released to follow the reactions of captivity bred lions that had become used to eating freshly killed carcasses provided for them.

The results were highly interesting and established that whilst the entire pride was captivity bred, they still retained an ability to track, hunt, and kill as well as wild lions could. The hierarchy within the pride proved to be the same as those in their natural habitats, so essentially, the cats hunted the same as they did in the wild. They separated and used multi-positioning flanking movement to ensure the prey was surrounded before the strike was done.

To a certain extent, the hunting was carried out by the lionesses within the pride. With fourteen days passing since any food was provided, the entire pride was becoming hungry. A natural impulse which sent a chemical reaction through them not entirely dissimilar to the infected. Feed, you must feed.

King was aptly named. King of the pride and the star attraction for the safari park. He dominated the vast grounds and controlled his territory with extreme aggression. There were other males within the pride, but they were kept firmly in check. King was the alpha, the leader. This was his pack, and King knew his pride were hungry. His own hunger was gnawing away at his stomach, but the lack of nutrition had done nothing to diminish the solidly packed muscle on the animal.

Legs like tree trunks, and paws the size of dinner plates. Shoulders rippling with muscle and a thick mane that served to accentuate his size. A beast of mythical proportions with a voice that matched his size.

The movement was noted as soon as it took place. The cats have the ability to intrinsically know their environment, and the noise and movement of the humans had been spotted instantly.

Without breeze or wind, it took longer for the scent of the humans to reach them. Humans were not part of their known food group, and if not for the smells that drifted on the super-heated currents of air, they may well have just watched with docile interest.

These humans, however, had been fighting and gone from battle to battle solidly for days. Their clothing was stained with the blood of the infected, a strong, pungent smell that carried far and was easily detected. That tang of blood drew the pride into formation. As one, they started moving in, interested and watchful at first. Strangers on the grounds. Humans normally stayed well away and watched from afar, but these humans carried the smell of blood. Blood meant meat; meat meant food. Food was everything.

That hunger prompted King to move with the pride. He was going to feast and be the first to do so. This was his territory and his pride, so this was his food. He would take this prey down.

'That definitely ain't flight,' Cookey comments at seeing the group of lions moving in towards us.

'Radiator's fucked,' shouts Blowers. Turning round, I can see the steam hissing from the front end as the four-wheel drive bounces down the slope, the rear wheels scoring plumes of dust into the air that hangs behind it like a dirty cloud.

An almighty roar comes from behind as the big male lion starts the charge. His mouth open as he bellows, clearly telling the other lions we are his dinnertime snack.

'Oh fuck ... oh fuck ...' Cookey mutters louder and louder as Milly giggles in delight at all the swear words being said around her.

'IN,' Clarence bellows out the window, slewing to a stop in a cloud of dust. We burst towards the vehicle, wrenching doors open. Blowers scoops Milly off her feet, who laughs with absolute pleasure. Launching her onto the back seat, he gets in, scrunching along as Cookey climbs in the other side. I go for the front passenger seat as Dave and Lani squeeze into the back, and Clarence is already putting his foot down as the doors are closing.

The lion launches at the side of the moving vehicle, still going slow and yet to pick speed up. The impact jolts the vehicle with a thunderous crash, rocking us on the already over-worked suspension.

'Go. Fucking go!' Blowers yells.

'I'm trying,' Clarence shouts back. The lions move in, one of them landing on the bonnet and swiping at the windscreen. Clarence jerks the wheel hard, veering to the right, and the lioness loses her grip and slides off.

'Radiator's gone,' Clarence informs us needlessly as he tries to peer through the hissing steam pluming out the front.

'Just keep going,' I mutter.

Suddenly, I dive to the right as the big lion takes another go at the side. The energy from him drives one huge front leg through the window, shattering it instantly as it stretches inside. Meredith reacts instantly, lunging from the back to sink her teeth into the paw. The lion roars with pain. Trying to move with the vehicle, it drops down, limping on the bleeding leg, while Meredith scrambles to get out the broken window. Grabbing a fistful of fur round her neck, I just about stop her going out, screaming for her to get back in the vehicle while she barks and snarls.

She hates the things. They tried to hurt her little one, so they have to die. They killed the man that was her pack, and they try to hurt this pack. Killing the things is a necessity and one that is done for protection.

Cats, though? Cats can fuck off. She hates cats. She hates the way they leave their scent everywhere and how offensive the stench is to her nose. The things she kills for necessity, but cats are done for blind, psychotic rage, an instinct buried deep that all cats have to be killed. Regardless of anything else, all cats must die.

These are big, but they smell like cats. They are cats. Big, nasty cats that want to fight. The urge to kill them takes over as she scrambles to get out the window. Getting her teeth into that big, meaty leg was good, but now she wants more. The pack leader is shouting for her to stop, but he doesn't know just how much she hates cats.

She really hates cats.

Cats must die.

'Fucking hell,' I scream out, trying to pull the dog back inside. 'Help!' yelping out, I see hands stretching over from the back to grab at her coat, tail and legs as we desperately try to pull her back in.

Another lion runs at the passenger window, or the gap where the bloody window was a few seconds ago. Meredith surges forward, fighting like crazy to attack it. The cat launches up with a wide, snarling mouth full of horrendously big teeth. Meredith is there, head out and savaging as she bites and gnashes. The sheer ferocity of her attack sends the cat dropping back as Clarence veers to the side again.

'What's got into her?' Clarence glances over with a pained look. The constant veering has plunged us into a swirling dustbowl that cuts our vision down and clouds the passenger window. 'Can't see a fucking thing,' he bellows.

'Keep going ... just keep moving ... MEREDITH, STOP IT!' I wrench her back with all my strength, but she fights on, digging her paws into my legs and side as she tries to wrestle free. Blowers dives in between the gap of the front seats, his hands stretching out to grab and hold as we become tangled in legs, tails, and bodies all wriggling and shouting.

With Blowers on top of me and the others leaning forward to try and help, I catch a glimpse through the entwined mess to see Milly bouncing up and down on the back seat, clapping her hands and laughing with pure delight.

'Shit!' Clarence shouts, having got a glimpse through the dust to see that we are heading further into the grounds and away from the slope.

'You said a bad word,' Meredith laughs. 'Everyone says bad words. Shit ... shit ... shit ...' she screams out, half-laughing at the same time.

'Milly, stop swearing,' I shout through the melee and the barking dog, 'and everyone else, stop bloody swearing too!'

'Mr Howie said a bad word,' Milly laughs.

'Wait till she meets Nick,' Blowers mutters through gritted teeth, somehow managing to get his arms wrapped over Meredith's backside and interlocking his hands under her stomach. She pays no heed, no heed whatsoever to so many hands holding her back. She could easily turn and start biting us, but thankfully, she remains fixated on the lions still charging in.

Smashing glass comes at the same time as a huge impact at the rear of the vehicle, showering Milly in the small, glittering fragments. Blowers and Cookey, both leaning forward to grab Meredith, scream as the dog twists from our grip to launch and clamber over the back seat to get at the lioness sticking her head through the rear window.

Bedlam. Complete and utter bedlam ensues as we all end up going with Meredith. She does the job and once more fends the cat off with a double row of big canine teeth that sink into a foot before resuming her efforts to get out the back window.

Six adults, one child, and a bloody great big dog crammed into a four-wheel drive that is now clunking and clanging with unhealthy noises. Not only that, but those bodies within said vehicle are clambering, screaming, and fighting to prevent the bloody great big dog from getting out.

'Where are we?' I yell out, unable to see anything, half jammed through the gap in the seats and mostly buried under everyone else's bodies.

'In a safari park,' Cookey shouts, still able to get a quip in despite the circumstances.

'I don't know,' Clarence muffled voice comes from the front. 'I'm looking for a fence or a way out.'

'INCOMING,' Dave dives on top of Milly as another impact from the driver's side rocks the vehicle. Claws dig into metal panels, filling the air with a sound like nails on a blackboard. Another impact from the back, then another from the passenger side. Meredith spins as she catches fleeting glimpses of big cats lunging through the choking dust.

'I need a poo!' Milly announces. 'Can we stop, please?'

'Not now,' Clarence bellows.

'Who are you?' Milly asks with a tone that suggests she should know everyone.

'Clarence,' Clarence shouts as I get the full impact of Meredith into my stomach as she spins to attack another window.

'My name is Milly,' Milly says happily. 'I like lions and cats and elephants and ...'

'Shit!' Clarence roars, and I feel the vehicle lurch violently to the side, followed by a massive impact to the passenger door.

'You alright?' Lani's face appears next to mine, except she's upside down, or maybe I'm upside down. One of us is upside down anyway.

'Fine, you?' I reply casually while trying to keep my hands on the leg I am gripping and being constantly battered by the crazed dog's tail.

'Yeah, you know,' Lani smiles, 'keeping busy.'

'Oh, that's good,' I grunt. 'Better to be busy.'

'ATTACK FROM THE REAR,' Dave's voice fills the confined space. Lani disappears, whipped away by Meredith deciding she is now going to try for the back window again, which means we all go with her.

'This place is huge,' Clarence informs us amidst the carnage of the rear section. 'And we're losing power,' he adds.

'Losing power?' I yelp. 'Find a way out then!'

'Yeah trying,' he remarks.

'Milly, go up front with Clarence,' Lani shouts. 'She's gonna get squashed in the back here ... axes and knives everywhere.'

'Milly, come up here,' Clarence calls out, followed swiftly by a small, shoe-clad foot squashing my face as she steps on me.

'I want to drive,' she settles on his lap, safely nestled between the side impact bars of his gorilla-like arms.

'Maybe later. Look for a fence.'

'Cookey, get your arse off my face,' I yell.

'That's my arse, Mr Howie,' Blowers shouts.

'Not surprised,' Cookey laughs as Meredith goes back to the front passenger window.

'FENCE!' Clarence shouts. 'BRACE!'

'On what? With what?' I scream out, but it's too late. The barking is drowned out by the front end colliding with something big and metallic, which I can only guess is another big chain-link fence.

'ANOTHER ONE!' Clarence bellows above the noise of twisting metal and groaning car panels. The sound comes back again, shuddering and jolting the vehicle violently, shaking us all over the place as he punches through.

It seems to go on for hours, a constant scream of metal being warped and torn apart. Then, suddenly, it's all over, and the vehicle coasts along quietly.

'Have we stopped?' I shout out, getting the eerie sensation of no longer being in motion.

'Yep,' Clarence answers clearly.

'Oh ... why?'

'Do lions like gorillas?' Clarence asks.

'Don't ... don't say it ...'

'Yeah ... about that,' he says drily.

Fighting through the limbs and bodies, I manage to pull myself through the gap and into the backseat, shaking my head before peering up over the back seat. The trail of destruction behind us is immense–two big chain-link fences torn apart, with the twisted remains poking up all over the place.

The lions have stopped on their side, clearly wary of passing over the metallic panels that lie blocking the route. They must be aware of the fence being electrified, and even now, with the power off, they still hold well back.

'Time to go,' I announce. 'Keep hold of the dog, someone.'

'I got her,' Blowers replies. The doors, impacted by the charging lions, have to be forced open from the warping of the frame as we clamber out, nursing bruised appendages. Clarence holds Milly in one arm and looks very at home in the gorilla enclosure. Stick a black fur coat on him, and he'd blend right in.

Meredith's eyes stay fixed on the trail behind us, as though daring that pride of cats to try and come after us.

We retrieve our axes from the car and set off, moving quickly away from the vehicle before the lions decide to try and get through. However, hunger is a powerful motivator, and within minutes, the lions are edging closer to the gaping hole.

Scurrying on, we stay together, advancing into lusher green pastures with long grass and sturdy trees covered in ropes with tyres attached.

Over another crest, and we start dropping down and out of sight of the fence line. A large, old-fashioned wooden shack lies nestled in the grounds, looking like something from a fairy tale. Cresting the apex, the gorillas are immediately obvious, clustered in a large group of about a dozen primates. They range in size from tiny tots, no bigger than Milly, to their very own Clarence, except their Clarence makes our Clarence look like scrawny teenager.

The male silverback is huge, with shoulders that seem to stretch away from an enormous, broad head and arms like a steroid-pumped wrestler. His chest is just staggering, so powerful, so strong, and he doesn't flinch at the sight of us rushing towards them.

There is no threat to him. He could snap any of us in half and use our limbs as toothpicks if he so desired. Even the sound of the fence crashing down doesn't seem to have perturbed them. Sitting in small groups close together, several are well into a grooming session, rummaging through their thick, black fur to find mites and bugs to eat.

They look as we approach, but that's it. We hold no greater interest to them than a small crowd walking down an average High Street on a Saturday afternoon, and I guess they are used to close human contact from living in this sanctuary for so long.

Even Meredith goes quiet. Nose down and sniffing the ground, she keeps glancing up to view the animals warily but fortunately doesn't growl or show her teeth.

'They relatives of yours, Clarence?' Cookey whispers.

'I knew one of you would say it,' he grumbles, still holding an enraptured Milly staring at the gorillas. 'This one needs a bath,' he adds, turning his head away from the small girl.

Slowing down, we take it easy and keep to furthest edge of the clearing. No one speaks other than very low whispers, and we keep our eye contact to a minimum.

However, going along with our current trend of everything fucking up, the big silverback slowly rises to his feet, showing us just how bloody enormous he really is, easily standing the same height as Clarence at well over six feet.

'He's got to be thirty stone,' Clarence mutters, 'easily ... Look at him!'

'Why is he getting up?' Lani whispers. The other gorillas start moving back away from us, some low noises sounding out. The way the females scoop the young up to hold close is so similar to human behaviour, it's staggering.

'Not us,' Dave says in a low voice and a glance behind. Turning slowly, I catch sight of the big alpha male lion standing proud on the crest of the hill. Squat and with the lush meadow rolling away beneath him, he looks every inch the king of all he purveys.

'Fuck,' Cookey mutters, 'fucking stand-off between a silverback and a lion ... No way ... no fucking way ...'

'Mr Howie, Cookey said rude words again ... you said–'

'Yes, I know, Milly. Cookey, don't keep swearing.'

'Sorry, sorry, Milly,' Cookey whispers. 'Who would win?'

'What, these two? The lion, easily,' Blowers replies.

'No way,' Clarence says. 'A silverback will beat a lion.'

'Get off, would it,' I scoff. 'A lion is made to kill. Look at it ...'

'Yeah, they're about the same weight,' Clarence whispers urgently, 'but the silverback has something like ten times the strength of a human male, and his arms are over two metres long.'

'What, each?' Cookey asks.

'No, you twat, the arm span,' Blowers hisses.

'Oh ... I'm with, Clarence. That gorilla would tear it apart,' Cookey says.

Still shuffling along, we keep tightly together, glancing back and forth between the gorilla and the lion. Neither of them move, but the lion has clearly breached the gorilla's territory. The lion, however, must be bloody hungry because, despite the size of the primate, he isn't moving away.

The gorilla moves forward, a clear sign of advancement to protect his pack. The lion looks down with an almost scornful look, and I can imagine the rest of his pride gathered behind him.

'Lani? What do you reckon?' Cookey asks.

'I don't care,' Lani hisses. 'I'm not getting drawn into another stupid conversation in the middle of another life-threatening situation. Can we just be quiet and get out of here in one piece.'

'Okay,' Cookey whispers. 'Dave? What do you think?' he asks, moving straight on as Lani rolls her eyes with frustration.

'First, we have to understand the skills and advantages

of each combatant,' Dave speaks in his flat tone. 'They both weight about thirty stone each, so weight is equalled out. The lion has enormous explosive strength to propel it forward for attack, whereas the gorilla has incredible static strength and could tear the lion apart with ease.'

'Told you,' Clarence cuts in.

'But,' Dave cuts in himself, 'the lion is designed to attack and fight. That's pretty much all it knows, so it has the advantage of aggression and experience.'

'Ha!' Blowers whispers in triumph. 'The lion wins.'

'Having said that,' Dave continues as we keep shuffling on down the side of the clearing, 'the gorilla effectively has four hands and incredibly dense muscle and bone. The lion would need to get a good grip and avoid being beaten by those arms if it stands any chance of winning.'

Seconds pass while we wait for him to continue. Only he doesn't. He just tails off into normal Dave silence.

'So?' I prompt him.

'So what?' he asks.

'Who would win?'

'I don't know,' he replies to a low chorus of groans from the lads.

'If you had to choose?' I press him.

'Why would I have to choose?' he asks.

'Say someone put a gun to your head and said pick one.'

'I'd kill him,' Dave answers promptly, which takes me back to that bloody conversation we had about the glass of water.

'Does it really matter?' Lani seethes. 'Can we just get out of here, please?'

'We are,' I protest. We watch in complete fascination as the lion starts a slow walk down the hill. The gorilla darts forward while making loud noises, then stands upright to wave its arms about. The other gorillas start yelping in high-pitched barks and yelps. The tension ramps up within seconds as the lion slowly ambles down the slope and shows no signs of being intimidated.

'We should run,' Lani whispers. 'Run now.'

'No,' Dave responds, 'don't draw attention, just keep moving slowly.'

'Is the monkey gonna play with the lion?' Milly asks in a voice that is far, far too loud, immediately getting shushed by every one of us.

'It's not a monkey. It's an ape,' Dave says once the shushes have ceased.

'Dave,' Lani warns, 'don't start them off again.'

'What's the difference, then?' Cookey asks to a low groan from Lani.

'Not sure,' Dave replies. 'The tail, I think ... Monkeys have tails, I think.'

Panic ripples through the gorillas, screaming and yelping in fear and fright at the sight of the big cat stalking towards them.

The silverback stands his ground, slamming his huge fists onto the ground while roaring and jumping about. The message is abundantly clear, but still the lion comes on. Step after casual step, head held steady, and eyes fixed on the big primate.

The silverback charges in and stops again, a threatening motion designed to send the predator scurrying off. Only the lion doesn't scurry off but keeps coming.

The action is obvious. The lion is hungry and wants food. He has his own pride to take care off. The silverback is the protector of his group, so the end result is predestined. A pause between them. The lion goes stock still. The gorilla the same. For a second, it looks like that might be it, but one of them must twitch or make a movement as they both suddenly charge, running at each other flat out.

The sight is indescribable, the two biggest animals I have ever seen about to attack each other. The lion leaps with predictability, but that's only from having watched so many documentaries. The gorilla, I guess, hasn't spent much time in front of the Discovery channel and maybe isn't aware of the lion's basic attack method.

He chooses to meet the attack full-on, with head down and shoulders ready to slam the beast back. The collision is a dull thud of solid meat hitting solid meat.

They go at it. Snarling, twisting fangs that lunge while paws swipe and lash out. The gorilla moves with incredible speed, beating those huge arms down again and again. Evenly matched, and neither has the advantage. The lion feints and comes in again. The gorilla presses the attack home, driving its arms into the beast's flanks with thuds we can hear from this distance.

The lion shows no reaction but rears up on hind legs with the front paws slashing down to rake the front of the gorilla. They break away to circle and snarl. Blood is clearly visible on the gorilla's chest from the deadly claws of the big cat. Bang, they go again. Both lunging at the same time to meet with a force that would see even the biggest men be killed outright.

Both take a beating. The lion must suffer broken ribs from the blows rained down, and how the hell its spine doesn't snap from the power of the gorilla's fists is beyond me. The lion uses those huge teeth with jaws extended to bite and savage, claws raking again and again. Blood sprays out as the rage and pain between them builds.

Still shuffling, I become aware of just how insignificant we really are. These creatures would spend their entire lives living peacefully in accordance with the rules laid down by nature. Neither wants to fight and neither does it for pleasure.

The lion needs to eat. The gorilla needs to defend his group. That's it. It is humbling and awe-inspiring at the same time. Our species would do anything to wipe each other out, wars, famine, disease, and violence every day, but here, right here, there is the true savagery of nature at all its grittiest best.

If we ceased to be right now, if we simply lay down to die and all our species did the same, life would just keep going. Gorillas would sit and groom each other. Lions would lie in the shade and sleep between meals.

These generations of animals will die, but their species will continue, and the newborns would never know of the race that once dominated this planet.

Entranced and unable to stop watching, we view the most awful of battles taking place. Lion against gorilla, and they are so evenly matched that the end is just un-knowable. The gorilla's strength is his greatest asset, and when he co-ordinates, he dominates the lion with ease, throwing him away like a disused tissue.

The lion is ferocious beyond compare, attacking again and again with ceaseless violence and a thirst for blood greater than the infected. The sounds are terrible, rendering all of us speechless, and I, for one, can feel a tear falling down my face from the majesty of the creatures fighting. Something about being attacked by the lions and the peaceful nature of the gorilla has me clearly on his side, willing the primate to be victorious.

Blood is spilt, flesh is torn, and bones are broken, but still they refuse to yield. The explosive energy expended again and again now takes its toll as both animals move slower, both of them breathing so hard but still lunging again and again. They will never yield. There is no option. Both of their groups depend on them to do this. Their very survival hinges on one of them winning.

With a move that makes me gasp, the lion launches with a roar that rolls over the ground. The gorilla is too slow to react. The lion sinks teeth into the gorilla's face, and they both go down. The lion has grip and refuses to let go. The gorilla beats and beats against the lion with bone-snapping power. Both of them sink, the strength waning as they cling to each other in the final throes. The lion just refuses to relinquish the bite. The gorilla screams, but still he fights until his thick arms loop over the lion's back and squeeze as the gorilla pushes up to stand upright.

Still the lion clings on, hanging from the gorilla's face by the power in its jaws. Blood sprays from the wounds, but the gorilla squeezes harder and harder, driving the lion's magnificent chest inwards.

Bones are crushed, lungs are restricted, and the lion cannot draw breath, but my god, that animal will never let go. Upright, they dance round in a movement that gets slower with every step. Sinking down, the gorilla gives one final hefty pull, snapping the spine of the animal with a strength unknown in nature.

The lion is killed outright and pushed away as his jaws finally unclamp. With a heave, the gorilla pushes it off, but the damage is done. The creature's face is ruined, eyes gone and punctured with wounds down to the bone. Blood pours out as it sucks in air in a desperate fight to stay alive.

Without realising it, we're all rooted to the spot. No longer shuffling or trying to get away, but witnesses to something that has probably never been seen before and probably never will be again. Tears stream down my face, and

I'm not the only one. All of us are choked at the sight. Even Clarence stares with misted eyes at the utter heartbreaking sadness of watching two magnificent beasts destroy each other.

'Gorilla, then,' Dave nods, the only one of us with a dry eye. Even Milly has turned to sink her head into Clarence's neck, but not Dave. The cold bastard watched the whole thing with professional disinterest, and for the most fleeting of seconds, I hate his coldness, and I hate him for the lack of compassion he has.

'We go now,' he prompts us all. I have to look away, simply unable to look back to watch the gorilla die. The rest of the pride will probably move in now, and the same thing will happen again as the females go at each other.

We don't shuffle now but start moving faster and faster. A brisk walk that builds to a jog as we run through the enclose, searching for an exit. In silence, in oppressive silence, and oppressive heat, we run and get away.

CHAPTER THIRTY-TWO

The van rolls to a gradual stop and waits. The driver watches the cluster of armed men stood between the two vast stone pillars. A high wall, newly topped with coils of razor wire, runs off in both directions.

With the engine idling, the driver waits for the men to approach him, absorbed in his own thoughts at what he'll say and whether to be completely honest or not.

'Vince,' one armed man nods. Stepping up to the open driver's window, he peers into the cab and takes in the silent form of Billy and the absence of the other man. 'You on your own, then?'

'Yeah,' Vince nods, still undecided whether to be truthful or lie. Whatever he says now will have to be the story he sticks with.

'Something happen, then?' the guard asks.

'Yeah,' Vince nods grimly, but with a lack of elaboration.

The guard nods and signals to the main gate. 'Open up ... Ere, Vince,' the guard calls out before Vince drives forward, 'you seen Terry and John? They were due back hours ago.'

'No, mate,' Vince shakes his head and slowly eases the van forward, waiting for the truck parked inside the gates to be moved. Sandbags stacked high by the entrance, with a garden shed hastily erected to serve as a guard hut.

Vince nods back, noticing the confused and puzzled looks as they see he is now alone. The guard that approached him shouts that he has a boy, which sends a ripple of fresh interest buzzing through the other guards as they move in to peer in the windows.

Billy stays quiet, watching the hard faces staring in at him. With Todd gone, he feels desperately alone and terrified. Vince is quiet and doesn't shout like the other man did, but he's still scary.

'You'll like it here,' Vince says, the first conversational words he has said since seeing Nick stood over his mate. 'It's nice,' he adds with a quick glance down at the lad.

Billy looks up but doesn't say anything, too frightened to speak or move.

'We got lots of nice food,' Vince tries to smile, but the humour isn't there, and it quickly dies off. 'There are other boys here too, so you got friends to play with.' Vince knows what questions the boy will be asked, so this is the last effort to imprint a memory in the boy's head. 'Comfy beds and loads of toys. Do you like football? We got football and games, and we got a pond with fish,' Vince explains. 'But the best thing,' he tries to entice some interest from Billy, 'is the swimming pool, eh? We got a swimming pool ... Do you like swimming ...?No? Suit yourself.'

The long road sweeps through green, manicured grounds of lush grass dotted with ancient oaks and willow trees. Benches rest under the shade offered by the hanging branches, but there is no sign of life here. Everything feels empty and void.

'Look at that, Billy,' Vince points forward with one paltry last-ditch attempt to impress the boy. Billy feels he is being instructed rather than requested, so sits up to look forward. The big house coming into view is impressive, grand and old-fashioned, like something from a movie. Chapsworth House is one of the best-known stately homes in the south, and unlike many others, it was privately owned and still used as a domestic residence.

'Got fish in there,' Vince points to the water fountain in the middle of the circular parking area, a big stone feature that pumps water from tiny spouts to trickle down into the wide, lily-covered bowl. The fact that the fish are soon to be dead from the lack of oxygenated water now the pump has been switched off is not imparted to Billy.

With the van stopped, Vince pauses as he stares at the big double doors, a final chance to think of what to say. The consternation is clear on his features as he opens the door, motioning with his head for Billy to come out. The passenger door had been locked shortly after driving off. No way was he going to risk losing both of them.

'Vince! You're back,' a man calls out. He has a deep, hard voice tinged with a cockney accent, 'and who have we got here, then?' The new man grins at the sight of Billy.

'This is Billy,' Vince calls out.

'Hello, Billy! Would you like a lollipop?' The man crouches and draws a wrapped lolly from a pocket, slowly stretching his hand out while giving Billy an enormous grin. 'My name is Larson. Well, that's not my first name. It's my surname, but everyone calls me Larson, and I don't mind,' Larson speaks quick and soft. 'You must be tired from all that driving. Come inside and have something nice to drink, yeah? Come on, Billy.' Larson stands up while holding his hand out for Billy to take, a smooth motion and now well practised.

Billy stares at the lollipop he is now holding. He didn't want to take the lollipop, but it was like he didn't have a choice, and he had to take the lollipop. Lilly always said he had to remember his manners. 'Thank you for the lollipop,' he says in a small voice.

'Hey! Billy has wonderful manners,' Larson grins at Vince. 'I am very impressed. Now you come with me, young Billy, because we have a lovely man you need to meet.'

Larson gently steps in to grasp Billy's hand, not a hard grip but with just enough force to prompt Billy into walking with him. 'You coming, Vince?'

'Nah, I was gonna get the van unloaded.'

'Best come in, Vince,' Larson says in a light tone, but the order is clearly understood. 'The gate guard said you were alone.'

'Yeah, er ...'

'Not now, Vince, that can wait,' Larson says, grinning down at Billy. 'This is called Chapsworth House, Billy. Some very rich people lived here, but they don't anymore, so we use it now. It's got tons of rooms and loads of really cool things inside. Did Vince tell you about the swimming pool?'

'I did,' Vince replies quickly. Walking behind them, he can feel the nerves starting to build and entering the confines of the house only adds to the worry.

'I was asking Billy. Wasn't I, Billy?' Larson grins down. Behind them, Vince winces slightly at the rebuke. They're not happy. Suddenly, the idea he had of just driving off somewhere very far away doesn't seem such a bad one.

'Well, Billy, this is what we call the main hall. Big, isn't it?' Larson chatters on, pointing certain bits out while Billy stares in wonder at the size of the rooms. A grand staircase sweeps up to the first floor. The floors are carpeted with thick, patterned rugs everywhere, and the walls are panelled in dark wood but with lots of brightly coloured paintings hanging. Children laughing from somewhere unseen floats through the air.

'Oohh, got another one, have we?' a large-built woman waddles from a room, wearing a white apron over an old-fashioned floral dress. She beams at Billy, her face ruddy and smiling with naturally smiling eyes.

'We have,' Larson replies happily. 'This is Billy, and he's got wonderful manners.'

'Has he now?' the woman grins like this news is the best she has ever heard. 'We like manners here.'

'Billy, this is Meryl. Meryl makes all our delicious food, and she makes scrummy puddings too.'

'Oh, get off,' Meryl laughs at the compliment. 'He just wants seconds,' she says to Billy, 'but you look like a boy with a good appetite, and I bet you're hungry, aren't you, my love?'

Billy smiles shyly for the first time since being taken and feels a sudden urge to rush in and hug the big woman.

'OOOHHH,' Meryl cries with a laugh, 'we got a smile then, Larson.'

'Did we?' Larson looks down. 'Well, look at that.'

Vince stands back, feeling very excluded from the goings on. He glances round like he's looking for an escape route.

'Well, we'll come back to see Meryl in a little while,' Larson says with a quick look at Vince.

'I'll have something nice to eat all ready for you,' Meryl grins. 'And some clean clothes too,' she remarks at the state of the young lad.

Moving away, the man leads Billy down a long hallway, pointing out portraits and funny paintings hanging on the walls. The chatter is constant and done with the same friendly, light tone.

Billy stares down behind to see where the nice big lady went. He doesn't want to go up here with this man, but Lilly said he has to do as he is told. Mummy and Daddy also said he shouldn't talk to strangers, but that's confusing now because these people are strangers, but he doesn't know anyone, so does that mean they are still strangers?

The shock of the previous evening, of seeing his father and Norman killed, has been buried deep. His young mind is unable to process the understanding of what he saw, and in the frontal parts of Billy's mind, he still considers his father and Lilly to be coming here to take him back.

'You'll like it here, Billy,' Larson says with a friendly tone. 'We've got a very special person for you to meet now. He is the man that has got all of this arranged just so we can look after all the children that got lost.'

Billy thinks he wasn't lost. He was lost once when he went to the big shopping centre with Mummy. It was a Saturday, and all the shops were full of people. He only let go of Mummy's hand for a few minutes as he wanted to look at the toys. When he couldn't see her, there was a funny feeling in his tummy, like he was very scared and didn't know what to do. All the people were strangers, and they ignored him. They were all talking to each other and walking about. He did what he was told and found somebody in a uniform to tell, then waited until his mummy came. She was crying when she got there, like she was really upset about something and kept telling Billy off for walking away but giving him hugs and kisses at the same time.

He wasn't lost last night. He was with his daddy and Lilly. Maybe the man thinks he was lost.

'And here we are,' Larson says, coming to a stop in front of a set of double doors. He grins down and knocks on the door, light taps that are done in quick succession. 'Doc, I've got young Billy here to meet you,' he calls out.

Billy waits, with his hand still being held by Larson. The house is clean, and the big windows let lots of light inside. He stares round with wide eyes which snap back to the door at hearing the heavy footsteps on the other side.

Larson grins again with clear delight in his eyes, but Billy doesn't like him. He keeps smiling too much.

Slowly, the door swings inwards, hinges creaking noisily into the quietness of the hallway. Billy feels the hand of Larson twitch and grip just that little bit harder.

'Hello, young man,' a deep voice rolls from the room into the hallway as Billy looks up at the face of the Doc staring down.

CHAPTER THIRTY-THREE

Turns out, the gorilla enclosure isn't that easy to break out from. High fences strong enough to withstand the strongest primates in the world prove to be quite difficult for us too.

There was a choice, of course. Going back the way we came involved meeting the lions again which, on reflection, didn't appear to be the best move.

As close as our species are to gorillas, the one thing we have is tool-use, and equipped with axes, we manage to get the big gates open by snapping through the locks and chains. That means the lion and gorilla enclosures are now breached, but is that such a bad thing? The animals stand a better chance of survival if they can get out to find food.

The path leads us down to what we thought was a service road. But then we saw the repeated signs telling people to stay within their vehicles and keep the windows closed. So we're on a road that leads through another part of the park and one that has animals within it. The only problem is, we don't know what kind of animals yet.

The very recent sight of the fight between the gorilla and the lion have left us quiet and withdrawn. We're all used to seeing death and have given it out many times, but this was different. It was the futility of it, the valiant struggle between two opposing species that just wanted to survive.

'Shit ... shit ... shit,' Milly sings, clearly no longer bothered by the gruesome sight we just witnessed.

'Milly,' Lani warns in a low voice, 'don't say rude words.'

'But you all say rude words,' Milly protests, 'and Mr Howie doesn't tell anyone off.'

'Right, listen in,' I say with a firm voice, 'there is to be no more swearing. Is that understood? Anyone who swears will be given a very bad punishment, got it?'

'Yes, Mr Howie,' Blowers replies seriously.

'Got it, sir,' Cookey nods.

'See,' Lani says, 'Mr Howie has told everyone off.'

'Will we see hefalamps?' Milly switches topic swiftly again.

'Hefalamps? Er ... oh, elephants!' Cookey works it out a few seconds behind the rest of us.

'We have to find a way out,' Lani explains.

'I like hefelamps. They eat bananas ... I like bananas ... Do you like bananas, Lani?'

'Yes, Milly, I like them very much.'

'Do you like bananas, Cookey?'

'I love bananas!' Cookey says, and so it goes, each of us being asked if we like bananas, which we all do.

'... and I like apples,' Milly announces. 'Do you like apples, Lani?'

'We all love apples, all of us. We all really like them,' Blowers tries cutting her off.

'Lani, do you like apples?' Blowers' strategy fails dismally, so while stalking through a new section of the safari park and keeping a very close eye out, we have to go through every fruit that Milly can think of, which is pretty much limited to bananas, apples, and oranges.

'What about pears?' Cookey asks mischievously to some muted groans.

'I don't like pears,' Milly replies, then lapses into a very rare silence.

'Oh,' Cookey seems deflated as Blowers sniggers next to him.

'You really need a wash, young lady,' Clarence exhales, carrying Milly along in one arm.

'Lani will wash me,' Milly tells us all. 'Cos you are men, and men shouldn't wash girls,' she says in a very serious voice. 'So Lani can wash me, and she can wash my hair and wash my face and brush my hair, and we can wear dresses.'

'Now that I'd love to see,' I snort at the thought of Lani in a summer dress.

'And what's wrong with that?' Lani asks with a pointed stare.

'Nothing,' I reply quickly, 'er ... no, er ... be lovely to see you in a dress just, er ... you know, er ... doesn't fit the current, er ... image.'

'Well recovered,' Clarence mutters.

'Thanks, mate.'

'I'm right here,' Lani protests. 'I can hear you both, and I look nice in a summer dress.'

'Oh, I'm sure,' I try harder at the recovery.

'I can't exactly run round the country, killing zombies in a frock, can I?' she insists.

'No, look, I didn't mean you–'

'Just because I wear trousers and boots doesn't mean I can't wear a dress.'

'Yes, I know. I was ... Look, forget it, okay? Sorry, I didn't mean to laugh.'

'Yes, well,' she huffs, 'maybe Milly and I will put some nice dresses on then.'

'That would be awesome,' Cookey laughs, 'but where would you put the meat cleaver?'

'And the pistol?' Blowers adds.

'Handbag?' Lani suggests to a round of snorts.

'Don't worry,' Dave cuts in with his telling-off voice, 'I'll keep watch for the animals behind us, shall I?'

'Cheers, Dave,' I say happily, turning round to see a shit load of small monkeys running after us.

'What are they?' I ask.

'Monkeys,' Dave replies.

'Really?' I ask.

'Yes, Mr Howie,' he nods seriously.

'Those are the naughty ones that run over the cars,' Cookey says.

'Naughty ones?' Blowers laughs. 'They naughty, are they? Mr Howie, you'll have to tell the naughty monkeys off.'

'Piss off,' Cookey sighs.

'Cookey,' I warn, 'what did I say about swearing?'

'Sorry, Mr Howie,' he apologises quickly. 'Sorry, Milly.'

'Can we stroke the monkeys?' Milly asks.

'I don't think so,' Lani replies.

'Lani ...?' Milly starts, and we all wait for the question, all of us watching the little girl and grinning when it finally comes out. 'Do you like monkeys?'

'Yes, Milly,' Lani laughs, 'I like monkeys. We each wait our turn again as she goes from person to person, asking the question.

'Milly, how old are you?' I realise none of us have asked.

'I am six,' she says proudly. Holding up one hand with

the fingers extended, she seems to think for a second before holding up one more finger from her other hand.

'Rhesus monkeys,' Dave, as ever, brings our attention back to the current situation. The little monkeys suddenly don't look quite so little as they run and scamper closer towards us. Ranging in size and weight, there are well over seventy of them, just a sea of bobbing, jumping, brown bodies.

'Dave!' I call out at seeing him draw his pistol.

'What?' he turns to look at me.

'You can't shoot them.'

'I was going to scare them,' he explains.

'Why? They won't hurt us,' I reply firmly. 'Come on, keep going.'

'Er ... you sure, Mr Howie?' Cookey asks warily. 'They ain't slowing down.'

'What? Get off! We just met lions and gorillas. What are little monkeys going to do? Trip us up?'

Walking on, we keep glancing round as they bound over. Then they're with us. Running and skipping between us while making little monkey chattering noises. Tons of them all over the place. Running alongside of us, then in front, and within a few seconds, they're getting in amongst us. We all grin and laugh at the sight, fascinated at being so close to so many apparently happy animals.

Apart from Meredith, who trots along with a look that suggests she might try for one any second.

'Monkeys!' Milly laughs with delight. 'That one is doing a poo! Can I touch one? Please, Clarence, can I touch one?'

'They might bite,' Clarence explains, and I've noticed he is holding Milly a little bit higher and a little bit closer. Even the lads have moved in closer to form a barrier between her and the monkeys.

We keep walking while the monkeys seem content to run alongside and amongst us. Then they start getting braver, and no doubt spurred on by the same hunger the lions have, they start jumping onto legs to grab at pockets.

'OI!' Cookey is the first to get attacked. Well, not attacked, but more of an attempt at sticky-fingered pilfering. Shooing the animal off, it scurries away, jabbering noisily, but the precedent has been set. The brave explorer monkey got onto the leg and off again without being injured. The sight is seen by many other monkeys who all now want to get onto legs and check pockets.

'FUCK OFF!' Blowers shouts as he gets one on each leg. Clarence hoists Milly onto his shoulders, the little girl laughing as she clutches his big, bald head with her tiny arms. With one hand now free, he gets ready to swat them away as they launch in.

Funny thing is, they don't go anywhere near the dog, only us. Meredith seems to understand the lack of threat and just walks along, watching everything with interest.

Dave doesn't seem bothered by it all but calmly flicks each one away as it pounces. For a second, I thought he might be cutting little monkey throats behind me. Lani clearly isn't impressed, and for the first time since we met, she shows her feminine side by yelping and giving little screams every time they touch her.

Recognising a chance to make up for my faux-pas and also seeing an opportunity to be heroic and brave, I step in and try to keep them away from her. She clings to my side, panicking and shaking whenever they jump up.

With so many and more of them joining in every second, it's all we can do to just keep moving and try and stop them all clinging on. One gets on my back and stays there, quite happily gripping hold of my hair while I try and prise another from Lani's leg. Another jumps to my shoulder, then another on my leg. Clarence gets swarmed, the big man having much more body for them clamber over, and Milly loves the sight, laughing until tears are falling down her face.

'Run!' I yell out. We try jogging but get hampered by the bouncy little shits running in front of us. They are so nimble and accurate that there is very little chance of actually kicking one by mistake. It's just completely disconcerting to be running amongst so many moving objects.

Running does nothing other than make us hotter. The monkeys certainly don't mind us running, and for a few minutes, it looks like we might be stuck with them until we find a way out. Then a mistake is made. A line is crossed, which changes everything in a split second. One of the monkeys, possibly a Cookey-type monkey that is always trying to push the boundaries, gets brave and tries to jump on Meredith.

Now, the dog seemed quite happy for us to get swarmed and surprisingly didn't show any real reaction, but one on *her*? Not happening. She erupts into a frenzied fury of snarling, barking, gnashing teeth. Hair on end, tail curled up, and suddenly the area is devoid of monkeys. Eighty or so brown bodies starbursting away and being chased by Meredith.

'Thank god,' Cookey gasps.

'Little sods,' Blowers groans. 'They were going for everything. One almost got my pistol out.'

'MEREDITH ... COME BACK,' Dave bellows as she goes haring off, chasing them. She slows down and starts trotting back, but not without the very occasional glance to see if they're trying it again.

'Good girl!' I say as she rejoins us, all of us giving her

some fuss and rubs. The jabbering sound dies off as they get further away. All of a sudden, the noise is getting louder again.

Spinning round, we see the carpet of brown bodies coming back at us and this time a lot faster.

'The hole,' Clarence mutters, 'the hole in the fence ...'

'Shit!' I exclaim as I see larger black and brown figures running behind the rhesus monkeys. 'Time to go.'

'Hold on tight,' Clarence reaches up to push Milly's hands firmer onto his head as we set off, jogging at a good pace as we follow the meandering road.

Screams, roars, and horrific snarls sound out in the distance behind us. Three species of animals kept well apart are now thrown into the pot. At least now, with three enclosures breached, there are plenty of trees and land for the primates to use in their escape of the lions.

'Giddy up, horsey,' Milly screams with pleasure at the bouncy ride on Clarence's wide shoulders.

'There,' Dave points ahead to a big set of gates set into the chain-link fence. 'Give me your axe.' I offer mine up, which he takes and sprints ahead, outstripping us with graceful ease. Reaching the obstacle, he swings and levers away, snapping something, then dragging the gates open way before we get to them.

Bursting through, we keep the speed up as Dave slams the gates closed behind us, shouting that the lock is ruined before running up to join us again.

We are certainly a lot fitter than we were two weeks ago, but my god, the heat is sapping my strength quicker than anything I have ever known before. Each day just gets hotter, and it seems so much worse out here, in the wide open land, with heat shimmers hovering over the surface of the road.

Gradually, we slow down to a fast walk, the conversation drying up as we focus on breathing. Dehydration becoming a very real issue as the sweat pours down our faces to drench our clothes.

Thankfully, we start to see buildings in the distance, large, roofed structures that indicate we're heading towards the centre of the park.

Heads down, but eyes up, we push on, all too aware that the last gate we came through is closed but not locked and could easily swing open.

'Over there,' Blowers gasps and points to a herd of something grazing further down the rolling pastures. Those clever monkeys will soon realise they can open that gate; then, the lions have four enclosures to roam and now a herd of something, maybe bison or some other big animals, to hunt.

'Zebras,' Blowers points out another herd of the distinctive black and white creatures moving amongst a strand of trees. Closer towards the main centre, we see other herds of animals, all in the same vast area. These are all grazing animals, and with so much space, they must have all been put together. Those lions will be feasting at some point.

The safari park is so bloody big, it seems to take ages to finally reach the buildings, and the last gate is quickly pulled shut as the others start sagging down to rest.

'Not yet,' I gasp at them. 'Café up there.' That gets them back on their feet quick enough.

A place like this will have somewhere to eat and drink, so we head on, going past the small creatures' buildings and into the main centre. The buildings are all locked and secure, but finding the advertisement-adorned café is easy enough. Then, with Clarence's feet and our axes, getting the doors open takes just seconds.

Inside the entrance, we finally rest, bent over or dropping down to get our breathing under control.

'Wait here,' Lani walks off, quickly followed by Dave. Disappearing out of sight, we wait for them to come back, knowing exactly what they've gone for.

'They're not chilled,' Lani calls out, coming back with an armful of bottles of water. Dave is right behind her with more. Caps get unscrewed and water glugged down, poured over faces and heads with pleasurable sighs and groans.

Milly drinks quickly, holding the bottle to her mouth with both hands while staring round at the inside of the building.

It's a wooden structure made from stained, dark timber to give it an old-time sort of theme with wooden tables and chairs dotted everywhere. Every wall has posters and pictures of the animals held within the park as well as posters advertising the feeding times and extra gold packages you can pay for. They also have expert talks given by guest television presenters.

Cleverly, they've put the gift shop within the main café building and stocked the outer edge, the one closest to the café, with all the brightest and most colourful objects to attract the attention of children. It certainly works, judging by the stares of Milly.

'Gift shop,' Cookey mentions. Obviously works on him too.

'They got toilets?' Clarence asks.

'Do you need a poo?' Milly asks seriously with an actual air of genuine concern.

'No, you need a wash if I'm going to be carrying you,' he replies kindly.

'I'll do it. You think they got clothes in there?' she nods at the gift shop.

'Probably,' I reply, 'at least t-shirts and things. Get her a sunhat too if they've got them or at least a baseball cap ...'

'Yes, okay, Mr Howie,' she groans. 'Anything else?'

'I'll come with you,' I get to my feet and follow Lani and Milly towards the shop.

'Cookey, see if you can find some food.'

'Why me?' he asks with a groan.

'You were the last one to swear,' I turn round to grin at him.

'Okay,' the amiable lad smiles and gets up.

Fortunately, the gift shop is not sectioned off from the café, and we just stroll through into the aisles packed with every type of object known to mankind, and all of them emblazoned, stencilled, or stitched with the park logo on them. Advertising works, I guess, and no doubt they wouldn't stock it if it didn't all sell.

'There,' I point to a clothing section at the far end.

'Can I get a toy please, Lani?' Milly asks.

'You can have whatever you want,' Lani smiles down, 'but after we get you washed and changed, okay?'

Milly clearly contemplates this for a second. 'Anything?' she asks in the negotiating phase of the discussions.

'Anything,' Lani repeats.

'Okay,' Milly accepts the terms and conditions as we reach the clothing stands. Any concern of not having clothes is quickly negated. They've got every possible type of clothing here.

'Shorts or trousers?' I ask Lani, holding a pair of each up. They're khaki safari colour with the logo stitched in but are good quality material.

'Trousers for now,' Lani replies. 'Keep her legs covered in this sun but take the shorts anyway. Actually, grab a bag, and we can get a few bits. Actually ...' she adds again, 'get a few bags so we can fill up.'

'That,' I announce with a pointed look, 'is a very good idea. See ... it's not just your body that I fancy.'

'Oh really?' Lani laughs. 'My mind too, yeah?'

'Oh yes,' I reply in what I hope is a serious tone.

'Just not summer dresses, though,' she arches on eyebrow before turning away.

They've got rucksacks a plenty here, and as with the clothes, they are good quality, with padded straps and waist and chest fasteners. The park logo on everything is a bit annoying, but what can you do?

'There's loads of grub in the kitchens,' Cookey announces, walking into the gift shop, with the others strolling behind him.

'Get some stuff if you need it,' I call out. 'There are bags here we can use. Get clean tops or whatever you need.'

'Leave space for water,' Dave instructs.

'Are you getting changed too, Lani?' Milly asks from behind an aisle.

'I am,' Lani replies. 'Help me find something.'

'Okay,' Milly replies. 'What about this?'

'Hmmm, I think it's a bit hot for a tiger costume.'

'Go on, Lani, put it on!' Cookey calls out.

'Ah, perfect,' Blowers shouts, 'big rack of sunglasses here.'

'Where?' Cookey springs up, looking round.

'Don't get mirrored glasses,' Dave orders. 'They can reflect sunlight.'

'Roger that,' Cookey replies, running about, looking for Blowers.

'Here,' I walk back into the middle area, carrying a load of black t-shirts, 'they've got the logo on them but ...'

'Doesn't matter,' Clarence strides over. 'Clean clothes ... They got my size?'

'Probably not,' I reply. 'Have a look.'

'We're ready,' Lani appears with Milly who is loaded down with armfuls of clothes. 'Here,' she grins and throws something at me. Ducking out the way, I pick the object up and laugh.

'Really?'

'Yes,' Lani grins.

'What is it?' Cookey calls out.

'A safari park toothbrush,' I reply, 'in zebra colours.'

Milly and Lani head off to the toilets. Milly's voice chattering the entire way as the rest of us mooch through the heap of clothes I dumped to find the right sizes.

With toothbrush in hand, I head off to the toilets with Dave, agreeing with the rest that we'll go first and then start on the food, which gives Cookey a reprieve.

'Clean toilets, Dave!' I remark as we walk into the sparkling clean gents. 'They even smell nice.'

'They do, Mr Howie,' he heads straight over to the sinks and starts stripping off while running the water. I go a few sinks up and start the same, peeling off the sodden, filthy top and catching a whiff of my armpits.

'I wonder if Nick's at the fort yet?'

'I hope so,' Dave replies.

'You worried?'

'About Nick?'

'Yes, Dave.'

'Not really. He's very capable and very intelligent. Good fighter too.'

'I guess, but I still don't like it. That Milly is pretty fearless,' I say conversationally, which isn't the best thing to do with Dave, seeing as he struggles with mundane chitchat.

Glancing down the row of sinks, I watch him repeatedly press the plastic lever to fill his hands with liquid soap before smashing the lot into his face and lathering it up in a vigorous, almost epileptic manner. He then washes his hair, his neck and down to his shoulders and armpits until the soap runs out. He reloads with soap and carries on, scrubbing himself so methodically that he's done within a couple of minutes, rinsing the soap off to stand back, and starts using paper towels to pat dry his body.

'She is,' he finally adds. Having recorded the last comment made by me but being unable to answer for fear of getting a mouthful of soap, he simply continued what he was doing until he could talk. The man is mesmerising to watch. Even something normally boring like washing is done so clinically it's fascinating.

'You think she's got something wrong with her?' I turn back to my own messier and less clinical washing, which involves getting lots of water everywhere, blinding myself with soap, and then trying to talk at the same time.

'Wrong?' he asks while I rinse the soap from my burning eye.

'Yeah, like autism or something, you know. She hasn't mentioned her family or her house or anything. Those questions she asks too, and the way she remembers our names so quickly.'

'There is a wide spectrum with autism, Mr Howie,' he says. 'She doesn't appear to lack social skills but ...' He pauses for a second, which is so unusual it makes me stop washing to stare at him. 'I think perhaps her awareness of danger or threat is different to a normal person.'

'Makes sense,' I nod in agreement before turning back to the mirror. As I unwrap the new toothbrush, I contemplate using the liquid soap as a toothpaste. It would taste disgusting, but it would certainly clean my mouth. Would it be harmful? I suppose if I didn't actually swallow it ... Would they put dangerous liquid soap in public restrooms?

'You okay, Mr Howie?' he asks directly, staring at me hovering my brush under the soap dispenser.

'Uh?' Catching me unawares, I shake my head and start brushing without the soap, but doing it without paste feels so wrong. In the end, I compromise and add the tiniest dollop of soap before quickly shoving the bristles in my mouth and going for it before I can change my mind.

It tastes fucking awful, really nasty, but I keep going. Attacking the bottom row, then the top, all whilst trying to hold my tongue away from my teeth and reminding myself not to swallow. It's very complicated and rather too much for my stupid head to process and results in a messy situation with soapy saliva dripping from my mouth whilst I try not to gag.

As I finish, I suddenly realise I am groaning from distaste. I get my mouth under the tap to rinse and realise Dave is staring at me with a very strange expression.

'What?' I ask with a shrug.

'Nothing,' he shrugs back. Bloody hell, it must be bad when even Dave looks at you like you're doing something weird. 'Your eye is all red,' he comments.

'Got soap in it.'

The psychological effect of washing and putting a clean t-shirt on is amazing. All of us feel a little pepped up from scrubbing the stale sweat away. Out of the harsh sun and drinking cans of sugary drink, we start on the tinned food from the kitchens, carrying them all out onto a big table in the café.

'Fort or Saxon first?' Clarence asks, happily shovelling a spoonful of cold beans into his mouth.

'Fort. We need Nick or a mechanic,' I reply. 'None of us can fix it, and I hate being separated from him too.'

'Mmm, definitely,' Blowers nods in agreement with a mouthful of something, 'we should get Nick first.'

'Are you ready, gentlemen?' Turning round, we see Lani stood at the entrance to the toilets. Judging by the time she has taken, there must have been one hell of a cleaning session going on in there.

She leads Milly out by the hand. The little girl grinning from ear to ear, freshly scrubbed, with wet hair tied back, she looks completely different.

'Look at you!' Cookey calls out.

'Wow!' I stand up and clap. 'You look so much better.'

'She does,' Clarence adds, 'all clean and fresh.'

'Do the clothes fit alright?' Blowers asks.

'Perfect,' Lani replies. Milly bursts away from her, prompting us all to jump up in panic at the thought of her running off again. Giggling, she heads straight to Clarence, jumping up at the last second with a high-pitched laugh.

'Come here, you,' Clarence pulls her up to sit on his lap. 'Now you smell much better.'

'I got new clothes,' Milly grins round at us all, 'and Lani has new clothes, and I have brown trousers, and Lani has brown trousers, and I have a black top, and Lani has a black top ...'

'Breathe, Milly,' Cookey laughs as the girl launches into a long, excited explanation.

'We've all got black tops on,' she shouts, jumping up and down in absolute glee. 'Clarence has a black one, and Mr Howie has a black one, and Dave has a black one ...' she goes round, naming everyone as I watch her closely. I still can't help but notice the way she feels the need to point everything out individually.

'You alright?' I ask Lani when Milly finishes off.

'Fine, brush your teeth, did you?'

'I did.'

'Mr Howie used soap on the toothbrush,' Dave imparts helpfully to a load of faces screwing up in disgust.

'Wasn't that bad,' I shrug. 'Milly, are you hungry?'

'I'm on it,' Clarence says, pulling tins over so Milly can start eating.

'Where's Meredith?' Lani asks.

'Under the table, scoffing,' Blowers answers, tucking back into his food.

'Have you given her beans again?' she asks. 'You know what beans do to her.'

'Not much choice really. She's got tuna mixed in with it,' Blowers replies.

'Have you been here before, Milly?' I ask the little girl munching away on a bowl of tuna, beans, and sweet corn all mixed together. She shakes her head seriously while busily loading the spoon up.

'Never?' I ask in surprise. Being so close to the safari park, I would have thought all the local kids would have visited.

'Do you have any brothers or sisters?' I ask gently, remembering the other bedroom in her house with the posters of teen bands. Milly shakes her head again as she focusses on chewing.

'Oh,' I nod. Keeping the tone light, I start opening another tin. 'There was another bedroom at your house with posters. Who's bedroom was that?'

'Carly,' she replies. I watch her closely. She doesn't appear upset or worried. In fact, she seems the same, quite content to eat away.

'Who is Carly? Is she a relative?'

She shakes her head again and looks round, grinning at Cookey who laughs at the single bean that drops from her mouth.

Giving Lani a confused look, I shrug. The girl is a mystery. Maybe we had the wrong house, and her name isn't even Milly. 'Is Milly your name?' I ask quickly.

'Yes, Mr Howie,' she laughs as though it's the stupidest question ever.

'So who is Carly?'

'My mummy and daddy's daughter,' she says as if the answer is obvious.

'I'm lost,' Cookey mutters.

'But ...' I scratch my head, trying to work out if I've missed something.

'Milly, if Carly is your mummy and daddy's daughter, then shouldn't she be your sister?' Lani asks.

'Mummy and Daddy want us to be sisters,' Milly says, still focussing on loading up her spoon. We wait for the additional comment to come, but it doesn't. She just carries on eating.

'So, why aren't you sisters, then?' Lani carries on.

'Cos Carly is mean. She calls me rude names,' Milly replies, 'and I don't want to be her sister. Mummy and Daddy said they took me, so we have to be sisters, but I don't like her.'

'Took you?' Lani leans forward, staring with interest. 'Milly, are you adopted?'

'Yes!' she laughs in that crazy, quick way while munching her little jaw up and down.

'Oh,' Cookey nods slowly, 'got it.'

'Do you miss them?' Lani asks in a soft voice. We all wait for the answer, staring over at the girl perched on Clarence's lap.

'Nope,' Milly sings. 'I like beans,' she announces. 'Clarence, do you like beans?'

Laughing, the big man says he does like beans, but I notice his arm wraps round her that little bit tighter, and Lani gives her a big, warm smile. We all sense something not quite right, but none of us know what to say about it. Does it matter now? That's the question. Her family are gone and probably never to be seen again. What happened before all this is over. It could be that she is like Dave and unable to build connections to people in the way others can. But then watching her now, interacting with all of us, it doesn't seem that way. For instance, she can maintain eye contact and read other people's facial expressions, laughing when they laugh or responding to Cookey when he pulls a funny face. And the way she ran straight to Clarence too. Maybe she was just remembering that he carried her for a while, but she could have just got her own chair. Meredith certainly seems to like her, moving out from under the table to sit next to Clarence and keeping both of her sharp eyes fixed on the girl.

'We're going to the place we live,' Lani says after a few minutes of general talking. 'Do you want to come with us?' the question is asked gently and easy like a test to see how she responds.

'Is Clarence going?' she twists to look up.

'I am,' he nods.

'Is Dave going?' She asks each of us in turn, that same method of wanting everyone to answer individually.

'So?' Lani asks when she gets round everyone. 'Do you want to come with us?'

'I do,' Milly says. 'Will I have a bedroom?'

'Er,' Lani looks to me, unsure of how to respond. 'I don't know,' she says slowly.

'Oh, I should imagine so,' I nod knowingly.

'Will Meredith have puppies?' she asks. 'My mummy's friend had a dog, and she had puppies.'

'Er, no ... er ... I don't think so,' I reply, and that's it, conversation over as she takes up staring round the room instead.

'We'd better go,' I announce. 'Everyone eaten and got water?' Murmurs of affirmation and nods all round.

'Me and Blowers got these for you, Milly,' Cookey pulls a pair of sunglasses from a pocket to hand over. Pink plastic frames with dark lenses, and her mouth drops open like it's the best present she has ever had. Hugging the grinning lads in turn, she slips them on and grins, getting smiles and comments in response.

'I like glasses,' she announces. 'Cookey ...?'

And so she starts again as we head out into the heat once more. One little girl surrounded by the hardest zombie killers possibly left in the country and one truly psychotic, fearless dog that trots by her side. Chatting away, she lifts our mood greatly, even Dave smiles at her, which just shows the effect she's already having on us.

We just need Nick and the Saxon back now, and everything will be fine.

CHAPTER THIRTY-FOUR

'Hey, sleepy, how are you?' Lilly smiles, wanting Todd to wake up feeling reassured that she is here, and they are safe. 'You've been asleep for ages,' she adds. Todd stretches and looks across at Nick driving the van. Even with the windows wide open, the heat is incredible, and sweat drips down his face, giving him that uncomfortable sticky feeling. Shifting to look out the front window, he stares at the houses rolling by.

'Need the toilet,' Todd says quietly, the shock from everything rendering him near silent. No Samantha or his father, just Lilly and this man.

'I'll pull over,' Nick says with a quick smile down at Todd. 'You thirsty, mate?' he asks in a friendly tone. Todd nods but doesn't answer, his eyes wide and scared, and despite the intense warmth, he looks pale, drawn, and sickly.

'Bushes or a wall?' Nick asks lightly.

'Pardon?' Todd asks.

'Would you like to have a wee behind a wall or behind a bush?' Nick smiles.

Looking up at Lilly for reassurance and seeing her smiling along, he thinks for a moment. 'Bush, please,' he says so politely they both just smile sadly.

'Your wish is my command,' Nick replies. 'Right, we need a big bush. Can you see one anywhere?' Seeing the fear on the boy's face, Nick tries to be jovial in a quiet, muted sort of way. The horror the child has seen has clearly shocked him to the core.

'There's one. What do you think, Todd?' Lilly points ahead to a large house set back from the road with thick bushes lining the edge of the front grounds.

'Yes, please.' Todd stares around at the passing scenery. Everything looks so calm and nice, quiet and shining in the sunlight.

With the van stopped, Lilly drops down to the pavement, stretching her arms wide with a big yawn. 'I'm so sleepy,' she shakes her head quickly.

'It's the heat,' Nick replies. Switching the engine off, he jumps down to quickly check the view up and down the street, pausing for a second before nodding that he is satisfied. Pulling his packet out, he taps a cigarette free and lights it in one smooth, well-practised movement.

'Better?' Lilly smiles, seeing the look of relief on his face.

'Much,' Nick nods with a guilty grin.

'Come on, then,' Lilly says. Holding a hand out for Todd, she helps him down and follows him towards the large grounds of the big house.

'I need a poo-poo,' Todd whispers. He didn't want to say it in front of Nick, the embarrassment too much.

'Okay,' Lilly ruffles his hair. 'You go, and I'll find some toilet roll. Make sure you keep your shorts out the way,' she says softly, 'don't get poo in them, okay?'

'Okay, Lilly.'

'Don't go far, though.'

'You won't watch, will you?' he asks with a frown.

'No, silly,' Lilly replies, 'of course, I won't.'

'But what about the toilet paper? You'll see me when you bring it?' Todd looks deeply worried at the prospect of being seen having a poo.

'Okay, wait here, and I'll get some now,' she rushes off, first checking the cab before running to the back. Opening the doors, she clambers inside for a few seconds, then re-appears holding a roll of toilet paper up with a big grin. 'There, see? Now, make sure you wipe properly, okay?'

'Okay.' Nodding, he takes the roll and darts off through the open gates of the driveway. He takes a hard right and crouches behind a row of dense bushes cut into precise squares with flat sides and tops with tiny, new shoots now threatening to ruin the shape so lovingly created.

'He alright?' Nick asks as Lilly wanders back.

'Needs a poo,' she smiles, 'didn't want either of us to watch him.'

'Fair enough,' Nick shrugs, 'I wouldn't want anyone watching me take a shit either. Shit ... I mean a poo,' he adds with a roll of his eyes. Lilly giggles at hearing the word poo from a grown man, especially one that blushes so easily.

'We can't be that far away now,' Nick suggests in an awful attempt to move the conversation along.

'No, I guess not,' Lilly nods. 'You thirsty? They've got loads of stuff in the back.'

'Definitely.' Strolling to the rear, he stands at the back doors while she climbs in to mooch through the bags of foods and provisions taken by the two men.

'Coke? Lilt, Dr Pepper ... Lucozade ...'

'Lucozade, please,' Nick cuts in. 'We drink loads of that

stuff in the Saxon. It's good for electrolytes and ... stuff,' he shrugs, his voice tailing off self-consciously.

'Stuff?' Lilly prompts him, 'what stuff?'

'You know, like all the salts and things you lose in this heat from sweating. It's the glucose in those that give you the quick energy hit. Even Dave drinks it, so it must be good.'

'You keep mentioning Dave like he's something special,' Lilly muses. Jumping down with another two bottles, she opens one to take a long drink.

'Oh, he fucking is,' Nick nods. 'Shit! Why can't I stop fucking swearing? I must have shitting Tourette's or something ...'

'Shitting Tourette's?' Lilly laughs.

'Yeah, shitting, arsing, bloody ...' gritting his teeth, with a smile threatening to spread across his face. Relenting, he grins, laughing at himself.

'Don't worry,' Lilly takes another swig, 'it's sweet that you keep trying to stop.'

Sweet? Did she just say sweet? Nick turns away quickly to take another drink. She definitely said sweet. She really did.

'What?' Lilly asks at seeing his reaction.

'Eh? What?' Nick asks too nonchalantly.

'You blush so easily,' she teases with a grin. An image of her father flashes across her mind, of Sam with that brute between her legs, of Norman grabbing at her last night, and Billy being pulled away. The smile fades as quickly as it came. Guilt pervades at being here, laughing with an attractive boy so soon after.

'Hey,' Nick is there, right in front of her and looking at her with a sad look, 'that happens.'

'What?' she asks, confused.

'The memories like that,' he says softly. 'You felt guilty for laughing when, er ... when all that bad shit just happened ...'

'Yes,' she looks down with another guilty start.

'We all get it,' Nick continues. 'But it's okay to laugh and smile, Lilly. It doesn't mean you don't regret anything, and it doesn't make it fucking hurt any less but ...' he shrugs, 'but it helps you get through the day, I guess.'

'Have you lost ...?' Lilly asks quietly, unable to finish the sentence.

'Loads,' Nick replies. Seeing the girl look so full of anxiety, he puts one hand on her shoulder. Immediately, she moves to place her own hand over his. Taking comfort from the contact, she closes her eyes for a second and almost nestles into his arm. 'But we're here,' Nick says. 'It's fuck awful and shit but ...' Seeing the tears start to fall down her face, he steps in, wrapping his arms round her shoulders.

'I'm sorry,' she bites the tears away. 'I keep doing this.'

'It's only twice,' Nick laughs softly. 'You're tired and exhausted. It's fucking hot, and fucking hell, Lilly, after what has just happened ... Shit, you cry as much as you want.'

'Maybe I should start swearing like you,' she chuckles.

'Nah, it wouldn't suit that posh voice. You'd sound like someone from a porno.' He freezes, realising what he just said, as though alluding to the fact that he may have actually seen pornography.

'Porno?' Lilly chuckles again. 'Posh porno, eh? Is that your thing?'

'What? Me? No, fuck no ... shit ... I never watched any. It was, er ... something Cookey said.'

'Would you like a shovel for that hole, Nicholas?' She looks up through tear-misted eyes and smiles sadly.

'Yeah,' he nods, 'a big one, please. You okay?'

'Fine. Thank you,' she says with real meaning, 'I don't know what we would have done without you.'

'You'd survive,' he shrugs, becoming painfully aware that the reassuring hug he offered is fast evolving into an embrace.

The scream, when it comes, rips through the air, making both of them flinch. High-pitched with anguish and pain and so unexpected they freeze for the most fleeting of seconds. Hearts boom with fright and adrenalin as Nick pulls away, his longer legs working as he pumps his arms, racing towards the garden ahead.

'TODD!' Lilly screams out, sprinting just behind Nick. 'TODD?'

The scream keeps going, one long, pitiful sound that chills her to the core. Though the gate, Nick turns quickly behind the thick hedgerow, pushing round a cluster of low ferns. He sees Todd on his front, his shorts round his ankles, and a crawler biting deep into his calf. Beating his arms against the ground, Todd wails in pain and terror. Nick surges in, kicking it off, but he's too late.

Snapping back, the infected rolls away from the blow. It has greying skin drawn tight over its cheekbones, eyes sunk and deep, with only a few wisps of matted hair left on his filthy scalp. The thing bares its teeth, gnashing to get at Nick.

No axe and no pistol, so he uses his feet, stamping down and kicking to get the zombie further away from Todd. Again and again with increasing force, he stamps the sole of his boot, snapping bones, the nose, and cheeks to bits.

'Todd!' Lilly drops down, clutching the boy in her arms as he cries in agony. 'Oh, Todd ... Oh my god!'

The neck snaps with the final hard kick, the head lolling

to one side as Nick looks round at the area, spotting the drag marks across the lawn and flowerbeds made by the zombie slowly pulling itself along. Furious inside that he didn't check the garden, that the one spot they choose has an infected in it.

'Todd,' Lilly sobs. Holding him tight, she fights the rising panic and uses one hand to grab at the ragged wound in an attempt to stem the bleeding.

'Let go.' Nick speaks low and urgent, yanking her hand free and checking the wound, a deep bite down to the bone. Two minutes at the most before he turns.

'Do something,' Lilly pleads, 'Nick ... do something, please.'

Moving round to the boy's head, he smiles down, soothing the hair plastered to his forehead. 'You're going to be okay,' Nick speaks clear and confident. Stroking the boy's head, he watches as the screams die out, leaving a terrified, little boy gasping with pain.

Remembering what Lani said, he smiles down. 'Everything is fine, Todd. It's just a tiny bite ... that's all, just a tiny cut that we clean up.' Todd looks up, locking his frightened eyes on Nick. He stares pitifully, hanging on the comfort offered. 'Does it hurt?' Nick asks.

Shaking his head. 'No,' Todd whimpers.

'See,' Nick smiles, 'it's getting better already. We'll just rest here for a minute, then we can go get something to drink. You're going to be alright, Todd. You feeling sleepy?'

Nodding slowly, Todd blinks with heavy eyelids. The infection courses through his system, already working to take the small body over.

'My tummy hurts,' Todd wriggles as the pain grips his insides.

'That's from all those fizzy drinks.' Nick soothes the

boy's head, watching as Lilly gently strokes his cheek. 'All those fizzy drinks, and you needed a poo. You have a nice sleep,' Nick forces himself to keep smiling. 'Have a nice sleep, Todd, and we'll carry you into the van, and then we can find Billy.' The boy writhes for a second, then gradually goes still. Eyelids fluttering as unconsciousness threatens to pull him under any second.

'Ssshhh,' Nick says softly, 'you sleep, Todd, have a nice sleep, and you'll feel better.'

'I want my mummy,' Todd snaps his eyes open, fighting against the urge pulling him under.

'I know,' Nick says. The lad is finished, dying in his arms. 'Todd,' he says softly, 'your mummy is at the place we're going to. She is waiting for you.'

Todd looks up with a fresh glimmer of hope in his eyes.

'That's right,' Nick swallows to stop the tears, 'she told me not to tell you because she wanted to surprise you, but she is there, and ... and I'm going to take you to see her, so you have a nice sleep, Todd, sleep and have nice dreams, and when you wake up, you'll be with your mummy.'

The boy smiles, a feeble twitch of the lips as the eyes start to defocus.

'And your mummy told me to tell you something,' Nick continues. 'She said to tell you she loves you very much, and she misses you. She has a great big cuddle waiting for you, and she is so proud of you, Todd, really proud, and she loves you with all of her heart.'

Sobs break from Lilly as she clamps her mouth shut, forcing herself to smile at Todd.

'That's right, Todd, Mummy is waiting, and she can't wait to see you. You sleep Todd, you've been so brave, such a brave boy.' Stroking his cheeks, they watch his eyes close for the last time. The small chest ceases movement as the infection takes the body.

'Todd?' Lilly whispers.

'It's done,' Nick mutters softly. 'We have to move away.'

'Todd?' Lilly drops closer to his face, Nick ready to react for the turn.

'Lilly, we have to move away,' he urges. Watching closely, he gives her a few seconds to drop her mouth and kiss his forehead, wet tears falling from her eyes to soak his pale, lifeless cheeks.

'Now, Lilly,' Nicks says firmer, 'we have to move now.'

'I can't,' Lilly sobs. Nick doesn't hesitate but grabs the girl by her shoulders, pulling her roughly away. 'Get off,' she screams out, pushing against him.

'No,' Nick growls. Keeping grip, he pulls the girl away from the body. 'Lilly, we have to move now.'

'Get your hands off me,' Lilly shouts, lashing out with her hands while sobbing hysterically.

'Lilly, please ...' Nick takes another blow to the head, wincing as it strikes the bruised bit she caused earlier.

'TODD ...' Lilly screams. Fighting to get free, she thrashes against Nick, pushing and pulling to get his hands off her arms.

She fights so hard that Nick has no choice. Sweeping her legs out as gently as possible, he lowers her to the ground, wrapping his arms round her chest to stop her breaking free, knowing she'll rush back to the boy.

'Look,' Nick shouts as the spasms start pulsing through Todd's body. 'LOOK,' he forces her head to face the re-animating corpse.

Lilly freezes, mesmerised by the intense violent fitting. She manoeuvres into a seated position, with Nick directly behind her, his arms wrapped tight round her chest and shoulders.

'Watch, Lilly,' he speaks into her ear, 'this is what happens. It isn't Todd that comes back ... understand? That isn't Todd now ... It's one of them. When it wakes up, it will attack us and try to bite. Just one bite, that's all it takes. Now we have to get up.' Grunting with effort, he gets his legs under and pushes up, lifting the girl with him until they're both standing.

Without realising, she grasps his arms in comfort, no longer trying to break free but pulling his arms tighter round her frame. The tears cease as she watches the shuddering corpse become lifeless again.

Nick pulls his arms free to move round in front of her, using his body as a shield.

'Go back to the van,' he orders.

'No,' she whispers close behind him.

'Go back,' he hisses, 'please, Lilly, just go now.'

'No, I'm staying.'

'Lilly, I'm going to kill it. Do you understand? I'm going to fucking kill it ... Go back to the fucking van.'

'No,' she growls with defiance.

Todd sits up, side on to Nick and Lilly. His red, bloodshot eyes snap open. Slowly, the head turns away, then slowly back towards them. Drool hangs from its mouth, and low growls sound from the throat as it lurches forward, gaining its feet.

Lilly squeezes the trigger on the pistol. She doesn't remember the motion of taking it out, but there it is, up and aiming. The reflex of her finger squeezing jolts the gun, the round striking Todd centre chest, and the power of the bullet slamming his light body back several feet.

The sudden gunshot makes Nick's ears ring, so close

and completely unexpected. Instantly, he sees the round strike the chest and knows the body will just get back up.

'The head,' he whispers. 'The chest doesn't do anything.'

'Okay,' her voice quavering, she takes aim with shaking hands, using both of them in an attempt to hold the gun level.

'Let me,' Nick says.

'No,' shaking her head firmly, she takes a deep breath as Todd sits back up, the wound in his chest bleeding heavily but nothing like it should be.

'They don't bleed like we do,' Nick whispers. 'They heal faster too. They don't eat or drink ... They move fast, and they will do anything to kill us ... They don't feel pain, nothing ...'

'I understand,' Lilly replies, her voice now dull and flat. Hands now steadier, she pulls the trigger, watching with shock as the round penetrates the forehead and removes the back of his skull. Pink mist flares for a second as the bushes beyond become drenched in gore and brain matter.

The body drops, dead again, and it's final this time. She lowers the gun slowly as Nick watches her closely. Neither of them speak for a minute. Lilly gently pushes the gun back into the holster and stares down at the ground.

'Lilly,' Nick asks gently, 'you okay?'

She nods before looking up at him. 'Yes,' swallowing, she thinks for a second. The confusion and hysteria have gone now. A weird calmness descends, a sensation of being numb. Like none of this was real. Snapping her head quickly, she takes another breath. She can see the pain in his eyes, the worry and genuine care. He reacted so quickly and knew exactly what to do. Beating that thing off before making her let go of Todd's leg.

Those things he said too, the kind words and the soft tone. How did he know to do that? He knew Todd was dying, but he had the presence to stay calm and ease the boy slowly away. One minute they were laughing and crying, then this, Todd's dead.

'Don't overthink it,' Nick urges. 'This is our fucking life now.'

She nods back, staring at him intently.

'If I could take any of this away from you, I would,' Nick continues. 'You don't deserve it ... Really, Lilly, I would do anything so you didn't have see this or ...' he shrugs, searching for the right words, 'but if you want to find your brother and protect him, this is what you have to do. It's fucked up and shitty as fuck but–'

'I understand,' she nods again, lifting her chin higher. 'Are they always like that?' she asks.

'No,' Nick shakes his head, drawing another cigarette out. 'Some can speak and look pretty normal, but so far,' he takes a drag and blows the smoke away, 'they've all got red eyes. That's what to look out for.'

'Okay,' she nods, 'what else?'

'Else?' he asks with a puzzled frown.

'What else do I need to know? Like you said,' she stares at him, 'if I'm going to protect Billy ...'

'Go for the brain,' Nick says quickly, 'gunshot or stab, an axe, or even something heavy, but go for the head. Or you cut them so bad they don't stop bleeding, but that's like a fucking artery, you know?'

'An artery, right.'

'Yeah, in the neck here,' Nick touches the sides of his own neck. 'Cut this open, and they bleed out, but there's arteries in the groin and other places too.'

'I know,' Lilly nods. 'Right, arteries or head.'

'And strike and move,' Nick almost smiles at the words of Dave and Mr Howie being repeated over and over. 'We'd better go. You sure you're okay?'

'Not really,' she sags for a second, 'but I haven't got any choice ...'

'Nope,' Nick shakes his head, 'none of us have. Fucking shit, ain't it?' He offers a hard grin with a shrug.

'It is,' Lilly replies slowly. 'It is very fucking shit.'

CHAPTER THIRTY-FIVE

'I tell you, we share this place, yes?' Lenski glares at the man. 'We have the space and ...'

'SHUT UP,' the man yells, his face glistening with sweat as the frustration gives way to a feeling of losing control.

'I'm telling you, Shaun, this is fucked up ... completely fucked up. We gotta do somethin, man.'

'Just shut up! All of you, shut the fuck up and let me think,' Shaun paces the room, trying to think. This was meant to be so easy. Hell, the first bit was easy. The lack of guards and the intense confusion of the place meant taking it was easier than a walk in the park. Not now, though. Everything was starting to go sour.

'Shaun, man ...'

'Ginge, if you say another word, I swear I'll cut your fucking throat,' Shaun hisses, his eyes bulging as much as the veins in his neck.

'Easy, man,' Ginge puts one hand up to placate him. Stepping back, he uses the hand to sweep the locks of red hair from his eyes. 'Shaun, man, I'm just like, you know,' Ginge shrugs, 'saying is all.'

'Yes, but the fucking problem is, is that you keep saying it,' Shaun screams. 'Saying and saying and fucking saying ...'

'Okay, man,' Ginge backs off, 'it's all you, bro.'

'Stop speaking like a fucking surfer,' Shaun glares with a look of pure violence. He is angry, backed into a corner, and everything is going wrong, but here is something he can yell at. The long-haired, ginger prick and the way he speaks. Yeah, that's something that can be shouted about.

'Man,' Ginge shakes his head sulkily, 'you bring me down, man. This is how I speak, bro ...'

Lenski watches the men interact, sensing a hint of desperation which can be exploited, but only by treading very carefully.

'Shaun, may I speak, yes?' she asks softly, changing her manner instantly and earning a quick glance from Sierra.

'No!' Shaun snaps.

'I see you are worried, yes,' Lenski pushes on, speaking rapidly. 'You are not the bad man. I see this,' she pauses for a second. 'You have the families too, yes? You need the food for them, and we need the food and the safe place too ...'

'I said shut it.'

'Please,' Lenski pleads, 'please hear me, yes? You have lost good men, and no more should die here ... My people, they just try to protect us. Let me speak with them and–' Her voice snaps off as the black, circular ends of a double-barrelled shotgun appear inches in front of her eyes.

'One more word,' Shaun mutters, holding the gun there, 'one more word ...'

'Okay,' Sierra shouts, 'we're sorry, okay ... We didn't mean nuffin.'

'Ginge, get rid of these two. I can't fucking think with them going on.'

'Alright, man, yeah, that's cool, you know. Come on, ladies, we gotta do what the man says.'

Leading the two women out, Ginge casts a final look at Shaun, seeing the worry etched onto his features and the way his finger keeps tapping at the trigger of his sawn-off shotgun.

Alone, he starts to pace, frantic with worry. He'd heard the fort was here, and like everyone else, he knew it was the safe place to head for. The only difference was that Shaun had designs to be in charge. He wanted to lead.

Shaun already had a large group of survivors with him and had managed to gather various shotguns, rifles, crossbows, and bladed weapons from farms during the journey south. They all looked to him. He was their leader. The prospect of handing his power over to someone else didn't appeal to him.

The initial recce of the fort showed him that the place was in chaos, with new groups arriving all the time. No sense of order or discipline anywhere. Just some little kids running about with guns. This wasn't what he was expecting. Like everyone else, the survivors' grapevine had been buzzing with how the fort was a government-controlled place of safety with law, order, hospitals, schools, food, and police. All of it run by Mr Howie and his team of soldiers.

The fort Shaun saw wasn't anything like that. From the edge of flatlands, he used his high-powered binoculars to watch all the soldier-types move out. Wondering when they were due to return, he kept watch, knowing his group was safely hidden in the abandoned houses nearby.

Some came back, then more left. Judging by the pile of bodies stacked up, this group had certainly been busy. This meant they had done the hard work and cleared the area off the zombies.

When none of them returned for several hours, he made his move.

The plan was simple. They were to present themselves as refugees much like everyone else. The women and children were to be at the front, obscuring the view of the armed men behind. With the gates wide open and the front area in a general scene of confusion, it was executed with perfection.

The women and children chattered noisily as they reached the front. Many of them calling out to ask questions as the young woman with the accent came out with the black girl. With so many voices calling out, they quickly became distracted. The men watched and waited for Shaun to give the signal and held still for long minutes. Letting the distraction grow, watching as the two women from the fort tried to get order from the new group, waiting as the few kids left nearby grew bored and lost interest. Moving slowly the men started filtering out from the main body of the group, just a few steps taken with the weapons held out of sight. A few rolls of the eyes, a few hands rubbing foreheads and temples, and the image of hen-pecked menfolk was superbly presented.

The take-over was almost instant. One second Lenski and Sierra were doing their best to answer questions and calm the scared and angry women down. The next second, they were surrounded by men holding weapons, pointing shotguns and rifles at them.

The children left behind, when the rest moved out to assist Howie and Maddox, were too slow to react. Seeing their two leaders so rapidly disarmed, they had no choice but to relinquish their own arms.

Shaun gave the order as his group swept through the gates. With the place occupied by new people not having any idea as to the established running order, there was no serious opposition. Control was taken, the fort secured, and that was it.

Easy.

Then it all went horribly wrong. The return of the first group marked the initial opportunity to explain how things were. One man posted outside with a gun, several more on the inside of the first gate, and the idea was simple–get them disarmed first, and then consideration would be given to whether access would be granted.

Shaun assumed he had factored for every eventuality, whereas in reality, he had not factored for shit. For instance, the lack of willingness on behalf of those coming back to be cowed by a single armed sentry, the experience they had of fighting, the aggression of coming from a very recent highly intense battle, the cohesive manner of their movement. None of that was factored.

What they got was a very angry Maddox and an equally angry Clarence who destroyed the armed sentry, gained entry to the first gates, then destroyed everyone else.

Those that got back inside spoke of how fast they moved, the brutality of their actions, and the violence dished out.

Since then, the situation had allowed to become stagnant. Shaun gathered his group to establish the next course of action. The overriding impression was that if the people out there would willingly kill the men behind the first gate, they sure as hell wouldn't hesitate to do the rest if they got inside.

Some suggestions of opening negotiations were put forward. Some ideas of fleeing out the back door, but they were quickly negated when the rear area was actually checked and found to consist of a very narrow strip and very deep water.

Hesitation to make a decision moved into reluctance and slowly morphed towards clear delay. Those outside made repeated efforts to gain contact, calling out for anyone to talk, banging on the gate and shouting.

Shaun forbade any of his team from answering. Instead, he waited, but not knowing what he was waiting for meant the waiting just stretched on through the long hours of the night.

The worry that he had made a very bad decision was nagging at him. He didn't think it through clearly enough. Of course, the fort occupants seen driving away had only been going *somewhere* to do *something*.

Of course, they would come back, and what the hell was he thinking? If they were strong enough to take and hold a fort in the first place, they wouldn't exactly roll over. It was just the thought of no longer being the leader of his group, of not being admired and listened to. He was an estate agent, a nobody from nowhere living a life of boredom and repetition. This was his chance to forge himself into something unique and strong.

Those two women at the front, Lenski and Sierra, had been taken to the old police offices and questioned by Shaun himself. His self-imposed feeling of importance was soon withered by the surly attitude of Lenski mixed with the passive aggression of Sierra.

You have no idea, no idea what you bitten off. The black

girl Sierra had said to him. That was the thing that really sunk worry into his gut. They weren't afraid or cowed for themselves, but rather they begged and pleaded for him to surrender now before it was too late.

He had the men with guns, he had the weapons, he had the upper hand, and he was in control, but *they* were begging *him* to stop while he had the chance. Their total confidence rippled through his group; whispers turned into muttered conversations. Quick glances became long stares of concern.

Give it up, yes? Before it too late. You stop now, and they not hurt you. Who the fuck had he picked a fight with? A combination of the SAS, Navy Seals, and Millwall football fans by the sounds of it.

Even those little kids outside kept tutting and shaking their heads, sucking their little bastard council estate teeth while retaining an air that his group had done something very, very bad.

'Shaun,' Derek walks in, nodding once in greeting, 'what did they say?'

'Same thing,' Shaun replies.

'Fuck,' Derek sighs, visibly sagging. 'Did they say who they were?'

'Not really. They don't need to,' Shaun mumbles. 'Look at what they did. They fucking slaughtered everyone out there within minutes ...'

'I fucking knew this was a bad idea,' Derek mutters. Leaning his back against a wall, he lowers the rifle to stare at the ground.

'Bollocks, Derek,' Shaun snaps, 'you were up for it as much as I was, so don't start trying to back out now.'

'I'm not,' Derek, seeing the angry look on Shaun's face, is quick to placate him. 'I'm with you, Shaun.'

'Yeah, you are, we all are, all of us, so don't fucking forget it.'

'But like,' Derek stammers, 'them fucking kids out there are putting the fear of god into our lot, saying shit about some big, hench bloke and someone called Maddox and...'

'And what?'

'Nothing,' Derek looks away.

'And what!?' Shaun demands.

'A ninja,' Derek spits it out. 'They keep saying they got a fucking ninja called Dave.'

'A what? A ninja? Don't be so bloody stupid,' Shaun huffs, shaking his head with disgust.

'S'wot they said,' Derek mutters, 'and we, well, we got kids, Shaun. You ain't got any kids and no wife, but we have.' Derek plucks the courage up to say what he was sent in for, 'We've got families, Shaun. It's alright for you being single an' all but ...'

'But what?' Shaun asks quietly. 'So it's okay for me to get killed but not you because you got kids, yeah? So you decided to breed a couple of brats, and that makes you better than me?'

'No,' Derek blanches, 'nothin' like that, Shaun ... but like, they're shitting themselves now, and like, they're saying this was your idea and ...'

'Keep going.'

'Well, and we could have just come in here anyway ... We didn't need to do all the guns and stuff and take it over ...' he adds quietly.

'Bit late, Derek,' Shaun locks eyes on the man, 'wouldn't you say?'

'Talk to 'em, then,' Derek pleads. 'Fucking hell, Shaun, just fuckin' talk to 'em and see what they say.'

'What do you think they will say? Hey, don't worry, we

won't do anything with our fucking ninja. Just open the gates and everything will be okay,' Shaun mimics a light tone, waving his free hand about. 'Yeah, we won't kill all of you ... Really, we won't.'

'We can make a deal,' Derek suggests. 'Like we let their people go or something.'

'Yeah, great idea,' Shaun mocks, 'we increase their numbers even more, making it easier for them to fight their way in.'

'Shaun, this place is huge. We don't got enough blokes to keep watch everywhere ... We got the women in some places, and they's fuckin' fumin' at us.'

'Hey, man,' Ginge strolls in with a roll-up hanging from his mouth. 'Hey, Derek, man.'

'Ginge, you alright?'

'Yeah, but like, you know this is fucked up, D-man, like some fucked-up shit.'

'For fuck's sake, Ginge, his name is fucking Derek. Stop fucking calling him D-man,' Shaun explodes. Ginge rolls his eyes quickly at Derek and lapses into silence.

'Shaun?' Derek asks lightly.

'I fucking heard you, Derek,' Shaun snaps.

'So, like? What we gonna do then?' Derek stammers. Turning to Ginge, he says, 'I said we should go talk to them.'

'Man, that's like a great idea,' Ginge nods with a big grin. 'Yeah, like we go and chat, man, shoot some shit and see what they say.'

'I need time to think,' Shaun says quietly, his manner distracted as he paces up and down the room, swinging the sawn-off in one hand. This is all fucked up. Even the thought of going out there to quell the rising issues is too much to deal with.

'Yeah, man,' Ginge nods in agreement, 'but like, Shaun,

man? You've had like ages to think, and like, it's almost daylight, you know?'

'FINE!' Shaun screams in temper. Speaking to them is about the only option left. What started out as a take-over has quickly become a feeling of being held prisoner. Using the constant nagging as a reason for giving in without being seen to be weak, he agrees to the negotiations.

'Like really, man?' Ginge nods stupidly.

'Yeah, man,' Shaun mimics him cruelly. 'Yeah, man, we'll go and fucking speak to them, man.'

'Cool,' Ginge nods, either missing the mocking or choosing to ignore it.

'Twat,' Shaun spits. Striding past the two men, he wrenches the door open before stomping down towards the front. Even with a face like thunder and keeping his eyes to the front, he spots the angry glances being sent his way. Murmured voices and whispered comments all add to the pressure he already feels.

'We're going to negotiate,' Derek announces, making Shaun wince. 'Just bear with us folks, and we'll get this all sorted.'

Folks? Get this sorted? Shaun bites down the urge to scream obscenities at the idiot, instead keeping his head fixed forward while marching towards the gate.

'Shaun, you alright, mate?' one of the armed men stationed there nods at seeing the three men approach.

'Fine,' Shaun snaps. 'Anything?'

'Nothing,' the man replies, 'quiet as fuck.

The three men stop. Shaun in the lead, with Ginge and Derek close behind him.

'Shaun's gonna talk to 'em,' Derek nods eagerly, 'like get some negotiations going.'

'That's great, Shaun, good luck,' the gate guard says earnestly.

'Yeah, great,' Shaun mutters. Time to switch on, time to get the old estate agent's juices going, selling all that real estate and making good money from commission. Yep, Shaun could sell an igloo to an Eskimo. *Everyone is watching Shaunie. They're all looking to you. Better make it good. Not too soft, don't show fear but not too hard either and make them think there is no hope. Give them a glimmer of hope, show them an escape route out of this mess.*

Thinking hard, he nods to himself, rubbing his hands down his trousers to wipe the sweat off, the sawn-off clamped under his armpit. Glancing up, he spots the first tendrils of light spreading across the sky. Hot, too hot. It's close in here, with no breeze or air.

Clearing his throat noisily, Shaun steps closer to the gate. No, if he speaks from here, they could try and shoot through it. Stepping aside, he turns to see everyone staring at him. Not just his own group, but everybody from the camp, by the looks of it. Thank fuck those two women are locked up.

Come on, Shaunie. Time to shine.

'Right,' he calls out in a firm voice, 'you listening out there? It's about time we had a little chat.' Happy with that. Nice, strong opening making him sound like the decision to talk is his own and not through force or being worried.

'We got loads of armed people in here, guns and ... more guns,' wincing, he moves on swiftly. Long years of intense wrangling with buyers, sellers, and all the people in between had given him good skills to know when to rush on and smooth over the verbal cracks. 'We got your people here too. They're all safe, and nobody has been hurt ... yet,' he adds menacingly. Yeah, good start. Shows them there's some intent if he's not happy.

Hmmm, they really should have said something back by now. Just silence. No sounds at all.

'You hear me out there?' he shouts. 'I said nobody has been hurt yet. That can soon change.'

Silence, long seconds of silence. Someone in the camp coughs, others shift position. A rifle butt knocks against someone's shotgun, followed by a muted 'excuse me'.

'Go ahead,' a voice calls out casually from the other side, 'you's fucked anyway.'

'What?' Shaun stares in shock at the inert gate as though that was the thing that spoke to him.

'You deaf or something?' the voice calls back. 'I said do what you want cos you's fucked anyway.'

'Oi ...' Shaun shouts, trying to make his voice sound less shocked and more aggressive.

'You ain't got no way out, bro,' Maddox shouts, using a hard street edge to his voice. 'There are no other exits, no other way out but through this door,' Maddox blends his voice skilfully, easing gradually from the *street voice* to the *educated voice* as the Bossman used to call it. He knows the effect will be disconcerting to them. 'So go ahead, kill everyone, kill everything ...'

'Now, hang on a minute–' Shaun blusters.

'But,' the single word silences Shaun instantly, clear and calm, yet full of authority. No panic in that voice, just complete confidence.

'But what?' Shaun asks, realising that by asking he just lost the power dynamic of the attempted negotiations.

'No buts,' a female voice calls out now. 'You're all going to die for what you've done, slowly, painfully, and every single one of you will suffer horribly ...' Paula is also used to negotiations and also very used to dealing with men.

'And we're going to feed you to the zombies,' Maddox adds. 'All of you. Your wives and children will go first while you watch.'

Shaun spins round at the muted ripples of consternation spreading through the crowd behind him. The voices are so clear, carrying easily to the far ends of the small, gathered crowd.

'And anyone that stands with you will suffer the same fate,' Paula shouts, 'and their families and their children too.'

'Shit, man, what the fuck?' Ginge stares in horror at Shaun.

'We'll burn your fucking fort to the ground. We'll kill everyone and leave nothing behind ... Everything you just said, we can do too,' Shaun bellows.

Silence again. He stares at the gate expectantly, waiting for the retort.

'Sorry, did you say something?' Paula shouts casually. 'We were talking.'

'I said we'll burn your house to the ground ...'

'Fort,' Derek interrupts.

'What?' Shaun snaps.

'Fort, you said house ... We're in a fort.'

'Derek, fuck off, you twat,' Shaun seethes. 'I said we'll burn your fort to–'

'You did say house,' the female voice cuts him off mid-flow.

'Yes, I bloody know, but it doesn't matter! House, fort, fucking caravan ... We'll burn it and everyone inside.'

'That includes you,' Maddox says.

'Yeah,' Shaun roars, 'yeah, us too.'

'Go ahead. Saves us a job,' Maddox says with an almost verbal shrug for effect.

'What's your name?' Shaun asks quickly. Personalise the conversation, take away the faceless entity, and start working on the person.

'My name?' Maddox asks.

'Yes, what is it?'

'My name is fuck you.'

'Right, is that how you want this to go? I can get some of your people here right now and fucking shoot them. Then for every minute you hang about out there, I'll shoot another one.'

'Like I said,' Maddox replies in a flat, almost bored voice, 'you do what you gotta do, but just one thing ... for every bruise on our people, I will cut a finger off, for every mark you leave, I will cut a toe off, for every open wound that bleeds, I will feed you those fingers and toes one at a time, and I will keep going until all of your people have neither fingers nor toes ... After that, I will start on tongues, and that's just your children.'

'Man,' Ginge shakes his head, 'we shouldn't of come here, you know, like, like ... this is bad shit, really bad shit.'

'They're fucking psychos, really ... really real psychos. We're fucked.'

'Psychos?' Paula calls out. 'No, not us ... That's the other ones. Mr Howie and Dave and their team ... We're very nice compared to them.'

Fresh murmurs course through the crowd at hearing the names now so familiar to them. Those murmurs easily reach the ears of Paula, Maddox, and the others grouped near the outside of the gate.

'They've held this place against everything,' Paula continues, aware of how many people must be listening.

'You saw the bodies at the top? The big stacks of bodies piled high. They killed every one of them. They've killed tens of thousands and most likely more than that. The zombies got inside that fort you are inside now. They turned all of their friends and families, and you know what they did?' she pauses for effect. 'They killed them. They cut them down without hesitation. Do you understand? They killed their own families to keep this fort. Do you think for one second they will let anyone else take it from them?'

'Shaun,' Derek mutters, 'mate, this is going bent ... seriously really ...'

'Listen to him, Shaun, man,' Ginge cuts in.

'Shut up,' Shaun hisses.

'This fort is a free place,' Maddox takes the flow up. 'Every man, woman, and child in there is there from their own free will. You get me, bro?' he slips easily into his urban twang with a hard edge. 'They could come and go as they please,' straight back out to normal voice. 'What you have done is create a tyranny, a tyrannical rule, whereby you are forcing people to be held against their will. We invited them in. We gave them shelter and promised them safety and food. What are you doing?' Maddox ends with the loaded question. 'Can they leave if they want?'

'What my colleague is saying,' Paula takes her turn, 'is that you tried to take something by force that would have been given to you freely. We would have taken you all in with open arms. We could feed you, give you clean clothes and running water. We have order and control. We have stability and people who want to work towards making a safe place for everyone.'

'But you gone and fucked all that up, bruv,' Maddox jumps in, 'fucked it up good and proper.'

The sense of panic in Shaun rises to the point of threatening to burst from the top of his head. Sweat pours down his face. His control is gone, slipping away through his fingers.

'Tell you what we'll do,' Paula says. 'Take an hour or two to discuss it with your people, let them know the women and children are free to stay here without duress or punishment. We understand the dangers out there and that many people will want to stay in big groups for safety. So you all have a chat and then let us know what you want to do.'

'Wait,' Derek blurts out, fearing the people outside are about to walk off. 'You said the women and children can stay. What about the men?'

Silence. Maddox giving Paula a shake of the head, telling her not to answer. She nods back, understanding his methods.

'Hey? You there?' Derek shouts again. 'I said what about the men?'

Still no reply. Just an empty silence.

'Man,' Ginge sweeps his long, greasy hair from his forehead, 'this is so bad, like, you know? Like so bad. It's a real downer for sure.'

'Ginge, 'Shaun seizes on the thing he can be angry about, 'you are a total prick, you know that? A complete total fucking surfer prick.'

'Hey, man,' Ginge shakes his head, the locks of hair falling back over the top of his head. 'Like, you know, Shaun,' he adds without saying anything at all.

'Shaun, we gotta talk about this,' Derek shuffles nervously from foot to foot. 'Really, Shaun, we really gotta talk about this, yeah?'

'Not here,' Shaun hisses, 'in the office.'

'Wait a minute,' one of the women in the crowd says, a

solid-built lady that was instrumental in causing the distraction outside. 'This concerns all of us now, so you ain't running off to discuss things behind our backs.'

'Yeah, bloody right,' someone adds firmly as murmurs of agreement grow.

'Fine, can we just go away from here at least,' Shaun concedes.

The group moves off. The people that were present before the new armed group arrived stay close to listen. Sensing this man is rapidly losing control, and having heard word for word what Maddox and Paula said, they stay quiet, waiting to see how it plays out.

Shaun pauses for a moment, gathering his thoughts. He stares back at the gate, wishing it was wide open so he could run through it and get as far away from here as possible.

Thinking frantically, he moves slowly behind the crowd, regretting ever coming here.

'Did we push it too far?' Paula whispers. Having moved away from the inside of the gate, they stand outside the fort, speaking in low voices. Maddox looks to Paula, then to Roy standing quietly as he follows the conversation, and finally to Darius nearby keeping a close eye on the inner section.

'No, I don't think so,' Maddox replies. 'They sound scared, and you heard all the other people in there talking.'

'I did,' Paula nods. 'You don't think he'll carry out the threat, then?'

'Kill people? No,' Maddox says firmly, 'definitely no way. Even if he wants to, I think the others will stop him. The men he's got with him have families in there, and we've given them a way out by saying the women and children can stay. Nah, he's shitting himself right now ...'

'I agree,' Roy interjects, 'he's going to be feeling more like a prisoner than a siege lord.'

'Siege lord?' Paula gives him a quick quizzical look.

'And I know what Sierra will be saying,' Darius cuts in. 'Lenski too ...'

'Plus the crew we left here,' Maddox nods at his friend. 'They ain't stupid. They'll be saying things to plant seeds and get them worried.'

'What now, then?' Paula yawns with a big stretch. Fighting all night, then having to deal with this, the exhaustion is starting to show.

'We wait,' Maddox says with that calm air of authority. He knows the outcome will be one of two actions–either they'll give up and come out of their own accord or they won't, and if they don't, then as soon as Howie gets back, they'll go in. Simple. 'Get some sleep, yeah?' Maddox says. 'Darius, you keep watch for now, bruv, get me if anything happens.'

'You sleeping too?' Paula asks with surprise. 'Aren't you worried for Lenski and the others.'

Maddox thinks before answering, the natural inclination to never admit a weakness and never display emotion. 'Worrying won't fix this. Being smart and thinking straight is what we need, and being too tired to do either won't help anyone. Get some rest. Darius, you on it, yeah?'

'I'm on it, Mads.'

He walks off, ending the conversation. His face doesn't betray a flicker of expression, but those intelligent eyes never stop searching, thinking, planning, and factoring every nuance that might happen. Lenski is the first woman he has ever got close to. Being a well-built, handsome man,

Maddox has enjoyed more than his fair share of attention from the opposite sex, but Lenski is different, all of this is different. New world, new rules.

For the first time in his life, he feels a nagging sensation deep inside that the person he loves is in danger, and there is nothing he can do to help. The cold, ruthless core of Maddox works swiftly to override that sensation. Lenski is exceptionally capable and intelligent, and she can look after herself.

It's all a game of chess, Maddox. Life is a game of chess. Know your opponent and know yourself; then, you can predict what he'll do next. Once you know that, you are in control.

The Bossman ended his reign badly, fucking up from smoking too much of his own produce, but the lessons he instilled in Maddox run deep. In order to plan, he needs a mind that is sharp. Sleep deprivation does not make a sharp mind.

Settling down in the shaded lee of the wall, he closes his eyes. Breathing deeply to help calm his mind, he slowly allows sleep to start pulling him under.

'He's an exceptional kid,' Paula whispers to Roy. Both of them resting against the wall some distance away, watching as he calmly rests.

'Yep,' Roy agrees. 'How old is he? Can't be more than twenty.'

'Must be about that. How are you doing?' She looks at the man next to her. She has known him for less than 24 hours, but it feels so much longer. The way he fought last night was incredible. First with his bow and arrow, cutting them down as they burst forward to attack the lines. In the dark, with so much noise and heat, he didn't miss once–an amazing feat of skill.

Even after that, when the time for projectile weapons was done and it came down to getting close, he didn't falter but pulled his sword out and stayed close to Paula throughout. Fit, strong, and athletic, and he stayed steady, not letting anger or fear control him.

'Me?' Roy asks. 'Yeah, I got this funny feeling in my back,' he shifts position with a worried look on his face, 'like a dull pain.'

'Where?' she asks softly.

'Behind my right lung. Like when I breathe in really deep, it hurts.'

'Okay, show me,' Paula slips into the calm doctor-type tones she knows will calm his worried countenance. Placing a hand on his back, she moves it around slowly as he shifts and wriggles.

'Up a bit ... No, not there ... Bit left ... too much, go back ... Yeah, that's it, just in there.'

'Does it hurt a lot?' Paula asks.

'No, it's a tiny pain really, but that's what tumours do. They just grow silently until they're the size of bowling balls.'

'I can't feel anything, Roy,' flattening her hand, she rubs all around the area, pushing harder, then more gently.

'Hmmm,' Roy sighs at the relaxing sensation produced by the inadvertent back rub.

'Twist round,' she orders gently. Smiling, she starts using both hands to rub his back on the premise of searching for growths. 'No ...' she says slowly, 'really can't feel anything here ...'

'Uh-huh,' Roy mutters, 'must be something there.'

'Want me to keep checking? Maybe down here?' She slowly works down his back, kneading and pressing into the muscles. Sitting cross-legged, his head starts dropping as his body relaxes. What a strange man, she muses, so competent, yet so afraid. What an awful life to have lived every day gripped with irrational fear and being unable to apply logical thinking. It must have dictated his entire life and defined who he was. Yet here he is, not only surviving the apocalypse but thriving. Healthy, fit, and fully in control. He has a complete lack of fear towards the infected, genuinely unbothered about them or anything else going on for that matter.

She's noticed too that he stays close to her, like they are a pair now, a team within a team. Howie has his lot, Maddox has his crews, and they all work together with Paula and Roy.

After what happened in the office on the night it started with that bastard Clarke, she made a decision to reject any form of human contact and do it alone. But as she glances round at the people resting quietly nearby, she realises that she has changed. These people are important to her now, important enough for her to risk her life for, safe in the knowledge that they would also risk their life for her. She is not alone anymore.

'Did you find something?' Roy asks. Paula blinks as she realises she's stopped rubbing and is scratching the back of her right hand absent-mindedly as she thinks. Looking down, she spots the swelling of a definite lump over the last knuckle of her little finger.

'Oh,' she mutters, taking a closer look.

'What?' Roy asks. Twisting round, he notices her staring at her hand. 'You alright?'

'Er, yeah,' she nods.

'Cor, fucking hell, that's a bit swollen,' he nods at her hand. 'Here, let me see,' gently, he pulls her hand closer to peer down closely. 'Insect bite,' he mutters. 'You got a tiny puncture in the skin, must be allergic to something. Is it itchy?'

'Yeah, I was scratching without realising.'

'Insect,' Roy nods confidently, 'maybe a little spider ... What!?'

'Don't say spider,' she shudders.

'You don't like spiders?'

'I'm terrified of them,' she half-grins, remembering the one in the mechanics' workshop toilet creeping towards her. She retells the story, putting herself as the idiot blundering about, whacking zombies while trying to evade a tiny, harmless creature. Chuckling at the story, Roy watches her speaking, absorbed by the self-effacing manner of this beautiful, confident woman.

More than once, he's been called misanthropic with his general distaste for all things humanity, and the thought of teaming up with anyone, even a beautiful woman, would have sent feelings of repulsion through him.

He was a good-looking man, fit and athletic, with a very intelligent mind, and deep down, he was also exceptionally kind. It was the anxiety that made him appear self-obsessed and selfish, and in turn, that tended to drive people away. They never understood and just kept saying things like *get over it, snap out of it, just don't think about it.* Only that wasn't possible–there was something wrong with his mind. He knew that, and as years went by, he just kind of accepted it.

A sensation would appear in his body, and his mind would go into meltdown with an immediate assumption it was some horrific, fatal disease. He was checked, given a clean bill of health, and would be fine for a few days until the next one started.

Like Paula, he rejected thoughts of teaming up with

anyone, instead embracing the solace in return for not being judged.

Again, he feels differently now. With Paula on hand to soothe his fears, he can concentrate on things other than himself. For the first time in years, he can work with other people towards a common aim. These people were very capable and willing to get stuck in; plus with everything going on, they haven't judged him.

He likes the quiet Mr Howie and the immense power oozing from him, same with Maddox. That youth is deeply intelligent and very tough. Dave, Clarence, and even those lads with them. They all seem, well ... they seem right. Right for this. The right people to deal with it. They cut down so many last night, more than he could ever imagine, and with Paula by his side, he didn't have to worry about covering his back.

This fort isn't his; it means nothing to him. He only came here thinking there would be doctors to check him over and find the many diseases that must have developed in the last two weeks. He could walk away, go find his van, and survive the way he was before, only something is stopping him. A sense of a mission started that has to be seen through. Secure the fort, re-establish control for Mr Howie and Maddox; then, he and Paula can go find some doctors and medical equipment. Yep, that's the plan. Isn't it? Is there another reason for staying here? There is something else deep down that has yet to surface into a tangible thought. Paula resumes the back rub, and that intangible thought floats a bit closer to the surface.

Maybe another reason for staying.

Maybe.

CHAPTER THIRTY-SIX

The chair is too big for him. His legs dangle with his feet still inches from the ground. Hands on his lap, he watches the man.

Never in his young life has Billy seen such a man before. His mind reeling from recent events, he just stares in wonder at the person in front of him.

'So, young Billy,' the Doc smiles, showing a great big mouth full of slightly crooked teeth. Billy doesn't know where to look. The teeth are big, his mouth is big, his nose is bigger than any nose he has seen before, and those eyes ... A light shade of blue edging into grey and so cold, yet so friendly at the same time. Almost hypnotic, and Billy stares in a trance-like state.

'How are you feeling?' The Doc asks in a deep voice that rolls from his mouth. 'I understand,' he says when Billie doesn't answer. He then stands upright, causing young Billy to crane his neck back just to look up.

'You need me here?' Larson asks from the door.

'No, no, I don't think so,' the Doc replies. 'I think Billy and I will be just fine.' The Doc crosses the room in three easy strides to stand next to Larson. Billy stares at the height difference. Being young and small means everyone looks big to Billy, but the Doc towers over Larson. He towers over everything.

Tall but not wide, with long arms and legs and huge hands with great big, long fingers and thick nails on the ends.

'Call if you need me,' Larson nods. Walking out, he pulls the door closed behind him, sealing Billy in the room with this strangest of men.

'Larson,' the Doc opens the door, calling after the man, 'tell Vince I will speak to him shortly.'

'Will do,' Larson nods. Billy watches this interaction, wondering why the Doc didn't just say that to Vince himself. Vince is stood right there, right next to Larson.

'Ah,' the Doc grins, turning back to Billy like he forgot he was there. Crossing back over the room, he pulls a wheeled chair out from under a desk and pushes it across the room, towards Billy.

'That's better,' he sighs as he eases himself into the chair. Still smiling, he watches Billy. 'One of the few disadvantages of being so tall,' the Doc explains. 'Get sore knees,' he adds with a conspiring wink.

'So, Billy, tell me about you,' a gentle question but a command, nonetheless. Billy doesn't know what to say but looks at the man's hair. Long and grey, and it hangs limply down to his shoulders. There was a man in Billy's town that had hair like that. Mummy said the man was homeless, which means he had lost his home. Billy thought this was odd as a house was very big, so how did he lose it? Unless he forgot where he put it, but then he could just ask someone to help find it, like he did when he couldn't find one of his toys.

'I understand,' the Doc repeats knowingly, 'you must be terrified, and I understand that, Billy. Really, I do. I'm a doctor, Billy. Do you know what that means?'

Billy nods, a small, tiny movement.

'Good,' the Doc beams, showing his crooked teeth again. 'A doctor is an expert who knows everything about the body–my body, your body, everyone's body. Like a mechanic that fixes cars, a doctor fixes bodies. That's what I do,' the Doc continues in a deep rumble. 'Now, do you know what is happening?'

The question is too broad for Billy to understand, so he simply stays quiet and watches the man.

'I shall tell you,' the Doc says. 'Do you know what a disease is, Billy? A disease is when some germs get inside your body and make you sick. Like when you get a cold and can't stop coughing or sneezing. That is like a disease. Some diseases, like the cold, are quite harmless and don't really hurt us because our bodies can do things that make them go away. Some diseases are stronger, and the body can't make them go away, but doctors have medicines, and we can use those medicines to make them go away.' The Doc pauses, taking a breath and nodding with a quick grin.

'What's happened out there, Billy, is that a new disease has got inside some of the bodies. That disease makes people very, very sick, and it makes them want to bite other people. When one person bites another person, it means the disease can move from the first body to the second body. Now, Billy, this disease is brand new. We have never known of this disease before. So we don't have any medicines for it. Do you understand, Billy? If someone gets this disease, there is nothing we can do to help them, and if we just leave them alone, they will bite other people, and then lots more will get the disease. So, I thought, being a doctor,' he nods, 'what we need, is a safe place away from all of the people with the disease. Next, I thought, *hey, who shall I invite to live in my safe place?* And you know what, Billy? I wanted children to come and live with me. Oh, adults can look after themselves. They are big and can run fast, but children, well, they are small and young and can't run so fast, so I want this safe place to be for the children. Children like you, Billy. We already have other children here, but I want more.' The Doc chuckles, holding his big hands spread out. 'Every room should be full of laughing children that are having fun. We have lessons,' the Doc drops into a serious tone. 'Lessons are important, and children should be taught to read and write, and yes, Billy, we have bedtimes too as children also need lots of sleep so they can grow big and strong, but we have nice food and lots of space to play and have fun!

'But in order to keep all these wonderful, happy children safe, we have to have guards, Billy, like the queen has people to make sure nothing bad happens to her. Well, we have the same thing. We have big, strong men with guns that are here to protect us, so there is no need to be frightened of them.' Leaning forward, the Doc drops into a whisper, 'I know some of them swear and say rude things, and that's very naughty, but sometimes we have to ignore things like that so we can all be safe.' The Doc sits upright, hands on his knees and beaming happily. When he doesn't say anything, Billy feels that he should speak now, but he can't remember if there was a question. Fidgeting nervously, he tries to think of everything the Doc just said. It all made sense, but he can't really remember it now.

'Now, onto the serious business,' the Doc adopts a mock serious manner. 'We don't want the disease to ever get into our safe place, do we, Billy?'

That is a question, and Billy nods first, then realises he should be shaking his head, so does that instead.

'That's right,' the Doc says, 'we don't want it here. We don't want that disease to get anywhere near my children, so we have some tests to make sure the disease doesn't get in here. Now, Billy, I have a couple of questions for you, and I need you to be really honest and not tell me any lies. Do you understand?'

Billy nods.

'Good, has anyone bitten you, Billy? Anyone at all, say, your mummy or daddy or even a friend, maybe a dog or cat? Anyone at all, has anyone bitten you?'

Billy shakes his head.

'Has anyone tried to bite you?'

Billy shakes his head.

'Good,' the Doc smiles, 'now, has anyone scratched you like a cat scratches with its sharp claws. Has anyone scratched you, Billy?'

Billy shakes his head.

'Has anyone tried to scratch you?'

Again, Billy shakes his head.

'Now, Billy, this is a disgusting question but very, very important one. Has anyone got blood on you? Blood that wasn't yours?'

Billy nods, earning a sudden interested look from the Doc.

'They have?'

Billy nods again.

'Who got blood on you, Billy? You can tell me, go on ...'

'The man,' Billy whispers.

'The man? What man, Billy?'

'The man that did wrestling with Sam, and he hurt Norman and my dad.'

'Wrestled with Sam? What does that mean, Billy? Who is Sam?'

'Sam was my sister's friend. The man pulled her pants down and wrestled with her, but she didn't like it, and she cried, so the man hit her.'

'Did he now?' The Doc says softly. 'And he hurt your daddy too and the other man Norman?'

Billy nods.

'Was it the man that brought you here, Billy? Was it Vince?'

Billy shakes his head.

'The man that was with Vince, he did all of that?'

Billy nods.

'What did Vince do?'

'He was watching,' Billy mutters, unable to take his eyes off the Doc's face.

'I see, and it was after the man wrestled with Sam and hurt your daddy and Norman that you got blood on you? Is that right?'

Billy nods.

'Right,' the Doc says slowly, 'hmmm, I think, Billy, that I need to talk to Vince for a minute. Can you wait here for me?'

Billy nods.

'Good boy,' the Doc smiles, but this time there isn't any humour in his eyes, 'you stay right there and don't move.' The Doc spins round on the chair and strides across the room, pulling the door firmly shut behind him.

Billy does as told and stays rooted to the chair. Outside the room he hears an angry voice and footsteps; then, a door slams shut. The angry voice shouts and another noise, like someone slapping their hand on the table. Someone yelps like they hurt themselves. Billy hears more hands on the table and more yelps. Then the yelping stops, and a big thud sounds out. The shouting carries on for a little while with more loud banging noises. Then it all goes quiet. Footsteps, door opens and closes, footsteps again, then silence.

After a minute, the door opens, and the Doc walks in. His face is flushed like he has run up and down the stairs. Billy notices some red ink has splashed on the bottom of his long, white coat. It looks like the coat doctors wear on TV but a lot dirtier. Mummy would tell him off if he got his coat that dirty.

Breathing hard, the Doc crosses the room and picks up a radio walkie talkie from the desk.

'Larson.'

'Here, Doc.'

'I've spoken to Vince. Can you please deal with him?'

'Will do, Doc.'

'Right,' the Doc takes a deep breath before turning to face Billy, 'I have spoken to Vince, and he has said he is very sorry for letting his friend hurt your daddy and the ... er ... other people. He said it will never happen again. Now, where were we? Oh yes, you got some blood on you, didn't you, Billy?'

Billy nods, watching the beads of sweat fall from the Doc's large, broad forehead.

'Now, although I am very, very sure the blood was not the diseased blood, we still need to give you a thorough check-up, just to be completely sure. Is that alright with you, Billy?'

Billy nods. At this current time, he would nod to anything.

'Have you seen a doctor before, Billy?'

'I had acheear.'

'You mean earache, so you saw a doctor because your ear hurt, yes?'

Billy nods.

'And I bet the doctor had a torch, and he looked in both your ears, yes?'

Billy nods, remembering the shiny object the doctor held in her hands.

'If you had a sore throat, the doctor would check your mouth, and if you had a bad foot, the doctor would check your foot, wouldn't they? So what I have to do, Billy, is I have check all of you. I need to check all of your body just to make extra sure that you don't have anything wrong with you. Do you understand?'

Billy nods, not really understanding.

'Good boy. Now you get your clothes off, and we'll get you all checked. Then after that, you can have some food with Mrs Meryl, and then you can meet the other boys and girls.'

Billy holds still, wondering what the doctor means. He said *get your clothes off,* and now he's looking like he's expecting Billy to do something.

Get your clothes off.

Billy eases forward to drop from the too-big-chair. Slowly, he grabs the bottom of his t-shirt and starts pulling it up. The Doc grins and nods before turning round to take something from his desk.

'Good boy, Billy, and the pants too ... That's it. I'm a doctor, Billy, and I have seen many, many naked people, so don't you worry about anything.'

Billy works at his button, wishing Lilly was here to help him. His mummy was with him when the doctor looked in his ears, but now he's alone. Slowly, he pulls his shorts and pants down to stand naked.

'Have you seen one of these before, Billy?' The Doc looks the boy up and down whilst holding out his stethoscope.

Billy nods, then shakes his head; he's seen them on television but not in real life.

'This is called a stethoscope.' The Doc drops down onto his knees in front of Billy and reaches towards him. 'Here, you put these bits in your ears like this,' he pushes the ends into Billy's ears. 'Ah, your ears are too small. Here, you hold them.' Billy reaches up to hold the end next to his ears.

'Now, this bit we put against the chest like this, and you can hear the heart working away,' the Doc places the round section against Billy's chest.

'Can you hear it, Billy?'

Billy nods, hearing a thump-da-thump.

'So that means that your heart is working properly,' the Doc grins. 'Now, try mine. Is my heart working properly, Billy?'

The Doc deftly undoes a button of his open-necked shirt to reveal a smooth, very pale chest. He stretches the stethoscope towards his chest, pulling Billy in closer.

'So your heart works okay, and my heart works okay. What else do we need to check?'

Billy stares awkwardly up at the Doc, unsure of what to say, so he just listens to the Doc's heart instead. The sound is much different to his own heart. The Doc's heart is booming much faster and harder.

'We have to listen to your lungs,' the Doc says. Taking the stethoscope end, he presses it once more to Billy's chest, then gently takes the ends from Billy to press into his own ears.

Billy waits as the Doc listens intently. 'Breath in for me, Billy. Nice, big breath. That's it ...'

The Doc leans in closer, dropping his head so it almost touches Billy's chest. Maybe being closer means the tube things work better. Billy glances down at the big bald patch on the top of the Doc's head and the white bits of skin his mummy always called dandyrough or something.

This close to the Doctor, Billy can smell the sweat coming from him. It's stale smell that isn't very nice, but the Doc stays there for a long time, just leaning in close and listening while Billy breathes in and out.

Eventually, he pulls away and takes the tube thing out from his ears. Pulling a thin torch from his top pocket, he clicks the end to make it light up.

'Now, we have to check you all over,' the Doc says. His face is red again, and he speaks a bit faster than he did before.

Billy stands quietly while the Doc pours over every inch of his skin. His back and chest, his arms and armpits, then his feet and legs. The Doc doesn't touch him but hovers really close, so close that Billy can feel his hot breath on his skin.

The Doc seems to spend ages looking at Billy's bottom, then round at his front bits.

'Got to be very careful here, Billy,' the Doc says breathlessly. 'The disease can get in places like this very easily, so we have to be very, very careful and keep a good watch.'

The Doc stares and stares, moving slowly to shine the torch from lots of different angles but still doesn't touch Billy. A couple of times, it's like the Doc *wants* to touch Billy, but he doesn't. His big hand just sort of stops and shakes a bit before dropping.

'Right,' the Doc calls out in a loud voice as he clambers back to his feet, 'I would say, young Billy, that you are all clear. Isn't that good?' The Doc turns away. Taking a tissue from his desk, he wipes the sweat from his face with trembling hands.

'But,' the Doc says with his back still turned to Billy. 'We have to keep checking to make sure the disease doesn't get here. Oh, you can get dressed again now, Billy,' the Doc adds as he turns back to see Billy still standing there naked.

'Larson, Billy is all clear. He needs to go down to Meryl for some food.'

'Okay, Doc, give me a minute.'

Pulling his wheeled chair back to his desk, the Doc doesn't glance at Billy but sits down to start leafing through a big book. Billy dresses quickly and waits.

'Wait outside, please, Billy,' the Doc says without looking round. 'Larson will be up for you in a minute.' His voice is different now, speaking like the teachers did at school when they were busy and didn't want to talk to you.

Closing the door behind him, Billy waits in the corridor like he was told to. A door further down opens, and he watches two men pulling another man out. Billy recognises the clothes that Vince was wearing and wonders what happened him? Maybe he fell down and cut his head.

One of the men carrying Vince glances up the corridor and spots Billy. 'Shit, go back, go back,' he urges his mate. Within a second, they've shuffled out of view, closing the door behind them.

Billy just waits, thinking that this place is very strange, but he's glad the disease hasn't got him. The disease sounds horrible, and Billy doesn't want to bite anyone either.

Quietly, he waits, thinking about the big, strange man in the white coat and wondering if Lilly will be here soon.

CHAPTER THIRTY-SEVEN

'That's the last one,' I say. Clambering into the big, zebra-striped Land Rover, I glance back at the gates now open.

'You sure about this?' Lani asks, 'I mean, nice idea but …'

'It's done now.'

'We couldn't just leave them locked up like that,' Cookey says, twisting round as though expecting to see herds of wild animals bursting from the gates in a mad dash for freedom.

'We might have just re-introduced wild predators to England,' Blowers says proudly. 'Now, that is cool.'

The decision to open the safari park was taken quickly. We all felt a sense of responsibility for the animals after seeing the lion and gorilla fight. That was our fault, and none of us wanted more animal death on our hands. The lions were able to move about now, so they could go through the broken enclosures, but that meant the prey animals had nowhere to go. So we opened everything.

Clarence found the keys to one of the safari vehicles, all of us laughing when he pulled up in the black and white striped Land Rover. Milly was safely secured inside with Clarence, and Meredith was tied up, using some rope we found. After that, it didn't take long, moving to each enclosure, breaking the locks, snapping chains, and pulling the gates open.

For a second or two, we did consider the snakes in the glass cabinets. The big pythons wouldn't have been a problem, but none of us fancied trying to release a more nimble cobra or rattlesnake.

Milly had a great time, a proper trip round the park, looking at all the animals while being held by Clarence. Bouncing up and down with absurd glee and asking us each in turn whether we liked certain animals.

The fleeting conversation we had earlier in the café was done and apparently gone. She hasn't said as much, but I think we all get the impression she was a bit neglected by her family.

Loaded up, we leave via the long exit road as we snake through the wooded copses to the main road.

'Ha!' Cookey bursts out laughing. 'Guess what we just saw?'

'What?' Blowers asks.

'Lions and tigers and bears ...' He looks round, waiting for someone to finish the sentence. 'Oh, come on ... Lions and tigers and bears ... Don't leave me hanging.'

'Not doing it,' Blowers shakes his head.

'Lani? Come on!'

'Nope, not a chance, Cookey.

'Clarence?'

'What do you think?'

'Dave, then, come on, Dave ...'

'What?'

'Finish it off ... Lions and tigers and bears ...?'

'And what?' Dave asks dully.

'Boss?' Cookey moves swiftly on, looking at me with a pleading look.

Smiling whilst shaking my head, I feel the stupid urge to say it.

'Don't do it, Mr Howie,' Blowers urges.

'I can't leave him hanging,' I say. 'Go on, then.'

'Ha! Lions and tigers and bears ...'

'Oh my,' in the end, it comes out with a laugh as Cookey cheers. Milly watches, enraptured at the young lad laughing at his own jokes.

'Lions and tigers and bears ...' Cookey repeats.

'Oh my,' I say louder, laughing at the groans coming from the others.

'Lions and tigers and bears ...' Cookey sings now.

'Come on, Milly,' I coax. 'Oh my!' She claps her hands in delight, waiting for Cookey to say it again so she can join in.

'Lions and tigers and bears ...'

'OH MY!' Milly and I shout the reply, both of us laughing.

'Come on,' Cookey yells, 'lions and tigers and bears ...'

'OH MY,' Lani joins in this time, and I can see Blowers is struggling not to say it. Even Clarence is starting to smile.

'Lions and tigers and bears ...'

'OH MY,' Blowers joins in, laughing, just leaving Clarence and a somewhat bemused Dave to go.

'Lions and tigers and bears ...'

'OH MY!' Clarence adds his deep voice to the chorus, even Meredith gives a high-pitched bark at the sudden explosion of noise.

'Dave, come on, Dave,' Cookey grins. 'Lions ... and ...' he

goes slowly as everyone turns to stare at Dave, 'tigers ... and bears ...'

Dave looks round at everyone slowly, his expressionless eyes giving nothing away. With a shrug, he turns away to stare out the window. 'Oh my,' he adds quietly with a rare wry smile.

'YES!' Cookey booms in victory. 'I got Dave to say oh my.'

'Do it again,' Milly giggles.

'Lions and tigers and bears ...'

'OH MY,' Milly yells, almost collapsing in a fit of giggles.

'Lions and tigers and Millies,' Cookey calls out.

'OH MY,'

'Shame we can't get the Saxon on the way,' I turn to Clarence, leaving Cookey and Milly singing in the back.

'We can go there, but unless you know how to fix it ...'

'Not a chance,' I reply. 'We need Nick, really. Christ, I bet even Maddox's lot will probably know more about engines and stuff than us.'

'You've not mentioned it much?' Clarence asks quietly.

'Which bit? Immune or one of the other things going on?'

'Fair point,' Clarence nods. 'Immunity, then ... Start with that.'

'What's to say?' I ask him. 'Like I said before, it doesn't change anything. Without doctors and scientists, it means nothing to us.'

'No, it does mean something. It means everything,' Clarence says seriously, turning to fix me with a keen glare. 'It explains why they shit themselves round you, explains why you can do that thing ...'

'What about Lani, then?'

'That I don't know,' Clarence concedes. 'The most likely explanation is that you've passed some kind if gene or antibody to her. Not as strong as yours, which is why she turned but got better, whereas you didn't turn at all.'

'Maybe. How we gonna test that, then? I kiss one of you and send you out to get bit?'

'Again, fair point,' Clarence sighs, 'but seriously, boss, maybe it's something we should be thinking about.'

'I know. It's been going through my head,' I reply. 'I was thinking like an insurance policy, in case one of you does get bitten, then it might help. Might be like Lani and resist it.'

'Right, insurance policy,' Clarence nods. 'We should do it.'

'But, mate, on the flip side, I could be a carrier, so could Lani. We could still infect you. Is that a risk worth taking?'

'Yes,' Blowers calls out, making me realise the back has fallen into silence following our conversation.

'Seriously?' twisting round, I look at the hard lad, only he isn't a lad really now. He, Cookey, and Nick are men now.

'Definitely,' Blowers nods. 'I've been thinking about it ... And don't even think of making any gay jokes,' he glares at Cookey.

'I didn't even think about it,' Cookey admits, 'but cheers for reminding me.'

'So you'd risk getting infected from me to see if you can ... I don't know ... resist the virus or ... ? Jesus, mate, what if it turns you?'

'Then you'll know,' Blowers replies.

'Risk one to save many,' Dave cuts in.

'No, I couldn't do it. I couldn't risk any of you.'

'Mr Howie,' Blowers leans forward. 'They are shi–' he

pauses with a glance at Milly, 'they are scared of you. We've all seen it again and again ...'

'And you kissed Lani, and Lani came back,' Cookey takes over. 'What Clarence said makes sense.'

'No. No, it can't be that simple. You telling me that my saliva is the cure for the zombie plague? Not a chance, lads, sorry.'

'Why not?' Clarence asks. 'If you'd told me two and a half weeks ago I would be running through a lion enclosure to save a little girl or running around with you lot, killing zombies, I would have laughed, but here we are.'

'The circumstances we find ourselves in are completely separate to whether or not my saliva gives you antibodies that resist the virus. There are so many factors to this. What about the body the heart came from? He could be the special one. He could be able to carry the virus but not transmit it.'

'Eye juice and fingers,' Lani says quickly.

'It was pitch black and very confusing,' I retort. 'Anything could have been happening then. 'We don't know enough. The risk of me passing saliva to one of you and infecting you is too great.'

'What about that cigarette yesterday,' Lani says, 'remember?'

'Yeah, I remember, but that still doesn't mean anything. You might not have got your saliva on it, and that was you to me, not the other way round.'

'So what if Lani made you immune? Maybe her saliva got into your system, and that's what protected you,' Clarence suggests.

'Maybe,' I shrug, 'it could be a thousand different things that led to it. Bloody hell, I could have eaten something three weeks ago that made me immune. It could be a random gene or a mutated string of DNA, or ... it could just be luck.'

'Luck?' Lani lifts one eyebrow. 'That two people in the same group are immune when the whole world is getting infected?'

'I agree. I totally agree, but the problem is *we just don't know*. Forgive me for raising this, Lani, but how do we know Marcy didn't do something to me? Pass me something, or I don't know, but the point is we don't know anything more than we did before, other than it *appears*,' I emphasise the word, 'that I cannot be turned, and it *appears* that Lani is resistant to it. I'm not going to risk infecting any of you, so unless you want to abduct some poor bloke off the street and hold him down while I kiss him, then drive about until we find an infected to throw at him ... then forget it.'

They lapse into silence, not sullen or sulky but thoughtful. Milly, unbelievably, stayed quiet during the conversation, watching us all intently before moving in closer to rest her head on Lani's lap.

'Have you had any sleep?' I ask Clarence, watching him yawn.

'No, but I'm okay,' he replies.

'Nah, pull over, mate. I'll drive the rest of the way.'

'Sure?'

'Yep. We'll need you awake and ready when we get back.'

He doesn't argue and brings the vehicle to a stop. He jumps out to walk round while I climb over and work out how to adjust the seat to bring it forward.

Within minutes, he's nodding off with his face turned to the open window. Using the rearview mirror, I see Lani staring out at the passing fields while gently stroking Milly's face. Sensing me watching her, she turns and smiles.

The lads stay quiet for once, all of us absorbed and knackered from the exertion and heat. On the back seat, I see Dave staring at me. Our eyes lock as the sunlight pours through the window, bathing his face in a golden glow. Shadows flit across his face, but he doesn't blink or move, just stares at me. I hated him earlier. I hated his coldness and inability to feel, but now I remember every sacrifice and risk he has taken for me. How utterly devoted he has been and risking his life again and again.

Last night while I was passed out, he chose to go outside and take that horde on his own. None of us would be here if it wasn't for that quiet man, and for the most fleeting of seconds, I get an overwhelming sensation that he knew I was immune all along. Realisation dawns as I remember all those times he's made odd comments about how I must be the one to survive.

Glancing back at him in the mirror, he's still staring at me. He nods once and smiles, a small twitch of the lips before turning to stare out the window.

Even if I am immune, it won't be me that saves everyone. It'll be Dave.

CHAPTER THIRTY-EIGHT

'Pathogen,' the Doc mutters to himself. Taking his reading glasses off, he rubs his eyes slowly. 'Definitely a pathogen.'

A pathogen causes disease in the host. The zombie virus is without doubt a disease that is spread from host to host, making it a communicable disease. It appears to be passed when bodily fluids from a host get into a healthy body.

That much is obvious. The infected zombie bites someone, and that person then gets infected. The disease is not airborne, nor does it appear to be able to survive once it is outside the host body. Does that make it parasitical? Or possibly even a parasitoid? If it requires the host to survive, like a parasite would, then surely that must make it parasitical in nature? The Doc rubs his eyes again. Christ, this is confusing.

So a parasite gets into the host and, in the worst case, eventually destroys the host by eating the organs, destroying the immune system, and so on. But this isn't a parasite.

A parasite can be a form of pathogen, but there are other forms of pathogen too. Pathogen is just the word used to describe anything that can produce disease.

Flicking back a few pages, the Doc starts reading the Introduction to Pathogens chapter again. He discovers the word prion and a description of how a prion propagates by transmitting a misfolded protein state. The prion enters a healthy system and converts the healthy cells into the disease replicated state by acting as a template.

'Got it,' the Doc grabs his pen to write the word prion on his notepad and underscores it several times. 'The zombie virus is a prion.' He knew he could work this out.

Oh wait, a prion can attach to a virus. Creutzfeldt-Jakob disease is a prion.

'Mad cow disease,' he says, finding the right page. Yes, of course, CJD was what everyone called it a few years ago. So that was a prion, was it? How interesting. But if prions and viruses are both forms of pathogens, then how can a prion be *attached* to a virus? Can they work together? Wouldn't that make the prion a parasite? If the prion was leapfrogging on the back of the virus, it would be parasitical, wouldn't it? No, a parasite eats the host, but the prion doesn't eat the virus it, just works with it.

Next to the underscored prion, he writes virus and underscores that too, then links them together with a single line with arrow heads at both ends.

Hmmm, it says here that smallpox, measles, rubella, Ebola and the flu are all types of pathogens, and they are definitely viruses. So yes, the zombie virus *is* a virus. Whether or not it has a prion on its back is another matter.

So if the virus is mutated by the prion when it gets into the host body, the prion converts all the other cells into replicas of the virus cells.

The mental image the Doc had of spending hours pottering about a sterilised and brightly lit laboratory, mixing stuff in test tubes and looking at slides under microscopes was rapidly disappearing. For a start, he didn't have a laboratory yet. His men were too busy gathering supplies and finding children.

Also, he didn't know what to put in the test tubes or under the microscopes. The movies always showed some wriggly things within the blood, and then someone worked out a way to kill the wriggly things and become the saviour of the human race.

He didn't even have any test subjects as there was nowhere to hold them yet.

He looks up sharply at the knocking on his door. Blinking, he rubs his eyes once more.

'Come in.'

'Doc,' Larson nods once as he walks in. Closing the door behind him, he crosses the room and sits in the chair Billy used.

'Everything okay?' The Doc asks.

'Fine,' Larson replies. 'Except for you killing Vince, that is,' he adds in a mild tone.

'Hmmm,' the Doc nods seriously, 'yes, I did go a bit far.'

'Again,' Larson adds quietly, 'that's the third time in as many days.'

'I was angry,' the Doc shrugs like it's no big deal, 'Billy told me what they did and ...'

'And what did Billy say?' Larson asks, crossing his legs to listen intently.

'He said the two men raped a girl and killed their fathers.'

'Right,' Larson lifts his eyebrows as if waiting for more.

'That's it,' the Doc says.

'So you killed him because they did what you said? I didn't get a chance to speak to Vince or ask him any questions, so I've got no new intelligence from the sector you gave them. I've no idea of where that boy came from. We don't know where Gordon is–'

'Gordon?' the Doc asks.

'Gordon, the other man that went out with Vince ...'

'Was that his name?' The Doc realises Gordon must have been the one Billy said was wrestling with his sister after pulling her pants down. He chuckles at the innocent way children explain some things.

'What's so funny?' Larson asks.

'Nothing, just something Billy said.'

'What did Billy say?'

'Ha, he said he saw the men wrestling with his sister, only she had her pants down while they were wrestling.'

'Right, and you find that funny?'

'Just the way he said it. You had to be there ... Anyway, so?'

'Doc, we need you,' Larson says with a sudden intensity. 'We need your expertise and your medical knowledge. You've got us this far, living in a nice, big house, with loads of food, and the idea of assigning sectors for the men to scavenge was brilliant, but you've got to stop killing them ... Hang on, Doc, I'm not criticising you, and I know you get angry sometimes, and that's fine, but if you keep doing it, they'll bugger off and leave us. They're already terrified of you. It won't be long before one goes out on duty and decides just not to come back. Then they'll all do it. You need them.'

'Okay,' the Doc sighs theatrically.

'They're just doing what you told them to. You said, *Go out to your sectors, go house to house, and get the food. If you see any children, bring them back. Anything else is down to you.* You said that, Doc ...'

'Yes, yes, I know I did,' the Doc sighs.

'So what was it this time?' Larson shakes his head and asks quietly.

'Billy was upset by what he saw them do,' the Doc explains. 'I saw Billy upset, and it upset me. So I went to talk with Vince, and he, well ... he just set me off ...'

'Set you off? How did he set you off?'

'Well,' the Doc looks away, 'his manner, his demeanour, the way he, he ... sneered and looked.'

'Vince wouldn't sneer at you,' Larson says with a patient tone. 'He was shit scared.'

'Well, it's done now.'

'Please, Doc, I'm asking nicely.'

'Yes, fine, I understand ... no more killing men. Yes, I've got it.'

'You're a big man, Doc, and you don't know your own strength.'

'Larson, I've said sorry, so can we drop it now?'

'Okay,' Larson relents, 'but if they all run off, don't go blaming me. You might let the lads have a few beers tonight? To take their mind of things.'

'Hmmmm, ok. Just a few, though. I mean it, Larson, I don't want my children getting woken up by drunken carousing into the early hours.'

'How was Billy anyway?'

'Fine, all checked and all clear.'

'And you're still checking them every couple of days?'

'Of course, we have to be vigilant.

'What about the men? They're going out into the world. Shouldn't they be checked too?'

'I've told you what to look for, so you do it,' the Doc snaps. 'I've got enough work to do without getting every man in here, dropping his pants to moon at me.'

Fine for the kids to do it, though, Larson muses but stays quiet.

'Speaking of which, any progress?' Larson asks nodding at the desk.

'Well, yes, actually,' the Doc's features light up at his chance to showboat. 'I have established the zombie virus is a pathogen, and in particular a prion attached to a virus that has mutated into the infection as we know it. Similar to CJD. You remember that outbreak? The papers crassly called it Mad Cow Disease.'

'Oh yeah, I remember,' Larson nods.

'CJD was a prion, which is a form of pathogen that enters the host body and acts as a template, tricking the cell structure to mutate and become like the infected cell. Now, CJD was a prion, but in this case, I am confident that we have a virus together with a prion. You know, a virus like smallpox or Ebola which are both communicable diseases. The virus transfers to new hosts, and the prion mutates the existing cells to convert them into the ... er ... the zombie cells,' the Doc speaks quickly, and he knows he sounds confident. These new words are brilliant. Larson will go back and tell the others the Doc was talking about prions and cells, and everyone will know how intelligent he is.

'Good work,' Larson nods appreciatively. 'What next, then?'

'Good lord, Larson, this takes time and study,' the Doc sighs. 'I need time to, er ... study the virus and establish just how it works.

'Then you can find the cure, right?'

'Or a vaccine, yes, but that takes time, and if I have so many other things to do, I can't ...'

'Got it,' Larson sighs. 'We'll leave you alone. Listen,

why don't I do the kids then for now so you can just focus on your studies?'

'No,' the Doc replies quickly, 'the children should be checked by a healthcare professional. When I do establish the vaccine, they will be the first to have it, so I need to make sure they are fit and healthy.'

'Fine. Right, I'll leave you to it, then. By the way, John and Terry never came back either.'

'Losses have to be expected, Larson,' the Doc pushes his glasses up his long nose.

'Just letting you know,' Larson adds before exiting the room.

The power dynamic between the two men was a strange, lilting beast of varying proportions. If anyone else spoke to either man the way they spoke to each other, there would be severe and violent consequences.

It was the Doc's idea to locate a place such as this, and it was Larson that found it. The actual taking of the premises was a joint enterprise as the occupants were killed and the bodies removed for burning.

Once the premises had been secured, it was then a matter of finding resources. The two men ferreted out survivors of a type and manner who were willing to overlook certain behavioural issues in return for safety and food.

As with the fort and Maddox within his compound, as with many secure locations established by survivors across the world, Chapsworth House evolved every day. The more men they got, the wider the scavenging took place, the more food was brought back, the more weapons sourced, the more guards they had and, of course, more children.

Larson knew why the Doc was so keen to have children in the house. Regardless of the explanations that they were the innocent casualties of this modern-day plague, that they were innocents to be protected so that when the vaccine or cure was found, they could be the first to receive it. Larson saw the change in the Doc's eyes when he talked about children. He could sense the excitement and hunger within the man.

Larson was a survivor, and he would survive come hell or high water. He would prevail at any cost, and the only real allegiance he had was to himself. For now, it suited his purpose to be with the Doc. Agreeing with the Doc and not questioning his motives meant he was kept happily in a bubble of pretence that everything was how he wanted.

The Doc, for his part, recognised a fellow psychotic when he saw one. Larson might speak with an air of calmness and sound full of common sense and judgement, but the Doc had seen first-hand just how violent the man could be.

Larson didn't ask why he wanted children here, and the only time he did raise an objection was when the Doc's actions threatened the stability of what they had built, like his frequent *temper tantrums* as the Doc called them. The same *temper tantrums* that had now seen several men being killed.

The Doc knew only too well what this new world meant. It meant anyone could be anything they wanted. Larson could have been a policeman, a soldier, or even a priest two weeks ago. It didn't matter what you were. It matters what you are now.

So he became the Doc. He had attended medical school, but his deviant interest in children had soon been noticed, and he was quietly removed. That was a long time ago when people didn't make a big fuss about it. Things like that weren't discussed in the open; they were dealt with quietly to avoid any embarrassment.

The Doc had joined other medical schools, but the world of medicine was a small one, and it never took long for him to be found out. Being six foot six made you stand out from the crowd and get noticed.

Before computerised record keeping and due to the lack of communication between agencies, the Doc was able to slip into various healthcare roles. He became a nurse and worked alongside charity organisations, but each time his odd manner was quickly identified, and he was removed.

Years went by, and slowly he convinced himself that his knowledge and abilities were far beyond what they were. The fact he had attended medical school, albeit for a very short time, served to perpetuate the ideology that he *was* medically trained.

Certainly field medicine, triage, and the basic treatment of wounds and injuries were easy to understand, and with his manner of professional elocution, he often passed for being far more trained and skilled than he really was.

While millions died during those first terrible few days of the outbreak, the Doc realised he could now be a doctor. He *was* a doctor, and he tended to injured, sick, and wounded people with the perceived professionalism of a real doctor. His physical size gave him presence. His deep voice gave him a serious countenance. His blue-grey eyes held people transfixed, and his explosions of utter fury brought those around him a propensity to walk on eggshells.

The anger hadn't always been there. He liked to think he was naturally a calm, intelligent, cultured, and refined man, but the expelling from medical school and the following years of being labelled a paedophile, a child molester, a freak deviant had slowly brought that anger to the front. In the old world, he couldn't do anything about it and was constantly biting his tongue and suppressing his violent tendencies.

He didn't have to do that now. So he didn't. He could be anything he wants to be, so he *is* a doctor, and he *can* get angry when he wants, and after so much death, the action of taking life is effectively meaningless.

Our worlds define us. The things we do, the places we go, the people we meet, and our experiences all contribute to who we become. The Doc, to a certain extent, was a result of his own life experiences, all apart from the fascination with children. That had always been there. In fact, it had been a part of him for so long he no longer questioned it.

To face your own demons and flaws conflicts with any self-image of being a good person. Often those flaws are ignored and buried deep. He wasn't a monster; he wasn't a sick paedophile. Those were labels for other people, not him. He was normal; he just loved children. His self-justification was so strong, he no longer believed there was anything wrong with him.

Re-reading the section on prions, he notices the frequent mention of proteins and starts thinking of the brightly coloured tubs of whey protein with the pictures of bodybuilders on the front. The internal image blends into him standing in a brightly lit, sterilised lab staring at wriggly things through a microscope and using a syringe to inject whey protein into petri dishes.

CHAPTER THIRTY-NINE

'Now you look a darn sight better, you do,' Meryl grins at Billy exiting the bathroom, scrubbed clean and in fresh clothes. He was uncomfortable being naked in front of the big Doctor man, but when Meryl told him to strip off, it didn't feel so bad. For a start, she didn't stare at him. She tutted and huffed at the grime on his skin and at the state of his hair before going away and coming back with clothes.

Chattering away in a constant stream of one-sided conversation, she set about scrubbing him from head to toe. She gave him a towel to dry off with before telling him to get dressed and come out when he's finished.

This was only time since being taken that he felt even the slightest bit comfortable. The nagging fear was still there, that awful tight ball in his stomach that made his mouth dry and his hands and legs tremble. But with Meryl there, the fear was a bit less.

Smiling sheepishly, he stands still like an automaton waiting for further instruction, lost in the vastness of the large kitchen.

Cases of tinned food stacked on the floor, and through

an open door to the pantry, Billy can see more foodstuffs jammed onto every shelf.

'Come on, sit yourself down,' Meryl instructs kindly, beckoning Billy to a large wooden table with a chair pulled out waiting for him. 'That's it, get yourself comfortable. Now drink this first. God knows how long you been out there in the heat, so you have this first.' Placing a large glass of water in front of him, she waits expectantly until he picks it up to take the first sip. 'Get it down, Billy,' she says as she bustles off, clanging about with a constant stream of chatter.

'Well, so we got another mouth to feed, have we? Oh yes, more mouths to feed means more work for Meryl, but I don't mind,' she says, throwing a big grin at him. Billy watches the woman moving about. The way everything clangs and bangs is re-assuring, reminding him of his own mother. There is something about the way Meryl dominates the space and moves naturally, like it's her environment which has been designed especially for her.

Big windows at the back of the room let the beautiful, warm light into the kitchen, and the view of sculpted grounds with large, flat lawns leading to rolling pastureland in the distance is peaceful.

'You see the river?' Meryl moves to join him looking out the window. 'All sparkly and inviting, isn't it?' she adds before moving off quickly back into her domain.

Billy takes it in, soaking up the wide expanse of water glittering from the sun's reflection. It does look inviting.

'You'll be down there later, no doubt,' Meryl interrupts his thoughts, 'having a swim and splashing about. The Doc, he likes his children to get outside and have fresh air, he does, says it's good for you and better than all thems computer games you play these days. Well, I say these days, but these days there ain't no computer games, is there?

Gone back to the old ways already, haven't we, Billy? Healthy food and lots of fresh air, eh?' Well, I say healthy food, but all we got is tinned food at the moment but plenty of it, so no one will be going hungry just yet. We can get some crops planted so's we got plenty for next year too. The Doc and Larson got it all figured out, they have.'

Switching to an internal monologue, she realises the situation they're all in. Vince wasn't a bad fella, just easily led and too willing to let others do as they wished. Didn't deserve that, though. The doctor is such a nice man most of the time, apart from what she hears he does with the kids and them temper tantrums he has. Well, that's what he calls them anyway. More like blind rage if you ask Meryl.

Strange, though, not a mark on any of the kids. She washes them regular, like, being so young and daft, half of 'em don't know how to wash properly, so she supervises often, and it gives her a chance to give them the once over. No bruises or marks anywhere. So whatever the Doc is doing with 'em is gentle enough. God almighty! If she knew two weeks ago that some filthy pervert was doing something bad to kiddies, she'd be straight on the phone to the police, but there ain't no police now. Just what they got here, and these kids are being well fed and got a safe bed at night. They ain't being physically harmed from what she can see, and those things don't know they're here either. Hell, she hasn't seen any of the walking zombie lot since she got here. There are plenty of tough men with guns to protect them all, so she keeps working. She feeds, cleans, and deals with any number of issues within the house, and the rest just has to be ignored cause there ain't anything she could do about it anyway.

Her aim is to not so much smooth over the cracks, as to take a huge trowel and smother the gaping holes with as much cement as possible. The children are shell-shocked, and despite the natural resilience of the young, they've all seen far too many horrors to be anywhere near normal yet. That'll take a long time, so for now, they just got to get through each day.

Glancing back at young Billy, she feels a pull on her heartstrings. So young and tiny, staring about with wide eyes at everything. He looks to be the same age as her little one was before, well, before all this happened. God knows what he's been through and then having to do whatever the Doc does with 'em. Well, she can't help that, but she can try and put a smile there now.

At the sink, she wets a cloth to wipe her face; the heat is incredible and so close. Muggy as you like. Everyone is listless and getting tired too, snapping at each other, and no wonder the Doc keeps losing his mind.

It's troubling times, that's for sure, so she does what she can to help, smiling and fussing over the children.

'There you go. Ain't nothing special, but it's food, and it'll fill your belly up.' Placing the plate down, she watches for his reaction. When it doesn't come, she reminds herself he's too young to notice the significance of having a sandwich to eat. Proper bread sandwich too. The adults notice it all right and love it when she makes fresh bread. Course it isn't anywhere near like the supermarkets had it. Bit too doughy and heavy, but it's bread all the same, and they soon wolf it down alright.

Billy tucks in. He doesn't feel the slightest bit hungry, but he knows his manners, and he knows Meryl wants him to eat, so he does. Picking up the sandwich, he takes the first bite. The bread is tough and chewy, but the jam inside is sweet and bursting with flavour.

After days of eating tinned and junk food, his appetite

soon comes back. Biting and chewing as he gets strawberry jam smeared round his mouth.

Sitting down with a steaming mug of black tea, Meryl watches him eat, grinning at the obvious pleasure he's getting from it.

'Good boy,' she nods at the empty plate. 'Now you can have a treat, but don't be expecting them all the time cause I don't give 'em out willy-nilly.' She pulls a packet of crisps from the large pocket on her apron. Billy doesn't want to tell her he doesn't want crisps. He's eaten more bags of potato chips in the last two weeks than ever before, but Billy knows his manners, so he dutifully eats them up, munching slowly through the packet while staring at the ruddy-faced woman.

'Will Lilly come here?' he asks, speaking for the first time. Meryl freezes for a split second, the grin remaining, but the happiness sliding off her face. She hates this bit when they ask about their families. She doesn't know who Lilly is, and she doesn't want to know. Knowing just makes it harder to deal with.

'We're very lucky to be here, Billy,' she says in a kind tone, 'very lucky, and we all lost our families, so we're all the same now. No more about the past. We gotta look to the future, so eat thems crisps up; then, you can go play with the other children.'

Billy nods. He doesn't feel very lucky right now. In fact, he feels very unlucky, but Lilly will come. His young mind can't quite grasp what happened during the night, but he does know Lilly wasn't there, and she didn't get hurt, so he knows she will come. She has to. She's his big sister, and that's what big sisters do.

CHAPTER FORTY

'Probably about a mile now.' Nick judges the distance on the map, then glances up to view the surrounding countryside. 'We should leave the van here and go on foot.'

'Okay.'

'There's a hill here. See the lines get closer together? We should aim for that so we can look down and maybe get a view of the house before we decide anything.'

'Got it,' she nods quickly. 'We'll need water in this heat.'

Grabbing bottles from the back, they empty an old rucksack found in the front cab before filling it with fluids and snack bars. With the van parked at the end of an old track, they lock up and set off, Nick checking the map positions before folding it away to light a cigarette, figuring this might be the last chance for a smoke for a while.

'You okay?' he asks mildly.

She nods, scanning the area ahead as they climb a fence into a wide field. Sticking to the hedgerow, they walk side by side over the hard, sun-baked earth.

Shock threatened to pull her under, but with Billy at risk, there is no choice but to swallow it down. What happened to Todd plays over and over in her mind, blending with images of Samantha on the ground with that monster between her legs, Norman bleeding, and seeing her father blown to bits. All of it whirling and blundering through her head but only serving to strengthen her resolve.

Those first-hand experiences of how quickly death can come increases the pressure to find Billy and make him safe.

Nick was so quick. He didn't hesitate and knew exactly what he was doing. If she is going to survive and protect her brother, then she has to very quickly become more like him, ruthless and hard.

Only that isn't everything he is. The kindness and compassion pour off the young man, the easy way he blushes, swears, laughs, and constantly checks that she's okay.

'Thank you again,' she gives voice to her thoughts.

'You don't have to keep saying it,' Nick replies. His thoughts were with his team, wondering where they were and what they were doing. Being separated like this was horrible, and above else, he wishes Mr Howie was here to deal with this. Clarence, Dave, Lani, and the lads, even the dog. Together they would get this sorted quickly. He still has that strange sense of knowing that they are all ok, but he wishes they were here by his side.

Swigging from a bottle of water, Nick glances up into the blue sky, hazy with an incredible sense of oppressive heat. Even the plants and branches wilt from the absurdly high temperatures. The sun scorches exposed skin, but with very little choice, they have to keep moving.

Rolling pastures of green fields become desert-like, with heat shimmers and a feeling of being baked in an oven.

The land starts to rise, gently at first but with increasingly more hostile terrain of devoted fields and furrowed lanes. Each step becomes an ankle-twisting hazard, and although only a mile has to be walked, it feels far greater.

Lapsing into silence, they aim for a thicket of trees at the crest of the hill with a deep longing to be amongst the shaded copse and out of the blistering sun. When they reach it, both are bathed in sweat, with clothes clinging to bodies and hair lankly plastered across their foreheads. The very air seems too thick to breathe, so they slump down amongst the fauna, trying to catch their breath.

Water is poured over heads and down throats, sweat rinsed off, but little comfort does it give. Nodding at each other, they push off, threading through the dense foliage to reach the edge of a sweeping, shallow valley. There, in the distance, nestles what can only be Chapsworth House. A huge, sprawling mansion surrounded by manicured gardens. At the rear of the property, beyond the rear lawns lies a glittering river, meandering through the scene.

A long driveway stretches from the front of the house towards a high wall and what looks like a gated entrance. They are too far away to be able to see any detail but can see the basic layout.

Movement at the gate. A vehicle approaches. Another van like the type they took in the town. The van pauses as tiny figures to move around it. When it moves off, Nick and Lilly track the movement as it heads slowly down the long driveway, stopping at the front.

Another small figure exits the house and stands near the front of the vehicle. Nick imagines a conversation taking place. The figure walks off, and the van moves round the side of the house, stopping at a set of doors.

Two people get out the van, open the rear doors, and start unloading items which are carried into the house and out of view.

Nick settles low and lets his eyes move gently over the vista before him. The figures at the gates must be guards, and there must be others at the front of the house. Scanning the grounds, he spots another two figures strolling from the river, towards the house. They stop in the middle of the grounds, and Nick watches as a large group come into view from the back of the house, heading towards the river.

Children, lots of children with two or three larger figures which must be adults. The group moves towards the two guards and stop. Words must be exchanged before they all head off, crossing the grounds before stopping just short of the water.

The black, insect-like figures seem to wait, with small movements indicating something is happening within the group. After a few minutes, a few start to filter off, crossing the last bit of land before disappearing out of sight.

With the glittering reflection from the surface of the water, neither Nick or Lilly can make out the figures swimming, but the action is obvious. Movement from the figures as they move in and out of the water. Fast movement of children running, chasing each other. In and out of the river they go. The adults with them stand close by and appear ready to react.

This doesn't look right. The house is beautiful, the grounds are large and well cared for. It looks serene and nice, and with the children playing in the river, it wasn't anything like either of them were expecting.

Chain gangs or something, sexualised predators intent on deviant activities maybe, but this? Children swimming under the watchful eyes of adults, and judging by the running motions, they are having fun too. Nick's mind works to fill in the blanks, and he can almost imagine the children's laughter, calling out as they splash and run. The adults standing close, smoking cigarettes while chatting amiably.

The two men from the van have stopped unloading and are standing talking to a larger figure. Things are stacked on the ground next to them which can only be the items taken from the vehicle. The larger person seems animated, waving their arms about as they talk. Within a couple of minutes, the larger figure disappears, then comes back out carrying something. Heading away from the house, the person stops and starts bending over, then standing back up.

'Putting washing out,' Lilly mutters at seeing light-coloured things being fastened to what must be a rope or wire.

The two men from the van walk over to the larger person. One of them stands still while the other helps hanging the clothes up.

'Your brother must be with that lot,' Nick says quietly.

'He loves swimming, but this ... this is ...'

'Not what you were expecting? Nah, me neither. Looks nice as fuck down there, like proper posh. I bet you had a house like that.'

'No!' Lilly exclaims.

'Yeah, with horses and llamas.'

'Llamas?'

'Don't posh people have llamas?'

'No, Nick, they don't, and I'm not posh.'

'You talk posh.'

'My dad was bankrupt, and we lived in a little flat near the town centre.'

'Oh shit, sorry, Lilly.'

'You didn't know.'

'But you still sound posh.'

'Yes, okay, Nicholas.'

'Fuck, don't call me Nicholas.'

'Stop saying I'm posh, then.'

'Nope.'

'Okay, Nicholas.'

'Okay, Lilly ... er ... Lillyander.'

'What? You made that up! That's not even a name.'

'It is ... Lillyander.'

'Whatever, Nicholas. Now, would you mind awfully if we focussed on rescuing my brother.'

'Awfully?'

'I said that on purpose.'

It helps making mindless, stupid jokes that cost nothing. It doesn't take the pain or fear away, but it helps to cope, giving a façade of being okay.

'I think that side entrance looks the best bet,' Nick says seriously. 'It looked like those men just walked in. They didn't stop to wait for someone to open up.'

'Agreed,' Lilly nods, 'do we wait for nighttime or ...?'

Nick tracks back to the area of the main gate and the figures moving around it. Counting four of them, he looks back at the river. There were two people there first; then, two or three adults came out with the children, so that makes about five. Nine people split between the gate and the rear, and if they can afford to have that many just on guard, then they must have a whole lot more inside.

The two men finish unloading the van, and one goes into the house while the other gets back into the vehicle, slowly turning round to drive towards the front of the house, then straight across to the far side, and out of view.

'Another one,' Lilly nudges his arm, pointing to the gate. A big, blue van is going through what looks like the same procedure as before. There is some movement at the gate; then, the van goes down the drive. The figure comes out the house, has a chat, then round to the side to unload. Nick nods. He was right. One of the figures went straight in, so that door can't be locked. More figures come out this time to help unload. One of them stands at the back of the van, handing items over to be carried inside.

'Too many,' he mutters quietly. Turning his head, he casts a sad look at Lilly. 'There's too many for just two of us.'

'We can wait for night and try sneaking in.'

'No way,' Nick shakes his head gently, 'they'll see us way before we get inside the house. Look at how many men they have. Four or five on that front gate, more out the back with the children, and every van looks like it has two people in it. Plus, we don't know how many vans are parked round the other side. That house could be full of men like those back in that town.'

'I'm not leaving Billy here,' Lilly hisses.

'We've got to be smart here,' Nick explains. 'If we go down there now, we'll be caught. Fact. No way round it. That bloke who took Billy saw me standing over his mate, so I'll probably be recognised, and even if they don't know you, there's no fucking way you can go down there.'

'Why not?'

'What you gonna do? Just walk in and ask for your brother back? Lilly, I don't mean this in a rude way, but like, er ... well, you're fucking stunning, really beautiful ... They'll take one look at you and ...'

'Norman,' Lilly sags.

'If that was the bloke that tried it on last night, then yeah, it'll be like that but probably worse.'

'What do we do? We can't just leave him.'

'If they took Billy from you like that, then all those kids would have been taken from people. This isn't just about Billy; this is about all those kids. We can't leave any of them there, but then we,' he motions between them, 'can't do fuck all with just two of us.'

'I can't–' Lilly starts to say.

Cutting her off quickly, Nick pushes on. 'Look, though, they're swimming,' Nick points down the hill. 'They ain't been fucking tortured or anything right now. They're running about and playing, which means they're fine.'

'For now.'

'Yeah, I know, but Billy only just got here, but some of those kids might have been here a while, and they're still running about and swimming. Those vans are going into the towns to bring food back, so they got loads to eat. I get it Lilly. Really, I do. We can't just leave them there without knowing they're okay, but we cannot fucking go down there with just two of us. Fuck, no, we could, but we'd probably get killed, and then Billy is fucked left, right, and centre. Mr Howie doesn't know where I am, so he can't come rescuing us. We gotta go down to the fort and find the others; then, we come back with my team and deal with this properly.'

'What if they don't want to come back?' Lilly asks with a look of pure fear on her face.

'They will,' Nick urges.

'They might not. They might see it as someone else's problem.'

'No, not a chance,' Nick replies firmly.

'How can you be so sure?'

'Cause I've been with them since this started,' Nick says with an earnest expression. 'I know what they're like. A few days ago we were walking through this fucking awful, shitty council estate right. It's night, and we've been all over the place, doing weird stuff, but anyway, as we go along, we hear a fucking shit loads of zombies attacking this place in the middle. Now, we could have just crept away. They didn't see us, and we could easily have slipped past them and been done, but we didn't. Mr Howie saw we had a chance to cut them down, so we went for it. Last night, we were out fighting for hours, and we left others in that car park we went to earlier. We were off down the road in the Saxon and could see there were fucking thousands of them trying to get into that car park. Again, we could have fucked off and gone somewhere else, but Mr Howie, well, he got that Saxon right through 'em so we could get to the top and help the others. See what I'm saying? There's no way he'll leave these kids here.'

'I can't, Nick,' Lilly says with a pleading look, her eyes brimming with tears. 'I can't just leave him.'

'We don't have a choice.'

'No, I'm not going anywhere without Billy.'

'Lilly, please listen to me. There are too many men down there. You've already seen what they did to your father and that girl ...'

'Sam.'

'Yes, her, sorry, I couldn't remember her name. If we get caught, which we will, there will be nobody left to come and help. Do you understand that?' Turning back to stare down the hill, he looks between the gate and the river. 'And how the hell are we going to get all those children out? We can't just take Billy and leave them.'

'Do you promise?' Lilly implores him, begging with her eyes for re-assurance that this isn't it, that they're not just walking away.

Shifting position, Nick puts his hand over hers, squeezing softly. 'I swear, Lilly. I totally fucking swear.'

'You keep on swearing,' she smiles sadly as a single tear rolls down her cheek.

'Sorry,' he flashes a quick grin. 'We will come back.

Even if we don't find the others, no matter what happens, I swear I will come back and get your brother.'

'Okay,' she whispers, seeing the honest intent in his eyes.

'They're okay,' Nick whispers. 'They're splashing about and having fun. Fuck, I wish I was down there, cooling off in the water.'

'It is rather hot,' she concedes.

'Rather hot? Oh, I say, it is rather warm, don't you know?' Nick puts on his poshest voice in an attempt to gain a smile.

'Very good,' Lilly nods primly. 'Nick, thank you, and I do believe you. I do, but I'm so scared.'

'Good,' Nick nods, 'fear keeps you alive.'

'Is that another of that Dave's sayings?'

'No,' Nick grins, 'I heard that one on telly. Dave would say *Nicholas, stop swearing and put that cigarette out, and is your kit cleaned, and have you shaved today?*'

'Does he really sound like that?'

'No, Dave's fucking great.' Snaking back, they gain the tree line and start heading away from the valley. An awful sadness steals through Lilly's heart.

'Lilly and Billy, eh?' Nick asks as they step free of the shade, into the blistering heat once more.

'Yeah, I know, believe it or not, my parents never thought about it. They always wanted him to be called William.'

'Oh, I get it,' Nick nods.

'He was William for years, then went to school on his first day, and the teacher called him Billy. Then all his classmates called him Billy, and it just stuck.'

'Hmmm, I was like that too.'

'Oh? How so? What was your nickname?'

'Wanker,' Nick says seriously.

'Really?' Lilly stares in horror.

'Nah, not really,' Nick grins. 'It was thicko when I was younger because I couldn't read or write; then, it just got worse as I got older as I still couldn't read or write, and now ... ha! I still can't read or write, and here I am, running around the countryside.'

'With a beautiful girl,' Lilly laughs.

'Alright, big-head,' Nick chuckles.

'No, you said it a minute ago ... *Look, Lilly, you's like crumpet, love,'* she deepens her voice, trying to make jokes as a way of masking the desperation.

'I never said that,' Nick laughs easily.

'True, you said *you's fucking stunning, you are.'*

'I don't speak like that. I don't sound like you, but I ain't that bad.'

'I am only joking, Nicholas.'

'Thank you, Lillyander.'

Nick can sense the despair coming from the girl and works to keep the chat light. Cookey and Lani are good at making conversation to put people at ease. Mr Howie always seems to know what to do. If the team were together now, a plan would have been made within five minutes. The boss would have stared down at the house with those brooding eyes, everyone would say they were up for it, and then with a few suggestions from Clarence and Dave, they'd be off.

'At least we're going downhill this time,' he comments quietly.

'True,' she replies. Glancing over, she can see the kindness in the young man as he hovers nearby, ready to offer a helping hand on the uneven ground. Everything he said made sense, and she works hard not to snap at him. He's right. If they mess it up, then Billy really is alone. It might take longer this way, but they stand a better chance of succeeding.

What if they don't come back, though? What if this Mr Howie says it isn't their problem or they have other things to do? Will Nick still come back or stay with them? He's promised now, but that could change for any reason.

Fretful and worried, she thinks frantically, tiredness sapping at her heavy legs as the images of the last day get stuck on replay in her mind. Norman pawing at her, the screams, and seeing Sam being raped, her father being killed, then following the boys back to the van. Those two men in the street, then trying to fight Nick. Todd being bitten and turning. It goes round and round, a never-ending video of lust and violence. Lust from Norman, lust from that rapist, and the violence of everything else. That's all this world is now, just sex and violence. Men want sex, so they take it. Men want food, so they take it. Not all men are like that. Nick hasn't once glanced at her in *that* way she has become so familiar with. He hasn't made any suggestive comments either. Well, other than saying she was beautiful.

He does think she's beautiful, then, and he said stunning too, which is a very high compliment. So he's not gay, but just very polite and well mannered. Handsome too, and he's got a lovely backside.

That's it. There's the hook to make sure he will come back. Make it so he wants to come back, give him something to come back for.

She's kissed boys and fumbled around a bit, but that's as far as it's ever gone. Naturally, at fifteen years old, she knows the birds and the bees, what sex is and, well, pretty much everything to do with it, apart from actually doing it.

How would she start? Now or later? Say something or

do something? What if he rejects her? No, he pretty much blushes every time she looks at him, and he did say she was beautiful *and* stunning.

It's got to be now. If she waits, she'll overthink it and never be able to do it. *He's very handsome, and it's not like it would be rape or anything, not if I'm giving it to him. It's not how I imagined the first time would be, but then it could also be far worse. He's kind and caring, and I have to make sure he'll come back.*

'Nick,' she blurts out. He snaps to face her, alarmed at the tone in her voice.

'What?' he asks urgently. Seeing the strange look on her face, he steps closer, staring with concern.

'Er ...' she stammers, her heart hammering like crazy. She fidgets for a second and almost backs out, but no, he has to come back, he has to want to come back.

'What the fuck!' Nick gasps as Lilly launches herself at him. Clumsily planting her lips on his, she pushes against his body.

Nick freezes. Things like this don't happen. Zombies, yeah. The apocalypse–definitely. All of that is fine, but beautiful women don't just throw themselves at you in the middle of fields.

She pushes harder, wrapping her arms round his waist to pull him in tight. 'Kiss me,' she murmurs, but the words don't sound right, not like when Nick has kissed women before and *sensed* them getting turned on.

Gently, he pulls away, and despite the bizarre circumstances, he finds his heart beating strong and hard, his face flushed as she looks up and locks those blue eyes on him. Her lips, as clumsy as they were, were soft and yielding.

'What?' she asks with a worried look. 'Don't you like me?'

'Yeah, yeah, course, but ... what you doing?'

'I want you,' she blurts. 'I really want you.'

'Want me? What, now? Like here?'

'Yes,' she nods, remembering that women who want to look seductive bite their bottom lip, so she tries to nibble on it suggestively, 'right here.'

'Seriously?' Nick stares in wonder at the girl as she chews on her lip. She looks amazing, with the way her blond hair falls round her shoulders, smooth skin, and those eyes which bore into him, causing his breath to catch.

'Come here,' she whispers.

'Lilly, this is ... well ... What the fuck!?'

'Come on, Nick, I really want you ...'

'What? Lilly, I ... Fuck me, what's going on?'

'Nothing, just all this heat and ... and you're so strong and handsome, and ... I don't know, I just really want to do it.'

'It?'

'Yes, sex. I want to do sex with ... I mean I want to have sex with you.'

'What?' Nick keeps repeating, his mind reeling.

'You said I'm beautiful,' she says in a quiet voice, stepping towards him.

'You are. I mean yeah, like you really fucking are,' Nick nods, willing himself to move back but being unable to do anything as she steps in close, 'but ...'

'But what?' she asks, trying to make her voice light. She can feel her legs trembling and her hands shaking, so she moves in quick again to plant her lips on his once more.

Nick wills and wills himself to break away, but it feels so nice. So soft and warm. He doesn't grab or do anything but just stands there and lets her kiss him. Her lips stay still, planted on his as though waiting for him to do something.

Fear of rejection keeps her locked on, a desperate worry that he'll get back to the fort and stay there with his team, and she'll be left alone to rescue Billy. Terrified and feeling completely helpless, something happens. He doesn't grab at her, he doesn't grope or do anything. He doesn't even really respond. But something changes.

His body is close, so warm and masculine, capable and ready for anything. He moves, just a tiny shift, but she finds herself shifting too. He moves again, a slight tremble that she detects through his lips; then, slowly, as gentle as a feather brushing against her skin, his lips move as he starts to kiss her back.

Her heart that was racing in fear a second ago now races from a different reaction. A closeness of two people alone and scared, both of them young and trapped in horrors that no person should ever go through. Emotions start pulsing through them. Terror, then adrenalin, exhaustion, and heat.

Contact. That's all it is. Just the act of two people putting their lips together, but it means so much more. Fleeting and random and done for every wrong reason, but all of those wrong reasons blend to become the right action. He kisses her slowly, and she kisses him back. Not from self-imposed duress, not because of wanting to lure him into coming back, not because of a need to give her body to him so he wants it again, but for another reason. She kisses him because it feels right, because she wants to kiss him.

He feels the change. The awkward force that shocked him is suddenly gone. Nick knows he's been exceptionally lucky to be with Mr Howie and the others and that if it wasn't for them, he'd probably be dead somewhere. This contact, this kiss, tells him why they fight. They fight because life is for living, because the race has to prevail and keep going.

He doesn't know when the shotgun and axe fall from his hands, but he knows when her fingers entwine in his. Electricity pulses through him and all from a slow, gentle, loving kiss.

Lilly feels the strength in his warm hands, the long fingers that squeeze with a gentle firmness. He could take her right now. He is strong enough to do what he wants, but he restrains himself with a gentleness that sends her heart soaring.

When the kiss ends, they stand still, eyes closed and lost in a feeling of pleasure that has become so rare in this new world.

Reality seeps back in as they become aware of the heat, of the uneven ground beneath them, of where they are.

'I'm sorry,' she whispers.

'Why?' Nick croaks, his voice low and husky.

'I ... I ... nothing,' she turns away with such a look of sadness it propels Nick to react, reaching out to gently take her wrist.

'What? What is it? Where did that come from?'

'I don't know,' she looks up at him, then quickly away. 'I'm scared, Nick, scared that you won't come back with me, so I thought I would ... let you have sex with me,' her voice tails off, squeezing her eyes closed from shame. 'You can if you want,' she blinks up at him again, 'I don't mind, really. I want to ...'

'Lilly,' he says softly, a sad smile forms on his lips.

'You can have sex with me now and later when you come back or whenever you want,' she rushes on. 'I don't mind, really. Nick, I ...'

'Stop,' Nick shakes his head as he stares at the girl, 'I don't ...' The smile grows until he can't stop himself from laughing softly. 'Shit, Lilly, for a second I thought you liked me. Fucking hell,' he groans, rubbing his forehead before reaching down to collect the weapons. 'Shit a brick …' he groans again, still shaking his head.

'I do like you,' Lilly blurts.

'Look,' he says, 'I gave you my word that I'll come back, and I meant it. Even if you run off now, and I never see you again, I will be coming back with Mr Howie and my team to see what's going on down there. Fucking hell, Lilly,' he laughs again, starting to walk off.

'Nick,' she rushes after him, 'I didn't mean I didn't like you … I do like you, but I was …'

'Scared, yeah, you said. Fucking hell. Well, for what it's worth, Lilly, that was a fucking amazing kiss, and you are stunning, but shit, well out of my league, but thank you,'

'Thank you?' She stumbles after him.

'Yeah, thank you. You kissed me for all the wrong reasons, but shit, it was still lovely, and I ain't never been kissed by anyone as pretty as you.'

'Nick, please just listen …'

'Have sex?' Nick says to himself. 'What would you have done if I went for it?'

'I said you can have it,' she mutters.

'Have it?' He turns with a hard look. '*It* isn't something that should be fucking given like that. I don't need to have sex with you, and you don't need to give me anything to make sure I come back.'

The darkness of the man flashes across his face, a fleeting glimpse of a rigid morality that, despite the temptation, still holds true and strong.

'I'm so sorry,' she walks after him, feeling completely ashamed of herself. She never meant to humiliate him or do anything to hurt him. The kiss *was* amazing. It was more than amazing, but to say that now will make it seem like more lies on top of lies.

'Don't worry,' he says kindly, all trace of the anger gone, 'you're worried about your brother.'

'Yes, I was, but ... I liked it too.'

'Okay, Lilly, look, I said I'll come back, so you don't have to say ...'

'I mean it, Nick,' she gasps. 'I really mean it.' But it does come out wrong, and it sounds false now.

'What a fucking day,' Nick sighs. That was the best kiss he has ever had. The nicest, the softest, the most meaningful kiss he was ever likely to have. Not cheap and horny but deep and emotional, touching him within his heart. She only did it for her brother, only so he'd come back. Shit! The most beautiful girl he has ever seen kisses him and offers him sex right here. Of all the things that could happen, of course, she didn't really mean it. *You thick fucker, thinking that someone like that would want to kiss you.*

He stops dead, something not right. Movement ahead, a sound maybe.

'Nick?'

'Sssshhh.' Pushing his fingers to his lips, he strains to listen. Not far from the van now, just beyond that hedge. Voices there, someone has found it.

Spinning round, he scans the area, but there is nowhere to go. If they look over the gate, they'll see them both, and the field is too big to cross. They'll never make it back to the wooded copse.

Grabbing Lilly, he pulls her down into the base of the hedge, covering her mouth with his hand. Male voices, at least two people. Now a third. A radio crackles with static. They've got radio contact with the house. With the shotgun and pistol, they could shoot their way out, but the people at the house will know something is happening.

'Listen,' he presses his mouth close to her ear, 'they've found the van, and they're going to find us. Take this.' He thrusts his axe into her hands. 'Go south and find the fort, find Mr Howie or Dave or Maddox, or a woman called Paula and tell them what happened. Ssshhh, just listen ... You tell Mr Howie I told you about how I operated Tower Bridge and made the zombies fall off. You tell them I told you I set fire to the ferry coming back from the Isle of Wight ... You tell them that and show them my axe ...'

'What are you doing?' she pulls his hand from her mouth, whispering back at him.

'I'm going to go out there. Stay here and stay down. Wait for us to go, then get away ... get away as quickly as possible but stay away from this road for a while. Lilly, just listen,' he cuts her protests off, 'we don't have a choice, okay? Stay here and for fuck's sake don't make a sound.'

Grabbing a water bottle, he twists the lid off, before pouring a tiny drop down the crotch of his trousers.

'Nick, please,' she whispers, 'they might go away.'

'Too late, they've seen the van, and they'll start searching any minute. I'll go out, and you get to the fort. Find a car and don't stop for anyone. Kill anything that comes anywhere near you, got it?'

She nods, terrified and rooted to the spot.

He starts to move, then drops back down. 'That kiss was amazing,' he grins. 'Really, you are so beautiful ... so just in case,' he darts in and plants a quick kiss on her lips, 'sorry, but you know ... like I said, it was fucking amazing.'

'Nick, don't go,' she tries to grab his wrist, but he's already up and moving off. 'I liked it. I really did.'

'Really?' He looks back. 'You mean that?'

'Honestly, really, I did.'

'Fucking awesome,' he grins, 'made my day that has. Now just stay quiet ...' He walks out from the hedge a few feet, going further into the field. 'Oh bollocks,' he calls out in a loud voice, 'fucking hell.'

'Who's that?' a deep male voice calls out.

'Eh?' Who's that?' Nick shouts back.

'Who the fuck are you?' a man appears at the gate holding a shotgun aimed at Nick pretending to wipe at the wet stain on his crotch like he just took a piss. A second man comes into view as Nick grins at them both before walking towards them. Still holding the shotgun but one-handed so he can't be seen as a threat.

Lilly lies flat, wriggling into the base of the hedge, she watches Nick walk towards the gate.

'Who the fuck are you I might ask,' Nick shouts back but in a friendly tone. 'You trying to nick my van?'

'Your van, is it?' the first man replies instantly.

'Is now,' Nick responds. 'Found it in a town a few miles away. Some bloke just got bit ... He said he was going to Chapswhich House or something ... Got shit loads of food in the back of it. The van, I mean ... Figured I'd try and find it.'

'That right, is it, nipper?' the man asks. 'What was his name then?'

'How the fuck would I know that?' Nick shakes his head. 'He just got bit, and it was too late for fucking introductions. Stocky bloke, brown hair, and loads of tattoos, had swallows tattooed on his hands.'

'Terry,' the second man says with a glance to the first man.

'Must be. That's their van,' the first man replies. 'Was there another bloke with him?'

'Didn't see anyone. You know him, then? This fella that got bit?'

'Yeah, sounds like Terry. He got them tattoos, 'cept he had another bloke with him, John.'

'Nah,' Nick replies easily, 'maybe he got bit somewhere else or something. Just the bloke with that tatts is all I saw ... What's this Chapstick house, then?'

'Chapsworth House,' the first man says.

'Yeah, that's it. That's what he said. You know it, then?'

'Yeah, could say that. You'd better come with us ...'

'Eh? Why, you gonna shoot me or something?' Nick asks. 'Speaking of which, he had this shotgun, that Terry fella.'

'Let's see,' the man holds his hand out.

'Fuck off!' Nick replies quickly. 'You two got guns, so why would I hand mine over?'

'Fair point,' the second man says.

'Alright, just hold it up so we can see it. Yeah, that's Terry's alright ... got his initials on the stock, see.'

'Oh yeah, didn't see them before,' Nick says.

'Right, well, you gotta come with us anyway. We're from Chapsworth House.'

'Are you?' Nick exclaims. 'That Terry bloke said I should go there, something about seeing a doctor. You need more blokes?'

'What happened to him?'

'What, Terry? Er ... well, don't get shitty, but you know ... he fucking turned, didn't he, so I, er ... you know.'

'Shot him?'

'Yeah, sorry if he was, like, your mate or something.'

'Forget it,' the first man shrugs. 'Shit happens nowadays.'

'Yeah, ain't that right?' Nick nods in agreement. 'Ere, you got a light? Lost mine. You want a smoke?'

Ice broken, he climbs over the gate, taking the two men safely away from seeing Lilly. He was right too; a third man stands back from the hedge, keeping watch quietly while holding a rifle.

'Alright, mate,' Nick nods in greeting.

'What you doing over there?' the third man asks.

'Needed a piss,' Nick laughs, pointing at the stain on his crotch, 'and I was fucking lost too. Map says that house is round here somewhere, but fucked if I could find it.'

The third man stares at the dark stain, then at Nick for a few seconds. Seemingly satisfied, he nods at the other two.

'Take him with you. I'll bring Terry's van.'

Her head spins, and there's an icy grip on her stomach. This is the second time within a few hours she's hidden in undergrowth, listening, but at least this time she can hear Nick talking to them. He sounds natural too, and judging by their tone of voice getting easier, she suspects they believe him.

It happened so fast, and again, he acted on instinct, knowing exactly what to do and saving her again. Sacrificing himself so she can get away. He could have sent her out or both of them. He could have chosen to fight or try and kill them, but he knew this was the best option.

Waiting silently, she listens to the doors slamming on vehicles. An engine starts, then another one, and within a minute, both of them have driven away, leaving her in the silence of the field.

At the gate, she peers round in case there's a trap or anyone left behind. No one here, so she clambers over, then remembers what Nick said about avoiding the road. Back in the field, she starts making her way back down the hill. Steady at first, but her speed increases to a gentle jog. The axe is surprisingly heavy but comforting at the same time. She is glad to have something of his still retained in her possession.

The exhaustion is terrible, sapping her energy to an all-time low. Legs feel heavy and unresponsive, but with no other choice, she wills herself to keep going. Step after step, the sun glaring down makes her feel sick. Water, keep drinking water, and she sips frequently.

Through fields and hedgerows, brambles, and navigating thickets of trees, she runs. The ground hard and unyielding, unforgiving on her hot, tired feet.

Can't stop, can't rest. Got to find a car and find the fort. Find Mr Howie and get them back here.

How can everything go so wrong so quickly? In the space of a day, she's seen her friend being raped and her father being killed. Then Todd was bitten and died slowly, only to come back as one of them.

The pressure is incredible, a panicked urge to do something. An action must be taken now. She wants to find a hole, crawl in, and sleep for days and weeks until this is all over, but that can't happen.

Bite the shock down and keep going. Only the strength of her will pushes her on now. With the initial adrenalin wearing off, the after-effects plummet her down to the depths of despair. A feeling of there being no hope, that Nick was the last chance she had to get her brother. She doesn't know Mr Howie or any of these people. What if they reject her? What if they think she hurt Nick and took his axe?

Mistake compounded by error compounded by fatigue.

Thoughts whirl and spin through her mind, threatening to pull her to the ground where she can weep and scream at the unfairness of it all. That won't get Billy back, though. It won't help Nick or anyone.

Onto the road now, easier going, and she pushes on. Forcing herself to alternate between jogging and walking. Gasping for air, sweating, and feeling sick from the exertion. The road just keeps on, long and twisting so that every hope of reaching a corner to find a house is taken away by the sight of more melting tarmac, more hedges, more fields.

The axe is heavy, the pistol jolts in the holster, irritating her every step. Her clothes, as thin as they are, feel heavy and cling to her frame. Hair soaked, plastered down her face. The water is gone, consumed within the first couple of miles. This is rural England, not the desert. The humidity eats away at the reserves of energy.

Two weeks ago, you wouldn't even think about taking a walk on a hot day like this. Granted, this country hasn't seen heat like this ever before but still. You'd know you can stop, call someone from your mobile, go to a café or shop. Get a bus or sit in the shade to cool down. There would be a cold shower later and some ice cream. Same place, same weather, but everything is dangerous now. The risk of exposure is serious, the risk of dehydration is real. There won't be an ambulance coming to administer fluids as they work to reduce the core body temperature.

As exhausted as her body is, her brain is still working to keep her alive. The power lines overhead are a signal that houses must be close. The information is taken in, processed, labelled, and sent to the front of her mind, where it screams and stamps its feet until noticed.

When it does register, she finds that extra speed, maintaining the jog now until the first property comes into view.

The end wall of a house, then another. A whole row of houses, country cottages, all picturesque and pretty.

Think, Lilly, you need a car that is easy to drive, and make sure it has fuel. The Land Rover was too old and difficult; the gears were impossible.

A BMW, nice and new. Sleek and powerful-looking. It sits outside one of the cottages in the middle. Pistol out, she stalks towards it, staring up at the windows of the houses she passes.

All of them have been entered, the doors a mixture of smashed in completely and just standing ajar like they've been left open by the owners. No time to pause and listen, move fast and keep going.

Up the path and straight into the house. Pistol up, aimed, and ready to be fired. Through the hallway, she goes, checking the small table for the vehicle keys. Finding nothing, she heads into the kitchen, large and spacious like something from a country magazine, with a big pine table in the middle.

Papers piled up on the table next to an open laptop, a large button calculator amongst pens and notepads. She recognises the type of letters instantly from the big, red words at the top of each page. Debt letters, demands for payments. The image of the occupier sat there on the night it happened, wading through bills and letters as they struggled to work it all out.

The futility of it, that none of it mattered, strikes her hard. Watching her father go through a nervous breakdown because of the financial pressure heaped on him.

At the sink, she twists the tap on, letting the water run while she mooches through the drawers and cupboards, searching for the keys.

Amongst the papers on the table, she finds them. A

single black key with a leather fob attached and the BMW symbol etched on.

Pushing her head under the tap, she lets the cool water cascade down her neck, soaking into her hair before rubbing the sweat from her face. A long drink, and she refills the water bottle before heading outside.

D-R-1-2-S. She stares at the automatic gear stick for a few seconds. R must be reverse. One and two must be the first gears. What do D and S mean? Turning the key, she checks the display, noting the tank is over half full.

Leather interior, and the black coloured car is incredibly hot inside, almost scorching the very air from her lungs.

A button on the side of the gearstick. She presses it in, but the thing won't move. She yanks harder, but still it won't budge. Frustration comes to the fore quickly, and she stamps down as she heaves at the stick. Her foot hits the brake, which releases the safety catch. The gearstick yanks down the far end, slotting into R. Handbrake off, and she pushes her foot on the accelerator. The Land Rover was diesel and slow to respond. This is a petrol-driven BMW and is not slow to respond. The engine engages at the slightest touch, sending the car veering backwards with shocking speed. In panic, she pushes her foot down harder. The engine roars from the pressure applied as the vehicle surges backwards into the road, across the road, off the road, slamming into the wooden five-bar gate opposite.

Airbags burst, deploying instantly from the sensors rigged throughout the vehicle. The engine management system cuts out, detecting an airbag deployment. It will now not restart until a full diagnostic check has been completed.

Useless. Modern and useless. She gets out, slamming the door shut before running towards the next cottage with a vehicle outside. This one also modern but with normal gears. The keys are found, the action repeated as she checks the fuel. Carefully this time, she selects reverse and applies gentle pressure while releasing the handbrake. The car backs out slowly as she negotiates the steering wheel.

Which way is south? Damn it! The map is in the van. Wait, she came from that direction, and they were heading south on their way to Chapsworth House, so yes, right. If she goes away from the direction she came, that should be south.

Windows down, air flow on full, and she pulls away. A fifteen-year-old girl forcing herself to keep the speed down for fear of having an accident.

CHAPTER FORTY-ONE

'Man, listen to the D-man, Shaunie. He, like, says it how it is, man.'

'Fuck me, I'm going to kill him ... I really am going to kill him,' Shaun glares at Derek with wide, angry eyes.

'Ginge, I'd be quiet for a bit, mate,' Derek says, trying to placate their angry leader.

'Don't take it out on him,' the large-built woman snaps.

'Yeah, man, like, you know. I'm just helping is all man.'

'I can't stand it. He's English ... Ginge, you're English, not some fucking gangster from Jamaica or ... or ... wherever that fucking voice comes from.'

'We need a decision,' the large woman shouts over the arguing. 'We've been going over this for hours ... What are we going to do?' she speaks slowly, through gritted teeth.

'If we let them in, we're fucked,' Shaun says for the umpteenth time. 'All the men are fucked ... They'll kill us. You heard them. They said the women and children will be fine ...'

'We should vote on it,' Derek suggests.

'Yes, Derek! I know you want to vote. You keep saying

you want to vote, but if we do vote, and the majority say we let them in, then you and I are going to be killed ... Do you understand that?'

'They might not?' Derek shrugs.

'YOU'S ALL FUCKED, INNIT?'

'Someone shut that fucking kid up,' Shaun snarls. 'If he shouts once more, then ...'

'Then what?' the large woman demands. 'You'll what? Kill him? Yeah, because that'll help our situation.'

'Man, why don't we like, you know, let everyone go if they want to go,' Ginge suggests. 'You know, like, don't let them be prisoners but set them free.'

'Set them free?' Shaun shakes his head. 'They ain't fucking pandas being released into the jungle.'

'He's got a point. It'll show we're nice people,' someone comments from the depths of the crowd gathered round Shaun.

'We are nice people,' Shaun replies. 'We're very nice people, but they ain't gonna think that.'

'Maybe they'll go away,' Ginge continues, 'like, you know, they'll get their people, and they'll, like, go away and find another fort.'

'HA, YOU DUMB FUCKER,' the youth laughs.

Ignoring the youth, they carry on, worried faces with worried expressions. Everyone too hot, too tired, and not knowing what to do.

'Where's that woman?' Derek asks. 'The Polish one. She seems alright. Ask her to go out and talk them down.'

'What?' Shaun exclaims.

'That, man,' Ginge nods emphatically, 'is like a really cool idea, you know.'

'It is,' the large woman adds. 'Derek, go and find her.'

'Oi,' Shaun cries out, 'we haven't decided anything yet.'

'We have,' the woman cuts him off. 'We listened to you so far, Shaun, and look at where we are?'

'Okay,' Shaun switches into his calm negotiator's voice, 'we shouldn't rush into anything now. Let's just stay calm and talk this through.'

'He's gone, man,' Ginge says needlessly. 'Like, the D-man has gone to get the girl.'

'Derek!' Shaun shouts. 'His fucking name is Derek.'

'Whatever, man,' Ginge shakes his head.

'Right, love,' the large woman takes centre position as Derek leads Lenski into the middle of the group. 'Your people out there said they'll let the women and children stay here, but what about the men?'

Lenski stays quiet. Scanning the group, she takes in the panicked expressions, sensing the palpable worry amongst them.

'They not hurt the woman or the children,' Lenski says in a clear, confident voice. 'They never hurt them. They are not those people that do those things.'

'What about us?' Shaun asks.

'You?' Lenski shrugs as though it matters little to her.

'Yeah, us?' Shaun repeats. 'What will they do to us?'

'You took this place. This is not your place to take. What you expect?'

'Shit, man, I knew this was bad karma,' Ginge reels from the flat-toned words of Lenski.

'What the fuck have you done, Shaun?' Derek wails. 'We're fucked now, fucking, fucking fucked ...'

'Get a grip,' Shaun snaps, thinking frantically. 'Has anyone seen them from the walls yet?'

Heads shaking, the armed men look at each other, then back to Shaun. 'They're right up against the wall,' one explains. 'We keep looking, but, well, unless we stick our heads right out over the edge and look down, we can't see 'em, and I for one ain't doing that.'

'Bloody right,' Derek nods, 'they're like proper trained for this shit. We're just ordinary people ... Fuck's sake, Shaun, you were an estate agent.'

Lenski stares at the crowd gathered round the flustering Shaun. He just asked if anyone can see them from the walls. If he can ask that, then the people from the walls must be down here. Casually, as though bored of the conversation, she looks up and round, scanning the firm line where the wall meets the open sky. Smooth all round, no people, no guards.

Yawning, she stretches her arms out and checks over her shoulder, at the back gate. That too has been left unattended.

How can she let them know outside? Tell them this is the time to do something?

'I speak with them, yes?' Lenski interrupts the chatter. 'Maybe they hear my voice, and they don't feel so bad. I tell them we are okay, and we see it gives you more time,' she adds with a nod at Shaun.

'Yeah,' the former estate agent seizes on the chance to once more appear as though in control, 'do that, but no fucking funny business. You tell 'em we haven't hurt anyone ...'

'Yeah, and say we're sorry, and they can have their fort back,' Derek blurts, getting a glare from Shaun.

'No, don't say that,' Shaun says quickly.

'Yeah, do say that,' Derek urges. 'Say we're really sorry, and like, we didn't mean it ...'

'Bloody hell,' the large woman snaps, taking a step forward, 'just tell them no one has been hurt, and we want to end this peacefully, alright?'

'I say this, yes,' Lenski nods at the woman.

'Yeah, yeah, good one,' Derek nods, flicking his gaze between the woman and Shaun.

'Okay, as you wish.' Lenski starts to walk off, wondering if anyone will grab her or tell her to slow down. For a second, it looks like the idiots might just let her go alone, and she starts eyeing the bolts on the inside, thinking how quickly she can get them all pulled back.

'I'll be right here,' Shaun jogs up to fall in step beside her.

'Of course,' Lenski nods, not showing any expression. Reaching the inside of the gate, she pauses, glancing at the man for permission to start. He stares back for a second, wondering what she wants before nodding and tapping his shotgun for effect which just earns a withering look from the unflappable Lenski.

'Maddox, you hear me, yes?'

The other side of the gate bursts into silent activity, arms waving at one another to get ready. Everyone presses in tight to the sides of the walls as they edge closer to listen. Maddox and Paula ease their way to either side of the gate, staring at each other intently. With Jagger and Mohammed returning, the numbers have swelled considerably, with hard-faced youths ready to do something.

'Yeah, I'm here,' Maddox replies. 'You okay, Lenski?'

'Yes, I am okay,' Lenski says slowly. Speaking slower than normal, she conveys the obvious message that people are listening to her.

'Good, what's going on?' Maddox nods at Paula.

'They have the meeting with *all* of their people, yes? *All* of the people they talk, and they worry, yes?'

Paula locks eyes with Maddox. Having only met Lenski once, she doesn't know her voice, but even she detects the inflection when she says *all.* All the people? She stares about, thinking intently before searching out Roy with her eyes. Motioning to him, she points two fingers at her own eyes, then points to the top of the wall. Roy nods once and starts moving back, staring up.

'They should be worried,' Maddox caught the inflection too, giving Paula a quick nod when he sees what she has asked Roy to do.

'They know this now,' Lenski's voice drifts through. 'They tell me to say none of the people have been hurt.'

'Good,' Maddox replies flatly.

'And they want the peaceful end, yes?'

Paula motions to Maddox, *keep her talking, keep them focussed.*

'Like what?' Maddox asks. 'They suggest anything, then?'

'I not know this, but ... they worry, yes? They worry the men will be killed, so they not wanting to come out.'

'Tell them to come out now, then, guns down and hands up, and maybe we can have that peaceful end.'

Roy runs back in from the outer gate, motioning to Paula the top wall is clear.

'Lenski, it's Paula ... Is everyone okay?'

'I say this already. Yes, the people are okay.'

'How do we know you're not being made to say that?'

'You don't know this,' Lenski replies, 'but I say this, yes? The people, they are just scared and worried.'

'So who is in charge in there?' Paula asks.

'Er ... the man, he is in charge. His name is Shaun, I think. He is here now.'

'Shaun? Can you hear me?' Paula asks, getting a nod from Maddox to continue.

'Yep,' Shaun calls out. Both Paula and Maddox recognising the same voice from earlier.

'How about it, then?' Paula asks. 'You're the boss in there, right? So you make the decision, just walk out now with guns down and arms up.'

'How do we know you won't kill all the men?'

'You don't,' Maddox snaps in a harsh tone. 'You don't know anything, but what else you gonna do?'

'Stay in here obviously,' Shaun retorts in a sarcastic tone.

Paula motions once more for Maddox to keep going before stepping away to join Roy.

'Can you take him out if we get you up there,' Paula points up at the wall.

'Yes,' Roy answers quick and flat. He has absolutely no doubts about his expertise with the bow. 'Unless he's behind cover, of course.'

'He's right behind that gate. There was no cover there.'

'Be fine then,' Roy nods. 'You sending me up there, then?' he adds with a grin.

'Er, yeah, I was thinking about it. Could you?' she asks.

'No problem, we just need a rope. I did have one in my fucking van, but my fucking van isn't here,' Roy thinks out loud while Paula notices once more that weird way he speaks so nicely but swears all the time. 'And a grappling hook too. You got any grappling hooks, Paula?' he asks with a glint in his eye.

'Yeah, in my purse.'

'Boat yards, anchors ... ropes ... We're right by the sea so ...' Roy twists round to stare out, over the flatlands.

'No time for that. We've got one chance while he's at the gate.'

'Righto,' Roy nods, 'well, unless you can teach me how to fly, I don't see ...'

'Come on,' she jogs off with a bemused Roy following in her wake. Motioning again for Maddox to keep them talking, she runs past, towards the many vehicles parked between the walls.

'Must be something here,' she murmurs to Roy trailing behind her. 'There ... that digger thing ... What if you stand on the bucket, and we lift it up?'

'Ha! Yeah right ... Oh, you're being serious, er ... well, er ... it would make too much noise,' Roy replies, more than slightly taken aback.

'Yeah, it would, wouldn't it?' Paula bites her lip.

'Ladders,' Roy points down to a battered flat-bed lorry with aluminium ladders roped onto the back.

'Too short. That wall is very high.'

'Put them on top of something then.' Roy moves forward, then turns, quickly waving at several youths watching them with interest. 'Move quietly and get those ladders down. Not a sound, though.'

The children burst away, glad to be doing something. Like ferrets, they pour over the flat-bed lorry, lithe fingers working deftly at the securing ropes. They are young but already have many years practise of breaking into properties and working silently to take what they could.

Roy gauges the distance between the top of the roof to the top of the wall. He looks at the ladders extending. They're still going to be too short.

'Rope,' he mouths at the children, 'get some rope.'

'You need a hand?' Darius appears, leaving Maddox trying to drag the conversation out at the gate.

'We want that ladder on that truck and some rope,'

Paula replies. Roy glances at her, startled at how she had already worked the plan out.

The ladder clunks ever so slightly as it strikes the side of the truck cabin, earning the child responsible a round of hard glares. With everything in position, the ladders are slid up to the fullest extension.

'Too short,' Roy tuts at the six-foot gap left between the top of the ladder and the wall.

'Rope,' Darius whispers, pointing to a young girl running towards them with blue, thin coiled rope.

'Great, but we got no way of fastening it to the wall, and it's too thin to grip too,' Roy says matter of fact.

'Leave it with me, bruv,' Darius strides off, whispering something to two children. They nod back and coil the rope out before hunkering down to start tying knots every few inches.

Roy clambers onto the truck, leaning down as Paula passes him the compound bow. At the foot of the ladder and staring up, he can't see a way of securing the rope to the wall.

'Mind out,' Darius whispers as the young girl who found the rope gets on top of the truck. With the end of the rope between her teeth and the rest played out down to the ground, she climbs the ladder with ease, pausing only briefly at the top before starting to go further up. Her small hands and feet find cracks and holes to propel her light body up. At the top, she scans left and right, with the blue rope still between her teeth, giving Roy an image of a young child-pirate.

With one smooth movement, she gains the top of the wall, immediately going flat to minimise her profile. Disappearing from view, they wait for just seconds until she appears, leaning over and giving a thumbs up.

'You're up,' Darius mouths.

'What?' Roy stares in shock at the rope dangling down the wall.

'It's tied on, bro,' Darius urges. 'Go ... fucking quick ...'

'How? Oh, never mind,' Roy blinks at the speed the girl did it. Little burglars extraordinaire, this lot. No wonder crime was so good to them if they can do stuff like this.

Bow looped over his shoulder, he starts up the ladder while his tongue starts the internal probe of his mouth. The far corner, on the bottom bit where the cheek meets the jaw. Yep, definitely a new lump. Fuck it. It's going to be a big-ass, giant tumour sucking the life out of him. Probing further, his face contorts as he tries to stretch his tongue into the corner, poking and prodding with the tip. The girl at the top stares in wonder at the strange man climbing up, pulling weird faces.

Gripping the rope, he starts the climb, hand over hand, using the knots put in place by the kids. Nearing the top, the girl twists round to check before nodding.

'Stay low,' she hisses as he negotiates the lip of the wall.

'I'm trying,' Roy whispers. Going flat, he lies still, grinning at the little girl giving him a big, toothy smile. 'Well done,' Roy nods.

'Cheers, mate,' the girl whispers.

'Mate? I'm old enough to be your dad,' Roy shakes his head. Crabbing along, he starts across the top of the flat-topped wall. The girl remains at the still, watching him as he gets closer to the inner edge.

Shifting position, he scans round, gaining a view of the inside of the inner gate. The Polish girl, Lenski, stands next to a man holding a long-barrelled gun. Other armed men are nearby but not too close.

Even from this distance, they look worried, casting

nervous glances at each other as they listen to the negotiations.

He senses movement behind him. He twists round to see the girl motioning for him to get on with it, clearly relaying a message sent from below.

Nodding back, he pulls the bow free, takes an arrow, and in one movement is up on one knee, with the arrow nocked and aimed.

Turning his head, he spots the girl holding her hand out flat, telling him to wait.

The girl watches Darius below holding his hand out flat. Darius stares along to Paula, watching her holding her hand out flat. In turn, Paula watches Maddox holding his the same way.

'It's all on you,' Maddox repeats, 'either you come out or you don't.'

'Why don't you come in without the weapons?' Shaun says again. 'You want us to come out unarmed, so why don't you come *in* unarmed. Then we can talk about it properly.'

'Last chance,' Maddox says, getting a thumbs up from Paula that Roy is ready.

'Eh? What's that fucking mean? Last chance or what? You gonna wreck your own gates to get in here? We'll kill everyone before you get a foot inside.'

'Remember this,' Maddox calls out, making sure his voice carries into the fort. 'You remember I gave you every chance.'

His flat hand changes to a thumbs up. Paula's copies his. Darius changes his own hand shape, which is then copied by the girl.

Heart rate slow, breathing normal. Nothing but the arrow exists. Roy sees the thumbs up, turns his head and looses. The arrow flies true and straight on a downhill trajectory that uses the force of gravity as much as the pressure given to its flight from the bow.

The arrow takes Shaun through the throat, pinning him to the wooden post behind him.

Maddox listens, hears a thud and strangled yelp, followed in an instant by screams coming from inside.

On his feet, and Roy breaks cover, the next arrow already nocked, pulled, and ready. The crowd of people react in stunned shock. Some scream out as others gape at the sight of their leader killed outright. A man steps out, holding a weapon, only to be taken off his feet by the arrow striking his chest, driving clean through his heart.

'GET DOWN,' Roy bellows. 'DROP THE GUNS NOW ... LENSKI ...'

Already reacting, she grasps the bolts ramming them back. Maddox wrenches the gate open. Grabbing Lenski, he pulls her through before striding in, pistol up and aimed. Paula is right behind him as Darius and the children burst in, storming into action.

'GUNS DOWN,' Maddox roars. The crews already inside spring to life. Ploughing into the crowd, they start striking and hitting at anyone holding a weapon. Roy screams from the wall. Paula charges forward, firing a round into the air. There's chaos but in a controlled and directed manner, an overwhelming assault to the senses. Two men killed within seconds, gunshots ringing out, people shouting orders. Children everywhere running amongst the group, hitting and grabbing guns from unsuspecting men.

'OKAY ... OKAY ...' Derek throws his gun down. Stretching his arms to the sky, he stands stock still, yelling at everyone else to do the same.

Within thirty seconds of the first arrow striking Shaun, the fort is taken back. The last of the armed men drop their weapons or have them ripped from their hands by hard-faced children.

Women screaming, children crying, and quickly they start dropping to their knees in a desperate attempt to show surrender.

'CLEAR?' Roy shouts from above.

'CLEAR,' Paula shouts back. 'Get those guns away,' she shouts at the children, motioning towards the weapons dropped to the ground.

'Wow ...' Ginge, being the only one left standing and holding his arms completely stretched to the sky, stares in stunned awe. 'Man ... that was like, you know ... wow.'

'Took your time,' Sierra walks out from the room she was locked in, grinning at Darius as she quickly walks over to kiss him.

Roy lowers his bow but keeps his eyes locked on the crowd below. Two lives taken. Two men killed without hesitation, and his only concern is that worrying sensation now in his tongue, aching a bit like it's strained. The fact that his tongue has been stretching over to the far corner of his mouth doesn't enter his head.

'That was great, mate,' the girl joins him at the edge of the wall.

'Thank you,' Roy replies quietly, 'and my name is Roy, not mate.'

'You teach me?'

'Pardon?'

'Teach me to do that?' she asks seriously.

'Takes years,' Roy mutters, watching the crowd closely, 'hours of practise every day.'

'I see you shooting them arrows at the zombies. You's well good, and I ain't goin' nowhere, so teach me, yeah?'

'Was that an actual sentence?' Roy asks with a quick shake of his head. 'What's your name?'

'Kizzie, innit?'

'Kizzie Innit? Unusual name.'

'Nah, bruv, it's just Kizzie.'

'Oh, right, yeah, sorry, er ... well, Kizzie, we'll have to see.'

'Don't brush me off,' the girl tuts.

'Kizzie, it really is hours every day and takes a long time to learn.'

'Yeah, so's when I'm older, I be as good as you, yeah?'

A flicker of irritation crosses Roy's face. Not at the interest the girl shows, but the way she speaks. 'Tell you what,' Roy says, 'we'll practise archery, but only if you start talking properly.'

'How's I gonna know that then, bruv?'

'I'll teach you, and for a start my name is Roy. Not bruv or mate, but Roy.'

The girl looks up at him with an expression of sublime confidence. 'Okay, Roy. Sweet, bruv. So we going down there now, yeah?'

'No, Kizzie, we're staying here to keep watch. The walls don't have anybody on them, you see. That was their mistake,' he nods at the large group kneeling on the ground. They left themselves undefended and open to attack, which is what we exploited.'

'Ah right,' the girl nods.

'Kizzie? You comin' down?' Darius peers up, using his hand to shield his eyes from the sun.

'Nah, bruv, me and Roy, we's defending so no fucker exploits the walls.'

'I think your man got an apprentice,' Darius jokes to Paula.

'Good for him,' Paula replies, wincing at the two dead bodies speared by arrows. Having walked back in, Lenski views Shaun's corpse with distaste before crossing to join Maddox in front of the group.

'I warn you of this, yes? You not say I did not try,' she calls out.

'We gave him a chance,' Maddox adds. 'It's done now.'

'What happens now then, love?' the large woman asks. 'You mind if I sit on my arse? I'm too fat to stay on my knees.' Without waiting for the answer, she shifts position, wincing from the pains in her legs as she stretches them out.

'CONTACT,' Roy shouts. 'VEHICLE COMING.'

'Darius, you stay with these. Maddox, you coming with me? ROY? YOU STAYING UP THERE?' Paula speaks fast, moving towards the gate.

'YEP, GOT GOOD RANGE,' Roy shouts.

Leaving Darius to oversee guarding of the group, they run towards the gate.

'Must be more refugees,' Paula mutters, watching the approaching vehicle in the distance. Standing quietly, they watch as the zebra-striped vehicle gets closer, exchanging confused stares at the sight of the strange-looking Land Rover.

'Is Howie, yes?' Lenski takes a step forward. 'Yes, is Mr Howie.' She nods, looking back at Maddox and Paula.

Relaxing slightly, they wait as the vehicle slows to a stop. The easily identifiable bulk of Clarence in the passenger seat.

Doors open as the group clamber down, Meredith jumping out first to run over with excited barks in greeting.

'Hello,' Milly shouts in advance of anyone else speaking.

'Er, hi,' Paula calls back with a bemused smile.

'Long story,' Howie says with a glance at the girl holding Lani's hand. 'Where's Nick?' he asks, staring back to the fort.

'Nick?' Maddox asks.

'Yeah ... is he not back yet?'

'No, no sign of him,' Maddox replies. He sees the look of worry cross their faces.

'Shit ... right ...' Howie stops a few feet from them, staring back over the flatlands.

'We got the fort back,' Paula says.

'Really?' Clarence asks.

'Got Roy onto the wall. He took their leader out and another man. Lenski got the gate open, and we went in.'

'Well done,' Howie says seriously, 'anyone hurt?'

'Just two of theirs,' Paula replies.

'They not hurt anyone,' Lenski adds. 'Where is Nick?'

'No idea, he didn't show at the car park, so we figured he'd come back here. Everyone, get water and food quickly, change clothes and wash if you need to. We're going back out. You got everything here?' He looks to all three in turn.

'Yeah,' Maddox nods, 'we got this. We'll get some more with you, yeah?'

'What's the situation in there?' Clarence asks.

'We only just took it, like a few minutes ago ... They're all kneeling in the dirt just inside the gate.'

'Boss? We need to sort them out first, then go get Nick. You got anyone good with vehicles? The Saxon broke down on the way out,' Clarence stares at Maddox.

'Only stealing them,' Maddox replies. 'Some of 'em are okay at stuff but ...'

'There might be someone who can do this. We have many come here now,' Lenski cuts in.

'Shit, Nick, where the hell are you?' Howie mutters. 'Let's get inside.'

'Mr Howie said a rude word,' Milly pipes up, announcing it to everyone. 'I'm Milly,' she grins.

Worried now. Very worried. Nick is strong and capable, and he'd know to get back here. Something has happened.

Leading the way, I stride towards the gate. The others right behind me, being introduced to Milly who talks non-stop but shows that skill again by instantly remembering everyone's names.

'Roy,' I nod up in greeting at the sight of the man on top the wall, bow in hand. He nods back as I cross through the gap into the fort.

Darius stands with a rifle aimed at a large group of people sitting and kneeling on the ground. Ordinary people of all shapes and sizes, men, women, and children, and all of them looking terrified.

Maddox's children are stood encircling the group, all of them armed with weapons, and despite how exhausted we all are and the fucking heat sapping away at everyone, they look keen-eyed and switched on.

All eyes fix on me as I approach the group. Dave right behind me with Clarence. The lads and Lani just behind them. Nodding at Darius, I stop just before the group and look down.

Two men have been killed by Roy. One of them pinned to a wooden post with an arrow through his neck; the other lies still on the ground with one through his chest.

'Jagger, did you see any sign of Nick on your way back?' I call out to the lad standing next to Mohammed.

'No, Mr Howie,' shaking his head, he looks at Mohammed.

'Is he missing?' Mohammed asks.

'Yeah,' I notice the ripple of attention spiking up in the group as Jagger says my name. Everyone now looks closely as they scan the group, spotting Dave and Clarence, then down to Lani. Meredith, still off the lead, makes no hesitation in plundering forward to snake through the group, sniffing at them. Some flinch away from the huge dog as we wait for her to finish her sniffing. The thought that some might be infected is already in my mind, and I know Dave has already drawn his pistol.

'Stay still,' I call out bluntly.

'Are you Mr Howie?' a large woman asks quietly.

'Mr Howie said to stay still,' Dave replies instantly.

Meredith trots through the group, wagging her tail as she sniffs at children before seeming to lose interest and trotting off to the side.

'Yes, I am,' I finally answer the woman who asked the question. 'This is Dave, Clarence, Lani, Blowers, and Cookey.' If my name is going to get banded about, then the others can have it too. 'What happened here?'

'Hey, man, like, we didn't mean no bad karma, man, you know. We were only, like, doing what Shaunie said, but the D-man said Shaunie didn't know what he was doing but ...'

'Do what?' I ask the man with dreadlocked, ginger hair, not really understanding what he just said.

'Sue, you tell 'em,' a man calls out from within the group.

'Are you Sue?' I ask the large woman.

'I am,' she replies in a confident voice. 'That idiot,' she points back to the man pinned to the post with the arrow through his neck, 'talked us into taking this place for ourselves ... God knows how he did it ... but he did, so ...'

'And you all went along with it?' I ask quickly. 'It's a big group to do what one man says.'

'He said we shouldn't be under control of someone else. He, like, got it in our heads that the women might get taken and the kids and stuff,' a man blurts out, nervous looking; he glances between me and Sue.

'Who are you?'

'Derek,' he replies.

'D-man,' the ginger-haired man adds for whatever strange reason.

'This place is free,' I call out. 'We don't hold anyone by force, and we don't turn anyone away. We have controls to keep the infection out, and we've already lost this place to the disease once, but we'd have taken you in.'

'We didn't know that,' Sue replies.

'But you see the people outside, yes? You see them queue and come in?'

'Shaun said they were probably having to give all their stuff over and weapons,' Derek says. 'Like, I know it sounds stupid, but he was really good at talking us into stuff.'

'Until the end when we realised what a prick he was,' Sue scoffs.

'Sue said a rude word,' Milly calls out. 'Mr Howie will tell you off now,' glancing over, I see Milly staring at me expectantly.

'Er, don't anyone swear,' I call out which seems to meet her approval. 'Or Milly will tell me off,' I add.

'What now?' Sue asks. 'They said before the woman and children will be safe.'

'We did say that before we got in,' Paula explains. I nod in understanding.

'Are you all from the same place?' I ask.

'No, just a couple of us,' Sue replies. 'More joined as we came down ... Shaun was in the first lot.'

'Darius, you stay with them, mate. Everyone else, with me, please.' I walk off, fully aware that I'm telling everyone what to do, but with Nick still not back, the pressure to get this sorted and back out is on.

'Right, ideas?' I ask the group gathered round me. 'We're not hurting anyone or killing anyone else.'

'I agree,' Paula says quickly, 'we said the women and children would be safe, so we should honour that. They're in a right mess, filthy and hungry too by the looks of it.'

'They eat lots when they come in,' Lenski explains, 'but then they worry, and they not wash, and the fort it too big for them to guard, so they worry and argue.'

'You've been with them the longest. What do you think?' Maddox asks his partner.

Thinking for a minute, Lenski turns to stare at the group. They know their fate is being discussed, so they stare over with concerned, fearful faces.

'Yes, they not the bad people. The man Shaun, he controlling them, but he lose the control at the end. The men, they are the husbands and fathers of the women and children, so they are the families ... They no different to the other people that come here,' she nods at the main camp and the groups standing about, watching with worried interest. 'They worry too,' she adds. 'Everyone, they worry. This is the safe place for all the people, so we not make them go.'

'How did they get in?' Dave asks in his blunt tone.

'We not have enough people here,' Lenski replies equally as blunt. 'You take too many last night, and they come and argue and make the scene ...'

'Distraction,' Maddox nods.

'Yes, they use the distraction,' Lenski says.

'That's twice now we've lost this place,' I say with a glance at Clarence. 'It can't keep happening.'

'We had no choice,' Maddox is quick to jump in. 'With that lot coming at us, we had to deal with it.'

'Yeah, I know,' I nod, 'but the infected could try something like that too.'

'I'll sort it. You leave it with me now,' Maddox says firmly. 'With my crews here, we can control the gates, the walls and make sure security is done properly.'

'Paula? What about you? What's your plans with Roy?' I ask her.

'Me? I haven't got a clue,' she laughs. 'Roy wants to find a doctor, you know, with his, er ...'

'Yeah,' I nod quickly, 'that's our priority too. Well, after finding Nick and getting the Saxon back and then finding more ammunition, maybe some more guns, and of course, we've still got the bodies to burn ... which now means more fuel.'

'Tell you what,' Paula says clearly, 'er ... if you don't mind me suggesting things?' She suddenly seems to become aware of everyone looking at her.

'Carry on,' I urge.

'Sure?' She looks at Maddox and Lenski.

'Sure, yes, you stay here, yes, we need the people like you,' Lenski nods firmly. An acceptance made, a transition of an agreement. Paula and Roy are now with us.

Relaxing, she smiles once before carrying on. 'Well, I was thinking that maybe,' she goes steady, clearly not wanting to be seen as bossy, 'Maddox does the security and organises getting those bodies burned, you lot go look for

Nick, and I'll take Roy to find ammunition ... Just tell me where to look, and we'll sort it.'

'Military bases, barracks, armouries,' Dave cuts in. 'There's a supply ship in Portsmouth harbour that we never emptied.'

'We can do that,' Paula says.

'Makes sense,' Lani nods at me, 'means we're free to find Nick ...'

'Do that then. Everyone happy?' I stare round at the nodding heads. 'Just leaves that lot to be spoken to. You happy if I say something?' This is getting awkward. Me not wanting to tread on Maddox's feet, him not wanting to do the same, now with Paula too. I guess it takes time for things to settle. Maybe we should have that council after all. Bloody hell, I can imagine Sergeant Hopewell cursing me from beyond.

In agreement, and we walk back to the group, all of them looking worried as they stare up.

'LIONS AND TIGERS AND BEARS,' Milly decides to shout.

'Oh my,' Cookey can't resist the add on.

'Paula, do you like lions and tigers and bears?'

'Pardon? Er ... yes, I think so.'

'Maddox, do you like lions and tigers and bears?'

The hard-faced man stares at me. I shrug and motion for him to answer.

'Er, yeah,' Maddox says slowly.

'Lenski, do you like lions and tigers a bears?' And so it goes on. Somehow the little girl keeps everyone waiting as she goes round the large group, asking everyone if they like lions and tigers and bears. Funny thing is, no one tells her to stop but just waits until she's finished. She even asks Sue and Derek, remembering their names from the brief introduction a few minutes ago.

'Right, I think she's finished,' I call out. 'This is a free place and will remain as such. You will not be held against your will, nor will you be expelled. You will all be searched for weapons, and they will be removed. Anyone with skills will be asked to work but not forced. Our food is held centrally so we can share everything with everyone. There has to be control in a place like this. More people will arrive, so although it looks big now, it will soon fill up. The people in charge here are the ones you can see standing with me. We don't own this fort, but we run it, and we do it for the good of everyone, and for now, it will stay like that. Any questions?'

'Man, like, you saying we can stay here?'

'He just said that, Ginge,' Sue mutters quietly.

'Yeah, I thought so, but like, you know, I wasn't expecting that ... Cool, man.'

'Mr Howie,' Sue calls my attention, 'we aren't bad, really. We just followed the wrong person. We want to stay, and we want to be involved. It *was* a bad idea what we did, and on behalf of everyone, I want to say how sorry ...' murmurs break out, heads nodding in agreement. Some of the men and women cry openly at the good news. Relief, exhaustion, stress, and tension all playing their part.

'We've got an hour or two of daylight left. Get these people checked for cuts, bites, or open wounds; then, we put the same controls in as before, but more guards on the gates. Keep them rotated so they stay switched on. Keep the walls covered and also ... check the vehicles in the gap because if you got in that easy, so will others.'

'Good point,' Paula says. 'I was thinking the same thing.'

'We learn as we go,' I sigh, about to ask Nick for a cigarette. 'My lot, get cleaned and ready to go.'

'Lenski, can we find a mechanic here?'

'Sierra, she has the lists, yes? I sort this.' She walks off, heading towards the police office.

'CONTACT,' Roy shouts, 'VEHICLE ...' Lenski stops mid-stride, turning round as she rolls her eyes, tutting at the relentless pace.

'Sierra?' She calls out. 'Mr Howie, he needs the mechanic, yes? You find this?'

'Mechanic? Ginge, ain't you a mechanic?' Derek from the kneeling group asks.

'Yeah, man,' Ginge nods, 'like, you know, yeah.'

'Really?' I ask him. 'You don't look like a mechanic.'

'My father had a garage, you know. I had to do it, like. I had no choice, man. I was oppressed.'

'Poor you,' I glare at him. 'Our vehicle has broken down.'

'A Saxon. Do you know them?' Clarence asks. 'An army vehicle, big armoured personnel carrier?' he adds at the blank look.

'Engines are engines,' Ginge shrugs, 'apart from, like, you know, the modern cars with computers and the diagnostic stuff.'

'Nah, this is old,' Clarence replies.

'Old is good,' Ginge shrugs.

'Good, you're coming with us, then.'

'Me? Whoa, man, like hang on here.'

'Want to stay here?' Clarence takes a big step forward. Folding his huge arms, he glares down at the poor man.

'Yeah, like whatever, man, glad to help, you know,' Ginge changes tack instantly. 'Need tools, man,' he adds.

'We'll find them on the way,' I reply.

'SINGLE VEHICLE AT SPEED,' Roy shouts, 'NOT SLOWING DOWN.' That gets us going. My team all breaking away, running towards the gate.

Outside, we stand ready, moving into a circular line as we watch the small hatchback roaring down the track towards us.

'Where's Milly?' I ask Lani as she moves into position next to me.

'Lenski's got her.'

'Fuck me, they're in a hurry,' Blowers mutters.

'Maybe they need a poo,' Cookey replies, earning a quick look from the rest of us. 'What?' he says with a grin.

The car leaves the braking to the very last second, bringing the anti-lock braking system into play, juddering the rear wheels as the car slews to a stop in a cloud of dust.

'Cor,' Cookey can't help himself at the sight of the beautiful girl clambering out of the driver's door. Seeing us, she scans the group, visibly staring first at Clarence, then Dave, and Lani before moving to lock eyes on me.

'She's armed,' Blowers shouts. We all draw quickly, taking aim as Dave moves out to the side.

'DROP THE WEAPON,' he roars.

'WAIT,' the girl screams, 'please ...'

'Blowers, move in and take the gun,' I raise my voice so the girl can hear. "Don't move ... just stay still ... Are you bit?'

'No, Nick sent me ...' she blurts out.

'Nick?' I exclaim.

'What did you say?' Blowers demands. 'Where is he?'

'Is he hurt?' Cookey walks forward. We all do as Dave deftly moves up behind her and slips the pistol from her holster.

'Please,' she holds her hands up, tears streaming down

her face. She is very pretty but looks utterly exhausted, literally swaying on her feet.

'Lani?' she asks Lani. 'Are you Lani? And you're Clarence, and you're Dave,' she nods at Dave standing next to her, staring at the pistol he took from her belt. 'You must Blowers and Cookey, and you're Mr Howie.'

'How do you know that?' I ask.

'Nick said to tell you he made Tower Bridge move so the zombies fell off, and the ferry from the island too, er ... he set it on fire ...'

'Okay, take it easy,' I speak calmly. 'What's happened? Where is he?'

'Oh god, is it you? Is it really you? Nick said to find the fort and find Mr Howie, that he'd know what to do.'

'You've found us,' Lani moves in close to the distressed girl. 'It's okay, just take a breath.'

'He said ...' she starts crying harder, gasping for breath, 'he said you'd know what to do.'

'We will,' Lani says softly. 'Mr Howie is right here. We're all right here ... Now, where's Nick?' You look exhausted. Are you injured?'

'No ... I haven't slept, and it's so hot ... but Nick and Billy.'

'Okay, take it easy. Lani, can you check her over with Paula and bring her through to the police office. Let's get her out the sun and some fluids inside her.'

'Come on,' Lani pulls the girl gently away.

'Wait!' she cries. Rushing back to the car, she leans in to draw a single-bladed axe out.

'That's Nick's,' Blowers says quickly.

'He made me take it to show you,' the girl says.

'Is he in danger? Right now, is he in danger?'

'No. Yes ... I, er ... they took him, but he seemed okay. I don't know,' she stammers.

'I'll take her in and get her calm,' Lani says. 'What's your name?'

'Lilly, I'm Lilly.'

'Come on, Lilly, you come with me.'

CHAPTER FORTY-TWO

'You look better,' Paula smiles kindly as the girl walks into the room. Pausing slightly, she takes in the many faces staring at her and smiles nervously.

'Sorry for earlier. I was a bit overcome with it all.' Her voice is refined and cultured, indicating a private education from a wealthy background.

'You feeling okay?' I ask, desperate to find out about Nick.

'Tired,' she smiles at me, 'I haven't slept for ... gosh, I don't even know how long it's been.'

'Here,' Cookey stands at the side, still on coffee-making punishment for his many mischievous misdemeanours. He passes her a steaming mug, and she's shown to a vacant seat. As she settles down, she keeps glancing nervously up at everyone.

'From what Lilly just told me, it sounds like Nick is okay for the minute,' Lani explains quickly, putting our minds at rest before looking at the girl. 'Tell us everything from the start,' she prompts.

'Everything?'

'Everything,' Clarence says. 'Takes a bit longer, but then we know all the facts.'

'Right, well,' she takes a deep breath and starts. The story that follows holds us captivated. Her elocution is so perfect, her pronunciation so clear that I can imagine everything as she relays it all.

An awful, truly horrific set of events, but she bravely fights the tears during the hardest parts, forcing herself to keep going. When she tells us how she hid in the undergrowth and watched her friend Sam being raped, then her father being killed, I know I am not the only one with a lump in my throat.

She tells us of how she tracks Billy and Todd back to the holiday cottage, driving the Land Rover after them, and finally how she met Nick in town.

She explains it all clearly, leaving few questions, and the attention becomes super focussed when she talks about meeting Nick. It even earns a chuckle when she says how she was punching him, mistaking him for one of the men.

Lilly tells how they went back to the car park, and she told Nick to stay and wait for us and that she didn't have time to lose, she had to leave immediately. He, as any of us would, made the decision to go with her.

As she tells me everything, I can't help but feel an immense pride in Nick. Clarence gives me a nod, and I can even see Dave leaning forward to take interest at how she says Nick handled everything. Blowers has a tight-lipped smile, and Cookey is hanging off every word she says.

Todd being bit and turned drops our eyes. The sadness and injustice of it all is terrible, and she has to stop for a few minutes to compose herself.

'He did the right thing,' I say gently.

'I know,' she nods and carries on. 'He was so fast, and ... he didn't panic or anything like that.'

'We've been through a lot together. Please, carry on,' I motion when she recovers her composure.

'Then we were on our back to the van when we heard the voices. Well, Nick heard them first. We hid by the hedge for a minute, and that's when Nick gave me the axe and said about Tower Bridge and burning a ferry from an island. He said to find you and tell you what happened.'

'What happened next?' I ask, completely engrossed.

Smiling sadly, she looks round at us. 'Nick got some water and poured it on his, er ... his groin area, then called out, asking who was there. They shouted back, and he pretended he had been for a wee,' the way she says it, using the word *wee,* and the image of Nick pretending he'd sprinkled on himself brings a few smiles from us. 'He said he'd found the van in that town, but that driver had been bitten. He said the man told him to go to Chapsworth House. He was very believable,' she nods emphatically. 'I could hear them speaking, and they seemed to believe him. It was like he was there because he was trying to find the house but was lost, and he was glad they had found him.'

'Good lad,' Clarence sits back, folding his arms, 'quick thinking.'

'Right,' sitting back too, I stare up at the ceiling whilst I run it back through my mind. 'So they saw the children playing in the river. They were guarded, which suggests they are being cared for, and the very act of letting them play in the water on a hot day speaks of at least some level of care being given. Sounds like a doctor has got control of this place and is getting his men to scavenge the houses, bring back the food and any children they find. Armed guards on the front gate, armed people at the rear, and a roving patrol too by the sounds of it.

'Well,' I pause to think for a second, 'if we go in all guns blazing, we run the risk of them hurting the children or Nick, so that's out. Stealth is the next idea. Sending Dave in on his own will get the job done. However, if they've got lots of men, and I'm not worried for Dave as he can take care of them, but the noise created will alert them ... Maybe we should go and speak to them?' I look round the table.

'Just turn up?' Blowers asks.

'That's what I was thinking, but no, after what Lilly said they did ... No, we need to get in, get the children and Nick, and get them out.'

'May I play devil's advocate for a minute?' Paula asks. 'How do we know that the actions those two men took outside in the town are the orders given by whoever is in the house, this Doc person or ...'

'True,' I nod, 'they could have been acting independently.'

'No, actually I'm not going to play devil's advocate,' Paula continues. 'Those children are old enough to say what happened to them, and Lilly said there looked to be a lot of them in the river, so those children are being taken back and telling whoever is in charge exactly what happened. This suggests,' she continues, 'that they are maybe ... I don't know ... sanctioning it, for want of a better word.'

'Agreed,' Clarence leans forward. 'I think we have to assume worst case scenario here. Children are being taken from families that were, to a certain degree,' he looks apologetically at Lilly, 'in a safe environment, with parents taking care of them. Certainly not under any immediate and direct threat, other than what was happening to Lilly with Norman.'

'But that was just me,' Lilly cuts in. 'They couldn't have known that, and it didn't involve Billy or Todd. They just found a peaceful sleeping camp.'

'Okay, so no negotiations then. That leaves us with one course of action, and that's to get inside and get them out.'

'That's me, then,' Dave says bluntly, 'but from what the young lady said, this house is big and well-guarded. Describe the layout to me again, please,' he directs the question at Lilly, listening intently while she goes through it.

'Got it, river at the back, a few hundred metres from the house, with some trees and bushes in the grounds that can give us cover. At the front, there is the long drive with armed guards at the gates and then what sounds like more of them at the front of the house. The delivery entrance to the side looks like the first point of entry.' She nods as I relay the details back to her.

'Multiple strikes, then,' Clarence says quietly, looking across at Dave.

'Yes,' Dave replies, 'the gate guards, the front of the house, and the rear at the same time as I go in through the side.'

'Won't that alert them?' Cookey asks.

'Distraction and diversion,' Clarence explains, 'the inside of the house will erupt in chaos, which gives Dave the opportunity to move through them.'

'I think,' I say, 'Dave should go in first, and the rest of us will be in position to strike and move when we hear the first contact from inside.'

'Yes, Mr Howie,' Dave nods.

'We need someone to go in with Dave. No offence, but

if I was a child and had some mad man running towards me with two big knives, I think I'd shit myself,' I suggest quietly.

'Fair point,' Clarence agrees with a smile.

'I'll go,' Roy speaks for the first time, sitting at the back and silently listening to the proceedings. We all twist round to stare at him, he nods back with a big smile. 'Bows are silent, and I can use a knife too.' He edges forward, shuffling his chair across the floor to be closer to the discussion, a keen, interested look on his face.

'Yeah, Dave with knives and Roy with his bow ... That's not gonna scare them any more, is it?' Paula says drily.

'Does it matter if we scare them?' Dave says. 'Getting them out is the priority.' Silence for a few seconds as we all absorb what he just said. Bloody hell, imagine Dave going at a bunch of terrified kids, bellowing at them to go with him. That'll be worse trauma than everything they've been through so far.

'Hmmm,' I nod diplomatically. 'Yes, we could ... or maybe a friendlier face?'

'I'll go,' Lilly cuts in firmly.

'No, not happening ...'

'He's my brother, so he'll trust me,' she cuts me off again.

'Lilly, we can't send you in with Dave and Roy. You haven't seen what Dave does when he gets going. No offence, Dave.'

'None taken, Mr Howie.'

'I don't care,' she says defiantly. 'It can't be any worse than what I've seen already.'

'It is. Trust me,' Cookey mutters.

'I think you take the girl, yes?' Lenski says. 'She is the sister, and the boy will be frightened, so seeing the sister will be good, yes? You protect the girl, and she take the children out.'

'Yes!' Lilly exclaims.

'No,' I retort, 'no way.'

'Hang on,' Paula holds a hand up. 'It's a good idea to take Lilly in with you. Dave might be stretched to protect her fully and ...'

'I won't,' Dave says a touch indignantly.

'So take a couple more in. We've got enough people now. Clarence or Maddox, or even I can lead against the gate guards. That leaves your lads or whoever to do the front and the rear. In fact,' Paula gears up. 'Roy can take the rear as he can eliminate them without noise, and I don't mean to be sexist, but a female face is going to soothe those children a lot more than one of you.'

'I can take them out at the back,' Dave says.

'You're going in the side door,' Paula replies.

'After I've taken the guards out,' Dave responds.

'No, right, listen in ...' I bring their attention to me. 'Maddox, you up for this?'

'Yeah, course,' he nods instantly.

'Right then. Maddox leads against the gate guards with his crews. Roy and Paula work well together, so you two take the back of the house. Clarence at the front with you two,' I nod at Blowers and Cookey. 'Me, Dave, Lani, and Lilly go through the side.'

'Four of us?' Dave asks.

'Yes, four of us. Dave, you deal with whatever comes at us and maybe lead them off with lots of noise. Lani and I will stay close to Lilly for protection and focus on getting the children out.'

'While Dave kills everyone,' Lani adds helpfully.

'Probably,' I nod glumly.

'Where does that river go?' Paula asks.

'Don't know,' I reply. 'Anyone?' Heads shake at me.

'Once we've got them out, we'll need a way of getting them away. We can't take vehicles close to the house, or they'll hear us coming, and we don't want to be running miles with loads of terrified children either.'

'Boats?' Dave asks with a look of alarm.

'It's an idea,' Paula looks round at everyone. 'Straight out the back and down to the river, get them on boats and away quickly. What?' she asks with a puzzled frown at everyone grinning at Dave.

'Dave doesn't like boats,' I explain.

'Great idea,' Clarence grins evilly.

'They can run,' Dave says quickly. 'We can park close, and it won't be that far.'

'Boats make sense, Dave,' I say.

'Or we just call the vehicles in once we're secure,' he suggests with a pleading look.

'It's not the sea, Dave. It's only a river.'

'That's not the point, Mr Howie,' he says unhappily.

'Is it deep enough for boats?' Maddox asks. 'It might be a shallow stream or a minor tributary running to a larger body of water.' Silence for a few seconds as everyone stares at the hardened ex-drug dealer gang leader speaking so eloquently.

'Good point, we'll need an advanced reconnaissance pathfinder expedition then,' I reply with a smile to Dave in memory of the last time I tried to sound all military outside the police station in Portsmouth.

'Dave again then,' Lani quips.

'Yep, reckon so. Lilly, you go with Dave and one other to drive you there, then show Dave the way in. Dave, you check the depth of the river and please don't kill anyone ...

Dave, I'm being serious, don't go attacking that house on your own.'

'Okay, Mr Howie.'

'Dave, seriously ... just check the river and the layout and get back here before nightfall. We'll get everything else ready and move out as soon as it's dark.'

'Okay, Mr Howie.'

'Paula and Roy, do you mind going with Dave and Lilly? Once you've established the depth, find us some boats to use. Stay discreet, don't engage with anyone, and no killing zombies unless you absolutely have to, and if you do, then for fuck's sake do it quietly.'

'Got it,' Paula nods seriously, 'leave it with us. Er... can I suggest something? Is it worth creating a diversion for when Dave goes in? An explosion or something like that? They must have a parking area, so we could rig something up on the vehicles. When that goes off, everyone knows to start the attack.'

'Dave? Clarence?'

'Yeah,' Clarence nods slowly, 'yes, could work ... one big diversionary explosion draws their attention. You go in the side, and we attack the other points.'

'Suppression and distraction, an overwhelming attack on their senses which will give the effect of a much larger force taking them out,' Dave says.

'Prisoners?' Maddox asks, 'if they surrender?'

'Kill them,' Dave replies quickly, too quickly.

'No! Don't kill them,' I almost shout. 'Suck it and see, mate, do what you think is right.'

'Kill them,' Dave nods again.

'Don't kill them,' I add. 'Dave, we can't just kill everyone.'

'We did at the refinery.'

'Yeah, but that was slightly different.'

'How?'

'Well, for a start, they'd murdered loads of people, and they started shooting at us.'

'We shot them first ... on the road outside.'

'They'd just killed those people, remember? They executed them.'

'These men have killed Lilly's father and the other people.'

'Yes, but ... and we didn't mean to blow the refinery up either.'

'Didn't we?' Clarence asks with a raised eyebrow.

'Eh?' I ask him with a touch of alarm.

'Dave has never missed a shot in his life,' Clarence mutters.

'It was their shots that blew it up. They were shooting at us ...' I exclaim. 'Anyway, we can't just rampage round the place, shooting everyone ... or stabbing them either,' I shoot a dark look at Dave sitting there with a look of pure innocence on his face.'

'Bringing this conversation back to some relevance ...' Maddox says, his deep voice ending our refinery debate. 'Use Jagger and Mohammed to set the explosives on the vehicles, just show them what to do. Darius is staying here this time to maintain protection on the fort.'

'But ...' Darius interjects with a pained expression.

'No buts, bruv,' Maddox waves him down. 'I need you in charge of security when we are not here. You get me?'

'Yeah,' Darius sighs.

'Darius, bruv, we can't lose this place again ...'

'Got it, Mads, won't happen.'

'Weapons?' Maddox turns back to the group. 'We're down to pistols and shotguns.'

'Got some rifles out there,' Roy suggests.

'Sawn-offs!' Cookey grins. 'Back to the sawn-offs ... Oh yeah!'

'There's no range on them,' Blowers tilts his head thoughtfully.

'We'll have to make do,' I counter. 'Blowers and Cookey, you two are on weapons detail. Get what you can. Darius, you speak with the lads and make sure you got enough here for defence. Clarence, while they check the ground,' I nod at Paula, 'can you find a mechanic and see if we can get the Saxon back here.'

'Yup, will do,' he yawns, stretching two huge arms out either side of his body.

'Another suggestion,' Paula leans in. 'Lilly here looks exhausted. She doesn't need to come with us. We'll find a map and find our own way. I think she should stay here and rest.'

'No, I'm fine,' Lilly says with a look of panic.

'Paula's right,' Lani interrupts. 'We'll need you tonight, so get some sleep.'

'But ...'

'Lilly, we all know what we're doing,' Lani reassures her. 'Your brother will be okay for another few hours. You're safe here, so get cleaned up, eat, and rest.'

'Lani, can you show Lilly to our rooms at the top please?' I say.

'Will do.'

'Okay, so the rough plan until Dave gets back is that Maddox leads against the gate guards, Paula and Roy at the rear, Clarence and the lads at the front. If ...' I pause and look round, 'Dave and the others see anything that changes the plan, we'll go through it again later. Everyone happy?'

Nods all round, chairs scrape across the rough concrete

floor, and voices murmur in low tones, instructions and suggestions being passed round.

Another day and another round of problems, but at least this time, I didn't have to deal with taking the fort back. Really, the very fact they took it back so easily is reassuring. The people here are capable to act without prompting, but more than that, they learn each other's strengths and weaknesses, and they work together.

Just watching them now, Maddox with Lenski and Sierra, Paula and Roy talking in muted tones, Clarence grinning at Blowers and Cookey as they make a beeline for Lilly, Lani watching them with a bemused look on her face, and then Dave staring back at me with that strange look he has sometimes.

Shrugging, I turn and walk outside into the searing heat and blistering sunshine, squinting my eyes up at the deep blue sky. A deeper shade of blue than I have ever seen before, almost purple in hue, but then I guess nightfall isn't that far off now, an hour or two at the most.

Looking down, I settle on the groups moving around within the fort and the hastily erected tents sagging across the ground.

'Penny for them,' Lani speaks as softly as her tread stealing up on me.

'More people and yet more people.'

'And they'll keep coming too,' she replies, 'to see the great Mr Howie and Dave.'

'And the Chinese girl,' I grin.

'Thai, I'm not Chinese ... Can we get a sign or business cards or something?'

'What, like calling cards to leave after each scrap? Today you have been slaughtered by the following persons ...'

'Yeah,' she nods, 'perfect. You worried?'

'About Nick? Yeah, course I am.'

'Me too, did you, er ... brush your teeth, then?'

'You know I did, at the safari place, with the soap?'

'Oh right.' She looks at me coyly as I feel her fingers entwining mine. 'Got five minutes then, Mr Howie? I, er ... need to discuss some important strategy and tactics with you ...'

'Bloody right ...' Giggling like idiots, we rush away into one of the old storerooms and dart round behind the door. With my back to the wall, Lani steps in, looking up at me underneath heavy eye lids, pink lips parting with a wry smile, our hands clasped together.

Her body feels warm and firm against mine, her teeth so white and even. The golden skin of her face is framed by silky, pitch-black hair. Gently, we move closer until our lips are barely touching. That final act of hesitation done to increase the pleasurable tease of the initial contact. Her breath on my lips, her fingers squeezing tight.

'Lani! Lani! Lani!' Milly bursts in through the door, spinning round with a mischievous giggle. Meredith comes bounding in behind her, wagging her tail as she moves round the little girl.

'Sorry,' a woman comes running in. 'I tried stopping her, but she keeps running off.'

'Yes, she does that,' I laugh as Milly runs to hug Lani.

'Lions and tigers and bears ...' Milly shouts.

'OH MY!' we both shout in chorus, exchanging rueful looks.

CHAPTER FORTY-THREE

The sun is hot, very hot, and sweat forms on his forehead. The fear and confusion are still there, but the mind has defences against trauma, and it reaches a point where the images seen, the sounds heard, and the memories recorded are buried deep to be dealt with later, or never at all.

Instead, Billy transforms quickly into an automaton, doing what he is told, going where he is instructed, and drinking when water is given to him. His young mind shuts down, he doesn't speak unless spoken to, he doesn't so much as smile as moves his lips in the formation of what a smile should be.

From the meal with the nice lady in the kitchen, he is taken upstairs to meet the other children. Young faces staring at him with the same wide-eyed looks of fear and confusion. Chatter from the youngest, boisterous swagger from the oldest, intent on dominating their environments. Some have been here for days. Others, like Billy, have just arrived and suffered the same overwhelming assault to the senses.

Ripped away from parents, siblings, guardians, and even

kind strangers caring for them to be taken to this strange house where each was thoroughly examined by the tall doctor. Eating food with the nice woman, made to wash and get clean, then told to play and have fun but all the time watched by men with guns. Men that didn't interact with them, men that stared with hard eyes and smoked cigarettes, men that had stale coffee breath and were covered in tattoos, men with scars and shaved heads.

Taken into a large playroom and left, Billy remained still for long minutes. Watching the others watching him. All of them boys. Staring round, he looked for girls as his mind instinctively sought the comfort and maternal instincts that only a girl can offer.

No girls. Just boys. Lots of boys with freshly scrubbed cheeks and dressed in freshly cleaned clothes. Some had bruises and cuts, evidence of the scrapes and dangers they suffered prior to their arrival.

Others are unblemished physically, but their eyes show how injured they really are.

'What's your name?' A bigger boy looms in front of Billy, his face a sneer of barely restrained temper.

'Billy,' he mutters quietly, his voice low and scared. Looking away from the bigger boy, he stares at his feet, sensing the immediate threat of a bully.

'Silly Billy,' the boy quips, 'silly Billy.'

Lilly used to call him silly Billy, but then he'd call her silly Lilly, so it didn't matter. The words don't bother him, but the tone the boy uses is rough and harsh.

'Silly Billy,' the boy repeats and pushes Billy in his chest, forcing him back a step. 'Are you a silly Billy?' The boy shoves again.

Billy doesn't say anything. There isn't anything to say. There are no adults in here, just lots of big chairs and lots of books, colouring pencils and brightly coloured toys strewn across the floor.

'You're boring.' The bigger boy stalks off, kicking out at a Lego house painstakingly put together by a young boy with glasses. The bespectacled child reacts the same as Billy, staring forlornly at the broken house while waiting for the bigger boy to go away.

Billy shuffles forward a few steps. Reaching down, he starts picking the plastic bricks up, gathering them into little piles of matching colours. Without speaking, the child blinks behind his glasses and slowly moves round to sit next to Billy. Working together, they start rebuilding the house, neither of them speaking but pushing red brick into red brick, then green into green, and so on. Eyes down, hands busy, minds occupied with something they both recognise and understand.

'Well, well,' the Doc bursts into the room with a flourish, 'look at you all playing nicely.' He stands tall, beaming down from his great height at the sullen faces. 'Young Billy is already playing with Simon. Making a Lego house? That's great. Great work, boys. Right, who's up for a swim in the river?' He waits for a chorus of cheers that never comes. Ignoring the slight, he strides round the room, towering over every child within.

'Come on, come on,' the Doc booms, 'let's get you into that refreshing water, eh?' Cajoling the boys up to their feet and out the room, they traipse out under the watchful gaze of the armed guards. The guards avoid all eye contact, looking everywhere but at the children.

Those young boys that try to make eye contact, to reach out for a friendly older face are rebuffed by that action alone. Not only under strict orders to avoid contact with the children, but all of the guards, as nasty and as rough as they may be, have an idea of what goes on behind the Doc's closed door. The world has fallen, but here there is food, shelter, and weapons. The Doc has promised them a vaccine or a cure too, and none of the boys look injured or hurt.

Word of Vince's sudden and violent demise spread through the house like a dose of dysentery. Confusion and apprehension grew. The orders were clear: scavenge the houses in the allocated sectors, bring back the food and any boys they find. Whatever else they did, found, kept, took was down to them.

Those that did think of leaving kept the thoughts to themselves. Larson was friendly with all of them, plying them with treats and special privileges in exchange for whatever gossip or rumour was circulating.

For his part, Larson knew it was only a matter of time before they started haemorrhaging manpower. Yeah they had food, shelter, and weapons, but they needed the company of women too. Something the Doc had expressly forbidden, with the exception of Meryl.

Give and take. Larson knew the name of the game and was prepared to ride it out. He sensed the Doc would relent sooner or later about women being allowed here.

From his position at the front of the house, he watched the Doc march the boys past. The absurdly tall medical man was singing jovially as he jokes the boys into swinging their arms and stamping their feet. Awkward and uncomfortable. Larson can see the boys are too stunned to do anything other than what they are told.

Sighing deeply, he shrugs and strolls slowly after them, watching as they exit the back of the grand house and onto the manicured lawns, heading down to the river. He knew what was coming next; he'd already seen it several times.

A look of distaste crosses his face. A man of very low principle and a born survivor, he will do what it takes to get by, but still, some things just leave a nasty taste in the mouth.

'That's it my lovely boys, down we go ... Afternoon Jacob!' The Doc waves happily at one of the guards strolling towards them.

'Afternoon, Doc,' Jacob nods before quickly turning away to scan the surrounding area, a wooden-stocked rifle across his shoulders.

The Doc checks the rear area–the guards are posted where they should be, spread out and vigilant but not actually watching. The sun is shining, the weather glorious and hot.

'Now, boys,' he brings them to a halt at the river's edge, the glittering surface meandering by with a gentle eddy. Lower than it should be, the water has gradually fallen during the weeks of incredible heat, dwindling to a wide but relatively shallow stretch of beautiful, crystal-clear water. 'We're all boys together, eh, so no shy boys here,' he grins round at the gathered youths. 'We don't need trunks or shorts, do we?' he calls out. 'Fresh air and exercise is what we need! Lots of fresh air to our bodies, so come on, strip off and let's get you into the water.'

Those here for longer start doing as bid, yanking t-shirts off and shoving shorts down. The new children are slower to respond. Hesitant to the point of shyness.

'Come on, you lot,' the Doc laughs. 'We're all men, so don't be shy. We've all got the same bits between our legs, haven't we?' Laughing, the Doc pulls his top off, exposing his long, pale torso already smothered in thick, white suncream. Dark, greying patches of hair line his chest and stomach, and his arms are skinny but long, with sinewy muscle. Clusters of thick, dark moles stand proud of his skin, and grinning, he starts on his trousers, pulling first one leg out, then the other before standing upright in a pair of pale blue y-fronts.

Silence for a second as he scans the boys already stripped off, hungry eyes lingering on the narrow chests and thin limbs of the youths.

'Hang on,' he holds one long bony finger up as though he suddenly thought of something very important, 'have you all got suncream on? The sun is very dangerous, you know ... Here, I brought some with me. Come and get a dollop and get it rubbed in.'

Again, the boys already experienced at the daily river ordeal dutifully edge closer with hands stretched out, waiting for the bottle of cream to be squeezed out.

Jacob turns slowly, his face dripping with sweat and from behind his dark glasses, he watches as the large group of boys all strip off. The Doc kneels down amongst them, and even on his knees, he towers over every single one of them. Those huge, meaty, yet bony hands rub cream into the under-developed bodies of the young boys.

Like Larson and all of the carefully selected men, Jacob bites down the surge of revulsion at the sight. He knows what's out there in the world. Surely this is better for the kids? At least here they are physically safe, safe from bodily harm.

'Billy,' the Doc singles the young lad out with what he thinks is a humorous look, 'come on, you little monster. Let's get you all lathered up and protected from that sun, eh?'

Billy does as he is told, standing patiently while the Doc rubs cream into his chest, arms, back, and legs. His dad used to do this, his mum too, and sometimes Lilly. They were always worried about him getting burnt, but then

Mum would spend hours lying in the sun, saying how nice it felt.

Mum never put suncream on his bottom, though, neither did Dad or Lilly. But then he always wore shorts outside and was never nuddy. Nuddy was only for bath-time or in the shower.

'Right,' the Doc stands up suddenly, his face flushed and red, 'into the water with you. Come on, splash about and have some fun ... Last one in is a rotten egg!'

The boys watch as the Doc strides into the water. His legs long and thin like his arms, knotted with sinewy muscle. There's a bulge in his pants now too. Some of the boys recognise this from seeing dads run to the bathroom first thing in the morning, others wonder what it is. The Doc seems to pay no attention and runs into the water, splashing about while yelling out in apparent glee.

In they go, slowly at first, but it is very hot, and the water is lovely and cool. Even the worse conditions cannot suppress the natural ability of children to laugh, and before long, not all, but some of them splash and jump as they feel the effects of the gloriously cooling liquid.

Shallow at the sides but deeper towards the middle, the river's current is gentle. Those that can swim lift their feet from the riverbed and feel themselves being moved gently away.

The Doc darts about, wading through the water to grab at boys, heaving them up into the air as he forces them to have fun. He demands them to smile and laugh, and all the time, his thick, strong hands hold on just that bit longer than they need to, and that bulge stays in his pants.

'Sir,' Jacob walks closer to the riverbank, calling out for the attention of the Doc while averting his eyes, finding something interesting just left of where the children were.

'What is it, Jacob?' the Doc shouts with a grin. Jacob knows that grin is one step away from all-out violence, and although the Doc is tall and rangy, without proper arms training, his strength is awesome. Coupled with his explosive ability to get violent at the merest perceived slight, it makes him a very dangerous man and one to be extremely careful around.

'Larson, sir, he just radioed and said they found someone in the grounds nearby. Young lad apparently, and er ... they're just bringing him in the front now.'

'Another young lad, eh? Well, well, this is a prodigal day.' The Doc swings a young boy over the surface of the water, making no effort to hide his erection.

'Er ... yes, sir,' Jacob nods. *Prodigal? Doesn't he mean prodigious? Either way, I'm not correcting him.*

'Tell Larson to keep the lad there, get him some food with our nice Meryl, and I shall be along shortly.'

'Sir, will do,' Jacob hurries away a few metres, fighting to keep his face a mask of neutrality. The Doc will find the cure. He will fix this and fix all of them. As soon as he has that vaccine or cure, Jacob is out of here. Middle of the night, grab a vehicle and drive, keep driving and get far away. For now, though, there is no choice but to stay and entertain that sick fucker's depraved desires. At least he's not hurting them, well, not obviously anyway.

'Weeeeee!' the Doc yells. Grasping a young boy by the wrists, he spins him round and round, knowing the angle of the youth's face is in eye-line with his crotch. Letting go quickly, the boy flies off to land with a splash in the middle of the river. The Doc already turning away to grab another one, urging the youngsters to climb on his back and play-fight.

'Right, that's me all done,' he sighs theatrically, 'I'm not as fit as you youngsters, that's for sure, eh?' Clambering out of the river, he walks slowly to a large towel and starts patting himself dry, presenting himself face on to the boys still splashing in the river. 'You stay here with Jacob, and I'll go meet our new boy, shall I? Everyone having fun, are they? What about you, Billy? Settling in okay?'

It's been a few hours at the very most. And in that time, he has had his *medical examination,* had some food, met the other boys, and come out here for a swim. Settling in doesn't cut it. It doesn't come close to the shell-shocked manner of Billy and the rest.

Blithely carrying on, the Doc beams as though Billy just said he was having the best time of his life. A genuine belief that the boys are now happier than before. They probably all lived on shitty council estates with parents that hated them, on benefits and smoking dope all day. Bah! They're going to be happy here, and that's for sure. Healthy food, lots of exercise and time to play–that's what they need. They can run about in the fresh air and have their very own doctor on hand to keep checking them over.

The self-justification runs deep, the roots of the refusal to accept there is something wrong with him have taken hold in every part of his being. In his mind, he is a doctor, he is a protector, and his flaws – well, they're just the eccentricities of a brilliant mind.

'Keep a good eye out, Jacob,' the Doc says, striding past with his clothes held under one arm.

'Will do, sir.' Jacob nods and makes a point of scanning the vista, then focussing on the children in the river. With the Doc gone from the water, the view isn't offensive, and in fact, the sight of children playing on a hot day is actually a nice thing to see. A thin smile threatens to tug at Jacob's lips.

'WHAT IS THAT?' the Doc roars. Jacob spins round, his heart ramping from normal to racing within a split second. His hands grip the weapon, index finger extending for the trigger. Halfway between Jacob and the house, two more guards undertake a patrol across the rear lawns. The Doc stands over them, glaring down with unremitting fury in his face.

Jacob winces at seeing one of the men trying to casually drop the still-lit cigarette in a hopeful but futile attempt to hide it from the Doc.

'I ... WILL HAVE ... ' The Doc speaks each word slow and loud as though struggling to even speak with the rage pulsing from him. 'NOONE SMOKING NEAR ... THE CHILDREN!' as he roars the last word, he steps in close, pushing the other man back with his chest.

Jacob sees it coming well before it happens. The Doc's long right arm crosses his waist and swings up and out with a vicious backslap, connecting with the guard's cheek. The noise snaps out clearly, a distinct crack. The guard is removed from his feet, spinning to one side as he sprawls out.

'DOC ... STOP...' Larson bursts out from a set of rear doors, sprinting across the lawn as the Doc starts striding towards the downed man. In his panic, he doesn't think to get up but starts crabbing back with a look of pure fear on his already bruised and rapidly swelling face.

'NO SMOKING,' the Doc reaches down with one smooth movement, gripping the man by the front of his shirt. He lifts him to his feet like a ragdoll. Jacob watches mesmerised at the strength in the man. There was no effort at all. He just bent over and picked him up, shaking him hard while the guard rattles and begs for forgiveness.

Reaching the scene, Larson slows down, throwing

quick, hard looks at the Doc, at Jacob, down to the boys in the river, then at the guard being shaken by those two huge hands.

'Doc, easy now ... remember what we said?'

'HE WAS SMOKING,' the Doc screams, spittle flying from his mouth to coat the guard being held in his grip.

'Okay, I understand, and I'll deal with it. Just put him down now, Doc ... You're, er ... well, the kids look scared.'

Jacob holds his breath as everyone waits for Doc's reaction. Even mentioning the children in any negative sense is likely to cause an explosion of violence.

It works, though. The Doc releases the man instantly. Turning to the river with a look of guilt, he waves out. 'It's okay, children, we're only playing ... Ha! Grown-ups like to play too.'

'Isn't that right, Rob?' Larson glares at the guard just released, standing there, looking terrified. He blinks slowly, first looking at Larson, then the Doc before seeming to see a light showing him a way out of this mess. One arm shoots up quickly, waving at the children, and he forces himself to smile while ignoring the flare of pain across his face.

'Just playing,' Rob shouts out.

'So, where's this new lad, then?' The Doc turns to Larson like nothing just happened.

'In here,' Larson doesn't flinch but nods back to the house. 'Rob, we'll speak later, carry on your patrol but ...'

'I got it. Sorry. I'm really sorry,' Rob mutters quickly.

Jacob finally releases the breath being held as the Doc walks off with Larson, leaving Rob nursing a swollen face.

'You alright?' Jacob asks quietly once the Doc and Larson slip out of view into the house.

'That fucking hurt,' Rob hisses. 'Shit, I think he fractured my cheek.'

'Lucky he didn't kill you, mate. What the fuck Rob?'

'I didn't think, mate. Fucking heat, fucking weather, fucking sweating, and shit, mate, how's it look?'

'Bad,' Jacob nods quickly, 'but for fuck's sake just keep going, take a big loop, and get some painkillers on the way back.'

'I feel sick, Jacob.'

'Rob, he catches you puking or fucking about, he'll kill you. Just swallow it down and get some Nurofen or something and stay out of his way.'

'Okay,' Rob breathes out.

'Larson will get you on the gate later so you're out of sight for a few hours.'

'I fucking hate it here, Jake.' Jacob stiffens at the sight of tears pricking the other man's eyes.

'Stop it, Rob ...'

'I can't stay here, Jake, this is fucked up ... He's a fucking psycho. Did you hear about Vince?'

'Yeah,' Jacob mutters, making a point of looking round in case he's being watched, 'but we ain't got a choice, have we, mate? Everyone feels the same. We stay till we get the vaccine or a fucking cure, then we go. Not now, though, so don't even look like you're thinking anything.'

'Them boys, Jake,' Rob shakes his head, the tears streaming freely down his face now, 'what's he doing to them?'

'Fuck off, Rob,' Jacob hisses. 'You fuck off right now, don't be a stupid cunt. Man up and deal with it. Here, take these and fucking go away.' Jacob hands his sunglasses over, the harsh words seeming to bring some resolve to the shaken Rob. Slipping them on, he grimaces, nods, then walks off to join his mate who quickly walked on.

'He was found on the hill, near the copse,' Larson

explains as they walk through the rear rooms, 'Young lad, on his own, but he had one of our vans with him.'

'What? He drove here?' The Doc asks, confused at how a young boy can drive a big van. Must be a plucky little chap being able to do that.

'Just in here.' Larson steps ahead, opening an internal door to a small drawing room. Two men with guns stand either side of the door on the inside.

Striding in, the Doc nods politely at Nick, then looks round with a slight look of puzzlement on his face.

'Where is he, then?' he asks Larson.

'That's him,' Larson nods at Nick.

'Oh,' the Doc looks crestfallen, his voice low and disappointed, 'I thought you said a young lad.'

'Oh, right,' Larson nods in understanding, 'sorry, Doc, my mistake. I meant a young lad like a young adult lad, not a, er, boy.'

'Oh,' the Doc sighs, 'well, we're here now. What's your name, young man?'

'Nick, sir,' Nick replies promptly. His face is devoid of expression at the sight of the exceptionally tall man walking in wearing nothing but underpants and dripping wet. He must have been swimming in the river with the children. He has long, grey, scraggly hair, but Nick notices the tight muscles and quickly guesses the man must be very strong. There's something else about him too, an energy coming off him. The two guards left in the room were reasonably relaxed a second ago, making small talk with Nick, but now they've stiffened to attention and refuse to look at him.

'Nice to meet you, Nick. Everyone here calls me the Doc. Seeing as I'm a Doctor, that's rather apt, wouldn't you say?'

'Of course, sir,' Nick nods firmly.

'This is Larson, and the other two are ... er ... Well, anyway, so what brings you here, Nick?'

'Me, sir?' Nick adjusts his position. 'I was, er, well, I was saying to those blokes that I found one of your men, I think. He'd been bitten, sir, by one of the zombies. He was in a bad way but told me to take the van and come here. I, er ... I got lost, though, and stopped for a piss when they found me,' Nick nods at the two men, both of them nodding in agreement but doing so at Larson, not at the Doc.

'Well, got bit, did he?' the Doc takes a seat opposite Nick. Easing his big frame into an armchair, he casually crosses his legs, putting one ankle over the other knee while he thinks. 'Bad luck, that's for sure,' the Doc nods. 'Where did he get bitten?'

'In the town, Sir,' Nick replies instantly, knowing the man means where on his body but wanting to appear nice and thick.

'Ha!' The Doc chuckles. 'I meant where on his body?'

'Sorry, sir, er ... on his leg, sir. It was a deep bite. I reckon he had about two minutes, maybe a couple more before he turned.'

'Yes, quite,' the Doc affects a cultured voice. 'Indeed. Well, these things will happen, but a shame, nonetheless. He was a great man.'

'There were two with the van, Doc,' Larson cuts in. 'Nick here says he didn't see the other man.'

'Really?' The Doc looks up, nodding thoughtfully. 'Well, I dare say something happened, and he ran off or got bitten himself.'

'Possibly,' Larson nods.

'Well, Nick, thank you for bringing our van back. Really, very kind of you. So tell me, where are you going?'

'Nowhere, sir,' Nick replies. 'I was just moving about,

trying to stay away from them, er ... finding food and shelter, maybe somewhere safe to be ... That kind of thing.'

'You're dressed like a squaddie,' Larson remarks casually. 'Were you serving?'

'No, sir, I just joined when it happened, er ... like the first training weekend, sir,' Nick gives the truth.

'Ah,' Larson nods, 'so you got the kit but not the training, right?'

'That's right, sir. Salisbury, sir ... whole place was infected, so I just legged it and been running ever since. Had a few scrapes here and there as you can tell from my, er ...'

'Yes, quite,' the Doc says, looking in distaste at the blood- and filth-stained clothes Nick is wearing. 'You've done well, though. Staying alive, I mean,' the Doc asks.

'Guess so, sir,' Nick nods.

'We've got an unusual establishment here, Nick,' the Doc puts on that refined voice again, settling back into his chair with his hands together in front like offering a prayer, 'a safe place; that's for sure. We haven't had any contact with the infected here, but what we have got is lots of children. We gather them up, you see, Nick. Larson and I send our men out to scavenge the houses for food, and they are under instruction to bring back any lost children they find on the way.'

'Right, sir, that's very good of you.'

'Yes, Nick, you see, we believe in the sanctity of childhood here, Nick. I'm, er... well, currently working on a cure for the infection, maybe a vaccine, and it is my plan to administer the cure to the children first. They are the future, Nick.'

'Yes, sir,' Nick nods affably.

'We have plenty of food, some generators for power,

fresh running water, and security for the boys. The duties are relatively easy, wouldn't you say, chaps?' The Doc smiles at the two armed men standing by the door.

'Very much, sir,' they both nod enthusiastically.

'Duties, sir?' Nick asks with a puzzled expression.

'I think what the Doc means,' Larson cuts in, 'is that we've obviously lost two men from that van, and we've had another slight issue resulting in one other being taken from us ...' Nick watches the exchange of looks between Larson and the Doc. 'So we're offering you a chance to stay with us. You work here, and we give you food and shelter.'

'Oh, right. Well, yeah, that's great,' Nick nods with a big smile.

'Course we don't know you,' Larson continues, 'so you'll be put with someone else for now until we know we can trust you. Basic duties at first then.' Larson tilts his head side to side. 'If you show promise, then we can see about adding to your duties. The ultimate goal for our men is to be on the scavenging crews. They get to go out and find food, find children and, er ... well, whatever else they get up to out there is down to them, if you catch my drift?'

'Yes, sir,' Nick nods and smiles again.

'Right, well, nothing else for me here,' the Doc stands up quickly, obviously bored. He nods at Nick before walking towards the door. 'Do you smoke, Nick?'

'Smoke, sir, yes, I do,' Nick replies.

'We have rules here. Do not engage with the children unless you have my direct consent, do not smoke near them or in sight of them, do not smoke in the house, do not swear in the house or near the children, understood?'

'Of course,' Nick nods. Bloody hell, no smoking *and* no swearing. This could be a very long day. Hope to fuck the others get here quickly.

'I'll be upstairs, Larson, got some studies to undertake. Tell me, Nick,' the Doc pauses at the door, 'do you know anyone called Mr Howie?'

'Mr who, sir?' Nick asks with a blank stare, fully aware of the penetrating gaze fixed on him from Larson.

'Never mind, all yours, Larson.' Closing the door behind him, the Doc exits the room, still dressed in his underpants but thankfully without the erection this time.

'Carry on, gents,' Larson nods at the two armed guards visibly relaxing with the Doc leaving the room.

'See ya, Nick,' one of them nods as they walk out.

'Later, mate,' Nick calls out. Remaining seated, he watches the door close again, then switches his gaze to Larson. That same penetrating stare, like he can see something inside.

'Drink, Nick?' Larson changes instantly, morphing into a friendly man with a natural, easy smile.

'Wouldn't mind,' Nick nods happily. *A cure? The Doc in his underpants said he was working on a cure, maybe a vaccine. Shit. Mr Howie is likely to send Dave in first, and Dave won't discriminate. He'll know Nick is inside and will kill everything that stands in his way, including the Doctor.*

'Something on your mind, son?' Larson asks with a concerned look at Nick.

'Eh? No, er ... just, er ... you know.'

'What?' Larson asks.

'Er, you know,' Nick nods, 'he was in his, er ... pants.'

'Oh, that!' Larson laughs, shaking his head. He walks behind Nick, opening cupboard doors to reveal well stocked shelves of soft drinks and bottled water. 'You'll get used to the Doc, Nick. He is a strange one but, er ... well, if he gets this cure for us, then ...'

'Oh, definitely,' Nick agrees. 'Sorry, I was just like, fuck ... Shit! Sorry, I didn't mean to swear.'

'Don't worry,' Larson laughs again. 'It's only the Doc you've got to worry about; the rest of us are easy going, but listen up, Nick, the Doc has a, er ... well, let's call it a temper problem, which can erupt like the proverbial Mount Vesuvius and at anything too.'

'Seriously?'

'Seriously, I only say this as when he goes, he has a habit of lashing out. He's a big man and doesn't know his own strength.' Pausing at the open doors, Larson looks back at Nick. 'Do what he says, don't smoke or swear, and don't talk to the children.'

'Got it,' Nick nods.

'Water or something sugary, Nick?'

'Sugary please, mate.'

'Coming up.'

'So how many kids have you got here?' Nick asks casually.

'Twenty-two, and we get more nearly every day too. All boys, no girls, and all from ages five to eleven.'

'Oh.'

'Oh indeed, Nick, don't ask. Don't question it, don't look at it, don't think about it,' Larson speaks fast as he opens two cans of Dr Pepper. 'You'll see weird stuff but show no reaction. Do what you're told, and you'll be looked after. We got food, drink, enough cigarettes and tobacco to open a cash-and-carry warehouse, and hopefully soon we'll get some women here too.'

'That's always a good thing,' Nick smiles at the right point.

'Here,' Larson hands him the can. Drinking from his

own, the standing man looks round the room, waiting for Nick to take his first sip.

Holding the can to his lips, Nick feels first the warm, syrupy liquid gushing into his mouth. Suddenly, a cold, sharp blade presses against his throat. Freezing mid-gulp, he holds position, not daring to move. His intelligent mind frantically goes through the conversation and what was said to trigger this reaction.

'We've got a good thing here, Nick,' Larson whispers in his ear, 'and no one is going to fuck it up. Do you understand? Don't nod, or you'll cut your own throat open. It was a rhetorical question. The Doc gets mad. He kills men nearly every day. He's already killed the one who brought young Billy back earlier.'

The name, Billy. Larson must know the connection, but how? With the knife pressed so hard, Nick can't move but holds stock still, waiting for the man to keep speaking.

'But the Doc isn't the only to watch, Nick. I'm here all the time, and I never lose my temper. I watch, and I listen, and when the time is right in my mind, I move fast and without hesitation. Now, the Doc asked you if heard of Mr Howie. You said no, didn't you, Nick? Only I swear I saw a little reaction in your face, a twitch, an absence of a twitch. Fuck, who cares, but it was there alright. I don't know who Mr Howie is. We've heard about him and his men, and I couldn't give a toss what he does, but what I do care about is why you would feel the need to lie.'

That was it. The *too natural* forced reaction when the Doc asked him. Larson is sharp, sharper than this knife pressed to his throat.

'So, Nick, just you and me now, big boy, and you *are* going to tell me exactly what you know.' The knife is removed, a flick-blade retracted back into the handle as

Larson takes his can, sips, and strolls round to sit down in the armchair vacated by the Doc.

Nick swallows and breathes out. Blinking hard, he puts the can down to rest on one knee.

'Like I said, Nick. I don't care about this Mr Howie or what he does. I just want to know why you lied.'

'I didn't,' Nick blurts out. 'I don't know anyone by that name.' An instinct tells Nick to maintain the story, that to give an inch now will bring disastrous results.

'Don't believe you,' Larson says quietly with a wry smile.

'Sorry,' Nick shrugs, 'I can't make something up ... I don't know him, never heard of him. Who is he?'

'You tell me,' Larson prompts.

'I don't know,' Nick shakes his head, 'sorry, mate.'

'You hearing me okay, Nick?' Larson leans forward, fixing his dark eyes on Nick. Unblinking, stern, focussed, and utterly in control, 'I don't care who he is. I don't care what he does. I just want to know why you lied about knowing who he is.'

'I didn't, mate,' Nick sighs. 'It's hot. I'm fucking tired and hungry. I got lost and fuck ... I'm in here with a huge, almost naked man asking me if I know someone. Shit, mate, sorry if I looked the wrong way or something, but ...' he shrugs again, staring back at Larson.

Larson jumps to his feet, the movement fluid, swift, and fast. Knife out, blade glinting in the sunlight which is streaming through the window. He doesn't say anything but advances slowly, the knife held at waist height.

'Shit, mate, put that fucking thing away,' Nick blanches. 'I don't know Mr fucking Howard or whoever the fuck he said.'

'Where did you come from?' Larson asks quickly.

'What?' Nick stares in confusion, 'the town where I found your man ...'

'Before that,' Larson motions with the knife, 'quick now, Nick, where were you before that?'

'North,' Nick shrugs, 'I told you. I was at Salisbury when it happened. I went north, thinking the land would be fucking open and less towns, but it's all shit, so I started heading south again.'

'Why? Answer me, Nick,' Larson demands, that gaze unflinching.

'I'm from Hampshire,' Nick blurts, 'near Winchester, so was heading that way, got no other place to fucking go.'

'Family?'

'None.'

'None?'

'No, none. No brothers, no sisters. Grandparents died, dad fucked off when I was a kid, so just me and Mum ... but she's a fucking bitch so ...'

'So why go back Nick? Why head this way? This isn't the way to Winchester.'

'I was north of that town,' Nick talks quickly, staring at the knife and noticing the steady hand that holds it, 'in the countryside, but I got hungry and dirty, so went into town to get stuff, found your bloke, and here I am.'

'Met many people?'

'No, kept myself to myself.'

'Really, Nick? A lone wolf traipsing through the countryside, surviving rather well by the looks of it, yet you happen to find one of my men having been bitten and decide to honour his dying request by bringing his van back to us.'

'Yes!' Nick exclaims. 'That's exactly it. Well, not the

honouring him bit, no offence, but I didn't know him. I'm hungry, lonely, and it's fucking frightening out there ...'

'So you came here?'

'Yes,' Nick nods.

'But you got lost, did you?' Larson pulls a pouty face. 'Got lost in the van and couldn't find the fucking big house marked on the map in said van.'

'Fuck's sake,' Nick groans.

'What?'

'I can't read or write. I can't read a fucking map, I was guessing. I know what the word Winchester looks like, so I was hoping to see it on a signpost.'

'What? Fuck off! There isn't anyone left these days that can't read or write.'

'Dyslexia,' Nick looks down at the ground, 'like really fucking bad Dyslexia, the army was about the only job I'd get. No one else would hire me.'

'What did you join?'

'Infantry, the exams are the easiest.'

'You talk alright,' Larson says.

'Yeah, but I can't read or write properly. I'm good with electrical stuff, mechanical stuff, engines and things like that but ...'

'But you can't read or write?'

'No,' shaking his head, he stares away from Larson.

'So you don't have any allegiance to anyone? Not missing, say, a brother or something and come looking for him?'

'No,' Nick repeats.

'You killed, Nick?'

'Yes,' Nick replies instantly, staring back up at Larson with his own dark, focussed stare.

'Oohh, you didn't ask whether I meant zombie or human.'

'Both.'

'Zombies are easy,' Larson shrugs, 'but people, Nick, people are living. They fight back, they scream and shout and are unpredictable, yet here you are, claiming to have killed them. Who did you kill, Nick?'

'One man, stabbed him. He found me sleeping and tried to take my food. Stabbed him through the chest and kept stabbing until he didn't move anymore.'

'Okay, and the zombies? How many of them you killed?'

Oh, mate, you have no fucking idea. 'A few, during the day when it first happened, and they were slow. Hid at night; then, they got quick in the day, so I hid then too.'

'Any good with a weapon?'

'What kind?'

'Firearms?'

'Not really, shotguns are easy but, er ... didn't get that far in basic training.'

'Hand weapons?'

'Okay,' Nick shrugs again, 'my kills came from knives so ...'

Larson doesn't speak but stares, holding Nick's gaze with a level look. A light starts to dawn in Nick's mind, a sensation, maybe an instinct or a prickling of an idea. They haven't checked him over, not asked him to strip off to be checked for bites or cuts. The questions thrown at him by Larson are straightforward. Bloody hell, even Cookey could talk his way out of this. That stare Larson keeps giving. That's all he has. Just that hard look. Hold his stare, and he'll believe anything. Incompetent and running on blind luck that they've found a place so isolated the infected simply haven't come this way.

The gate guards were behind sandbags, for fuck's sake. Like sandbags are going to stop a swarm of charging infected pumped to the eyeballs with whatever chemicals the infection is using to drive them. The distance from the main gate to the house is too big. If the gate is overrun, there is no way of getting re-enforcements to them. The walls surrounding the house looked high but again would pose no challenge. Nick could scale them easily enough, which means–anyone could.

Even here, with armed men walking about, the house is wide open, with the Doc walking about in his underpants fresh from swimming in a river with a bunch of little boys.

Don't question it, don't look at it, don't think about it, that's what Larson said. A grown man swimming in his pants with little boys taken from their families, and we're not supposed to question it? Larson also said the scavenge crews can do what they like once they're out of here, which means they effectively had permission to rape and kill the way they did with Lilly and her family.

The serenity of the place, the quietness of the area, the rich furnishings of wonderful opulence all dulled his mind into thinking this actually might be a decent place.

Rotten to the core and run by a bunch of idiots getting by on luck and violence for the benefit of a doctor promising them a cure on the basis that he can fiddle with small children.

All of this swims through Nick's mind. The neural pathways of his brain might be wired slightly differently to others; the ability to recognise and learn the written word somehow doesn't work in his head, but he is very intelligent and highly savvy, with a keen instinct for human nature.

He had fourteen days of dealing with the most extreme of situations, and all the time watching, learning, absorbing. Seeing the sheer, unadulterated effort and depth of planning that Mr Howie applies to everything they do. How he thinks, weighs options, listens and watches and then decides for the benefit of everyone.

Larson holds that stare while Nick blankly looks on. All these thoughts whirl within a split second. A sub-conscious conclusion is drawn, but he doesn't show it. He remains passive, hoping he appears to be the slightly daft, affable lad he looks like.

'I'm happy,' Larson nods at length. 'You seem the right person for us, Nick.' A firm nod, and Larson extends a hand, offering an equally firm grip. 'You'll fit in well here, son. Good to have you on board. Sorry about the questioning, but you just never know, and it pays to be vigilant. The Doc does what he can to fix this, and I make sure the place is safe.'

Utter fool. You are a complete fucking tool, mate.

'Yeah, sure,' Nick nods, 'I understand completely. I'm, er ... just glad you're happy to have me.'

'More than happy, Nick,' Larson nods again with a sincere look. 'I was in the services. A few of our blokes were too, but er, well, I can't really say what I did in the army, you know, son, classified and all that,' he gives a quick wink.

Classified? Now? After all this going on? Dave doesn't even try and hide what he did now and talks quite openly about it, and he's more autistic than Rain-Man.

'Wow,' Nick nods in admiration, 'sounds intense, mate.'

'Yeah, let's just say I saw things ... did things ... went places, you get me?'

'Yeah, sure,' Nick keeps the nod going, staring in admiration and awe at the older man.

'Right, come with me, Nick,' Larson leads them out of the room, across the hall, and through the kitchen, introducing him briefly to Meryl before leading Nick through the back doors and out onto the rear lawns. 'I've got things to do,' Larson explains. 'I'll get you paired up with Jacob, he's been here for a while and is a good hand. Jacob! This is Nick. He just joined us.'

'Nick,' Jacob nods in serious greeting.

'Hello, mate,' Nick holds his hand out to shake.

'He's all cleared,' Larson explains to Jacob. 'Been through the Q and A session with him, passed with flying colours. Stick with him, show him the ropes, and I'll see you both later.'

'Okay,' Jacob mutters.

'Where's your glasses?' Larson asks, noticing the armed guard squinting in the sun.

'Gave them to Rob. His face was swelling up.'

'Good thinking. We'll rotate him onto the gate in a minute. Keep an eye on those kids and get some coffee when they go back inside.'

'Will do,' Jacob nods. Standing quietly, he watches Larson retreat back into the house before eyeing Nick warily for a few seconds. Seemingly satisfied, he turns back to stroll towards the riverbank.

'Doc tell you about the kids?'

'Er, yeah,' Nick replies, 'something about don't talk to them, don't like engage or ...'

'Yep, don't do anything. Just stand here and keep watch. Larson tell you about the Doc's temper?'

'Yeah, but fuck that, mate. He said he's getting a cure ready.'

'Don't swear, Nick,' Jacob warns quickly.

'There's no one here.' Nick looks round at the wide-open lawn leading down to the riverbank, the house well out of ear shot.

'Doesn't matter, just don't do it.'

'Okay, sorry, Jacob.'

'For your sake, Nick, not mine, come on,' the older man walks steadily towards the riverbank, and the children now moving about quietly without the Doc's perverted exuberance making them jump about. 'He's working on something. Don't know what, but he keeps saying he's getting closer. I heard he was on about identifying what kind of virus it is today, telling Larson about different types of pathogens and things. Clever bloke.'

'Yeah, definitely,' Nick nods, unsure of what to do with his hands after two weeks of carrying a weapon everywhere. To hide his fidgets, he shoves them into his pockets, feigning a young lad's slouch instead. 'These the boys, then?' Nick nods at the youths.

'They are,' Jacob sighs. 'Don't look at them, Nick, look round them, look through them, look to the sides and beyond, but don't look at them.'

'Why not?'

'Cos the Doc gets angry if you do. He already broke a man's cheek today.'

'Shit, really?' Nick asks in surprise, wondering why this man is opening up to him. Jacob doesn't know if Nick is a stooge, a real newcomer or anything else. He looks troubled, though, troubled and deeply worried with big, heavy bags under his bloodshot eyes.

'There's quite a few,' Nick comments, making a point of turning to scan the area.

'Over twenty now, and we get more every day.'

'Just boys, though?'

'Yep.'

'Why boys? Why not girls?'

'He likes boys,' Jacob says darkly, a fleeting shadow crossing his face.

'Oh,' Nick says as if only just realising, 'oh shit, really? Like... you mean he *likes* boys?'

'We just guard,' Jacob ignores the question. 'And that's it. Look, Nick,' Jacob glances at the young lad, 'world's fucked, innit? Everything, everyone. We're lucky to be somewhere like this.' Nick watches the man attempt to justify it and can sense the turmoil within him.

'You, er, you go out on these scavenges, then?' Nick asks as a way of changing the conversation.

'Sometimes,' Jacob replies slowly, 'some of the blokes love it. They empty the houses and do all sorts of things, come back and boast about it at night when we have a few drinks.'

'What sort of things?' Nick asks with a grin.

'Use your imagination. There ain't no women here, Nick, so the blokes got to find what they can.'

'Oh, fuck ... that's bad,' Nick says, hoping he's judged it right.

'Not my thing,' Jacob says quickly. 'I like women, don't get me wrong but ...'

'Why no women? Is that another one of the Doc's rules?'

'Yep,' Jacob sighs again. Rubbing his stubbled chin, he checks the boys playing in the river and smiles briefly, an act noticed by Nick but left unremarked upon.

'What did you do before this?' Nick asks casually. The itch for a cigarette is starting, his hands keep twitching to draw the packet from his pocket.

'Had a building firm a few years back but lost it when the recession hit. I was labouring here and there, fucking handyman cutting grass. Missus left a couple of years ago, took our boy and went home.'

'Home?'

'Polish, from Poland,' Jacob adds needlessly.

'How old is your son?'

'Eight,' Jacob growls.

Nick glances at the boys in the water, then at Jacob, understanding where the conflict comes from. Not just something disgusting that has to be tolerated but something the man can relate to, his own child being the same age as those under the care of the paedophile doctor.

'Sorry, mate,' Nick mutters, 'you er ... thought about trying to find them?'

'Course,' Jacob nods, 'look, forget it Nick. This ain't your concern.'

'Sorry, Jacob, didn't mean to piss you off.'

'Stop swearing.'

'Sorry.'

'What you smiling at?'

'You reminded me of someone else. They were always telling me off for swearing too.' Staring at the man, Nick feels an instinct forming, a confidence to push further. 'Can I ask you a question, Jacob?'

The older man looks at him, an expression of almost pleading etched onto his weathered face, pleading that the young man stops now before it gets too painful.

'Why do you stay?' Nick asks quietly.

'I'm loyal to the Doc,' Jacob says quickly. 'I just want to do my job, and that's it.'

'Yeah, course,' Nick winces, thinking that he pushed it too far too quickly.

An uneasy silence descends between them. Nick's

confused at why the man stays when he could just take off and try find his family. Why be here, watching this happen?

Exhaling another deep breath, Jacob steps in closer and speaks in a low voice. 'He doesn't hurt them,' he says quickly. 'I ain't seen no bruises or anything. They're quiet and like, you know, subdued, but shit, what else do you expect? I think he just likes looking at them.'

'Fucking sick,' Nick mutters.

'It is, but there's worse that can happen, Nick. You understand, yeah? He could be raping 'em or hurting 'em, but I don't think so. He just gets 'em to strip off and stand there while he examines them. He swims with 'em every day with a hard on in his pants.'

'Stop,' Nick urges, feeling the first surge of anger coursing up.

'Listen, Nick, if he gets a cure, that can save everyone. If he gets a cure or a vaccine, I can take it with me and find my son. Save him, you know? And like I said, he ain't hurting 'em, not physically.'

'What if he did?' Nick asks quickly. 'What if he was hurting them? What would you do?'

Jacob stares back with genuine pain in his eyes. 'I'm loyal, Nick. I just want to do my job.'

'What would you do, Jacob?'

'You hear me, nipper? I'm loyal see. I don't want no trouble from anyone.'

'Okay, Jacob.'

'How old are you? What, twenty? Twenty-one?'

'Something like that,' Nick replies, looking at the children.

'You seem older,' Jacob remarks, 'a lot older.'

'Hard life,' Nick grins.

'I don't know what I'd do,' Jacob says, his eyes locked on Nick. 'I know what I'd want to do but ...'

'Yeah.'

'No, I shouldn't have said that. I'm talking bollocks, this heat, yeah? Makes you say weird things.'

'Don't worry, Jacob. I won't say anything, I promise.' Nick can feel the desperation and fear coming from the armed guard. He looks so stoic and unflappable but is clearly crumbling inside.

'He's coming,' Jacob changes instantly. Standing straight, he assumes the poker-faced look with almost expert precision. Nick doesn't turn immediately but quickly removes his hands from his pockets to hold them together in front. Adopting the same serious expression, he scans the area, viewing the hill that he and Lilly were hiding on just a little while ago.

Did she get away okay? As long as she makes it to the fort and finds the boss, then everything will be okay. That kiss, what was all that about? Offering herself like that so he would help her.

'WHERE'S MY LOVELIES!?' the Doc's voice booms out across the lawn. Dressed in clothes again, he strides towards the river, completely ignoring Nick and Jacob as he walks past.

Grinning with genuine belief that the children will be happy to see him, he badgers and jokes them out of the water, urging them to run around on the lawn so the sun can dry their bodies.

Nick watches the glint in his eye, the way he leers at the wet bodies. All the boys' underpants, which are now soaked through from the river, have become effectively see-through.

It's sickening and repulsive. What should be a happy sight of children having fun is destroyed by the perverted lust evident on the Doctor's face. His long, gangly frame lolloping behind the boys as he gently slaps bottoms and scoops them up to hold for a few seconds.

The size of the man and his exuberance makes the children meek in his presence. The very essence of childhood seems to fade from them as though too afraid or too cowed to reveal any character or personality. The sight makes Nick think of Nazis and how they cowed people into submission, that the mere presence of them, the power they gave off was enough to subdue the masses.

'Look away,' Jacob whispers, jolting Nick to turn quickly and make a point of scanning the back of the house.

On the pretence of turning slowly, Nick gains glimpses of the Doctor rounding the children up. He gets them into two lines, with the smallest at the front, clearly a feeble excuse that gives him reason to physically move them into place, rubbing his hands over their bare skin. With a loud, jovial order, he leads them off at the march, shouting "one-two, left-right" while comically swinging his long arms.

Only it isn't comical. Sinister is the word. Perverted. Nick swallows the surge of anger down again. Not yet. Wait for the others.

The Doc marches the children across the lawn and through rear doors, into the grand mansion house, leaving Jacob visibly relaxing as his shoulders sag, his face suddenly looking ten years older.

'Coffee,' the guard mutters. Nick follows him across the short grass to the side of the house and through a service door. From the bright sunshine into a gloomy room, Nick blinks to adjust his vision, aware of the low murmur of adult male voices.

Men are sitting in easy chairs, on benches, and old, wooden dining chairs. All of them sipping from old, faded, chipped mugs. The stench of coffee, stale body odour, unwashed bodies hangs in the air. Tobacco too, but not from being smoked. The men here have smoked somewhere else and brought the smell in with them.

Tattoos, heads that were once shaved short but now growing longer from the lack of clippers and power to run them. Thick arms, thick necks, and broken teeth. Tough men from hard backgrounds, gnarled hands used to physical labour. Lean men with hard stares, the type that Nick used to see propping up the bars at the local pub.

Jacob nods as he walks in but doesn't stop to engage in conversation, instead heading to the far end where he checks the water temperature in a large pan by sticking his finger in.

'Just boiled, Jake,' a man calls out, then quickly goes back to his conversation. A few glances at Nick but nothing of interest. *Drink the coffee, guard the house, protect the children, and go out to rape and kill who you want.*

They were in the old servants' quarters with stone walls and small windows. Nick stands near Jacob, watching him making drinks while discreetly looking round the room. Eight men in here. There will probably be a few more patrolling, plus the ones on the gate and others out scavenging houses.

'Got a few men here, then,' Nick remarks casually.

'About twenty, maybe twenty-five,' Jacob replies. 'Get a new one every couple of days, and we lose one every couple of days too. Quite a few today from what I've heard.'

Twenty-five. That'll keep Dave busy for all of five minutes. Nick looks away with a fleeting vision of these chatting men having their throats cut open within the next few hours.

'We'll go outside.' Jacob picks the two steaming mugs

up, once again leading Nick through the room and out into the sunshine. 'Can't smoke in the house,' he adds over his shoulder.

Outside, they cross the path and skirt round the offside of a low outbuilding. Several garden chairs gather round a plant pot full of cigarette butts. Taking a seat, Jacob passes one steaming mug over to Nick before easing himself over to one side as he works to free a pack of smokes from his pocket.

Nick is a step ahead of him. He's gagging for a smoke, and it's in his mouth, lit, and inhaled before Jacob has even got his packet out.

'Cheers,' Nick lifts his mug.

'Alright,' Jacob sighs again, something he keeps doing. They were the sighs of a man with the weight of the world on his shoulders. Stretching his legs out, Jacob lights his cigarette and closes his eyes, drawing deeply before blowing it away.

'They seem alright,' Nick remarks, working to keep his tone casual.

'Few are,' Jacob coughs from the harshness of the cigarette smoke. 'I'll point the decent ones out as we go round.'

'Yeah, cheers,' Nick nods, taking a seat opposite Jacob. 'This is alright,' he looks round at the chairs, 'nice little smoking area.'

'Larson,' Jacob says dully, 'he talks the Doc round on a few things. We can have a couple of beers in the evening as long as we ain't on the guard rota, but don't get pissed and don't get noisy.'

'Got it.'

They sip at the black coffee and smoke cigarettes. Nick looks about but keeps glancing back at the other man, seeing the worry on his face, the way he holds himself tucked in, the eyes staring out blankly.

'What's your son called?'

'Eh?' Jacob looks up quickly. 'Oh, er ... Lucas.'

'Nice name,' Nick nods. 'They went to Poland then, you said?'

'Yeah,' Jacob nods. A few seconds of silence pass before he speaks again. 'We were alright, you know, like we were getting on okay, but times were hard, and she missed her family. We kept in contact, phoning and Skyping every day. I was going to go out there and see her next week but ...'

Staying quiet, Nick sips at his coffee and lights another cigarette, letting his ears and senses settle to the background noises the way Dave showed them all. Listening without listening.

'Happened, didn't it?' Jacob offers a grim smile.

'You can still go there. Plenty of cars about, and the channel isn't that wide from Dover,' Nick says quietly.

'Yeah, like I said, I'm loyal here, and I want to do my job.'

'Course,' Nick mutters.

'You know where they are?'

'In Poland? Yeah, course, been there a few times.'

'You know the way, then?'

'I do.' Jacob stares across at Nick, not the same stare offered by Larson but a quiet, thoughtful look. 'What about you, nipper? Where you from?'

'Just outside Winchester,' Nick repeats what he said earlier. 'Just joined the army when it happened, was on the first weekend training thing. Legged it from Salisbury, then just kept going, found the van then ...'

'The van?' Jacob asks with a puzzled glance. Nick relays

the story given to Larson and the others, keeping the facts brief and retelling it casually.

'John and Terry,' Jacob nods. 'Tattoos on his hands, yeah?'

'Yeah,' Nick replies, 'they mates of yours?'

'Them two? No.'

'Ah, right, you said some are to be avoided.'

'They are, and them pair were arseholes. Vince and Derek too. Mind you, Vince weren't that bad, but Derek was a nasty bit of work. The Doc did Vince in earlier.'

'What for?' Nick remembers the man he shot calling out for Vince.

'No idea, he doesn't need a reason.'

'You think there's other places like this?' Nick asks lightly.

'Guess so,' Jacob mutters, 'but have they got a doctor with a cure?'

'Probably not,' Nick concedes.

'Thing is,' Jacob leans forward, dropping his voice after quickly checking all around, 'I don't know anything about science, but I saw programmes on telly, all with test tubes and computers, microscopes, and people in white suits in labs and stuff, but we don't have any of that here. Nothing, no equipment, no lab or anything. You know.' Jacob drops his voice even lower, 'We don't even have any of them things here, you know, to get samples from or test or something. Maybe I watched too many movies, but surely you gotta have the actual disease or virus or whatever it is to examine, and how do you examine it without equipment?'

'Dunno,' Nick whispers, 'big house, though. Maybe he's got some stuff tucked away.'

'Nah, I been in every room. We have to do a daily checks, and I don't go out scavenging, see. Larson likes me, so he gets me to do things like that. No lab, no equipment. Mind you, though, Nick, I'm loyal, see. I'm not saying the Doc don't know what he's doing, not at all, you know ...'

'Jacob, don't worry,' Nick urges softly, 'I won't repeat a word you tell me, not to Larson or anyone. You got my word on that, mate.'

'Forget it,' Jacob sits back with a look of mild panic on his face, 'heat, innit, gets to your head and makes you say stupid things. I'm loyal, Nick, loyal, see. I won't upset anyone or do anything stupid. I like it here.'

He knows he's stepped too far now and panics, trying to take it back, worried that Nick will report him to Larson or worse yet–the Doc. The young lad seems different, though, and he's got a hard look about him, something trustable and decent.

'So how's he finding a cure, then?' Nick asks, trying to bring the conversation back.

Jacob shrugs, already worried he's gone too far. 'Another coffee, Nick?'

'Yeah, please, er ... what now? I mean, what we got to do now?'

'Nothing, just be here. Someone else is on patrol for a bit. We get another turn later, but right now, we just sit down and drink coffee.'

'Sounds good to me,' Nick smiles.

'We'll have a walk round in a bit.' Jacob stands and pauses for a second as if he wants to say something, then changes his mind, offering a grim smile instead.

'I'll come with you.' Nick gets up to walk with him, suddenly aware that the conversation they just had might be repeated by Jacob. If he is really worried about being seen as disloyal, then snitching on Nick asking loads of questions would cement his position.

Jacob chuckles, shaking his head, 'Now you're worried that *I'll* say something. Pair of twats, ain't we?'

'Didn't even enter my mind,' Nick says, rolling his eyes.

'So you're alright then, are you, Nick?'

'Fine, mate,' Nick replies, slightly confused.

'No, I mean, *you're alright, yeah?*'

'Oh, yeah, I get it Yes, Jake, I am alright. You got nothing to worry about, mate.'

'Okay, hope so. Only just met you but,' Jacob shrugs, 'everything's fucked up. Don't know who to trust. Being careful what you say all the time.'

'Yeah, I bet.' An urge rises in Nick to tell Jacob about the fort and Mr Howie, that there are others out there who offer a different way, that the old principles and morals haven't vanished, but they're here and stronger than ever. Jacob would fit in well at the fort. He's turned a blind eye to the Doc's perverted nature, but only on the justification that he's waiting for the cure so he can leave and save his family. A hard pill to swallow by any degree but relatable, nonetheless, and Nick can see the intense conflict in the man and the slow erosion of his soul.

Nick glances at the gun and the way Jacob keeps it close. Mr Howie will send Dave in first, that's obvious. Maybe Clarence too. This lot, as tough and as hard as they look, don't stand a chance against the team. Meredith, Dave, Clarence, Lani, and the lads. Not to mention Mr Howie when he gets into that mood. Anyone that stands before them will be cut down. Anyone that opposes them will be dealt with swiftly and without hesitation. Once Lilly tells them what happened to her and her family, about the rape, the murders, taking the young boys, and then seeing the boys here at the house, well, nothing short of a disaster will prevent them coming.

'Are there any others like you, Jacob?'

'Like me?' Jacob asks quietly, both of them standing by the garden chairs, watching each other closely. No effort to move off and make more coffee has been made.

'Decent ... like you,' Nick holds the gaze and speaks in a quiet but level voice. Eyes locked, both of them feeling the pressure to say more, to offer to help to each other, to form an alliance, but both too wary to take that step.

'No,' Jacob shakes his head sadly, 'there have been, but they went, left or ...'

'The Doc?'

'And Larson,' Jacob nods, whispering now, with that pleading look in his eyes. Nick watches, his own eyes narrowing as he detects the prickle of tears in the older man's eyes.

'Feels like we're both waiting to say something,' Nick nods, urging the other man to take the plunge.

Jacob shrugs, the dilemma evident. His mouth forms words, but no sounds come out. His hands grip the weapon; angst and turmoil pulsing through his body.

'I'm loyal,' Jacob croaks without conviction.

'You want to see your son,' Nick says softly. 'Lucas, you want to see Lucas.'

'Yeah.' A single tear rolls down a weathered cheek.

'There are others, Jake,' Nick whispers so quietly that Jacob has to step closer; his eyes alert now and locked on Nick. 'Others that aren't like this.' The gamble is taken, the dice thrown, but this isn't a game of chance. Nick has calculated the odds and knows the risk is worth taking. It's that or Jacob will die at the hands of Dave later.

'Who?' Jacob asks, the sound hardly made.

Nick pauses, unsure of how to proceed. What to say and how to say it. How does he go now? The wrong thing said could result in a serious risk being posed to the others.

'Nick, tell me,' Jacob steps in even closer, glancing about to be sure they're alone, 'what others? Where?'

The second wave of instinct hits Nick, but this wave is contrary to the first one, an instant feeling of an error made.

'Nick, I swear I ain't gonna say nothin', mate,' Jacob urges, his face a mask of emotion that contorts his features. A glimmer of hope, a fleeting idea that there might be something else out there. 'I hate it here, Nick. I want out. I fucking hate the Doc, and I swear if he hurts one of those boys, I'll kill him. I'm only here for the cure; then, I'm gone. Nick, please ...'

'Stay close to me, Jacob,' Nick whispers. 'I can't say anything. I won't say anything but stay close to me at all times.' Nick watches as Jacob nods quickly, his expression intense and hanging off every word the young lad says.

This is it. Will Jacob press for more information or be satisfied at that. Nick watches him, watches the light flicker in the other man's eyes. The atmosphere between them is charged, electric almost.

'Okay,' Jacob whispers, 'don't tell me, don't say anything, but just know, yeah, that I ain't like these people here. I didn't do no rapes or murder. You want the gun?' Jacob almost holds it out, ready and willing to hand it over.

'How's that gonna look?' Nick grins. His easy smile returns as the confidence that he took the right risk pays off.

'Yeah, course,' Jacob nods, almost smiling himself. 'Alright, what can I do?'

'Nothing, mate, just stay close, that's all ... Er, they got an armoury here?'

'Larson has 'em all in his room. The blokes got shotguns and rifles with 'em, but the rest is kept safe.'

'His room's locked?'

'All the time,' Jacob nods. 'Keeps the key in his pocket. Nick, you ain't thinking of doing something yourself, are you? I mean, they'll fucking tear you apart.'

'No,' Nick shakes his head quickly, 'just stay close.'

Looking round, Jacob steps away, forcing himself to look normal. 'We'd better get some more coffee so we look normal, maybe get something to eat too. You hungry?'

'Funny that,' Nick grins. 'I'm starving as it happens.'

CHAPTER FORTY-FOUR

'You two move out and keep watch,' Clarence watches as Jagger and Mohammed move swiftly away from the Transit van. Both of them carry sawn-off shotguns as they position themselves a few metres away from the forlorn and empty Saxon. Tools, hastily sourced from the fort, were shoved in the rear of the van as they drove quickly through the deserted roads, into the town where the Saxon was left. Clarence winced at the trail of destruction his explosion of temper left earlier.

'Wow, man,' Ginge nods comically, his red, dreadlocked hair bobbing away as he looks with wide eyes at the big army vehicle, 'that's like, you know, a proper big army thing, yeah?'

'It is. Now fix it,' Clarence growls.

'Man, you don't understand that, like, you know, I gotta see what's wrong with it before I fix it. What happened? Did it, like, you know, make noise or what, man?'

'The power went,' Clarence shrugs. 'No noises or bangs, just went.'

'Slow or fast?' Ginge asks.

'Quick,' Clarence replies, 'just died.'

'Man, that sounds like a fuel problem. Maybe a fuel line or something, like, you know?'

'Know what?'

'Was there, like, you know, diesel on the road or ...?'

'No,' Clarence snaps, 'nothing.'

'Well, okay, man,' Ginge grins, 'that's helpful, you know? I'll go take a look, then.'

'You do that. If you get it working, then I might not shoot you.' Deadpan delivery, face as devoid of expression as Dave. Voice deep, eyes glaring. Ginge gulps, smiling nervously before thinking that maybe it wasn't a joke.

'Lads,' Clarence calls out to the two slightly older lads who are rapidly evolving into two trusted and capable youths, 'if he does anything you don't like, runs off, shouts out, whatever ... shoot him.'

'You got it, hench man,' Jagger nods seriously. Having already spoken to the lads, Clarence made it clear he wanted the dreadlocked mechanic frightened to the point of doing whatever it takes to get the Saxon running.

'Here, this is it,' Paula runs her finger along the blue line on the map. 'This has to be it,' she murmurs. Folding the map out fully, she spreads it across the hot bonnet of the four-wheel drive. Tracing the line of the river, she curses mildly when a drop of perspiration falls from her head onto the paper. 'Yep, Chapsworth House. This is the river, then.'

'Not deep enough,' Dave says dully. At the side of the bridge they're parked on, he looks down into the gentle current sweeping by.

'Sure?' Paula asks gently, believing the man but also

fully aware of how he reacted in the offices earlier when boats were mentioned.

'Definitely too fucking shallow,' Roy says lightly. Placing his hands on the top of the barrier, he leans forward to look down, then starts staring at the back of his right hand, quickly bringing it up to examine closely.

'No boats, then,' Paula says with a smile at Dave.

'Good,' Dave nods, 'unless it gets deeper further on, but then we don't have time to find out. Nor would we have time to find boats and bring them to the deepest part.'

'Agreed,' Paula says quickly, 'so what's the next plan, then?'

'We'll go by land,' Dave says, moving across to the map spread out over the front of the vehicle, 'take me to here, and I'll run in for a look, then run back.' He points to a spot a couple of centimetres from the property marked Chapsworth House on the map. 'If that spot gets compromised, then fall back half a mile and keep going.'

'Okay, Dave. Roy? You okay?' she calls out, spotting Roy with that worried look on his face while staring at the back of his own hand.

'Got a bruise,' he replies in a meek voice, 'can't remember hitting it. Probably a disease of the blood or ...'

'We've all got bruises, Roy,' Paula adopts the gentle tone, 'and you did climb up that rope, remember? You probably knocked it on the way up.'

'Oh yes, that rope, yes,' Roy grins with relief. 'I'd forgotten all about that. Righto, so what's the plan, Dave?' He walks over in a jaunty manner, grinning happily at the news that he isn't dying of some incurable blood disease.

'I'll explain on the way. You driving?'

'Really don't mind,' Roy grins. 'Yeah, I'll drive, and you

relax so you can plan and plot and come up with crazy wild ideas for everyone,' he laughs.

'Okay, Roy,' Paula chuckles.

Dave looks from one to the other as he climbs into the back, settling himself into the hot leather seats. They like each other, these two. Just like Mr Howie and Lani and Clarence and Mr Howie's sister. Before she got killed and turned, then had her throat cut open by Dave, that is.

People are strange, Dave muses. Smiling and grinning at each other. Why don't they just say they like each other and be done with it?

'No way, that cannot be right.' I stare at the thermometer, then across to Lani.

'What's it say?' Maddox strolls over with Lenski at his side.

'Er,' leaning in closer, I count the black bars, 'forty-two degrees Celsius. Did you hear that? Forty-two degrees! Shit ... that's got to be a record.'

'No wonder everyone is wilting,' Lani sighs, 'and that's in here, out of the sun.'

'How's it looking, then?' I ask the two lads, Blowers and Cookey.

'Same as before,' Blowers replies, 'down to sawn-offs and pistols. Luckily we got tons of shotgun cartridges, and we got a few rifles but only single-shot ones.'

'Clarence has got Dave's sniper rifle from the Saxon, though,' Cookey adds, 'for later, if we need it.'

'Close up and dirty, then,' I sigh.

'What is the close and dirty?' Lenski asks with a puzzled glance.

'He means the fighting,' Maddox says. 'Sawn-off shotguns are brutal at close range but no good for anything over a few metres away. Security is back up,' he says, looking at me. 'Got a crew on the wall with rifles and shotguns, a few at the back inside and outside, and a whole crew outside, plus another one stationed inside the inner gate. We'll get a daily password, and no one gets inside without it.'

'Good idea, mate,' I nod at him.

'Medical tents are functioning. We got that male nurse and his wife checking new people. We'll need more, but it'll do for now.'

'Why you say this like you do this?' Lenski glares at Maddox. 'I do all these things, yes? But you steal the lemonlight.'

'Lemonlight?' Maddox grins, an instant transformation that changes his face, giving him a completely different personality.

'What?' Lenski glares round at the smiles.

'It's limelight,' Lani comments.

'Oh, this funny, yes?' She glares first at Maddox, then at me, which abruptly wipes the smirk from my face. Give me a horde of zombies to fight any day over getting on Lenski's bad side.

'Er, Lilly alright?' I ask Lani to change the subject.

'In our rooms,' Lani replies. 'I had to shoo these two away,' she nods at Blowers and Cookey, 'which was very bloody hard until I told them how old she is.'

'How old is she?' I ask.

'Fifteen, boss,' Blowers pipes up.

'You're shitting me?' I exclaim.

'No way,' Maddox shakes his head, earning a swift dig in the ribs from Lenski.

'That's what she said. She, er, she said something else

too,' Lani drops her voice. 'She was so worried Nick would desert her, she offered herself to him, you know ... sexually.'

'Fuck,' I gasp.

'He turned her down too,' Lani explains with no little touch of pride.

'Good lad,' I raise my eyebrows. Nick was high in my estimations before, but now? Now he's off the chart. Mind you, I know in my heart that we'd all do the same. Even Blowers and Cookey, for all their banter, wouldn't do that.

'Poor girl,' Lenski sighs, 'we all see these things, yes, but she see them in the one day: father, friend, and her brother, plus the man try and touch her.'

'She'll cope,' Maddox lifts his head. 'She got to.'

'I know this, but still it sad,' Lenski lifts one shoulder. 'We lose the boys last night, and I sad. We lose the people today, and I sad. Roy, he kill the two men and ... It never end, no?'

'One day,' Lani mutters, staring at me.

'Shit,' Cookey gasps, snapping our attention to him. He stands completely still, staring at the dirty pane of lead-lined glass giving a smudged view of outside. Slowly, his arm lifts to point one finger at a single fat droplet of water rolling down the glass. 'Rain.'

CHAPTER FORTY-FIVE

On the sixth day there was rain. A squall. A passing cloud laden with moisture. The rain fell, and within a few hours, all signs of it were gone, evaporated back into the superheated atmosphere.

The cessation of mankind has had multiple effects. Every school student learns that people take oxygen in and exhale carbon dioxide. Every student learns that carbon dioxide contributes to the warming effect of the planet.

Only humanity didn't cease. A large proportion of it ceased being human, but they didn't go away. The infected still take oxygen in. The only way to keep the body moving is to draw air in so the lungs can still enrich the infected blood that pumps through the infected heart.

Cars. Factories. Aircraft. Ships. Trains. Motorbikes. Furnaces. Generators. Power stations. Within twenty-four hours, they all stopped. The fumes were no longer being pumped into the air. The smog started to clear, to lift. Cities whose atmosphere caused absurdly high rates of asthma and other breathing related problems, started to change. The air became cleaner day after day, and after two weeks, the stench of those fumes is barely noticeable.

In every language still spoken on the planet, the phrase '*new world, new rules*' is repeated over and again. An acceptance that what was is no more. *This is a new time, and there are new rules.*

Everything can change, and maybe Mother Nature is aware of the abrupt change to the surface of her planet. Maybe, like any good manager, she recognises the opportunity to make alterations, to change things, to have a good clean out.

The surface is dirty and littered with corpses. The world is stained with the stench of death and dried blood, gore and innards slowly cooking in the heat or freezing in the cold.

A famous scientist once said Mother Nature can *and will* do what it takes to heal herself.

Maybe that time is now. Maybe all these things have happened for a reason.

Maybe Mother Nature will take this chance to cleanse.

Maybe.

Or maybe it's just a storm. Something that would have happened regardless of the dead rising.

Reconnaissance: observation of an area to gain information.

From the broiling, rolling clouds gathering on the horizon, one cloud is sent forward. Small and hardly visible, yet loaded with enough moisture to generate a single fat drop of rain. That drop is expelled, sent through the atmosphere to plummet at terminal velocity towards the ground.

From the fort, the bastion of civilisation that already has seen many good men and women fall to protect it, one small man is sent forward to view the ground in preparation of the planned attack. The attack that seeks to recover the disabused children ripped from the loving embrace of their families to place them back into a secure and ordered environment.

From the horde that gathers quietly in the forests north of the fort, one infected is sent forward. The assumption that all the infected were drawn into the area for the attack of the previous evening is wrong. That attack came from the southeast of England. More infected are available. More are summoned. More are gathered, and quietly they wait. With chemical enforced patience, they remain steady and resolute.

With each passing day, their form becomes less and less human. Skin drawn and tight, teeth dirty, and the thin lips pulled back in a never-ending snarl ready for the bite.

Eyes sunken and hollow but still with that bloodshot, red appearance. Hands claw, limbs twitch, and drool hangs. Hundreds, thousands gather in the shade of the deep woods. More arrive from the north. They use hedgerows and valleys for stealth. Quiet. Unnoticed.

Determined.

CHAPTER FORTY-SIX

'You fixed it yet, bro?'

'No, like you know, man, I ...'

'What's up, bruv? You ain't fixed it yet? You's gonna get killed.'

'Hey, man, that's, like, oppressing me, like, my soul and how I work, you know ...'

'You's should have it fixed by now, bruv.'

'Innit, bruv, you wanna die, do ya?'

'What? No, man ...'

'He wants to die, Jagger.'

'He does, Mo Mo. He wants it bad.'

Ginge sweats, Ginge focusses, Ginge works harder as the two youths continue the unrelenting banter. The problem was simple, a fuel line connector shaken loose from all the constant battering. Finding it was difficult due to the vehicle being military specification and not the same as most road going vehicles.

The job would normally have taken at least half a day, with the Saxon hoisted on a ramp, various parts stripped away, and all the time the bill for labour costs growing at an alarming rate. But Jagger and Mohammed, as young and annoying as they may be, turn out to be great motivators. Ginge works quickly with the ever-increasing threat of being killed, shot, stabbed, hung, strangled, drowned, or choked on his own bollocks. He finds the fault and starts working to fix it.

'Make it good,' Clarence orders once the hippy mechanic shouts that he's found the issue and can fix it. 'If it breaks again, I'll come for you.'

'Done, man. Like, you know, I fixed it, and like, it ain't gonna break again, man, like a proper fix that is for sure.' Sliding out from underneath the vehicle, he stands up, smiling coyly while wiping the sweat from his face.

'Well done that, man,' Clarence booms, giving him a manly slap on the arm, which sends the mechanic sprawling off to one side.

Inside the vehicle, Clarence winces at the heat built up from being sat baking in the sun all day. Ignition on, and it fires up. The huge roar of those defiant engines screams into the quiet, deserted town centre.

Clarence smiles, like welcoming a comrade back into the unit. Patting the wheel gently, he murmurs *welcome back,* then motions for the others to get in.

'Shame that, bruv,' Jagger tuts, 'I was looking forward to slicing you up.'

'See if it holds first,' Clarence adds evilly, enjoying the revenge on the man for daring to take their fort by force.

Clarence's mind runs through the plan. Get back to the fort, get the gear loaded back in, then see what Dave, Paula, and Roy came up with. Wait till dark, then we're off. Get Nick, get the kids, get back to the fort again, and see what else happens. Shaking his head at the never-ending tasks laid out in front of him, he yawns and rolls his neck. The heat saps at his energy, causing little bites of annoyance to grow into an irritation. He is fed up with wiping the sweat from his face, fed up with drinking so much water just to replace the lost fluids, fed up with being so bloody hot all the time.

It can't hold. This weather surely can't keep on like this. Two weeks of solid, blistering sunshine that gets hotter every day.

On cue, the shadow covers the ground, a veritable darkening of the skies. Leaning forward, he peers through the windscreen to the heavens, seeing the rolling, deep grey clouds streaked with huge patches of almost pure blackness.

Dusk falls in an instant. The clouds blot the blue sky away. The electricity in the air charges up, hairs on his arms and neck prickle. Static fills the very air he breathes.

Foreboding, dark, and dangerous. A sight of awe-inspiring power of a thing yet to come. The men are unable to speak, the air too thick. Clarence presses his foot down to drive power to the engine, racing faster to head back before all hell breaks loose.

CHAPTER FORTY-SEVEN

He runs. He likes running. Fast, sleek, and fluid in his movements, he stays low, surging alongside the hedgerows. Having memorised the map, he knows the direction to head for, going for the higher ground that Lilly explained.

Sweat forms. This is an unusual occurrence for Dave, whose body is so finely tuned as to be nearing perfection in physical form. Breathing harder, he pushes on. Nick is within that place, and Nick is part of the team. Mr Howie won't stop until Nick is back with them.

The children are important but only in the sense that Dave has been told they are important. Knowledge not emotion. Mr Howie says this has to be done, so it gets done.

Into the copse, vaulting downed tree trunks, dodging low branches until he reaches the edge, drops down, and scurries forward quickly.

Big house and exactly as described by Lilly. Lawns to the rear, the water of the river glistening as it goes by. Ground to the front stretching out to a high wall that runs round the perimeter to the main gate, an old, stone-built thing with two huge pillars and a cluster of sandbags stacked in a semi-circle.

Small figures move around the sandbags. Armed guards. Several of them, but the distance between the gates and the house is huge. Dave watches, almost tutting at the absence of a fall-back point or a second tier of defences between the gate and the house. No visible patrols, no sentry points.

Two people sat behind a shed off to the side of the house, must be a smoking area. Almost tutting again, he imagines Nick sitting there, smoking like he always does.

Dave watches them stand up, something in the movement of one of them. Nick. No doubt about it. Dave knows his team well, and that is Nick, standing there, talking to the other man. They stay still, then move closer, talking so they stay unheard. Maybe an ally? Maybe someone willing to help when it goes off.

Dave nods to himself, a very small, slight movement. Be aware that one of them might be willing to help. Either way, Dave knows the house is as good as taken. Not vanity or conceit, but pure confidence that he can do what others cannot do.

Entering a property this size and killing so many people is not something that bothers Dave. Taking life has never bothered Dave. What bothers him is the thought that in these very worst of times, there are people who will prey on the weak and vulnerable.

Nick is there. Nick is part of the team. Nick is to be taken back. Frowning, he knows he could go down now and get the job done with ease. No, the children. Remember the children. This isn't just to get Nick out but to save the children too. He could get to Nick with ease but not the children, not without alerting the people inside to his presence, and like Mr Howie said, Dave charging at a bunch of terrified kids with two bloodied knives wouldn't work that well.

Time to go. Recce complete. Scurrying back, he simply follows his access route in. Building speed up and staying low, he races downhill and onto the level ground.

Just before reaching the waiting vehicle, he glances up at the huge, sprawling clouds filling the horizon. A never-ending wall of dark greys and blacks. The back of Dave's neck starts to tingle.

'See that?' he comments on reaching the four-wheel drive. Barely out of breath, he gets in the back and does his seatbelt up.

'Yeah,' Paula nods from behind the driver's wheel.

'Go.'

No one speaks for the same reasons that Clarence finds affecting him, the air is too thick, too charged, too electric.

Hairs rise, and Paula finds a sudden, dull pain forming in the back of her head. It's the same dull pain she always gets before a storm, and as with Clarence, she finds her foot pressing down harder to make the journey back to the fort.

CHAPTER FORTY-EIGHT

Solitary it stands, scans the area, then moves forward with a loping gait. Tall and thin, no excess fat on this infected. Tight muscles that cling to the bone and show clear underneath the drawn skin.

Grey in pallor, it's a sickening hue of withering human but animated, full of energy, and driven to push forward and scout the land.

Five miles north of the fort, there is a wooded copse, a forest as ancient as the land itself. Oak trees that have been growing since records began. Protected by conservationists and home to many unique species, it now acts as a temporary refuge for the newest species on the Earth.

The infection calculated the loss of the previous evening. It factored there was a possibility that Howie and the others would evade it.

Howie *was* taken, but the connection couldn't be made. In the darkness and confusion, even the infection couldn't seek him out. Scent wouldn't work with so many bodies moving and so much blood split.

It starts to understand why the hosts fear him. Why,

despite the chemicals, pheromones, and endorphins pumped into the bodies, they still react.

He is unique. He is different. There is a dark spot of knowledge here. Even from the collected conscious of the infected, from the hive mind ability, the infection cannot understand what makes him unable to turn.

The infection felt both the host pushing the heart into his mouth at the same time as it felt being pushed through the organisms within the heart. It was inside of him. The blood pumped into his mouth, absorbed into his soft tissue. He swallowed it into his stomach lining where it was absorbed, but that was it, that's where it ended.

Immunity. The infection knows what immunity is, and if Howie was content to live his days quietly, without issue, there would be no further attempts to take him. Only he won't. Like the proverbial fly in the ointment, he keeps coming back, showing up here and there as he inflicts greater and greater losses on the hosts.

It doesn't want Howie now. Howie cannot be taken, so instead, he will be killed. At whatever cost, his life will be ended.

They must be exhausted. The infection understands they will be tired, hot, drained, and therefore, they will be slower and less dynamic.

The infection factored all of this before the battle of the previous evening, so it built reserves. Stockpiling resources to be used.

In the wooded copse, five miles north of the fort, is the next group to be despatched. Under cover of night, they will charge, quietly, without fuss or noise, and they will gain that fort and destroy it.

The infection makes the head turn up. It looks through

the red, bloodshot eyes at the gathering clouds so vast filling the sky as they race across the heavens.

A storm will not only provide cover but will provide water to the hosts, re-energising them.

The time is close. The solitary infected makes his way south, moving through streets, roads and lanes, across fields, and all the time picking out the best cover to be used by the masses behind him. All the way down it goes, right to the countryside bordering the bay that curves round to the fort so solid and proud.

Not for long.

CHAPTER FORTY-NINE

Walking quietly down the long corridor of the top floor, the two men come to a sudden stop. Staring at each other with wide eyes, they hear something happening, happening now.

Nick doesn't breathe; it's too early for them to come now. It's gloomy but not night yet. The noise is awful and from all around them. A constant drumming cacophony that comes screaming out of the silence.

Slowly, Jacob loses the look of intense concern and starts to smile, a slow grin that spreads across his face. 'Rain,' he mutters.

As soon as the word exits his mouth, Nick recognises the sound for what it is. Sustained, intense rainfall. An old house with large windows. The drumming effect of the fat raindrops smacking into the large panes echoes through the grand building.

On a tour of the house, Jacob pointed out the various rooms, showing Nick the layout and focussing on the route from the servants' quarters where they drank coffee to the area designated for the boys.

The Doc's rooms are noted, along with those used by

Larson. The guards make use of the servants' smaller bedrooms on the top floor.

They descend quickly. Moving swiftly through the house, they are joined by others coming out of rooms to head outside and see the rain. The big double front doors have already been opened, with a small cluster of men standing in the shelter of the overhang.

A blur of purple sky ahead. Solid sheets of rain that fall with thunderous effect onto the hardstanding. It's so loud they have to speak in raised voices, shouting at one another in amazement at the spectacle.

Nick feels the intense heat still hanging in the air. Pausing for a second, he first extends one hand out to feel the water cascading down, then ventures out to stand in the downpour. The effect is shocking–the warm, soft water drenches him completely in an instant. Hair soaked through, his clothes cling to his lean, muscular frame. He closes his eyes, and for a second, everything else is forgotten. Rain. Pure and clean.

Others move out to join him, Jacob staying close to the younger man. It's like standing under a shower, but like a shower unknown in his lifetime. Perfectly warm, perfectly refreshing, perfectly soaking.

Hearing noise, Nick opens his eyes to see the crowd outside the house growing. The Doc ran to gather the children, hastily leading them outside to stand with the others. Squeals of pleasure erupt from the boys as for a few minutes all thoughts of loss, pain, and suffering are gone.

Nick closes his eyes again, and a sudden, intense feeling of being lonely hits him. Away from the others, the separation tugs at his heart. He still doesn't know for sure if everyone made it through the battle of the car park. Listening to the sound of the rain striking the ground, he misses them more than ever. The image of Lilly swims into his mind. The way she offered herself to him. What would that have been like?

He would never do that, never take advantage in such a manner, but Nick is but a young man with the dreams and hopes that young men have. Lilly is beautiful beyond words, so the desire, the dream, the wonder of allowing himself to imagine it is allowed. The kiss, although maybe given under duress by her, was both magical and intense, yet soft and over far too quickly.

Where is she now? Is she standing in the rain, thinking of him? Where are the others? What are they doing right now?

He realises that he's homesick. Not for a place, but for his team, his family.

Stay strong and wait. They'll come soon.

CHAPTER FIFTY

I watch her young face turn up to the sky. The rain drenches her in an instant. Her blonde hair gets plastered to her face. She looks so alone, so frightened but resolute at the same time. Is she thinking of her brother? Of Nick in the house?

I feel Lani's hand push into mine, our fingers entwine as we stand beneath the deluge. Everyone stands beneath the deluge.

Blowers, Cookey, Maddox, and Lenski. Everyone. The whole fort stands still and faces the heavens.

The rain is massaging and warm, soft, yet just hard enough to stimulate, and in this heat, it feels like nothing I have ever felt before. Refreshing and cleansing, pure and sweet.

I'm not the only one who opens their mouth to catch the falling drops. Only this isn't the average rainfall. This a deluge of the greatest intensity I have ever felt. My mouth fills with water. I swallow and do it again. It tastes amazing. No pollution, no chemicals, nothing but clean water.

Someone laughs nearby as a child jumps in the puddles

already forming. Someone else cheers, and I hear the sounds of people being happy. Maybe only for a few minutes, but it's enough to lift the spirits.

Ominous, though. Portentous even. My heart rate suddenly increases, hammering in my chest, breathing coming hard and fast. Everything slows. Blowers with his face turned up, rivulets of water pouring down his stubbled chin. Meredith lapping at a puddle, and her pink tongue seems to flick in and out so slowly.

Lani runs her hands through her long, silky hair, sweeping it clear from her face. Electricity pulses through my body, making me feel sick. Hairs standing on end, and a tightening in my stomach.

Searching, looking all around. Something bad comes this way. Headlights at the front as the gates are swung open. The Saxon drives in, slowly becoming visible through the sheets of rain. The driver's door opens as Clarence jumps down to join the others staring up at the sky.

The bulk of the Saxon hides the four-wheel drive tucked behind. It drives out and round, pulling up alongside. Paula and Roy step out to smile and laugh at the feel of the rain drenching them in an instant.

Swallowing, I can feel the pressure building inside me. I want to shout, roar, and scream out loud. Something bad comes this way.

Dave watches me, unblinking, unflinching. Water runs freely down his head to stream from his chin. Something bad comes this way.

He knows it.

His eyes search mine as I look to him. Turning slowly, Blowers is no longer facing up but staring at me, his dark eyes locked on mine too. Cookey does the same. Lani and Clarence too. All of us feel that pressure, that static building stronger by the second. Maddox, Lenski, Paula, Roy, and now Lilly. They all stare across at me, towards me, watching, waiting.

Something.

I don't know what.

Bad.

What bad? I don't know what it is.

Comes this way.

The air breaks. It breaks with noise so deep, so full of bass, with a roar that makes me feel so small and insignificant it brings tears to my eyes. Thunder.

From every direction, it comes at once. Not from the distance but right above us and at the same time all around us. Low but high, close and far. It rolls and booms, jarring my organs. Screams and cries, people hit the ground in fear as the sound continues. It rolls and echoes and never goes away. Getting deeper, more powerful, building to a point where surely the planet will split and fracture into tiny pieces.

There is no action to be taken. The noise, the sensation, the feeling of the thunder driving through our bones renders us to the point of amoebas.

Thunder and lightning. Except in this case there is no *and*. Thunder. Lightning. Both together, at the same time. Co-ordinated and exact.

Light fills the dark sky. Forks of pure, white energy burn onto my retina so the shape of them remains for seconds. More come. Forks all around us. Crackling and flashes as the heavens explode in light.

Suddenly dark. Night came without any hesitation. The clouds blacken the sky to be revealed in their almighty glory by the electric flashes that seem to split the sky every few seconds.

Thunderous war drums boom round and round. A sight so great, so mesmerising it takes my breath away.

A huge, thick fork screeches down into the fort, a solid beam of jagged, blue-white light that seems to dance along the ground. Tents explode as the metal frames heat within a split second. The wooden outbuildings erected as make-shift kitchens burst into flames at the gentlest lick from the serpent's forked tongue.

Sparks and flames shoot into the air. Another fork hits the visitor centre with enough energy to burst the one remaining pane of glass left proudly in the window. The smell is incredible, like singed hair but metallic and sulphuric too. Static everywhere, like tingling on the ends of my fingers. Speaking is negated as the thunder rolls back and forth, seemingly feet above our heads.

People screaming and running, but there's no point. The flames caused by the lightning are doused quicker than any fire service could ever do. There are a billion hoses on full spray in the clouds above, and nothing can stay alight under that much water.

A fork hits the centre of the fort, the point gouging divots of earth as it snakes, dances, and scores a path. Someone gets hit and is ripped from his feet to be sent spinning off into the darkness. It's coming this way, and we've seen enough action now to know when to stop and stare and when to run. So we run. Star-bursting, we explode away in all directions as the crackle whips by.

'OFFICE,' Dave roars at the top of his voice. Even so close, he sounds muted, like he's trying to compete with the giants of the sky. They mock and laugh in return, rolling out a series of deep, explosive, rolling drums.

Heads down, we run. The ground covered in a layer of water that flares up with every step. Clarence, the closest, gets there first and wrenches the door open. Standing outside, he almost lifts everyone off their feet as he shoves them inside.

Slamming the door, we stand dripping, breathing hard like we've been running for hours. The thunder is still going, but the roof above our heads is thick stone and deadens the noise enough that we can hear each other shouting. Flashes of lightning burst into the darkness, giving us a harsh strobe like effect.

There's another noise, but from within now, it takes a few seconds, but I gradually become aware of Meredith howling with her nose turned up and her long neck stretched out. Mournful and haunting, she keeps going until Lani drops down next to her, literally tugging at her to stop.

'RIVER IS NO GOOD,' Paula shouts, waving her hand under her chin to emphasise her point.

'RECCE?' I shout, my voice cracking from the exertion.

'DONE,' Dave is easier to hear, 'AS LILLY SAID.'

Lilly, she's still with us. The plucky kid ran with everyone else to get inside the offices.

'SAXON?'

'FIXED,' Clarence bellows with a thumbs up.

'WE GO NOW, THE STORM,' I point at the sky, 'GOOD COVER.'

Nods all round, everyone in agreement.

'SAME PLAN?' Maddox shouts.

'DAVE?'

'YES.'

'SAME PLAN?'

'I SAID YES, MR HOWIE.'

Funny bugger, I swear he does it on purpose. 'WE'LL TALK ON THE WAY. LET'S GO.'

Sprinting to the armoury, we grab shotguns, both sawn-offs and long-barrelled. Dave grabs his sniper rifle while Clarence takes the GPMG from on top of the Saxon. No ammunition, but the sight of it might make a difference.

All around us, the thunder booms and rolls. The risk of being struck by lightning is very real, especially given the fact we're about to load into a huge metal can. Is it earthed? What will happen if lightning hits it?

Still, the storm is perfect cover for what we're about to do. The noise of it, the spectacle, the reduced visibility all work in our favour.

The Saxon is loaded up with me in the driver's seat, Clarence in the passenger, and my team in the back. Another van is loaded with Maddox, Roy, Paula, and the two youths Jagger and Mo Mo.

'Wait,' Clarence jumps back outside and runs off while I get the engine started, trying to peer through the gloom and watching another jagged fork strike the top of the seaward side wall. It's an incredible sight and truly frightening.

The rear doors open to reveal a very sad-looking, ginger, dread-locked man being launched in. Door closes, and the big man is climbing back into the passenger seat, giving me a thumbs up.

'Nice one.' I nod back at the terrified man staring up at the hard faces from his hands and knee. He looks round, then stops dead at the sight of Meredith holding her nose inches from him.

Blowers visibly tuts. Grabbing hold of his shirt, he pulls him onto a seat and says something to him.

That's it, loaded up and ready to go. Pulling away, I

navigate a wide turn to face back the right way and start heading towards the main gates, the second van close behind me.

'Fuck,' I gasp at the sight before us. The hard, compacted earth, baked so dry after two weeks of such intense heat, isn't absorbing the rain. Instead, it pools and gathers on the surface, giving an appearance of a huge lake stretching out in front of us. The noise of the rain striking the Saxon is constant, a drumming, pattering sound. That coupled with the thunder and constant flashes gives everything a static, surreal feel.

Edging forward slowly, I aim for where the road will be, knowing there are two big ditches here somewhere that are now unseen. After so many trips up and down this road, I find it instantly and start moving away.

'Keep an eye out the back in case the van gets stuck,' I yell out, hearing as someone opens the rear doors to watch. A huge thunderclap literally vibrates the Saxon on its springs, followed a split second later by huge, twisting, jagged bolts of pure energy strobing the sky.

Just hang on, Nick. Not long now, mate. Hold tight and wait for us.

CHAPTER FIFTY-ONE

'You got any spare clothes?' Jacob asks. Back in the house, and the young boys were quickly removed once the thunderous claps and bolts of light started. There were screams of fear as the sheer awesome sound and light show terrified the children to their cores.

'I'll be alright,' Nick replies. 'It's still hot, so they'll dry.'

The Doc ushered the boys into the house, yelling in delight at them to run and get to safety. He led them up the stairs like a heroic saviour of children, picking two of the smallest up but refusing to let any of the guards help.

Left in the hallway, Nick and Jacob stand away from the others to watch the storm through one of the large display windows, marvelling at the power of the storm hitting so quickly.

'It's everywhere,' Nick observes as the thunder booms and rolls, seemingly from every direction at the same time. The barbs of lightning bring the vista to daylight for split seconds, burning the image onto retinas.

'Long time coming,' Jacob has to shout over the noise of the pelting rain and thunder, 'Feel this heat, though?' Jacob asks, watching as Nick nods. 'Means the worst is yet to come. Feels like it's getting hotter too, humid and static, yeah?'

'Yeah,' Nick nods in agreement, the air feels almost thick and syrupy. His head is clogged with a dull pain, and he can feel the static, the hairs on his neck and arms prickling.

'It will get much worse,' Jacob nods, staring back out the window. 'No wind yet either.' He bites his bottom lip, blinking as a fork strikes the ground just metres away. 'Thunder is the air being split by the lightning. Hear that crackle, then the sonic booms?'

Glancing over he, sees Nick staring at him closely. 'The lightning hits which does something to the air, like positive and negative ions or something. Anyway that displaces the air so fast it creates that sonic boom, like an aircraft but ...'

'Yeah,' Nick nods, 'how do you know that?'

'Read up on it for my kid,' he shrugs. 'He asked me what thunder and lightning was, so I figured I should know. I hope I got it right,' he adds quickly.

'Sounds good, mate,' Nick smiles. Perfect weather. This noise and the reduced visibility will hide the approach of the others when they come. They'll be on their way now, setting out in vehicles, with Dave sat in the back, sharpening his knives, whilst Cookey cracks crap jokes that still make everyone smile. Clarence will be up front so everyone has a bit more space in the back, probably with Lilly and Lani sat together while the lads gawp at her.

'You look like you're waiting for something,' Jacob whispers quickly between a break in the thunder.

Nick looks and smiles sadly. He likes Jacob more with every passing minute. They've only just met, but the older man has taken a huge gamble in trusting him and opens up more every few minutes. He hasn't questioned Nick about anything but just stayed close. The way Jacob explains things: who to avoid, the dangerous men, the easy going, lazy ones, and the layout of the house in such detail that Nick knows the man suspects something is going to happen soon.

'Tonight?' Jacob asks hopefully. 'Just tell me where you want me when it happens, yeah?'

Indecision keeps Nick silent, unsure of exactly how much to tell the man. It could still be a trap. He was placed with Jacob by Larson. This man could be faking all the misery and upset, but it doesn't feel that way, and sometimes you just have to go with your gut.

'Well, my glorious men,' the Doc booms, walking jauntily down the stairs. 'The boys are with the lovely Meryl. Poor little mites were terrified. I would say,' he stops halfway down the last flight of stairs, a perfect position to hold court to the men gathered in the grand hallway. 'This weather breaking is cause for celebration. Who agrees with me?'

Deep voices murmur in agreement, a muted, restrained response from men too wary of the psychotic doctor to do anything else.

'Come now,' the Doc laughs, 'I expected more of a rousing cheer. Well, if you don't want beer and liquor and, dare I say, some of the fine single malt whiskey, then fine ... Oh, that got your attention, didn't it? I say again ... Who agrees with me?'

The responding cheers echo through the cavernous room, deep voices yelling in happiness. Someone whistles as Nick takes in the various broken-toothed smiles, almost as ugly as the infected.

'Larson, my good man, let's get these men a drink.'

'Right you are, Doc,' Larson appears at the edge, leaving Nick wondering if he had always been there or just arrived. 'Everyone with me, then.'

'What about the guards?' Nick asks Jacob quietly.

'Rotation is done for the evening,' Jacob replies. 'The gate guards will stay there till morning, and just a few left on patrol. 'Ere, Mick,' Jacob calls out to a passing man with old-style, faded, green tattoos on his neck, 'you on patrol tonight?'

'Yeah,' Mick scowls at the prospect of not being able to drink.

'Me and the lad will do it. I promised Larson I'd show him round.'

'Bloody hell, Jacob, I don't need asking twice, mate. Nice one!' Mick grins, grabbing his mate to give him the good news.

'Cheers, Jacob and whatever your name is,' another thickset man calls out from the crowd.

'Nick. No worries,' Nick calls back with a smile.

'What's that?' Larson steps in, looking between the two pairs.

'Jacob said he'll show Nick round and do our patrol tonight. Means we can have a drink, yeah?' Mick explains with a sudden, worried look that Larson will refuse it.

'Good on you, Jacob,' Larson nods firmly. 'Everything okay then, Nick? Settling in alright?'

'Fine, thank you,' Nick nods, thinking it's only been a couple of hours and how can he possible have *settled* in yet.

'Take it easy tonight, Mick,' Larson warns in a low growl, 'don't get drunk, you hear me?'

'Course not,' Mick murmurs. A strange, subdued response from such a hard-looking man. The scars and marks on his body speak of countless fights and scraps, yet he instantly defers to Larson. They all do, nodding respectfully as they file past, into one of the big downstairs rooms.

Jacob and Nick tag along, watching as the Doc uses a key to open the door to a walk-in cupboard. Grinning and calling out jovially, he starts passing out cases of beer, bottles of wine and spirits. Men queue up and wait for the drinks to get passed round.

Scanning between them, Nick notices the puzzled look Larson aims at the Doc. Clearly confused as to why the big man is letting everyone drink now.

This isn't like him. He normally hates it when the men want a drink, but here he is, passing it out like a veritable Santa at the office Christmas party. Larson watches the way the tough guards defer even more to the Doc, speaking only when spoken to and nodding respectfully the whole time. Animals can recognise a dangerous predator amongst them.

The storm rages and builds with intensity and power. Candles, lit throughout the main corridors, flicker and dance, casting soft illuminations against the walls. Windows patter as the rain lashes against them; rolling claps and booms accompanied by the flashes of sheet and fork lightning.

Maybe the storm has eased the pressure? Everyone has been feeling the heat build, and along with it, tempers have been getting frayed and short. The Doc's explosion at Vince is a prime example, resulting in the man being beaten to death. Guilt? Could be. Maybe the Doc has stewed on their earlier conversion and then smacking that poor guard's face later. Maybe he's picked up on the sulky, terrified manner of the men and decided to show a different side.

Either way, it's a good thing and long overdue. Wait till he gets a few drinks inside him, then he can ask about getting some women in here. Meryl can't cook morning, noon, and night for everyone, and none of this lot can boil an egg. Plus, there's the laundry too. Everything needs hand-washing now, and the boys could do with some maternal types here to put 'em at ease.

That Nick is a good lad. Thick and obviously low on the intelligence scale, but that just makes the nipper eager to please his elders and betters. Look at him now, gooning over Jacob in a desperate attempt to please him and earn favour. Can't read or write? Jesus, what is the world coming to if the youth can't even get a proper education.

Still, the thicker, the better. Easier to manipulate and control. Give 'em some food, a few wenches to fuck, and a bit of freedom, and they'll keep coming back. Yeah, maybe a few get lost here and there, not returning from the scavenging, or, of course, the Doc losing his rag and killing them, but loses are to be expected.

Thinking of the Doc, he is already knocking them back. Larson frowns at those big hands gripping a can of lager. It doesn't look right that a man of such learning, from such a dignified profession drinks from a can like normal men. Surely he should be drinking wine or even pouring the beer into a glass first, but there he is, glugging away.

First can finished, and the Doc crushes the aluminium container while giving a big belch, then wiping his mouth with the back of his hand.

'You alright?' Larson asks quietly, motioning for the Doc to step away from the men. More have come in now. Those hanging about the servants' quarters being quickly called and summoned to the impromptu party. Muted conversations start to lift, but many a wary glance is still thrown towards the Doc and Larson.

'Fine, Larson,' the Doc beams with a film of sweat covering his pale, meaty face.

'This such a good idea?' Larson says bluntly. 'You drinking down here with the men?'

'What?' the Doc laughs. 'Why on earth not? Oh, I get it. Yes, my temper,' the Doc mimics the smaller man. 'I'll have you know, Larson, that I am a happy drunk and not at all violent.'

'Okay, Doc,' Larson smiles slowly. 'Studies going okay?'

'Takes time, my good man. It's not something that can just be ...' he waves one huge hand in the air, '... plucked out of the sky. Study, research, and time.'

'Test subjects, then? We any closer to needing any?' Having asked before, he probes further, wanting to know when they'll need to capture some control specimens of infected.

'All in good time,' the Doc pulls the ring back on another can.

'Equipment, then?' Larson pushes. 'You want me to start looking for stuff? Like microscopes or ... I don't know.'

'Yes, yes, look, my man, the weather has finally broken. We've got well stocked supplies and a house full of happy, healthy boys, so let's just enjoy tonight, eh? Switch off and have a couple of drinks.'

Nodding with a quick grin, Larson steps back as the Doc brushes past him, heading to a group of tattooed men laughing quietly. The fact that they're laughing at all is amazing, showing humour in the presence of the Doc.

Alright for you to switch off, Larson thinks darkly, *you're not the one running everything. Guards to sort out, patrols, and making sure no one upsets you or even looks at the boys the wrong way. I've still got Vince's body to dump too.*

More laughter from nearby, a joke cracked, and men smirking in response. The Doc moves over to the laughing group, and instantly they return to being poker-faced. *What was the joke,* the Doc asks. Larson watches as one man quietly re-tells it. Nervous glances and worried looks as the Doc listens intently. The atmosphere charges to the point of being almost as energised as the storm outside. The punch-line, a brief pause of bated breath. The joke teller visibly wilts, seeing his life flash before his eyes.

Then the Doc roars with laughter, a huge sound produced by a big set of lungs, and it fills the room. Genuine laughter too. The other men join in, laughing more from relief than from hearing the joke a second time.

Whack. The Doc slaps the shoulder of the man telling the joke, a hard hit but one done from camaraderie. The joke teller flinches from the contact, spilling his drink over the Doc's shoes. Silence. The Doc guffaws and takes a big gulp, not noticing the spillage, and even Larson realises he is holding his breath.

He's on his third can already, and it's strong lager too. Mind you, the Doc is a big man, so maybe he can hold it well. Noticing it getting louder, Larson scans the groups quietly, watching the inhibitions start to fade as the alcohol flows faster.

The Doc throws one arm up, shouting that they need nibbles and aperitifs. 'What kind of cocktail party is this?' he shouts with mock anger. 'Larson, my good man, we are in need of nibbles, I say.'

'Leave it with me,' Larson mutters, almost thankful for a reason to leave the room. Exiting, he nods at Jacob and Nick, a conciliatory nod of men who can't really join the party, the designated drivers that have to go along with the jokes and banter.

'We'll do a sweep,' Jacob says quietly to a return nod from Larson. Leaving the room, the three soon separate as Larson heads upstairs to find Meryl.

'Never seen him drink before,' Jacob remarks as they walk through to the side delivery entrance of the servants' quarters.

'You mean the Doc?'

'Yeah,' Jacob nods. Out of the room, he allows the worry to show on his face, a strange morphing as he drops the guard and allows his features to reflect his true emotions. In the guard room, where the men gathered earlier to drink coffee, Jacob automatically goes to the side door and checks the thick bolts on the inside are driven home. A thick wooden door, ancient and built to withstand a hard battering. Nick almost winces, suspecting this would be the preferred point of entry for Dave.

With his hand on the top bolt, Jacob turns to stare, noticing the flicker of concern on the younger lad's face. They hold, eyes locked, nothing said. Nick watches as Jacob keeps his hand firmly grasped on the lever of the bolt. Dull laughter echoes down the hallway, a rolling boom of thunder still so loud it makes them both flinch. Flashes of lightning strobe the room. Still nothing said.

Slowly, Jacob nods and pulls the bolt back, his eyes fixed on Nick. His hand drops to the middle bolt and repeats the action, drawing it open to slide the solid metal tube out of the locking mechanism. Eyes still locked as Jacob bends down, groping for the third bolt. Without looking what he's doing, his hand flails up and down, side to side, constantly missing the bolt.

'Fuck it,' Jacob mutters, shaking his head. 'You want these left open, yeah?' he asks with a smile.

'Maybe,' Nick laughs at the absurdity of them both still refusing to say anything outright.

'S'the way I'd come in if er ... I was going to try anything sneaky ... Not that I would, of course, Nick. I'm loyal to the Doc.'

'Yeah, you said that, Jacob.'

'Just so we understand each other then–best leave this door open to let some air in. Stuffy in here ...'

'Good idea, mate. I was thinking the same. Maybe leave the light on too?'

'What, this lamp here? The one we're about to walk past and forget to turn off?'

'Yeah, that one.'

'Where now?' Jacob asks. The power shifts, the older man now looking to the newcomer for leadership. They've only known each other a few hours, but the transition is smooth. Almost at breaking point, Jacob was urging himself to stay strong and do his job, get the cure and get out. Nick has a presence, though, an undefined power to him that speaks of something good and decent, and in sheer desperation, Jacob throws caution to the wind and makes the decision, 'I'm in. Whatever it is, I want out of here.'

'Okay,' Nick replies, 'like I said, just stay close no matter what happens.'

'Got it.'

'Other than that, we should do whatever is normal.'

'Yeah,' Jacob nods, a glimmer of hope now alight in his eyes. Maybe? Maybe there is a way out of this. Maybe he doesn't have to stay here and be aware of little boys being abused. He can get away and find his wife and son. No, he *will* get away and find them.

'I'm gagging, Jacob. Can we have a fag here?'

'The Doc wants food for the men,' Larson says from the doorway of the makeshift dormitory. There are beds down both sides of the long room. Double beds, single beds, camp beds, and all of them covered in colourful blankets and duvets. Toys everywhere, and lots of little faces clustered round the maternal figure of Meryl sitting on the floor with her back to a big footboard, reading a story from a book.

'Boys, this'll have to wait,' she says with a sad smile. 'You get into bed now, and I'll come back up later to check on you. Go on now, into bed ... I'll be right out,' she calls out.

Larson waits quietly, letting her know this should be done sooner rather than later, watching as the kind woman ushers the boys to their beds and noticing the newest arrival Billy looking even more lost and confused than before.

'You come with me,' Meryl takes the small boy's hand, leading him to the last bed on the right. 'That's it, get in there, and I'll be back soon.'

'He's drinking,' Larson mutters as Meryl steps out, closing the door behind her. She pauses, nods once, and walks on without saying a word. Sighing deeply, she flinches at another booming clap of thunder shaking the house. Violent bolts of lightning score the grounds outside. If the Doc is drinking, they'll all probably be drinking, and that's all she needs–a house full of terrified boys and drunk, violent men.

Well, the supplies are good, so they can have what they want. In fact, the more food the better to soak the alcohol up. Sandwiches would be better–lots of bread, but unless they can wait a few hours while she bakes some, it will have to be snack food instead.

Larson watches her slip down the stairs. In the darkness of the main corridor, he takes in the flickering candlelight and the huge walls illuminated for the split second of lightning flashes.

Hot and close still, and the humidity must be off the chart. Movement catches his eye. The candles all flicker in a row from the closest to the furthest. A draft but from where?

Then the noise comes. A sudden, intense howling of wind that builds within a few seconds. It gusts through the house, rattling windows and slamming any unlocked doors.

Echoes of drunk men guffawing float between the gaps of noise created by nature. The Doc's voice is easily recognisable.

Staring at the stairs, he slowly looks away to the doors of the Doc's rooms, wondering if he locked them up.

No, he didn't. The door swings open easily. The tiny squeak from the hinges is lost in the cacophony of noise from outside. It's dark in here, no candles. Larson pulls the small LED torch from his pocket and shines the beam round the room.

The examination bed is on one side, the easy chairs and the desk on the other side. Leaving the door slightly ajar, he crosses to the desk. The torch light sweeps over the books stacked up, slips of paper acting as bookmarks. He looks at medical books, encyclopaedias, pharmacy books, and all manner of surgical and medicinal publications.

How close is he? Larson starts flicking through the hand scribbled notes on the jotters. Seeing how scrawly his handwriting is, he smiles as he remembers the age-old joke about doctors having appalling handwriting

Medical terms underlined and scored. *Pathogen. Disease. Infection. Cure.* Basic words that anyone who had seen a medical reality television show would know. Flicking through, he notices the same words are repeated over and over.

On the top page there are new words, the same ones the Doc was talking about earlier. *Prions, parasitoids, protein.*

Marked on the same jotter, there is a reference to a page number and section. The closest book is folded open and left face down. Picking it up, Larson notes the page number is the same as the one on the jotter. A yellow highlighter pen has been used to mark certain words, the same words as on the jotter. *Prion. Protein. Parasitoids.*

Flicking his gaze between the jotter and the pages of the medical book, he remembers what the Doc said earlier.

'***CJD was a prion, which is a form of pathogen that enters the host body and acts as a template, tricking the cell structure to mutate and become like the infected cell. Now, CJD was a prion ...***'

There it is, the same passage in this book. Not word for word but as good as. Grabbing another book, he opens to the pages marked by the slips of paper: *Understanding Basic Medical Terms, Medical Terminology for Students, Basic Field Triage, Level One Training for the First Aider.*

More pages marked on how to apply bandages, dressing, clean wounds, check for broken bones, and recognising brain injuries.

Realisation hits. A sinking feeling that starts in the pit of his stomach, knotting his insides up. Fake. A fucking fraud. A dirty, paedophilic, child abusing cunt posing as a doctor to touch up little kids.

Stick with me, Larson. I'll get us a cure. I'll make us famous.

The words he said in the beginning, the tone, the

implied confidence that he can fix this, can find the cure, and make a vaccine.

I just need time to study.

Dirty bastard. The fact the fraudster tricked him so he could fiddle with boys doesn't bother him. Being tricked, full stop. The blow to his self-belief that he could read people and see through them.

'Larson?' He spins round, startled at his name being called. Jacob and that new lad are standing in the doorway, watching him. 'Everything alright? We, er ... we saw the door open?'

'Yeah,' Larson gasps, 'fine ...'

'Doc downstairs still, is he?' Jacob asks, knowing the answer and already cursing himself for asking the question. Close the door and leave, whatever is going on is nothing to do with him.

'He's a fucking fraud,' Larson spits, unable to contain the rage building. 'He isn't a fucking doctor. The cunt is a fraud, a dirty fucking ... fucking ...'

'What?' Jacob asks, his mouth dropping open.

'Close the fucking door,' Larson snaps. 'The bastard is a fraud. He isn't a fucking doctor. All these books, all these notes ain't about finding a cure. They're all about basic fucking, cunting, shitting, medical shit,' spitting with fury, he glares at the desk.

'Those kids,' Larson seizes on the thing that he knows will anger even the hardest of men. All of them have not only turned blind eye, but actively facilitated the Doc being able to abuse the children on the basis he was going to fix mankind. 'He fiddled with those kids while we waited for him to get the cure ... fucking fucker ...' Larson is seething with rage that blinds him to the point of carelessness.

'Easy, Larson,' Jacob steps forward, holding a placating hand out in an effort to calm him.

'Easy? Easy, Jacob? Fuck that. What the fuck have we been doing here? Dirty cunt ...' He turns back to the desk, shining his torch at the notes as he reads aloud some of the basic words and phrases.

Jacob glances at Nick, a questioning look on his face. Nick nods, equally worried and sensing the explosion about to come off Larson. If he does blow, if he does react, it could jeopardise everything. Mr Howie *will* come tonight. Nick knows it. If Larson starts going nuts now, it could cause problems? Or could it? Can it be beneficial somehow? Cause confusion or mayhem which the others can take advantage off? It's full dark now, and the storm not only rages but builds with power every passing minute. They should be here any minute. But then what if they don't come?

The first nagging doubt descends into Nick's mind. He could have got it completely wrong. He banked on Lilly getting safely to the fort, counting on everyone being okay. Nick hasn't seen any of them since the middle of the fight in the car park. What if they're all dead or injured? That feeling, that bond between them that told him everyone is safe could be wrong, could be a side effect of the heat making him delirious.

The Doc is drunk on strong lager. The chemicals soak into his system and for such a big man, he can't hold his drink very well. The nibbles Meryl brought are being devoured as the pile of empty beer cans grows larger by the second. The howling wind, the thunder and lightning, all ignored as the men drink and drink, becoming raucous and animated. The jokes get course, the language becomes foul as the drunken atmosphere gets wilder.

The Doc grins at the nearest group of men, any sense of keeping the familiarity down, of keeping that sterile distance is gone. He's one of the men now, one of the lads, a fellow drinker that can swear and cuss, tell rude jokes and behave badly.

There's an itch, though. Alcohol does that. It lessens the inhibitions. That itch. It won't go away. This has happened before when he got drunk, which is how he ended up serving time in that sex offenders' hospital and being put on that god-awful sex offenders register, telling them where he lived, letting them come into his house and check his computer. Bastards.

Ah, that itch it just won't go away. Those poor boys, sleeping innocently upstairs. They're probably terrified of the storm and the howling wind outside. God, that thunder hasn't stopped one bit, getting worse if anything, and the rain! Never seen rain like it.

Blasted itch. An urge, a demand, a nasty desire that nags and nags. He knows what he wants, but it's a step too far.

He's the Doc, though. He can do what he wants when he wants. He owns this house and everyone inside it. He's going to find the cure and the vaccine and fix everyone. He'll be worshipped then, and his dirty little secret won't matter. Hell! Mothers will be queuing up to hand their sons over. Yeah, that's right, *I am the Doc, and I can do what I want.*

'Ere, Doc, what about getting us some women 'ere, then?' a big bruiser asks drunkenly. Squat and ugly, with scars on top of scars and faded tribal tattoos down his neck. He is a victor of many fights on the terraces and in the streets after the games. Poland, Germany, Italy. He's fought for his club all over the world, with weapons and with his bare hands. A big man but quick and with a violent streak and a list of convictions to match.

There is a difference between psychotic and naturally violent. A big difference. The naturally violent know right from wrong. To them, violence is almost a sport, a team game to be done when the time is right. You don't kill the opponent, but fuck him up, make him bleed, and maybe break a few bones, but killing? That just means a life sentence.

Psychotic don't care. They just don't care about the consequences. The rage comes, and it must be fed, instantly and without hesitation.

The Doc crosses the room within a split second and drives the point of his large thumb deep into the other man's eye, bursting the pressurised ball within. Screaming, he doesn't go down but quickly backs away, flailing to get the digit from his eye socket. The Doc goes with him, primal rage takes over, blow after blow is given. Fists, elbows; then, as the man goes down, feet are used. He doesn't stop but kicks and stamps at the head until all that remains is a bloodied, dead mess.

'I'M THE DOC,' he screams over and over. 'THE DOC. I'M THE DOC.'

The men watching could tear him apart within seconds if they worked together, but so great is the fear the man brings, they do nothing. The other men watch quietly as all conversation ceases. Cans get put down, men back away fearfully. Not one word is spoken other than the screams given by the Doc.

He stamps and stamps. The skull caves in, but still it doesn't scratch that itch. It does nothing to feed the urge he feels inside. They won't touch me. They won't do anything. Immunity from everything he has, immunity from prosecution, from being judged, from being stopped.

The world is his for the taking. Standing back, he glares round the room, towering over every man present. Eyes wild and unblinking, unaware of the gore stuck to his shoes, uncaring even.

'DRINK THEN,' he roars, 'DRINK. THIS IS WHAT YOU WANTED, SO DRINK.' He picks on one man stood slightly away from the others. Nervously, the man lifts a random can from the table and sips at the edge. Others do the same. Sullen but terrified, they lift cans and drink, not one man even daring to glance at the corpse lying at their feet.

'Enjoy your night, gentlemen. I shall retire and bid you a good evening.' The Doc speaks gently, with the forced tones of a cultured man, but still he's holding that central position as though daring anyone to speak.

Eventually, he walks towards the door, head held high, one hand sweeping the scraggly, grey hair away from his neck.

Breathing hard from the exertion of stamping a man to death, his head swims from the aftereffects of the violence and alcohol. Heart thumping hard, which only serves to give him the sensation of being untouchable.

The sweat flows freely down his face, caught by the flickering illumination of the candles and the flashes of pure energy strafing the sky. To the beat of the rolling thunder, he mounts the stairs, long legs ascending with ease. Hand gripping the rail as the first layer of conscious thought grasps the idea of tucking the boys in while the deeper levels know exactly what he's intending once he's in that room.

At the top of the stairs, he holds still, resting for a minute while he gets his breathing under control. Absentmindedly his hand tugs at the collar of his shirt, pulling it away from his neck. Rolling his head, he eases the tension in his neck. Flashes of light all add to the overwhelming sense of power dripping from his fingers.

Lips twitching with unabated, lustful hunger, he advances towards the door. Step after heavy step. Fingers twitching at the prospect of grasping that door handle and turning it slowly. Eyes now fixed and staring.

It's dark within the room, the boys lie huddled under sheets. Too hot to be covered but too scared to lie on top. Tears stream down faces, small chests heave with quiet sobs, images of parents of siblings and relatives, of the lives they lost dance through their minds. Billy sucks his thumb, something he hasn't done for years. Lilly will come. Lilly will come. He holds that thought, knowing she'll come for him.

The thunder rocks the house, vibrating the very foundations. Lightning forks outside the unsheathed windows. Howling wind roars through every gap and crevice, shaking the old, wooden frames. The boys hear noises of monsters everywhere, but the greatest danger is yet to come as slowly the door handle creaks.

Boys hold their breaths, longing to see the large, friendly shape of Meryl silhouetted in the frame. Swinging open on creaking hinges, they stare into the darkness, waiting, longing, terrified.

'My boys,' the huge figure of the Doc looms in the frame. Flashes of light race across the sky, lighting his drunk, grotesque features, showing the hunger evident on his face as he steps inside and quietly closes the door.

CHAPTER FIFTY-TWO

'I can't go any faster,' I call out.

'Eh? No one said anything,' Clarence stares at me.

'I know, but this feels so slow.'

'Better to get there in one piece,' Clarence mutters. Well, I say mutters but more shouts due to the noise of the storm, 'And we could go faster, but the van behind us can't.'

Sheets of rain lash the road ahead; visibility is reduced to just a few metres. The powerful headlights just bounce the light back off the water, giving a dazzling effect. The route ahead is now featureless. The surface water has pooled so deep as to present a lake. The road is straight, so we keep heading on, ever mindful of much less ground clearance of the van behind us.

'Man, like you know, this thing is built for this,' Ginge calls out. 'Like deep water and bad things, man, you know. Like it can take it.'

'Got to be near the estate now,' I lean forward to peer out, straining to get a glimpse of the ruined area. A wall looms ahead. The dark shape of the side of a house maybe? But no, it's too big.

I can't make it out. There wasn't anything this big here before. Dave saw to that when he blew the estate up. What is that?

Slower now, edging forward as crackling static fills the Saxon. Suddenly, a fork of lightning shoots down straight in front of us. The glimpse is less than a second, but it's enough to have my foot on the brake instantly. Despite the slow speed, the Saxon lurches to a halt, jarring everyone inside.

'What?' Clarence shouts. Dave moves up to stand behind and view out the front. They all do.

'No, no way,' I mutter, 'not possible.'

'What isn't?' Lani urges.

Lightning again, long and sustained as several separate forks hit, one after the other, giving a series of strobe-like flashes of illumination, revealing everything in perfect, gory detail.

Gasps sound out behind me. A wall in front of us stretches as far as we can see. Six feet in height and solidly built, with no gaps. Meredith growls, deep and resonant. Lips pulling up, she locks eyes on towards the front.

They've done this before. No. *It* has done this before. In the car park last night, they did this, using their own fallen to make a corpse wall. But this one is bigger and better made.

When the lightning strikes again, we all look to where the enormous mounds of bodies were stacked up, waiting to be burnt. We know they'll be gone, but visual evidence is needed.

They are gone. Instead, the human remains have been made into bricks–limbs and torsos jammed together.

'How did you not see this?' I shout at Clarence.

'Wasn't there,' he growls. 'I saw the fucking mounds. It wasn't built yet.'

'It wasn't,' Dave cuts in. 'When we came back, it was normal.'

'They did this in what? Half an hour?'

'Looks that way,' Clarence mutters.

'Where the fuck they coming from? We got thousands again last night,' Cookey asks. 'Where? Where from?'

'I told you,' Dave says flatly, 'there will be millions. The population was at fifty million when it started ... A few thousand kills is nothing.'

'Not now, though. We've got to get Nick,' Lani says. 'Punch through, just go ...' she urges.

'We can't leave the fort.'

'It's moving,' Dave cuts in again.

'What?' I shout in disbelief. We wait in silence for another flash of light. At the same time as thunder splits the air apart, we see a multitude of forks hitting the wall. It is moving, inching closer every second. The weight of it must be immense. There must be thousands not only holding it in place but pushing it along. More than that as the numbers of the killed in those mound were well into the thousands. Staggering in scale, terrifying in the noise of the storm.

A vicious wind starts to pick up, a low, groaning noise that quickly grows to a wild howl. It's so powerful it buffets the Saxon on its hinges. Crackle and static from the radio. The atmospheric conditions so bad it's rendering the transmission from the van just a few feet behind us to a broken hiss.

'TURN BACK,' Clarence transmits again and again. Closer now. The wall keeps coming. So solidly made, it sends little waves of surface water scooting in front of it.

No GPMG, no assault rifles, no grenades, no cannon,

no anything. Fucking sawn-off shotguns, a few pistols, some axes, and an angry dog. And Dave. As good as he is, even he can't fight of thousands by himself.

'We can't stop them. They're too wide. We'll have to go back,' I twist round to stare at the others.

'I can't,' Lilly says firmly.

'Listen,' Lani snaps, 'you're with us now. You go out, and you'll be dead in minutes.'

'But ...'

'No buts,' I cut her off. 'We stay together.'

'And do what?' Clarence asks with a shrug. 'And what with?'

'Fuck knows, but we'll figure it out as we go. Dave, how long till they reach the fort?'

'At that speed?' He pauses. 'An hour, maybe an hour and a half.'

'No boats,' I say more to myself.

'Boss, we can't put people in boats in this wind.'

'Van's turned round,' Cookey yells from peering out the back. I start the turn, driving backwards onto what I know is solid ground. Pausing at the turn, we all stare across at the wall of infected, knowing our friends and families are within it.

Think, Howie. Think. There will be a way. Even if we destroy that wall, that still leaves the several thousand that must be beyond it, and we're cut off from the mainland now, stuck on this spit of land.

With a sinking feeling of abandoning Nick and cursing foully, I turn back, towards the fort. Nobody speaks, and even the sound of the big engine is lost to the calamitous noise outside. The wind is getting stronger by the second, howling over the flatlands so much it whips the surface spray up into waves that roll and crest with no discernible pattern.

Visibility is down to the lowest so far, and within a few metres, the wall is lost from view. Surely even they can't keep pushing a wall of bodies that size in this weather.

Slowing down, we watch as the van ahead of us slowly navigates the treacherous route. The rear doors get ripped open, yanking them from Cookey's hands. Shouts inside as they all work to pull them closed, heaving with every bit of strength they have.

Clarence clambers over, into the back, moving swiftly to grasp the doors and heave them closed. Just before they slam shut, we see the corpse wall shuffling into view. It looks dark, black, and fucking big. Grotesquely made from shapes so easily identified as once being of the human form.

It's the coordination that staggers me. That not only must they be pushing at the same time but also holding the bodies in place as they do. Human remains are soft, and after so many days left festering in big mounds in the increasing heat, they will be gooey as anything. Pushing them will just cause those at the base to fall apart. Surely the whole thing can't be lifted clear off the ground?

Can it?

CHAPTER FIFTY-THREE

Physics. Matter and energy.

The wall is the matter to be moved. The hosts are the energy. Apply mathematics and a logical execution of weight to body ratio and the wall is lifted.

Howie was right, the base layer of bodies would get squashed, dragged, and fall apart. This was accounted for once human bricks were slotted into place.

The expenditure of energy is vast. The host bodies now use sustained strength to hold the wall clear of the ground. The weight is distributed evenly between every host body.

Thousands of pairs of hands lift while thousands of pairs of hands hold the bricks in place. Together those thousands move forward in perfect synchrony.

Like a Roman Testudo. Soldiers interlocking their shields and stepping in perfect time to present a solid unbroken line towards the enemy, so they shuffle left and right, left and right. If they wore hobnail boots on a parade square, the timing would be perfect.

The wall is ever so slightly angled back, towards the hosts. This has been calculated to prevent the bodies falling forward. The tallest hosts are used to apply pressure to the top of the wall, and in doing so, they prevent bodies falling out.

It will take time to advance the distance, but the infection has time. The infection knows there is nowhere for the inhabitants of the fort to go. The weather is too wild to allow an escape via the sea.

There weren't enough bodies to stretch fully from one side of the flatlands to the other, but fortunately, the reduced visibility means the survivors couldn't see that. The appearance of a solid, unbroken wall was enough to send them scuttling back.

To use the terminology favoured by this region of survivors: Howie is fucked.

CHAPTER FIFTY-FOUR

'I'm saying we sit on it, do nothing, and wait till tomorrow,' Larson says. Calm now, the wild fury ebbing away as he starts scheming and plotting. To take action now, while everyone is so drunk, could be disastrous.

'And I agree,' Jacob sighs, repeating himself for the third or fourth time. Ten minutes they've been in here, talking quietly, and still Larson goes on, almost like he's trying to convince Jacob and Nick of his plans, get them on side, and form allegiances.

Nick listens patiently, knowing that every minute wasted is a minute closer to Mr Howie coming, but the night is getting on now, so where are they? Figuring the weather must be delaying them, he leans against the wall and closes his eyes for a second. It's still so hot and clammy, and he sweats just standing here.

'Yeah,' Larson nods quickly, 'we see who's with us; then, we strike. Get rid of him. Quickly, though, cos he's strong, unpredictable, and quick too.'

'Course, Larson, tomorrow. We'll get it all sorted then, but now's not the time, is it? Not with everyone drinking,'

Jacob reinforces the message, noticing the discrete nod from Nick. Stall for time, keep him calm, and just wait.

'Dirty bastard,' Larson groans, 'a fucking cure, a fucking vaccine ... a fucking ... WHAT the fuck is that?' Larson yelps at the strangled yell wailing down the corridor between the thunderous claps booming from the sky.

'The boys,' Jacob spins round to lunge out the door and sprint down the corridor, with Nick and Larson right behind him.

'COME HERE,' the Doc orders. Loud, angry, and drunk. It floats clearly down the hall from the boys' room, bringing Jacob to a sudden stop. The instinct has already been ingrained not to stop the Doc doing what he wants, ignore everything, and turn a blind eye.

'Wait,' Larson hisses from right behind them, 'don't go in ... Listen, we got to be cool about this.'

'NOOOO,' a terrified wail from a young boy whilst others cry in abject fear. More scream and add to the terror from within. Lightning flashes across the three men as they come to a stop outside the door. Nick gets ready, his eyes fierce and determined, staring between the two men.

'I said TOUCH IT,' the Doc roars from the other side of the closed door. 'TOUCH IT NOW!'

'I'm going in,' Nick growls.

'You ain't!' Larson snaps, stepping in front of Nick.

'Get out the way,' Nick stares at the guard leader, eyes fixed and unblinking.

'Who the fuck do you think you are?' Larson hisses. 'Fuck off, you little cunt. We ain't going in there, are we, Jacob? I said ... are we, Jacob?'

'THAT'S IT ... TOUCH IT ... TOUCH IT PROPERLY.'

'Move,' Nick snarls.

'Jacob, get this fucker away from me. We wait till tomorrow.'

'Larson, we can't ...'

'What, Jacob?' Larson turns on the other guard. 'We can't what?'

'We can't leave them,' Jacob mutters, torn between what to do. The sounds of crying are clear. The boys are being terrorised, but Jacob has seen what the Doc can do. The man terrifies him, his temper and brutal violence. The size of him, with those huge hands and the wild eyes he gets.

'We fucking can, and we fucking will,' Larson snaps, stepping to the side to block Nick trying to move past him. 'Do that again, nipper, and I'll fucking have y–' the words cut off as Nick lunges in with a quick headbutt, slamming his forehead into Larson's nose. As the man staggers, Nick moves in with quick, hard punches, striking into the man's face until he goes down under a flurry of blows.

Once down, Nick jumps back, unaware of the shock on Jacob's face at the speed the young lad moved at. Grabbing the door handle, he wrenches it open, surging into the big dormitory.

The sight that greets him is one of pure evil. The Doc, the huge, rangy, sinewy man standing centrally amongst the boys forced into kneeling positions in a circle around him.

Bright forks and violent, crackling sheets burst through the sky, one after the other. He is naked from the waist down but still has his shoes on; trousers and pants dumped nearby. Standing there with a swollen erection while he moves from boy to boy, forcing them to reach out and touch him.

'GET OUT,' The Doc roars with intense fury. 'LARSON ...' the Doc slaps the boy touching him, a back handed strike that sends the boy flying off to hit a wooden footboard with a sickening crunch of bones. 'GET OUT, GET OUT,' the Doc rages again, turning towards Nick with his manhood standing proud. Boys scream and cry, cowering down from the attack, the lightning, the sexual assault, and the wind howling to rattle the wooden-framed windows.

'Cunt.' Nick moves forward, fists clenched, and eyes fixed on the huge form of the fraudulent doctor.

'Nick!' Jacob shouts in warning, trying to reach out and pull the lad away.

'HERE ... UP HERE ...' Larson screams at the top of his voice, 'GUARDS UP HERE...' Bleeding heavily from his nose, he flicks his gaze quickly between the open door to the dormitory and the stairs.

Jacob holds the shotgun, but the man is struck senseless, rooted to the spot in shock as he watches Nick charge weaponless at the half naked man.

With a yell, the Doc feels the psychotic rage descend once more. To be disturbed at this time, to be seen doing this, and he will unleash hell on this young newcomer. The temper flares and breaks as he lashes out with one shoe-clad foot, slamming into the face of a child, which sees him careering away like a doll.

The boys become objects to be trashed, things that are in his way. Full of perverted sexual craze, he starts rampaging with blind ferocity.

Nick moves fast, seeing the damage being wrought. Charging full on, he lunges at the Doc with a roar, only to be grabbed and lifted bodily off the ground by two strong hands and flung aside, sailing through the air to land in a crumpled, sprawling heap.

Refusing to be stunned, Nick twists as he strikes the

ground. Rotating his body to face up and expecting to see the Doc coming in for the after-attack.

Thunder booms within the room, too close and too loud. The shotgun blast drowns every other sound as Jacob pulls the trigger at the first guard appearing at the top of the stairs. The shaven-headed, drunk man is taken from his feet by the power of the pellets striking him in his chest. Larson lunges for Jacob, weaving to the side as Jacob pulls the trigger for the second barrel.

Nick and the Doc land in a heap, fighting viciously as more guards appear at the top of the stairs. The Doc, in full on rage now, stamps and kicks his way through the room. Still half naked and erect, the blood hammers through his system. Lust, fury, violence, and psychosis erupt as he grabs beds and launches them with ease across the room. Boys are sent flying, some crawling away sobbing from blind terror.

The Doc stalks towards Nick, smashing everything in his path. There is bedlam at the top of the stairs as Jacob fends Larson off to gain his feet and stagger into the dormitory, slamming the door shut.

This has all gone wrong, horribly wrong. Jacob has made it clear which side he chooses, firing at his own comrades and killing one of them. He then tried to shoot Larson and made the deadly mistake of missing.

Miraculously, Jacob still holds the shotgun, and his panicked fingers work to break the barrel in an effort to reload. All the time, he pushes his back against the door, trying to prevent it being opened.

Where the hell is Dave? Where is Clarence to come charging into the room full of Viking fury to tear the Doc to pieces? Where is Meredith, launching through the eye with her fearless courage?

'Fuck,' Nick gasps, staring up at the demented man coming at him with a wild, feral look.

CHAPTER FIFTY-FIVE

'Maddox, we need the gates barricaded from the inside, both gates ...'

'On it,' he turns away, shouting orders at his crews who are already bursting away.

'Weapons from the armoury, get everything out and ready and all the ammunition, shotguns, sawn-offs, rifles, fucking everything,' I shout at Blowers who is just a few feet away. The noise of the storm drowns out my normal voice, and I haven't got time to be repeating myself.

The rain drives down, and despite the high walls, the gusts of wind are incredible in strength. Tents have already been ripped from the ground to get buffeted against the side. The howling, whistling noise of the wind, coupled with the thunder, is a full-on assault of the senses. The rain lashes in from every direction from the twisting wind.

Surface water stands everywhere, the ground simply too hard and dry to absorb it.

'They can't get through or round, so they'll go over,' I shout at the people gathered round me. 'Spread the word.

We need everyone on the walls, let them come over the first one so we can fire down with whatever we've got left; then, we meet them on the top of the inner walls. There's no way out of this, they're coming ...'

Fucking shotguns and rifles. That's it, oh, and a few pistols too, but against thousands? We are royally fucked, and we know it.

We can't even punch out with vehicles. The water on the ground outside is too deep for nearly all our vehicles now.

Sorry, Nick, we were coming, mate, I promise. That hurts more than anything. Not that they're coming for us again, but that we left Nick on his own. I really cannot see a way out of this, not this time. There's too many, and without weapons, we simply don't have a hope in hell.

Yeah, Dave can kill faster than anything alive, but he can't stop all of them. They'll get inside, and they'll take everyone.

'That's it,' I shout at the waiting faces, 'there's no plan this time, no way out. We fight until the last one falls ...'

'Again,' Dave adds. Everyone stares at him, but he just looks back blandly and shrugs. He stares at me and smiles. A sudden, startling grin that stuns every single one of us.

'What?' he asks as though we're all idiots. 'It doesn't end here.'

'Dave ... I ... fucking speechless, mate.'

'That'll be a first then,' Lani quips, a quick roll of her eyes.

Taking a step closer to me so she can be heard over the storm, Lilly stares with unsuppressed concern. 'I have to get out. I am getting out ... Billy is on his own, and I promised Nick ...'

'There's no way through ...'

'Listen, thank you for everything you have done, but I have to leave,' she cuts me off, speaking politely but very firmly.

'Lilly, I get it. Nick is one of us, and leaving him alone is against everything we stand for, but there is simply no way through this. We might stand a chance punching through with the Saxon, but that means taking people from here which we just can't do.'

'What about Dave?' she demands on the verge of panic. 'You said ... Nick said he can do anything ...'

'We can't lose Dave from here,' I reply as softly as possible, given the fact of having to shout.

'I wouldn't leave,' Dave adds.

'I'll go,' Roy steps in, shouting to be overheard, he looks first at Lilly then at me. 'One won't make that much difference against so many, and my bow is no good in this weather anyway.'

'Yes! Please, Mr Howie, please ... I have to get Billy, and you can't just leave Nick on his own.'

'Stop saying it like that,' Lani flares up, 'and grow up. We'd never leave any of our team anywhere, and any one of us would risk everything to save a child, but we've hundreds of people here to defend.'

'Oh god,' the girl cries, 'I just can't leave him. Please, Mr Howie, let Roy come with me, please.'

'Roy, you sure?' I ask, trying to work out the motivation behind it.

'Definitely,' he nods, 'the storm is good cover, and I've got night vision glasses–that gives me an advantage. If you can make a hole with the Saxon to get me through in a van ...'

'Just take the Saxon.'

'No point, Mr Howie, can't fit loads of children in that thing.'

'You can,' Clarence cuts in. 'They'll fit, and it's about the only thing we've got that'll get through that lot and keep going in this weather. This wind will have a van over on its side.'

'No offence, Roy, but what's one man going to do against a house full of people?'

'No offence, Mr Howie, but the girl is right. She made a promise, and you can't leave her brother alone. If we all die here tonight, he'll be left on his own. We have to get the girl out ... If nothing else, I can get a message to Nick, letting him know the situation here, and also, no offence again, Mr Howie, but the inside of a house is dry, and I *can* use my bow.'

'Do it,' Clarence urges, 'it's worth a shot if even one of us gets through to Nick.'

'Okay, now then ... You go right now while we have a chance. Get the Saxon ready, and both of you, listen. You tell Nick we tried coming for him, you tell him that no matter what happens to us to keep going and stay strong, and you tell him how proud I am of him.'

'Me too,' Clarence adds, 'all of us.'

'Got it,' Roy nods.

'Thank you,' Lilly throws her arms round my neck, 'thank you, Mr Howie.'

'You stay by Nick, you hear me? Do what he says and stay close to him.'

'I will, I promise.'

'Go, go now ...'

'CLEAR THE GATES,' Maddox walks off, shouting

ahead. Blowers moves quickly. Getting two sawn-offs and a load of shotgun cartridges, he hands them over.

We push them into the Saxon, and we slam the doors closed. The youths moving quickly to clear the vehicles from the gate.

Heading down to the front, we watch as the outer gates are swung open to reveal the lake that is now the flatlands. Roy revs the powerful engine with a determined look on his face, and I notice Paula biting her bottom lip in concern at him going. Did he say goodbye to her? If he did, I must have missed it.

'GO, GO FAST, AND GET THROUGH,' Clarence roars as Roy nods back, the night-vision goggles already on his forehead, ready to be pulled down.

Surging away, the vehicle quickly gathers speed, powering through the surface water with ease. No sign of the infected yet, but visibility is reduced so much, they could be thirty metres away, and we wouldn't see them.

The Saxon disappears into the gloom. After a split second, a dull thud reaches us and the screaming pitch of the Saxon being forced. Straining our ears, we listen as the sound of the engine gets further away.

'They got through,' Dave nods.

'Sure?'

'Definitely got through,' he adds confidently.

Sighing, I stare out for a few seconds, feeling like shit for leaving Nick on his own. Turning back, I look into the fort and the people gathered there, and for a second, I wonder if it's really worth it. Is this place worth the cost? So many good people have died defending it. Maybe we should just leave it, let the infected have it, let anyone who wants it have it. We could find somewhere else, somewhere far away in the middle of nowhere. Why here? Why this place? Why this fort?

That's it, though, too many sacrifices have been made for us to walk away now. Not that we could walk away if we wanted to, not with that fucking lot coming at us.

Still, Dave says it doesn't end here, so it must be true.

CHAPTER FIFTY-SIX

'Brace yourself,' Roy shouts as the wall comes suddenly into view from the gloom of the pelting rain. Lilly grabs whatever she can grasp and uses her feet to push her back into the seat. With his foot on the floor, Roy knows they'll have one chance at this. They need to be straight on with maximum power. His determination peaks as the details of the corpse wall get picked out by the headlights.

The impact is bone-jarring but thankfully over in a few seconds. The weight, power, and speed of the vehicle decimate the small section, sending bodies flying off as it bursts through. The sight of the thousands of infected on the reverse side is staggering, but again, Roy pushes on, knowing that to slow now will be disastrous.

Rocking on the suspension as they plough over everything in their path, they make headway, slamming bodies aside with loud thunks as the thick metal plating of the front end explodes heads and breaks bones with ease.

Then it's done. They burst through, with just the apparent lake in front of them; waves getting whipped up by the howling wind.

'We're through,' Roy shouts, glancing over at Lilly who's sat with her eyes tightly closed. She blinks them open and looks about as a small grin spreads across her face. Breathing a sigh of relief, she nods at the driver.

'Thank you,' she says in earnest. 'I ...'

'It's okay,' Roy shrugs it off. For the first time in many years, he feels a pang of guilt that his own selfish actions have forced him to lie and deceive.

Since the meeting with Lilly in the offices and hearing about a doctor, he hasn't stopped thinking about it. A real doctor that can examine him and check his ailments. A proper, medically trained, actual doctor. He stayed quiet, biting down the urge to leave instantly and head that way. When the team did move out, coming up against the wall was devastating for him.

Offering his services to get Lilly out was a natural step, but now, actually being out and away leaves a nasty taste in his mouth. He didn't even say goodbye to Paula or to any of the others either. They just loaded up and left.

He has an uncomfortable moment of self-reflection. After so many years of suffering anxiety and obsessive behaviour, he has become adept at masking emotions and strives to satisfy the never-ending urge to be medically examined.

They are good people, though. Good people trying to do their best and, for the most, succeeding at it. Mr Howie is amazing, the way he listens to everyone, yet has that presence, that power which just oozes from him. Maddox too, so young but so self-assured, so very capable and ready to do what it takes. All of them have unique skills which bring something to the group.

Paula fits in perfectly with them. Her ability to plan ahead and execute those plans is fantastic. They would never have got through last night if it wasn't for Paula. Actually, they would never have got through last night if it wasn't for all of them.

Maddox and his energy, his crews so willing to fight for him. Paula and her planning. Mr Howie and his team, so experienced and deadly. Even Roy taking the runners down with his bow, then taking his sword up at the end.

Team. It was a team effort. A real, true team that stuck together and achieved something only *because* they worked together.

And here he is, deserting them on the pretence of helping Lilly and Nick while all the time thinking of himself and his desire to be near a doctor.

This young girl is willing to sacrifice her own life to save her brother, and he could see the torment in Howie's eyes at being forced to leave Nick on his own.

He realises he is selfish and self-obsessed. Well, that changes right now. *I might have left for the wrong reasons, but I can see this through for the right ones. Find Nick and get the children, that's what matters.*

For the first time in his adult life, he stops probing the inside of his mouth, he stops feeling for lumps, he stops tensing the various parts of his body in an effort to detect what's hurting and what feels wrong. There is a task to be done, a job at hand, and people are counting on him.

He never said goodbye to Paula, and more importantly, he never said thank you to her either.

A determined focus descends on the man. Almost like being seated in the driver's position of the Saxon does something, changes him. The good of Howie and those who have sat here leave a presence that absorbs into his system, banishing the selfishness away.

Gripping the wheel, he stares ahead, unaware that the dark, brooding look the team have has now settled behind his intelligent eyes.

CHAPTER FIFTY-SEVEN

'EYES FRONT,' Dave bellows at the very top of his voice. Everyone hears him, the gods above the thunder probably hear him. Fucking hell, Nick has probably just heard him.

Eyes snap forwards. We are on top of the inner wall now, and for long minutes we've waited until the wall shuffles into view. Solid and unbroken, with no sign of where the Saxon went through.

So big, so bloody big. Just the sight of it is evil. Something from the worst nightmare you could ever imagine, a monstrosity dragged up from hell.

Driving torrential rain, howling wind that threatens to knock us off our feet, thunder booming so close overhead we keep flinching and ducking. Forks of lightning bursting in jagged flashes that give daylight for a split second.

From our height advantage, as the wall gets closer, we start to see the infected beyond it. Shapes at first, shadows of darker patches which gradually take form. When they become clear, it serves to lessen the fear, for we know this isn't some magical thing being moved by a means unknown.

There are thousands of infected pushing it. No need too

because we don't have the weapons to hurt them at this range, but fuck it, let them exhaust themselves pushing a needless defensive wall.

'Look,' Lani prods me in the shoulder, motioning for me to look away to the side. Waves. Big, rolling waves pound and crash into the side of the fort. As I watch, I realise they are getting bigger, more violent by the second.

It's like something from a movie or a documentary about faraway places. The sea is immense, with enormous waves cresting with white foam whipped by the wind. A living thing that we have only seen as a calm, placid beast for the last two weeks. To think we were swimming in these same waters a little while ago is amazing.

The storm moves up a gear and gets worse. Staggering from the wind, I have to bend over to stay upright and watch as Lani grabs hold of Clarence. Dave simply adjusts his position to let the wind flow round him and doesn't take his eyes off the wall.

Blowers and Cookey grin like idiots at the wind. I watch amazed as Cookey gives Blowers a little shove and watches him stagger away in the wind, pissing himself with laughter at the sight. Even now, with all this going on, they still piss about, and I get a pang of sadness at knowing Nick would be joining in with them.

Meredith stands with her head held high, eyes closed, and enjoying the sensation of the wind against her face. Her coat is soaked from the rain, but it isn't cold. If anything, it's still too hot.

The wall inches forward.

The angles of the two walls means we lose sight as the corpse wall disappears under the lea of the outer wall. The infected spread behind them keep going forwards as though walking through the wall.

Nothing happens, and for a second, we wonder if that's it–they're just going to wait there in siege until we either starve or give up. I catch confused glances from people trembling in fear on the inner wall.

We know what they're going to do, so we wait for the first one to appear. Single and solitary, a pair of clawed hands grasps the top of the outer wall. The rest of the body soon follows, a snaking figure with skin grey and drawn in deathly pallor and lank dark hair that would have once framed a beautiful face.

It looks about while growling and hissing, searching for the next move. The infection watches through those eyes, and then more hands appear, more heads, and more bodies of the infected.

Slow and steady, they crest that wall. I was expecting a violent, fast surge, but not so. Almost like they know we can't fight back from our position.

The fear that ripples through the people gathered on the inner wall is visible. Men and women alike shake with terror at the unearthly sight.

The human corpse wall is now being used as a ladder, a climbing frame of limbs and torsos. They spread out low along the wall in a never-ending surge. Gunshots ring out as shotguns take pot shots. The range is close enough, and a few drop, which prompts others to commence firing, and soon the cacophony of small arms fire adds to the thunder overhead, the muzzle flashes dull against the superior flashes of the forked lightning.

The wind increases, a violent, solid thing that seems full of fury and rage and hell bent on seeking revenge on us for our level of wanton destruction.

Looking round, I see none of my team are firing, neither is Maddox or a few of his select people. Paula refrains as well. Instead, we watch while everyone else takes shots and makes themselves feel better by killing the few they can get, hoping to stem the tide.

They soon fill the first wall and start dropping down, literally plummeting down to the alley between the walls. The first few are seriously injured from the impact but clearly sacrifice themselves to provide a soft landing for those that follow.

The infected drop to land on the soft bodies. Staggering away uninjured, they move towards the base of the inner wall.

The flow is thick now, like ants crawling along a log, swarming over any object in their way.

I roll my head side to side and start to ease the tightness in my shoulders. Hefting the axe, I feel the reassuring weight of it, the shaft firm within my grasp. Others start doing the same, getting battle-ready. Grim faces watch and assess, hearts start beating faster now, flooding our bodies with adrenalin.

Lani holds her meat clever steady. Dave, as always, completely composed. A look of pure calmness settles on his face whilst his two knives rest with the blades turned up against his forearms.

Blowers and Cookey side by side, both shaking water out their eyes. Meredith grows visibly in front of my eyes as the hair on the back of her neck stands up. Her feet are planted, lips pulled up, and eyes–the same as us–are fixed, dark, and ready.

'Dave, get everyone to spread out,' I call out.

'SPREAD OUT ACROSS THE WALL ... SPREAD OUT NOW,' his voice dominates the scene and makes me smile. They must have heard that, those thousands of infected coming at us. How many times now have they heard Dave bellowing the orders I give. Sure, the odds this time are overwhelmingly against us, and there really is no way out of this, but we stand together. We'll kill many, of that there is no doubt, but when our blades become dull and our arms become heavy, they will still outnumber us by the thousands.

'It doesn't end here? Is that what you said, Dave?' I ask with a pointed look.

He turns and smiles, a sudden, quick movement that lights his face up. Nodding at me and then, staring defiantly to the whole team, to everyone. Lightning behind him, thunder overhead, and Dave is a god of war. He was born to do this, born to destroy.

'THIS,' he roars after sucking a huge lungful of air in, and his voice matches that of the thunder, rolling and booming for all to hear, ' IS NOT THE END.' My god, the man is transformed. He isn't the small, quiet man we all know. He is alive, energy fiercely burning within him. 'THIS IS A FIGHT LIKE ANY OTHER, AND WE WILL PREVAIL ... WE WILL SURVIVE ... YOU SEE THAT MAN.' He holds one knife out in my direction, his arm rock-steady and his face shining. That voice of his is unlike anything I have ever known.

Everyone stares at me, every man and woman on the top of this wall stare directly at me, 'HE IS MR HOWIE, AND THEY FEAR HIM ...'

The ways he says it, with that voice growing louder by the second, holds everyone captivated. 'HE CANNOT BE TURNED ... HE IS IMMUNE ... HE IS MR HOWIE, AND THEY ...' he holds the other knife out to the infected scaling the outer wall, '... THEY CANNOT HURT HIM.'

Thanks, Dave. Thanks a lot, mate, really appreciate that pep talk you just did there. Now everyone is staring at me with wonder and awe in their faces, apart from Lani who just rolls her eyes. Blowers and Cookey grin at the sight, knowing how bloody uncomfortable this is for me.

I tell you what, though. It's worked. Backs are stiffer, jaws are set, and weapons are gripped–knives, sticks, and anything else that can be taken up with such short notice.

I give everyone a firm-lipped smile and nod while thanking the gods it's pissing down with rain, which'll hide the deep blush on my face.

'STAND FAST AND STAND READY,' Dave bellows, clearly getting into the swing of being the spokesperson for the latest fort battle. 'IT DOESN'T END HERE.'

'We're fucked, aren't we?' Lani mutters nearby.

'Yep,' I reply, 'completely.'

'Agreed,' Clarence adds.

'Fucking funny, though,' Cookey grins.

'Is ...' Blowers nods. 'Secret's out now,' he laughs.

'S'alright, we're gonna be wiped out in a few minutes anyway,' I shrug.

'Nah, Dave said we're gonna be alright,' Clarence says in a slightly sarcastic tone. 'Yeah, our hundred, maybe two hundred against their thousands.'

'Oh well, we're here, so best get on with it. Lads, for what it's worth ... What?' I stop as Lani starts smirking.

'Nothing,' Lani replies.

'You're laughing at me.'

'You always say that thing ... *Lads, for what it's worth, it's been a pleasure ...*' she mimics my voice.

'I do not,' I exclaim indignantly.

'You so do,' she shouts. 'I'm surprised you don't have some speakers up here to play rock music and get everyone holding hands while staring wistfully out to sea with your hair flapping in the wind.'

'Don't hold back, Lani,' I say with a hurt tone.

'Well,' she recoils, 'it's all so bloody macho, so ... so ... well, just blokey ...'

'Er ... we're blokes,' Cookey says.

'I'm not. Paula isn't, and neither is Meredith.'

'So what would you prefer?' I ask her.

'What?' she asks.

'Go on. So instead of the honourable speech thing, what else should I do?'

'I don't know, just something normal that isn't so ... so ... clichéd,' she shrugs at the end.

'Clichéd? I'm not clichéd. Am I? Lads?'

'No, boss,' Clarence shakes his head, 'not at all.'

'I don't think so,' Blowers decides. 'I never noticed it.'

'Oh, right, well, clearly I'm wrong then.'

'Lani, are you on your period?' Cookey asks, taking a swift step away as we all burst out laughing.

'No, I'm not!' she shouts. 'Men! Can't have an opinion without being accused of being menstrual.'

'Mental more like.' The lad can't help himself, darting out of reach of both women glaring at him.

'Cookey! One more comment from you...'

'Sorry, Lani,' he smiles sweetly, 'sorry ... Lani ... Sorry, Lani ... Lani? Sorry, Lani.' He steps closer and closer with the look of a child on his face, facing down but peering up with sad puppy eyes. She huffs and puffs for a second but crumbles and starts smiling, then grinning until she bursts out laughing.

'Ah,' Cookey shouts, 'you love us really.'

'Yeah, I do,' Lani laughs, 'bloody idiot.'

'Paula,' he turns the charm round with a big grin.

'Don't even try it,' she snaps.

'Paula, sorry, Paula ... Paula? Sorry, Paula,' he goes full puppy dog mode now, drooping his shoulders and making his eyes wide. 'Paula? I am sorry, Paula ... Don't be angry ...' he shuffles closer, looking at the ground; then glancing up, he gives a little huff as though about to cry. Blowers almost wets himself at the sight. Even I'm laughing hard and can hear Clarence chuckling away.

'Yes, alright!' Paula tries snapping but can't help herself and laughs, shaking her head at the absurdity of it all.

'Yes!' Cookey shouts. 'You love us too, don't you, Paula? Don't you, Paula? Don't you ...?'

'Yes,' she shouts, 'I love you all.' She shouts at the very moment the thunder stops, making everyone turn to face her with puzzled glances.

'Alex!' Dave shouts.

'Yes, Dave. Sorry, Dave,' he steps back in, beside Blowers.

'We have a big horde coming at us, Alex.'

'Yes, Dave.'

'So now is not the time for high jinks.'

'No, Dave. Sorry, Dave.'

'Anymore and you'll be brewing up for the rest of your life.'

'Which is about twenty minutes, by the looks of it.'

'Alex!'

'Sorry, Dave, I didn't mean it.'

'You'll be lucky to see the next twenty minutes if you carry on like that.'

'Yes, Dave.'

'Dave, were you ever a sergeant by any chance?' Clarence calls out.

'No, rank didn't really apply in my unit.'

'Oh, shame. Suits you,' the big man says as he hefts his axe. 'Not long now, by the looks of it.'

Turning back, I blanch at the sight of the infected now pouring over the wall and dropping onto the soft layer of bodies underneath. Dave edges forward to look down, nodding as he does so.

'They doing it again?' I ask.

'They are, Mr Howie, using themselves as a base to climb ... DON'T JUST STAND THERE, SHOOT THEM,' he shouts at a group stood nearby, rooted to the spot in fear. They physically jump at his voice and quickly aim down to recommence the firing.

'If anyone gets away from this, find Nick,' I call out.

'Will do,' Blowers nods seriously. The joking is done now, the humour gone. We grip our weapons and wait as the wind builds to what must be hurricane force. The rain pelts so hard it almost stings, like pinpricks jabbing again and again at our skin.

The thunder builds stronger and deeper, rolling claps that split the air apart with forked lightning. A huge, jagged flash crackles the air, lancing down to strike the top of the outer wall, flinging infected aside like they are made of paper. The static in the air from being so close is bizarre like standing near one of those Tesla machines.

'Howie,' Lani calls my name as softly as the roaring noise will allow. Turning round, she's next to me, smiling up with kindness in her eyes. She kisses me softly on the lips. 'I love you,' she mouths. For a second, I am lost as my heart soars and booms like the thunder above.

'I love you too ... with all my heart, I love you ...'

'INCOMING,' Dave's voice roars from behind me, but I hold still, pausing as I refuse to let those filthy fucking things take this away.

'Always and forever, Lani.' Our eyes hold as the line bursts to activity. 'Whatever happens ...'

'Go ...' she looks at me with such intensity, it strikes my soul, 'go now, Howie, do your thing, do it ... do it now ... They need you...' She speaks quickly, searching my eyes for the spark that drives the infected away. 'There it is. There's my Howie,' she says as the rage starts building inside me. The growling, hissing, fetid stench of them offends me. They've driven Nick apart from the group, they've used my family's and friends' remains as a fucking ladder, and they just ruined the happiest moment of my life. They will pay.

Rolling my head, I lift my axe high in challenge as I walk towards the infected cresting the top of our wall.

My spine ripples as electric current runs down my arms, strength floods into my legs, and my vision becomes crystal clear. I can see every drop of rain as it falls and feel every variance of the wind as it buffets my face.

Breathing harder, heart booming. They can't turn me. My grip is strong on the axe shaft. You failed to turn me. Striding forward, I see the first hands grip the ledge. The alley between the walls is thick with them, and more are coming, pouring over the outer wall.

Running down, I burst in front of the line with my axe raised and ready, timing it perfectly as the first one gains his feet to bare those filthy teeth at me. An uppercut takes him clean off his feet and sends him sailing high into the air to fall slowly down amongst his own kind.

The first blood of the battle is spilt, and they surge up hard, reaching for the ledge to start levering themselves over.

Roaring, we attack with sheer brutality, hacking, stabbing, and killing anything that crests our wall. Men with sticks batter them; women with kitchen knives stab down into faces.

Clawed hands reach out and grab ankles, ripping people from their feet to pull them down into the seething mass beneath.

Fury erupts on both sides. The wind, the rain, the thunder and lightning, it's all forgotten as the battle begins. Lani to one side, Dave to the other, and my team stretched out. Meredith comes into her own and savages with immense speed and precision, biting fingers and hands clean off as she rags and gnashes.

It only takes a few seconds for them to push us back. The surge is so strong we have no choice but to give ground. If anything, though, it serves us better as fighting down was harder. Now we're on the same level and can use our vast experience of hand-to-hand combat.

The tempo of the fight gets faster and faster. Driving deep amongst them, like water, I glide to be where I need to be. They fall away from me, my axe becomes light as a feather, and as with before, it is an extension of my body. I do not think, nor do I really see them. They are there, and I am here, but every blow is where it needs to be.

The power grows, and I get faster and stronger. It grows more, and yet I speed up again, slicing left, right, forward, and round. They are slow now, so very slow, and the faster I get, the more they wilt back. They physically pull away from me, faces contorted with hungry rage becoming twisted in fear. They scream and wail as I cut them down.

Still it grows, far stronger than ever before, and still, I get faster. I can feel pure energy pouring from me.

They fear you, Howie.

They do fear me. I am Howie, and you fear me. It's

suddenly like I can tap into what I felt before. By opening my mind and accepting what I am, I allow the full scope of my energy to come in. It floods through me and tingles every cell in my being.

A feeling of calm euphoria comes over me, and I go deeper, cutting whole sections down. Dave is off to my side, spinning gracefully, but it looks slower than before. He does everything the same as before but slower. Only it isn't him being slower, it's me being faster. My speed matches his, and for the first time, I match him kill for kill. He glances over and smiles, his eyes full of pride and love. We fight closer until we're side by side.

'Finally,' he mutters.

Then together, we go to work.

I do not know how much time passes us by. All I am aware of is the axe, Dave, and the infected. That's it. Dave and I move together as one. We drive a path through them, laughing and smiling. Dave is actually laughing as we work side by side. He throws his head back and laughs in the face of these foul creatures. His knives flick out, my axe hammers home, and nothing can touch us.

We go right through the middle and come out by the edge. Grinning, we turn round and start back in. They die and fall, never to get back up. Blood everywhere, gore coating us as Meredith breaks into our gap and joins our spree. Leaping to tear throats out, her teeth wrenching and slashing left, right, and front. She is so strong and so fast. Perfectly built to use her weight, strength, and violence to destroy these things.

. . .

Like surfing on a wave, I let the power of it pull me along and instead of letting the fear grip me at the sight of the huge wall of water above me, I simply let it be.

I can't leap like Dave, nor can I twist, pivot, or move like him. I will never, never have his grace or fluidity of movement. It's the same with Meredith. The pair of them were born to do this, designed by nature to be as perfect as they can be.

The infected cease to be anything that was once human. They are simply things to be taken away from here.

The storm rages overhead, a brutal storm of power unknown, certainly never seen before in this country, and while that storm displays the true awesome might of nature, we fight to survive.

I know men and women all around me are dying. The survivors from the fort so bravely fighting are getting taken down. Blowers and Cookey fight with their usual savagery, constantly covering each other's flanks and backs. Lani is fast, moving more and more like Dave, letting her athleticism outmanoeuvre them as she whips that cleaver back and forth. Clarence goes for the full berserker, a rampaging bull elephant of immeasurable strength.

Paula is amongst them, fighting with fear and determination. The emotion of the battle is clear on her face, but she fights and moves well.

Maddox is incredible, fast and strong, and with just one knife, he stabs and cuts anything that gets close to him. It's the same with his youths, especially Jagger and Mohammed. Vicious and small, they dance and skip, fighting together.

. . .

But. They are still too many. Even now, in this zone and matching Dave with his kill rate, we cannot ever hope to hold them back, let alone stand a chance of success.

All we can do is keep going, that's it. That's all we have.

CHAPTER FIFTY-EIGHT

Panic everywhere. The boys screaming and running, some hiding under beds, and others sat completely still, too stunned to do anything. Carnage and noise fill the room as the Doc rampages with the thunder booming outside.

Fumbling, Jacob feels panic grip him. Trying to reload the shotgun, it slips from his hands and bounces away from the door. It bursts open in the sudden absence of anyone holding it closed, and he gets knocked flying forwards.

Rolling away, he tries to scoop the gun up on the way but misses. Shoulder slamming into the wall, he scurries towards the shotgun as the guards burst into the room.

With a speed that belies his size, the Doc crosses the room and grabs hold of Nick. Two strong hands grip Nick's neck to lift him bodily from the floor. Gripping the Doc's wrists, Nick feels his feet leaving the ground and the almighty pressure on his throat. He is unable to draw breath and knows the Doc could snap him like a twig.

The rage is too much though to allow for conscious thought or planning. The Doc could kill Nick outright right there, but he doesn't. Instead, he launches Nick off to the side with a strangled roar.

Nick sees the disaster unfolding as he flies through the room. Guards pour into the room, drunk and angry. Larson, right in the middle, still bleeding heavily. Children scatter everywhere, and at least one of them is lying on the floor unmoving.

Nick lands on something hard and feels it splintering underneath his weight. Something wooden that thankfully breaks his drop. Winded and dazed, he lifts his head to see the Doc charging for him again.

'Fuck it,' he gasps, rolling off to the side, wondering where the hell Jacob is and why he let the others in.

Jacob is on his feet, shotgun grasped but useless as a firearm, the cartridges now scattered all over the dark room. He uses it as a club instead, swinging out at the guards. All of them are too drunk to have thought to grab their own weapons, so for a few seconds Jacob is able to fend them off by taking wild swings that connect with a few skulls.

Stamping down, the Doc narrowly misses Nick's head as he rolls away. Another stamp, and Nick rolls again, rolling over and over to escape those hard feet trying to drive his skull in.

Striking the wall, he has nowhere left to go, so he springs to his feet, ignoring the dizziness and pain. Leaping off to the side to avoid the Doc lashing out, Nick is not quick enough, and he feels a hand grab the back of his hair, ripping him off his feet again as he gets launched back to where he landed a minute ago.

Landing amongst whatever he broke during his last descent, he gets a fleeting idea of what it must be like for the zombies when Clarence starts throwing them about, not nice, not nice at all.

Scrabbling to get back up, his hand presses down on something hard. A signal gets sent from his brain to that hand to grip it, take hold, and bring it up as he stands.

Without realising it, Nick grasps the object as he gets up, darting off to avoid the incoming psychotic man.

This time he moves further away, crossing to the other side of the room. Seeing a boy sitting stunned on the floor, he reaches down and pushes the lad hard under the nearest bed before dancing back towards the windows.

Jacob swings out again, but these men are good at one thing, and that's fighting while drunk. Many a bar room brawl has been enjoyed, and they take to it like a duck to water. Charging in, feinting left and right to take Jacob off his feet. The darkness causes confusion, only the strobe-like effect of the storm giving any illumination. The noise is immense from the thunder, the wind, the boys screaming, the Doc roaring, and the men all shouting. They hit each other in the chaos as Jacob lashes out as hard as he can.

Nick gains the area by the window, staggering from the repeated quick succession of blows. Fucked this up. No sign of Howie or Dave, and unless they get inside this very room within the next minute, there'll be no point.

The Doc will kill him, the men will kill Jacob. Then Larson will tell them about the Doc, and they'll all go at it. The Doc'll kill a few of them, but they'll get him down, and then what? What happens to these boys left with whatever psychotic nutters are here?

I'm fucked. Royally and completely fucked. Still, that kiss with Lilly was worth it. He allows himself a slight smile as the Doc comes at him once more. He's still half naked, and bizarrely, he still has a fucking hard-on too. Dirty fucker.

Without conscious thought, Nick hefts the thing held in his hand. It's part of an old-style, wooden desk with a metal frame, heavy and well made. Funny thing is, it feels the same kind of weight as his axe. Same length too roughly, and something is stuck on the end. Glancing down, he notices a chunk of metal. Same shape, same weight, same length.

It's a weapon, and a weapon he knows well. He has spent hours on the GPMG, more hours spent with assault rifles, shotguns, pistols, but above all else, many hours spent gripping a weapon like this.

Fourteen days of fighting. Fourteen days of learning from people like Dave and Clarence. Fourteen days of running. Fourteen days of killing.

Dyslexia is a disability and has no relationship with intelligence. Nick is highly intelligent, with exceptional hand to eye coordination. He is young, fit, and now highly experienced at close quarters fighting.

The infected were human, so they move like humans. They charge forward on two legs and lunge in with unrestrained fury. They are pumped full of chemicals, chemicals that drive them wild with rage, lust, and hunger. Just like the Doc.

All those days and all those fights. Nick, without knowing it, has had more fights than any man in this room, more than any of the guards. More than all of them put together, and his fights were not drunken punch-ups, but life and death battles.

He can hear Mr Howie's voice right now, roaring with defiance *we will not yield, we are the righteous, and we will fight.*

He switches to a two-handed grip and goes forward to meet the charge, roaring as the anger of battle erupts within him. The Doc keeps going, the psychosis giving him supreme confidence that none can stand before him.

A feint left, and the weapon lashes out with a killing blow. Only the weapon isn't an axe but a wooden shaft with a piece of blunt, broken metal on the end which strikes the Doc to the side of his neck.

Nick expects the blade to bite deep, but it doesn't. He recovers quickly, compensating for lack of blade and goes in again. Only Mr Howie and Clarence use the double-bladed axes, the rest use single blade with the heavy, flat end on the reverse side.

The adjustment is made as Nick slams the heavy metal into the back of the Doc's knee, forcing him to drop the leg. As the big man goes down, Nick is already going with the next swing, slamming into the Doc's shoulder.

The Doc screams with fury, never before has someone struck him like this. His size, speed, and temper have always seen him demolish everything. The axe hits again, this time in the middle of his back, which sends him sprawling out. Screaming in pain, he rolls too late as Nick takes his turn to stamp down, connecting his heavy assault boot to the Doc's exposed groin and his rapidly deflating penis.

Pain explodes in his groin as he doubles over, instinct screaming to move, move now before the next blow comes. He surges up, biting down the agony. Nick dodges back in full fight mode.

He swings again and smashes the blunt metal club into the Doc's face, the satisfying crunch and splinter of bones telling him his aim was true, blood spraying out everywhere.

He kicks hard now, the flat of his boot into the Doc's face. The Doc reels back from the blow as Nick steps in and swings the weapon down hard onto the top of his skull. He does it again and again, and he keeps going as the skull gives way, sending shards of bone deep into the Doc's twisted brain. His death is quick, but Nick doesn't take any chances and keeps going until the next flash of lightning shows him the man is clearly very dead.

With a roar, he jumps back, weapon up and ready for the next zombie to lunge in. Jacob is down on the floor, with men all over him. Nick charges in. Swinging the axe, he whacks the first one out of the way before launching into the rest.

Lashing out left, right, and front, he breaks bones, noses, skulls, limbs as he kicks and stamps with a speed unknown to these men. It's human instinct to compare yourself to others, and in Nick's case, he has Dave. Comparing himself to Dave, he feels slow and sluggish, untrained and without fluidity of movement.

Here, alone, against normal people, he is a whirling dervish of power and strength. He is where he needs to be as he tracks and identifies the next opponent. These men react slower than zombies, and Nick soon clears space around Jacob on the floor.

Back they go, driven by a young man wielding a bit of wood with a lump of metal on the end. Men are killed outright, skulls fractured, and spines snapped.

In fear, they drop away, heading towards the door, intent on getting shotguns. Larson screams into his radio for back-up, but the atmospheric conditions ruin the transmission.

Nick pauses as the last one heads towards the door, checking the area is clear before reaching down to check on Jacob.

'Mate,' Nick shakes him roughly, 'Jacob ...'

'I'm alright,' Jacob mumbles. 'It were just a kicking ...' He gets up quickly, wincing at the pain in his sides and head from the repeated blows of fists and feet. His forearms feel the most battered from covering his head to defend against the many drunken hits.

'Boys, listen to me ... get under the beds and hide, stay quiet ... come on, do it now ... Billy? Where is Billy?' Nick paces into the room, staring into the gloomy shadows.

'Billy? Your sister Lilly sent me here. Billy?'

'Here,' a little voice calls out from the end of the room.

'Where? Where are you?' Nick asks, unable to see anything.

'Here,' the voice repeats. There's no time for this. They have to press the attack before the guards get organised.

'All of you, get under the beds and hide. Stay here and wait ... Billy, your sister said she loves you, and we'll get you out very soon ... Jacob, we gotta finish this now.'

'Yep,' Jacob reloads the shotgun, snapping it shut.

'Now, we go right now.' Nick runs towards the door, knowing every second lost is a second closer the guards get to their guns.

In the hallway, he heads towards the stairs. He can hear Larson screaming at them to get armed and get back here.

Too late, too fucking late.

Hang on. Larson. His rooms.

'Jacob, quick ...' Nick bursts away, heading towards the end of the corridor. 'Which one? I can't remember?'

'Which one what?' Jacob staggers out of the room, holding his ribs.

'Larson's room? Which one?' Nick shouts.

'There ... that one, no next one up ...'

He pushes the handle down and throws his shoulder against it, but there's no give. Fuck it. Stepping back, he remembers what Clarence said about aiming for the locks. This is only an internal door, so the only lock will be at the keyhole. With a yell, he kicks out, impacting hard against the door. It splinters but holds. Breathing in, he does it again and again, slamming his foot repeatedly against the door until finally it gives with a crunching noise.

'Nick ...' Jacob shouts with alarm.

'Hold them cunts off,' Nick shouts back, allowing himself the luxury of swearing. 'No fucking swearing, my sweaty fucking arse,' he mutters, shouldering the door aside.

Inside is dark, too dark to see. There's no light, and thick curtains cover the windows. Fumbling, tripping, and swearing louder with every second, he rips back the curtains, tearing them from the fixtures.

It's still bloody dark, but he holds still, waiting for the next flash of lightning to come. There's thunder, rain, very strong wind ... but no fucking lightning.

'NICK!'

'Coming,' he shouts, wanting to stare at the window like he would be able to see where the lightning is. Staring into the room, he waits for the flash to illuminate.

'NICK!' louder now, more urgent.

'Come on, you fucking cunt,' Nick hisses. It comes so suddenly and without warning that he almost blinks at the retina burn it causes. Squinting, he tries to remember what he saw. Nothing, it was over too fast, and he didn't register anything.

Another flash and thunder roars as the windows shake in their frames. The jagged forks do as bid and provide light for Nick to see. They are overly helpful and strike the house in a series of ear-splintering crunches. Glass is blown in somewhere as the wind gets even more ferocious.

There's something in the corner, something with a long barrel. A shotgun. In the dark, his fingers work quickly to feel the holes, swearing under his breath when his fingers find no resistance from cartridges.

'Fucking empty ... Lighter!' Shoving a hand in his pocket, he draws the plastic tube out to slide his thumb over the bevelled metallic wheel. Instant flame, weak and flickering but enough. Casting about, he finds a whole stack of shotguns on the floor next to boxes of cartridges. All of them long-barrelled but better than nothing.

Working to rip a box of shells open, he loads two shotguns and grabs more shells before running out the door.

'Jacob, you ever shot anyone before?'

'What?'

'Have you ever shot anyone?' Nick asks again.

'No, no, I fucking have not.'

'Right, you load then, and I'll fire.'

'You serious?'

'Deadly, mate. Here, have these and don't fuck about this time ...' Nick hands the shells over along with one of the guns.

'You shot people before, then?'

'Loads, hundreds ... fuck, probably thousands ... maybe more than that actually,' Nick shrugs. 'You ready, then?'

'For what?'

'Going down,' Nick nods at the stairs.

'You fucking nuts or something?' Jacob glares at him in horror.

'Fucking probably,' Nick grins. 'Nice being able to swear again, isn't it?'

He turns and starts down the stairs, pausing to make sure Jacob is right behind him. Shotgun up and aimed like an assault rifle, and he takes the steps quickly.

The first shot is fired by Nick, catching a man running past the bottom of the stairs. The short range and power take him clean off his feet as the pellets shred his torso. Down he goes, screaming in agony, but Nick has already tracked away, sweeping left and right as he takes the steps, one after the other.

'Reload,' swapping over, he brings the fresh shotgun up to his shoulder. He steps off the bottom step and into the hallway. Spotting movement to the left, he moves, aims, and fires, drops down to one knee to find his next target, moves, and fires again. Three down so far.

'Jesus fucking hell ...' Jacob gasps as Nick shouts for the next gun.

'RUN, YOU CUNTS,' Nick roars, 'RUN BEFORE I SLAUGHTER YOU ALL ... I AM NICK, AND I WILL KILL YOU.' Ha! Hope Dave doesn't mind him stealing the words.

A shot blasts from the end of the room. Its rifle, badly aimed by a drunk man, and the shot goes wide, tearing a chunk of plaster out of the wall. Nick pivots and fires both barrels in quick succession, nodding at the scream of pain he hears coming back.

Jacob works with nervous fingers to reload the guns as Nick takes shot after shot, shooting through doors and at anything he hears or sees. He is stunned by the complete lack of hesitation that the young lad shows and the speed at which he reacts.

They hear shouting from other rooms, panicked yells of confusion. With a nod, Nick leads Jacob to the open front door and out into the driving torrential rain.

'What about the boys?' Jacob asks, thinking they're making a run for it.

'We'll come back in the side ... Look out!' he shouts in alarm as two guards burst from the front door behind them. Nick drops quickly to take aim as Jacob ditches one shotgun and pulls the trigger of the second one he holds. The spread of the pellets hits both men, flinging them back as they drop to the floor. Jacob stalks up to them, takes aim, and fires quickly, killing one of the writhing figures before using the butt of the weapon to slam down on the other's head.

Turning to face Nick with water cascading down his face, he realises what he just did. He killed and took the lives of two men. The wind whips at this shirt tails, but there is a grim determination in his eyes. He breaks the gun and quickly reloads with fresh shells, all trace of the trembling hands gone now.

'Fuck the side, back in the front,' Nick yells, knowing the idea must be blown out now. They sprint back into the hallway, both of them diving for cover as multiple shots ring out. The men have organised themselves but fired too quickly. Without choice, Nick and Jacob go for the stairs, vaulting them two by two as they race to the top, splinters of bullets hitting to the sides and behind them.

'YOU'RE FUCKED,' Larson screams from somewhere on the ground floor. 'HEAR ME? FUCKED ...'

'Is there another staircase?' Nick asks at the top.

'Down the end ...' Jacob nods down the corridor, past the Doc's and Larson's rooms.

Too late. They hear the crash of a door being kicked open, then the internal corridor door swings inwards. Nick fires quickly as more shots come from downstairs, forcing them to retreat towards the boy's dormitory. The impetus is lost as the guards, sobering up fast from the very real threat of death, become organised and rally under the cohesive orders of Larson.

Holding outside the dormitory door, they take turns firing at the stairs and down the corridor, reloading quickly to snap the guns shut as they frantically think of a way out.

The storm increases in volume, power, and energy. With the windows smashed, the wind races through the old house, slamming doors and causing the window frames to tremble ever more violently. There's the smell of burning in the air, smoke from an unseen fire.

The radio on Jacob's belt keeps crackling, Larson trying again and again to transmit to the gate guards, knowing they'll be sober and well armed. The static bursts with his repeated efforts, but those repeated efforts start paying off as even without any words getting through, the odd gunshot is clearly heard, the tone of Larson's panicked voice, and the fact there are repeated efforts to transmit made.

Nick takes all this in, knowing the gate guards will be heading down soon, which is the last thing they need. Fresh, sober men, trusted to work the main gate, will pose a very serious problem. These people have no care for the boys within that room. With the Doc dead and Larson spreading the word of how the Doc was a fraud, the men will want quick riddance of Nick and Jacob, and they'll do it by any means.

'What's he saying?' The men huddle together in the garden shed, hastily erected outside the main gates to Chapsworth House. The storm outside rages with increasing fury, threatening to tear the flimsy shed apart.

'No idea,' one of the guards replies, 'must be the storm fucking the signal up.'

'Why's he keep calling? Somethin' going on?' someone else asks. Six of them all stare at the radio held by their group leader.

'Pissed, ain't they? Probably fucking about.'

'Nah, fuck off! They wouldn't do that–the Doc has a radio ...'

'Shit, you hear that?' They all step in as another burst of static fills the room. They clearly hear the distinct sound of gunshots and Larson's voice, broken, unclear, but panicky.

'Fuck, right ...' the leader stares round at the shocked faces, 'fucking get down there. Tony, get the van.'

'We all going?' Tony asks.

'Fuck yeah, someone shooting in the big house. Fuck yeah, we're all going,' the leader replies. 'Don't just fucking stand there, you prick, get the fucking van!'

Tony moves, pausing as a strong gust of wind pushes the thin, wooden door into the frame, preventing the man from pushing it open. Others join him, forcing the door ajar. Suddenly, the wind changes direction and removes the door from the hinges, pulling it high into the air where it dances on the currents like a feather, leaving several men face down on the floor.

'Fuck,' Tony gasps as the door is removed from sight. With the door gone, the wind decides the shed is the next thing to play with. Starting with the weakest part of the structure, the howling gale starts testing to see how much power is needed to take the roof off.

The men stare up, hearing the creaks and groans from the timber ceiling above their heads. The whole structure judders with the power of the storm.

A slight punch to the chest makes Tony take a step back, thinking some debris glanced off him. The others stare at him in utter shock.

'What?' Tony asks. 'Oh ... oh fuck.' Looking down at the end of the arrow shaft sticking out of his chest, he stupidly tries to turn to see if it's sticking out his back, like a dog chasing its tail. The awareness brings pain, a searing agony that drops him instantly.

Another arrow thuds into a second guard, pinning him against the side of the shed. Within a second or two, another arrow flies through the door, hitting the same man, securing him firmly to the wall of the shed.

Several metres away and lost in the gloom of the storm, sits the Saxon, reversed towards the shed, with the rear doors wedged open. Roy kneels inside the rear section, night-vision goggles on his forehead as he stares out across the short distance to the guard hut.

The crackle of the radio by his side bursts to life. It is a mass-produced radio that was sold in the hundreds of thousands across the country. It also uses the same set frequencies over short range distance as the radios inside the house.

Roy simply had to twist the dial through the stations to find the channel used by Chapsworth House. The static-filled hiss of repeated transmissions told him something was going on. The gunshots and shouts he heard in the broken crackles told him even more.

Decision made. Saxon quickly moved into position. The wind is exceptionally strong, and the rain is hard, but inside the vehicle, the bow string is dry, and the outside elements can be taken into account.

The first arrow was a test. The men inside the shed had no clue that single long-shafted arrow flew over the top as Roy watched for wind direction, fall, and positioning.

The next one was true, the bow held with the arrow nocked and ready. Breathing easy, hands steady, and he waited for the door to open. When the wind ripped it away, he had a clear sight to the interior. The first one taken down. The second one, he put two into his chest just to be sure.

Now he waits, knowing that the men have little choice for he can see the wind working at the structure. The shed was obviously put in place after the event happened when the weather was fine and glorious. It's a nice shed, but it's been plonked down and not secured to the ground in any way.

Now, despite the combined weight of the men inside, it is in very real danger of being plucked away.

What do they do? Do they risk being struck by another arrow or risk a nice nighttime flight in a garden shed.

People are so stupid, Roy muses quietly. *Go out the back. The shed is thin–a few kicks will have you through the rear panels.*

Loosened, an arrow flies across the ground, the barbed point entering the eye socket of the man peering round. Holding his hand out, Roy feels another arrow being pressed into his palm by Lilly kneeling silently next to him.

Three down. The only problem is he doesn't know how many are in there. Five to seven, he guesses, going from what Lilly said she could see and the size of the shed.

'Oh fuck ... fuck ... shit ... Who is out there? What the fuck is this?'

'Shut up! Shut the fuck up!' the leader shouts as the three remaining men lie on the floor of the shed, keeping well clear of the door.

'Fucking arrows, someone shooting fucking arrows ... like Robin fucking Hood ...'

'We gotta make a run for it,' the leader shouts.

'Fuck off, John. You think I'm going out there?'

'It's a fucking arrow, not a machine gun. He can't get all three of us at the same time,' John retorts.

'He's got a point,' the third man shouts, missing the unintentional pun that would have been seized on and ragged senseless by a joking Cookey.

'Well, I ain't going first,' the worrier announces.

'Use Tony,' John shouts. 'We get behind Tony, yeah?'

'Tony? He's fucking dead, you stupid cun–' worrier shouts in panic.

'That's the idea,' John roars. 'They won't fucking hurt him, will they?'

'Yep, nice one,' worrier nods quickly, 'fucking do it now, then, go on grab him. You're the closest ... FUCK!' Worrier cries as John reaches out to grab Tony's ankle and finds an arrow appearing in Tony's calf, just inches from his grip.

John huffs as he tugs Tony's corpse across the floor, manipulating the dead weight to use as a shield.

'Right.' John and the third man lift dead Tony to his feet and hold him propped up. 'We get Tony in the door, then fucking go for it ... We'll go left, and you go right,' John shouts to worrier.

'NO,' Worrier shouts, 'fucking leaving me on my own. I'm going left with you, and he can go right.'

'Fucking hell, you prick,' John shouts in anger, 'does it fucking matter?'

'If it doesn't matter, then you go right, and us two will go left. I ain't going right on my own ...'

'Fine, you two go right, and I'll go left,' John sighs.

'Your left or my left?' worrier asks.

'We're going to be facing the SAME FUCKING WAY,' John roars, losing his patience.

'Alright, fucking hell, John,' worrier whines.

'Go left with me,' John whispers into the ear of the third silent man.

'What was that?' worrier shouts.

'I said Tony is a fat cunt, and he's too heavy ... You ready?'

'No, but fuck it ... I ain't staying in here.'

Tony is presented to the doorway. Immediately, an arrow thuds into his chest, rocking the two men holding him from the force of the impact.

Worrier gets behind them as John gives a three count. Tony is pushed bodily forward as they scurry behind him.

Ditching the body with a yell, all three burst away to the left while yelling at each other to go right. The first arrow takes the silent third man through the neck, leaving John and worrier trying to run while pushing and shoving at each other.

'FUCK!' John yelps in pain, going down from the arrow sent into his meaty thigh. Clutching the wound, he writhes in pain as another one strikes his other leg.

'COME BACK,' John roars as worrier makes good his escape. The third arrow hits his right arm in the bicep, pinning the limb to his torso. Pain explodes from the three barbed shafts sticking from his body.

A pause; then the fourth takes him through the neck, severing his windpipe and opening the main artery.

With the weight suddenly removed, the wind plucks the shed from the ground and casts it about for a few seconds before deciding to slam it against the big, solid wall. It smashes to pieces, the noise lost in the thundering boom overhead. The bodies within fly off to land on the sodden lawn, water gathering all about.

In the Saxon, Roy holds ready to fire. The one that ran off went away from the house. The chances are he's running as fast as he can and won't stop until he runs out of breath.

'Can you drive?' Roy asks gently, his tone one of complete calmness. 'Take us down the road to the house, go quickly but carefully.'

Lilly moves quickly, clambering over to drop into the driver's seat. The engine is still running, and she pulls the Saxon round in a long, wide circle to face back, towards the house.

Through the gates, she navigates the driveway, going as fast as she dares without headlights, the frequent flashes of lightning illuminate the grounds enough to keep on the right route.

Roy fastens his leg quiver using the thick Velcro straps. Selecting his chosen arrows, he quickly runs his hand down each one, checking for any signs of being warped.

'Go for the side,' Roy shouts, remembering what he was told earlier.

'The front door is open,' Lilly shouts back as the front of the house comes clearer into view.

'Side, please,' Roy replies. The radio still crackles with panicked transmissions. He can make out a male voice screaming for someone called John to *get his fucking arse down here,* gunshots clear in the background noise, sharp cracks of rifles, and solid bangs of shotguns.

Should be interesting, Roy thinks as he tests the string for any moisture. This will have to be quick, out of the vehicle and into the side door. Can't afford to stand in the rain and get the string wet.

Always wanted to use this, Roy checks the small lightweight box on the bow, watching as the pure straight line of the green laser shines out. With the night-vision goggles on, the light from the laser red-dot sight is perfect. Not something he ever used when hunting the zombies as he didn't want to give his position away but close quarters within a house should be ideal.

'Stay here ...' Roy calls out as the girl brings the Saxon to a jarring halt.

'No way,' Lilly says, already over the seats.

'You'll get in my way,' Roy says bluntly. 'People in there are shooting guns, and I don't need someone else running about.'

'I'm coming,' Lilly hisses.

'Idiot,' Roy growls, 'stay behind me then and don't say a word. Stay quiet and don't get in my way.'

'Fine!'

'What's that?'

'Nick's pistol. He gave it to me.'

'Do you know how to use it?'

'Yes, thank you,' Lilly answers primly, 'Nicholas showed me how.'

'Okay, just don't shoot me.'

'I'll try not to,' Lilly mutters, then immediately feels a stabbing pang of guilt. 'Roy, sorry, I didn't mean that ...'

'Don't worry,' Roy sighs, 'come on, let's find your brother.'

CHAPTER FIFTY-NINE

It matters nothing, this speed and ability to kill is rendered useless against so many. Already we've killed and killed, but a quick glance at the outer wall shows they're still coming over in droves.

The wind is so strong now. Violent gusts take people off their feet to sail a few feet in the air before they land heavily on the soaking ground. Infected and human alike are chosen and plucked away. The water on the top of the wall gathers in deep puddles, making the ground treacherous. The thunder is so loud we can't hear the shouts of each other. The flashing of intense light makes it hard to see.

Noises boom all around me. The thunder echoes off the big concrete walls, but another sound starts to rise, a crashing noise that too becomes more regular as it builds into a distinct sound of its own.

One word from Dave explains it, his voice being the only thing remotely audible above the wind, 'WAVES.'

Shit, no bloody way. It surrounds the fort on three sides, so I risk a quick glance at the sea and can see that Dave is right. I thought the storm above our heads was bad, but that's just noise, water, and light. Yeah, the lightning has killed a few already and blasted some minor chunks from the wall, but the sea, that is a raging beast alive with an intense hatred.

The infected lay siege on one side, but the sea does the three sides. It throws huge, rolling waves with no discernible pattern that slam and crash into the walls. Now I'm aware of it, I start to hear just how bad it is, even feeling the vibration beneath my feet as they slam into the wall.

That staggers me. The fact that waves are hitting the outer wall with such ferocity that I can feel it while standing on the top of the inner wall is incredible.

I gain several moments' peace before I glance back to the rear of the fort. Spray erupts over the edge of the wall every few seconds. Those walls are several meters high; the sheer *power* of the waves renders me speechless.

A surge of infected occupies me for a few seconds. I remove one head and spilt the others apart with my deadly axe. I move back a few steps and look again to the sides. With only the lightning to see by, I get such brief glimpses, but they show me just how dangerous this whole environment has become. The sea is challenging us, probing at this tiny spit of land sticking out as though it shouldn't be here. The sea doesn't want this land here; it wants a nice, gentle, curving bay without any protrusions. It starts working to remove it, like a carpenter sanding down a bulging knot on his otherwise perfect length of wood. But the sandpaper doesn't do it quick enough, so he breaks out the power tools, plugs them in, and laughs like a maniac.

The sea comes at us on all three sides. Bursting higher and higher as those waves become bigger mountains and deeper valleys.

It gets so powerful that I'm not the only one seeing it

now. All across the top of the wall, men and women glance at the waves bursting higher, at the huge crashing noise each surge of tidal water brings.

The infected don't care but keep coming as the wind gets worse and starts plucking them off the outer wall. The storm has just increased massively, like what we had before was the entrée, the starter soup in nature's restaurant. The bowls have been cleared, and the main course is coming.

What comes defies belief. It is an act of God, of Mother Nature at her very worst. What power we as mankind thought we possessed is nothing. We are but a speck of dirt in comparison to what she can do. Elements, just elements is all they are. Wind, rain, thunder, and lightning, but they are combined and unleashed to their full majestic might, and we are nothing.

I realise now we have been humoured throughout our history of so-called domination of the planet. She could remove us anytime she wishes to do so. Atom bombs, wars, mining, and taking away the vast resources of oil, gas, and coal, all of those things are tiny compared to what she can do, and what's more, I get the strong impression this, what I see now in front of me, is nowhere near the fullest fury she can reveal.

Waves take the spit of land. One minute they're crashing into the walls, then simply it's as though the sea swells, and they go over it. Huge, rolling mini tsunamis burst across the spit from both sides to meet in the middle with an explosion of water and noise.

Bigger they get, and more they come, one after the other in a relentless, ceaseless surge of tidal immensity. The pounding against the walls increases; the vibrations beneath our feet physically shake us. The wind, playful before, becomes spiteful and mean, and we have no choice but to drop down low. Dave is shouting, but the noise is lost, his breath gently taken away by the gusts.

The infected take the full brunt. Refusing to lie down, they continue surging towards us, and the defiance they dare to show Mother Nature sees her wreaking vengeance with awful precision.

First, the waves surge past the front of the outer wall. One minute the ground is covered in bodies charging towards us; the next, and there is water and nothing more. All of those bodies, all of those thousands of infected are swept casually away.

Next, she shows displeasure at anything trying to stand up. Even crouching down, we're being rocked and moved, but standing, and you become a kite to be played with. Infected are lifted and taken high into the air, tossed about on the twisting, conflicting currents.

Crawling to each other, we grasp wrists and legs as we hang on for dear life. Weapons down, and nothing matters now. The battle is done. Clarence is the anchor we all aim for, and gradually we build something heavy. Maddox and his crews head towards us, snaking across the ground with windswept faces full of fear and awe. Dave, down low, simply grabs the big man's wrist and stares out to see everything going on, his face alive with interest as he watches something inherently more powerful and deadly than he.

Paula is with us. Lani by my side. The lads grip onto each other, no doubt making gay jokes about the closeness of their bodies. Even Meredith is lying down in the lea side of Clarence with a few arms wrapped round her chest.

Scrabbling along, going hand to hand while gripping anything I can hold, I edge towards the lip of the wall and peer down. The outer gates are leaking water quicker than a tap left on full. The weight of the vehicles jammed behind it just manages to keep them closed, but there are enough holes for the sea to get through, and quickly the alley starts to fill.

The first bodies left on the ground are lifted by the low rise. Dragged along, they start knocking into the infected that got down into the alley. More water surges in, and the walls act as the sides of a bath, trapping the water as it fills, rising higher and higher with every second.

With Dave at my side, both of us peer down and still. The fucking things try to climb up, not to escape the water, but to get at us.

Still, they come, only to get plucked away the second they stand up, until the ripple of the idea spreads amongst their hive mind, and they change tactic. Staying low as they crest the wall, and the fight is back on. A low fight, a battle done with bodies no higher than a crouch.

Dave goes at them, using one hand to stab and slash out and the other to take hold of whatever he can grip. The axes become unwieldy down on our bellies, so we draw knives and go for it.

All of us adopt Dave's method of fighting one handed whilst we struggle to hold on to each other. Barred teeth still come at us in crab-like surges. The faces of the infected appear more violent and deranged than ever before. The fighting becomes gritty and brutal. Clarence is the only one strong enough to use his axe, and he swings it in big sweeps left and right, tearing chunks of flesh from heads.

Meredith hunts like a lioness. Staying low, she crabs towards the target until close enough to run in, grip, savage, and drop down again.

A glimpse to the rear shows me the back gate has been smashed open, water pouring through the gap like a giant fire hose.

Feeling safer now, we fight with renewed confidence. Their numbers are finite again and limited. With the water rising in the alley between the walls and the kills we give out, we know we can get through this.

Perhaps that's it, perhaps that glimmer of knowledge brings a very slight sense of complacency, but disaster befalls us as Cookey screams in agony.

Fighting outwards and being on the ground reduces our ability to scan all sides, and the infected take advantage to swarm in.

With the noise of the storm and the howling wind, it takes us a few seconds to realise Cookey has let go of whoever he was clinging onto. Combined yells, as whipped away by the wind as they are, still reach me as I turn to see Cookey twisting round to beat at the female infected biting into his thigh.

Our group implodes as we dive towards him. Hampered by the strong wind and being unable to stand, we have to roll, crouch, and dive forward.

Blowers is the closest and reacts with incredible violence, literally diving onto the back of the female infected to pull her off with his bare hands. Getting his arms round her throat, he squeezes with all his might and snaps the head left and right, copying the motion he has seen done so many times by Dave and Clarence.

With the neck broken, he twists first to check we're getting to Cookey, then spins to face the rest of the horde off.

The banter gets harsh sometimes, and Cookey is relentless of his jibes towards Blowers, but never in my life have I seen two closer mates, and right now, Blowers shows that closeness by plunging in to attack multiple infected on his own. His boxing training shows, and even being on his stomach, he smacks and pummels their faces with brutally hard blows, using his feet to kick and force them away.

Dave propels himself over Cookey to dive into the midst, joining Blowers to protect the lad and fight them back. We all converge, forming a protective barrier round a very shaken Cookey, lying on his back with his hands pressed round the bite wound on his thigh.

Maddox gets his crews in tight round us and starts beating out, gradually forming a larger circle around us as our team falls back to gather round the injured lad.

Like a father, I love my team equally for they each bring something unique that makes us complete. Clarence has his strength and years of experience. Dave is Dave, nothing more needs to be said. Lani anchors us, brings reason and common sense with a ferocity of love for me, for all of us. Nick is gifted in ways he will never know. The unassuming lad is so clever, so quick, and so very capable, and if he only knew the loss we feel at his absence. His ability with machines, devices, mechanical and electrical things has saved us time and again.

Blowers, a strong, young man so ready to laugh, joke and put people at ease but so ready to step up and take the role of corporal. Always knowing what needs to be done and always one step ahead of me. Hard too, with a street toughness that makes him a highly formidable opponent.

Humour defines humanity. Without humour, we are but another species. Cookey has that rare gift of bringing humour. He shows his heart every day without fear of rejection or judgement. He cries openly and without shame, but he laughs more than he cries. He laughs, and he makes us laugh.

In the direst, darkest of times, there has always been

Cookey to make a quip, crack a joke, make an observation or comment that so many times has had us clutching our sides.

Together we are strength. Together we have unity and can survive and achieve. All of those things are a combination of what we each bring, and Cookey, he is our spirit. He is the spirit of humanity.

His face drains of blood, trembling, with tears already pricking in his eyes to roll down his cheeks to join the streams of rainwater. He stares at me with wide eyes, showing the innocence of his kind heart.

Not my Cookey, the kindest, warmest one of us all who just minutes ago had us all laughing as he joked about while facing impossible odds. Cookey who never once doubted what we were doing, never flinched, never moaned, never complained but did everything we asked of him and did it with a smile.

My heart sinks to plummet down through my stomach. Blowers pushes to gain Cookey's side. His face a mask of emotions that even he, the hard-faced lad that he is, finds impossible to cover up. Tears stream, and his bottom lip quivers, trembling with fear. With shaking hands, he gently lifts Cookey's head to stare down with nothing but love and horror.

This hits us hard, harder than anything we've been through so far. None of us care about the battle now, and the storm becomes a thing in the distance. Here, on this sodden ground, we cradle and stare down at the shocked face of one of our own.

'Mr Howie,' Cookey stares up at me. We lean in close as our bodies protect him from the wind. 'Don't let Blowers bum me when I'm gone,' he tries to joke, but it chokes off in a sob. His hand reaches out, bloodied and slick from gripping the wound, but I take it within my own as Lani grips his other one.

A hot wetness to the side of me, a forceful push, then Meredith is amongst us, staring down with her big, brown eyes.

Tears from all of us. Clarence red-eyed and swallowing. Lani streaming. Blowers sobbing, and the salt of our emotions mixes with the sweetness of the rain.

'Show me,' I croak and bend down as many hands work to gently turn him onto his side. The wound is clear, with a nasty bite to the fleshy, meaty rear of his thigh. Not deep, and under normal circumstances, a quick bandage would see it covered and protected. But now, with the infected blood coursing through his system, he has but minutes at the most.

'I'm sorry,' he gasps. Rolled onto his back again, and he stares first at me, then at Lani, and finally up at Blowers.

'Don't be,' I gasp as Lani sweeps his hair from his forehead.

'Mate,' he looks up at Blowers, 'I'm so sorry, mate.'

'Not you,' Blowers sobs, 'please not you.'

'It's alright, mate. It's done now. It's over,' Cookey smiles. 'Don't be fucking soft.'

'Fuck you, Cookey,' Blowers chokes.

Cookey chuckles softly, a soft sound that rocks his body. 'You love me really, Blowers.'

Shit, that does it for me. No way am I letting this fucking infection take him, no matter what it takes.

'Cut me, Dave.' The small man reacts instantly, his hand flicking out to score a perfect, shallow cut across my palm. 'Deeper, make it bleed more,' I demand, and he flicks again, opening the wound with surgical precision.

'Hold tight, mate,' I squeeze his hand while I push my

injured palm under his leg and feel for the wound. Finding it, I grip hard and knead at his thigh, forcing my blood into his cut. Clarence gets his hand over the top of mine and clamps hard, driving my palm into his leg.

Gritting his teeth, Cookey lies back with his eyes clamped shut. Hands hold him gently as I knead and push in a desperate effort to do something.

'Me, do it,' Lani shouts at Dave, holding her hand open. Again, within a second, she has a perfect cut across her palm. 'Sorry, Cookey,' she smiles while lifting his hand towards Dave.

'Do it,' Cookey clenches his eyes closed as Dave opens his skin. Lani presses her hand to his, tears and blood mingling with the rain as we press our bleeding wounds to his. Desperate to do anything to save his life, and without doubt, if I could offer myself right now for Cookey to have his life, I would do it. That prayer races through my mind, willing whatever it is Lani and I have to work on Cookey.

'The dog,' Blowers shouts, 'she's immune too.'

'Fuck off, Blowers,' Cookey says through gritted teeth. 'We had that conversation, yeah, you can't just take the dog's blood and put it in yours,' he mimics Blowers' voice which has us all smiling stupidly as Dave leans in and whips the point of his blade over the back of Cookey's free hand.

'Stop stabbing me!'

Blowers grabs Meredith's head and guides her into the back of Cookey's hand. While I massage the back of his leg and Lani pushes her cut hand into his, so Meredith starts licking at the third wound. Her long tongue takes firm, controlled licks of the open cut. The fact that she might have infected blood in her mouth from all the bites doesn't register at that moment.

'How long?' I glance up at Dave, knowing he will be timing it.

'Two minutes,' he says without a blink.

'COME ON,' I bellow at the top of my lungs, screaming into the sky for the gods to save him. Whatever we have, whatever *thing* that the three of us possess must be worth something. It must be.

'Two and a half,' Dave announces.

'Yes, come on, Cookey,' Clarence grins.

'I'm not doing anything?' Cookey glances up with a confused look.

'Just keep doing it then,' Blowers pleads. 'How long now?'

'Three minutes,' Dave replies.

'No way,' Cookey stares at me, 'no fucking way ...'

'Yes, mate,' I grin. 'Any pain?'

'No ...' he shakes his head, 'just my leg ... and the cut where Dave got me ...'

'Stomach?' Lani asks.

'Nothing,' Cookey says in a weak voice as though not daring to believe it.

'Three and a half,' Dave says.

'Yes! Come on!' I scream with a big grin and feel Clarence pushing his hand harder over the top of mine as though to make it work better.

'You okay?' Blowers asks with a hopeful gaze at his best mate.

'Fine,' Cookey nods with fresh tears forming in his eyes.

'Really, Cookey?' Blowers voice breaks with a sob. 'Don't fuck about now, mate. You really okay?'

'I'm fine, Blowers, mate ... I feel fine.'

'Mr Howie?' Blowers looks at me like I have all the

answers, like I will know right at this very point whether Cookey will live or not.

'Four minutes,' Dave announces.

'Mate,' I push my free hand round the back of Cookey's neck, 'four minutes, Cookey. You hear that? Four minutes.'

'No way,' he sobs, staring at me while his hand hooks over my wrist.

'Yes, mate,' I feel a fresh outpouring of tears from my eyes.

'Four and a half,' Dave adds.

'Cookey,' I grin through the sobs, 'you're immune ...'

Just by saying it, just by muttering those words, it makes it a reality. None of us know anything. He could be infected, or it could be another dirty trick from the infection, but it doesn't matter. What does matter is that right now Cookey has that weight lifted off him and is given his life back.

Blowers sags down, his head held low as he heaves to get himself under control. Clarence and I slowly pull bloodied hands away as Lani leans in to kiss Cookey on the forehead.

For once, Cookey doesn't crack jokes but closes his eyes as his own bottom lip trembles. Like it's too good to be true, we hold there for another minute, all of us bent low to hug the lad, and none of us speaking.

Such as my mind is, I can't help but realise that Dave will still have his knife drawn and ready, but even he, the most emotionless man ever to walk the earth, leans forward to gently stroke Cookey's cheek. An act of such gentle care that it takes my breath away. Cookey has his eyes closed and will never know that gesture came from Dave, but that is as close to Dave showing love as you could ever hope to see.

'Six minutes, and you're fine,' Dave breaks the silence, 'get up and get back to work.'

Laughing with delight, Cookey snaps his eyes open and stares up. The sadness gone, the fear evaporating as he locks eyes on Blowers.

'Ha! Fuck you, Blowers ... I'm immune ...'

'Oh god,' Blowers shakes his head, 'he's gonna go on about this forever.'

'Fucking right, I am,' Cookey sits up, grinning. 'You must be well jel that Mr Howie was massaging my arse.'

'Such a twat,' Blowers shouts through a grin that stretches ear to ear.

Clarence tears a strip of material from the bottom of his t-shirt and quickly loops it round Cookey's leg, tying it off with enough pressure to stop the bleeding.

Whatever this means, Cookey not becoming infected, there isn't time to contemplate it now. The fighting is still all around us, and without my team joining in, the others have become beaten back.

With renewed energy, we go back to doing what we do best. With fresh hope in our hearts for now we know four of us cannot be turned.

CHAPTER SIXTY

'What we gonna do?' Jacob mutters as he snaps the shotgun open to push two more fresh cartridges in the tubes.

'Fuck knows,' Nick replies grimly. 'Can you get those kids out the windows?'

'Nailed shut. The Doc had 'em done so they wouldn't run off.'

'Fuck it, we're trapped, then.'

'You said your people were coming,' Jacob hisses.

'Must be the storm,' Nick says with a sense of isolation descending in his mind. 'They might still come.'

'Yeah right,' Jacob mutters, 'bit fucking late now.'

'YOU TWO ... PUT THE GUNS DOWN!' Larson bellows from the ground floor.

'WE JUST WANT TO GET THE BOYS OUT,' Nick shouts. 'THAT'S IT ...'

'COME DOWN THEN, AND WE'LL TALK ABOUT IT,' Larson shouts.

'I KNOW YOU, LARSON,' Jacob roars. 'YOU'LL KILL US.'

'I WON'T ... I PROMISE ...'

Staring at Jacob, Nick watches as the older man shakes his head. 'He will,' Jacob whispers.

'YOU COME UP,' Nick shouts, 'COME UP SO WE CAN TALK.'

'FUCK THAT,' Larson bellows, 'YOU'RE BOTH FUCKED.'

'See,' Jacob sighs.

'We just got to hold on as long as we can,' Nick whispers urgently. 'They'll come. I know they will.'

'We don't have much choice really, do we?' Jacob mutters as they both make ready to fire again.

Side door unlocked and slightly ajar, the lights inside are off, and Roy can see perfectly with his night-vision equipment.

Lilly is right behind him, holding the pistol in the two-handed grip Nick showed her, gun lowered pointing at the floor, treading carefully.

Roy goes slow, each step measured and checked before proceeding. Being inside now, the noise of the storm is muffled enough to gain sounds of the house. He hears shouts from inside, an exchange of words between two or three people, the tone demanding.

Edging closer to the internal door, he pauses and listens before taking hold of the handle to start pressing down. The bow held in his left hand, the arrow already knocked into the string.

Easing the door open, it creaks and groans, but the storm masks the sound. Dropping down to one knee, he stares into a long corridor–a door open at the other end, leading into an illuminated area, the main hallway probably.

Two men kneel at the end of the corridor by the door. Both of them armed and watching out into the main hallway area.

'COME ON, LADS,' a voice sails down clearer now. 'THERE'S NO WAY OUT OF HERE. YOU'RE BOTH FUCKED ... COME DOWN NOW, OR I SWEAR WE'LL KILL THOSE FUCKING KIDS.'

'GET FUCKED,' another voice replies instantly.

'That's Nick,' Lilly breathes softly in his ear, her voice trembling with excitement at hearing him alive. The boys must be alive too if the other man is threatening to hurt them.

'COME UP AND GET THEM, YOU CUNT,' Nick roars. 'COME ON, FUCKTARD ...'

The boys are upstairs with Nick, Roy nods gently, processing the information. How many men? He can take these two easily, but how many are left after that?

Drawing an arrow from the quiver, he props it against his thigh, ready to reload, and he draws the string back, pulling the tension into the mechanism.

Waiting, he pauses for the right moment. Either that man shouting or thunder breaking–something to mask the noise.

Thunder comes first, a big, rolling clap that vibrates the house. The arrow takes less than a second to cross the distance. The headshot kills the man instantly. Second arrow nocked, drawn, and loosed, and as the other man turns, he too is taken out.

Both down without any noise other than their weapons falling to the ground. With the two men kneeling, the weapons only dropped a couple of feet, and the sound was hopefully lost with the thunderous booms from outside.

Roy ebbs forward, the next arrow already nocked and under strain. Closer to the door, he can see the illumination is coming from a couple of big candles, one straight ahead and one off to the right.

Take the candles out, and it gets dark, which gives him the advantage. As before, he draws another arrow to rest against his thigh and calculates the distance and any wind coming from the open front door.

Whoosh, and the candle is out. The arrow slices through the tiny wick and embeds in the wall beyond it. Second arrow up, he crabs out, taking the risk of exposure to go for the second candle. Shouts and shots ring out, panicked shots from men holding the triggers too tight and jumping when the candle goes out.

On the move, he has to take a rapid shot, missing the wick but striking the actual wax candle. Roy sighs, not content with the scrappiness of his shot. The thing bursts apart, which achieves the same aim, plunging the big hallway into relative darkness.

He bursts out, the laser sight probing the blackness as he sweeps round. The night vision gives him a clear view of men starbursting in panic. With constant movement, he takes the first shot, dropping a guard with a clear neck penetration.

Nocked and ready. Stepping to the side, he hears a gunshot from the corridor behind him. Lilly, catching sight of movement, fires into the darkness, knowing she will be adding to the confusion and hoping to hell she doesn't hit Roy.

'NICK,' Roy roars, then fires again, another clean shot

through the chest which takes a tattooed guard clean off his feet.

'UPSTAIRS,' Nick shouts back, 'ABOUT SEVEN OR EIGHT OF THEM LEFT. A FEW UP HERE TOO. WE'VE GOT THE BOYS SAFE IN A ROOM.'

'RIGHTO,' Roy bellows, the young lad giving him all the information he needs. Noises fill the hallway, doors slamming, men running and shouting. A shot from close by but aimed into the darkness. Roy spins, drops, and looses, the arrow taking the man through his groin, causing him to drop the rifle he was holding. The second one hits his chest, straight through the heart. Moving again, Roy aims for the corridor as he hears Lilly crossing the hall in a dash for the stairs.

Covering her run, he pauses, hearing the thuds of her feet as she races up.

'INCOMING, NICK ... DON'T FIRE,' Roy bellows quickly. Straining, he hears her voice as she gets to Nick. Good, that's her sorted. Now it's just a hunt, the same as ever before. He switches the laser red dot sight off and starts moving off.

'Lilly!' Nick gasps as the girl reaches the top of the stairs and races across the landing. Jacob takes aim down the corridor in case of anyone trying to take a shot.

'Nick,' she runs into his arms, throwing her own around his neck.

'Billy's in there. He's fine ...' Nick says quickly. 'I knew you'd come.'

'Just me and Roy. The things attacked the fort,' she blurts out. 'Roy's killed the men at the gate with his bow and another few downstairs.'

'Take this,' Nick pushes the shotgun into her hands,

gently pulling the pistol out of her grip. 'You got that spare magazine?'

'Here. What are you doing?' she asks.

'I'll help Roy. You two, stay here. Get the boys ready to come out if I shout to move, okay?'

'Okay,' Lilly nods.

'Jacob, stay with her.'

'Will do, Nick,' the older man replies. He was right. They did come. Someone called Roy has already killed all the men at the gate and a couple downstairs, with a bow? Jesus, who are these people?

Lilly breaks away. Pushing the door open, she enters the dark room. 'Billy? It's me ...'

Billy reacts instantly and breaks cover to run across the room, throwing himself at his big sister. She drops to her knees, gripping him in her arms as she cries tears of relief into his hair.

'It's okay,' she rubs his back. 'We're going to get you out of here. Are you hurt?'

Billy shakes his head, the sobs and utter terror rendering him unable to speak.

'I need your help, Billy. We've got to get all these boys over to the door so we can get out ... Will you help me? Everyone, come over here. We're going to get you out to a safe place. Come on quickly,' gently, she urges the boys out the dark and ruined room. Dead bodies litter the ground. Lilly gets glimpses through the room. There are guards and two boys lying near each other. Another man, naked from the waist down, huge and frighteningly ugly, lies further away.

Slowly, she coaxes the boys out from under beds and hiding in the corners, getting them all into a group by the door.

Shocked to the core and utterly traumatised, the soft female tones of Lilly give the children just enough strength to respond and get into position.

Shots ring from outside the door as Jacob fires down the hallway. Hearing noise, he doesn't take a chance but lets tip before taking a quick step back into the doorway to reload.

'Roy?' Nick calls out. rushing down the stairs with pistol held ready.

'Over here,' Roy replies.

'Where?'

'Bottom of the stairs and off to the right.'

'I'll go left then. Don't shoot me.'

'I got the night vision. You don't shoot me.'

'Yeah, no promises,' Nick mutters, venturing off into the corridor. He clears room by room, exactly how Dave showed him. Pistol up and tracking where he looks.

Roy does the same but not from training. He's skilled with the weapon he carries and seen enough movies to have an idea of how it works. Room by room, they go, but no movement, no noise, no shouting now, nothing.

Within minutes, the downstairs has been checked, each room given the all-clear. With only two of them and such a big house, the chances are the men have hidden, but it doesn't matter.

'Get the vehicle round to the front,' Roy whispers. 'I'll cover from here.'

Nick runs off, out the front door, and into the rain. The wind instantly hits him with such power it almost takes him off his feet. Bending forward, with one hand shielding his eyes, he fights to gain ground, moving gradually round the front of the house, towards the corner.

Seeing the silhouette of the Saxon from the forks of lightning, he heads towards it. Movement from the side door as someone bursts out running for the driver's side. Pistol up, aimed, and he fires two quick, successive shots. The man is flung back against the side of the vehicle and slumps to the ground.

In the Saxon, and he starts the engine, pulling away to drive round to the front. Eyes stinging from the weather, and his whole body drenched from the torrential downpour.

Reversing to get the rear doors as close as possible, he jumps down and races into the hallway. 'Ready,' he murmurs.

'Get them down. I'll stay here,' Roy whispers back.

Nick vaults the stairs, rising quickly to the first floor where he sprints across the landing. Inside the room, with Jacob watching down the corridor, he finds Lilly waiting with a large group of terrified boys.

'Vehicle's out the front. We need to get everyone down and into the back ... Jacob and I will cover you as you go down the stairs, and we'll come down behind you ... Jacob, you hear that, mate?'

'Yep.'

'Lilly, you got to keep them fucking moving, don't fucking stop.'

'Okay,' she replies.

'Shit, sorry, I didn't mean to swear. Right ... Jacob, you ready?'

'Hang on,' Jacob steps out and fires both barrels down the hall. Wood and plaster shredded, he breaks the gun and slams two more shells in. 'Now,' he grunts, snapping the shotgun closed.

Nick steps out into the corridor, taking aim with the pistol as Lilly starts urging the boys out and across the hallway.

Out they go, terrified, crying and sobbing but doing as told. Ushered across the landing and down the stairs.

Roy, at the bottom, glances up to see the group descending. He crosses closer to the front door and checks outside as the first children reach the bottom.

Filing past him into the rain, Lilly leads them to the back of the Saxon, helping them up and into the vehicle. One after the other, they get heaved in.

Nick and Jacob work a retreat. Facing back, they go gradually down the stairs behind the children. A noise from somewhere, a door crashes open and shots ring out. Jacob fires both his barrels, knowing there is nothing to aim for but sending a clear message.

As though waiting for him to use both his barrels, a man runs into view at the top of the stairs, already firing as another one joins him, opening up with a double-barrelled shotgun.

Nick takes the first one out, taking two shots and having to readjust his aim, but the second man has dived out of sight.

'WE'RE GOING,' Nick shouts. 'JUST LET US GO ... KEEP THE HOUSE AND THE FOOD ... KEEP ALL OF IT ... LET US LEAVE ...'

'DON'T COME BACK,' a deep voice roars.

'WE WON'T,' Nick replies. 'NOT EVER ... ALL YOURS ... WE JUST WANTED THE BOYS ...'

Silence.

'YOU GET MORE CHILDREN HERE, AND WE WILL COME BACK,' Jacob adds.

There's still no response, but they get to the bottom of the stairs and out into the rain without further incident. Roy holds position inside the front door to protect his bow from the rain.

The children are loaded up, crammed in but with enough room for Lilly and Jacob to squeeze in.

'Roy,' Nick runs back. The two men race for the front, Nick taking the driver's seat as Roy clambers in beside him.

Doors shut, engine ready, foot down, and they're away. No one speaks until they reach the gates and speed off onto the main road heading south.

'Everyone alright?' Nick calls out.

'Fine, can't believe we did it!' Jacob shouts back.

'Lilly?'

'Fine, thank you ... Thank you for doing this,' she says with earnest.

'How's Billy?' Nick asks.

'Shocked, not speaking, but I don't think he's hurt.'

'What was at the fort, then?' Nick turns to Roy, listening as Roy quickly explains the situation.

'We'll go there first,' Nick says at length after listening. 'If it's no good, we'll head off.'

'They had no weapons, Nick, nothing other shotguns, and there were thousands of them ...'

'Yeah,' Nick replies quickly, 'but they have Dave ...'

Sighting down the barrel, he holds the rifle steady and breathes out, a long exhalation of air that brings his heart rate down. The boys being taken isn't an issue. In fact, life will be much easier without them. The Doc is dead, and a high number of the guards have been taken down. A power vacuum has been created, and one that Larson fully intends to manipulate to his advantage. A smaller team is much easier to manage.

He could let them go, but something tells him that

young man won't leave it at that. He doesn't know who Nick is or the other man firing arrows so expertly, but he does know these are dangerous people, and if they come back? Well, that can't be allowed to happen.

Steady now. Breathing easily, he waits flat on his stomach in the deep puddle at the corner of the house. Absorbed by the shadows, unseen, and waiting. The powerful rifle is ready, the safety off. All he needs is one clean shot, and that young man will be taken down.

Watching as the children are loaded, the pretty blonde woman lifting them into the back of the vehicle. That idiot with the bow moving in and out of the front door, and Jacob, that fucking traitor, he'll pay for this.

Ignoring the rain pelting his face, blocking out the driving wind and thunderous crashes, he applies the first miniscule amount of pressure on the trigger. Nick moves back and forth, scurrying left and right as he gets the children out of the house. The pattern has been set. As Nick moves out from the rear doors, he can take his shot straight through the back of his head.

The pressure on the trigger is increased. Breathing out in one long, steady exhalation, he pauses, frozen in stature as his stomach drops through his arse.

Swallowing hard, he dares not move. The cold, hard press of the barrel firm against the back of his head brings everything to a halt.

'Let them go,' the voice says quietly from behind him. Larson nods, instantly moving his finger off the trigger. He gently slides his hand away, showing the other person he will comply.

'Can I get up?' Larson asks. No reply but the firm prod of the barrel in the back of his skull gives the answer clearly. 'He was a fake,' Larson adds in a hoarse whisper. 'The Doc, he was a fake ... You hear that? We all put up with him and for what?'

'Ssshhh,' the voice sounds out as the speaker watches the children being manhandled into the rear of the army truck. The way the rescuers lift those children with care, the way that blonde woman hugs the little boy so tight. The soft tones they use, the sheer violence they threw against those that did their children harm. These are good people, and letting these children go now is the right thing.

The Doc was a fake. They all went along with it for the promise of a cure or a vaccine, convincing themselves it was for the greater good. The children weren't bruised or hurt, or were they? Not all injuries leave marks, not all assaults leave bruises. Things could have happened in his offices, and they all knew, yet chose not to challenge it.

The last of the children are loaded in, and the two people wait in the pouring rain as the Saxon pulls slowly away to navigate the long driveway.

'What now?' Larson asks as the vehicle disappears into the gloom of the storm.

'We all knew,' the voice says sadly, 'but we did nothing.' The guilt hits with such overwhelming force that it instantly negates any hope of ever going away. You can't be witness to something like that and then keep going like nothing happened.

'Evil triumphs when good people do nothing,' the voice mutters.

'Wait!' Larson detects the finality of the tone and screams out, twisting round in a final, desperate bid to save himself. The shot is so quick the sound doesn't even register, just blackness that takes all form of life away. Larson's head is taken from his body as the first barrel of the shotgun explodes an inch from his skull.

Tears stream as a heart breaks. *There is no going back from this. There is no forgiveness.* The barrel is pushed into the mouth as an arm stretches out to feel for the trigger.

God, I am sorry for all my sins done here. I am sorry for what I am about to do. Please keep those children safe.

Meryl sighs deeply. Holding the image of her own little boy firmly in her mind, she smiles sadly and pushes the trigger.

CHAPTER SIXTY-ONE

'Dave!' My voice isn't loud enough for him to hear me. He's fighting close by but facing away from the last surge of infected heading towards the survivors huddled together near the vehicle ramp.

With the sea bursting over the flatlands and Cookey back on his feet, we know the battle is ours. With limited numbers, they can't possibly hope to beat us now, but as ever before, still they try.

The sea pours through the gaps of the outer gate, rapidly filling the alley. Already it is several feet deep by the gate and pushing out to both side. Water gets through the inner gate as the fort interior starts to flood.

The rear gate went a little while ago, and with the huge waves crashing against the back wall, that too is rapidly flooding.

Enough of them left to cause us a problem. Hundreds had gained the alley and are now climbing the wall to attack us and have not learnt to stay low to avoid being plucked by the extraordinary strength of the gales battering us.

Fear has frozen one group of survivors to the spot.

Huddled together on the floor, I can just see them through the driving rain. Figures clinging on for dear life, eyes squeezed shut as they pray for it to end.

The infected have seen them, and a smaller group break away to start crawling at the group of people.

I scream and shout, but with the noise as it is, there is no way they can hear me. There are seconds to go before the horde reach them, so with no other option, I get onto all fours and scrabble in desperation to cut them off. But it's too slow. I'm too slow like this, and I'll never get there. Still screaming at them to get out the way, I risk moving on to two legs in an effort to get there faster.

The very second my hands leave the ground, the wind hits my legs and flips me over like I weigh nothing at all. Somersaulting head over arse while screaming, my axe is gone, my knife dropped, and I land smack amongst the horde.

For a second nothing happens. I'm slightly dazed, and they're looking at me like *where the fuck did he just come from?*

Flat on my back, surrounded by infected on their stomachs. Twisted, gruesome features leer at me, and now the dried blood has been washed off, I can see them clearly. Their pallor is sickly, skin so tightly drawn you can see the cheekbones pushing against the flesh. Teeth bared, yellow and dirty. Hair, whatever hair they have left, is straggly, lank, and plastered to scalps from the torrential downpour.

'Hi,' I nod in greeting, hoping maybe, just maybe they'll remember I'm the bloke that had the heart shoved in his gob, and maybe, just maybe I've suffered enough, and they'll leave me alone.

Not so. With growling hisses, they start descending like the nasty, fetid pack of undead wolves they are. Sensing my solace, isolated and without a weapon, they come in hard and fast.

But hey, guess what, motherfuckers? I'm immune, so I can take a couple of bites. That changes everything. It changes the way I fight, it changes the fear I have of them, it changes my methods of attack and defence, and it means I don't have to be so careful about where their mouths are.

Grinning like a twat, I laugh into the air and actually relish the prospect of an all-out scrap. Their attention is on me now, not the terrified survivors clinging onto each other with their bloody eyes clamped shut.

The first one goes straight for the bite. Arms back and head forward, he dives in. A scrawny, emaciated-looking thing, and I punch him hard on the nose, feeling the crack as the bone breaks. Fresh blood bursts from his nostrils only to be quickly rinsed away by the rain. Another blow onto his nose, then another, and I keep going. Hard, quick punches that batter his face senseless and probably cut my knuckles in the process.

One comes from the other side, so I stretch out and get my hand round its throat, squeezing hard while I keep up the punches to the first one. Two more come towards my feet, so I start cycling to batter them senseless with the hard soles of my combat boots.

Oh yes! This is fucking amazing. I'm fighting four at the same time. Unarmed and on my own, and I'm punching one in the face, strangling another whilst kicking the shit out of two more. Only problem is, there is more than four infected in this horde, and I've run out of limbs to deal with the others.

Bollocks, getting slightly overwhelmed now. The one being strangled is shifting his entire body weight onto my arm, slowly sinking down, towards my face. The bastard being punched doesn't give in either. Despite his face now being mangled, he keeps coming in for a lunge, so I get that hand to his throat and start squeezing him too.

Shit, two being strangled while kicking at the same two down there, and more still crawling in. Not good, not good at all.

With a yell, I drive my hands towards each other and smash their heads together. That does nothing other than apparently irritating them and causing them to start thrashing about in a rather unnecessarily violent manner.

The infected in my left hand drops down to smother my chest, and in the confusion, he bites into his mate's shoulder. The bitten one starts thrashing more wildly, and I think the one biting gets impression it's me thrashing about, so he bites harder, driving his teeth into flesh.

Fuck me, they're biting each other now. These things are pumped up like nothing I've seen before. Demented to the point they're biting anything they can reach.

I realise there's weight on my legs. I'm being pinned by an infected sprawling in to join the feast. This time I go fucking nuts. Heaving, bucking, striking out, I throw myself in all directions so they can't get a hold of me. Sharp pain on my thigh as some rancid fucker bites into me. With the violence pulsing through my system, I wrench my leg up at the same time as I bring my arm down to smash and batter the thing away. Old and almost decaying-looking, the infected biting into me must be eighty years old, and how the fuck it got over the wall, I'll never know, but here it is, chomping away on my leg. The pain is intense, so I go full-on nuts, thrashing and beating until I feel the flesh tearing and the bones breaking. Eyes clamped shut, I heave the thing away from me, but the pain is still there. Scanning quickly, I can see the body lying next to me but no fucking head. Shit, the fucking head is still on my leg. Screaming, I grab at the old skull and try to prise it away, wrenching it free to throw at the next one looming in. If I don't do something quickly, I'm going to be fucked.

More weight on my legs, more on my stomach. Completely pinned now, and I'm starting to worry maybe I didn't think this through properly.

Then she's there. Meredith. A flying blur of wet, black fur that adds her weight to the pile already on top of me. She's death on four legs. Huge canine teeth lashing left and right, shredding any infected that gets near me. It's almost like that scene from the film Crocodile Dundee when the Aussie man gets mugged by the thugs wielding a small flick-knife, and he shows off by pulling out his own huge knife.

Meredith sees their lips pulled back showing teeth. *They ain't teeth. These are fucking teeth.* She growls, pulling her own lips back. Hers are far better and far more deadly.

Within seconds, they're gone from on top of me, and I'm able to twist round to start fighting again. The two of us go at it, fists, feet and teeth, but with the space created, I can see one of them has broken away from the group and is almost at the group of petrified survivors.

As they still haven't moved, I have no time to do anything than get up and try to reach him before he reaches them. Once again on all fours, crawling. Meredith works at my back, keeping them away.

Diving forward, I grab at his ankle just as he grabs at the nearest person and starts pulling them towards his open mouth. Screaming wails erupt as the group start a tug of war, trying to pull the woman away from the infected, who is now inching his teeth towards her foot.

Out of options again, I stand up and fight the wind to get one arm under his throat. A gust of wind so strong lifts me off the ground, my only anchor being the arm I have round the infected thing's neck.

Stronger it gusts, and gently he starts to rise, the wind lifting both of us from the ground. We rise that extra couple of feet and hit the strongest thermals. Like a kite, we get pummelled into the air, me screaming while holding onto the infected, round his throat.

Sailing over the heads of the others, Clarence glances up with a confused look on his face that quickly morphs into worry.

The edge of the wall is rapidly approaching, and just for a fleeting second, I wonder if the thermals over the alley are going to be different from the thermals over the top of the wall.

Yep, they are. There are no thermals at all actually, and we plummet as soon as we get gusted over the edge. Down into the darkness of the no man's land between the walls.

We land on a pile of soft, squelchy bodies that burst open from impact of the drop. With the wind knocked out of me again, I writhe and keep writhing as I try and move to find out where I am. It's so dark down here, but with the walls so high, the noise of the storm is muted a little.

With a sudden jolt, I realise I'm still holding onto the infected I was grasping when we came down. He's not dazed but already fighting to break free so he can turn round and rip my throat out.

Body parts scattered around me, corpses stacked against the wall as an ad hoc climbing frame for the infected to use, the water level rising by the second as the sea batters at the front gates and pours through the gaps.

Gripping hard, and I squeeze with every ounce of strength in my arms. He thrashes and bucks, but he's done for. Thirty seconds later, I release the lifeless body. Struggling upright, I push against the water and floating bodies to figure out a way back up.

Apparently Clarence wasn't the only one to see me coming down here. Several bodies drop from the top wall to land close by. Thuds and sploshes as the heavy bodies splash into the water or amongst the corpses.

I'm still surrounded by zombies and still without a weapon, and worse, I'm waist deep in treacherous water covered in floating bodies and the debris from all of our vehicles.

The first one bursts from the water with a roar. How overly dramatic. I mean, come on. Why roar? We're all down here about to have a scrap after god knows how many scraps over the last two weeks, and this one has to give it large by roaring as it comes up through the surface of the water.

Mind you, he looks the part. Big and covered with thick muscles that stand defined from the sudden loss of protein shakes over the last two weeks.

'Fuck you,' I shout and give him the middle finger again, 'I'm immune, motherfucker ... Hear that? IMMUNE!'

Yeah, he's going to beat the living shit out of me, and his mates are getting up now too. Backing away, I have to push the heavy, floating bodies out the way, bloated from the water and swollen to grotesque shapes that barely register as human.

They form a semicircle, coming at me–the big fucker front centre with his ugly mates ranged off to the sides. Hemmed in by the walls and the water surging in through the gates behind and more of our vehicles floating further behind me.

Reaching out, my hand gropes something furry. Fearing a rat, I jerk it away and glance down to see the bearded face of Big Chris floating by; the skin torn, and jagged throat now washed clean and deathly white. His features are bloated, but there's no mistaking who it is, and the beard is still so black, glistening from the water.

Lightning overhead flashes, a trick of the eye, and I swear for a split second he looks alive, like he's about to open his eyes and laugh.

These bodies down here are from the estate, taken by these fucking things to be used as objects. Sarah will be amongst them, Terri too. Ted and Steven. Our lads from Salisbury, Tucker, Jamie, and Curtis.

My mind snaps alert, and I realise I'm not backing away now but wading forward. My eyes set on that big infected at the front. Fists clenched, and my eyes unblinking as the water pummels down from above. Wind whips at my hair and stings my eyes, but I refuse to take my gaze off him.

It surges up within me, that feeling I had a few minutes ago when I was fighting with Dave. I embrace it, feeling the strength that floods into my limbs, seeing my vision sharpen and focus and hearing my blood screaming for vengeance. Charging at each other, both of us hell-bent on destroying the other. The infection knows I'm immune. It must know. It shoved a still beating heart into my mouth, but here I am, fit, fighting, and unturned. Lani and now Cookey too. Three of us that had that deadly disease pushed into our systems only to reject it, kill it, and work on like nothing happened. Not just immune but untouched, unbothered, unaffected, and un-fucking-remitting in our desire to stop them.

I remember a big bastard like you. Two weeks ago one your size came at me in the street. I was scared and tried to drive away, panicked and flapping. I only just survived, and that was nothing more than pure luck. I remember being wedged almost upside down in the car, trying to operate the foot pedals with my hands. Terrified and incompetent, bumbling from disaster to catastrophe.

But that was two weeks ago, and a lot can happen in a fortnight. No fear now, you fucker, no fear at all. Just pure, blind rage that drives me on with savage ferocity.

The impact is like running into a tree. Punches and kicks will do nothing to this one, and he knows it. His arms wrap round my body and lift me up at the same time as he starts crushing me. The pain is immense as the air is driven from my lungs. With my arms pinned to my side, I can't fight out or do anything other than flail my dangling legs about.

He roars with victory, stretching his head back to scream into the sky, bellowing that he alone will defeat the annoying little prick Howie. Fuck you. I've got a mouth too, and you ain't the only one that can bite, so I drive my face into his big, meaty neck. I pull my own lips back and take a huge bite into the big Adam's apple poking out. It is the most disgusting and foul thing I have ever done. The flesh tears with amazing ease as I bite and gnash. Copying Meredith, I thrash my head side to side while biting in deeper and deeper. Blood bursts and pours down my throat, hot and metallic, but I keep going, tearing his fucking throat out with my teeth, widening the bite to go further left and right until I get an artery and tear the thing apart with my teeth.

He releases then as the sudden pressure loss from his once sealed system drains the strength from his arms. He goes down. and I remain standing, victorious. You like biting people? Well, I can bite too.

As he sinks beneath the waves, I glance up to see the infected staring at me. Not advancing, not retreating, but staring, and I can feel the fear coming off them.

'Did you like that?' I growl. Locking eyes on the closest, I can feel the hot blood pouring down my chin. 'Guess what?' I ask with a glance round from face to face. 'Rules just changed.'

I'm up, bursting from the water as I lunge at the closest. He flinches and tries to pull away, which is something I have never seen an infected do before, but it's too late, and I'm on him. No weapons, no knives or axes, no guns. Just me with two hands, two feet, and a mouth.

Landing solidly, I take him off his feet, driving him down beneath the water. Plunging beneath the surface, I grope for his face and use my thumbs to drive into his eyes while I savage his throat with my teeth. Like a wild animal, I fight, and I kill. Surging back up, I use my feet to stamp down repeatedly on his head while screaming into the sky.

They change as the fear is replaced with pure, demented fury, a visible reaction to whatever dose of chemicals being used to drive them is increased dramatically.

They come at me as I go at them. Wild, unabated, and furious, we fight. Teeth biting, fingers gouging, hands strangling. Teeth bite into my right shoulder, but I don't feel the pain now–the blood lust of battle is too strong.

They take me off my feet, and it's my turn to get driven down beneath the surface of water. Dark and tidal, the waves are getting stronger, buffeting us all left and right. We slam into walls, vehicles, and bodies. The saltwater gets into my mouth, making me gag and swallow more. Eyes stinging so much it renders me blind.

Something lands amongst us, something very big and very heavy, that starts hauling bodies away with the ease of a Nordic giant. I feel a hand grip the back of my shirt and launch me several feet away to land on the top of a floating car.

I cough and gag as the saltwater is puked from my body. Slowly, my vision clears to reveal Clarence battering them away. More infected must have come down, for their numbers are greater now. The giant swats and breaks necks. Lifting one up, he goes for the human battering trick as he fends them off.

A streak of darkness, a splash of water that plumes up between Clarence and the infected. Dave bursts from the surface with his knives drawn, and instantly they are upon him.

Sod this. I'm not missing out, so I slide off the car, find my feet, and start heading in, towards the fight.

The infected move in. Spurred on by the burst of action, they charge for Clarence. I grab one and take him down under the water, gripping his throat while I squeeze the life out of him and ram my knee into his stomach. I know that won't hurt him, but the reflex action is to breath in, and what with him being under water and all ... well, he kind of drowns quicker.

That tactic worked well, so I try it again, grabbing one as he lunges in and using my body weight to pull him down. Clarence is splashing about somewhere nearby, cracking skulls with his hands.

Hands to throat, knee striking stomach, but this bastard keeps his mouth shut and finds his feet, pushing us both up and out of the water.

Using the flat part of my palm, I strike his nose. It breaks, so I keep going. Right and left, hard blows that stagger him backwards. I feel his cheekbones break and use my left hand to grip his thick hair while my right hand builds power as I get used to the action.

Pulling him down with my left as my right hand

pummels him, I get his head back under the water and hold him down.

Something hits me hard, a heavy weight on my back and a sharp, searing pain on my shoulder. Sinking beneath the waves, I twist and feel the teeth biting into me. Unable to generate power under the water, I have to fight every instinct not to breath in or open my mouth.

It's a woman with long hair, and I try getting a grip to pull her head away. She twists and contorts, getting on top of me, using her body weight to hold me on the ground, well beneath the surface.

Knees striking up, kicking, thrashing as I desperately try to get her off me. Another searing pain as she bites me again. Fucking idiot must be on autopilot.

Reaching up, my hands feel something. I grab and pull, hoping to pull myself up. Whatever it is I grip comes down instead, so I pull it harder, realising it's one of the bodies floating on the surface.

Twisting, I manage to pull it between us. She bites down again and again, but this time her teeth sink into the rotten flesh of the corpse, and it gives me a chance to beat my way out.

Feet stamping down, I feel the beloved ground and push up, driving my legs to push my head out of the water.

The corpse is still between us, and she tries to leap over it. A flash of lightning gives a split second of light to the scene. Once again, it flashes over the features of Big Chris as he gently bobs between me and the female infected, proving that even in death, he can still save my life.

As she comes over him, I reach out and grab two fistfuls of hair and simply pull her head under the water while moving backwards. Unable to gain her feet, I keep jerking left and right while holding her face down in the water.

'MR HOWIE,' Dave shouts and throws a knife. It strikes the body of Chris with the blade sinking into his chest. Wincing, I realise Dave had no way of knowing he just used Chris as a dartboard.

Handle gripped, and I pull it out, this time nodding an apology at the corpse of the big man. Just in time too as the last one charging at me comes in quick. Diving forwards with a howl, I stab out, driving the point of the blade deep into the chest. Twisting the handle, I pull the knife out as it keeps the forward charge up. Puncture wounds pucker his side. In and out, the blade sinks deep into his stomach and chest before I finally get a clean shot at his neck, stabbing through the main artery.

With his life blood pumping high into the air, I let go and move out of the way, watching as he folds up and sinks beneath the water.

The water is deeper now, above my waist and almost at my chest. Glancing up, I see both Dave and Clarence have finished and are stood facing towards the gates.

I wade towards them, but there is a tide now, the water is streaming past me with more power than a few seconds ago.

Thunder still rips through the sky, but between those booms and the crackles of lightning, another awful noise of grinding metal reaches me. The gates bow from the force of the water on the other side, and the vehicles jammed into that space are now being lifted and crushed, unable to resist the ever-increasing force and weight of the sea.

If those gates go, this whole alley will be flooded within seconds. With the sea claiming the flatlands, the fort is getting battered from all sides, and suddenly the threat of death doesn't come from the infected undead but from the very thing that saved us just minutes ago.

Unbiased she is, Mother Nature holds no allegiance to man nor beast, giving life and taking it without fear or favour.

'CLIMB,' Clarence shouts, wading across the width of the alley. Dave and I respond the same, wading with effort to reach the side of the inner wall.

As the infected earlier, we have no choice but to use the stacked and fallen corpses as a ladder. Screeching sounds of metal warping against metal come from the gates.

With the rising tide starting to lift the obstacles put in place behind the outer gates, we know it's only a matter of time before those gates burst open.

Splitting up, we start the climb, our feet sliding into the soft, squidgy bodies, hands gripping whatever we can find, gore and body parts coming away under our fingertips. Dave, as ever, climbs like a monkey and gets up quickly. Clarence and I don't fare so well and struggle with the cascading water pouring down on us and the bodies slipping and shifting under our weight.

Clarence and I are only halfway up when the gates finally yield to the pressure of the waves battering them.

Screeching metal, huge thumps and bangs boom out as the makeshift barricade is lifted and pushed down the alley, towards us. Huge vehicles, vans, and trucks surging along as the tidal wave propels them down the alley.

We can both see what will happen and lock eyes as the first of the vehicles impacts on the base of the corpse wall we're climbing up. Another vehicle behind it, then another, and the concertina effect removes the bodies from the bottom.

Like a deck of cards, the wall starts to crumble, and Clarence, being closer to the surge than me, is the first to go.

As the bodies start tumbling down, he nods goodbye and slides to plummet into the roaring mess beneath us.

Glancing up, and I can see hands reaching down. I could make it. I could move quick, grab a hand, and get pulled up, but that isn't our way.

With Clarence being so big, I catch sight of his enormous frame landing in a gap between two vehicles. The bodies falling after him push him down under the surface. The tidal pressure forces the vehicles closer until they're colliding, and there's no way out of it. He's trapped under water with several tons of vehicles over his head.

A gap off to the side. It's the only chance, and I take it without hesitation. Pushing off from the wall, I feel myself drop, landing on a mixture of hard-edged car and soft, yielding bodies.

Twisting onto my front, I slide across the bonnet and slip headfirst into the pulsing, pitch-black water so foul and littered with hard objects that bang into me from all sides.

Groping about, I feel body after body and have to work my hands to the head, feeling for Clarence's bald skull. It's so dark, but opening my eyes makes them burn with excruciating pain. Diesel and chemicals leaking from the vehicles are mixing with the salty water, and already I'm feeling light-headed and weak.

Something here, warm and hard. His bald head. His arms reach up, feeling for my hands. I guide his grip and pull, tugging and forcing his body out of the confined space. No good. He doesn't budge but tries to push me away, telling me to go now while I still can.

I need air, so I break away and rise to the small gap left between the vehicles. Sucking in a huge lungful, I push back down and head under the constantly shifting vehicles, using my hands to grip wheels and exhaust pipes to get along. Finding his head again, I press my lips against his and start blowing a steady stream of air out. He gets the idea and holds still while I fill his lungs with the air from my own.

Once done, I work down his body, feeling the obstacles trapping him in place. The vehicles have trapped bodies underneath them which have piled up on top of one of Clarence's legs. Tugging and pulling in a swaying motion, my chest longs to draw air. I try and find something that will shift position, anything that will move and give me leverage.

Again I need air, so to the surface, giving a quick prayer that the small gap is still there. Back under and to Clarence first, giving him air before I start groping for limbs and torsos.

Finally something shifts, only a few inches, but by straining, pushing, then pulling, I work it free of the pile. Upside down, with my feet against the underside of the car, I prise with all my strength until the body finally slips free.

Fearing I'll black out, I head back up and draw more air in as a violent surge moves us along by a couple of feet.

Pummelled by the water, I cling on to a wheel and wait for a second, hoping it will settle again. The water is coming from the waves which are hitting the front wall. Those waves will keep coming, so I have a few seconds between each crashing wave.

Down again, and the shifting has freed some of the bodies, just a few to grip and heave, and finally his leg gets free as another crashing sensation hits the wall and sends a vibration through the water. Within a second, we feel the fresh surge and get thrown about, colliding with each other, with vehicles, and dead bodies pounding us from all sides.

Scrabbling in panic, we fumble and pull ourselves along underneath the vehicles, trying to find a gap, but the constant wave surges have pushed them all together.

Clarence grips my hand and guides me to a smooth metal surface, trying to show me something, so I grope about until I find a familiar object. A car door handle. One of the vehicles must have rolled onto its side. Grasping the handle I wrench the door open, sensing more than feeling Clarence trying to do the same. Slowly it gets prised enough, and the big man is pushing me inside the pitch darkness of the inside of a flooded car.

Seats, steering wheel, gear stick, I pull myself over them to reach the other door, working along the inside to find the handle. I find it and push, slowly creating a gap.

Then I'm being propelled through the gap by Clarence pushing me from behind. Up I go, and I clear the door to flop down on the side. Reaching back in, I help pull Clarence free as he sucks in air with frantic gulps. We look about at the scene of devastation around us.

Aware that we could get sucked under by a wave again at any second, we get on top of the car and start scrabbling along. Slipping, sliding, and doing everything we can to try and get to safety.

'ROPE,' we hear Dave's voice above, turning to see many hands waving at us. Heading that way, we feel the vehicles moving beneath our weight, precarious and ready to tip, roll, or slide away. Eventually, we find the thick rope hanging down.

'GO,' I scream at Clarence.

'YOU,' he gasps, 'GO FIRST.'

'GO, JUST FUCKING GO ... NOW!' With that, he grips and starts climbing. He is strong, but he's also very heavy, and the exertion on his drained and oxygen-depleted muscles must be terrible. Through will power alone, he gets up that rope, with me right beneath his feet.

With both of us clinging on, we feel it start to lift. We're being hauled in. Waves batter into and through the ruined gates. The alley fills as every object is lifted from the ground to be sent crashing into every other object and the sides. Knuckles get skinned as we are lifted up the side of the course wall. Water cascading down, thunder booming everywhere, lightning forks that flash with long, jagged sword-like points.

Hands grip my arms and lift; more under my armpits and onto my belt. Clarence is already pulled over, and I join him, wrenched the last few inches to get safely onto the top of the wall where I lie flat-out, panting and feeling the rain pelting at my face.

'Said I'd bloody kiss you,' I gasp at the big man lying next to me.

CHAPTER SIXTY-TWO

Only there isn't time to rest. There is never any time to fucking rest. Maybe two, three minutes we lie still until the sense of danger and urgency once more has us up and moving.

Crawling, we all start aiming for the top of the vehicle ramp, snaking along to get beneath the top of the wall. More survivors are left than I hoped for, many more. People are getting better at fighting back. Even the meek, mild, and downright terrified can pick something sharp up and use it to stab out.

Mind you, if it hadn't been for the flatlands flooding, we wouldn't have stood a chance. Thinking of which, with the outer gate gone, the inner gate can't be far behind.

We crawl and snake past survivors hugging and holding each other. They're grouped together in one long human chain of closeness. Men hold other men, and everyone clinging on in abject terror at the noises and sensations battering our nerves.

Reaching the ramp, we crab down enough to huddle together and view the inside of the fort. The rear gate is busted in and rapidly flooding with each wave that crashes against the back wall. Already a deep layer of water covers the ground, and it's going to get worse as the night goes on.

The roof of the visitor centre has already been shorn off and lying off to one side, smashed to pieces. None of the tents or other flimsy structures remain anywhere.

The inner gate holds. Darius, or whoever took care of it, made sure they used big, heavy vans, and the digger has been put there too.

'The children are in the locked rooms. We need to get them out and up here on the ramp in case the inner gate goes ... Then we find a way of blocking that rear gate up,' I shout the instructions and watch as they get passed along the line. Men start breaking away to crawl down, glancing down at the rear wall and the debris floating about.

'Kids first, then everything else after ... Go.' We jump up and start running down into the fort. Off the top wall, the wind is just slack enough not to rip us from our feet. We get to ground level and start wading through the water, tripping and falling as our feet get snagged on the tents and things floating about.

The children are screaming with terror at the prospect of drowning when we reach them, the water already seeping through to drip and cause minor, menacing floods.

We work quickly, ushering and carrying the little ones to the ramp where they are gathered at the halfway point.

'There's water pouring in the front, but it looks solid enough for now,' a man shouts at me, having just run down to the front gates.

'Okay, you know about these things, yeah?' I ask him, still having to shout to be heard over the noise.

He nods. 'Structural engineer. Kevin.' He holds a hand out.

'Kevin,' I nod quickly. 'Howie. Guess what?'

'What?' he asks with concern.

'You're now in charge. Tell us what you want, and we'll do it ... Clarence, Maddox, this is Kevin, structural engineer ...'

'Kevin,' Clarence nods. 'You told him he's in charge?'

'Just done it.'

'Where do you want us?' Clarence repeats.

'Alex!' Dave shouts at seeing Cookey and Blowers walking past.

'Yes, Dave?'

'You might be immune, but you're still on brew duty. Either get it done or find someone who can ...'

'Yes, Dave.'

'Right, Kev,' I grin at him, 'tell us what you need?' The poor man stares out at the many faces waiting for their instructions, utterly overwhelmed.

Kevin is a nervous man, and after the events of the evening, no one can blame him. He quickly finds his feet as boss, though, after he realises that the group in front of him only kill zombies and bad people.

Work groups are organised. Materials from the visitor centre roof are stripped down and used under Kevin's supervision to build a make-shift dam to block the gate at the rear.

Constant checks are done at the front, and orders are given to keep the area clear in case it buckles.

Cookey is soon relieved of his brew-making responsibility as everyone starts working at the tasks they are capable off. More tea than we can handle is brewed up, with a never-ending flow coming out in any liquid-holding receptacle found available.

Blowers leads a room clearance party, getting everything off the floor and onto the shelves, tables, and chairs. Generators are lifted and put under constant use to boil water. Gas bottles are exhausted to heat and boil more water.

With the threat of the infected gone for now, the storm continues to rage. In fact, it builds and becomes worse, with an increasing ferocity to the driving rain and the wind. The thunder rolls and booms. The lightning stays with us all through those dark hours, but we work. Oh, we work.

The brews give us something to share, a few seconds of stolen rest as we gather to sip at the beverages. Jokes shared, banter gets thrown, weak at first as people struggle with the terrible events that befell us, but the camaraderie grows. The new arrivals to the fort soon understand that this is their place too; this is home for all of us. Characters start to step forward, leaders and doers and, of course, the whiners and shirkers.

Paula works with us at first but is soon claimed by Lenski to help with the overall planning and organisation, a role she seems perfect for.

The hours of darkness pass by. The storm rages, but within these walls, a sense of safety starts to build. That we've survived the very worst that can be thrown at us.

As the first grey streaks enter the torn sky, so the storm appears to move on. Not abating or weakening but simply going somewhere else for now. A vast monster that, I am sure, will sweep across many lands. I can only hope it aids others as it has done with us tonight.

Frequently we speak of Nick, of where he is, if Roy and Lilly made it to them. As the flooding eases, so we start thinking of moving out. As tired as we all are, we cannot rest until we know Nick is safe.

All of our vehicles are ruined, and the Saxon was taken by Roy, but we'll swim or wade if we need to. Gathering in the offices, we leave Kevin the unenviable task of working out if it's safe to open the front gates so we can get out, and if not, then to find a way out.

'Everyone okay?' I walk in last from speaking with Kevin to find everyone gathered. The exhaustion evident on their faces, bodies smeared with grime, and clothes soaked to the skin.

Nods returned, and I notice Paula, Maddox, Lenski, Darius, and Sierra are all seated amongst my team, not separate and on their own but together. Unity.

'So,' I grab a mug of something black and hot and remain standing. 'Cookey, then,' I grin, the first chance we've had to talk properly.

'Yes!' Cookey grins, 'feels like winning the lottery.'

'You just liked having your arse groped by Mr Howie,' Blowers says.

'I did,' Cookey nods, 'and it was very nice. Thank you, Mr Howie.'

'You're welcome.'

'So we all immune, then?' Cookey asks with that expectant gaze that assumes I know the answer to every possible question.

'All immune?' Lenski asks, reminding me we haven't had time to explain the events of the last day or so.

It's run through quickly, the briefest facts outlined so everyone understands everything. No secrets now, nothing held back. Lani, me, and now Cookey, and Meredith, of course.

There's a long silence after I tail off. Everyone deep in thought. Why us? Why us three? Or is it just us three?

'Nick?' Cookey asks, breaking the silence

'Kevin is seeing how we can get out. You all happy to go once we find a way?'

'Of course,' Blowers nods.

'No doubt, boss,' Cookey says in a rare serious voice.

'I'm in,' Paula adds, 'er ... if that's okay, that is.' She suddenly looks awkward, like she invited herself to a party.

'Ah, you love us, Paula!' Cookey quips.

'Definitely, we'd love to have you with us,' I add once the laughter dies down.

'Not just for this either,' Lani is quick to say, 'but all the time. God knows I need another woman with this lot.'

'I'd like that,' Paula smiles, 'thank you.'

'So what this mean?' Lenski asks. 'You immune and Lani and now Cookey. I don't understand this.'

'Neither do we,' Clarence says.

'We still don't know anything,' I shrug. 'We're still in the same situation we were before, without doctors, without scientists, without tests ...'

'We'll get there,' Maddox cuts in. 'The fort will get cleared up, you'll find Nick, and after that ... plenty of time,' he says with confidence.

'Until that lot come again,' Blowers says, 'which will be in about half an hour, I reckon.'

'Not yet,' Dave says flatly. 'They'll need time to regroup.'

'Guys?' Kevin bursts in. 'You better see this.' The urgent tone in his voice has us all scrambling to our feet. Weapons grabbed, and we start jogging, the tiredness gone in an instant.

Outside the wind has gone completely, the rain has

stopped, and it actually looks like the sun will be coming through again.

'Jesus, mate,' I whistle. The inner gates stand open, with a large pool of water sitting on the surface and the vehicles all moved back.

'The walkway between the walls is still deep, but it'll drain,' he calls out. Running together, we reach the front of the fort and push through the gap between the gates.

'Fucking hell,' Cookey is the first to say something as we stand in silence, staring at the sea in front of us.

There's a small strip of land in front of the main gates, but that's it. The rest is water stretching away to the estate in the distance. Unbroken sea from left to right. The flatlands gone, taken away.

With the storm gone now, the sea is flat and calm, just a gentle sway of the waves as they roll by.

'Will it stay like that?' I ask Kevin.

'I've been out a few metres, and it's deep. There might be some shallower points, but ... time will tell. It'll either stay as it is, or it will drain anyway to be like it was before. I just don't know.'

'Be better if it doesn't,' Maddox says quietly. 'This is perfect.'

'It is,' I nod in agreement, 'completely cut off ... like an island.' I turn back to look up at the solid walls of the fort.

'No bodies,' Lani remarks, nodding at the sea.

'They'll be well gone,' Clarence replies. 'They'll be popping up on beaches all over the place.'

'Still loads in the walkway between the walls,' Kevin explains.

'We'll get that cleared,' Maddox says. 'Nothing that can't be fixed.'

'We've got incoming,' Dave says in his flat tone.

'Where?' I ask, scanning the view ahead but seeing nothing.

'Over there. Boats ... several of them,' he points away to the left, at the sweeping bay. Straining my eyes, I can't see anything.

'You sure?' I ask, which is pointless as Dave doesn't even speak unless he's sure.

'Yes, Mr Howie.'

'See 'em!' Lani calls out.

'Fuck me, I need glasses,' I rub my eyes and try again, somewhat reassured to see Clarence and the lads doing the same thing.

'Do zombies use boats?' Cookey asks.

'How the hell would we know that?' Blowers asks.

'Just asking,' Cookey shrugs. 'Didn't Marcy use boats to get over from the–'

'Who?' Lani asks with a very barbed tone, followed by a few coughs and shuffling feet.

'Yeah, so, a beautiful morning, then ...' I say lightly.

'Yes, lovely,' Lani adds in the same light tone.

'Sorry, Lani,' Cookey says quietly.

'Don't worry ...'

'You're not holding a meat cleaver behind my head, are you?'

'That again?' Lani sighs. 'Really?'

'Yep, got them now,' I say as the small, black dots come into view.

It takes ages for the small line of boats to get into better view. Low-powered engines putter through the gentle waves, the sounds of them reaching us well before we get any view of the occupants.

Dave walks forward a few steps, shielding his eyes to

stare at the boats. Someone stands in the lead boat, arms held high, waving back and forth.

'Nick,' Dave announces.

'WHAT? Really?' I go forward to the edge of the water. We all do. It's almost too much to hope. We crowd round until our feet are wading into the shallows.

'NICK!' Dave bellows. We start waving, arms held high as he stands at the front, waving back. Then there he is, the boats close enough for him to be seen clearly. Three small boats, each filled with children. Nick in the first with Lilly, Roy in the last one, and another man in the middle one.

'I DIDN'T BREAK IT,' Nick shouts, pointing at where the flatlands were.

'BET YOU DID,' Cookey bellows back.

We start wading out, surprised at how warm the water is. Nick brings the boats in close enough for us to grab and pull in. Everyone helps to pull until the first one grounds out gently.

Jumping down, I see he looks a bit battered and bruised but otherwise good. That brilliant smile of his plastered to his face.

'Mate!' I grab him for a hug. 'Really missed you, Nick. Thank god you're okay.'

'You too, boss,' he smiles sheepishly. 'Is everyone okay?'

'Fine, mate, loads to tell you, but we'll do that later. Are you okay? Any injuries? Are you hurt?'

'Fine, Mr Howie, really ...' He gets mauled by everyone in turn. Blowers and Cookey are genuinely delighted, and I'm not the only one with a tear in my eye at having him safely back with us.

Watching Lilly, I can see she doesn't take her eyes off Nick the whole time, staring at him in awe as he gets greeted so very warmly by everyone. There's long hugs and tears, Clarence giving him a bear grip, and Lani kissing his cheek. Even Maddox shakes his hand, and Paula gives him a hug. Having him back with us, seeing him here in the flesh, safe and sound, I can't express what it feels like.

Pure joy is the closest term I can think of. Absolute, pure happiness.

'Right,' I smile into the boats, seeing the terrified children staring wide-eyed. They look pale and sickly. 'You are all safe here. No one will hurt you, I promise. Come on, let's get you out.'

A human chain is formed as we unload the first boat, lifting the children out to be passed along until they're safely on the beach. The second boat gets pulled up, and the same process is repeated with the man handing the children over. He too looks battered and bruised.

'Mr Howie, that's Jacob ... He was a guard at the house, but he's okay,' Nick says. I stare up at the man. His eyes speak of sadness, of deep conflict, but I trust my team, and if Nick says he's okay, then I won't question it.

'Jacob, I'm Howie, nice to meet you. Thank you for helping Nick.'

'Mr Howie, my pleasure,' he replies solemnly, 'and it was Nick that helped me. He saved these kids ...'

'Nah,' Nick gives his shy smile, 'fucking team effort.'

'Nick,' Lilly calls out.

Wincing, Nick turns quickly, 'Sorry!'

'You said to tell you,' she points out.

'Tell him what?' Cookey asks with interest.

'Don't tell hi–'

'When he swears,' Lilly states. 'He said he wants to stop.'

The damage is done. Nick winces again as both Cookey and Blowers look like all their birthdays came at once.

'Did he now?' Cookey calls out.

'Nick? Not swearing? No chance...' Blowers bursts out laughing.

'Mr Howie, Roy was amazing, really amazing ... I'll tell you later, but bloody hell,' Nick speaks quickly and quietly.

'You just swore,' I smile quickly. 'Was he? He did alright, then?'

'More than alright,' Nick nods.

'Roy,' I nod as the third boat gets pulled in, 'thank you for getting Nick back to us.'

'S'alright,' he shrugs, 'he did most of the work ... Paula!' He jumps out deftly, wading through the shallows as he heads straight to Paula.

She grins warmly at seeing him, walking forward as though to hug him. 'Hey,' she calls out, 'are you okay?'

'No,' Roy whimpers, 'I think I've got a lump.'

'Right,' she hardly breaks pace, sliding effortlessly into concern, 'where?'

'In here,' Roy opens his mouth, 'in my cheek, where the cheek meets the jaw ... See it? Is it huge?'

'You mean here?' She gently touches his jaw, smiling when he winces in pain.

'Yeah, my god, you can see it from the outside!'

'It's a bruise, Roy, you've bruised your jaw ... Big battle last night? Remember that?'

'Oh, right,' Roy probes his jawline, fingering the tender spot. 'Right here, yeah?'

'Yes, Roy,' Paula says gently, 'bit swollen but definitely bruised.'

'Oh, thank god, I was so worried,' Roy sags with relief.

'Anytime,' Paula smiles, but with a hint of sadness in her eyes.

'Great,' Roy nods, still fingering his jaw. 'A bruise ... Er, Paula?'

'Yes, Roy?' she asks with patience.

'I didn't say goodbye yesterday. Sorry about that. I'm not very good with people ... Er ... you okay? Everything alright?'

Her face lights up, a visible change as she smiles at him. 'Yes,' she replies, 'fine, and you?'

'Yeah,' he nods, unsure of what to do, 'fine. Er ... weird night, but we got the kids out.'

'Come here,' Paula laughs, grabbing him for a hug. 'Glad you're back,' she says softly.

'Anyone got a smoke?' Nick asks. 'Mine got fucking–. Shit! Sorry, Lilly. Mine got ruined.'

'He's been like that the entire way here,' Jacob smiles fondly.

Heading inside, Lenski soon gets some of the mothers formed into a work party to take care of the boys.

'LANI!' Milly breaks free of a group as she hurtles towards us. 'It was raining, and there was thunder and lightning and everything!' Milly shouts as she launches herself into Lani's arms.

'Yes! I saw it,' Lani laughs.

'Clarence, do you like rain?' she asks immediately, holding her arms out for the big man to take her from Lani.

'I do,' he smiles as we all wait to see who will be next. Instead, she peers at Lilly, then at Nick, and finally down at the little boy being held by Lilly.

'Who are you?' Milly demands.

'I'm Nick, and this is–'

'My name is Milly, and this is Lani, and this is Clarence, and he is Cookey, and he is Blowers, and we have a dog called Meredith. You can fuss her if you want, and he is Dave, and that is Mr Howie, and he's in charge of everyone, like a teacher ...'

'Wow,' Nick shakes his head, staring in shock at the little girl proudly being held by a grinning Clarence.

'Who are you?' Milly turns to Lilly and the boy.

'Hello, Milly,' Lilly says politely. 'I'm Lilly, and this is my brother Billy ...' I can almost hear the cogs turning, the delight spreading across her face as she throws her head back and laughs excitedly.

'Milly and Lilly and Billy,' Milly sings. 'Milly and Lilly and Billy!'

'Lions and tigers and bears ...' Cookey shouts.

'OH MY!' Milly responds, clapping her hands in glee.

'Lilly, do you like rain?'

And so it goes on. We have to wait until Milly has done the rounds, asking everyone if they like rain, then if they like thunder, and finally if they like lightning. That's before she tells everyone about the trip to the zoo.

Billy looks shocked to the core, but the pressing questions posed by Milly leave no room for hesitancy. Something about the way the little girl asks the questions means you just have to answer.

Wriggling to be put down instead of asking, Milly gets to the ground and runs to hug Meredith sitting patiently watching everyone. Throwing her arms round the huge dog's neck, it's hard to believe that dog was tearing throats out just a few hours ago. She looks blissfully happy now, being fussed and hugged by the girl.

'This is Meredith,' Milly says to Billy. 'She likes boys and girls, but she doesn't like the zombos.'

'Zombies,' Lani corrects.

'Or the zombies ... She doesn't like them ... You can stroke her if you want.'

We move back to the offices, but this time with Nick, Roy, and Lilly with us. Having got her exhausted brother to sleep, Lilly was finally convinced that he'll be safe and joined us to find out what happened.

Nick gives most of the account until he starts explaining what happened when he got to the house. At that point, Jacob comes in for a very hard time as we understand he knew what was going on within the house.

He handles it well and explains his reasons for doing so, drawing a picture from his pocket of a woman and boy. He states clearly that the boys were never physically hurt, but there is pain in his eyes when he says it. He breaks down, sobbing hard as he relives what he had to see and hear, the killings given out by the Doc and Larson, the perversion, and the overwhelming desire to get the cure and try and find his family.

He makes it clear he doesn't want anything from us, that getting out with Nick was all he wanted, and his intention is to leave and find his family.

After that, Nick explains the rest, with some help from Lilly, Jacob, and the odd bit from Roy, all the way through to the house clearance at the end and getting back to the estate and seeing the flatlands flooded.

In turn, we explain our events of the day, seeing Milly and going off for miles, chasing her. Nick smiles with genuine humour at hearing how we all tried catching her and failed dismally.

All of them listen enraptured as we all go through the night's events, the storm, the flooding, and the infected charging over the walls.

Nick grins like a maniac when we explain what happened to Cookey.

We drink coffee, eat food brought to us, and talk. We talk about everything since we last saw each other.

We talk until we can't stop yawning, and Clarence starts dozing off. Meredith is already flat out on her side, snoring peacefully.

'Our rooms?' Nick asks. 'They flooded?'

'Only the main room got wet,' Blowers replies. 'The others were alright. With the doors open, it'll dry out quick.'

'Good, because I am fucked,' Nick yawns.

'Nicholas,' Cookey warns.

'Don't swear, Nicholas,' Blowers adds.

'Sorry about this, Lilly,' Nick says quickly, 'but you two can fuck right off.'

'Er, right, well, I better leave you to your, er ... meeting. Thank you for everything you did, Nick, and thank you to all of you and Roy ...' Lilly starts standing up, speaking very politely.

'Get off!' Cookey bursts out laughing. 'Stay with us for a bit. You don't have to go anywhere.'

'Honestly, sit down,' Lani urges. 'We'll find you some rooms in a minute.'

'She can stay with us,' Nick stretches, then realises what he just said, going bright red in the face as he stares wide-eyed at Lilly. 'Shit, I didn't mean like ... Fuck it! I meant ...'

'Ah, go on, Nick ...' Cookey laughs.

'Piss off, I just meant ... Fuck it! You know what I meant.'

'Not swearing going well then, mate?' Blowers asks.

'I know what you meant, and thank you, that's a very kind offer,' Lilly says sweetly, 'but I should stay with Billy.'

'We're going to have to find a bigger space,' I say. 'We

need more rooms now ... That's if Paula and Roy are staying?' I look over at them. 'We'd like you to stay, genuinely.'

'We take your room, yes?' Lenski says. 'Maddox and me, Darius and Sierra. We have those rooms. The armoury, it have some more rooms with the big space, so we move the weapons to the engineer rooms, and you have the armoury rooms, yes? I do this already,' she adds with a grin.

'Lenski!' Maddox exclaims.

'What! I do these things. They need to be done, yes? The guns I get Jagger and Mo Mo to move with the crews. Your stuff I move, and our stuff I move. You have the bigger space now with the bigger rooms. You have more people so ... the engineer rooms, they have the big lock, so it better for the guns ...'

'That,' I say, 'is wonderful. Thank you very much, Lenski.'

'Is no bother. You sleep now, yes? I work to do.'

'You need to sleep too,' Maddox says with a frown.

'I sleep soon,' she shrugs. 'We need to get the boats to the estate, yes? How the people going to get here without the boats? We make the ferry, I think, and we use the radios to talk ...'

'Whoa,' Maddox shakes his head, 'later, yeah? Please ... later ...?'

'Okay,' Lenski concedes, 'we talk this later. You have the rooms now. So, Paula and Roy, are you staying, yes? I need to know this. I have the rooms made for you.'

'Er,' Paula glances at Roy, 'I think so. I want to stay ... Roy? You staying for a bit?'

'Yes,' Roy announces.

'Great!' Paula adds to Roy's rather short answer. 'We'd love to stay.'

'I take you now, yes? I show you the room?'

'Now? Room? One room?' Paula asks.

'You have the two rooms,' Lenski replies, and I swear I see a very masked look of disappointment flash across both their faces. 'One is for the day, and one bedroom, but they make the two bedrooms. This is decision for you. Come now, I show you, yes?'

'Kit, weapons, and then sleep,' Dave announces as Lenski starts to lead Roy and Paula out. Groans escape from the lads with coy smiles as Dave gives them one of his glares.

Drifting off, we start heading out of the offices and into the fort. Some activity is taking place, but mostly people are dropping wherever they can find a dry spot. With the sun up, the weather is fine and warm, not hot like before. Amazingly, the sky is clear and a gorgeous blue colour, with no sign of the ferocious storm from the night before.

'Where you going, Nick?' Cookey calls out at seeing Nick walking off with Lilly.

'Leave him alone,' Lani cuts in quick, pulling Cookey round.

'Nicely done,' I comment as we enter our new bigger rooms. A table and chairs have been put in the main room, and checking the side rooms, we see bedding has been brought down.

'Lenski gets things done,' Blowers mutters.

'She bloody does, mate,' I reply.

'Mr Howie and I are having this room,' Lani announces, selecting the furthest room along.

'Lani, do you call Mr Howie *Mr Howie* when you're alone?' Cookey asks.

'I do. He insists on it,' Lani replies seriously. 'Very strict is our Mr Howie.'

'We got our own gas stove for brewing up,' Cookey nods at the burners on the shelves at the end.

'Twat, those were in our rooms before,' Blowers sighs.

'Were they? Oh yeah ...'

'You should know. You used them enough,' Blowers says.

'Hello, sunshine!' Cookey laughs as Nick walks in.

'You can fuck off,' Nick grins easily.

'Did you walk her home safely?' Blowers asks.

'Yes, I did,' Nick sticks one finger up.

'Tell you what, mate,' Cookey says seriously, 'she's a stunner for a fifteen-year-old.'

'Yeah, fifteen, nice one,' Nick shakes his head. 'Am I sharing with someone?' he asks with a nod towards the rooms.

'She is, mate, fifteen,' Blowers says.

'Fuck off!' Nick laughs. 'Fifteen ... yeah right!'

'She is,' Cookey says. 'Really, Nick, she's fifteen.'

'Piss off, yeah right, like I would be kissing a fifteen-year-old girl ...'

'You kissed her?' Blowers asks in shock.

'Well, yeah, but I didn't mean it like I was bragging ... like not like that ... She's really nice ...'

'We know you're not like that, Nick,' Lani says, 'but she is fifteen.'

'Eh?' Nick looks over at me for confirmation, the blood draining from his face when I nod. 'Fifteen? She's fucking fifteen?'

'Didn't she tell you?' I ask gently.

'No, boss, she bloody didn't ... She's really fifteen? Fucking hell! I thought she was like eighteen or nineteen.'

'She looks it,' I reply. 'Easy mistake, but yeah, fifteen, mate.'

'Oh fuck ... I kissed her,' Nick slumps into one of the chairs. 'She was offering herself and everything ...'

'Yeah, we heard,' I move over to sit down as Clarence glares at the two lads, daring them to make any quips now.

'Shit ... I kissed a fifteen-year-old girl ... fuck ... What if I had ...?'

'But you didn't,' Clarence says gently. Sitting down, he lifts his feet to rest on the table. 'And you only kissed her, Nick.'

'Nick, it's okay,' Lani says. 'You're only, what? Five or six years older? It doesn't matter. She told us she offered herself to you.'

'And that,' I stare at Cookey, 'doesn't get repeated outside these rooms.'

'No, course not,' Cookey nods seriously. 'Nick, you alright, mate? You want a brew, mate? Don't worry, Nick, she looks well older than fifteen, and a kiss don't mean anything.'

'I killed real people tonight,' he suddenly stares up at me. 'I beat men to death and shot some more. Not the fucking zombies but real people ...'

'I know, mate,' I nod gently. 'You did what had to be done.'

'And you did it well,' Dave cuts in, 'very well, Nick. If it wasn't for you, it would have been much worse.'

'Nick, don't take it to heart, son,' Clarence leans forward. 'We've had to kill before, the refinery ... We took lives there.'

'I know,' Nick nods, 'but ... I don't know ... I was on my own, making all the decisions, and I had to do it ...'

'Nick, there are twenty or so children in our fort that don't have to be abused anymore because of the actions you took. You did that, Nick. Not me or Dave or Clarence. You did it because it was the right thing to do.'

'Our way,' Nick says softly.

'That's right,' Clarence says, 'that's our way, the way we do things ... We do them because right now no one else will ...'

'And what's more,' I add, 'we're all here because we do those things. I don't know what all this means, but three of us are immune, maybe all of us. Something tells me this isn't over by a long shot yet.'

'It isn't,' Dave adds his voice.

'So that means we've got to do what it takes to get through this. We're the good guys now ... We're the ones that people will turn to. Word is spreading fast about who we are. Everyone who turns up here now seems to have heard of us.'

'They asked about us at the house,' Nick nods. 'I didn't say anything.'

'We're famous,' Cookey smiles, 'and I'm immune, so fuck you, Blowers.'

'Okay, mate, too tired to respond,' Blowers yawns.

'Sleep,' I announce, 'we'll talk more when we get up. You okay, Nick?'

'Yeah, fine.'

'Lenski's put you in with us, by the looks of it,' Cookey says. 'You alright with that, mate?'

'Not really. Blowers will try and touch my arse again.'

'In your dreams,' Blowers laughs.

The lads go off after Lani gives Nick a quick hug and tells him he's done nothing wrong. Clarence pats him on the shoulder before moving off to his room.

Lani and I finally get into ours, and she quickly pushes the two mattresses together. Wasting no time, she pulls her top off and starts unbuckling her trousers before sitting down to unlace her boots.

'Your eyes are going to fall out in a minute, Mr Howie,' she says without glancing up.

'Sorry,' I smile and start undressing.

'That's okay, Howie,' she adds with a grin.

'You told Cookey you call me Mr Howie all the time.'

'Do you want me to, then?' she asks softly, both her boots off, and she tugs her trousers free of her ankles. The rain has done one more thing for us–it has left us clean after a long fight, probably giving us the best wash since this all happened.

'Nah, it's okay, unless you want to, that is ...?' I tug my boots off and pull the sodden socks off my feet.

'I quite like calling you Mr Howie,' she says, 'and then just Howie when we're alone ... It sort of fits ... Does that make sense?'

'Not really,' I reply and get a wet sock thrown at my face.

'Ooh, that looks sore.' In her bra and panties, she crawls over to look at my shoulder. 'Does it hurt?'

'My whole body hurts,' I groan, 'head to fucking toe.'

'Oh, you poor thing,' she says softly as I push my trousers down and kick my feet free.

'I need lots of care,' I groan, 'special care and warm kisses.'

'Warm kisses?' she asks as I lay back. Staring up at her sitting next to me, I reach out and find her hand, fingers entwining. 'I think we can do more than warm kisses,' she adds as she bends down towards me.

ALSO BY RR HAYWOOD

Washington Post, Wall Street Journal, Audible & Amazon Allstar bestselling author, RR Haywood. One of the top ten most downloaded indie authors in the UK with over four million books sold and nearly 40 Kindle bestsellers.

GASLIT

The Instant #1 Amazon Bestseller.

A Twisted Tale Of Manipulation & Murder.

Audio Narrated by Gethin Anthony

A dark, noir, psychological thriller with rave reviews across multiple countries.

*A new job awaits. **Huntington House** needs a live-in security guard to prevent access during an inheritance dispute.*

This is exactly what Mike needs: a new start in a new place and a chance to turn things around.

It all seems perfect, especially when he meets Tessa.

*But **Huntington House holds dark secrets**. Bumps in the night. Flickering lights. Music playing from somewhere.*

Mike's mind starts to unravel as he questions his sanity in the dark, claustrophobic corridors and rooms.

Something isn't right.

There is someone else in the house.

The pressure grows as the people around Mike get pulled into a web of lies and manipulation, forcing him to take action before it's too late.

-

DELIO. PHASE ONE

***WINNER OF "*BEST NEW BOOK*" DISCOVER SCI-FI 2023**

#1 Amazon & Audible bestseller

A single bed in a small room.

The centre of Piccadilly Circus.

A street in New York city outside of a 7-Eleven.

A young woman taken from her country.

A drug dealer who paid his debt.

A suicidal, washed-up cop.

The rest of the world now frozen.

Unmoving.

Unblinking.

"Brilliant."

"A gripping story. Harrowing, and often hysterical."

"This book is very different to anything else out there - and brilliantly so."

"You'll fall so hard for these characters, you'll wish the world would freeze just so you could stay with them forever."

*

FICTION LAND

****Nominated for Best Audio Book at the British Book Awards 2023***

***Narrated by Gethin Anthony**

***The #1 Most Requested Audio Book in the UK 2023**

***Now Optioned For A TV Series**

***#1 Amazon bestseller**

#1 Audible bestseller

"Imagine John Wick wakes up in a city full of characters from novels – that's Fiction Land."

Not many men get to start over.

John Croker did and left his old life behind – until crooks stole his delivery van. No van means no pay, which means his niece doesn't get the life-saving operation she needs, and so in desperation, John uses the skills of his former life one last time... That is until he dies and wakes up in Fiction Land. A city occupied by characters from unfinished novels.

But the world around him doesn't feel right, and when he starts asking questions, the authorities soon take extreme measures to stop him finding the truth about Fiction Land.

*

EXTRACTED SERIES

EXTRACTED

EXECUTED

EXTINCT

Blockbuster Time-Travel

#1 Amazon US

#1 Amazon UK

#1 Audible US & UK

Washington Post & Wall Street Journal Bestseller

In 2061, a young scientist invents a time machine to fix a tragedy in his past. But his good intentions turn catastrophic when an early test reveals something unexpected: the end of the world.

A desperate plan is formed. Recruit three heroes, ordinary humans capable of extraordinary things, and change the future.

Safa Patel is an elite police officer, on duty when Downing Street comes under terrorist attack. As armed men storm through the breach, she dispatches them all.

'Mad' Harry Madden is a legend of the Second World War. Not only did he complete an impossible mission—to plant charges on a heavily defended submarine base—but he also escaped with his life.

Ben Ryder is just an insurance investigator. But as a young man he witnessed a gang assaulting a woman and her child. He went to their rescue, and killed all five.

Can these three heroes, extracted from their timelines at the point of death, save the world?

*

<u>THE CODE SERIES</u>

The Worldship Humility

The Elfor Drop

The Elfor One

#1 Audible bestselling smash hit narrated by Colin Morgan

#1 Amazon bestselling Science-Fiction

"A rollicking, action packed space adventure..."

"Best read of the year!"

"An original and exceptionally entertaining book."

"A beautifully written and humorous adventure."

Sam, an airlock operative, is bored. Living in space should be full of adventure, except it isn't, and he fills his time hacking 3-D movie posters.

Petty thief Yasmine Dufont grew up in the lawless lower levels of the ship, surrounded by violence and squalor, and now she wants out. She wants to escape to the luxury of the Ab-Spa, where they eat real food instead of rats and synth cubes.

Meanwhile, the sleek-hulled, unmanned Gagarin has come back from the ever-continuing search for a new home. Nearly all hope is lost that a new planet will ever be found, until the Gagarin returns with a code of information that suggests a habitable planet has been found. This news should be shared with the whole fleet, but a few rogue captains want to colonise it for themselves.

When Yasmine inadvertently steals the code, she and Sam become caught up in a dangerous game of murder, corruption, political wrangling and...porridge, with sex-addicted Detective Zhang Woo hot on their heels, his own life at risk if he fails to get the code back.

*

The Undead. The First Seven Days

The Undead. The Second Week.

The Undead Day Fifteen.

The Undead Day Sixteen.

The Undead Day Seventeen

The Undead Day Eighteen

The Undead Day Nineteen

The Undead Day Twenty

The Undead Day Twenty-One

The Undead Twenty-Two

The Undead Twenty-Three: The Fort

The Undead Twenty-Four: Equilibrium

The Undead Twenty-Five: The Heat

The Undead Twenty-Six: Rye

The Undead Twenty-Seven: The Garden Centre

The Undead Twenty-Eight: Return To The Fort

The Undead Twenty-Nine: Hindhead Part 1

The Undead Thirty: Hindhead Part 2

The Undead Thirty-One: Winchester

The Undead Thirty-Two: The Battle For Winchester

The Undead Thirty-Three: The One True Race

Blood on the Floor

An Undead novel

Blood at the Premiere

An Undead novel

The Camping Shop

An Undead novella

*

A Town Called Discovery

The #1 Amazon & Audible Time Travel Thriller

A man falls from the sky. He has no memory.

What lies ahead are a series of tests. Each more brutal than the last, and if he gets through them all, he might just reach A Town Called Discovery.

*

THE FOUR WORLDS OF BERTIE CAVENDISH

A rip-roaring multiverse time-travel crossover starring:

The Undead

Extracted.

A Town Called Discovery

and featuring

The Worldship Humility

*

www.rrhaywood.com

Find me on Facebook:

https://www.facebook.com/RRHaywood/

Find me on TikTok (The Writing Class for the Working Class)

https://www.tiktok.com/@rr.haywood

Find me on X:

https://twitter.com/RRHaywood

Printed in Dunstable, United Kingdom

63938169R00442